# THE ESSAY

# THE ESSAY

## Michael F. Shugrue
College of Staten Island

Macmillan Publishing Co., Inc.

New York

Macmillan Publishing Co., Inc.
866 Third Avenue, New York, New York 10022

Collier Macmillan Canada, Ltd.   PE 14/7
                                  E 77

**Library of Congress Cataloging in Publication Data**

Main entry under title:
The Essay.
1. College readers. I. Shugrue, Michael Francis.
PE1417.E77        808.84        80-14862
ISBN 0-02-410380-2


Printing: 1 2 3 4 5 6 7 8     Year: 1 2 3 4 5 6 7

## ACKNOWLEDGMENTS

Copyright works, listed in the order of appearance, are printed by permission of the following.

Renata Adler, The Movies Make Heroes of Them All, From *A Year in the Dark,* by Renata Adler. Copyright © 1969 by Renata Adler. Reprinted by permission of Random House, Inc.

Woody Allen, "My Speech to the Graduates." © 1979 by The New York Times Company. Reprinted by permission.

Aristotle from "Poetics" translated by Ingram Bywater, from *The Oxford Translation of Aristotle,* edited by W.D. Ross vol. 11 (1925). Reprinted by permission of Oxford University Press.

Richard Armour, "The Transcendentalists," from *American Lit Relit,* published by McGraw-Hill Book Company. Copyright © 1969, by Richard Armour. Reprinted with permission.

W. H. Auden, "Work, Labor, and Play" from *A Certain World* by W. H. Auden. Copyright © 1970 by W. H. Auden. Reprinted by permission of Viking Penguin, Inc.

Russell Baker, "Purging Stag Words," © 1974 by The New York Times Company. Reprinted by permission.

James Baldwin, "If Black English Isn't A Language, Then Tell Me What Is?" © 1979 by The New York Times Company. Reprinted by permission.

Bruno Bettelheim, "Dear Lord, make me dumb," from *The Informed Heart*. Reprinted by permission of Macmillan Publishing Co., Inc. Copyright © 1960 by The Free Press, a Corporation.

Heywood Broun, "A Study in Sportsmanship," "Dying for Dear Old ——" by Heywood Hale Broun, copyright 1925; reprinted by permission of Bill Cooper Associates.

Pearl Buck, "A Debt to Dickens," appeared in Saturday Review. Copyright 1936.

Rachel Carson, "What Makes Waves," from *The Sea Around Us*. Copyright © 1950, 1951, 1961 by Rachel L. Carson. Reprinted by permission of Oxford University Press, Inc.

Shirley Chisholm, "Women and Their Liberation" from *Unbought and Unbossed,* published by Houghton Mifflin Company. Copyright © 1970 by Shirley Chisholm. Reprinted by permission.

Malcolm Cowley, "Examination Paper" and "The Long Furlough." From *Exile's Return* by Malcolm Cowley. Reprinted 1934, 1935, 1941, 1951 © renewed 1962, 1963 by Malcolm Cowley. Reprinted by permission of Viking Penguin Inc.

Joan Didion, "On Keeping a Notebook" from *Slouching Towards Bethlehem* by Joan Didion. Reprinted by permission of Farrar, Straus & Giroux, Inc. Copyright © 1966 by Joan Didion.

Annie Dillard, "A Field of Silence." Reprinted by permission of the author and her agent, Blanche C. Gregory, Inc. Copyright © 1978 by Annie Dillard.

Loren Eiseley, "The Illusion of the Two Cultures." Copyright © 1978 by the estate of Loren Eiseley. Reprinted by permission of Times Books, a division of Quadrangle/The New York Times Book Co., Inc. from *The Star Thrower* by Loren Eiseley.

William Faulkner, Nobel Prize Award Speech. Reprinted from *The Faulkner Reader*. Copyright 1954 by William Faulkner (Random House, Inc.). By permission of the publisher.

E. M. Forster, "Art for Art's Sake." Copyright 1949 by E. M. Forster; renewed 1977 by Donald M. Parry. Reprinted from *Two Cheers for Democracy* by E. M. Forster by permission of Harcourt Brace Jovanovich, Inc.

Vicki Goldberg, "The Undressed Man." © 1979 by Vicki Goldberg. Originally published in Saturday Review.

Germaine Greer, "The Stereotype" from *The Female Eunuch* by Germaine Greer. Copyright © 1970, 1971 by Germaine Greer. Reprinted by permission of McGraw-Hill Book Company.

Aldous Huxley, "Madness, Badness, Sadness" from pp. 299–308 from *Collected Essays of Aldous Huxley*. Copyright © 1956 by Aldous Huxley. Reprinted by permission of Harper & Row, Publishers, Inc.

Ada Louise Huxtable, "The Queens that Ruled Seas and Set Styles," © 1980 by The New York Times Company. Reprinted by permission.

Jane Jacobs, "The Uses of Sidewalks: Contact," from *The Death and Life of Great American Cities,* by Jane Jacobs. Copyright © 1961 by Jane Jacobs. Reprinted by permission of Random House, Inc.

Alfred Kazin, "Epilogue 1945" from *Starting Out In the Thirties,* © Alfred Kazin. Reprinted by permission of the author.

Helen Keller, "Three Days to See." Copyright © by The Atlantic Monthly Company, Boston, Mass. Reprinted with permission.

Martin Luther King, Jr., "Letter From Birmingham Jail—April 16, 1963" from *Why We Can't Wait* by Martin Luther King, Jr. Copyright © 1963 by Martin Luther King, Jr. Reprinted by permission of Harper & Row, Publishers, Inc.

Niccolo Machiavelli, "The Morals of the Prince." Reprinted by permission of

H. L. Mencken, "The Incomparable Buzz-Saw," Copyright 1920 by Alfred A. Knopf, Inc. and renewed 1948 by H. L. Mencken. Reprinted from *A Mencken Chrestomathy*. Edited and annotated by H. L. Mencken, by permission of Alfred A. Knopf, Inc.

Jessica Mitford, "Women in Cages," Copyright © 1972 by Jessica Mitford. Reprinted from *Kind and Usual Punishment: The Prison Business*, by Jessica Mitford, by permission of Alfred A. Knopf, Inc.

Michel Eyquem de Montaigne, "It is Folly to Measure the True and False by Our Own Capacity" from *The Complete Works of Montaigne: Essays, Journal, Letters* translated by Donald M. Frame with the permission of the publishers, Stanford University Press. Copyright © 1943 by Donald M. Frame. © 1957 by the Board of Trustees of the Leland Stanford Junior University.

Michel Eyquem de Montaigne, "Of Idleness," (same credit as immediately preceding entry.)

Joyce Carol Oates, "New Heaven and Earth." Reprinted by permission of the author and her agency, Blanche C. Gregory, Inc. Copyright © 1972 by Joyce Carol Oates.

George Orwell, "Politics and the English Language" from *Shooting An Elephant and Other Essays* by George Orwell, copyright 1950 by Sonia Brownell Orwell; renewed 1978 by Sonia Pitt-Rivers. Reprinted by permission of Harcourt Brace Jovanovich, Inc.

Katherine Anne Porter, "The Necessary Enemy" excerpted from the book *The Collected Essays and Occasional Writings of Katherine Anne Porter.* Copyright © 1948 by Katherine Anne Porter/originally published in Mademoiselle as "Love and Hate." Reprinted by permission of Delacorte Press/Seymour Lawrence.

Reynolds Price, "The Heroes of Our Times," appeared in Saturday Review, December 1978.

Mario Puzo, "Meet Me Tonight in Dreamland" reprinted by permission of Candida Donadio & Assoc., Inc. Copyright © 1979 by Mario Puzo.

Bertrand Russell, "Functions of a Teacher" from *Unpopular Essays*. Copyright © 1950 by Bertrand Russell. Reprinted by permission of Simon & Schuster, a Division of Gulf & Western Corporation.

Tom Wolfe, "Mauve Gloves & Madmen, Clutter & Vine" from *Mauve Gloves & Madmen, Clutter & Vine* by Tom Wolfe. Copyright © 1975 by Tom Wolfe. Reprinted by permission of Farrar, Straus and Giroux, Inc.

Virginia Woolf, "Professions for Women" and "Death of the Moth," from *The Death of the Moth and Other Essays* by Virginia Woolf, copyright 1942 by Harcourt Brace Jovanovich, Inc.; copyright 1970 by Marjorie T. Parsons, Executrix. Reprinted by permission of the publisher.

# Preface

In compiling this anthology of short, nonfiction works, I have tried to illustrate and define a literary form: the essay. Since Montaigne first published his *Essais,* or trials, in 1580, the essay has been with us as a staple of prose. In all probability, the production of essays outnumbers, especially today, that of all the other genres of literature, and the student of composition usually encounters and experiments with the essay form before he or she ventures into the regions of fiction, poetry, or drama. It is a natural beginning. The essay is primarily an expression of personal opinion and depends less for its effect on wide research and deep, mature understanding of humanity than do other brands of writing. At the same time, the essay does involve the fundamentals of the writer's craft: organization, diction, tone, description, narration, argument, and exposition. And no one will argue that research and understanding endanger the essay writer's success. I firmly believe the essay form deserves close examination and that its practitioners are worthy of emulation, particularly in the case of anyone setting out to improve his or her writing capability.

This collection contains 102 essays that range from classical Greek models to contemporary commentary. Forty-one of the selections were written before 1900. They represent major authors and works in the history of the genre's development. British and American authors predominate in the collection because the craft of their prose is not distorted by the interpretations of translators. But I have included selections from the classical and continental traditions for their intrinsic interest and their significance to contemporary and historical authors, who frequently allude to them. The essays vary from 300 to 10,000 words. Twenty essays are less than 1,000 words long and should prove readily comprehensible to the reader beginning a study of the essay form. Twenty essays are longer than 4,000 words. They offer the challenge of extended discussion. Of the rest of the works included, the majority fall between 1,500 and 3,500 words, lengths readers may expect to find in most of today's periodical literature.

I have arranged the essays alphabetically by authors. The method recommends itself as the least prescriptive and the most convenient; works can be located easily, and authors represented by more than one selection are not dismembered according to rhetorical categories or publication dates. For those who want to approach the essay historically or theoretically, I have provided secondary tables of contents, one chronological and one rhetorical. The latter indicates a major form of development used in a given selection, but the classifications are necessarily arbitrary. Inevitably, some pieces fit as well into one category as another, but the division does suggest openings for discussion and analysis of the ways an essay can be organized.

For convenience, I have used the conventional rhetorical classes of exposition, argument, narration, and description. The student of composition who learns to recognize and discuss these classifications will appreciate the essays more fully and will better understand the author's strategy that controls each selection. From appreciating an author's strategy to implementing a strategy of one's own is a rational development in the process of writing.

Brief biographical and critical headnotes to each essay introduce the author and indicate the focus and rhetorical method of the work. The suggestions for discussion and writing that follow each essay direct attention to the rhetorical principles and devices used in it. Some questions and comments involve two works by the same author; some refer to other essays treating the same or similar themes and ideas; and some encourage the recognition of other essays using similar methods of development, rhetorical devices, and points of view. For unfamiliar allusions, foreign phrases, and unusual vocabulary, I have provided textual notes. The reader is advised, however, to have a dictionary at hand. A glossary of rhetorical terms is also included.

I hope the material in this collection will be a source of pleasure and interest. The ideas and rhetorical skills of these authors will reward their discovery. They should, moreover, be taken as guides and stimuli to one's own writing that shows increasing skill, power, and ease.

# PERSONAL ACKNOWLEDGMENTS

I should like to thank President Edmond L. Volpe, College of Staten Island, City University of New York, and the Research Foundation of City University for the opportunity to undertake this project. I am grateful to Carl A. Barth, Russell K. Heiman, Robert E. Jackson, and Spencer Means for research and editorial assistance. Most of all, I owe a special debt of gratitude to D. Anthony English for his encouragement and sound editorial advice.

Michael F. Shugrue
*The College of Staten Island*

# Contents

# Chronological
# Contents

# Rhetorical
# Contents

The following arrangement of essays will suggest ways in which readers can approach the selections. The classifications are not, of course, rigid, and many selections might fit as easily into one category as another.

## EXPOSITION

Exposition is the most commonly used of the traditional four forms of discourse: exposition, argument, narration, and description. Expository writing sets out to present ideas in a clear, straightforward, objective manner.

The six most frequently used methods of development in expository writing are classification, example, definition, analysis, cause and effect, and comparison and contrast.

## ARGUMENT OR PERSUASION

Argument attempts to persuade a reader to accept the writer's view-point or position. Logical argument appeals to the reason or intellect of the reader while persuasive argument appeals primarily to the reader's emotions. Logical argument uses three methods to develop a position: induction, deduction, and analogy.

# NARRATION

Narration tells a story or presents a sequence of events that occurred over a period of time. If the story is significant in itself, it is narration. If a story illustrates a point in exposition or argument, it may be called illustrative narration. If a story outlines a process step by step, it is designated as expository narration.

# DESCRIPTION

Description presents a factual information about an object or experience (objective description) or reports an impression or evaluation of an object or experience (subjective description).

# INTRODUCTION

Traditionally, the essay has been of moderate length, written in prose, and has presented a view based on the writer's thought and experience rather than on formal study. Usually, the essay depends less on fact than it does on the revelation of the author's point of view. By nature the essay is essentially tentative and discursive. The essayist, then, is a person speaking his or her mind, sometimes vigorously and argumentatively, sometimes wittily and personally.

The word "essay" became current in France in 1580 when Montaigne's highly personal reflections on individuals and their behavior were first published as *Essais* or trials. The word came into English in 1597 with the publication, under the title of *Essayes,* of Francis Bacon's aphoristic generalizations on the human condition.

During the seventeenth century in England, two main currents marked the development of the essay. One preserved Montaigne's intention of conveying a moment of personal reflection on a subject uppermost in the author's mind. Montaigne's truly discursive method was frankly personal and frequently autobiographical, quoted aptly from classical as well as modern writers, and used anecdotes, witticisms, and aphoristic moralizing. The other current in the century, derived in part from Bacon, pursued general human truth and sought to enlighten readers morally. The range of the essay extended from imitations of Montaigne's intimate, informal, and graceful essays to models of Bacon's dogmatic, formal, and expository pieces. By 1665, in one of many commentaries on the essay as a form, Ralph Johnson in his *Scholar's Guide* could describe the essay as "a short discourse about any virtue, vice, or other commonplace."

Neoclassical interest in England in such forms as the Platonic dialogue, the *Meditations* of Marcus Aurelius, and the character

1

sketches of Theophrastus, well-known in the ancient world, also contributed to the development of the essay form. Although there were some notable poetic essays, such as Alexander Pope's "An Essay on Criticism" and "An Essay on Man," the essay was, from the beginning, primarily a prose form. In the eighteenth century, the rise of journalism and the increase in periodical literature helped to spread and popularize the essay. Even today, in fact, most of the essays we encounter appear in the daily newspapers and magazines we read.

The eighteenth century produced notable essayists writing for the journals and magazines of the day. In their *Tatler* and *Spectator* papers, Joseph Addison and Richard Steele provided an opportunity to study the familiar essay in all its variety, subtlety and permanently delightful form. Other outstanding periodical essayists in the period included Henry Fielding, Oliver Goldsmith, Dr. Samuel Johnson, and Jonathan Swift.

In the nineteenth century, popular essayists like Charles Lamb and William Hazlitt continued to give vitality and personal style to the familiar essay. Other essayists, like Matthew Arnold, Thomas Carlyle, Thomas Huxley, and Thomas Macaulay, wrote more seriously and at greater length about the conduct and responsibilities of men and women. Their thoughtful, extended essays on such subjects as education became models for later serious essayists.

In America, the work of authors like Washington Irving proved to their contemporaries in the United States and abroad that writing by an American could be as charming and worthwhile as writing by anyone else. Men and women like Ralph Waldo Emerson, Margaret Fuller, Abraham Lincoln, and Henry David Thoreau showed their ability to express subtly penetrating ideas with persuasive directness in the essay form.

The essay has remained a vital literary form in our own century. Such outstanding stylists as E. B. White, for example, have demonstrated the essayist's ability to say complicated things simply and personally. As readers, our best continuing allegiance has been given to essayists who write seriously on matters that concern us. Martin Luther King's pleas for civil rights and Germaine Greer's keen perceptions about women's liberation continue to interest and challenge readers of the essay.

Even the modern essayist ordinarily develops an idea or captures an experience by using one or more of the traditional forms of discourse.

Exposition is the most commonly used of the traditional four forms of discourse: exposition, argument, narration, and description. Expository writing sets out to present ideas in a clear, straightforward, objective manner. The six most commonly used methods of development in expository writing are classification, example, definition, analysis, cause and effect, and comparison and contrast. The *Glossary* in this volume will explain their methods of development in greater detail.

Argument attempts to persuade a reader to accept the writer's viewpoint or position. Logical argument appeals to the reason or intellect of the reader while persuasive argument appeals primarily to the reader's emotions. Logical argument uses three methods to develop a position: induction, deduction, and analogy.

Narration tells a story or presents a sequence of events which occurred over a period of time. If the story is significant in itself, it is narration. If a story illustrates a point in exposition or argument, it may be called illustrative narration. If a story outlines a process step-by-step, it is designated as expository narration.

Description presents factual information about an object or experience (objective description) or reports an impression or evaluation of an object or experience (subjective description).

These methods of development help the essayist shape ideas. The writer also often uses figurative language (similes and metaphors, for example), literary and historical allusions, and other rhetorical devices to add interest and richness to a selection.

A reader who is aware of the rhetorical techniques used by an essayist will be able to understand and appreciate more fully the ideas and emotions expressed in a piece of writing. Thoughtful analysis and class discussion can also help the student writer make wise decisions about how best to organize and present his or her ideas and experiences.

The following essays, then, are presented in order to introduce the reader to significant essayists and essays, to foster careful analysis of the essay as a literary form, and to stimulate student writing.

# HENRY ADAMS

## The Dynamo and the Virgin

Henry Adams (1893-1918) was the grandson of President John Quincy Adams and the great grandson of President John Adams. A diplomat, historian, and man of letters, he published the *History of the United States During the Administrations of Jefferson and Madison* (1889-1891). The masterpieces of his later years, which outline his theory of historical change, are *Mont-Saint-Michel and Chartres* (1904) and *The Education of Henry Adams* (privately printed in 1906), from which "The Dynamo and the Virgin" is taken.

In this famous chapter, filled with historical allusions, Adams contemplates the mechanical devices displayed at the Great Exposition in Paris in 1900. He finds in the power and energy of the dynamo a potent new force which reminds him of the power the symbol of the Virgin Mary exercised in earlier centuries in Europe.

Until the Great Exposition of 1900 closed its doors in November, Adams haunted it, aching to absorb knowledge, and helpless to find it. He would have liked to know how much of it could have been grasped by the best-informed man in the world. While he was thus meditating chaos, Langley[1] came by, and showed it to him. At Langley's behest, the Exhibition dropped its superfluous rags and stripped itself to the skin, for Langley knew what to study, and why, and how; while Adams might as well have stood outside in the night, staring at the Milky Way. Yet Langley said nothing new, and taught nothing that one might not have learned from Lord Bacon,[2] three hundred

---

[1] Samuel P. Langley (1834-1906) was an American astrophysicist.
[2] Francis Bacon (1561-1626), an English philosopher of science, wrote *The Advancement of Learning* (1605).

years before; but though one should have known the "Advancement of Science" as well as one knew the "Comedy of Errors," the literary knowledge counted for nothing until some teacher should show how to apply it. Bacon took a vast deal of trouble in teaching King James I and his subjects, American or other, towards the year 1620, that true science was the development or economy of forces; yet an elderly American in 1900 knew neither the formula nor the forces; or even so much as to say to himself that his historical business in the Exposition concerned only the economies or developments of force since 1893, when he began the study at Chicago.

Nothing in education is so astonishing as the amount of ignorance it accumulates in the form of inert facts. Adams had looked at most of the accumulations of art in the storehouses called Art Museums; yet he did not know how to look at the art exhibits of 1900. He had studied Karl Marx and his doctrines of history with profound attention, yet he could not apply them at Paris. Langley, with the ease of a great master of experiment, threw out of the field every exhibit that did not reveal a new application of force, and naturally threw out, to begin with, almost the whole art exhibit. Equally, he ignored almost the whole industrial exhibit. He led his pupil directly to the forces. His chief interest was in new motors to make his airship feasible, and he taught Adams the astonishing complexities of the new Daimler motor, and of the automobile, which, since 1893, had become a nightmare at a hundred kilometres an hour, almost as destructive as the electric tram which was only ten years older; and threatening to become as terrible as the locmotive steam-engine itself, which was almost exactly Adams's own age.

Then he showed his scholar the great hall of dynamos, and explained how little he knew about electricity or force of any kind, even of his own special sun, which spouted heat in inconceivable volume, but which, as far as he knew, might spout less or more, at any time, for all the certainty he felt in it. To him, the dynamo itself was but an ingenious channel for conveying somewhere the heat latent in a few tons of poor coal hidden in a dirty engine-house carefully kept out of sight; but to Adams the dynamo became a symbol of infinity. As he grew accustomed to the great gallery of machines, he began to feel the forty-foot dynamos as a moral force, much as the early Christians felt the Cross. The planet itself seemed less impressive, in its old-fashioned, deliberate, annual or daily revolution, than this huge wheel, revolving within arm's-length at some vertiginous speed, and barely murmuring—scarcely humming an audible warning to stand a hair's-breadth further for respect of power—while it would not wake the baby lying close against its frame. Before the end, one began to pray to it; inherited instinct taught the natural expression of man before silent and infinite force. Among the thousand symbols of ultimate energy, the dynamo was not so human as some, but it was the most expensive.

Yet the dynamo, next to the steam-engine, was the most familiar of exhibits. For Adams's objects its value lay chiefly in its occult mechanism. Between the dynamo in the gallery of machines and engine-house outside, the break of continuity amounted to abysmal fracture for a historian's objects. No more relation could he discover between the steam and the electric current than between the Cross and the cathedral. The forces were interchangeable if not reversible, but he could see only an absolute *fiat* in electricity as in faith. Langley could not help him. Indeed, Langley seemed to be worried by the same trouble, for he constantly repeated that the new forces were anarchical, and specially that he was not responsible for the new rays, that were little short of parricidal in their wicked spirit towards science. His own rays, with which he had doubled the solar spectrum, were altogether harmless and beneficent; but Radium denied its God—or, what was to Langley the same thing, denied the truths of his Science. The force was wholly new.

A historian who asked only to learn enough to be as futile as Langley or Kelvin,[3] made rapid progress under this teaching, and mixed himself up in the tangle of ideas until he achieved a sort of Paradise of ignorance vastly consoling to his fatigued senses. He wrapped himself in variations and rays which were new, and he would have hugged Marconi and Branly[4] had he met them, as he hugged the dynamo; while he lost his arithmetic in trying to figure out the equation between the discoveries and the economies of force. The economies, like the discoveries, were absolute, supersensual, occult; incapable of expression in horse-power. What mathematical equivalent could he suggest as the value of a Branly coherer? Frozen air, or the electric furnace, had some scale of measurement, no doubt, if somebody could invent a thermometer adequate to the purpose; but X-rays had played no part whatever in man's consciousness, and the atom itself had figured only as a fiction of thought. In these seven years man had translated himself into a new universe which had no common scale of measurement with the old. He had entered a supersensual world, in which he could measure nothing except by chance collisions of movements imperceptible to his senses, perhaps even imperceptible to his instruments, but perceptible to each other, and so to some known ray at the end of the scale. Langley seemed prepared for anything, even for an indeterminable number of universes interfused—physics stark mad in metaphysics.

[3] William Thomson, Lord Kelvin (1824–1907), was a British physicist.
[4] Guglielmo Marconi (1874–1937) invented the wireless telegraph. Edouard Branly (1846–1940) invented the first detector for radio waves.

Historians undertake to arrange sequences,—called stories, or histories—
assuming in silence a relation of cause and effect. These assumptions, hidden
in the depths of dusty libraries, have been astounding, but commonly unconscious and childlike; so much so, that if any captious critic were to drag them
to light, historians would probably reply, with one voice, that they had never
supposed themselves required to know what they were talking about. Adams,
for one, had toiled in vain to find out what he meant. He had even published
a dozen volumes of American history for no other purpose than to satisfy
himself whether, by the severest process of stating, with the least possible
comment, such facts as seemed sure, in such order as seemed rigorously consequent, he could fix for a familiar moment a necessary sequence of human
movement. The result has satisfied him as little as at Harvard College. Where
he saw sequence, other men saw something quite different, and no one saw
the same unit of measure. He cared little about his experiments and less about
his statesmen, who seemed to him quite as ignorant as himself and, as a rule,
no more honest; but he insisted on a relation of sequence, and if he could
not reach it by one method, he would try as many methods as science knew.
Satisfied that the sequence of men led to nothing and that the sequence of
their society could lead no further, while the mere sequence of time was
artificial, and the sequence of thought was chaos, he turned at last in the
sequence of force; and thus it happened that, after ten years' pursuit, he found
himself lying in the Gallery of Machines at the Great Exposition of 1900, his
historical neck broken by the sudden irruption of forces totally new.

Since no one else showed much concern, an elderly person without
other cares had no need to betray alarm. The year 1900 was not the first to
upset schoolmasters. Copernicus and Galileo[5] had broken many professorial
necks about 1600; Columbus had stood the world on its head towards 1500;
but the nearest approach to the revolution of 1900 was that of 310, when
Constantine set up the Cross. The rays that Langley disowned, as well as
those which he fathered, were occult, supersensual, irrational; they were a
revelation of mysterious energy like that of the Cross; they were what, in
terms of mediaeval science, were called immediate modes of the divine
substance.

The historian was thus reduced to his last resources. Clearly if he
was bound to reduce all these forces to a common value, this common value
could have no measure but that of their attraction of his own mind. He must

---

[5]Both Copernicus (1473-1543) and Galileo (1564-1642) taught that the earth revolved
around the sun.

treat them as they had been felt; as convertible, reversible, interchangeable attractions on thought. He made up his mind to venture it; he would risk translating rays into faith. Such a reversible process would vastly amuse a chemist, but the chemist could not deny that he, or some of his fellow physicists, could feel the force of both. When Adams was a boy in Boston, the best chemist in the place had probably never heard of Venus except by way of scandal, or of the Virgin except as idolatry; neither had he heard of dynamos or automobiles or radium; yet his mind was ready to feel the force of all, though the rays were unborn and the women were dead.

Here opened another totally new education, which promised to be by far the most hazardous of all. The knife-edge along which he must crawl, like Sir Lancelot in the twelfth century, divided two kingdoms of force which had nothing in common but attraction. They were as different as a magnet is from gravitation, supposing one knew what a magnet was, or gravitation, or love. The force of the Virgin was still felt at Lourdes, and seemed to be as potent as X-rays; but in America neither Venus nor Virgin ever had value as force—at most as sentiment. No American had ever been truly afraid of either.

This problem in dynamics gravely perplexed an American historian. The Woman had once been supreme; in France she still seemed potent, not merely as a sentiment, but as a force. Why was she unknown in America? For evidently America was ashamed of her, and she was ashamed of herself, otherwise they would not have strewn fig-leaves so profusely all over her. When she was a true force, she was ignorant of fig-leaves, but the monthly-magazine-made American female had not a feature that would have been recognized by Adam. The trait was notorious, and often humorous, but any one brought up among Puritans knew that sex was sin. In any previous age, sex was strength. Neither art nor beauty was needed. Every one, even among Puritans, knew that neither Diana or the Ephesians nor any of the Oriental goddesses was worshipped for her beauty. She was goddess because of her force; she was the animated dynamo; she was reproduction—the greatest and most mysterious of all energies; all she needed was to be fecund. Singularly enough, not one of Adams' many schools of education had ever drawn his attention to the opening lines of Lucretius, though they were perhaps the finest in all Latin literature, where the poet invoked Venus exactly as Dante invoked the Virgin:—

"Quae quoniam rerum naturam *sola* gubernas."
Since thou alone govern the nature of things

The Venus of Epicurean philosophy survived in the Virgin of the Schools:—

"Donna, sei tanto grande, e tanto vali,
Che qual vuol grazia, e a te non ricorre,
Sua disianza vuol volar senz' ali."
Lady, thou art so great in all things
That he who wishes grace and seeks not thee,
Would have his wish fly upwards without wings.

All this was to American thought as though it had never existed. The true American knew something of the facts, but nothing of the feelings; he read the letter, but he never felt the law. Before this historical chasm, a mind like that of Adams felt itself helpless; he turned from the Virgin to the Dynamo as though he were a Branly coherer. One one side, at the Louvre and at Chartres, as he knew by the record of work actually done and still before his eyes, was the highest energy ever known to man, the creator of four-fifths of his noblest art, exercising vastly more attraction over the human mind than all the steam-engines and dynamos ever dreamed of; and yet this energy was unknown to the American mind. An American Virgin would never dare command; an American Venus would never dare exist.

The question, which to any plain American of the nineteenth century seemed as remote as it did to Adams, drew him almost violently to study, once it was posed; and on this point Langleys were as useless as though they were Herbert Spencers[6] or dynamos. The idea survived only as art. There one turned as naturally as though the artist were himself a woman. Adams began to ponder, asking himself whether he knew of an American artist who had ever insisted on the power of sex, as every classic had always done; but he could think only of Walt Whitman; Bret Harte, as far as the magazines would let him venture; and one or two painters, for the flesh-tones. All the rest had used sex for sentiment, never for force; to them, Eve was a tender flower, and Herodias[7] an unfeminine horror. American art, like the American language and American education, was as far as possible sexless. Society regarded this victory over sex as its greatest triumph, and the historian readily admitted it, since the moral issue, for the moment, did not concern one who was studying the relations of unmoral force. He cared nothing for the sex of the dynamo until he could measure its energy.

Vaguely seeking a clue, he wandered through the art exhibit, and, in his

[6] Herbert Spenser (1820–1903) was a British philosopher.
[7] Herodias, the wife of King Herod, caused the death of John the Baptist.

stroll, stopped almost every day before St. Gaudens's General Sherman,[8] which had been given the central post of honor. St. Gaudens himself was in Paris, putting on the work his usual interminable last touches, and listening to the usual contradictory suggestions of brother sculptors. Of all the American artists who gave to American art whatever life it breathed in the seventies, St. Gaudens was perhaps the most sympathetic, but certainly the most inarticulate. General Grant or Don Cameron had scarcely less instinct of rhetoric than he. All the others—the Hunts, Richardson, John La Farge, Stanford White—were exuberant; only St. Gaudens could never discuss or dilate on an emotion, or suggest artistic arguments for giving to his work the forms that he felt. He never laid down the law, or affected the despot, or became brutalized like Whistler by the brutalities of his world. He required no incense; he was no egoist; his simplicity of thought was excessive; he could not imitate, or give any form but his own to the creations of his hand. No one felt more strongly than he the strength of other men, but the idea that they could affect him never stirred an image in his mind.

This summer his health was poor and his spirits were low. For such a temper, Adams was not the best companion, since his own gaiety was not *folle;* [crazy]; but he risked going now and then to the studio on Mont Parnasse to draw him out for a stroll in the Bois de Boulogne, or dinner as pleased his moods, and in return St. Gaudens sometimes let Adams go about in his company.

Once St. Gaudens took him down to Amiens, with a party of Frenchmen, to see the cathedral. Not until they found themselves actually studying the sculpture of the western portal, did it dawn on Adams's mind that, for his purposes, St. Gaudens on that spot had more interest to him than the cathedral itself. Great men before great monuments express great truths, provided they are not taken too solemnly. Adams never tired of quoting the supreme phrase of his idol Gibbon[9] before the Gothic cathedrals: "I darted a contemptuous look on the stately monuments of superstition." Even in the footnotes of his history, Gibbon had never inserted a bit of humor more human than this, and one would have paid largely for a photograph of the fat little historian, on the background of Notre Dame of Amiens, trying to persuade his readers—perhaps himself—that he was darting a contemptuous look on the stately monument, for which he felt in fact the respect which every man

---

[8] August Saint-Gaudens (1848-1907) was a famous American sculptor. Adams mentions other prominent American artists and architects.
[9] Edward Gibbon (1737-1794) wrote *The Decline and Fall of the Roman Empire* (1776-1788).

of his vast study and active mind always feels before objects worthy of it; but besides the humor, one felt also the relation. Gibbon ignored the Virgin, because in 1789 religious monuments were out of fashion. In 1900 his remark sounded fresh and simple as the green fields to ears that had heard a hundred years of other remarks, mostly no more fresh and certainly less simple. Without malice, one might find it more instructive than a whole lecture of Ruskin.[10] One sees what one brings, and at that moment Gibbon brought the French Revolution. Ruskin brought reaction against the Revolution. St. Gaudens had passed beyond all. He liked the stately monuments much more than he liked Gibbon or Ruskin; he loved their dignity; their unity; their scale; their lines; their lights and shadows; their decorative sculpture; but he was even less conscious than they of the force that created it all—the Virgin, the Woman—by whose genius "the stately monuments of superstition" were built, through which she was expressed. He would have seen more meaning in Isis[11] with the cow's horns, at Edfoo, who expressed the same thought. The art remained, but the energy was lost even upon the artist.

Yet in mind and person St. Gaudens was a survival of the 1500's; he bore the stamp of the Renaissance, and should have carried an image of the Virgin round his neck, or stuck in his hat, like Louis XI. In mere time he was a lost soul that had strayed by chance into the twentieth century, and forgotten where it came from. He writhed and cursed at his ignorance, much as Adams did at his own, but in the opposite sense. St. Gaudens was a child of Benvenuto Cellini[12] smothered in an American cradle. Adams was a quintessence of Boston, devoured by curiosity to think like Benvenuto. St. Gaudens's art was starved from birth, and Adams's instinct was blighted from babyhood. Each had but half of a nature, and when they came together before the Virgin of Amiens they ought both to have felt in her the force that made them one; but it was not so. To Adams she became more than ever a channel of force; to St. Gaudens she remained as before a channel of taste.

For a symbol of power, St. Gaudens instinctively preferred the horse, as was plain in his horse and Victory of the Sherman monument. Doubtless Sherman also felt it so. The attitude was so American that, for at least forty years, Adams had never realized that any other could be in sound taste. How many years had he taken to admit a notion of what Michael Angelo and Rubens were driving at? He could not say; but he knew that only since 1895 had he begun to feel the Virgin or Venus as force, and not everywhere even

[10] John Ruskin (1819–1900) was an English art critic.
[11] Isis was an Egyptian fertility goddess whose statue stood at Edfu.
[12] Benvenuto Cellini (1500–1571) was an Italian Renaissance sculptor.

so. At Chartres—perhaps at Lourdes—possibly at Cnidos if one could still find there the divinely naked Aphrodite of Praxiteles—but otherwise one must look for force to the goddesses of Indian mythology. The idea died out long ago in the German and English stock. St. Gaudens at Amiens was hardly less sensitive to the force of the female energy than Matthew Arnold at the Grande Chartreuse.[13] Neither of them felt goddesses as power—only as reflected emotion, human expression, beauty, purity, taste, scarcely even as sympathy. They felt a railway train as power; yet they, and all other artists, constantly complained that the power embodied in a railway train could never be embodied in art. All the steam in the world could not, like the Virgin, build Chartres.

Yet in mechanics, whatever the mechanicians might think, both energies acted as interchangeable forces on man, and by action on man all known force may be measured. Indeed, few men of science measured force in any other way. After once admitting that a straight line was the shortest distance between two points, no serious mathematician cared to deny anything that suited his convenience, and rejected no symbol, unproved or unproveable, that helped him to accomplish work. The symbol was force, as a compass-needle or a triangle was force, as the mechanist might prove by losing it, and nothing could be gained by ignoring their value. Symbol or energy, the Virgin had acted as the greatest force the Western world ever felt, and had drawn man's activities to herself more strongly than any other power, natural or supernatural, had ever done; the historian's business was to follow the track of the energy; to find where it came from and where it went to; its complex source and shifting channels; its values, equivalents, conversions. It could scarcely be more complex than radium; it could hardly be deflected, diverted, polarized, absorbed more perplexingly than other radiant matter. Adams knew nothing about any of them, but as a mathematical problem of influence on human progress, though all were occult, all reacted on his mind, and he rather inclined to think the Virgin easiest to handle.

The pursuit turned out to be long and tortuous, leading at last into the vast forests of scholastic science. From Zeno[14] to Descartes, hand in hand with Thomas Aquinas, Montaigne, and Pascal, one stumbled as stupidly as though one were still a German student in 1860. Only with the instinct of despair could one force one's self into this old thicket of ignorance after

---

[13] Matthew Arnold (1822-1888) was an English poet and critic who wrote "Stanzas from the Grand Chartreuse" (1855).

[14] Adams lists famous philosophers and writers whose works he had studied: Zeno (fifth century B.C.), Descartes (1596-1650), St. Thomas Aquinas (1225?-1274), Montaigne (1533-1592), and Pascal (1623-1662).

having been repulsed at a score of entrances more promising and more popular. Thus far, no path had led anywhere, unless perhaps to an exceedingly
modest living. Forty-five years of study had proved to be quite futile for the
pursuit of power; one controlled no more force in 1900 than in 1850, although the amount of force controlled by society had enormously increased.
The secret of education still hid itself somewhere behind ignorance, and one
fumbled over it as feebly as ever. In such labyrinths, the staff is a force almost
more necessary than the legs; the pen becomes a sort of blindman's dog, to
keep him from falling into the gutters. The pen works for itself and acts like
a hand, modelling the plastic material over and over again to the form that
suits it best. The form is never arbitrary, but is a sort of growth like crystallization, as any artist knows too well; for often the pencil or pen runs into
side-paths and shapelessness, loses its relations, stops or is bogged. Then it
has to return on its trail, and recover, if it can, its line of force. The result of
a year's work depends more on what is struck out than on what is left in; on
the sequence of the main lines of thought, than on their play or variety. Compelled once more to lean heavily on this support, Adams covered more thousands of pages with figures as formal as though they were algebra, laboriously
striking out, altering, burning, experimenting, until the year had expired, the
Exposition had long been closed, and winter drawing to its end, before he
sailed from Cherbourg, on January 19, 1901, for home.

I. **Suggestions for Discussion:**
   1. Why did the dynamo become a "symbol of infinity" for Adams?
   2. What was the role of the Virgin Mary in medieval Europe? According
      to Adams, why has she never played a similar role in the United
      States?
   3. What roles do Samuel Langley and Augustus Saint-Gaudens play in the
      education of Henry Adams? How does he characterize them?
II. **Suggestions for Writing:**
   1. Describe what impressed you most about a local, state, or international
      fair you have visited.
   2. Write an essay agreeing or disagreeing with Adams's assertion that
      American education, is as far as possible sexless. Was that observation
      more true in his time than it is in ours?

# JOSEPH ADDISON

## Tatler 249—The Adventures of a Shilling

Joseph Addison (1672-1719) had a distinguished career as a statesman, classical scholar, and man of letters in eighteenth-century England. During a career as diplomat, member of Parliament, and eventually secretary of state, he published poetry (*The Campaign* in 1704), tragedy (*Cato* in 1713), and the essays for which he is best known in the *Tatler* and *Spectator* periodical papers.

In the following essay, a conversation with a friend leads Addison to narrate a dream about the picaresque adventures that might have befallen an English coin in the seventeenth and eighteenth centuries.

No. 249. Saturday, Nov. 11, 1710.

> Per varios casus, per tot discrimina rerum, Tendimus . . .
> Through various hazards and events we move.
> —Virgil, *Æneid,* I, 204.

*From my own Apartment, Nov. 10.*

I was last night visited by a friend of mine who has an inexhaustible fund of discourse, and never fails to entertain his company with a variety of thoughts and hints that are altogether new and uncommon. Whether it were in complaisance to my way of living, or his real opinion, he advanced the following paradox, that it required much greater talents to fill up and become a retired life than a life of business. Upon this occasion he rallied very agreeably the busy men of the age, who only valued themselves for being in motion, and passing through a series of trifling and insignificant actions. In the heat of his discourse, seeing a piece of money lying on my table, "I defy," says he, "any of these active persons to produce half the adventures that this twelve-penny-piece has been engaged in, were it possible for him to give us an account of his life."

My friend's talk made so odd an impression upon my mind, that soon after I was a-bed I fell insensibly into a most unaccountable reverie, that had neither moral nor design in it, and cannot be so properly called a dream as a delirium.

Methought the shilling that lay upon the table reared itself upon its edge, and turning the face towards me, opened its mouth, and in a soft silver sound gave me the following account of his life and adventures:

"I was born," says he, "on the side of a mountain, near a little village of Peru, and made a voyage to England in an ingot, under the convoy of Sir Francis Drake. I was, soon after my arrival, taken out of my Indian habit, refined, naturalised, and put into the British mode, with the face of Queen Elizabeth on one side, and the arms of the country on the other. Being thus equipped, I found in me a wonderful inclination to ramble, and visit all the parts of the new world into which I was brought. The people very much favoured my natural disposition, and shifted me so fast from hand to hand, that before I was five years old, I had travelled into almost every corner of the nation. But in the beginning of my sixth year, to my unspeakable grief, I fell into the hands of a miserable old fellow, who clapped me into an iron chest, where I found five hundred more of my own quality who lay under the same confinement. The only relief we had, was to be taken out and counted over in the fresh air every morning and evening. After an imprisonment of several years, we heard somebody knocking at our chest, and breaking it open with a hammer. This we found was the old man's heir, who, as his father lay a-dying, was so good as to come to our release: he separated us that very day. What was the fate of my companions, I know not: as for myself, I was sent to the apothecary's shop for a pint of sack. The apothecary gave me to an herb-woman, the herb-woman to a butcher, the butcher to a brewer, and the brewer to his wife, who made a present of me to a nonconformist preacher. After this manner I made my way merrily through the world; for, as I told you before, we shillings love nothing so much as travelling. I sometimes fetched in a shoulder of mutton, sometimes a play-book, and often had the satisfaction to treat a Templar[1] at a twelvepenny ordinary, or carry him with three friends to Westminster Hall.

"In the midst of this pleasant progress which I made from place to place, I was arrested by a superstitious old woman, who shut me up in a greasy purse, in pursuance of a foolish saying, that while she kept a Queen Elizabeth's shilling about her, she should never be without money. I continued here a close prisoner for many months, till at last I was exchanged for eight-and-forty farthings.

"I thus rambled from pocket to pocket till the beginning of the Civil

---

[1] Lawyers who went to the law courts in Westminster Hall.

Wars, when, to my shame be it spoken, I was employed in raising soldiers against the King; for being of a very tempting breadth, a sergeant made use of me to inveigle country fellows, and list them in the service of the Parliament.

"As soon as he had made one man sure, his way was to oblige him to take a shilling of a more homely figure, and then practise the same trick upon another. Thus I continued doing great mischief to the Crown, till my officer chancing one morning to walk abroad earlier than ordinary, sacrificed me to his pleasures, and made use of me to seduce a milkmaid. This wench bent me, and gave me to her sweetheart, applying more properly than she intended the usual form of, 'To my love and from my love.' This ungenerous gallant marrying her within few days after, pawned me for a dram of brandy, and drinking me out next day, I was beaten flat with a hammer, and again set a-running.

"After many adventures, which it would be tedious to relate, I was sent to a young spendthrift, in company with the will of his deceased father. The young fellow, who I found was very extravagant, gave great demonstrations of joy at the receiving the will; but opening it, he found himself disinherited and cut off from the possession of a fair estate, by virtue of my being made a present to him. This put him into such a passion, that after having taken me in his hand, and cursed me, he squirred me away from him as far as he could fling me. I chanced to light in an unfrequented place under a dead wall, where I lay undiscovered and useless during the usurpation of Oliver Cromwell.

"About a year after the King's return, a poor cavalier that was walking there about dinner-time fortunately cast his eye upon me, and, to the great joy of us both, carried me to a cook's-shop, where he dined upon me, and drank the King's health. When I came again into the world, I found that I had been happier in my retirement than I thought, having probably by that means escaped wearing a monstrous pair of breeches.[2]

"Being now of great credit and antiquity, I was rather looked upon as a medal than an ordinary coin; for which reason a gamester laid hold of me, and converted me to a counter, having got together some dozens of us for that use. We led a melancholy life in his possession, being busy at those hours wherein current coin is at rest, and partaking the fate of our master, being in a few moments valued at a crown, a pound, or a sixpence, according to the situation in which the fortune of the cards placed us. I had at length the good luck to see my master break, by which means I was again sent abroad under my primitive denomination of a shilling.

"I shall pass over many other accidents of less moment, and hasten to

---

[2] The shilling showing Oliver Cromwell had two shields commonly called breeches.

that fatal catastrophe when I fell into the hands of an artist, who conveyed me under ground, and with an unmerciful pair of shears cut off my titles, clipped my brims, retrenched my shape, rubbed me to my inmost ring, and, in short, so spoiled and pillaged me, that he did not leave me worth a groat. You may think what a confusion I was in to see myself thus curtailed and disfigured. I should have been ashamed to have shown my head, had not all my old acquaintance been reduced to the same shameful figure, excepting some few that were punched through the belly. In the midst of this general calamity, when everybody thought our misfortune irretrievable, and our case desperate, we were thrown into the furnace together, and (as it often happens with cities rising out of a fire) appeared with greater beauty and lustre than we could ever boast of before. What has happened to me since the change of sex[3] which you now see, I shall take some other opportunity to relate. In the meantime I shall only repeat two adventures, as being very extraordinary, and neither of them having ever happened to me above once in my life. The first was, my being in a poet's pocket, who was so taken with the brightness and novelty of my appearance, that it gave occasion to the finest burlesque poem in the British language, entitled from me, 'The Splendid Shilling.' The second adventure, which I must not omit, happened to me in the year 1703, when I was given away in charity to a blind man; but indeed this was by a mistake, the person who gave me having heedlessly thrown me into the hat among a pennyworth of farthings."

I. **Suggestions for Discussion:**
   1. Which of the adventures of the shilling do you find most amusing? Why?
   2. Demonstrate that Addison has a good eye for details.
   3. Why is some knowledge of English history in the seventeenth and eighteenth centuries valuable for an understanding of Addison's dream or reverie? Cite references which were not clear to you.
II. **Suggestions for Writing:**
   1. Narrate the adventures of a Susan B. Anthony dollar in the United States.
   2. Describe the physical appearance of any United States coin.

---

[3] The shilling now showed the head of King William III rather than the likeness of Elizabeth.

# RENATA ADLER

## The Movies Make Heroes of Them All

Renata Adler (1938–    ) is a well-known American journalist and film critic. In addition to articles and reviews in *The New Yorker* and the *New York Times,* she has published such books as *Toward a Radical Middle,* (1969), *Speedboat* (1976), and *A Year in the Dark* (1968), from which the present selection is taken.

Reviewing two films in the *New York Times,* she uses example to discuss the impact which screen violence has on viewers.

The motion picture is like journalism in that, more than any of the other arts, it confers celebrity. Not just on people—on acts, and objects, and places, and ways of life. The camera brings a kind of stardom to them all. I therefore doubt that film can ever argue effectively against its own material: that a genuine antiwar film, say, can be made on the basis of even the ugliest battle scenes; or that the brutal hangings in *The Dirty Dozen* and *In Cold Blood* will convert one soul from belief in capital punishment. No matter what film-makers intend, film always argues yes. People have been modeling their lives after films for years, but the medium is somehow unsuited to moral lessons, cautionary tales or polemics of any kind. If you want to make a pacifist film, you must make an exemplary film about peaceful men. Even cinema villains, criminals and ghouls become popular heroes overnight (a fact which *In Cold Blood,* more cynically than *The Dirty Dozen,* draws upon). Movies glamorize, or they fail to glamorize. They cannot effectively condemn—which means that they must have special terms for dealing with violence.

I do not think violence on the screen is a particularly interesting question, or that it can profitably be discussed as a single question at all. Every action is to some degree violent. But there are gradations, quite clear to any child who has ever awakened in terror in the night, which become blurred whenever violence is discussed as though it were one growing quantity, of which more or less might be simply better or worse. Violence to persons or animals on film (destruction of objects is really another matter) ranges along what I think is a cruelty scale from clean collision to protracted dismemberment. Clean collision, no matter how much there is of it, is completely innocent. It consists, normally, of a wind-up, a rush, and an impact or series of impacts; and it includes everything from pratfalls, through cartoon smashups, fistfights in westerns, simple shootings in war films, multiple shootings in gang films, machine gunnings, grenade throwings, bombings, and all manner of well-timed explosions. Most often, thorough and annihilating though it may be, a film collision has virtually no cruelty component at all. It is more closely related to contact sport than to murder, and perhaps most nearly akin, in its treatment of tension, to humor. I am sure that such violence has nothing to do with the real, that everyone instinctively knows it, and that the violence of impact is among the most harmless, important, and satisfying sequences of motion on film.

Further along the cruelty scale, however, are the individual, quiet, tidy forms of violence: poisonings and stranglings. Their actual violence component is low, they are bloodless but, as any haunted child knows, their cruelty component can be enormous. The tip-off is the sound track; abrupt, ingratiating, then suddenly loud, perhaps including maniacal laughter—the whole range of effects that the radio-and-cinema-conditioned ear recognizes as sinister—to approximate the nervous jolt of encounters with violence in reality. Further yet along the scale are the quick and messy murders with knives or other instruments (some uncharacteristically ugly impact scenes also fall into this category) and finally, the various protracted mutilations.

I do not know whether scenes of persons inflicting detailed and specific physical sufferings on other persons increase the sum of violence in the world. There are probably saints who dote upon amputations, and certainly sadists who cannot stand the sight of blood. But I think the following rules are true: violence on the screen becomes more cruel as it becomes more particular and individual; and it is bad in direct proportion to one's awareness of (even sympathy with) the detailed physical agonies of the victim. What this amounts to, of course, is a belief that films ought to be squeamish. In life, it is different: awareness of the particular consequences of acts is a moral responsibility and a deterrent to personal cruelty.

The difference between film and life on this point, I suppose, is this: that an audience is not responsible for the acts performed on screen—only for watching them. To be entertained by blasts, shots, blows, chairs breaking over heads, etc., is not unlike being entertained by chases, bass drums, or displays of fireworks; to be entertained by their biological consequences is another thing entirely. An example, again from *The Dirty Dozen:* in one scene, a demented soldier, rhythmically and with obvious pleasure, stabs a girl to death; in another, a chateau full of people is blown up by means of grenades dropped down gasoline-drenched air vents, and nearly everyone else is mowed down by machine-gun fire. In real life, or in ethics seminars, one person dying slowly is less monstrous than a hundred blowing sky high. Not so, I believe, on film, for none of the deaths was real, and only one was made cruel and personal. The style of the Armageddon was most like the style of an orchestra; the style of the stabbing was too much like violence in fact. And while I don't suppose that anyone will actually go out and emulate the stabbing, I don't think dwelling on pain or damage to the human body in the film's literal terms can ever be morally or artistically valid either. Physical suffering in itself is not edifying, movies celebrate, and scenes of cruel violence simply invite the audience to share in the camera'a celebration of one person's specific physical cruelties to another.

I. **Suggestions for Discussion:**
   1. When does Adler believe that violence on the screen is objectionable. Do you agree? Explain.
   2. Comment on her assertion that films ought to be "squeamish." Do you agree? Explain.
   3. How much do you learn about the two films that prompted her review? What more would you want to know in order to decide whether or not to see the films?
II. **Suggestions for Writing:**
   1. Discuss the violence in a recent film you have seen.
   2. Based on your own experience viewing films, argue for or against her notion that film is unsuited to moral lessons.

---

# WOODY ALLEN

## My Speech to the Graduates

---

Woody Allen (1935–      ), the American actor, comedian, director, film-maker, and writer, is best known for such outstanding films as *Annie Hall* (1977), *Interiors* (1978), and *Manhattan* (1979). His humorous essays have appeared in the *New York Times, The New Yorker,* and in such collections as *Getting Even* (1971) and *Without Feathers* (1975).

In the following parody of a commencement address, Allen faces
a world of gloom and chaos with humorous platitudes and endless
good will.

---

More than any other time in history, mankind faces a crossroads. One
path leads to despair and utter hopelessness. The other, to total extinction.
Let us pray we have the wisdom to choose correctly. I speak, by the way, not
with any sense of futility, but with a panicky conviction of the absolute
meaninglessness of existence which could easily be misinterpreted as pessi-
mism. It is not. It is merely a healthy concern for the predicament of modern
man. (Modern man is here defined as any person born after Nietzche's edict
that "God is dead," but before the hit recording "I Wanna Hold Your Hand.")
This "predicament" can be stated one of two ways, though certain linguistic
philosophers prefer to reduce it to a mathematical equation where it can be
easily solved and even carried around in the wallet.

Put in its simplest form, the problem is: How is it possible to find
meaning in a finite world given my waist and shirt size? This is a very difficult question when we realize that science has failed us. True, it has conquered many diseases, broken the genetic code, and even placed human
beings on the moon, and yet when a man of 80 is left in a room with two
18-year-old cocktail waitresses nothing happens. Because the real problems
never change. After all, can the human soul be glimpsed through a microscope? Maybe—but you'd definitely need one of those very good ones with
two eyepieces. We know that the most advanced computer in the world does
not have a brain as sophisticated as that of an ant. True, we could say that of
many of our relatives but we only have to put up with them at weddings or
special occasions. Science is something we depend on all the time. If I develop
a pain in the chest I must take an X-ray. But what if the radiation from the
X-ray causes me deeper problems? Before I know it, I'm going in for surgery.
Naturally, while they're giving me oxygen an intern decides to light up a cigarette. The next thing you know I'm rocketing over the World Trade Center in
bed clothes. Is this science? True, science has taught us how to pasteurize
cheese. And true, this can be fun in mixed company—but what of the H-
bomb? Have you ever seen what happens when one of those things falls off a
desk accidentally? And where is science when one ponders the eternal riddles? How did the cosmos originate? How long has it been around? Did
matter begin with an explosion or by the word of God? And if by the latter,
could He not have begun it just two weeks earlier to take advantage of some
of the warmer weather? Exactly what do we mean when we say, man is
mortal? Obviously it's not a compliment.

Religion too has unfortunately let us down. Miguel de Unamuno writes blithely of the "eternal persistence of consciousness," but this is no easy feat. Particularly when reading Thackery. I often think how comforting life must have been for early man because he believed in a powerful, benevolent Creator who looked after all things. Imagine his disappointment when he saw his wife putting on weight. Contemporary man, of course, has no such peace of mind. He finds himself in the midst of a crisis of faith. He is what we fashionably call "alienated." He has seen the ravages of war, he has known natural catastrophes, he has been to singles bars. My good friend Jacques Monod spoke often of the randomness of the cosmos. He believed everything in existence occurred by pure chance with the possible exception of his breakfast, which he felt certain was made by his housekeeper. Naturally belief in a divine intelligence inspires tranquility. But this does not free us from our human responsibilities. Am I my brother's keeper? Yes. Interestingly, in my case I share that honor with the Prospect Park Zoo. Feeling godless then, what we have done is made technology God. And yet can technology really be the answer when a brand new Buick, driven by my close associate, Nat Persky, winds up in the window of Chicken Delight causing hundreds of customers to scatter? My toaster has never once worked properly in four years. I follow the instructions and push two slices of bread down in the slots and seconds later they rifle upward. Once they broke the nose of a woman I loved very dearly. Are we counting on nuts and bolts and electricity to solve our problems? Yes, the telephone is a good thing—and the refrigerator—and the air conditioner. But not every air conditioner. Not my sister Henny's, for instance. Hers makes a loud noise and still doesn't cool. When the man comes over to fix it, it gets worse. Either that or he tells her she needs a new one. When she complains, he says not to bother him. This man is truly alienated. Not only is he alienated but he can't stop smiling.

The trouble is, our leaders have not adequately prepared us for a mechanized society. Unfortunately our politicians are either incompetent or corrupt. Sometimes both on the same day. The Government is unresponsive to the needs of the little man. Under five-seven, it is impossible to get your Congressman on the phone. I am not denying that democracy is still the finest form of government. In a democracy at least, civil liberties are upheld. No citizen can be wantonly tortured, imprisoned, or made to sit through certain Broadway shows. And yet this is a far cry from what goes on in the Soviet Union. Under their form of totalitarianism, a person merely caught whistling is sentenced to 30 years in a labor camp. If, after 15 years, he still will not stop whistling they shoot him. Along with this brutal fascism we find its handmaiden, terrorism. At no other time in history has man been so afraid to cut his veal chop for fear that it will explode. Violence breeds more violence and it is predicted that by 1990 kidnapping will be the dominant mode of social interaction. Overpopulation will exacerbate problems to the breaking point. Figures tell us there are already more people on earth than we need to move even the heaviest piano. If we do not call a halt to breeding, by the year 2000 there will be no room to serve dinner unless one is willing to set the table on the heads of strangers. Then they must not move for an hour while we eat. Of course energy will be in short supply and each car owner will be allowed only enough gasoline to back up a few inches.

Instead of facing these challenges we turn instead to distractions like drugs and sex. We live in far too permissive a society. Never before has pornography been this rampant. And those films are lit so badly! We are a people who lack defined goals. We have never learned to love. We lack leaders and coherent programs. We have no spiritual center. We are adrift alone in the cosmos wreaking monstrous violence on one another out of frustration and pain. Fortunately, we have not lost our sense of proportion. Summing up, it is clear the future holds great opportunities. It also holds pitfalls. The trick will be to avoid the pitfalls, seize the opportunities, and get back home by six o'clock.

I. **Suggestions for Discussion**:
   1. Discuss Allen's use of exaggeration and understatement as sources of humor.
   2. What real social problems does Allen address?
   3. Discuss the ways in which Allen's choice of allusion and vocabulary contribute to the effectiveness of his parody.

II. **Suggestions for Writing**:
   1. Write and deliver a humorous speech to your graduating class.
   2. Prepare and deliver a serious graduation address in which you identify two or three major social or personal problems facing today's graduates, and offer your solutions.

---

## ARISTOTLE

### From the Poetics

---

Aristotle (384–322 B.C.) studied at Athens under Plato and later tutored Alexander the Great. In such influential works as the

*Poetics* and the *Politics,* he discussed logic, moral philosophy, metaphysics, poetics, physics, zoology, politics, and rhetoric.

In this difficult and justly famous selection from the *Poetics,* Aristotle carefully defines the characteristics of a perfect tragedy.

---

. . . Tragedy, then, is an imitation of an action that is serious, complete, and of a certain magnitude; in language embellished with each kind of artistic ornament, the several kinds being found in separate parts of the play; in the form of action, not of narrative; through pity and fear effecting the proper purgation of these emotions. By 'language embellished,' I mean language into which rhythm, 'harmony,' and song enter. By 'the several kinds in separate parts,' I mean, that some parts are rendered through the medium of verse alone, others again with the aid of song.

Now as tragic imitation implies persons acting, it necessarily follows, in the first place, that Scenic equipment will be a part of Tragedy. Next, Song and Diction, for these are the means of imitation. By 'Diction' I mean the mere metrical arrangement of the words: as for 'Song,' it is a term whose full sense is well understood.

Again, Tragedy is the imitation of an action; and an action implies personal agents, who necessarily possess certain qualities both of character and thought. It is these that determine the qualities of actions themselves; these— thought and character—are the two natural causes from which actions spring: on these causes, again, all success or failure depends. Hence, the Plot is the imitation of the action—for by plot I here mean the arrangement of the incidents. By Character I mean that in virtue of which we ascribe certain qualities to the agents. By Thought, that whereby a statement is proved, or a general truth expressed. Every Tragedy, therefore, must have six parts, which parts determine its quality—namely, Plot, Character, Diction, Thought, Scenery, Song. Two of the parts constitute the means of imitation, one the manner, and three the objects of imitation. And these complete the list. These elements have been employed, we may say, by almost all poets; in fact, every play contains Scenic accessories as well as Character, Plot, Diction, Song, and Thought.

But most important of all is the structure of the incidents. For Tragedy is an imitation, not of men, but of an action and of life—of happiness and misery; and happiness and misery consist in action, the end of human life being a mode of action, not a quality. Now the characters of men determine their qualities, but it is by their actions that they are happy or the reverse.

Dramatic action, therefore, is not with a view to the representation of character: character comes in as subsidiary to the action. Hence the incidents and
the plot are the end of a tragedy; and the end is the chief thing of all. Again,
without action there cannot be a tragedy; there may be without character. . . .

These principles being established, let us now discuss the proper structure of the Plot, since this is the first, and also the most important part of
Tragedy.

Now, according to our definition, Tragedy is an imitation of an action,
that is complete, and whole, and of a certain magnitude; for there may be a
whole that is wanting in magnitude. A whole is that which has beginning,
middle, and end. A beginning is that which does not itself follow anything by
causal necessity, but after which something naturally is or comes to be. An
end, on the contrary, is that which itself naturally follows some other thing,
either by necessity, or in the regular course of events, but has nothing following it. A middle is that which follows something as some other thing follows
it. A well constructed plot, therefore, must neither begin nor end at haphazard, but conform to the type here described. . . .

Unity of plot does not, as some persons think, consist in the unity of
the hero. For infinitely various are the incidents in one man's life, which cannot be reduced to unity; and so, too, there are many actions of one man out
of which we cannot make one action. Hence the error, as it appears, of all
poets who have composed a Heracleid, a Theseid, or other poems of the kind.
They imagine that as Heracles was one man, the story of Heracles ought also
to be a unity. . . .

It is, moreover, evident from what has been said, that it is not the function of the poet to relate what has happened, but what may happen—what is
possible according to the law of probability or necessity. The poet and the
historian differ not by writing in verse or in prose. The work of Herodotus[1]
might be put into verse, and it would still be a species of history, with metre
no less than without it. The true difference is that one relates what has happened, the other what may happen. Poetry, therefore, is a more philosophical
and a higher thing than history: for poetry tends to express the universal,
history the particular. The universal tells us how a person of given character
will on occasion speak or act, according to the law of probability or necessity; and it is this universality at which Poetry aims in giving expressive names
to the characters. The particular is—for example—what Alcibiades did or
suffered. . . .

---

[1] Herodotus (c. 480–425 B.C.) wrote a prose masterpiece history of the Persian wars.

Of all plots and actions the episodic are the worst. I call a plot episodic in which the episodes or acts succeed one another without probable or necessary sequence. Bad poets compose such pieces by their own fault, good poets, to please the players; for, as they write for competing rivals, they draw out the plot beyond its capacity, and are often forced to break the natural continuity. . . .

Plots are either simple or complicated; for such too, in their very nature, are the actions of which the plots are an imitation. An action which is one and continuous in the sense above defined, I call Simple, when the turning point is reached without Reversal of Fortune or Recognition: Complicated, when it is reached with Reversal of Fortune, or Recognition, or both. These last should arise from the internal structure of the plot, so that what follows should be the necessary or probable result of the preceding action. It makes all the difference whether one event is the consequence of another, or merely subsequent to it.

A reversal of fortune is, as we have said, a change by which a train of action produces the opposite of the effect intended; and that, according to our rule of probability or necessity. Thus in the *Oedipus*,[2] the messenger, hoping to cheer Oedipus, and to free him from his alarms about his mother, reveals his origin, and so produces the opposite effect. . . .

A Recognition, as the name indicates, is a change from ignorance to knowledge, producing love or hate between the persons destined by the poet for good or bad fortune. The best form of recognition is coincident with a reversal of fortune, as in the *Oedipus*. . . .

As the sequel to what has already been said, we must proceed to consider what the poet should aim at, and what he should avoid, in constructing his plots; and by what means Tragedy may best fulfil its function.

A perfect tragedy should, as we have seen, be arranged on the simple not the complicated plan. It should, moreover, imitate actions which excite pity and fear, this being the distinctive mark of tragic imitation. It follows plainly, in the first place, that the change of fortune presented must not be the spectacle of a perfectly good man brought from prosperity to adversity: for this moves neither pity nor fear; it simply shocks us. Nor, again, that of a bad man passing from adversity to prosperity: for nothing can be more alien to the spirit of Tragedy; it possesses no single tragic quality; it neither satisfies the moral sense, nor calls forth pity or fear. Nor, again, should the downfall

---

[2]One of two plays by Sophocles (496–406 B.C.) about a man who unwittingly kills his father and marries his mother.

of the utter villain be exhibited. A plot of this kind would, doubtless, satisfy the moral sense, but it would inspire neither pity nor fear; for pity is aroused by unmerited misfortune, fear by the misfortune of a man like ourselves. Such an event, therefore, will be neither pitiful nor terrible. There remains, then, the character between these two extremes—that of a man who is not eminently good and just, yet whose misfortune is brought about not by vice or depravity, but by some error or frailty. He must be one who is highly renowned and prosperous—a personage like Oedipus, Thyestes, or other illustrious men of such families.

A well constructed plot should, therefore, be single, rather than double as some maintain. The change of fortune should be not from bad to good, but, reversely, from good to bad. It should come about as the result not of vice, but of some great error or frailty, in a character either such as we have described, or better rather than worse. The practice of the stage bears out our view. At first the poets recounted any legends that came in their way. Now, tragedies are founded on the story of a few houses—on the fortunes of Alcmaeon, Oedipus, Orestes, Meleager, Thyestes, Telephus, and those others who have done or suffered something terrible. A tragedy, then to be perfect according to the rules of art should be of this construction. Hence they are in error who censure Euripides just because he follows this principle in his plays, many of which end unhappily. It is, as we have said, the right ending. The best proof is that on the stage and in dramatic competition, such plays, if they are well represented, are most tragic in their effect; and Euripides, faulty as he is in the general management of his subject, yet is felt to be the most tragic of poets. . . .

As in the structure of the plot, so too in the portraiture of character, the poet should always aim either at the necessary or the probable. Thus a person of a given character should speak or act in a given way, by the rule either of necessity or of probability; just as this event should follow that by necessary or probable sequence. It is therefore evident that the unravelling of the plot, no less than the complication, must be brought about by the plot itself, and not by Machinery[3] —as in the *Medea,* or in the Return of the Greeks in the *Iliad.* Machinery should be employed only for events external to the drama—either such as are previous to it and outside the sphere of human knowledge, or subsequent to it and which need to be foretold and announced; for to the gods we ascribe the power of seeing all things. Within the action there must be nothing irrational. If the irrational cannot be excluded, it

---

[3] Machines were used in the theater to show the gods flying in space. The term now refers to any implausible way of solving the complications of a plot.

should be outside the scope of the tragedy. Such is the irrational element in the *Oedipus* of Sophocles. . . .

The Chorus too should be regarded as one of the actors; it should be an integral part of the whole, and share in the action, in the manner not of Euripides but of Sophocles. As for the later poets, their choral songs pertain as little to the subject of the piece as to that of any other tragedy. They are, therefore, sung as mere interludes—a practice first begun by Agathon. Yet what difference is there between introducing such choral interludes, and transferring a speech, or even a whole act, from one play to another? . . .

I. **Suggestions for Discussion:**
  1. How does Aristotle define tragedy?
  2. What kind of character should be portrayed in a tragedy?
  3. What kind of plot is suitable for a tragedy?
II. **Suggestions for Writing:**
  1. Apply Aristotle's criteria to a play that you have watched in the theater, on film, or on television.
  2. Write an essay demonstrating that an implausible ending detracts from the impact and effectiveness of a play.

---

# RICHARD ARMOUR

## The Transcendentalists

---

Richard Armour (1906–   ), formerly professor and dean at Scripps College, has published dozens of books satirizing and parodying literature, history, medicine, and higher education. His academic spoofs include such popular books as *It All Started with Columbus* (1953), *American Lit Relit* (1964), and *English Lit Relit* (1969).

The following parody of literary criticism is Armour's humorous introduction to Ralph Waldo Emerson, Henry David Thoreau, and other nineteenth century American writers known as Transcendentalists.

---

After Irving, Cooper, and Bryant, the literary center of the United States moved from New York to New England. On Moving Day, roads were clogged with hundreds of poets, novelists, essayists, and editors, loaded down with the tools of their trade.[1]

The Transcendentalists were a group of New Englanders who looked upon themselves as mystics and were looked upon by others as queer. They formed a club, originally called the Aesthetic Club, or possibly Anaesthetic Club, where they sat around and talked about Immanuel Kant.[2] "I believe there was seldom an inclination to be silent," said one of the members. This is a Bostonian's way of saying that everybody talked at once.

One practical result of discussions at the Club was establishment of Brook Farm, a socialistic community where agriculture and the arts mingled, it being common practice to milk a cow with one hand while painting a landscape or writing a poem with the other. Mostly, however, unpleasant chores were assigned to a committee and forgotten, life being so beautiful that everyone was too busy looking at it to work. Despite emphasis on the individual, there was belief in mutual helpfulness. It was, as Emerson said, "an attempt to lift others with themselves." The sight of a Brook farmer struggling to lift himself with one hand and a friend with the other sometimes startled passersby.

## Ralph Waldo Emerson

The leader of the Transcendentalists was Ralph Waldo Emerson. Ralph (as few dared call him) came of a long line of Puritan ministers, which explains a great deal. He himself was a preacher for a while, and even after he left the pulpit continued preaching, as anyone knows who has read his essays.

Emerson lived most of his life in Boston and in Concord. In the latter he occupied a house that had been built for his grandfather and was therefore referred to as "the Old Man's."[3] It was there that Emerson wrote his book *Nature,* which is about nature. There too, during a heavy rainstorm, he made his famous pronouncement: "Nature is not fixed but fluid."

A versatile writer, Emerson wrote both prose and poetry. It has been said that there are poetic passages in his prose and prosaic passages in his poetry. No doubt he did this on purpose, to confound his critics.[4] However,

---

[1] Pens, erasers, paperweights, and rejection slips.
[2] "If Kant can't, nobody can," they were wont to say admiringly.
[3] Mistakenly referred to today as the Old Manse.
[4] "Confound my critics!" Emerson often said.

his poetry can easily be distinguished, even when it is not distinguished poetry, by such lines as:

> I like a church; I like a cowl;
> I love a prophet of the soul.

If you mispronounce either *cowl* or *soul,* but not both, it rhymes perfectly.

Many of Emerson's essays were first delivered as lectures. These lectures (for which he was well paid—see his essay "Compensation") took him all over the United States and to Europe. In England he was entertained by famous writers. One of them, George Eliot, jotted this somewhat cryptic entry in her diary: "He is the first *man* I have ever met." She was living at the time with George Henry Lewes, and it is a good thing she kept the key to her diary on a string around her neck.[5]

Emerson has been described as "a deep-seated genius," which is the kind of remark about a writer's physical appearance that a literary critic should never make. It would be kinder to say something about his Over-Soul, which might have been big and baggy but didn't show.[6]

In his essays,[7] Emerson urges reliance on self, which he refers to as Self-Reliance. In fact self was so important to him that when he traveled in Europe he wrote in his journal, after a hard day's sightseeing, "Wherever we go, whatever we do, self is the sole subject we study and learn." Some think he might have saved all that money and stayed home.

Anyone who has difficulty understanding Emerson will be helped by the following explanation: "The Kantian tripartition supplied the epistemological terminology for Emersonian transcendentalism." Suddenly it all becomes clear.

## Henry David Thoreau

The No. 2 Transcendentalist, whose number was up before Emerson's (he lived to be only forty-five), was Henry David Thoreau.[8] Thoreau grew up in Concord, where his father was a manufacturer of lead pencils. Since the youth could have all the rejects that couldn't be sold, it is no wonder he became a writer.

[5] George Eliot, it should be noted, was *not* a man.
[6] Or did it? Emerson himself refers to the Over-Soul as "the lap of immense intelligence."
[7] Entitled, with Emerson's customary flair for the unusual, *Essays, First Series* and *Essays, Second Series.*
[8] At first his name was David Henry Thoreau, but apparently he got himself mixed up.

Rather than earn money, it was Thoreau's idea to reduce his wants so that he would not need to buy anything. As he went around town preaching this ingenious idea, the shopkeepers of Concord hoped he would drop dead. Nor did his refusal to pay taxes endear him to local officials. Shuddering at the prospect of having a crank like Thoreau in the county jail, always demanding his special health-food diet, they paid his taxes and considered themselves fortunate.

Thoreau built himself a cabin on the shores of Walden Pond, near Concord, at a cost of $28.12½.[9] At least that is what he told the county tax assessor when he came to appraise the place. Thoreau was his own architect, carpenter, plasterer, and electrician, and he did without plumbing.[10]

Why Thoreau went to live alone at Walden, where he stayed two years and two months, he once explained as follows: "I wanted to live deep and suck out all the marrow of life." The picture of this rugged individualist crouched in a hole he had dug near his cabin, working away on a bone, is likely to linger for many a day.

Emerson, who enjoyed comfort, wrote of Thoreau somewhat irascibly: "I tell him a man was not made to live in a swamp, but a frog. If God meant him to live in a swamp, he would have made him a frog." Thoreau, who loved frogs just as he did ants and beetles, accepted this as a compliment and on summer evenings took to croaking softly.

Out of his experiences Thoreau wrote *Walden,* which hymns the pleasures of being alone with nature—away from newspapers, telephones, and Ralph Waldo Emerson. "If the bell rings, why should we run?" asks Thoreau. Callers who knocked on the door of his cabin often went away, thinking he was not home. Actually, he was getting out of his chair, but slowly.

It is probably unnecessary to say that Thoreau, preoccupied with eliminating what he called "superfluities," never married.[11]

## Other Transcendentalists

Other Transcendentalists included Orestes Brownson, who, fortunately, was not on a first-name basis with many persons, and Bronson Alcott. Alcott founded Fruitlands, an experiment in vegetarian living, which broke up after

---

[9] Thoreau not only cut corners, he cut pennies.

[10] There were woods all around the place.

[11] "As for taking Henry's arm," said one of his friends, "I should as soon think of taking the arm of an elm tree." Thoreau was a lovable fellow, but there was something a little wooden about him.

a few months. One night at dinner, when the Fruitlanders were eating squash and turnip greens for the fourteenth time that week, the scent of roast beef drifted in from a neighboring farmhouse.

With the failure of Fruitlands, Alcott was in financial straits, but, being a man of high ideals, he refused to permit just anyone to support him. Almost the only person who passed his rigorous standards was his daughter, Louisa May Alcott, who had made a fortune with her *Little Women,* a sweet tearful saga of four sisters.[12]

There was also Margaret Fuller, whom the male Transcendentalists accepted as an intellectual equal. Fortunately for her, these eccentrics were more interested in brains than beauty. As editor of the Transcendentalist publication, the *Dial,* she displayed a blend of idealism and practicality by paying nothing to its contributors. Of course, the fact that the paid circulation of the *Dial* never exceeded 250 may have limited her funds.

## I. Suggestions for Discussion:

1. Using your own research, indicate how much accurate information Armour gives about any of the Transcendentalists he discusses.
2. Discuss his use of specific details, including footnotes, as a major source of the humor in his essay.
3. Compare his observations about these nineteenth-century American authors with Samuel Clemens's observations about James Fenimore Cooper, p. 88.

## II. Suggestions for Writing:

1. Using Armour's essay as a model, write a humorous biographical sketch of a well-known literary, political, or sports figure.
2. Write a humorous sketch about the activities of a friend or acquaintance.

---

# MATTHEW ARNOLD

## The Duties of a Professor

---

Matthew Arnold (1822-1888) served as Inspector of Schools in England from 1851-1883 and as Professor of Poetry at Oxford from 1857-1867. In addition to his poetic works, he was recog-

[12] The term *sob sister* was first applied to Beth and her damp siblings.

nized for such prose works as *Essays in Criticism* (1865 and 1888), *Culture and Anarchy* (1869), and *The Study of Celtic Literature* (1867), from which the following selection is taken.

In this brief selection, Arnold argues that a deep commitment to learning on the part of university professors will make young people feel the worth and power of education.

---

It is clear that the system of professorships in our universities is at the present moment based on no intelligent principle, and does not by any means correspond with the requirements of knowledge. I do not say anyone is to blame for this. Sometimes the actual state of things is due to the wants of another age—as for instance, in the overwhelming preponderance of theological chairs; all the arts and sciences, it is well known, were formerly made to center in theology. Sometimes it is due to mere haphazard, to the accident of a founder having appeared for one study and no founder having appeared for another. Clearly it was not deliberate design which provided Anglo-Saxon with a chair at Oxford, while the Teutonic languages, as a group, have none, and the Celtic languages have none. It is as if we had a chair of Oscan or of Aeolic Greek[1] before we had a chair of Greek and Latin. The whole system of our university chairs evidently wants recasting, and adapting to the needs of modern science.

I say, *of modern science;* and it is important to insist on these words. Circumstances at Oxford and Cambridge give special prominence to their function as finishing schools to carry young men of the upper classes of society through a certain limited course of study. But a university is something more and higher than a great finishing school for young gentlemen, however distinguished. A university is a member of a European confraternity for continually enlarging the domain of human knowledge and pushing back in all directions its boundaries. The Statutes of the College of France, drawn up at the best moment of the Renaissance and informed with the true spirit of that generous time, admirably fix for a university professor, or representative of the higher studies of Europe, his aim and duty. The *Lecteur Royal* is left with the amplest possible liberty: only one obligation is imposed on him—to promote and develop to the highest possible pitch the branch of knowledge with which he is charged. In this spirit a university should organize its professorships; in this spirit a professor should use his chair. So that if the Celtic languages are an important object of science, it is no objection to giving them a chair at Oxford or Cambridge, that young men preparing for

---

[1] Oscan was the ancient language of Italy and Aeolic Greek the ancient language of Greece.

their degree have no call to study them. The relation of a university chair is with the higher studies of Europe, and not with the young men preparing for their degree. If its occupant has had but five young men at his lectures, or but one young man, or no young man at all, he has done his duty if he has served the higher studies of Europe; or, not to leave out America, let us say, the higher studies of the world. If he has not served these, he has not done his duty, though he had at his lectures five hundred young men. But un-doubtedly the most fruitful action of a university chair, even upon the young college student, is produced not by bringing down the university chair to his level, but by beckoning him up to its level. Only in this way can that love for the things of the mind, which is the soul of true culture, be generated—by showing the things of the mind in their reality and power. Where there is fire, people will come to be warmed at it; and every notable spread of mental activity has been due, not to the arrangement of an elaborate machinery for schooling but to the electric wind of glowing, disinterested play of mind. "Evidences of Christianity!" Coleridge used to say, "I am weary of the world! Make a man feel the want of Christianity." The young men's education, we may in like manner say, "I am sick of seeing it organized! Make the young men feel the want, the worth, the power of education."

I. **Suggestions for Discussion:**
   1. Discuss the principal obligations of a university professor, according to Arnold.
   2. In what ways will a professor attract students?
   3. Compare and contrast Arnold's views of the life of the university with those of John Henry Newman in "What Is a University," p. 421.
II. **Suggestions for Writing:**
   1. Using your own experience and observations, list the important quali-ties of a successful college teacher.
   2. Write an essay discussing the principal duties of a successful student.

---

# W. H. AUDEN

## Work, Labor, and Play

---

Wystan Hugh Auden (1907-1973) was born in England but be-came an American citizen in 1946. An essayist and playwright, he is best known for his poetry, which won him many awards, including the Pulitzer Prize. His *Collected Shorter Poems* appeared in 1967 and his *Collected Longer Poems* were published in 1969. A selection of his reflections and observations entitled *A Certain World: A Commonplace Book* appeared in 1970.

In this lucid essay, Auden distinguishes among work, labor, and play. He defines a worker as one who is personally interested in the job society pays him or her to do.

---

So far as I know, Miss Hannah Arendt[1] was the first person to define the essential difference between work and labor. To be happy, a man must feel, firstly, free and, secondly, important. He cannot be really happy if he is compelled by society to do what he does not enjoy doing, or if what he enjoys doing is ignored by society as of no value or importance. In a society where slavery in the strict sense has been abolished, the sign that what a man does is of social value is that he is paid money to do it, but a laborer today can rightly be called a wage slave. A man is a laborer if the job society offers him is of no interest to himself but he is compelled to take it by the necessity of earning a living and supporting his family.

The antithesis to labor is play. When we play a game, we enjoy what we are doing, otherwise we should not play it, but it is a purely private activity; society could not care less whether we play it or not.

Between labor and play stands work. A man is a worker if he is personally interested in the job which society pays him to do; what from the point of view of society is necessary labor is from his own point of view voluntary play. Whether a job is to be classified as labor or work depends, not on the job itself, but on the tastes of the individual who undertakes it. The difference does not, for example, coincide with the difference between a manual and a mental job; a gardener or a cobbler may be a worker, a bank clerk a laborer. Which a man is can be seen from his attitude toward leisure. To a worker, leisure means simply the hours he needs to relax and rest in order to work efficiently. He is therefore more likely to take too little leisure than too much; workers die of coronaries and forget their wives' birthdays. To the laborer, on the other hand, leisure means freedom from compulsion, so that it is natural for him to imagine that the fewer hours he has to spend laboring, and the more hours he is free to play, the better.

---

[1] Hannah Arendt was a distinguished political philosopher at the New School in New York who published *The Human Condition* in 1958.

What percentage of the population in a modern technological society are, like myself, in the fortunate position of being workers? At a guess I would say sixteen per cent, and I do not think that figure is likely to get bigger in the future.

Technology and the division of labor have done two things: by eliminating in many fields the need for special strength or skill, they have made a very large number of paid occupations which formerly were enjoyable work into boring labor, and by increasing productivity they have reduced the number of necessary laboring hours. It is already possible to imagine a society in which the majority of the population, that is to say, its laborers, will have almost as much leisure as in earlier times was enjoyed by the aristocracy. When one recalls how aristocracies in the past actually behaved, the prospect is not cheerful. Indeed, the problem of dealing with boredom may be even more difficult for such a future mass society than it was for aristocracies. The latter, for example, ritualized their time; there was a season to shoot grouse, a season to spend in town, etc. The masses are more likely to replace an unchanging ritual by fashion which it will be in the economic interest of certain people to change as often as possible. Again, the masses cannot go in for hunting, for very soon there would be no animals left to hunt. For other aristocratic amusements like gambling, dueling, and warfare, it may be only too easy to find equivalents in dangerous driving, drug-taking, and senseless acts of violence. Workers seldom commit acts of violence, because they can put their aggression into their work, be it physical like the work of a smith, or mental like the work of a scientist or an artist. The role of aggression in mental work is aptly expressed by the phrase "getting one's teeth into a problem."

## I. Suggestions for Discussion:
1. Discuss the distinctions Auden makes between work and labor.
2. What effects have technology and the division of labor had on the modern worker, according to Auden? List other effects as well.
3. What dangers of boredom does Auden identify?

## II. Suggestions for Writing:
1. Using Auden's definitions of work, labor, and play, analyze one or more professions or vocations you have considered.
2. Describe ways you have found to avoid boredom.

# SIR FRANCIS BACON

## Idols of the Mind

### from *The New Organon*

Sir Francis Bacon (1561–1626) was a lawyer, essayist, philosopher, and statesman. Lord Chancellor of England in 1618, he returned to literary and philosophical study after having been charged with bribery in the House of Lords in 1621. Among his best-known works are *The Advancement of Learning* (1605), *The New Organon* (published in Latin in 1620), and his fifty-eight *Essays* (1597, 1625).

In the famous essay about human understanding which follows, Bacon defines four classes of idols or false notions which beset people's minds: Idols of the Tribe, Idols of the Cave, Idols of the Marketplace, and Idols of the Theatre.

## XXIII

There is a great difference between the Idols of the human mind and the Ideas of the divine. That is to say, between certain empty dogmas, and the true signatures and marks set upon the works of creation as they are found in nature.

## XXXVIII

The idols and false notions which are now in possession of the human understanding, and have taken deep root therein, not only so beset men's minds that truth can hardly find entrance, but even after entrance obtained, they will again in the very instauration of the sciences meet and trouble us, unless men being fore-warned of the danger fortify themselves as far as may be against their assaults.

## XXXIX

There are four classes of Idols which beset men's minds: To these for distinction's sake I have assigned names,—calling the first class *Idols of the Tribe;* the second, *Idols of the Cave;* the third, *Idols of the Market-place;* the fourth, *Idols of the Theatre.*

## XL

The formation of ideas and axioms by true induction is no doubt the proper remedy to be applied for the keeping off and clearing away of idols. To point them out, however, is of great use; for the doctrine of Idols is to the Interpretation of Nature what the doctrine of the refutation of Sophisms is to common Logic.

## XLI

The Idols of the Tribe have their foundation in human nature itself, and in the tribe or race of men. For it is a false assertion that the sense of man is the measure of things. On the contrary, all perceptions as well of the sense as of the mind are according to the measure of the individual and not according to the measure of the universe. And the human understanding is like a false mirror, which, receiving rays irregularly, distorts and discolours the nature of things by mingling its own nature with it.

## XLII

The Idols of the Cave are the idols of the individual man. For every one (besides the errors common to human nature in general) has a cave or den of his own, which refracts and discolours the light of nature; owing either to his own proper and peculiar nature; or to his education and conversation with others; or to the reading of books, and the authority of those whom he esteems and admires; or to the differences of impressions, accordingly as they take place in a mind preoccupied and predisposed or in a mind indifferent and settled; or the like. So that the spirit of man (according as it is meted out to different individuals) is in fact a thing variable and full of perturbation, and governed as it were by chance. Whence it was well observed by

Heraclitus that men look for sciences in their own lesser worlds, and not in the greater or common world.

## XLIII

There are also Idols formed by the intercourse and association of men with each other, which I call Idols of the Market-place, on account of the commerce and consort of men there. For it is by discourse that men associate; and words are imposed according to the apprehension of the vulgar. And therefore the ill and unfit choice of words wonderfully obstructs the understanding. Nor do the definitions or explanations wherewith in some things learned men are wont to guard and defend themselves, by any means set the matter right. But words plainly force and overrule the understanding, and throw all into confusion, and lead men away into numberless empty controversies and idle fancies.

## XLIV

Lastly, there are Idols which have immigrated into men's minds from the various dogmas of philosophies, and also from wrong laws of demonstration. These I call Idols of the Theatre; because in my judgment all the received systems are but so many stage-plays, representing worlds of their own creation after an unreal and scenic fashion. Nor is it only of the systems now in vogue, or only of the ancient sects and philosophies, that I speak; for many more plays of the same kind may yet be composed and in like artificial manner set forth; seeing that errors the most widely different have nevertheless causes for the most part alike. Neither again do I mean this only of entire systems, but also of many principles and axioms in science, which by tradition, credulity, and negligence have come to be received.

But of these several kinds of Idols I must speak more largely and exactly, that the understanding may be duly cautioned.

## XLV

The human understanding is of its own nature prone to suppose the existence of more order and regularity in the world than it finds. And though there be many things in nature which are singular and unmatched, yet it devises for them parallels and conjugates and relatives which do not exist. Hence the fiction that all celestial bodies move in perfect circles; spirals and dragons being (except in name) utterly rejected. Hence too the element of Fire with its orb is brought in, to make up the square with the other three which the sense perceives. Hence also the ratio of density of the so-called elements is arbitrarily fixed at ten to one. And so on of other dreams. And these fancies affect not dogmas only, but simple notions also.

## XLVI

The human understanding when it has once adopted an opinion (either as being the received opinion or as being agreeable to itself) draws all things else to support and agree with it. And though there be a greater number and weight of instances to be found on the other side, yet these it either neglects and despises, or else by some distinction sets aside and rejects; in order that by this great and pernicious predetermination the authority of its former conclusions may remain inviolate. And therefore it was a good answer that was made by one who when they showed him hanging in a temple a picture of those who had paid their vows as having escaped shipwreck, and would have him say whether he did not now acknowledge the power of the gods,—"Aye," asked he again, "but where are they painted that were drowned after their vows?" And such is the way of all superstition, whether in astrology, dreams, omens, divine judgments, or the like; wherein men, having a delight in such vanities, mark the events where they are fulfilled, but where they fail, though this happens much oftener, neglect and pass them by. But with far more subtlety does this mischief insinuate itself into philosophy and the sciences; in which the first conclusion colours and brings into conformity with itself all that come after, though far sounder and better. Besides, independently of that delight and vanity which I have described, it is the peculiar and perpetual error of the human intellect to be more moved and excited by affirmatives than by negatives; whereas it ought properly to hold itself indifferently disposed towards both alike. Indeed in the establishment of any true axiom, the negative instance is the more forcible of the two.

## XLVII

The human understanding is moved by those things most which strike and enter the mind simultaneously and suddenly, and so fill the imagination;

and then it feigns and supposes all other things to be somehow, though it cannot see how, similar to those few things by which it is surrounded. But for that going to and fro to remote and heterogeneous instances, by which axioms are tried as in the fire, the intellect is altogether slow and unfit, unless it be forced thereto by severe laws and overruling authority.

## XLVIII

The human understanding is unquiet; it cannot stop or rest, and still presses onward, but in vain. Therefore it is that we cannot conceive of any end or limit to the world; but always as of necessity it occurs to us that there is something beyond. Neither again can it be conceived how eternity has flowed down to the present day; for that distinction which is commonly received of infinity in time past and in time to come can by no means hold; for it would thence follow that one infinity is greater than another, and that infinity is wasting away and tending to become finite. The like subtlety arises touching the infinite divisibility of lines, from the same inability of thought to stop. But this inability interferes more mischievously in the discovery of causes: for although the most general principles in nature ought to be held merely positive, as they are discovered, and cannot with truth be referred to a cause; nevertheless the human understanding being unable to rest still seeks something prior in the order of nature. And then it is that in struggling towards that which is further off it falls back upon that which is more nigh at hand; namely, on final causes: which have relation clearly to the nature of man rather than to the nature of the universe; and from this source have strangely defiled philosophy. But he is no less an unskilled and shallow philosopher who seeks causes of that which is most general, than he who in things subordinate and subaltern omits to do so.

## XLIX

The human understanding is no dry light, but receives an infusion from the will and affections; whence proceed sciences which may be called "sciences as one would." For what a man had rather were true he more readily believes. Therefore he rejects difficult things from impatience of research; sober things, because they narrow hope; the deeper things of nature, from superstition; the light of experience, from arrogance and pride, lest his mind should seem to be occupied with things mean and transitory; things not commonly believed, out of deference to the opinion of the vulgar. Numberless in short are the ways, and sometimes imperceptible, in which the affections colour and infect the understanding.

## L

But by far the greatest hindrance and aberration of the human understanding proceeds from the dullness, incompetency, and deceptions of the senses; in that things which strike the sense outweight things which do not immediately strike it, though they be more important. Hence it is that speculation commonly ceases where sight ceases; insomuch that of things invisible there is little or no observation. Hence all the working of the spirits inclosed in tangible bodies lies hid and unobserved of men. So also all the more subtle changes of form in the parts of coarser substances (which they commonly call alteration, though it is in truth local motion through exceedingly small spaces) is in like manner unobserved. And yet unless these two things just mentioned be searched out and brought to light, nothing great can be achieved in nature, as far as the production of works is concerned. So again the essential nature of our common air, and of all bodies less dense than air (which are very many), is almost unknown. For the sense by itself is a thing infirm and erring; neither can instruments for enlarging or sharpening the senses do much; but all the truer kind of interpretation of nature is effected by instances and experiments fit and apposite; wherein the sense decides touching the experiment only, and the experiment touching the point in nature and the thing itself.

## LI

The human understanding is of its own nature prone to abstractions and gives a substance and reality to things which are fleeting. But to resolve nature into abstractions is less to our purpose than to dissect her into parts; as did the school of Democritus, which went further into nature than the rest. Matter rather than forms should be the object of our attention, its configurations and changes of configuration, and simple action, and law of action or motion; for forms are figments of the human mind, unless you will call those laws of action forms.

## LII

Such then are the idols which I call *Idols of the Tribe;* and which take their rise either from the homogeneity of the substance of the human spirit, or from its preoccupation, or from its narrowness, or from its restless motion, or from an infusion of the affections, or from the incompetency of the senses, or from the mode of impression.

## LIII

The *Idols of the Cave* take their rise in the peculiar constitution, mental or bodily, of each individual; and also in education, habit, and accident. Of this kind there is a great number and variety; but I will instance those the pointing out of which contains the most important caution, and which have most effect in disturbing the clearness of the understanding.

## LIV

Men become attached to certain particular sciences and speculations, either because they fancy themselves the authors and inventors thereof, or because they have bestowed the greatest pains upon them and become most habituated to them. But men of this kind, if they betake themselves to philosophy and contemplations of a general character, distort and colour them in obedience to their former fancies; a thing especially to be noticed in Aristotle, who made his natural philosophy a mere bond-servant to his logic, thereby rendering it contentious and well nigh useless. The race of chemists again out of a few experiments of the furnace have built up a fantastic philosophy, framed with reference to a few things; and Gilbert also, after he had employed himself most laboriously in the study and observation of the loadstone, proceeded at once to construct an entire system in accordance with his favourite subject.

## LVI

There are found some minds given to an extreme admiration of antiquity, others to an extreme love and appetite for novelty; but few so duly tempered that they can hold the mean, neither carping at what has been well laid down by the ancients, nor despising what is well introduced by the moderns. This however turns to the great injury of the sciences and philosophy; since these affectations of antiquity and novelty are the humours of partisans rather than judgments; and truth is to be sought for not in the felicity of any age, which is an unstable thing, but in the light of nature and experience, which is eternal. These factions therefore must be abjured, and care must be taken that the intellect be not hurried by them into assent.

## LVIII

Let such then be our provision and contemplative prudence for keeping off and dislodging the *Idols of the Cave,* which grow for the most part either out of the predominance of a favourite subject, or out of an excessive tendency to compare or to distinguish, or out of partiality for particular ages, or out of the largeness of minuteness of the objects contemplated. And generally let every student of nature take this as a rule,—that whatever his mind seizes and dwells upon with peculiar satisfaction is to be held in suspicion, and that so much the more care is to be taken in dealing with such questions to keep the understanding even and clear.

## LIX

But the *Idols of the Market-place* are the most troublesome of all: idols which have crept into the understanding through the alliances of words and names. For men believe that their reason governs words; but it is also true that words react on the understanding; and this it is that had rendered philosophy and the sciences sophistical and inactive. Now words, being commonly framed and applied according to the capacity of the vulgar, follow those lines of division which are most obvious to the vulgar understanding. And whenever an understanding of greater acuteness or a more diligent observation would alter those lines to suit the true divisions of nature, words stand in the way and resist the change. Whence it comes to pass that the high and formal discussions of learned men end oftentimes in disputes about words and names; with which (according to the use and wisdom of the mathematicians) it would be more prudent to begin, and so by means of definitions reduce them to order. Yet even definitions cannot cure this evil in dealing with natural and material things; since the definitions themselves consist of words, and those words beget others: so that it is necessary to recur to individual instances, and those in due series and order; as I shall say presently when I come to the method and scheme for the formation of notions and axioms.

## LX

The idols imposed by words on the understanding are of two kinds. They are either names of things which do not exist (for as there are things left unnamed through lack of observation, so likewise are there names which result from fantastic suppositions and to which nothing in reality corresponds), or they are names of things which exist, but yet confused and ill-defined, and hastily and irregularly derived from realities. Of the former kind are Fortune, the Prime Mover, Planetary Orbits, Element of Fire, and like fictions which owe their origin to false and idle theories. And this class of idols is more easily expelled, because to get rid of them it is only necessary that all theories should be steadily rejected and dismissed as obsolete.

But the other class, which springs out of a faulty and unskillful abstraction, is intricate and deeply rooted. Let us take for example such a word as *humid;* and see how far the several things which the word is used to signify agree with each other; and we shall find the word *humid* to be nothing else than a mark loosely and confusedly applied to denote a variety of actions which will not bear to be reduced to any constant meaning. For it both signifies that which easily spreads itself round any other body; and that which in itself is indeterminate and cannot solidise; and that which readily yields in every direction; and that which easily divides and scatters itself; and that which easily unites and collects itself; and that which readily flows and is put in motion; and that which readily clings to another body and wets it; and that which is easily reduced to a liquid, or being solid easily melts. Accordingly when you come to apply the word,—if you take it in one sense, flame is humid; if in another, air is not humid; if in another, fine dust is humid; if in another, glass is humid. So that it is easy to see that the notion is taken by abstraction only from water and common and ordinary liquids, without any due verification.

There are however in words certain degrees of distortion and error. One of the least faulty kinds is that of names of substances, especially of lowest species and well-deduced (for the notion of *chalk* and of *mud* is good, of *earth* bad); a more faulty kind is that of actions, as *to generate, to corrupt, to alter;* the most faulty is of qualities (except such as are the immediate objects of the sense) as *heavy, light, rare, dense,* and the like. Yet in all these cases some notions are of necessity a little better than others, in proportion to the greater variety of subjects that fall within the range of the human sense.

## LXI

But the *Idols of the Theatre* are not innate, nor do they steal into the understanding secretly, but are plainly impressed and received into the mind from the play-books of philosophical systems and the perverted rules of demonstration. To attempt refutations in this case would be merely inconsistent with what I have already said: for since we agree neither upon principles nor upon demonstrations there is no place for argument. And this is so far well, inasmuch as it leaves the honour of the ancients untouched. For they are no wise disparaged—the question between them and me being only as to the way. For as the saying is, the lame man who keeps the right road outstrips the runner who takes a wrong one. Nay it is obvious that when a man runs the wrong way, the more active and swift he is the further he will go astray.

But the course İ propose for the discovery of sciences is such as leaves but little to the acuteness and strength of wits, but places all wits and understandings nearly on a level. For as in the drawing of a straight line or a perfect circle, much depends on the steadiness and practice of the hand, if it be done by aim of hand only, but if with the aid of rule or compass, little or nothing; so is it exactly with my plan. But though particular confutations would be of no avail, yet touching the sects and general divisions of such systems I must say something; something also touching the external signs which show that they are unsound; and finally something touching the causes of such great infelicity and of such lasting and general agreement in error; that so the access to truth may be made less difficult, and the human understanding may the more willingly submit to its purgation and dismiss its idols.

## LXII

Idols of the Theatre, or of Systems, are many, and there can be and perhaps will be yet many more. For were it not that now for many ages men's minds have been busied with religion and theology; and were it not that civil governments, especially monarchies, have been averse to such novelties, even in matters speculative; so that men labour therein to the peril and harming of their fortunes,—not only unrewarded, but exposed also to contempt and envy; doubtless there would have arisen many other philosophical sects like to those which in great variety flourished once among the Greeks. For as on the phenomena of the heavens many hypotheses may be constructed, so likewise (and more also) many various dogmas may be set up and established on the phenomena of philosophy. And in the plays of this philosophical theatre you may observe the same thing which is found in the theatre of the poets, that stories invented for the stage are more compact and elegant, and more as one would wish them to be, than true stories out of history.

## LXVII

A caution must also be given to the understanding against the intemperance which systems of philosophy manifest in giving or withholding assent; because intemperance of this kind seems to establish Idols and in some sort to perpetuate them, leaving no way open to reach and dislodge them.

This excess is of two kinds: the first being manifest in those who are ready in deciding, and render sciences dogmatic and magisterial; the other in those who deny that we can know anything, and so introduce a wandering kind of inquiry that leads to nothing; of which kinds the former subdues, the latter weakens the understanding. For the philosophy of Aristotle, after having by hostile confutations destroyed all the rest (as the Ottomans serve their brothers), has laid down the law on all points; which done, he proceeds himself to raise new questions of his own suggestion, and dispose of them likewise; so that nothing may remain that is not certain and decided: a practice which holds and is in use among his successors.

## LXVIII

So much concerning the several classes of Idols, and their equipage: all of which must be renounced and put away with a fixed and solemn determination, and the understanding thoroughly freed and cleansed; the entrance into the kingdom of man, founded on the sciences, being not much other than the entrance into the kingdom of heaven, whereinto none may enter except as a little child.

I. **Suggestions for Discussion:**
  1. In your own words, define the Idols of the Tribe, Cave, Marketplace, and Theatre.

2. Illustrate each of the Idols with examples from contemporary life.
3. Discuss Bacon's use of examples and illustrations to clarify his ideas.

## II. Suggestions for Discussion:

1. Use your own experience as the basis for an essay about the dangers of the Idols of the Cave.
2. Discuss Idols of the Marketplace that you observe operating in the United States today.

---

# RUSSELL BAKER

## Purging Stag Words

---

Russell Baker (1925–    ) has written witty and insightful essays for the *New York Times* since 1962. His books include *Our Next President* (1968), *Russell's Almanac* (1972), and *The Upside-down Man* (1977).

In this brief essay, Baker discusses efforts to remove sexism from language. Using many examples, he concludes that non-sexist alternatives often result in "windiness in an age when most of us already talk like politicians on television."

---

Everybody at some time has probably felt blood pressure rise and pulse when loaded words have been used to diminish him. The laborer who is called "a hardhat," the poor white who is called "a redneck," the black man who is called "boy," the intellectual who is called "an egghead," the liberal who is called "a bleeding heart," the policeman who is called "a pig"—all these and many others are painfully aware how brutally the English language can be used to humiliate them.

In such instances, words become weapons. Their victims see English as an enemy to be disarmed and, so, when they acquire political muscle one of their first goals commonly is to purge the language.

This is what feminists are now struggling to do in their assault on the heavily masculine freight that has been built into English from the time of the Angles, the Saxons and the Normans. When sensible adults are called "the weaker sex," or "the girls," they are apt to feel at least mildly ridiculed and possibly assaulted.

Hearing men refer to "the little woman," "the better half," "the ball and chain" or "a sweet young thing" may make them suspect they are being crushed in a velvet vise. Not surprisingly, then, the feminist movement is heavily engaged in a language purge.

It is not easy once they get beyond putting the taboo on "weaker sex," "ball and chain," "sweet young thing" and similar ancient clichés that were ready for retirement anyhow, for masculine primacy is deeply entrenched in English.

Some of the difficulties are illustrated in McGraw-Hill's "Guidelines for Equal Treatment of the Sexes in McGraw-Hill Book Company Publications," an admirable analysis of how firmly modern English confines women to the masculine mentality. The author, Timothy Yohn, describes the mental trap very persuasively but is less successful in suggesting how to break out.

The most awkward problem arises with all those words that are compounds of "man." Mr. Yohn tackles "Congressman" and suggests "member of Congress" as a better alternative. His "businessman" becomes "business executive" or "business manager." His "fireman" is a "fire fighter," his "mailman" a "mail carrier," his "salesman" a "sales representative," "salesperson" or "sales clerk," his "insurance man" an "insurance agent," his "statesman" a "leader" or "public servant," his "chairman" a "presiding officer," "the chair," "head," "leader," "coordinator" or "moderator," his "cameraman" a "camera operator" and his "foreman" a "supervisor."

In almost every case the alternative for the "sexist" word to be purged is either a longer word or a combination of words. Instead of "sexism," we have verbosity. It is a dilemma that feminists will have no trouble resolving, but whether it is a good idea to encourage more windiness in an age when most of us already talk like politicians on television is arguable.

One of feminism's goals, presumably, is to establish woman's right, too, to speak in words of one syllable. It will be a pity if everybody has forgotten how by the time equality is finally attained.

The trouble with most of Mr. Yohn's "nonsexist" alternatives—although "fire fighter" isn't bad—is that they abolish "man" only to bring on a Latin-root substitute, and Latin-root words tend to be not only pompous but also vague and long-winded.

Feminists with a classic turn of mind might object that the "or" endings on "operator," "supervisor," "moderator" and "coordinator" smack heavily of the masculine "or" ending common on Latin nouns and are, thus, merely "sexist" words concealed in a toga.

Ideally, someone should invent brand new words that are devoid of gender implication in their job descriptions without weighting the language down like lead settling into swamp water. A scouring of the dictionaries might even turn up some good old words that would serve.

Mr. Yohn suggests one when, in cautioning against "language that assumes all readers are male," he rules out "you and your wife" and suggests, instead, "you and your spouse." The trouble with "spouse" is that nobody but a lawyer can say it with a straight face. It belongs to W. C. Fields and dry wits in sawdust saloons, and in the plural who could resist saying, "you and your spice"?

Why not "you and your mate," Mr. Yohn? "Mate" has the strength of one unequivocal syllable. It also has sex in it, without gender, and that's what we are looking for, isn't it?

## I. Suggestions for Discussion:

1. Explain what Baker means when he writes that "words become weapons." Are the examples he cites effective? Explain.
2. Give examples of sexist language mentioned by Baker. Add examples from your own observation and experience.
3. What kinds of problems does Baker find with proposed efforts to eliminate sexism in language? Evaluate the solutions he offers.

## II. Suggestions for Writing:

1. Illustrate and defend your own solutions to such sexist terms as Congressman, businessman, and chairman.
2. Describe an incident in which words were used, either consciously or unconsciously, as weapons.

---

## JAMES BALDWIN

### If Black English Isn't a Language, Then Tell Me, What Is?

---

James Baldwin (1924–     ), the American essayist, novelist, and playwright, is the author of many books, including *The Fire Next Time* (1963), *Notes of a Native Son* (1956), and his latest novel, *Just Above My Head* (1979). He has long been an outspoken proponent of black civil rights.

In this blistering attack on American attitudes toward black people, Baldwin relates the development of black English to the history and experience of blacks in the United States. He cites many examples of black English words that have gained wide acceptance.

---

ST. PAUL DE VENCE, France—The argument concerning the use, or the status, or the reality, of black English is rooted in American history and has absolutely nothing to do with the question the argument supposes itself to be posing. The argument has nothing to do with language itself but with the *role* of language. Language, incontestably, reveals the speaker. Language, also, far more dubiously, is meant to define the other—and, in this case, the other is refusing to be defined by a language that has never been able to recognize him.

People evolve a language in order to describe and thus control their circumstances, or in order not to be submerged by a reality that they cannot articulate. (And, if they cannot articulate it, they *are* submerged.) A Frenchman living in Paris speaks a subtly and crucially different language from that of the man living in Marseilles; neither sounds very much like a man living in Quebec; and they would all have great difficulty in apprehending what the man from Guadeloupe, or Martinique, is saying, to say nothing of the man from Senegal—although the "common" language of all these areas is French. But each has paid, and is paying, a different price for this "common" language, in which, as it turns out, they are not saying, and cannot be saying, the same things: They each have very different realities to articulate, or control.

What joins all languages, and all men, is the necessity to confront life, in order, not inconceivably, to outwit death: The price for this is the acceptance, and achievement, of one's temporal identity. So that, for example, though it is not taught in the schools (and this has the potential of becoming a political issue) the south of France still clings to its ancient and musical Provençal, which resists being described as a "dialect." And much of the tension in the Basque countries, and in Wales, is due to the Basque and Welsh determination not to allow their languages to be destroyed. This determination also feeds the flames in Ireland for among the many indignities the Irish have been forced to undergo at English hands is the English contempt for their language.

It goes without saying, then, that language is also a political instrument, means, and proof of power. It is the most vivid and crucial key to identity: it reveals the private identity, and connects one with, or divorces one from, the larger, public, or communal identity. There have been, and are, times, and places, when to speak a certain language could be dangerous, even fatal. Or, one may speak the same language, but in such a way that one's antecedents are revealed, or (one hopes) hidden. This is true in France, and is absolutely true in England: The range (and reign) of accents on that damp little island make England coherent for the English and totally incomprehensible for everyone else. To open your mouth in England is (if I may use black English) to "put your business in the street": You have confessed your parents, your youth, your school, your salary, your self-esteem, and, alas, your future.

Now, I do not know what white Americans would sound like if there' had never been any black people in the United States, but they would not sound the way they sound. *Jazz,* for example, is a very specific sexual term, as in *jazz me, baby,* but white people purified it into the Jazz Age. *Sock it to me,* which means, roughly, the same thing, has been adopted by Nathaniel Hawthorne's descendants with no qualms or hesitations at all, along with *let it all hang out* and *right on*! *Beat to his socks,* which was once the black's most total and despairing image of poverty, was transformed into a thing called the Beat Generation, which phenomenon was, largely, composed of *uptight,* middle-class white people, imitating poverty, trying to *get down,* to get *with it,* doing their *thing,* doing their despairing best to be *funky,* which we, the blacks, never dreamed of doing— we *were* funky, baby, like *funk* was going out of style.

Now, no one can eat his cake, and have it, too, and it is late in the day to attempt to penalize black people for having created a language that permits the nation its only glimpse of reality, a language without which the nation would be even more *whipped* than it is.

I say that this present skirmish is rooted in American history, and it is. Black English is the creation of the black diaspora. Blacks came to the United States chained to each other, but from different tribes: Neither could speak the other's language. If two black people, at that bitter hour of the world's history, had been able to speak to each other, the institution of chattel slavery could never have lasted as long as it did. Subsequently, the slave was given, under the eye, and the gun, of his master, Congo Square, and the Bible—or, in other words, and under these conditions, the slave began the formation of the black church, and it is within this unprecedented tabernacle that black English began to be formed. This was not, merely, as in the European example, the adoption of a foreign tongue, but an alchemy that transformed ancient elements into a new language: *A language comes into existence by means of brutal necessity, and the rules of the language are dictated by what the language must convey.*

There was a moment, in time, and in this place, when my brother, or my mother, or my father, or my sister, had to convey to me, for example, the danger in which I was standing from the white man standing just behind me, and to convey this with a speed, and in a language, that the white man could not possibly understand, and that, indeed, he cannot understand, until today. He cannot afford to understand it. This understanding would reveal to him too much about himself, and smash that mirror before which he has been frozen for so long.

Now, if this passion, this skill, this (to quote Toni Morrison) "sheer intelligence," this incredible music, the mighty achievement of having brought a people utterly unknown to, or despised by "history"—to have brought this people to their present, troubled, troubling, and unassailable and unanswerable place—if this absolutely unprecedented journey does not indicate that black English is a language, I am curious to know what definition of language is to be trusted.

A people at the center of the Western world, and in the midst of so hostile a population, has not endured and transcended by means of what is patronizingly called a "dialect." We, the blacks, are in trouble, certainly, but we are not doomed, and we are not inarticulate because we are not compelled to defend a morality that we know to be a lie.

The brutal truth is that the bulk of the white people in America never had any interest in educating black people, except as this could serve white purposes. It is not the black child's language that is in question, it is not his language that is despised: It is his experience. A child cannot be taught by anyone who despises him, and a child cannot afford to be fooled. A child cannot be taught by anyone whose demand, essentially, is that the child repudiate his experience, and all that gives him sustenance, and enter a limbo in which he will no longer be black, and in which he knows that he can never become white. Black people have lost too many black children that way.

And, after all, finally, in a country with standards so untrustworthy, a country that makes heroes of so many criminal mediocrities, a country unable to face why so many of the nonwhite are in prison, or on the needle, or standing, futureless, in the streets—it may very well be that both the child, and his elder, have concluded that they have nothing whatever to learn from the people of a country that has managed to learn so little.

## I. Suggestions for Discussion:

1. What definition of language does Baldwin offer?
2. Cite specific examples of black words and phrases that have come into common use. Add to Baldwin's list from your own knowledge.
3. On what grounds does Baldwin claim that black English permits the nation its only glimpse of reality?

4. Compare the tone of Baldwin's column with that of Martin Luther King, Jr. in "Letter from Birmingham Jail," p. 293.

II. **Suggestions for Writing:**

1. Choosing illustrative examples, demonstrate Baldwin's point that language reveals the speaker.
2. Argue for or against Baldwin's claim that the bulk of white people in America never had any interest in educating black people.

---

# BRUNO BETTELHEIM

## Dear Lord, Make Me Dumb

### from *The Informed Heart*

---

Bruno Bettelheim (1903–     ), born in Vienna, survived the Nazi holocaust and became an American citizen in 1944. While a psychoanalyst at the University of Chicago, he published a number of significant studies of parents and children and of the significance of the holocaust, including *The Informed Heart* (1960), from which the following selection is taken.

In this brief selection, Bettelheim argues that German citizens who were not deeply secure in themselves reverted to childish behaviors as a way of coping with the constant threat of the Gestapo and the Nazi concentration camps during World War II. Such behaviors cost individuals their self-respect and all feelings of independence.

---

Like the prisoners in the concentration camps, almost all German citizens had to develop defenses against the threat of the Gestapo and the concentration camp. Unlike the prisoners they did not form organizations of their own. This, they felt, would only have made arrest a more likely fate. Prisoners inside the camps were quite aware of this, and said that the concentration camp was the only place inside Germany where one could discuss politics without immediate danger of betrayal and imprisonment. Because organized defense was extremely hazardous, German citizens relied mostly on psychological defenses. These were similar to the ones developed by prisoners, though not as deep reaching or elaborate.

Basically there was a limited choice of ways for German subjects to deal with the problem of the camps in the early years. They could try to deny their existence. This was difficult because the Gestapo itself publicized them. They could try to believe that the camps were not as bad as they imagined, and this many Germans tried to believe. But this too was difficult because again and again the newspapers warned them they could either behave or wind up in a concentration camp. The simplest way to deal with the problem was to assume that only the scum of society was sent there, and that what they got they deserved. But only a small segment of the population could make itself believe that.

Those Germans who were outraged by the terror they had to submit to, also had to admit to themselves that their own government was vile, which further undermined their self respect. To any person who clung to his morality or some self respect, recognizing the true character of the concentration camps implied an obligation either to fight a regime that created and maintained them, or at least to take a firm inner stand against it.

In the absence of effectively organized opposition, which appeared only after military defeat became obvious, open fight was both suicidal and pointless unless one's life was endangered. Nevertheless some few among the university students preferred the incredible odds against resistance to evading what they considered their moral obligation. Apart from open fight there were some things many people could do and a few did, such as hiding or tendering other help to anti-Nazis or Jews.

But even taking a decisive inner stand required readiness to give up present and future position; to risk economic security; in some cases to risk the emotional security that comes from living closely with one's family. Again only those few could run such a risk who felt secure in themselves about how little either possessions or status meant to them, and how secure they were in their emotional attachments to those closest to them, no matter what might happen. But this, until most of us have reached the higher integration needed for life in the mass state, is a security only few of us possess.

So it can readily be seen how living under such conditions weakens self respect and finally brings about the disintegration of the individual. It is less readily seen how this leads with near necessity to a deep split in the personality, and with it the destruction of autonomy.

The terror spread by the existence of the camps, and the various actions, made every German who was not deeply secure in himself wish to remain not just silent, but to show no action or reaction whatsoever that might displease those in power. It was just as in the camps: while the good child may be seen and not heard, the German citizen had to be unseen and also dumb.

It is one thing to behave like a child because one is a child: dependent, lacking in foresight and understanding, taken care of by bigger, older, wiser adults, forced by them to behave, but occasionally able to defy them and get away with it; most important of all, feeling certain that in time, as one reached adulthood oneself, all this would be righted. It is quite another thing to be an adult and have to force oneself to assume childish behavior, and for all time to come. The need to force it on oneself probably has deep psychological consequences that do not hold for the child's being forced to it by others.

It was not just coercion by others into helpless dependency; it was also a clean splitting of the personality. Man's anxiety, his wish to protect his life, forced him to relinquish what is ultimately his best chance for survival: his ability to react appropriately and to make decisions. But giving these up, he was no longer a man but a child. Knowing that for survival he should decide and act, and trying to survive by not reacting—these in their combination overpowered the individual to such a degree that he was eventually shorn of all self respect and all feelings of independence.

## I. Suggestions for Discussion:

1. What kinds of defenses did German citizens develop against the threat of the Gestapo and the concentration camps?
2. Why did some citizens behave like children?
3. What were the psychological consequences of childish behavior?

## II. Suggestions for Writing:

1. Discuss the way you handled an encounter with a rigid, authoritarian figure at some time in the past. Would you react in the same fashion again?
2. Using your own experience or observations, describe the way in which people you knew reacted to the demands of authority in the military service, in boarding school, or in camp.

---

# ANNE BRADSTREET

## To My Dear Children

---

Anne Bradstreet (1612–1672) came to Massachusetts from England in 1630. While raising her family in Puritan New England,

she wrote poetry and the brief spiritual autobiography presented
here.

Writing in sickness to her children, she describes her own spiritual
growth and the doubts that occasionally assailed her. She urges
her family to accept tribution as an opportunity to understand
God's ways and to learn to love God more fully.

---

> This book by any yet unread,
> I leave for you when I am dead,
> That, being gone, here you may find
> What was your living mother's mind.
> Make use of what I leave in love
> And God shall bless you from above.

*My dear children,*

I, knowing by experience that the exhortations of parents take most effect when the speakers leave to speak, and those especially sink deepest which
are spoke latest—and being ignorant whether on my death bed I shall have
opportunity to speak to any of you, much less to all—thought it the best,
whilst I was able to compose some short matters (for what else to call them I
know not) and bequeath to you, that when I am no more with you, yet I may
be daily in your remembrance (although that is the least in my aim in what I
now do), but that you may gain some spiritual advantage by my experience.
I have not studied in this you read to show my skill, but to declare the truth—
not to set forth myself, but the glory of God. If I had minded the former, it
had been perhaps better pleasing to you—but seeing the last is the best, let
it be best pleasing to you.

The method I will observe shall be this—I will begin with God's dealing
with me from my childhood to this day.

In my young years, about 6 or 7 as I take it, I began to make conscience of my ways, and what I knew was sinful, as lying, disobedience to
parents, etc. I avoided it. If at any time I was overtaken with the like evils, it
was as a great trouble. I could not be at rest till by prayer I had confessed it
unto God. I was also troubled at the neglect of private duties, though too
often tardy that way. I also found much comfort in reading the Scriptures,
especially those places I thought most concerned my condition, and as I
grew to have more understanding, so the more solace I took in them.

In a long fit of sickness which I had on my bed I often communed with my heart, and made my supplication to the most High who set me free from that affliction.

But as I grew up to be about 14 or 15 I found my heart more carnal, and sitting loose from God, vanity and the follies of youth take hold of me.

About 16, the Lord laid His hand sore upon me and smote me with the smallpox. When I was in my affliction, I besought the Lord, and confessed my pride and vanity and He was entreated of me, and again restored me. But I rendered not to Him according to the benefit received.

After a short time I changed my condition and was married, and came into this country, where I found a new world and new manners, at which my heart rose. But after I was convinced it was the way of God, I submitted to it and joined to the church at Boston.

After some time I fell into a lingering sickness like a consumption, together, with a lameness, which correction I saw the Lord sent to humble and try me and do me good: and it was not altogether ineffectual.

It pleased God to keep me a long time without a child, which was a great grief to me, and cost me many prayers and tears before I obtained one, and after him gave me many more, of whom I now take the care, that as I have brought you into the world, and with great pains, weakness, cares, and fears brought you to this, I now travail in birth again of you till Christ be formed in you.

Among all my experiences of God's gracious dealings with me I have constantly observed this, that He hath never suffered me long to sit loose from Him, but by one affliction or other hath made me look home, and search what was amiss—so usually thus it hath been with me that I have no sooner felt my heart out of order, but I have expected correction for it, which most commonly hath been upon my own person, in sickness, weakness, pains, sometimes on my soul, in doubts and fears of God's displeasure, and my sincerity towards Him, sometimes He hath smote a child with a sickness, sometimes chastened by losses in estate—and these times (through His great mercy) have been the times of my greatest getting and advantage, yea I have found them the times when the Lord hath manifested the most love to me. Then have I gone to searching, and have said with David, Lord search me and try me, see what ways of wickedness are in me, and lead me in the way everlasting, and seldom or never but I have found either some sin I lay under which God would have reformed, or some duty neglected which He would have performed. And by His help I have laid vows and bonds upon my soul to perform His righteous commands.

If at any time you are chastened of God, take it as thankfully and joyfully as in greatest mercies, for if ye be His ye shall reap the greatest benefit by it. It hath been no small support to me in times of darkness when the Almighty hath hid His face from me, that yet I have had abundance of sweetness and refreshment after affliction, and more circumspection in my walking after I have been afflicted. I have been with God like an untoward child, that no longer than the rod has been on my back (or at least in sight) but I have been apt to forget Him and myself too. Before I was afflicted I went astray, but now I keep Thy statutes.

I have had great experience of God's hearing my prayers, and returning comfortable answers to me, either in granting the thing I prayed for, or else in satisfying my mind without it; and I have been confident it hath been from Him, because I have found my heart through His goodness enlarged in thankfulness to Him.

I have often been perplexed that I have not found that constant joy in my pilgrimage and refreshing which I supposed most of the servants of God have; although He hath not left me altogether without the witness of His holy spirit, who hath oft given me His word and set to His seal that it shall be well with me. I have sometimes tasted of that hidden manna that the world knows not, and have set up my Ebenezer[1] and have resolved with myself that against such a promise, such tastes of sweetness, the gates of hell shall never prevail. Yet have I many times sinkings and droopings, and not enjoyed that felicity that sometimes I have done. But when I have been in darkness and seen no light, yet have I desired to stay myself upon the Lord.

And, when I have been in sickness and pain, I have thought if the Lord would but lift up the light of His countenance upon me, although He ground me to powder, it would be but light to me; yea, oft have I thought were I in hell itself, and could there find the love of God toward me, it would be a heaven. And, could I have been in heaven without the love of God, it would have been a hell to me; for, in truth, it is the absence and presence of God that makes heaven or hell.

Many times hath Satan troubled me concerning the verity of the Scriptures, many times by atheism how I could know whether there was a God; I never saw any miracles to confirm me, and those which I read of how did I know but they were feigned. That there is a God my reason would soon tell me by the wondrous works that I see, the vast frame of the heaven and the earth, the order of all things, night and day, summer and winter, spring and autumn, the daily providing for this great household upon the earth, the pre-

---

[1] Samuel set up a stone called Ebenezer to commemorate a Hebrew victory over the Philistines.

serving and directing of all to its proper end. The consideration of these things would with amazement certainly resolve me that there is an Eternal Being. But how should I know He is such a God as I worship in Trinity, and such a Saviour as I rely upon? Though this hath thousands of times been suggested to me, yet God hath helped me over. I have argued thus with myself. That there is a God I see. If ever this God hath revealed himself, it must be in His Word, and this must be it or none. Have I not found that operation by it that no human invention can work upon the soul? Hath not judgments befallen divers who have scorned and contemned it? Hath it not been preserved through all ages maugre[2] all the heathen tyrants and all of the enemies who have opposed it? Is there any story but that which shows the beginnings of times, and how the world came to be as we see? Do we not know the prophecies in it fulfilled which could not have been so long foretold by any but God Himself?

When I have got over this block, then have I another put in my way, that admit this be the true God whom we worship, and that be His Word, yet why may not the Popish religion be the right? They have the same God, the same Christ, the same word: they only interpret it one way, we another.

This hath sometimes stuck with me, and more it would, but the vain fooleries that are in their religion, together with their lying miracles and cruel persecutions of the saints, which admit were they as they term them, yet not so to be dealt withal.

The consideration of these things and many the like would soon turn me to my own religion again.

But some new troubles I have had since the world has been filled with blasphemy, and sectaries, and some who have been accounted sincere Christians have been carried away with them, that sometimes I have said, Is there faith upon the earth? and I have not known what to think. But then I have remembered the works of Christ that so it must be, and if it were possible, the very elect should be deceived. Behold, saith our Saviour, I have told you before. That hath stayed my heart, and I can now say, Return, O my Soul, to thy rest, upon this rock Christ Jesus will I build my faith; and, if I perish, I perish. But I know all the Powers of Hell shall never prevail against it. I know whom I have trusted, and whom I have believed, and that He is able to keep that I have committed to His charge.

Now to the King, immortal, eternal and invisible, the only wise God, be honor and glory for ever and ever. Amen.

[2] Despite.

This was written in much sickness and weakness, and is very weakly and imperfectly done; but, if you can pick any benefit out of it, it is the mark which I aimed at.

I. **Suggestions for Discussion**:
   1. What is Anne Bradstreet's purpose in writing this autobiographical essay?
   2. What doubts about her faith does she discuss? Does her choice of examples and illustrations move you as a reader? Explain.
   3. Discuss her use of biblical allusions.

II. **Suggestions for Writing**:
   1. Write an autobiographical account of a period of tribulation or suffering in your own life.
   2. Describe a situation in which your religious beliefs brought you consolation.

## HEYWOOD BROUN

### A Study in Sportsmanship

Heywood Broun (1888–1939) was an American columnist, dramatic critic, reporter, and sportswriter who helped found the American Newspaper Guild.

In the following essay, originally published in 1925, Broun argues that college football is taken too seriously and that winning games costs players and fans too high a price.

A young man is being supported by two comrades as he limps across a field. It would not be stretching a point to call him a boy, as he is just past nineteen. His face is grimed and bloody and one foot drags behind him. He is crying. Not because of his injury, mind you, for this is a deeper hurt. A cause for which he has fought is going down in defeat. After the grave disaster of this afternoon his team has lost all claim to the football championship of Cambridge, New Haven, and Princeton, N.J.

He is young, you say, and will soon get over the tragedy which has come upon him. I am not so sure of that. I remember the man who dropped the punt during my Freshman year at Harvard. Everybody thought Yale would win easily, but the crimson line was holding beyond all expectations. The score was 0 to 0 and then this man came into the game. The first play to follow was a punt by the Yale fullback. This man had the ball squarely in his arms. He dropped it. Down flashed a Yale end and in six rushes the ball was carried over the line. There was no further scoring. Yale won.

All this happened in November, and in June there wandered about the yard an unhappy soul who was known to all his fellows as "the man who dropped the punt." He was a senior and it may be that graduation brought some release, although it must have been hard for him to find a spot in the United States to which the news of his mishap had never carried. Fate had been harsh to him but not unscrupulous, exactly. He did drop the punt. The true protagonist of the tragedy was another. He might have been spared, for at the time his brother dropped the punt this one had not yet matriculated at Harvard. That made no difference. The tradition endured. During his four years of college life he was known universally as "the brother of the man who dropped the punt."

And in all seriousness I advance the surmise that there are middle-aged men in this country who have been a little embittered and shaken for thirty years because of the fact that in some critical football game they acquitted themselves badly. The team on which they played was beaten.

I don't think this is a fantastic assumption. Unless he grows up to be President, or defendant in an important murder trial, the college football player is likely to receive far more extensive and searching newspaper publicity during his undergraduate days than at any other period of his life. He is called upon to face an emotional crisis in his life and to be watched by seventy thousand as he faces it. On the following day several million people will read of what he did. The quarterback who calls for a plunge through center will be publicly denounced as dull-witted if the play is piled up just short of the goal line. To stumble in the spotlight never did anybody any good, and if the man who fails happens to be nineteen years old he may get an ego bruise which will leave him permanently tender. And if he succeeds brilliantly he may be no better off. The American community is cluttered with ineffective young men who gave their souls to learn dropkicking and then found that there was no future in it.

The football player is not permitted to take any big game casually. Emotionalizing his men is accepted by the coach as a necessary part of his functions. "I was assigned to work on a big halfback," a former football star at Harvard told me. "He was a good defensive player but in the early games he didn't seem to show much fire. He was a lonely sort of fellow and it took me some time to find a line to get going on. We talked awhile and he told me that he came from Weston, Massachusetts. I said to him, 'My brother lives in Weston, and when you get in that game to-morrow I want you to play so that he and everybody else in Weston will be proud of you. You don't want to disgrace my brother in Weston, do you?'

"It was perfectly true that I did have a brother in Weston," my football friend continued, "and the angle I took worked all right. In fact it worked a little too well. After I'd been talking about Weston for quite a time this big halfback began to cry. I couldn't get him to stop. He was crying the next morning when we got out to the field and the doctor wouldn't let him attend the talk before the game. The doctor had to walk him up and down the sidelines to get him quieted down. Still he did go in and play a whale of a game."

I've always wanted to get an exact transcript of the parting words of a head coach to his men or his subsequent speech between the halves. I do know one but it was delivered to the squad of a comparatively small college. Just before the North Carolina eleven took the gridiron against Harvard their coach said to his players. "I want you boys to remember that every man on the Harvard team is a Republican."

But in this case oratory failed. The game was a conventional Republican landslide. More effective was an address delivered to another Southern team which invaded the North. On this occasion the coach relinquished his privilege of providing the last words and called an old gentleman into the locker room. And the voice of the veteran rang out like a trumpet call. He spoke of the Civil War and of how the South had held the Yankees back for four years. There was a line not to be split by any Yankee plunger. And the sons of Rebs could do it again. The man called on the excited youngsters to remember Stonewall Jackson and Robert E. Lee. They remembered and played gloriously but later there was hard feeling, for the discovery was made that the old man had never served with any of the great commanders whom he mentioned but had actually marched with Sherman from Atlanta to the Sea.

Coaches are fond of saying, "I want you boys to fight and to keep on fighting." If asked to explain his precise meaning the coach would undoubtedly answer with complete sincerity, "I told them to play hard." But it does not always work that way. Only too often the instructions are taken all too literally. Football grows cleaner but Spotless Town is still a long march ahead. And when a young man deliberately injures an opposing player by the use of foul tactics there are accessories before the fact. Graduates who insisted loudly that "Dear Old—" must have a winning team, and coaches who said that defeat would sully the honor of the institution, must share in the blame. It isn't possible to rouse impressionable youth right up to the point of being ready to die for "Dear Old—" and not have a few of them, in the heat of battle, come to the decision that some of the foe ought at least to be maimed for the same good cause.

In spite of the stiff penalty provided by the rules, slugging continues. The officials can't see everything. Again and again players are tackled after they have crossed the sidelines and the whistle has blown. Men who are down get jumped upon. To be sure there is a difference between hard football and dirty football. When one watches the big games from way up on the rims of bowls and stadiums he is likely to have a good deal of trouble in detecting just where honest ardor ceases and foul play begins. I have observed, however, that star players tend to get injured a little more often than those of slighter worth. To be sure, the burdens of attack and defense fall more frequently to the stars, but this is not the only reason. Football, even under strict observance of the rules, permits the practice of disarming the enemy by injuring his most conspicuous players.

And in addition to physically dirty play there are other devices not wholly glamorous. A great college coach taught his scrub team to curse the varsity players most foully through an entire week of practice. "It worked well," explained a veteran of that eleven. "When we got into the big game that Saturday I never paid any attention to the names they were calling me. I don't care about being called names like that, but the practice made me used to it. The coach told us not to listen to anything but the signals and to go through with our assignments. They did all the cursing and we won the game."

And if all this is well founded, why is college football looked upon as the very flower and pattern of the highest sporting ideals in America? I don't know why. I like to watch college football and I can get emotional about it, but when I want moral stimulus and confirmation for my faith in the fundamental romanticism of man I go to see professional baseball. There have been scandals in the big leagues and even the most worthy and honest player is paid for his performances on the diamond. That doesn't matter. The distinction between the amateur and the professional cannot be reduced to a simple formula. In any field of endeavor your true and authentic amateur is a man who plays a game gleefully. I have never seen any college player who seemed to get half so much fun out of football as Babe Ruth derives from baseball. Ruth is able to contribute this gusto to his game spontaneously. Nobody makes him a set speech in the dressing room before he embarks to meet his

test. The fans will not spell out "N-E-W Y-O-R-K" with colored handkerchiefs
to inspirit him. There will be no songs about hitting the line. Indeed, Ruth
will not even be asked to die for the cause he represents.

Instead of running out at top speed, Babe Ruth may be observed am-
bling quite slowly in the general direction of the diamond. He approaches a
day's work. This thing before him is a job and it would not be fitting for him
to run. But a little later you may chance to see a strange thing happen. The
professional ball players take up their daily tasks. Soon, in the cause of duty,
Ruth is called upon to move from right center all the way to the edge of the
foul line. And now he is running. To the best of my knowledge and belief
there is no current gridiron hero who runs with the entire earnestness of
Ruth. Once I saw him charge full tilt against the wall of the Yankee Stadium.
It was a low wall and Ruth's big body was so inextricably committed to forward motion that a wall was insufficient to quell the purpose inhering in the
moving mass. And so his head and shoulders went over the barrier and, after
a time, his feet followed. The resulting tumble must have been at least as
vicious as any tackle ever visited upon a charging halfback. But for Ruth there
was no possibility of time out. He could not ask so much as the indulgence of
a sponge or a paper drinking cup. Shaking the disorders out of his spinning
head, he tumbled himself back over the wall again and threw a runner out at
the plate.

It is my impression that in the savage charge up to the wall and over,
Ruth was wholly in the grip of the amateur spirit. If he had stopped short of
the terrific tumble his pay would have still continued. To me there is nothing
very startling in the fact that young men manage to commit themselves
wholeheartedly to sport without hope of financial return. That is a commonplace. Recruiting volunteer workers for any cause is no trouble at all. I grow
more sentimental over a quality much rarer in human experience. I give my
admiration utterly to that man who can put the full sweep of effort into a job
even though he is paid for it.

The bleeding right-tackle making a last stand on the goal line is to me a
lesser figure than Walter Johnson staving off the attack of the Giants in the
final game of the World's Series. For, as I look at it, the bleeding tackle is
fighting merely for the honor and glory of his college. My mind will not
accept him as a satisfactory symbol of any larger issue. But when Johnson
pitched I felt that the whole samurai tradition was at stake. Once I shook
hands with Walter Johnson and he remarked that the late summer had been a
handicap for pitchers. Nothing more was said and I got no direct personal
emanation from the man which convinced me that I was in the presence of
true greatness. It never was the real Johnson but only the fictional one which

captured my imagination. He was the Prince of Pitchers and the Strikeout King. From Montana he came to the big leagues to throw a baseball faster than it had ever been thrown before. And as a boy I read of how the hands of his catcher were bruised and maimed by the ordeal of receiving this mighty delivery.

And so Johnson became a demigod, and I am always sad when the gods die. I saw Johnson sicken under torture as the Giants scourged him. I watched him driven to the dugout in defeat. And then I saw him come back from his cavern revivified with all his old magic. This demigod was alive again and before me was played out a solar myth. So it had been with Buddha and Osiris. There is resiliency in the soul of man and he may lie down to bleed awhile and return refreshed. College football is just a game; professional baseball can rise to the height of a religious experience.

And it is a religion with only the scantiest bonds of ritual. It is incumbent upon the faithful to stretch in the seventh inning. Beyond complying with that one easy ceremony, the roofer has no responsibility in this Quaker meeting. If he chooses to sit silent that is permissible. Only when the spirit truly summons him is there any necessity of shouting. And so I find the emotion of a big-league ball game far more genuine and deep rooted than at any college football encounter. All shade and sensitivity is sacrificed in football by the pernicious practice of regimentation. "A long cheer with three Harvards on the end," cries the man in the white sweater through his megaphone. It is entirely possible that at the precise moments he calls upon me and my fellows to declare ourselves there is stored up in none of us more than a short cheer. It may even be that we have no inclination to cheer at all. Still, the duty is heavy upon us and we must render lipservice.

Before the afternoon is done the vilest sort of hypocrisy will be forced upon us. When the team in blue comes out upon the gridiron we shall all be called upon to render them a long cheer and to add three "Yale's" for courtesy. This is in violation of the deeper feelings of the human heart. We wish no success to Yale. At the mass meeting eloquent speakers have pointed out that it is imperative to the honor of Harvard that Yale shall be turned back from our gates. Already we have sung of our intention to smash, bleach, and ride them down. And here we are called upon to cheer them. It is all too distracting. Ambivalency is not a condition which one cares to celebrate at the top of his voice.

The psychology of baseball is much more simple and more honest. The Washington rooter makes no pretense of wishing the Giants well. He pays them the compliment of thorough-going opposition. In the first game of the last World's Series two home runs were made by New York players. It was as if a lace handkerchief had been tossed into the Grand Canyon. This was an aggressive silence. A sincere horror and anguish struck forty thousand people into a muteness which fairly throbbed. They made no dishonest pretense of polite applause but maintained instead an honorable silence.

And yet your baseball player and your baseball fan never take defeat in any such tragic spirit as the football collegian. Finality is so long delayed. The game which is lost may be cancelled by victory on the succeeding day. And all this serves to create in the mind of the impressionable a picture of life more accurate than that which is conveyed by football. Defeat is a portion of every man born into the world. He must learn to accept it and, if he is to amount to much in his community, he must get from every check a certain stimulus to appeal from the decision. There is no use crying over spilt milk because it is no great trouble to run around the corner and get another bottle. As our Salvation Army friends say, "A man may be down but he's never out." That won't do for a football proverb. A team can be both. Princeton, let us say, has just run rings around Harvard. The final whistle has blown. From this there can be no appeal. The issue may not be tried again. The teams will not meet for another year and then many a new figure will be in the lineup of either side. Here is a finality which is disturbing. The Harvard rooters have no recourse except to say that football is not so terribly important and that anyway Harvard still has a better English department.

I arranged that my small son should first come into contact with sport by watching professional baseball. One reason is wholly unconnected with ethics. When he asks questions I am better prepared to answer them. But beyond that I don't want him to think of a game as something which leaves two or three young men stretched on their backs in the wake of every smashing play. I cannot think up any good reason, suitable to his immature years, why these young men should submit to such an ordeal. The chairman of the football committee at a great Eastern University explained to a mass meeting that preparedness was the chief justification for intercollegiate football. He said that unless the young men of America submitted to the arduous discipline and drill of training and the hard knocks of fighting football, we should have no adequate officers for our next war. But I won't want to use that reasoning on my small son. I have tried to enlist him in the determined ranks of those who insist that there will be no next war.

Only once did I ever hear of an official football speech which met with my entire approval. It was made by a Harvard captain. His team had lost to Yale but by a smaller score than was expected. It had been a fast and interesting game. At the dinner when the team broke training the captain said, "We lost to Yale but I think we had a satisfactory season. We have had fun out of football and it seems to me that ought to be the very best reason for playing the game."

A shocked silence followed his remarks. He was never invited to come to Cambridge to assist in the coaching of any future Harvard eleven. His heresy was profound. He had practically intimated that being defeated was less than tragic.

I. **Suggestions for Discussion:**
1. Analyze each of the arguments Broun raises against college football. Are some arguments stronger than others? Explain.
2. Discuss the details and illustrations Broun uses to bolster his arguments.
3. On what grounds does Broun claim that the psychology of baseball is simpler and better than that of football? Do you agree? Explain.

II. **Suggestions for Writing:**
1. Defend or attack Broun's charges against college football.
2. Write an impassioned half-time speech which a coach might give to bolster his team's spirits.

---

# PEARL S. BUCK

## A Debt to Dickens

---

Pearl S. Buck (1892-1973), the American novelist and essayist, lived in China for many years. She received the Pulitzer Prize for her novel about China, *The Good Earth,* and in 1938 was awarded the Nobel Prize for Literature.

In the following essay, she recounts her early life in China and discusses the important part that the novels of Charles Dickens played in her development as a person.

---

I have long looked for an opportunity to pay a certain debt which I have owed since I was seven years old. Debts are usually burdens, but this is no ordinary debt, and it is no burden, except as the feeling of warm gratitude may ache in one until it is expressed. My debt is to an Englishman, who long ago in China rendered an inestimable service to a small American child. That child was myself and that Englishman was Charles Dickens.[1] I know no better way to meet my obligation than to write down what Charles Dickens did in China for an American child.

First, you must picture to yourself that child, living quite solitary in a remote Chinese countryside in a small mission bungalow perched upon a hill among the rice fields in the valleys below. In the near distance wound that deep, treacherous, golden river, the Yangtse, and some of the most terrifying and sinister, as well as the most delightful and exciting moments of that child's life, were spent beside the river. She loved to crawl along its banks upon the rocks or upon the muddy flats and watch for the lifting of the huge four-square nets that hung into the moving yellow flood, and see out of that flood come perhaps again and again an empty net, but sometimes great flashing, twisting silver bodies of fish. She lingered beside villages of boat folk, and saw them live, the babies tied to a rope and splashing in the shallower waters. But she saw babies dead thrown into the deep waters. She wandered small and alien among the farm folk in the earthen houses among the fields. She accepted a bowl of rice and cabbage often at meal time and sat among the peasants on the threshing floor about the door and ate, usually in silence, listening and listening, answering their kindly, careless questions, bearing with shy, painful smiles their kind, teasing laughter at her yellow curls and unfortunate blue eyes, which they thought so ugly. She was, she knew, very alien. Upon the streets of the great city where sometimes she went she learned to accept the cry of foreign devil, and to realize she was a foreign devil. Once when she was very, very small, before she knew better, she turned as worms will, and flung back a word she had learned among the boat folk when they quarrelled. It was a word so wicked that the youth who called her foreign devil ran howling with terror, and thereafter she went more contentedly, not using the word any more because of its great wickedness, but knowing she had it to use if she needed it very much.

She grew from a very tiny child into a bigger child, still knowing she was alien. However kindly the people about her might be, and they were much more often kind than not, she knew that she was foreign to them. And she wondered very much about her own folk and where they were and how they looked and at what they played. But she did not know. In the bungalow were her parents, very busy, very, very busy, and when she had learned her lessons in the morning quickly, they were too busy to pay much heed to her and so she wandered about a great deal, seeing and learning all sorts of things. She had fun. But very often she used to wonder, "Where are the other chil-

---

[1] Charles Dickens (1812–1870) was a famous and enormously popular English novelist.

dren like me? What is it like in the country where they live?" She longed
very much, I can remember, to have some of them to play with. But she never
had them.

To this small, isolated creature there came one day an extraordinary
accident. She was an impossibly voracious reader. She would like to have had
children's books, but there were none, and so she read everything—Plutarch's
*Lives* and Fox's *Martyrs,* the Bible, church history, and the hot spots in Jonathan Edwards's sermons, and conversations out of Shakespeare, and bits of
Tennyson and Browning which she could not understand at all. Then one day
she looked doubtfully at a long row of somber blue books on a very high
shelf. They were quite beyond her reach. Later she discovered this was because they were novels. But being desperate she put a three-cornered bamboo
stool on top of a small table and climbed up and stared at the bindings and
in faded black titles she read *Oliver Twist,* by Charles Dickens. She was then
a little past seven years old. It was a very hot August day, in the afternoon
about three o'clock, when the household was asleep, all except the inde-
fatigable parents, and they were very, very busy. She took *Oliver Twist* out
of his place—it was fat and thick, for *Hard Times* was bound with it—and in
great peril descended, and stopping in the pantry for a pocket full of peanuts,
she made off to a secret corner of the veranda into which only a small, agile
child could squeeze, and opened the closely printed pages of an old edition,
and discovered her playmates.

How can I make you know what that discovery was to that small,
lonely child? There in that corner above the country road in China, with
vendors passing beneath me, I entered into my own heritage. I cannot tell
you about those hours. I know I was roused at six o'clock by the call to my
supper, and I looked about dazed, to discover the long rays of the late afternoon sun streaming across the valleys. I remember twice I closed the book
and burst into tears, unable to bear the tragedy of Oliver Twist, and then
opened it quickly again, burning to know more. I remember, most significant
of all, that I forgot to touch a peanut, and my pocket was still quite full when
I was called. I went to my supper in a dream, and read as late as I dared in
my bed afterward, and slept with the book under my pillow, and woke again
in the early morning. When *Oliver Twist* was finished, and after it *Hard
Times,* I was wretched with indecision. I felt I must read it all straight over
again, and yet I was voracious for that long row of blue books. What was in
them? I climbed up again, finally, and put *Oliver Twist* at the beginning, and
began on the next one, which was *David Copperfield.* I resolved to read
straight through the row and then begin at the beginning once more and read
straight through again.

This program I carried on consistently, over and over, for about ten years, and after that I still kept a Dickens book on hand, so to speak, to dip into and feel myself at home again. Today I have for him a feeling which I have for no other human soul. He opened my eyes to people, he taught me to love all sorts of people, high and low, rich and poor, the old and little children. He taught me to hate hypocrisy and pious mouthing of unctuous words. He taught me that beneath gruffness there may be kindness, and that kindness is the sweetest thing in the world, and goodness is the best thing in the world. He taught me to despise money grubbing. People today say he is obvious and sentimental and childish in his analysis of character. It may be so, and yet I have found people surprisingly like those he wrote about—the good a little less undiluted, perhaps, and the evil a little more mixed. And I do not regret that simplicity of his, for it had its own virtue. The virtue was of a great zest for life. If he saw everything black and white, it was because life rushed out of him strong and clear, full of love and hate. He gave me that zest, that immense joy in life and in people, and in their variety.

He gave me, too, my first real glimpse of a kindly English God, a sort of father, to whom the childlike and the humble might turn. There was no talk of hell in his books. He made Christmas for me, a merry, roaring English Christmas, full of goodies and plum puddings and merriment and friendly cheer. I went to his parties over and over again, for I had no others. I remember one dreadful famine winter the thing that kept me laughing and still a child was *Pickwick Papers*. I read it over and over, and laughed, as I still laugh, over the Wellers and the widow and Mr. Pickwick and all his merry company. They were as real to me as the sad folk outside the compound walls, and they saved me.

And he made me love England. I have no drop of English blood in my veins. I have German and Dutch and French ancestors, I was born in the United States of American parents, and I have spent my life in China. But part of me is English, for I love England with a peculiar, possessing love. I do possess something of England. When I went there years later, London was my city and the countryside I knew. I was not strange. The people were my own people, too. England is the mother of a certain part of my spirit. I can never take sides against England or the English. It is not only that we speak a common tongue and that we are the same race. There is far more than that. I know English people. I love English people. I have grown up among them. I am used to them. They have been my companions for many years. They are forever my friends. When several years ago in China there was a period of misunderstanding of certain British policies, I steadfastly refused to agree with the distrust expressed by some of my Chinese friends toward England. I was sure of the quality of the English people and of their integrity. What they said they would do, they would do. And they did. Their armies were peacefully withdrawn when the necessity of protection was over, they did not proceed to the conquest the Chinese thought was inevitable, and more than any Western power they have steadily shown their honesty of purpose toward the Chinese. After it was over, my Chinese friends said wondering, "You were right." And I replied, "I knew I was."

This is what Charles Dickens did for me. His influence I cannot lose. He has made himself a part of me forever.

I. **Suggestions for Discussion:**
  1. Under what circumstances did Buck read Dickens?
  2. What did Buck learn from Dickens?
  3. Discuss Buck's description of her early life in China.

II. **Suggestions for Writing:**
  1. Write an essay discussing the impact which a particular book or film has had on you.
  2. Briefly describe an unusual place you have visited. Use sensory details to bring your description to life.

---

# SAMUEL BUTLER

## A Bumpkin or Country-Squire

---

Samuel Butler (1612–1680), the English poet and character writer, is famous for his long, learned satiric poem, *Hudibras* (1663–1678). His character sketches, which satirized English manners and mores, were not published until 1759.

In this brief character sketch, Butler uses many details to draw an exaggerated picture of the coarse, crude habits of a seventeenth century English country squire.

---

A bumpkin or country-squire is a clown of rank and degree. He is the growth of his own land, a kind of Autochthonus,[1] like the Athenians, that sprung out of their own ground; or barnacles that grow upon trees in Scot-

---

[1] A native inhabitant.

land: his homely education has rendered him a native only of his own soil, and a foreigner to all other places, from which he differs in language, manner of living, and behaviour, which are as rugged as the coat of a colt that has been bred upon a common. The custom of being the best man in his own territories has made him the worst everywhere else. He assumes the upper end of the table at an ale-house, as his birthright; receives the homage of his company, which are always subordinate, and dispenses ale and communication, like a self-conforming teacher in a conventicle.[2] The chief points he treats on are the memoirs of his dogs and horses, which he repeats as often as a holder-forth, that has but two sermons; to which if he adds the history of his hawks and fishing, he is very painful and laborious. He does his endeavor to appear a drole, but his wit being, like his estate, within the compass of a hedge, is so profound and obscure to a stranger, that it requires a commentary, and is not to be understood without a perfect knowledge of all circumstances of persons and the particular idiom of the place. He has no ambition to appear a person of civil prudence and understanding, more than in putting off a lame infirm jade for sound wind and limb; to which purpose he brings his squirehood and groom to vouch; and, rather than fail, will outswear an affidavit-man. The top of his entertainment is horrible strong beer, which he pours into his guests (as the Dutch did water into our merchants when they tortured them at Amboyna) till they confess they can drink no more; and then he triumphs over them as subdued and vanquished, no less by the strength of his brain, than his drink. When he salutes a man, he lays violent hands upon him, and gripes and shakes him, like a fit of an ague: and, when he accosts a lady, he stamps with his foot, like a French fencer, and makes a longee at her, in which he always misses his aim, too high or too low, and hits her on the nose or chin. He is never without some rough-handed flatterer, that rubs him, like a horse, with a curry-comb, till he kicks and grunts with the pleasure of it. He has old family stories and jests that fell to him with the estate and have been left from heir to heir time out of mind; with these he entertains all comers over and over, and has added some of his own times, which he intends to transmit over to posterity. He has but one way of making all men welcome that come to his house, and that is by making himself and them drunk; while his servants take the same course with theirs, which he approves of as good and faithful service, and the rather because, if he has occasion to tell a strange improbable story, they may be in readiness to vouch with the more impudence and make it a case of conscience to lie as well as drink for his credit. All the heroical glory he aspires to, is but to be reputed a most potent and victorious stealer of deer and beater-up of parks, to which purpose he has

[2] An illicit meeting.

compiled commentaries of his own actions that treat of his dreadful adventures in the night, of giving battle in the dark, discomfiting keepers, horsing the deer on his own back, and making off with equal resolution and success. He goes to bawdy-houses to see fashions; that is, to have his pocket picked, and the pox into the bargain.

I. **Suggestions for Discussion:**
   1. Discuss the fairness of Butler's character sketch. Does Butler deliberately ignore favorable qualities? Explain.
   2. Discuss Butler's choice of details in the sketch.
   3. Compare Butler's sketch with that of Henry Fielding in "The Education of English Youth," p. 179.

II. **Suggestions for Writing:**
   1. Describe what you think might be the bumpkin's good qualities.
   2. Write a sketch of an unusual character whom you know or have observed.

---

# THOMAS CARLYLE

## The Execution of Louis XVI

---

Thomas Carlyle (1795-1881), the English social critic and historian, is known for such works as *Sartor Resartus* (1833-1834), *Past and Present* (1843), and the *History of Frederick the Great* (1858-1865). John Stuart Mill, the English philosopher who had been asked to read the manuscript of the first volume of *The French Revolution,* accidentally burned it, forcing Carlyle to rewrite his text before publication in 1837. The following selection is taken from volume three of that history.

Carlyle's majestic prose is eminently suited to his story of the death of King Louis XVI during the French Revolution. Vivid details enrich the account.

---

To this conclusion, then, hast thou come, O hapless Louis! The Son of Sixty Kings is to die on the Scaffold by form of Law. Under Sixty Kings this same form of Law, form of Society, has been fashioning itself together, these thousand years; and has become, one way and other, a most strange Machine. Surely, if needful, it is also frightful, this Machine; dead, blind; not what it should be; which, with swift stroke, or by cold slow torture, has wasted the lives and souls of innumerable men. And behold now a King himself, or say rather Kinghood in his person, is to expire here in cruel tortures;—like a Phalaris shut in the belly of his own red-heated Brazen Bull![1] It is ever so; and thou shouldst know it, O haughty tyrannous man: injustice breeds injustice; curses and falsehoods do verily return 'always *home*,' wide as they may wander. Innocent Louis bears the sins of many generations: he too experiences that man's tribunal is not in this Earth; that if he had no Higher one, it were not well with him.

A King dying by such violence appeals impressively to the imagination; as the like must do, and ought to do. And yet at bottom it is not the King dying, but the man! Kingship is a coat: the grand loss is of the skin. The man from whom you take his Life, to him can the whole combined world do *more*? Lally[2] went on his hurdle; his mouth filled with a gag. Miserablest mortals, doomed for picking pockets, have a whole five-act Tragedy in them, in that dumb pain, as they go to the gallows, unregarded; they consume the cup of trembling down to the lees. For Kings and for Beggars, for the justly doomed and the unjustly, it is a hard thing to die. Pity them all: thy utmost pity, with all aids and appliances and throne-and-scaffold contrasts, how far short is it of the thing pitied?

A Confessor has come; Abbé Edgeworth, of Irish extraction, whom the King knew by good report, has come promptly on this solemn mission. Leave the Earth alone, then, thou hapless King; it with its malice will go its way, thou also canst go thine. A hard scene yet remains: the parting with our loved ones. Kind hearts, environed in the same grim peril with us; to be left *here*! Let the Reader look with the eyes of Valet Cléry, through these glass-doors, where also the Municipality watches; and see the cruellest of scenes:

'At half-past eight, the door of the anteroom opened: the Queen appeared first, leading her Son by the hand; then Madame Royale and Madame Elizabeth: they all flung themselves into the arms of the King. Silence reigned for some minutes; interrupted only by sobs. The Queen made a movement to lead his Majesty towards the inner room, where M. Edgeworth was waiting unknown to them: "No," said the King, "let us go into the dining-room, it is

---

[1] Phalaris was a tyrant who executed criminals by placing them in a bronze bull and then having a fire lit under it.
[2] Baron de Lally-Tollendal (1702–1766) was beheaded in France for supposed treasonable dealings with England.

there only that I can see you." They entered there; I shut the door of it, which was of glass. The King sat down, the Queen on his left hand, Madame Elizabeth on his right, Madame Royale almost in front; the young Prince remained standing between his Father's legs. They all leaned towards him, and often held him embraced. This scene of woe lasted an hour and three quarters; during which we could hear nothing; we could see only that always when the King spoke, the sobbings of the Princesses redoubled, continued for some minutes; and that then the King began again to speak.'—And so our meetings and our parting do now end! The sorrows we gave each other; the poor joys we faithfully shared, and all our lovings and our sufferings, and confused toilings under the earthly Sun, are over. Thou good soul, I shall never, never through all ages of Time, see thee any more!—NEVER! O Reader, knowest thou that hard word?

For nearly two hours this agony lasts; then they tear themselves asunder. 'Promise that you will see us on the morrow.' He promises:—Ah yes, yes; yet once; and go now, ye loved ones; cry to God for yourselves and me!—It was a hard scene, but it is over. He will not see them on the morrow. The Queen, in passing through the ante-room, glanced at the Cerberus Municipals; and, with woman's vehemence, said through her tears, *'Vous etes tous des scélérats.'*[3]

King Louis slept sound, till five in the morning, when Cléry, as he had been ordered, awoke him. Cléry dressed his hair: while this went forward, Louis took a ring from his watch, and kept trying it on his finger; it was his wedding-ring, which he is now to return to the Queen as a mute farewell. At half-past six, he took the Sacrament; and continued in devotion, and conference with Abbé Edgeworth. He will not see his Family: it were too hard to bear.

At eight, the Municipals enter: the King gives them his Will, and messages and effects; which they, at first, brutally refuse to take charge of: he gives them a roll of gold pieces, a hundred and twenty-five louis; these are to be returned to Malesherbes,[4] who had lent them. At nine, Santerre says the hour is come. The King begs yet to retire for three minutes. At the end of three minutes, Santerre again says the hour is come. 'Stamping on the ground with his right foot, Louis answers: *"Partons,* Let us go." '—How the the rolling of those drums comes in, through the Temple bastions and bulwarks, on the heart of a queenly wife; soon to be a widow! He is gone, then, and has not

---

[3] To the officers of the Municipal Government, she says, "You are all scoundrels."
[4] Chrétien Guillaume de Lamoignon de Malesherbes (1721–1794), one of the king's ministers, defended him at his trial and was guillotined in 1794.

seen us? A Queen weeps bitterly; a King's Sister and Children. Over all these Four does Death also hover: all shall perish miserably save one; she, as Duchesse d'Angoulême, will live,—not happily.

At the Temple Gate were some faint cries, perhaps from voices of pitiful women: '*Grâce! Grâce!*' Through the rest of the streets there is silence as of the grave. No man not armed is allowed to be there: the armed, did any even pity, dare not express it, each man overawed by all his neighbours. All windows are down, none seen looking through them. All shops are shut. No wheel-carriage rolls, this morning, in these streets but one only. Eighty-thousand armed men stand ranked, like armed statues of men; cannons bristle, cannoneers with match burning, but no word or movement: it is as a city enchanted into silence and stone: one carriage with its escort, slowly rumbling, is the only sound. Louis reads, in his Book of Devotion, the Prayers of the Dying: clatter of this death-march falls sharp on the ear, in the great silence; but the thought would fain struggle heavenward, and forget the Earth.

As the clocks strike ten, behold the Place de la Révolution, once Place de Louis Quinze: the Guillotine, mounted near the old Pedestal where once stood the Statue of that Louis! Far round, all bristles with cannons and armed men: spectators crowding in the rear; D'Orléans Égalité there in cabriolet. Swift messengers, *hoquetons*,[5] speed to the Townhall, every three minutes: near by is the Convention sitting,—vengeful for Lepelletier.[6] Heedless of all, Louis reads his Prayers of the Dying; not till five minutes yet has he finished; then the Carriage opens. What temper he is in? Ten different witnesses will give ten different accounts of it. He is in the collision of all tempers; arrived now at the black Mahlstrom and descent of Death: in sorrow, in indignation, in resignation struggling to be resigned. "Take care of M. Edgeworth,' he straitly charges the Lieutenant who is sitting with them: then they two descend.

The drums are beating: '*Taisez-vous,* Silence!' he cries 'in a terrible voice, *d'une voix terrible.*' He mounts the scaffold, not without delay; he is in puce coat, breeches of grey, white stockings. He strips off the coat; stands disclosed in a sleeve-waistcoat of white flannel. The Executioners approach to bind him: he spurns, resists; Abbé Edgeworth has to remind him how the Saviour, in whom men trust, submitted to be bound. His hands are tied, his head bare; the fatal moment is come. He advances to the edge of the Scaffold,

---

[5] Guardsmen.
[6] Louis Michel Lepelletier de Saint-Fargeau (1760–1793) had been assassinated after voting for the king's death.

'his face very red,' and says: 'Frenchmen, I die innocent: it is from the Scaffold and near appearing before God that I tell you so. I pardon my enemies; I desire that France—' A General on horseback, Santerre or another, prances out, with uplifted hand: '*Tambours!*'[7] The drums drown the voice. 'Executioners, do your duty!' The Executioners, desperate lest themselves be murdered (for Santerre and his Armed Ranks will strike, if they do not), seize the hapless Louis: six of them desperate, him singly desperate, struggling there; and bind him to their plank. Abbé Edgeworth, stooping, bespeaks him: 'Son of Saint Louis, ascend to Heaven.' The Axe clanks down; a King's Life is shorn away. It is Monday the 21st day of January 1793. He was aged Thirty-eight years four months and twenty-eight days.

Executioner Samson shows the Head: fierce shout of *Vive la République* rises, and swells; caps raised on bayonets, hats waving: students of the College of Four Nations take it up, on the far Quais; fling it over Paris. D'Orléans drives off in his cabriolet: the Townhall Councillors rub their hands, saying, 'It is done, It is done.' There is dipping of handkerchiefs, of pike-points in the blood. Headsman Samson, though he afterwards denied it, sells locks of the hair: fractions of the puce coat are long after worn in rings.—And so, in some half-hour it is done; and the multitude has all departed. Pastry-cooks, coffee-sellers, milkmen sing out their trivial quotidian cries: the world wags on, as if this were a common day. In the coffee-houses that evening, says Prudhomme,[8] Patriot shook hands with Patriot in a more cordial manner than usual. Not till some days after, according to Mercier, did public men see what a grave thing it was. . . .

At home this Killing of a King has divided all friends; and abroad it has united all enemies. Fraternity of Peoples, Revolutionary Propagandism; Atheism, Regicide; total destruction of social order in this world! All Kings, and lovers of Kings, and haters of Anarchy, rank in coalition; as in a war for life. England signifies to Citizen Chauvelin, the Ambassador or rather Ambassador's-Cloak, that he must quit the country in eight days. Ambassador's-Cloak and Ambassador, Chauvelin and Talleyrand, depart accordingly. Talleyrand, implicated in that Iron Press of the Tuileries,[9] thinks it safest to make for America.

England has cast out the Embassy: England declares war,—being

---

[7] Drums!
[8] L. M. Prudhomme (1752–1830) and L. S. Mercier (1740–1814) were French revolutionary journalists.
[9] Charles Maurice Talleyrand-Périgord (1754–1838) went to the United States because of suspicions against him raised by letters found in the king's records.

shocked principally, it would seem, at the condition of the River Scheldt. Spain declares war; being shocked principally at some other thing; which doubtless the Manifesto indicates. Nay we find it was not England that declared war first, or Spain first; but that France herself declared war first on both of them;—a point of immense Parliamentary and Journalistic interest in those days, but which has become of no interest whatever in these. They all declare war. The sword is drawn, the scabbard thrown away. It is even as Danton said, in one of his all-too gigantic figures: 'The coalized Kings threaten us; we hurl at their feet, as gage of battle, the Head of a King.'

**I. Suggestions for Discussion:**
   1. Discuss Carlyle's use of detail to give immediacy to the scene he depicts.
   2. Discuss his use of dialogue and exclamation.
   3. What impact did the death of Louis XVI have on England?

**II. Suggestions for Writing:**
   1. Write a narrative account of the death of a prominent person about whom you have read.
   2. Write a newspaper account of the death of Louis XVI.
   3. Compare Carlyle's account of the death of Louis XVI with Thomas Macaulay's account of the death of Monmouth, p. 324.

---

## RACHEL CARSON

### What Makes Waves

from *The Sea Around Us*

---

Rachel Carson (1907–1964) was a marine biologist and early ecologist. She wrote movingly about the sea in such books as *The Edge of the Sea* and *The Sea Around Us* (1950), from which the present selection is taken. In *Silent Spring* (1962), she warned of the dangers of insecticides to the environment.

In the following essay, she analyzes the life and physical characteristics of a typical wave formed by the action of wind on water.

---

As long as there has been an earth, the moving masses of air that we call winds have swept back and forth across its surface. And as long as there has been an ocean, its waters have stirred to the passage of the winds. Most waves are the result of the action of wind on water. There are exceptions, such as the tidal waves sometimes produced by earthquakes under the sea. But the waves most of us know best are wind waves.

It is a confused pattern that the waves make in the open sea—a mixture of countless different wave trains, intermingling, overtaking, passing, or sometimes engulfing one another; each group differing from the others in the place and manner of its origin, in its speed, its direction of movement; some doomed never to reach any shore, others destined to roll across half an ocean before they dissolve in thunder on a distant beach.

Out of such seemingly hopeless confusion the patient study of many men over many years has brought a surprising amount of order. While there is still much to be learned about waves, and much to be done to apply what is known to man's advantage, there is a solid basis of fact on which to reconstruct the life history of a wave, predict its behavior under all the changing circumstances of its life, and foretell its effect on human affairs.

Before constructing an imaginary life history of a typical wave, we need to become familiar with some of its physical characteristics. A wave has height, from trough to crest. It has length, the distance from its crest to that of the following wave. The period of the wave refers to the time required for succeeding crests to past a fixed point. None of these dimensions is static; all change, but bear definite relations to the wind, the depth of the water, and many other matters. Furthermore, the water that composes a wave does not advance with it across the sea, each water particle describes a circular or elliptical orbit with the passage of the wave form, but returns very nearly to its original position. And it is fortunate that this is so, for if the huge masses of water that comprise a wave actually moved across the sea, navigation would be impossible. Those who deal professionally in the lore of waves make frequent use of a picturesque expression—the "length of fetch." The "fetch" is the distance that the waves have run, under the drive of a wind blowing in a constant direction, without obstruction. The greater the fetch, the higher the waves. Really large waves cannot be generated within the confined space of a bay or a small sea. A fetch of perhaps 600 to 800 miles, with winds of gale velocity, is required to get up the largest ocean waves.

Now let us suppose that, after a period of calm, a storm develops far out in the Atlantic, perhaps a thousand miles from the New Jersey coast where we are spending a summer holiday. Its winds blow irregularly, with sudden gusts, shifting direction but in general blowing shoreward. The sheet

of water under the wind responds to the changing pressures. It is no longer a
level surface; it becomes furrowed with alternating troughs and ridges. The
waves move toward the coast, and the wind that created them controls their
destiny. As the storm continues and the waves move shoreward, they receive
energy from the wind and increase in height. Up to a point they will continue
to take to themselves the fierce energy of the wind, growing in height as the
strength of the gale is absorbed, but when a wave becomes about a seventh as
high from trough to crest as the distance to the next crest, it will begin to
topple in foaming whitecaps. Winds of hurricane force often blow the tops
off the waves by their sheer violence; in such a storm the highest waves may
develop after the wind has begun to subside.

But to return to our typical wave, born of wind and water far out in the
Atlantic, grown to its full height on the energy of the winds, with its fellow
waves forming a confused, irregular pattern known as a "sea." As the waves
gradually pass out of the storm area their height diminishes, the distance
between successive crests increases, and the "sea" becomes a "swell," moving
at an average speed of about 15 miles an hour. Near the coast a pattern of
long, regular swells is substituted for the turbulence of open ocean. But as
the swell enters shallow water a startling transformation takes place. For the
first time in its existence, the wave feels the drag of shoaling bottom. Its
speed slackens, crests of following waves crowd in toward it, abruptly its
height increases and the wave form steepens. Then with a spilling, tumbling
rush of water falling down into its trough, it dissolves in a seething confusion
of foam.

An observer sitting on a beach can make at least an intelligent guess
whether the surf spilling out onto the sand before him has been produced by
a gale close offshore or by a distant storm. Young waves, only recently
shaped by the wind, have a steep, peaked shape even well out at sea. From
far out on the horizon you can see them forming whitecaps as they come in;
bits of foam are spilling down their fronts and boiling and bubbling over the
advancing face, and the final breaking of the wave is a prolonged and deliberate process. But if a wave, on coming into the surf zone, rears high as
though gathering all its strength for the final act of its life, if the crest forms
all along its advancing front and then begins to curl forward, if the whole
mass of water plunges suddenly with a booming roar into its trough—then
you may take it that these waves are visitors from some very distant part of
the ocean, that they have traveled long and far before their final dissolution
at your feet.

What is true of the Atlantic wave we have followed is true, in general,
of wind waves the world over. The incidents in the life of a wave are many.

How long it will live, how far it will travel, to what manner of end it will come are all determined, in large measure, by the conditions it meets in its progression across the face of the sea. For the one essential quality of a wave is that it moves; anything that retards or stops its motion dooms it to dissolution and death.

## I. Suggestions for Discussion:

1. Define the height, length, and period of a wave. Are Carson's definitions clear and sufficiently detailed? Comment.
2. Why does the height of a wave increase as it approaches the shore?
3. Discuss the process by which a wave is born, moves, and dies. Does Carson's analysis leave any unanswered questions in your mind? Explain.

## II. Suggestions for Writing:

1. Based on your observations and research, write an essay about a process in nature like a snowfall, the formation of smog, or an eclipse of the sun or moon.
2. Describe a process with which you are familiar, such as changing a tire or using a computer terminal.

---

# SHIRLEY CHISHOLM

## Women and Their Liberation

---

Shirley Chisholm (1924–    ) is a member of Congress from New York's Twelfth Congressional District. She has been an outspoken advocate of black and of women's rights.

In the following essay, she compares the discrimination against women in our society with that experienced by black Americans. She exhorts women to assert their rights vigorously and, in particular, urges them to become involved in politics.

---

When a young woman graduates from college and starts looking for a job, one question every interviewer is sure to ask her is "Can you type?" There is an entire system of prejudice unspoken behind that question, which is rarely if ever asked of a male applicant. One of my top assistants in my Washington office has always refused to learn to type, although not knowing how has been an inconvenience, because she refused to let herself be forced into a dead-end clerical job.

Why are women herded into jobs as secretaries, librarians, and teachers and discouraged from being managers, lawyers, doctors, and members of Congress? Because it is assumed that they are different from men. Today's new militant campaigners for women's rights have made the point that for a long time society discriminated against blacks on the same basis: they were different and inferior. The cheerful old darky on the plantation and the happy little homemaker are equally stereotypes drawn by prejudice. White America is beginning to be able to admit that it carries racial prejudice in its heart, and that understanding marks the beginning of the end of racism. But prejudice against women is still acceptable because it is invisible. Few men can be persuaded to believe that it exists. Many women, even, are the same way. There is very little understanding yet of the immorality involved in double pay scales and the classification of the better jobs "for men only." More than half the population of the United States is female, but women occupy only 2 percent of the managerial positions. They have not yet even reached the level of tokenism. No woman has ever sat on the Supreme Court, or the AFL-CIO council. There have been only two women who have held cabinet rank, and at present there are none. Only two women now hold ambassadorial rank in the diplomatic corps. In Congress, there are one woman senator and ten representatives. Considering that there are about 3.5 million more women in the United States than men, this is outrageous.

It is true that women have seldom been aggressive in demanding their rights and so have cooperated in their own enslavement. This was true of the black population for many years. They submitted to oppression, and even condoned it. But women are becoming aware, as blacks did, that they can have equal treatment if they will fight for it, and they are starting to organize. To do it, they have to dare the sanctions that society imposes on anyone who breaks with its traditions. This is hard, and especially hard for women, who are taught not to rebel from infancy, from the time they are first wrapped in pink blankets, the color of their caste. Another disability is that women have been programmed to be dependent on men. They seldom have economic freedom enough to let them be free in more significant ways, at least until they become widows and most of their lives are behind them.

That there are no female Supreme Court justices is important, but not as important as the fact that ordinary working women by the millions are subjected to the most naked and unjustified discrimination, by being confined to the duller and less well-paid jobs or by being paid less than men for doing the same work. Here are a recent year's figures from the Labor Department: white males earned an average of $7179 a year, black males $4508, white women $4142, and black women $2934. Measured in uncontestable dollars and cents, which is worse—race prejudice or antifeminism? White women are at an economic disadvantage even compared to black men, and black women are nowhere on the earnings scale.

Guidance counselors discriminate against girls just as they have long done with young black or Puerto Rican male students. They advise a black boy to prepare for a service-oriented occupation, not a profession. They steer a girl toward her "natural career," of being a wife and mother, and plan an occupational goal for her that will not interfere too much with that aim. The girl responds just as the average young black does, with mute agreement. Even if she feels vaguely rebellious at the limitations being put on her future before it has even begun, she knows how the cards are stacked against her and she gives in.

Young minority-group people do not get this treatment quite as much as they did, because they have been radicalized and the country has become more sensitive to its racist attitudes and the damage they do. Women too must rebel. They should start in school, by rejecting the traditional education society considers suitable to them, and which amounts to educational, social, and economic slavery.

There are relevant laws on the books, just as there are civil rights laws on the books. In the 91st Congress, I am a sponsor of the perennial Equal Rights Amendment, which has been before every Congress for the last forty years but has never passed the House. It would outlaw any discrimination on the basis of sex. Men and women would be completely equal before the law. But laws will not solve deep-seated problems overnight. Their use is to provide shelter for those who are most abused, and to begin an evolutionary process by compelling the insensitive majority to reexamine its unconscious attitudes.

The law cannot do the major part of the job of winning equality for women. Women must do it themselves. They must become revolutionaries. Against them is arrayed the weight of centuries of tradition, from St. Paul's "Let women learn in silence" down to the American adage, "A woman's place is in the home." Women have been persuaded of their own inferiority; too many of them believe the male fiction that they are emotional, illogical, unstable, inept with mechanical things, and lack leadership ability.

The best defense against this slander is the same one blacks have found. While they were ashamed of their color, it was an albatross hanging around their necks. They freed themselves from that dead weight by picking up their blackness and holding it out proudly for all the world to see. They found their own beauty and turned their former shame into their badge of honor. Women should perceive that the negative attitudes they hold toward their own femaleness are the creation of an antifeminist society, just as the black shame at being black was the product of racism. Women should start to replace their negative ideas of their femininity with positive ones affirming their nature more and more strongly.

It is not female egotism to say that the future of mankind may very well be ours to determine. It is a fact. The warmth, gentleness, and compassion that are part of the female stereotype are positive human values, values that are becoming more and more important as the values of our world begin to shatter and fall from our grasp. The strength of Christ, Gandhi, and Martin Luther King was a strength of gentleness, understanding, and compassion, with no element of violence in it. It was, in short, a *female* strength, and that is the kind that often marks the highest type of man.

If we reject our restricted roles, we do not have to reject these values of femaleness. They are enduring values, and we must develop the capacity to hold them and to dispense them to those around us. We must become revolutionaries in the style of Gandhi and King. Then, working toward our own freedom, we can help the others work free from the traps of their stereotypes. In the end, antiblack, antifemale, and all forms of discrimination are equivalent to the same thing—antihumanism. The values of life must be maintained against the enemies in every guise. We can do it by confronting people with their own humanity and their own inhumanity whenever we meet them, in the streets, in school, in church, in bars, in the halls of legislatures. We must reject not only the stereotypes that others have of us but also those we have of ourselves and others.

In particular, I am certain that more and more American women must become involved in politics. It could be the salvation of our nation. If there were more women in politics, it would be possible to start cleaning it up. Women I have known in government have seemed to me to be much more apt to act for the sake of a principle or moral purpose. They are not as likely as men to engage in deals, manipulations, and sharp tactics. A larger proportion of women in Congress and every other legislative body would serve as a reminder that the real purpose of politicians is to work for the people.

The woman who gets into politics will find that the men who are already there will treat her as the high school counselor treats girls. They see her as someone who is obviously just playing at politics part-time, because, after all, her real place is at home being a wife and mother. I suggested a bright young woman as a candidate in New York City a while ago; she had unlimited potential and with good management and some breaks could become an important person to the city. A political leader rejected her. "Why invest all the time and effort to build up the gal into a household name," he asked me, "when she's pretty sure to drop out of the game to have a couple of kids at just about the time we're ready to run her for mayor?"

Many women have given their lives to political organizations, laboring anonymously in the background while men of far less ability managed and mismanaged the public trust. These women hung back because they knew the men would not give them a chance. They knew their place and stayed in it. The amount of talent that has been lost to our country that way is appalling. I think one of my major uses is as an example to the women of our country, to show them that if a woman has ability, stamina, organizational skill, and a knowledge of the issues she can win public office. And if I can do it, how much more hope should that give to white women, who have only one handicap?

One distressing thing is the way men react to women who assert their equality: their ultimate weapon is to call them unfeminine. They think she is antimale; they even whisper that she's probably a lesbian, a tact some of the Women's Liberation Front have encountered. I am not antimale any more than I am antiwhite, and I am not antiwhite, because I understand that white people, like black ones, are victims of a racist society. They are products of their time and place. It's the same with men. This society is as antiwoman as it is antiblack. It has forced males to adopt discriminatory attitudes toward females. Getting rid of them will be very hard for most men—too hard, for many of them.

Women are challenged now as never before. Their numbers in public office, in the professions, and in other key fields are declining, not increasing. The decline has been gradual and steady for the last twenty years. It will be difficult to reverse at first. The women who undertake to do it will be stigmatized as "odd" and "unfeminine" and must be prepared to endure such punishment. Eventually the point will be made that women are not different from men in their intelligence and ability and that women who aspire to important jobs—president of the company, member of Congress, and so on—are *not* odd and unfeminine. They aspire for the same reasons as any man—they think they can do the job and they want to try.

For years to come, most men will jeer at the women's liberation groups that are springing up. But they will someday realize that countless women, including their own wives and especially their daughters, silently applaud the liberation groups and share their goals, even if they are unable to bring themselves to rebel openly. American women are beginning to respond to our oppression. While most of us are not yet revolutionaries, the time is coming when we will be. The world must be taught that, to use the words of Women's Liberation activist Robin Morgan, "Women are not inherently passive or peaceful. We're not inherently anything but human. And like every other oppressed people rising up today, we're out for our freedom by any means necessary."

**I. Suggestions for Discussion:**
1. In what sense must women become revolutionaries, according to Chisholm? Do you agree? Explain.
2. Compare and contrast the search for equal rights in American society by women and by blacks.
3. To what extent has the situation Chisholm described in 1970 changed?
4. Compare Chisholm's advice to women with that offered by Virginia Woolf in "Professions for Women," p. 597.

**II. Suggestions for Writing:**
1. Using your experiences and observations, discuss the current state of efforts by women to gain equal rights.
2. Write a brief biographical sketch of a woman who has succeeded in politics. Did she have to overcome special obstacles?

## SAMUEL LANGHORNE CLEMENS

### Fenimore Cooper's Literary Offenses

Samuel Langhorne Clemens (1835–1910), who wrote under the pseudonym Mark Twain, is one of America's most important humorists and social critics. His experiences on the Mississippi River and in the American west gave him source material for such major works as *Roughing It* (1872), *The Adventures of Tom Sawyer* (1876), *Life on the Mississippi* (1883), and *The Adventures of Huckleberry Finn* (1884).

The essay that follows is a long and very funny analysis of James Fenimore Cooper's popular frontier novel, *The Deerslayer* (1841).

Clemens gleefully ridicules the absurdities he notes in plot, setting, and character.

---

*The Pathfinder* and *The Deerslayer* stand at the head of Cooper's novels as artistic creations. There are others of his works which contain parts as perfect as are to be found in these, and scenes even more thrilling. Not one can be compared with either of them as a finished whole.

The defects in both of these tales are comparatively slight. They were pure works of art.    *—Prof. Lounsbury*

The five tales reveal an extraordinary fulness of invention.

. . . One of the very greatest characters in fiction, "Natty Bumppo." . . .

The craft of the woodsman, the tricks of the trapper, all the delicate art of the forest, were familiar to Cooper from his youth up.    *—Prof. Brander Matthews*

Cooper is the greatest artist in the domain of romantic fiction yet produced by America.    *—Wilkie Collins*

It seems to me that it was far from right for the Professor of English Literature in Yale, the Professor of English Literature in Columbia, and Wilkie Collins, to deliver opinions on Cooper's literature without having read some of it. It would have been much more decorous to keep silent and let persons talk who have read Cooper.

Cooper's art has some defects. In one place in *Deerslayer,* and in the restricted space of two-thirds of a page, Cooper has scored 114 offences against literary art out of a possible 115. It breaks the record.

There are nineteen rules governing literary art in the domain of romantic fiction—some say twenty-two. In *Deerslayer* Cooper violated eighteen of them. These eighteen require:

1. That a tale shall accomplish something and arrive somewhere. But the *Deerslayer* tale accomplishes nothing and arrives in the air.

2. They require that the episodes of a tale shall be necessary parts of the tale, and shall help to develop it. But as the *Deerslayer* tale is not a tale, and accomplishes nothing and arrives nowhere, the episodes have no rightful place in the work, since there was nothing for them to develop.

3. They require that the personages in a tale shall be alive, except in the case of corpses, and that always the reader shall be able to tell the corpses from the others. But this detail has often been overlooked in the *Deerslayer* tale.

4. They require that the personages in a tale, both dead and alive, shall exhibit a sufficient excuse for being there. But this detail also has been overlooked in the *Deerslayer* tale.

5. They require that when the personages of a tale deal in conversation, the talk shall sound like human talk, and be talk such as human beings would be likely to talk in the given circumstances, and have a discoverable meaning, also a discoverable purpose, and a show of relevancy, and remain in the neighborhood of the subject in hand, and be interesting to the reader, and help out the tale, and stop when the people cannot think of anything more to say. But this requirement has been ignored from the beginning of the *Deerslayer* tale to the end of it.

6. They require that when the author describes the character of a personage in his tale, the conduct and conversation of that personage shall justify said description. But this law gets little or no attention in the *Deerslayer* tale, as "Natty Bumppo's" case will amply prove.

7. They require that when a personage talks like an illustrated, gilt-edged, tree-calf, hand tooled, seven-dollar Friendship's Offering in the beginning of a paragraph, he shall not talk like a negro minstrel in the end of it. But this rule is flung down and danced upon in the *Deerslayer* tale.

8. They require that crass stupidities shall not be played upon the reader as "the craft of the woodsman, the delicate art of the forest," by either the author or the people in the tale. But this rule is persistently violated in the *Deerslayer* tale.

9. They require that the personages of a tale shall confine themselves to possibilities and let miracles alone; or, if they venture a miracle, the author must so plausibly set it forth as to make it look possible and reasonable. But these rules are not respected in the *Deerslayer* tale.

10. They require that the author shall make the reader feel a deep interest in the personages of his tale and in their fate; and that he shall make the reader love the good people in the tale and hate the bad ones. But the reader of the *Deerslayer* tale dislikes the good people in it, is indifferent to the others, and wishes they would all get drowned together.

11. They require that the characters in a tale shall be so clearly defined that the reader can tell beforehand what each will do in a given emergency. But in the *Deerslayer* tale this rule is vacated.

In addition to these large rules there are some little ones. These require that the author shall

12. *Say* what he is proposing to say, not merely come near it.

13. Use the right word, not its second cousin.

14. Eschew surplusage.

15. Not omit necessary details.
16. Avoid slovenliness of form.
17. Use good grammar.
18. Employ a simple and straightforward style.

Even these seven are coldly and persistently violated in the *Deerslayer* tale.

Cooper's gift in the way of invention was not a rich endowment; but such as it was he liked to work it, he was pleased with the effects, and indeed he did some quite sweet things with it. In his little box of stage properties he kept six or eight cunning devices, tricks, artifices for his savages and woodsmen to deceive and circumvent each other with, and he was never so happy as when he was working these innocent things and seeing them go. A favorite one was to make a moccasined person tread in the tracks of the moccasined enemy, and thus hide his own trail. Cooper wore out barrels and barrels of moccasins in working that trick. Another stage-property that he pulled out of his box pretty frequently was his broken twig. He prized his broken twig above all the rest of his effects, and worked it the hardest. It is a restful chapter in any book of his when somebody doesn't step on a dry twig and alarm all the reds and whites for two hundred yards around. Every time a Cooper person is in peril, and absolute silence is worth four dollars a minute, he is sure to step on a dry twig. There may be a hundred handier things to step on, but that wouldn't satisfy Cooper. Cooper requires him to turn out and find a dry twig; and if he can't do it, go and borrow one. In fact the Leather Stocking Series ought to have been called the Broken Twig Series.

I am sorry there is not room to put in a few dozen instances of the delicate art of the forest, as practiced by Natty Bumppo and some of the other Cooperian experts. Perhaps we may venture two or three samples. Cooper was a sailor—a naval officer; yet he gravely tells us how a vessel, driving toward a lee shore in a gale, is steered for a particular spot by her skipper because he knows of an *undertow* there whch will hold her back against the gale and save her. For just pure woodcraft, or sailorcraft, or whatever it is, isn't that neat? For several years Cooper was daily in the society of artillery, and he ought to have noticed that when a cannon ball strikes the ground it either buries itself or skips a hundred feet or so; skips again a hundred feet or so—and so on, till it finally gets tired and rolls. Now in one place he loses some "females"—as he always calls women—in the edge of a wood near a plain at night in a fog, on purpose to give Bumppo a chance to show off the delicate art of the forest before the reader. These mislaid people are hunting for a fort. They hear a cannon-blast, and a cannon-ball presently comes rolling into the wood and stops at their feet. To the females this suggests nothing. The case is very different with the admirable Bumppo. I wish I may never know peace again if he doesn't strike out promptly and *follow the track* of that cannon-ball across the plain through the dense fog and find the fort. Isn't it a daisy? If Cooper had any real knowledge of Nature's ways of doing things, he had a most delicate art in concealing the fact. For instance: one of his acute Indian experts, Chingachgook (pronounced Chicago, I think), has lost the trail of a person he is tracking through the forest. Apparently that trail is hopelessly lost. Neither you nor I could ever have guessed out the way to find it. It was very different with Chicago. Chicago was not stumped for long. He turned a running stream out of its course, and there, in the slush in its old bed, were that person's moccasin-tracks. The current did not wash them away, as it would have done in all other like cases— no, even the eternal laws of Nature have to vacate when Cooper wants to put up a delicate job of woodcraft on the reader.

We must be a little wary when Brander Matthews tells us that Cooper's books "reveal an extraordinary fulness of invention." As a rule, I am quite willing to accept Brander Matthews's literary judgments and applaud his lucid and graceful phrasing of them; but that particular statement needs to be taken with a few tons of salt. Bless your heart, Cooper hadn't any more invention than a horse; and I don't mean a high-class horse, either; I mean a clothes-horse. It would be very difficult to find a really clever "situation" in Cooper's books; and still more difficult to find one of any kind which he has failed to render absurd by his handling of it. Look at the episodes of "the caves;" and at the celebrated scuffle between Maqua and those others on the table-land a few days later; and at Hurry Harry's queer water-transit from the castle to the ark, and at Deerslayer's half hour with his first corpse; and at the quarrel between Hurry Harry and Deerslayer later; and at—but choose for yourself; you can't go amiss.

If Cooper had been an observer, his inventive faculty would have worked better, not more interestingly, but more rationally, more plausibly. Cooper's proudest creations in the way of "situations" suffer noticeably from the absence of the observer's protecting gift. Cooper's eye was splendidly inaccurate. Cooper seldom saw anything correctly. He saw nearly all things as through a glass eye, darkly. Of course a man who cannot see the commonest little everyday matters accurately is working at a disadvantage when he is constructing a "situation." In the *Deerslayer* tale Cooper has a stream which is fifty feet wide, where it flows out of a lake; it presently narrows to twenty as it meanders along for no given reason, and yet, when a stream acts like that it ought to be required to explain itself. Fourteen pages later the width of the brook's outlet from the lake has suddenly shrunk thirty feet, and become "the narrowest part of the stream." This shrinkage is not accounted for. The stream has bends in it, a sure indication that it has alluvial banks, and cuts them; yet these bends are only thirty and fifty feet long. If Cooper had been a nice and punctilious observer he would have noticed that the bends were oftener nine hundred feet long than short of it.

Cooper made the exit of that stream fifty feet wide in the first place, for no particular reason; in the second place, he narrowed it to less than twenty to accommodate some Indians. He bends a "sapling" to the form of an arch over this narrow passage, and conceals six Indians in its foliage. They are "laying" for a settler's scow or ark which is coming up the stream on its way to the lake; it is being hauled against the still current by a rope whose stationary end is anchored in the lake; its rate of progress cannot be more than a mile an hour. Cooper describes the ark, but pretty obscurely. In the matter of dimensions "it was little more than a modern canal boat." Let us guess, then, that it was about 140 feet long. It was of "greater breadth than common." Let us guess, then, that it was about sixteen feet wide. This leviathan had been prowling down bends where it had only two feet of space to spare on each side. We cannot too much admire this miracle. A low-roofed log dwelling occupies "two-third's of the ark's length"—a dwelling ninety feet long and sixteen feet wide, let us say—a kind of vestibule train. The dwelling has two rooms—each forty-five feet long and sixteen feet wide, let us guess. One of them is the bed-room of the Hutter girls, Judith and Hetty; the other is the parlor, in the day time, at night it is papa's bed chamber. The ark is arriving at the stream's exit, now, whose width has been reduced to less than twenty feet to accommodate the Indians—say to eighteen. There is a foot to spare on each side of the boat. Did the Indians notice that there was going to be a tight squeeze there? Did they notice that they could make money by climbing down out of that arched sapling and just stepping aboard when the ark scraped by? No; other Indians would have noticed these things, but Cooper's Indians never notice anything. Cooper thinks they are marvelous creatures for noticing, but he was almost always in error about his Indians. There was seldom a sane one among them.

The ark is 140 feet long; the dwelling is 90 feet long. The idea of the Indians is to drop softly and secretly from the arched sapling to the dwelling as the ark creeps along under it at the rate of a mile an hour, and butcher the family. It will take the ark a minute and a half to pass under. It will take the 90-foot dwelling a minute to pass under. Now, then, what did the six Indians do? It would take you thirty years to guess, and even then you would have to give it up, I believe. Therefore, I will tell you what the Indians did. Their chief, a person of quite extraordinary intellect for a Cooper Indian, warily

watched the canal boat as it squeezed along under him, and when he had got
his calculations fined down to exactly the right shade, as he judged, he let go
and dropped. And *missed the house*! That is actually what he did. He missed
the house, and landed in the stern of the scow. It was not much of a fall, yet
it knocked him silly. He lay there unconscious. If the house had been 97 feet
long, he would have made the trip. The fault was Cooper's, not his. The error
lay in the construction of the house. Cooper was no architect.

There still remained in the roost five Indians. The boat has passed under
and is now out of their reach. Let me explain what the five did—you would
not be able to reason it out for yourself. No. 1 jumped for the boat, but fell
in the water astern of it. Then No. 2 jumped for the boat, but fell in the
water still further astern of it. Then No. 3 jumped for the boat, and fell a
good way astern of it. Then No. 4 jumped for the boat, and fell in the water
*away* astern. Then even No. 5 made a jump for the boat—for he was a Cooper
Indian. In the matter of intellect, the difference between a Cooper Indian and
the Indian that stands in front of the cigar shop is not spacious. The scow
episode is really a sublime burst of invention; but it does not thrill, because
the inaccuracy of the details throws a sort of air of fictitiousness and general
improbability over it. This comes of Cooper's inadequacy as an observer.

The reader will find some examples of Cooper's high talent for inaccurate observation in the account of the shooting match in *The Pathfinder*.
"A common wrought nail was driven lightly into the target, its head having
been first touched with paint." The color of the paint is not stated—an important omission, but Cooper deals freely in important omissions. No, after
all, it was not an important omission; for this nail head is a *hundred yards*
from the marksman and could not be seen by them at that distance no matter what its color might be. How far can the best eyes see a common house
fly? A hundred yards? It is quite impossible. Very well, eyes that cannot
see a house fly that is a hundred yards away cannot see an ordinary nail head
at that distance, for the size of the two objects is the same. It takes a keen
eye to see a fly or a nail head at fifty yards—one hundred and fifty feet. Can
the reader do it?

The nail was lightly driven, its head painted, and game called. Then the
Cooper miracles began. The bullet of the first marksman chipped an edge of
the nail head; the next man's bullet drove the nail a little way into the target—
and removed all the paint. Haven't the miracles gone far enough now? Not to
suit Cooper; for the purpose of this whole scheme is to show off his prodigy,
Deerslayer-Hawkeye-Long-Rifle-Leather-Stocking-Pathfinder-Bumppo before
the ladies.

"Be all ready to clench it, boys!" cried out Pathfinder, step-ping into his friend's tracks the instant they were vacant. "Never mind a new nail; I can see that, though the paint is gone, and what I can see, I can hit at a hundred yards, though it were only a mosquito's eye. Be ready to clench!"

The rifle cracked, the bullet sped its way and the head of the nail was buried in the wood, covered by the piece of flattened lead.

There, you see, is a man who could hunt flies with a rifle, and command a ducal salary in a Wild West show to-day, if we had him back with us.

The recorded feat is certainly surprising, just as it stands; but it is not surprising enough for Cooper. Cooper adds a touch. He has made Pathfinder do this miracle with another man's rifle, and not only that, but Pathfinder did not have even the advantage of loading it himself. He had everything against him, and yet he made that impossible shot, and not only made it, but did it with absolute confidence, saying, "Be ready to clench." Now a person like that would have undertaken that same feat with a brickbat, and with Cooper to help he would have achieved it, too.

Pathfinder showed off handsomely that day before the ladies. His very first feat was a thing which no Wild West show can touch. He was standing with the group of marksmen, observing—a hundred yards from the target, mind: one Jasper raised his rifle and drove the centre of the bull's-eye. Then the quartermaster fired. The target exhibited no result this time. There was a laugh. "It's a dead miss," said Major Lundie. Pathfinder waited an impressive moment or two, then said in that calm, indifferent, know-it-all way of his, "No, Major—he has covered Jasper's bullet, as will be seen if any one will take the trouble to examine the target."

Wasn't it remarkable! How *could* he see that little pellet fly through the air and enter that distant bullet-hole? Yet that is what he did; for nothing is impossible to a Cooper person. Did any of those people have any deep-seated doubts about this thing? No; for that would imply sanity, and these were all Cooper people.

The respect for Pathfinder's skill and for his *quickness and accuracy of sight* (the italics are mine) was so profound and general, that the instant he made this declaration the spectators began to distrust their own opinions, and a dozen rushed to the target in order to ascertain the fact. There, sure enough, it was found that the quartermaster's bullet had gone through the hole made by Jasper's, and that, too, so accurately as to require a minute examination to be certain of the circumstances, which, however, was soon established by discovering one bullet over the other in the stump against which the target was placed.

They made a "minute" examination; but never mind, how could they know that there were two bullets in that hole without digging the latest one out? for neither probe nor eyesight could prove the presence of any more than one bullet. Did they dig? No; as we shall see. It is the Pathfinder's turn now; he steps out before the ladies, takes aim, and fires.

But alas! here is a disappointment; an incredible, an unimaginable disappointment—for the target's aspect is unchanged; there is nothing there but that same old bullet hole!

"If one dared to hint at such a thing," cried Major Duncan, "I should say that the Pathfinder has also missed the target."

As nobody had missed it yet, the "also" was not necessary; but never mind about that, for the Pathfinder is going to speak.

"No, no, Major," said he, confidently, "that *would* be a risky declaration. I didn't load the piece, and can't say what was in it, but if it was lead, you will find the bullet driving down those of the Quartermaster and Jasper, else is not my name Pathfinder."

A shout from the target announced the truth of this assertion.

Is the miracle sufficient as it stands? Not for Cooper. The Pathfinder speaks again, as he "now slowly advances towards the stage occupied by the females:"

"That's not all, boys, that's not all; if you find the target touched at all. I'll own to a miss. The Quartermaster cut the wood, but you'll find no wood cut by that last messenger."

The miracle is at last complete. He knew—doubtless *saw*—at the distance of a hundred yards—that his bullet had passed into the hole *without fraying the edges*. There were now three bullets in that one hole—three bullets imbedded processionally in the body of the stump back of the target. Everybody knew this—somehow or other—and yet nobody had dug any of them out to make sure. Cooper is not a close observer, but he is interesting. He is certainly always that, no matter what happens. And he is more interesting when he is not noticing what he is about than when he is. This is a considerable merit.

The conversations in the Cooper books have a curious sound in our modern ears. To believe that such talk really even came out of people's mouths would be to believe that there was a time when time was of no value to a person who thought he had something to say; when a man's mouth was a rolling-mill, and busied itself all day long in turning four-foot pigs of thought into thirty-foot bars of conversational railroad iron by attenuation; when subjects were seldom faithfully stuck to, but the talk wandered all around and arrived nowhere; when conversations consisted mainly of irrelevances, with here and there a relevancy, a relevancy with an embarrassed look, as not being able to explain how it got there.

Cooper was certainly not a master in the construction of dialogue. Inaccurate observation defeated him here as it defeated him in so many other enterprises of his. He even failed to notice that the man who talks corrupt English six days in the week must and will talk it on the seventh, and can't help himself. In the *Deerslayer* story he lets Deerslayer talk the showiest kind of book talk sometimes, and at other times the basest of base dialects. For instance, when someone asks him if he has a sweetheart, and if so, where she abides, this is his majestic answer:

> "She's in the forest—hanging from the boughs of the trees, in a soft rain—in the dew on the open grass—the clouds that float about in the blue heavens—the birds that sing in the woods—the sweet springs where I slake my thirst—and in all the other glorious gifts that come from God's Providence!"

And he preceded that, a little before, with this:

> "It consarns me as all things that touches a fri'nd consarns a fri'nd."

And this is another of his remarks:

> "If I was Injin born, now, I might tell of this, or carry in the scalp and boast of the expl'ite afore the whole tribe; or if my inimy had only been a bear"—and so on.

We cannot imagine such a thing as a veteran Scotch Commander-in-Chief comporting himself in the field like a windy melodramatic actor, but

Cooper could. On one occasion Alice and Cora were being chased by the French through a fog in the neighborhood of their father's fort:

> *"Point de quartier aux coquins!"* cried an eager pursuer, who seemed to direct the operations of the enemy.
>
> "Stand firm and be ready, my gallant 60ths!" suddenly exclaimed a voice above them; "wait to see the enemy; fire low, and sweep the glacis."
>
> "Father! father!" exclaimed a piercing cry from out the mist; "it is I! Alice! thy own Elsie! spare, O! save your daughters!"
>
> "Hold!" shouted the former speaker, in the awful tones of parental agony, the sound reaching even to the woods, and rolling back in solemn echo. " 'Tis she! God has restored me my children! Throw open the sally-port; to the field, 60ths, to the field; pull not a trigger, lest ye kill my lambs! Drive off these dogs of France with your steel."

Cooper's word-sense was singularly dull. When a person has a poor ear for music he will flat and sharp right along without knowing it. He keeps near the tune, but it is *not* the tune. When a person has a poor ear for words, the result is a literary flatting and sharping; you perceive what he is intending to say, but you also perceive that he doesn't *say* it. This is Cooper. He was not a word-musician. His ear was satisfied with the *approximate* word. I will furnish some circumstantial evidence in support of this charge. My instances are gathered from half a dozen pages of the tale called *Deerslayer*. He uses "verbal," for "oral"; "precision," for "facility"; "phenomena," for "marvels"; "necessary," for "predetermined"; "unsophisticated," for "primitive"; "preparation," for "expectancy"; "rebuked," for "subdued"; "dependent on," for "resulting from"; "fact," for "condition"; "fact," for "conjecture". "precaution," for "caution"; "explain," for "determine"; "mortified," for "disappointed"; "meretricious," for "factitious"; "materially," for "considerably"; "decreasing," for "deepening"; "increasing," for "disappearing"; "embedded," for "enclosed"; "treacherous," for "hostile"; "stood," for "stopped"; "softened," for "replaced"; "rejoined," for "remarked"; "situation," for "condition"; "different," for "differing"; "insensible," for "unsentient"; "brevity," for "celerity"; "distrusted," for "suspicious"; "mental imbecility," for "imbecility"; "eyes," for "sight"; "counteracting," for "opposing"; "funeral obsequies," for "obsequies."

There have been daring people in the world who claimed that Cooper could write English, but they are all dead now—all dead but Lounsbury. I don't remember that Lounsbury makes the claim in so many words, still he makes it, for he says that *Deerslayer* is a "pure work of art." Pure, in that connection, means faultless—faultless in all details—and language is a detail. If Mr. Lounsbury had only compared Cooper's English with the English which he writes himself—but it is plain that he didn't; and so it is likely that he imagines until this day that Cooper's is as clean and compact as his own. Now I feel sure, deep down in my heart, that Cooper wrote about the poorest English that exists in our language, and that the English of *Deerslayer* is the very worst than even Cooper ever wrote.

I may be mistaken, but it does seem to me that *Deerslayer* is not a work of art in any sense; it does seem to me that it is destitute of every detail that goes to the making of a work of art; in truth, it seems to me that *Deerslayer* is just simply a literary *delirium tremens.*

A work of art? It has no invention; it has no order, system, sequence, or result, it has no lifelikeness, no thrill, no stir, no seeming of reality; its characters are confusedly drawn, and by their acts and words they prove that they are not the sort of people the author claims that they are; its humor is pathetic; its pathos is funny; its conversations are—oh! indescribable; its love-scenes odious; its English a crime against the language.

Counting these out, what is left is Art. I think we must all admit that.

I. **Suggestions for Discussion**:
   1. Discuss some of the rules of literary art Clemens accuses Cooper of violating.
   2. What objections does Clemens raise to Cooper's episode on the river in *Deerslayer*? Are they fair? Explain.
   3. What faults does Clemens find in Cooper's story of the shooting match in *The Pathfinder*?
   4. Discuss whether or not Clemens treats Cooper's novels fairly.

II. **Suggestions for Writing**:
   1. Write a humorous analysis of a short story you have read. Carefully select details that support your critical observations.
   2. Read a selection by Cooper and write a rejoinder to Clemens, if you think one in order.

# SAMUEL LANGHORNE CLEMENS

## On the Decay of the Art of Lying

With tongue in cheek, Clemens worries about a decline in courteous lying and a growing prevalence of the brutal truth. He would have his readers learn to lie thoughtfully, healingly, and charitably.

Essay, for discussion, read at a meeting of the Historical
and Antiquarian Club of Hartford, and offered for
the thirty-dollar prize. Now first published.*

Observe, I do not mean to suggest that the *custom* of lying has suffered any decay or interruption—no, for the Lie, as a Virtue, a Principle, is eternal; the Lie, as a recreation, a solace, a refuge in time of need, the fourth Grace, the tenth Muse, man's best and surest friend, is immortal, and cannot perish from the earth while this Club remains. My complaint simply concerns the decay of the *art* of lying. No high-minded man, no man of right feeling, can contemplate the lumbering and slovenly lying of the present day without grieving to see a noble art so prostituted. In this veteran presence I naturally enter upon this theme with diffidence; it is like an old maid trying to teach nursery matters to the mothers in Israel. It would not become me to criticise you, gentlemen, who are nearly all my elders—and my superiors, in this thing—and so, if I should here and there *seem* to do it, I trust it will in most cases be more in a spirit of admiration than of fault-finding; indeed if this finest of the fine arts had everywhere received the attention, encouragement, and conscientious practice and development which this Club has devoted to it, I should not need to utter this lament, or shed a single tear. I do not say this to flatter: I say it in a spirit of just and appreciative recognition. [It had been my intention, at this point, to mention names and give illustrative specimens, but indications observable about me admonished me to beware of particulars and confine myself to generalities.]

No fact is more firmly established than that lying is a necessity of our circumstances—the deduction that it is then a Virtue goes without saying. No virtue can reach its highest usefulness without careful and diligent cultiva-

*Did not take the prize.

tion—therefore, it goes without saying, that this one ought to be taught in the public schools—at the fireside—even in the newspapers. What chance has the ignorant, uncultivated liar against the educated expert? What chance have I against Mr. Per—against a lawyer? *Judicious* lying is what the world needs. I sometimes think it were even better and safer not to lie at all than to lie injudiciously. An awkward, unscientific lie is often as ineffectual as the truth.

Now let us see what the philosophers say. Note that venerable proverb: Children and fools *always* speak the truth. The deduction is plain—adults and wise persons *never* speak it. Parkman, the historian, says, "The principle of truth may itself be carried into an absurdity." In another place in the same chapter he says, "The saying is old that truth should not be spoken at all times; and those whom a sick conscience worries into habitual violation of the maxim are imbeciles and nuisances." It is strong language, but true. None of us could *live* with an habitual truth-teller; but thank goodness none of us has to. An habitual truth-teller is simply an impossible creature; he does not exist; he never has existed. Of course there are people who *think* they never lie, but it is not so—and this ignorance is one of the very things that shame our so-called civilization. Everybody lies—every day; every hour; awake; asleep; in his dreams; in his joy; in his mourning; if he keeps his tongue still, his hands, his feet, his eyes, his attitude, will convey deception—and purposely. Even in sermons—but that is a platitude.

In a far country where I once lived the ladies used to go around paying calls, under the humane and kindly pretence of wanting to see each other; and when they returned home, they would cry out with a glad voice, saying, "We made sixteen calls and found fourteen of them out"—not meaning that they found out anything against the fourteen—no, that was only a colloquial phrase to signify that they were not at home—and their manner of saying it expressed their lively satisfaction in that fact. Now their pretence of wanting to see the fourteen—and the other two whom they had been less lucky with— was that commonest and mildest form of lying which is sufficiently described as a deflection from the truth. Is it justifiable? Most certainly. It is beautiful, it is noble; for its object is, *not* to reap profit, but to convey a pleasure to the sixteen. The iron-souled truth-monger would plainly manifest, or even utter the fact that he didn't want to see those people—and he would be an ass, and inflict a totally unnecessary pain. And next, those ladies in that far country—but never mind, they had a thousand pleasant ways of lying, that grew out of gentle impulses, and were a credit to their intelligence and an honor to their hearts. Let the particulars go.

The men in that far country were liars, every one. Their mere howdy-do was a lie, because *they* didn't care how you did, except they were undertakers. To the ordinary inquirer you lied in return; for you made no conscientious diagnosis of your case, but answered at random, and usually missed it considerably: You lied to the undertaker, and said your health was failing— a wholly commendable lie, since it cost you nothing and pleased the other man. If a stranger called and interrupted you, you said with your hearty tongue, "I'm glad to see you," and said with your heartier soul, "I wish you were with the cannibals and it was dinner-time." When he went, you said regretfully, "*Must* you go?" and followed it with a "Call again;" but you did no harm, for you did not deceive anbody nor inflict any hurt, whereas the truth would have made you both unhappy.

I think that all this courteous lying is a sweet and loving art, and should be cultivated. The highest perfection of politeness is only a beautiful edifice, built, from the base to the dome, of graceful and gilded forms of charitable and unselfish lying.

What I bemoan is the growing prevalence of the brutal truth. Let us do what we can to eradicate it. An injurious truth has no merit over an injurious lie. Neither should ever be uttered. The man who speaks an injurious truth lest his soul be not saved if he do otherwise, should reflect that that sort of a soul is not strictly worth saving. The man who tells a lie to help a poor devil out of trouble, is one of whom the angels doubtless say, "Lo, here is an heroic soul who casts his own welfare into jeopardy to succor his neighbor's; let us exalt this magnanimous liar."

An injurious lie is an uncommendable thing; and so, also, and in the same degree, is an injurious truth—a fact which is recognized by the law of libel.

Among other common lies, we have the *silent* lie—the deception which one conveys by simply keeping still and concealing the truth. Many obstinate truth-mongers indulge in this dissipation, imagining that if they *speak* no lie, they lie not at all. In that far country where I once lived, there was a lovely spirit, a lady whose impulses were always high and pure, and whose character answered to them. One day I was there at dinner, and remarked, in a general way, that we are all liars. She was amazed, and said, "Not *all*?" It was before "Pinafore's" time, so I did not make the response which would naturally follow in our day, but frankly said, "Yes, *all*—we are all liars; there are no exceptions." She looked almost offended, and said, "Why, do you include *me*?" "Certainly," I said. "I think you even rank as an expert." She said, "'Sh–'sh! the children!" So the subject was changed in deference to the children's presence, and we went on talking about other things. But as soon as the young people were out of the way, the lady came warmly back to the matter and said, "I have made it the rule of my life to never tell a lie; and I have never departed from it in a single instance." I said, "I don't mean the least harm or disrespect, but really you have been lying like smoke ever since I've been sitting here. It has caused me a good deal of pain, because I am not used to it." She required of me an instance—just a single instance. So I said—

"Well, here is the unfilled duplicate of the blank which the Oakland hospital people sent to you by the hand of the sick-nurse when she came here to nurse your little nephew through his dangerous illness. This blank asks all manner of questions as to the conduct of that sick-nurse: 'Did she ever sleep on her watch? Did she ever forget to give the medicine?' and so forth and so on. You are warned to be very careful and explicit in your answers, for the welfare of the service requires that the nurses be promptly fined or otherwise punished for derelictions. You told me you were perfectly delighted with that nurse—that she had a thousand perfections and only one fault: you found you never could depend on her wrapping Johnny up half sufficiently while he waited in a chilly chair for her to rearrange the warm bed. You filled up the duplicate of this paper, and sent it back to the hospital by the hand of the nurse. How did you answer this question—'Was the nurse at any time guilty of a negligence which was likely to result in the patient's taking cold?' Come—everything is decided by a bet here in California: ten dollars to ten cents you lied when you answered that question." She said, "I didn't; *I left it blank!*" "Just so—you have told a *silent* lie; you have left it to be inferred that you had no fault to find in that matter." She said, "Oh, was that a lie? And how *could* I mention her one single fault, and she so good?—it would have been cruel." I said, "One ought always to lie, when one can do good by it; your impulse was right, but your judgment was crude; this comes of unintelligent practice. Now observe the result of this inexpert deflection of yours. You know Mr. Jones's Willie is lying very low with scarlet-fever; well, your recommendation was so enthusiastic that that girl is there nursing him, and the worn-out family have all been trustingly sound asleep for the last fourteen hours, leaving their darling with full confidence in those fatal hands, because you, like young George Washington, have a reputa—However, if you are not going to have anything to do, I will come around to-morrow and we'll attend the funeral together, for, of course, you'll naturally feel a peculiar interest in Willie's case—as personal a one, in fact, as the undertaker."

But that was all lost. Before I was half-way through she was in a carriage and making thirty miles an hour toward the Jones mansion to save what was left of Willie and tell all she knew about the deadly nurse. All of which was unnecessary, as Willie wasn't sick, I had been lying myself. But that same day, all the same, she sent a line to the hospital which filled up the neglected blank, and stated the *facts,* too, in the squarest possible manner.

Now, you see, this lady's fault was *not* in lying, but only in lying in-judiciously. She should have told the truth, *there,* and made it up to the nurse with a fraudulent compliment further along in the paper. She could have said, "In one respect this sick-nurse is perfection—when she is on watch, she never snores." Almost any little pleasant lie would have taken the sting out of that troublesome but necessary expression of the truth.

Lying is universal—we *all* do it; we all *must* do it. Therefore, the wise thing is for us diligently to train ourselves to lie thoughtfully, judiciously; to lie with a good object, and not an evil one; to lie for others' advantage, and not our own; to lie healingly, charitably, humanely, not cruelly, hurtfully, maliciously; to lie gracefully and graciously, not awkwardly and clumsily; to lie firmly, frankly, squarely, with head erect, not haltingly, tortuously, with pusillanimous mien, as being ashamed of our high calling. Then shall we be rid of the rank and pestilent truth that is rotting the land; then shall we be great and good and beautiful, and worthy dwellers in a world where even be-nign Nature habitually lies, except when she promises execrable weather. Then—But I am but a new and feeble student in this gracious art; I cannot instruct *this* Club.

Joking aside, I think there is much need of wise examination into what sorts of lies are best and wholesomest to be indulged, seeing we *must* all lie and *do* all lie, and what sorts it may be best to avoid—and this is a thing which I feel I can confidently put into the hands of this experienced Club—a ripe body, who may be termed, in this regard, and without undue flattery, Old Masters.

## I. Suggestions for Discussion:

1. What does Clemens mean by judicious lying? Give some examples of your own.
2. Comment on Clemens's statement that an habitual truth-teller is simply an impossible creature.
3. Define the "silent lie."
4. What kinds of lying does Clemens recommend? Give examples of your own.

## II. Suggestions for Writing:

1. Describe a situation you have encountered in which a lie was prefer-able to the truth.
2. Make a list of the lies you have heard in the last week and comment on their impact and effect.

# SAMUEL TAYLOR COLERIDGE

## Two Kinds of Mystics

from *Aids to Reflection*

Samuel Taylor Coleridge (1772–1834) was a major poet and critic in the English Romantic Movement. With his friend William Wordsworth, he published the *Lyrical Ballads* in 1798, which contained his greatest poem, *The Rime of the Ancient Mariner.* His major critical work, the *Biographia Literaria,* was published in 1817.

In the following brief but difficult selection from *Aids to Reflection* (1825), Coleridge contrasts two kinds of mystics. He uses a parable about two pilgrims visiting the same oasis in the desert but perceiving and responding to it in different ways in order to distinguish two kinds of sensibility.

I shall endeavor to describe two ranks of mystics in a sort of allegory or parable. Let us imagine a poor pilgrim benighted in a wilderness or desert, and pursuing his way in the starless dark with a lantern in his hand. Chance or his happy genius leads him to an *oasis* or natural garden, such as in the creations of my youthful fancy I supposed Enos, the child of Cain to have found. And here, hungry and thirsty, the way-wearied man rests at a fountain; and the taper of his lantern throws its light on an over-shadowing tree, a boss of snow-white blossoms, through which the green and growing fruits peeped, and the ripe golden fruitage glowed. Deep, vivid, and faithful are the impressions, which the lovely imagery comprised within the scanty circle of light, makes and leaves on his memory. But scarcely has he eaten of the fruits and drunk of the fountain, ere scared by the roar and howl from the desert he hurries forward; and as he passes with hasty steps through grove and glade, shadows and imperfect beholdings and vivid fragments of things distinctly seen blend with the past and present shapings of his brain. Fancy modifies sight. His dreams transfer their forms to real objects: and these lend a substance and an outness to his dreams. Apparitions greet him; and when at a distance from this enchanted land, and on a different track, the dawn of day discloses to him a caravan, a troop of his fellow-men, his memory, which is itself half fancy, is interpolated afresh by every attempt to recall, connect, and piece out his recollections. His narration is received as a madman's tale. He shrinks from the rude laugh and contemptuous sneer, and retires into himself. Yet the craving for sympathy, strong in proportion to the intensity of his convictions, impels him to unbosom himself to abstract auditors; and the poor quietist becomes a penman, and, all too poorly stocked for the writer's trade, he borrows his phrases and figures from the only writings to which he has had access, the sacred books of his religion. And thus I shadow out the enthusiast Mystic of the first sort; at the head of which stands the illuminated, Teutonic theosopher and shoemaker, honest Jacob Behmen . . . .

To delineate a Mystic of the second or higher order, we need only endow our pilgrim with equal gifts of nature, but these developed and displayed by all the aids and arts of education and favorable fortune. He is on his way to the Mecca of his ancestral and national faith, with a well-guarded and numerous procession of merchants and fellow-pilgrims, on the established track. At the close of day the caravan has halted: the full moon rises on the desert: and he strays forth alone, out of sight but to no unsafe distance; and chance leads him, too, to the same oasis or islet of verdure on the sea of sand. He wanders at leisure in its maze of beauty and sweetness, and thrids his way through the odorous and flowering thickets into open spots of greenery, and discovers statues and memorial characters, grottoes, and refreshing caves. But the moonshine, the imaginative poesy of Nature, spreads its soft shadowy charm over all, conceals distances, and magnifies height, and modifies relations; and fills up vacuities with its own whiteness, counterfeiting substance; and where the dense shadows lie, makes solidity imitate hollowness; and gives to all objects a tender visionary hue and softening. Interpret the moonlight and the shadows as the peculiar genius and sensibility of the individual's own spirit: and here you have the other sort: a Mystic, an enthusiast of a nobler breed—a Fenelon. But the residentiary, or the frequent visitor of the favored spot, who has scanned its beauties by steady daylight, and mastered its true proportions and lineaments, he will discover that both pilgrims have indeed been there. He will know, that the delightful dream, which the latter tells, is a dream of truth; and that even in the bewildered tale of the former there is truth mingled with the dream.

## I.  Suggestions for Discussion:
  1.  Compare and contrast the two pilgrims whom Coleridge describes.
  2.  Discuss the effectiveness of Coleridge's parable as a means of clarifying the distinctions between the two kinds of mystics.

3. Discuss Coleridge's diction and tone in this selection. Would his ideas have been clearer to you if he had used more concrete, more specific language? Explain.

II. **Suggestions for Writing**:

1. Write a straightforward analysis of Coleridge's two kinds of mystics.
2. Write a parable or simple story that has a deeper significance or meaning.

---

# MALCOLM COWLEY

## Examination Paper

### from *Exile's Return*

---

Malcolm Cowley (1898–      ) is a distinguished American editor, essayist, poet, historian, and translator. From 1956 to 1959 and from 1962 to 1965, he was president of the National Institute of Arts and Letters. His autobiographical *Exile's Return,* from which the present selection is taken, was first published in 1934.

In this very brief selection, Cowley considers how a young writer responds to and learns from the work of celebrated authors.

---

People who read books without writing them are likely to form a simple picture of any celebrated author. He is John X or Jonathan Y, the man who wrote such a fascinating novel about Paris, about divorce, about the Georgia Crackers—the man who drinks, who ran off with the doctor's wife—the bald-headed man who lectured to the Wednesday Club. But to writers, especially to young writers in search of guidance, the established author presents a much more complicated image.

Their impressions of the great author are assembled from many sources. It is true that his books are a principal source, but there must also be considered his career, the point from which it started, the direction in which it seems to be moving. There is his personality, as revealed in chance interviews or as caricatured in gossip; there are the values that he assigns to other writers; and there is the value placed on himself by his younger colleagues in those kitchen or barroom gatherings at which they pass judgment with the harsh finality of a Supreme Court—John X has got real stuff, they say, but Jonathan Y is terrible—and they bring forward evidence to support these verdicts. The evidence is mulled over, all the details are fitted together like the pieces of a jigsaw puzzle, until they begin to form a picture, vague and broken at first, then growing more distinct as the years pass by: the X or Y picture, the James Joyce, Ezra Pound or T. S. Eliot picture. But it is not so much a picture when completed: it is rather a map or diagram which the apprentice writer will use in planning his own career.

If he is called upon to review a book by Joyce or Eliot, he will say certain things he believes to be accurate: they are not the things lying closest to his heart. Secretly he is wondering whether he can, whether he should, ever be great in the Joyce or Eliot fashion. What path should he follow to reach this goal? The great living authors, in the eyes of any young man apprenticed to the Muse, are a series of questions, an examination paper compiled by and submitted to himself:

1. What problems do these authors suggest?
2. With what problems are they consciously dealing?
3. Are they my own problems? Or if not, shall I make them my own?
4. What is the Joyce solution to these problems (or the Eliot, the Pound, the Gertrude Stein, the Paul Valéry solution)?
5. Shall I adopt it? Reject it and seek another master? Or must I furnish a new solution myself?

And it is as if the examiner had written: *Take your time, young man. Consider all questions carefully; there is all the time in the world. Don't fake or cheat; you are making these answers for yourself. Nobody will grade them but posterity.*

I.  **Suggestions for Discussion:**
1. According to Cowley, why do established authors present a complicated image to young writers in search of guidance?
2. Discuss the five questions on Cowley's examination paper.
3. Compare Cowley's advice on learning to write with that given by Eudora Welty in "The Point of the Story," p. 573 or by Mary McCarthy in "Settling the Colonel's Hash," p. 368.

II. **Suggestions for Writing:**
1. Using an author whom you have read recently, write an essay answering Cowley's five questions for yourself.
2. Discuss whether or not Cowley's five questions would help in learning another subject or skill.

# MALCOLM COWLEY

## The Long Furlough

### from *Exile's Return*

In this essay, Cowley describes in fascinating detail what life was like for World War I veterans living in Greenwich Village in New York.

After college and the war, most of us drifted to Manhattan, to the crooked streets south of Fourteenth, where you could rent a furnished hall-bedroom for two or three dollars weekly or the top floor of a rickety house for thirty dollars a month. We came to the Village without any intention of becoming Villagers. We came because living was cheap, because friends of ours had come already (and written us letters full of enchantment), because it seemed that New York was the only city where a young writer could be published. There were some who stayed in Europe after the war and others who carried their college diplomas straight to Paris: they had money. But the rest of us belonged to the proletariat of the arts and we lived in Greenwich Village where everyone else was poor.

"There were," I wrote some years ago, "two schools among us: those who painted the floors black (they were the last of the aesthetes) and those who did not paint the floors. Our college textbooks and the complete works of Jules Laforgue gathered dust on the mantelpiece among a litter of unemptied ashtrays. The streets outside were those of Glenn Coleman's early paintings: low red-brick early nineteenth-century houses, crazy doorways, sidewalks covered with black snow and, in the foreground, an old woman bending under a sack of rags."

The black snow melted: February blustered into March. It was as if the war had never been fought, or had been fought by others. We were about to continue the work begun in high school, of training ourselves as writers, choosing masters to imitate, deciding what we wanted to say and persuading magazines to let us say it. We should have to earn money, think about getting jobs: the war was over. But besides the memories we scarcely mentioned, it had left us with a vast unconcern for the future and an enormous appetite for pleasure. We were like soldiers with a few more days to spend in Blighty: every moment was borrowed from death. It didn't matter that we were penniless: we danced to old squeaky victrola records—*You called me Baby Doll a year ago; Hello, Central, give me No Man's Land*—we had our first love affairs, we stopped in the midst of arguments to laugh at jokes as broad and pointless as the ocean, we were continually drunk with high spirits, transported by the miracle of no longer wearing a uniform. As we walked down Greenwich Avenue we stopped to enjoy the smell of hot bread outside of Cushman's bakery. In the spring morning it seemed that every ash barrel was green-wreathed with spinach.

It was April now, and the long furlough continued. . . . You woke at ten o'clock between soiled sheets in a borrowed apartment; the sun dripped over the edges of the green windowshade. On the dresser was a half-dollar borrowed the night before from the last guest to go downstairs singing: even at wartime prices it was enough to buy breakfast for two—eggs, butter, a loaf of bread, a grapefruit. When the second pot of coffee was emptied a visitor would come, then another; you would borrow fifty-five cents for the cheapest bottle of sherry. Somebody would suggest a ride across the bay to Staten Island. Dinner provided itself, and there was always a program for the evening. On Fridays there were dances in Webster Hall attended by terrible uptown people who came to watch the Villagers at their revels and buy them drinks in return for being insulted; on Saturdays everybody gathered at Luke O'Connor's saloon, the Working Girls' Home; on Sunday nights there were poker games played for imaginary stakes and interrupted from moment to moment by gossip, jokes, plans; everything in those days was an excuse for talking. There were always parties, and if they lasted into the morning they might end in a "community sleep": the mattresses were pulled off the beds and laid side by side on the floor, then double blankets were unfolded and stretched lengthwise across them, so that a dozen people could sleep there in discomfort, provided nobody snored. One night, having fallen asleep, you gave a snore so tremendous that you wakened to its echo, and listened to your companions drowsily cursing the snorer, and for good measure cursed him yourself. But always, before going to bed, you borrowed fifty cents for breakfast. Eight hours' foresight was sufficient. Always, after the coffee pot was drained, a visitor would come with money enough for a bottle of sherry.

But it couldn't go on forever. Some drizzly morning late in April you woke up to find yourself married (and your wife, perhaps, suffering from a dry cough that threatened consumption). If there had been checks from home, there would be no more of them. Or else it happened after a siege of influenza, which that year had curious effects: it left you weak in body, clear in mind, revolted by humanity and yourself. Tottering from the hospital, you sat in the back room of a saloon and, from the whitewood table sour with spilled beer, surveyed your blank prospects. You had been living on borrowed money, on borrowed time, in a borrowed apartment: in three months you had exhausted both your credit and your capacity to beg. There was no army now to clothe and feed you like a kind-hateful parent. No matter where the next meal came from, you would pay for it yourself.

In the following weeks you didn't exactly starve; ways could be found of earning a few dollars. Once a week you went round to the editorial offices of the *Dial,* which was then appearing every two weeks in a format something like that of the *Nation.* One of the editors was a friend of your wife's and he would give you half a dozen bad novels to review in fifty or a hundred words apiece. When the reviews were published you would be paid a dollar for each of them, but that mightn't be for weeks or months, and meanwhile you had to eat. So you would carry the books to a bench in Union Square and page through them hastily, making notes—in two or three hours you would be finished with the whole armful and then you would take them to a second-hand bookstore on Fourth Avenue, where the proprietor paid a flat rate of thirty-five cents for each review copy; you thought it was more than the novels were worth. With exactly $2.10 in your pocket you would buy bread and butter and lamb chops and Bull Durham for cigarettes and order a bag of coal; then at home you would broil the lamb chops over the grate because the landlady had neglected to pay her gas bill, just as you had neglected to pay the rent. You were all good friends and she would be invited to share in the feast. Next morning you would write the reviews, then start on the search for a few dollars more.

You began to feel that one meal a day was all that anyone needed and you wondered why anyone bothered to eat more. Late on a June day you were sitting in Sheridan Square trying to write a poem. "Move along, young fella," said the cop, and the poem was forgotten. Walking southward with the Woolworth Building visible in the distance you imagined a revolution in New York. Revolution was in the air that summer; the general strike had failed in Seattle, but a steel strike was being prepared, and a coal strike, and the railroad men were demanding government ownership—that was all right, but you imagined another kind of revolt, one that would start with a dance through the streets and barrels of cider opened at every corner, and beside each barrel a back-country ham fresh from the oven; the juice squirted out of it when you carved the first slice. Then—but only after you had finished the last of the ham and drained a pitcher of cider and stuffed your mouth with apple pie—then you would set about hanging policemen from the lamp posts, or better still from the crossties of the Elevated, and beside each policeman would be hanged a Methodist preacher, and beside each preacher a pansy poet. Editors would be poisoned with printer's ink: they would die horribly, vomiting ink on white paper. You hated editors, pansipoetical poets, policemen, preachers, you hated city streets . . . and suddenly the street went black. You hadn't even time to feel faint. The pavement rose and hit you between the eyes.

Nobody came to help, nobody even noticed that you had fallen. You scrambled to your feet, limped into a lunch wagon and spent your last dime for a roll and a cup of coffee. The revolution was postponed (on account of I was hungry, sergeant, honest I was too hungry) and the war was ended (listen, sojer, you're out of that man's army now, you're going back behind the plow, you gotta get rich, you son of a bitch). The war was over now and your long furlough was over. It was time to get a job.

**I. Suggestions for Discussion:**
1. What was life like for Cowley and his friends in Greenwich Village? Consider their physical surroundings and their lifestyles.
2. How did Cowley and his friends make spending money? Do the examples given by Cowley suggest other possibilities? Explain.
3. What factors led Cowley and his friends to realize that it was time to begin earning a regular living?

**II. Suggestions for Writing:**
1. Describe a colorful area in which you once lived. Has it changed since then?
2. Write about an unconventional experience or period of time in your own life.

---

# DANIEL DEFOE

## An Academy for Women

### from *An Essay on Projects*

---

Daniel Defoe (1660?–1731) was one of the most prolific writers in the English language. He merged fact and fiction in his realistic

novels, the best known of which are *Robinson Crusoe* (1719),
*Moll Flanders* (1722), and *A Journal of the Plague Year* (1722).

In the following selection from *An Essay on Projects* (1698), the
ever practical Defoe outlines in specific detail plans to establish
an academy to educate young women. He defends his belief that
"a woman well bred and well taught . . . is a creature without
comparison."

---

I have often thought of it as one of the most barbarous customs in the
world, considering us as a civilized and a Christian country, that we deny the
advantages of learning to women. We reproach the sex every day with folly
and impertinence, while I am confident, had they the advantages of education
equal to us, they would be guilty of less than ourselves.

One would wonder, indeed, how it should happen that women are
conversible at all, since they are only beholden to natural parts for all their
knowledge. Their youth is spent to teach them to stitch and sew or make
baubles. They are taught to read indeed, and perhaps to write their names or
so, and that is the height of a woman's education. And I would but ask any
who slight the sex for their understanding, what is a man (a gentleman, I
mean) good for that is taught no more?

I need not give instances, or examine the character of a gentleman with
a good estate and of a good family and with tolerable parts, and examine
what figure he makes for want of education.

The soul is placed in the body like a rough diamond, and must be
polished, or the lustre of it will never appear: and it is manifest that as the
rational soul distinguishes us from brutes, so education carries on the distinction and makes some less brutish than others. This is too evident to need any
demonstration. But why then should women be denied the benefit of instruction? If knowledge and understanding had been useless additions to the sex,
God Almighty would never have given them capacities, for He made nothing
needless. Besides, I would ask such what they can see in ignorance that they
should think it a necessary ornament to a woman? or how much worse is a
wise woman than a fool? or what has the woman done to forfeit the privilege
of being taught? Does she plague us with her pride and impertinence? Why
did we not let her learn, that she might have had more wit? Shall we upbraid
women with folly, when it is only the error of this inhuman custom that
hindered them being made wiser?

The capacities of women are supposed to be greater and their senses quicker than those of the men; and what they might be capable of being bred to is plain from some instances of female wit, which this age is not without; which upbraids us with injustice, and looks as if we denied women the advantages of education for fear they should vie with the men in their improvements.

To remove this objection, and that women might have at least a needful opportunity of education in all sorts of useful learning, I propose the draught of an Academy for that purpose.

I know it is dangerous to make public appearances of the sex. They are not either to be confined or exposed; the first will disagree with their inclinations and the last with their reputations, and therefore it is somewhat difficult; and I doubt a method proposed by an ingenious lady in a little book called "Advice to the Ladies" would be found impracticable, for, saving my respect to the sex, the levity, which perhaps is a little peculiar to them, at least in their youth, will not bear the restraint; and I am satisfied nothing but the height of bigotry can keep up a nunnery. Women are extravagantly desirious of going to heaven, and will punish their pretty bodies to get thither; but nothing else will do it, and even in that case sometimes it falls out that nature will prevail.

When I talk, therefore, of an academy for women, I mean both the model, the teaching, and the government different from what is proposed by that ingenious lady, for whose proposal I have a very great esteem, and also a great opinion of her wit; different, too, from all sorts of religious confinement, and, above all, from vows of celibacy.

Wherefore the academy I propose should differ but little from public schools, wherein such ladies as were willing to study should have all the advantages of learning suitable to their genius.

But since some severities of discipline more than ordinary would be absolutely necessary to preserve the reputation of the house, that persons of quality and fortune might not be afraid to venture their children thither, I shall venture to make a small scheme by way of essay.

The house I would have built in a form by itself, as well as in a place by itself.

The building should be of three plain fronts, without any jettings or bearing-work, that the eye might at a glance see from one coin to the other; the gardens walled in the same triangular figure, with a large moat, and but one entrance.

When thus every part of the situation was contrived as well as might be for discovery, and to render intriguing dangerous, I would have no guards, no eyes, no spies set over the ladies, but shall expect them to be tried by the principles of honour and strict virtue.

And if I am asked why, I must ask pardon of my own sex for giving this reason for it:—

I am so much in charity with women, and so well acquainted with men, that 'tis my opinion there needs no other care to prevent intriguing than to keep the men effectually away; for though inclination, which we prettily call love, does sometimes move a little too visibly in the sex, and frailty often follows, yet I think, verily, custom, which we miscall modesty, has so far the ascendant over the sex, that solicitation always goes before it.

> Custom with women 'stead of virtue rules;
> It leads the wisest and commands the fools;
> For this alone, when inclinations reign,
> Though virtue's fled, will acts of vice restrain.
> Only by custom 'tis that virtue lives,
> And love requires to be asked before it gives.
> For that which we call modesty is pride;
> They scorn to ask, and hate to be denied.
> 'Tis custom thus prevails upon their want;
> They'll never beg what asked they easily grant;
> And when the needless ceremony's over,
> Themselves the weakness of the sex discover.
> If then desires are strong and nature free,
> Keep from her men and opportunity;
> Else 'twill be vain to curb her by restraint,
> But keep the question off, you keep the saint.

In short, let a woman have never such a coming principle, she will let you ask before she complies, at least if she be a woman of any honour.

Upon this ground I am persuaded such measures might be taken that the ladies might have all the freedom in the world within their own walls, and yet no intriguing, no indecencies, nor scandalous affairs happen; and in order to this the following customs and laws should be observed in the colleges, of which I would propose one at least in every county in England, and about ten for the City of London.

After the regulation of the form of the building as before:—

(1.) All the ladies who enter into the house should set their hands to the orders of the house, to signify their consent to submit to them.

(2.) As no woman should be received but who declared herself willing, and that it was the act of her choice to enter herself, so no person should be confined to continue there a moment longer than the same voluntary choice inclined her.

(3.) The charges of the house being to be paid by the ladies, every one that entered should have only this encumbrance, that she should pay for the whole year, though her mind should change as to her continuance.

(4.) An Act of Parliament should make it felony without clergy for any man to enter by force or fraud into the house, or to solicit any woman, *though it were to marry,* while she was in the house. And this law would by no means be severe, because any woman who was willing to receive the addresses of a man might discharge herself of the house when she pleased; and, on the contrary, any woman who had occasion, might discharge herself of the impertinent addresses of any person she had an aversion to by entering into the house.

### *In this house,*

The persons who enter should be taught all sorts of breeding suitable to both their genius and their quality, and in particular music and dancing, which it would be cruelty to bar the sex of, because they are their darlings; but besides this, they should be taught languages, as particularly French and Italian; and I would venture the injury of giving a woman more tongues than one.

They should, as a particular study, be taught all the graces of speech and all the necessary air of conversation, which our common education is so defective in that I need not expose it. They should be brought to read books, and especially history, and so to read as to make them understand the world, and be able to know and judge of things when they hear of them.

To such whose genius would lead them to it I would deny no sort of learning; but the chief thing in general is to cultivate the understandings of the sex, that they may be capable of all sorts of conversation; that their parts and judgments being improved, they may be as profitable in their conversation as they are pleasant.

Women, in my observation, have little or no difference in them, but as they are or are not distinguished by education. Tempers indeed may in some degree influence them, but the main distinguishing part is their breeding.

The whole sex are generally quick and sharp. I believe I may be allowed to say generally so, for you rarely see them lumpish and heavy when they are children, as boys will often be. If a woman be well-bred, and taught the proper management of her natural wit, she proves generally very sensible and retentive; and without partiality, a woman of sense and manners is the finest and most delicate part of God's creation; the glory of her Maker, and the great instance of His singular regard to man, His darling creature, to whom He gave the best gift either God could bestow or man receive. And it is the sordidst piece of folly and ingratitude in the world to withhold from the sex the due lustre which the advantages of education gives to the natural beauty of their minds.

A woman well bred and well taught, furnished with the additional accomplishments of knowledge and behaviour, is a creature without comparison; her society is the emblem of sublimer enjoyments; her person is angelic and her conversation heavenly; she is all softness and sweetness, peace, love, wit, and delight. She is every way suitable to the sublimest wish, and the man that has such a one to his portion has nothing to do but to rejoice in her and be thankful.

On the other hand, suppose her to be the very same woman, and rob her of the benefit of education, and it follows thus:—

If her temper be good, want of education makes her soft and easy.

Her wit, for want of teaching, makes her impertinent and talkative.

Her knowledge, for want of judgment and experience, makes her fanciful and whimsical.

If her temper be bad, want of breeding makes her worse, and she grows haughty, insolent, and loud.

If she be passionate, want of manners makes her termagant and a scold, which is much at one with lunatic.

If she be proud, want of discretion (which still is breeding) makes her conceited, fantastic, and ridiculous.

And from these she degenerates to be turbulent, clamorous, noisy, nasty, and the devil.

Methinks mankind for their own sakes, since, say what we will of the women, we all think fit one time or other to be concerned with them, should take some care to breed them up to be suitable and serviceable, if they expected no such thing as delight from them. Bless us! what care do we take to breed up a good horse and to break him well, and what a value do we put upon him when it is done, and all because he should be fit for our use; and why not a woman? Since all her ornaments and beauty without suitable behaviour is a cheat in nature, like the false tradesman who puts the best of his goods uppermost that the buyer may think the rest are of the same goodness.

Beauty of the body, which is the women's glory, seems to be now unequally bestowed, and Nature, or rather Providence, to lie under some scandal about it, as if it was given a woman for a snare to men, and so make a kind of a she-devil of her; because, they say, exquisite beauty is rarely given with wit, more rarely with goodness of temper, and never at all with modesty. And some, pretending to justify the equity of such a distribution, will tell us 'tis the effect of the justice of Providence in dividing particular excellences among all His creatures, share and share alike, as it were, that all might for something or other be acceptable to one another, else some would be despised.

I think both these notions false, and yet the last, which has the show of respect to Providence, is the worst, for it supposes Providence to be indigent and empty, as if it had not wherewith to furnish all the creatures it had made, but was fain to be parsimonious in its gifts, and distribute them by piecemeal for fear of being exhausted.

If I might venture my opinion against an almost universal notion, I would say most men mistake the proceedings of Providence in this case, and all the world at this day are mistaken in their practice about it. And because the assertion is very bold, I desire to explain myself.

That Almighty First Cause which made us all is certainly the fountain of excellence, as it is of being, and by an invisible influence could have diffused equal qualities and perfections to all the creatures it has made, as the sun does its light, without the least ebb or diminution to Himself, and has given indeed to every individual sufficient to the figure His providence had designed him in the world.

I believe it might be defended if I should say that I do suppose God has given to all mankind equal gifts and capacities in that He has given them all souls equally capable, and that the whole difference in mankind proceeds either from accidental difference in the make of their bodies or from the foolish difference of education.

From accidental difference in bodies. I would avoid discoursing here of the philosophical position of the soul in the body. But if it be true, as philosophers do affirm, that the understanding and memory is dilated or contracted according to the accidental dimensions of the organ through which it is conveyed, then, though God has given a soul as capable to me as another, yet if I have any natural defect in those parts of the body by which the soul should act, I may have the same soul infused as another man, and yet he be a wise man and I a very fool. For example, if a child naturally have a defect in the organ of hearing, so that he could never distinguish any sound, that child shall never be able to speak or read, though it have a soul capable of all the accomplishments in the world. The brain is the centre of the soul's actings, where all the distinguishing faculties of it reside; and it is observable a man who has a narrow contracted head, in which there is not room for the due and necessary operations of nature by the brain, is never a man of very great judgment; and that proverb, "A great head and little wit," is not meant by nature, but is a reproof upon sloth, as if one should, by way of wonder, say, "Fie, fie! you that have a great head have but little wit; that's strange! that must certainly be your own fault." From this notion I do believe there is a great matter in the breed of men and women—not that wise men shall always get wise children, but I believe strong and healthy bodies have the wisest children, and sickly, weakly bodies affect the wits as well as the bodies of their children. We are easily persuaded to believe this in the breeds of horses, cocks, dogs, and other creatures, and I believe it is as visible in men.

But to come closer to the business, the great distinguishing difference which is seen in the world between men and women is in their education, and this is manifested by comparing it with the difference between one man or woman and another.

And herein it is that I take upon me to make such a bold assertion that all the world are mistaken in their practice about women; for I cannot think that God Almighty ever made them so delicate, so glorious creatures, and furnished them with such charms, so agreeable and so delightful to mankind, with souls capable of the same accomplishments with men, and all to be only stewards of our houses, *cooks and slaves.*

Not that I am for exalting the female government in the least; but, in short, I would have men take women for companions, and educate them to be fit for it. A woman of sense and breeding will scorn as much to encroach upon the prerogative of the man as a man of sense will scorn to oppress *the weakness of the woman.* But if the women's souls were refined and improved by teaching, that word would be lost; to say, the weakness of the sex as to judgment, would be nonsense, for ignorance and folly would be no more to be found among women than men. I remember a passage which I heard from a very fine woman; she had wit and capacity enough, an extraordinary shape and face, and a great fortune, but had been cloistered up all her time, and for fear of being stolen, had not had the liberty of being taught the common necessary knowledge of women's affairs; and when she came to converse in the world, her natural wit made her so sensible of the want of education, that she gave this short reflection on herself:—"I am ashamed to talk with my very maids," says she, "for I don't know when they do right or wrong. I had more need go to school than be married."

I need not enlarge on the loss the defect of education is to the sex, nor argue the benefit of the contrary practice; it is a thing will be more easily granted than remedied. This chapter is but an essay at the thing, and I refer the practice to those happy days, if ever they shall be, when men shall be wise enough to mend it.

**I. Suggestions for Discussion:**
1. On what grounds does Defoe want to establish an academy for women? Discuss whether or not you find his reasons sound and clearly stated.
2. Comment on the feasibility of Defoe's plans for the academy. Does his use of details help give respectability to the plan? Explain.
3. What changes would you make in Defoe's plans?

**II. Suggestions for Writing:**
1. Propose your own plans for a model school for young men and women.
2. Argue either for or against the notion that women will benefit more than they will lose from being educated separately from men.

---

## THOMAS DE QUINCEY

### The Literature of Knowledge and the Literature of Power

---

Thomas De Quincey (1785–1859) was an English essayist and critic whose experiences with opium led him to write *Confessions of an English Opium Eater* (1822), which gave him fame. He published many essays, sketches, and translations. "On the Knocking at the Gate in Macbeth" (1822) is one of his best known literary essays.

De Quincey's famous essay on "The Literature of Knowledge and the Literature of Power" explains the difference between works like cookbooks, which communicate knowledge and teach the reader, and works like great poems, which move the reader and have enduring value from generation to generation. De Quincey's comparisons are quite clear despite his long paragraphs and many references.

---

Books, therefore, do not suggest an idea coextensive and interchangeable with the idea of Literature; since much literature, scenic, forensic, or didactic (as from lecturers and public orators), may never come into books, and much that *does* come into books may connect itself with no literary interest. But a far more important correction, applicable to the common vague idea of literature, is to be sought not so much in a better definition of literature as in a sharper distinction of the two functions which it fulfills. In that great social organ which, collectively, we call literature, there may be distinguished two separate offices that may blend and often *do so,* but capable, severally, of a severe insulation, and naturally fitted for reciprocal repulsion. There is, first, the literature of *knowledge;* and, secondly, the literature of *power.* The function of the first is—to *teach;* the function of the second is—to *move:* the first is a rudder; the second, an oar or a sail. The first speaks to the *mere* discursive understanding; the second speaks ultimately, it may happen, to the higher understanding or reason, but always *through* affections of pleasure and sympathy. Remotely, it may travel towards an object seated in what Lord Bacon calls *dry* light; but, proximately, it does and must operate,—else it ceases to be a literature of *power,*—on and through that *humid* light which clothes itself in the mists and glittering *iris* of human passions, desires, and genial emotions. Men have so little reflected on the higher functions of literature as to find it a paradox if one should describe it as a mean or subordinate purpose of books to give information. But this is a paradox only in the sense which makes it honourable to be paradoxical. Whenever we talk in ordinary language of seeking information or gaining knowledge, we understand the words as connected with something of absolute novelty. But it is the grandeur of all truth which *can* occupy a very high place in human interests that it is never absolutely novel to the meanest of minds; it exists eternally by way of germ or latent principle in the lowest as in the highest, needing to be developed, but never to be planted. To be capable of transplantation is the immediate criterion of a truth that ranges on a lower scale. Besides which, there is a rarer thing than truth,—namely, *power,* or deep sympathy with truth. What is the effect, for instance, upon society, of children? By the pity, by the tenderness, and by the peculiar modes of admiration, which connect themselves with the helplessness, with the innocence, and with the simplicity of children, not only are the primal affections strengthened and continually renewed, but the qualities which are dearest in the sight of heaven,—the frailty, for instance, which appeals to forbearance, the innocence which symbolises the heavenly, and the simplicity which is most alien from the worldly,—are kept up in perpetual remembrance, and their ideals are continually refreshed. A purpose of the same nature is answered by the higher literature, viz., the literature of power. What do you learn from *Paradise Lost?*[1] Nothing at all. What do you learn from a cookery-book? Something new, something that you did not know before, in every paragraph. But would you therefore put the wretched cookery-book on a

[1] John Milton's famous epic poem (1667).

higher level of estimation than the divine poem? What you owe to Milton is
not any knowledge, of which a million separate items are still but a million
of advancing steps on the same earthly level; what you owe is *power,*—that
is, exercise and expansion to your own latent capacity of sympathy with the
infinite, where every pulse and each separate influx is a step upwards, a step
ascending as upon a Jacob's ladder from earth to mysterious altitudes above
the earth. *All* the steps of knowledge, from first to last, carry you further on
the same plane, but could never raise you one foot above your ancient level
of earth: whereas the very *first* step in power is a flight—is an ascending movement into another element where earth is forgotten.

Were it not that human sensibilities are ventilated and continually
called out into exercise by the great phenomena of infancy, or of real life as
it moves through chance and change, or of literature as it recombines these
elements in the mimicries of poetry, romance, &c., it is certain that, like any
animal power or muscular energy falling into disuse, all such sensibilities
would gradually droop and dwindle. It is in relation to these great *moral*
capacities of man that the literature of power, as contradistinguished from
that of knowledge, lives and has its field of action. It is concerned with what
is highest in man; for the Scriptures themselves never condescended to deal
by suggestion or co-operation with the mere discursive understanding: when
speaking of man in his intellectual capacity, the Scriptures speak not of the
understanding, but of "*the understanding heart,*"—making the heart, *i.e.* the
great *intuitive* (or non-discursive) organ, to be the interchangeable formula
for man in his highest state of capacity for the infinite. Tragedy, romance,
fairy tale, or epopee, all alike restore to man's mind the ideals of justice, of
hope, of truth, of mercy, of retribution, which else (left to the support of
daily life in its realities) would languish for want of sufficient illustration.
What is meant, for instance, by *poetic justice*?—It does not mean a justice
that differs by its object from the ordinary justice of human jurisprudence;
for then it must be confessedly a very bad kind of justice; but it means a
justice that differs from common forensic justice by the degree in which it
*attains* its object, a justice that is more omnipotent over its own ends, as
dealing—not with the refractory elements of earthly life, but with the elements of its own creation, and with materials flexible to its own purest pre-
conceptions. It is certain that, were it not for the Literature of Power, these
ideals would often remain amongst us as mere arid notional forms; whereas,
by the creative forces of man put forth in literature, they gain a vernal life
of restoration, and germinate into vital activities. The commonest novel, by
moving in alliance with human fears and hopes, with human instincts of
wrong and right, sustains and quickens those affections. Calling them into

action, it rescues them from torpor. And hence the preeminency over all authors that merely *teach* of the meanest that *moves,* or that teaches, if at all, indirectly *by* moving. The very highest work that has ever existed in the Literature of Knowledge is but a *provisional* work: a book upon trial and sufference, and *quamdiu bene se gesserit.* Let its teaching be even partially revised, let it be but expanded,—nay, even let its teaching be but placed in a better order,—and instantly it is superseded. Whereas the feeblest works in the Literature of Power, surviving at all, survive as finished and unalterable amongst men. For instance, the *Principia* of Sir Isaac Newton was a book *militant* on earth from the first. In all stages of its progress it would have to fight for its existence: 1st, as regards absolute truth; 2dly, when that combat was over, as regards its form or mode of presenting the truth. And as soon as a La Place,[2] or anybody else, builds higher upon the foundations laid by this book, effectually he throws it out of the sunshine into decay and darkness; by weapons won from this book he superannuates and destroys this book, so that soon the name of Newton remains as a mere *nominis umbra,* but his book, as a living power, has transmigrated into other forms. Now, on the contrary, the Iliad, the Prometheus of Aeschylus, the Othello or King Lear, the Hamlet or Macbeth, and the Paradise Lost, are not militant, but triumphant for ever as long as the languages exist in which they speak or can be taught to speak. They never *can* transmigrate into new incarnations. To reproduce *these* in new forms, or variation, even if in some things they should be improved, would be to plagiarise. A good steam-engine is properly superseded by a better. But one lovely pastoral valley is not superseded by another, nor a statue of Praxiteles by a statue of Michael Angelo. These things are separated not by imparity, but by disparity. They are not thought of as unequal under the same standard, but as different in *kind,* and, if otherwise equal, as equal under a different standard. Human works of immortal beauty and works of nature in one respect stand on the same footing: they never absolutely repeat each other, never approach so near as not to differ; and they differ not as better and worse, or simply by more and less: they differ by undecipherable and incommunicable differences, that cannot be caught by mimicries, that cannot be reflected in the mirror of copies, that cannot become ponderable in the scales of vulgar comparison.

Applying these principles to Pope[3] as a representative of fine literature

---

[2] Pierre Simon Marquis de Laplace (1749–1827), a French mathematician and astronomer, is here contrasted with Sir Isaac Newton (1642–1727), the English mathematician, astronomer, and philosopher who published his *Principia Mathematica* in 1686.
[3] Alexander Pope (1688–1744) was an English poet and critic.

in general, we would wish to remark the claim which he has, or which any
equal writer has, to the attention and jealous winnowing of those critics in
particular who watch over public morals. Clergymen, and all organs of public
criticism put in motion by clergymen, are more especially concerned in the
just appreciation of such writers, if the two canons are remembered which we
have endeavoured to illustrate, viz. that all works in this class, as opposed to
those in the literature of knowledge, 1st, work by far deeper agencies, and,
2dly, are more permanent; in the strictest sense they are κτήματα ἐς ἄει:[4] and
what evil they do, or what good they do, is commensurate with the national
language, sometimes long after the nation has departed. At this hour, five
hundred years since their creation, the tales of Chaucer never equalled on this
earth for their tenderness, and for life of picturesqueness, are read familiarly
by many in the charming language of their natal day, and by others in the
modernisations of Dryden, of Pope, and Wordsworth. At this hour, one
thousand eight hundred years since their creation, the Pagan tales of Ovid,
never equalled on this earth for the gaiety of their movement and the capricious graces of their narrative, are read by all Christendom. This man's people
and their monuments are dust; but *he* is alive: he has survived them, as he
told us that he had it in his commission to do, by a thousand years; "and
*shall* a thousand more."

All the literature of knowledge builds only ground-nests, that are swept
away by floods, or confounded by the plough; but the literature of power
builds nests in aerial altitudes of temples sacred from violation, or of forests
inaccessible to fraud. *This* is a great prerogative of the *power* literature; and
it is a greater which lies in the mode of its influence. The *knowledge* literature,
like the fashion of this world, passeth away. An Encyclopaedia is its abstract;
and, in this respect, it may be taken for its speaking symbol—that before one
generation has passed an Encyclopaedia is superannuated; for it speaks
through the dead memory and unimpassioned understanding, which have not
the repose of higher faculties, but are continually enlarging and varying their
phylacteries. But all literature properly so called—literature κατ᾽ ἐξοχὴν,—for
the very same reason that it is so much more durable than the literature of
knowledge, is (and by the very same proportion it is) more intense and elec-
trically searching in its impressions. The directions in which the tragedy of
this planet has trained our human feelings to play, and the combinations into
which the poetry of this planet has thrown our human passions of love and
hatred, of admiration and contempt, exercise a power for bad or good over
human life that cannot be contemplated, when stretching through many gen-

[4] Forever there.

erations, without a sentiment allied to awe.[5] And of this let every one be assured—that he owes to the impassioned books which he has read many a thousand more of emotions that he can consciously trace back to them. Dim by their origination, these emotions yet arise in him, and mould him through life, like forgotten incidents of his childhood.

## I. Suggestions for Discussion:

1. What is it, according to De Quincey, that we gain from reading Milton's *Paradise Lost* that no "cookery" book could teach us?
2. Discuss the validity of De Quincey's claims for the "literature of power." Does he misrepresent or exaggerate the claims he makes for specific works? Explain.
3. What claims can be made for the "literature of knowledge" that De Quincey does not mention?

## II. Suggestions for Writing:

1. Identify from your own reading, viewing, and listening examples of what you might call the "literature of power." Explain the basis for your choices.
2. Compare and contrast De Quincey's discussion of the "literature of power" with E. M. Forster's discussion of "Art for Art's Sake," p. 183.

---

# ALEXIS DE TOCQUEVILLE

## The Sovereignty of the People in America

from *Democracy in America*

---

Alexis De Tocqueville (1805–1859) was a French aristocrat who visited America in 1831 to learn about American democratic

---

[5] The reason why the broad distinctions between the two literatures of power and knowledge so little fix the attention lies in the fact that a vast proportion of books,—history, biography, travels, miscellaneous essays, &c.,—lying in a middle zone, confound these distinctions by interblending them. All that we call "amusement" or "entertainment" is a diluted form of the power belonging to passion, and also a mixed form; and, where threads of direct *instruction* intermingle in the texture with these threads of *power*, this absorption of the duality into one representative nuance neutralises the separate perception of either. Fused into a *tertium quid*, or neutral state, they disappear to the popular eye as the repelling forces which, in fact, they are. [De Quincey's note.]

customs. His *Democracy in America* (1840) is considered the most important commentary on American institutions written by a foreigner.

In this admiring essay from *Democracy in America,* De Tocqueville argues that popular sovereignty arose in the United States as a result of the American Revolution, and he describes how admirably it works.

---

Whenever the political laws of the United States are to be discussed, it is with the doctrine of the sovereignty of the people that we must begin.

The principle of the sovereignty of the people, which is always to be found, more or less, at the bottom of almost all human institutions, generally remains there concealed from view. It is obeyed without being recognized, or if for a moment it be brought to light, it is hastily cast back into the gloom of the sanctuary.

"The will of the nation" is one of those phrases which have been most largely abused by the wily and the despotic of every age. Some have seen the expression of it in the purchased suffrages of a few of the satellites of power; others, in the votes of a timid or an interested minority; and some have even discovered it in the silence of a people, on the supposition that the fact of submission established the right to command.

In America, the principle of the sovereignty of the people is not either barren or concealed, as it is with some other nations; it is recognized by the customs and proclaimed by the laws; it spreads freely, and arrives without impediment at its most remote consequences. If there be a country in the world where the doctrine of the sovereignty of the people can be fairly appreciated, where it can be studied in its application to the affairs of society, and where its dangers and its advantages may be judged, that country is assuredly America.

I have already observed that, from their origin, the sovereignty of the people was the fundamental principle of most of the British colonies in America. It was far, however, from then exercising as much influence on the government of society as it now does. Two obstacles—the one external, the other internal—checked its invasive progress.

It could not ostensibly disclose itself in the laws of colonies which were still constrained to obey the mother country; it was therefore obliged to rule secretly in the provincial assemblies, and especially in the townships.

American society at that time was not yet prepared to adopt it with all its consequences. Intelligence in New England, and wealth in the country to the south of the Hudson, (as I have shown in the preceding chapter,) long exercised a sort of aristocratic influence, which tended to keep the exercise of social power in the hands of a few. Not all the public functionaries were chosen by popular vote, nor were all the citizens voters. The electoral franchise was everywhere somewhat restricted, and made dependent on a certain qualification, which was very low in the North, and more considerable in the South.

The American Revolution broke out, and the doctrine of the sovereignty of the people came out of the townships, and took possession of the State. Every class was enlisted in its cause; battles were fought and victories obtained for it; it became the law of laws.

A change almost as rapid was effected in the interior of society, where the law of inheritance completed the abolition of local influences.

As soon as this effect of the laws and of the Revolution became apparent to every eye, victory was irrevocably pronounced in favor of the democratic cause. All power was, in fact, in its hands, and resistance was no longer possible. The higher orders submitted without a murmur and without a struggle to an evil which was thenceforth inevitable. The ordinary fate of falling powers awaited them: each of their members followed his own interest; and as it was impossible to wring the power from the hands of a people whom they did not detest sufficiently to brave, their only aim was to secure its good-will at any price. The most democratic laws were consequently voted by the very men whose interests they impaired: and thus, although the higher classes did not excite the passions of the people against their order, they themselves accelerated the triumph of the new state of things; so that, by a singular change, the democratic impulse was found to be most irresistible in the very States where the aristocracy had the firmest hold. The State of Maryland, which had been founded by men of rank, was the first to proclaim universal suffrage, and to introduce the most democratic forms into the whole of its government.

When a nation begins to modify the elective qualification, it may easily be foreseen that, sooner or later, that qualification will be entirely abolished. There is no more invariable rule in the history of society: the further electoral rights are extended, the greater is the need of extending them; for after each concession the strength of the democracy increases, and its demands increase with its strength. The ambition of those who are below the appointed rate is irritated in exact proportion to the great number of those who are above it. The exception at last becomes the rule, concession follows concession, and no stop can be made short of universal suffrage.

At the present day the principle of the sovereignty of the people has acquired, in the United States, all the practical development which the imagination can conceive. It is unencumbered by those fictions which are thrown over it in other countries, and it appears in every possible form, according to the exigency of the occasion. Sometimes the laws are made by the people in a body, as at Athens; and sometimes its representatives, chosen by universal suffrage, transact business in its name, and under its immediate supervision

In some countries, a power exists which, though it is in a degree foreign to the social body, directs it, and forces it to pursue a certain track. In others, the ruling force is divided, being partly within and partly without the ranks of the people. But nothing of the kind is to be seen in the United States; there society governs itself for itself. All power centres in its bosom; and scarcely an individual is to be met with who would venture to conceive, or, still less, to express, the idea of seeking it elsewhere. The nation participates in the making of its laws by the choice of its legislators, and in the execution of them by the choice of the agents of the executive government; it may almost be said to govern itself, so feeble and so restricted is the share left to the administration, so little do the authorities forget their popular origin and the power from which they emanate. The people reign in the American political world as the Deity does in the universe. They are the cause and the aim of all things; everything comes from them, and everything is absorbed in them.

I. **Suggestions for Discussion:**
  1. What obstacles to popular sovereignty existed before the American Revolution? How specific is De Tocqueville in his discussion of these obstacles?
  2. What effects did the extension of electoral rights have on the young republic?
  3. To what extent does recent American history support or challenge De Tocqueville's assertion that the people reign in the American political world as the deity does in the universe?

II. **Suggestions for Writing:**
  1. From your own experience or reading, analyze a political situation in which the popular will either did or did not prevail.
  2. Identify and discuss current dangers to popular sovereignty in America.

# JOAN DIDION

## On Keeping a Notebook

### from *Slouching Toward Bethlehem*

Joan Didion (1935–     ) is an American essayist, novelist, and film scriptwriter. The selection that follows is taken from *Slouching Toward Bethlehem* (1966). Her latest book, a collection of essays called *The White Album,* was published in 1979.

Using many examples and details, she discusses why she keeps a notebook.

" 'That woman Estelle,' " the note reads, " 'is partly the reason why George Sharp and I are separated today.' *Dirty crepe-de-Chine wrapper, hotel bar, Wilmington RR, 9:45 a.m. August Monday morning."*

Since the note is in my notebook, it presumably has some meaning to me. I study it for a long while. At first I have only the most general notion of what I was doing on an August Monday morning in the bar of the hotel across from the Pennsylvania Railroad station in Wilmington, Delaware (waiting for a train? missing one? 1960? 1961? why Wilmington?), but I do remember being there. The woman in the dirty crepe-de-Chine wrapper had come down from her room for a beer, and the bartender had heard before the reason why George Sharp and she were separated today. "Sure," he said, and went on mopping the floor, "You told me." At the other end of the bar is a girl. She is talking, pointedly, not to the man beside her but to a cat lying in the triangle of sunlight cast through the open door. She is wearing a plaid silk dress from Peck & Peck, and the hem is coming down.

Here is what it is: the girl has been on the Eastern Shore, and now she is going back to the city, leaving the man beside her, and all she can see ahead are the viscous summer sidewalks and the 3 A.M. long-distance calls that will make her lie awake and then sleep drugged through all the steaming mornings left in August (1960? 1961?). Because she must go directly from the train to lunch in New York, she wishes that she had a safety pin for the hem of the plaid silk dress, and she also wishes that she could forget about the hem and the lunch and stay in the cool bar that smells of disinfectant and malt and make friends with the woman in the crepe-de-Chine wrapper. She is afflicted by a little self-pity, and she wants to compare Estelles. That is what that was all about.

Why did I write it down? In order to remember, of course, but exactly what was it I wanted to remember? How much of it actually happened? Did any of it? Why do I keep a notebook at all? It is easy to deceive oneself on all those scores. The impulse to write things down is a peculiarly compulsive one, inexplicable to those who do not share it, useful only accidentally, only secondarily, in the way that any compulsion tries to justify itself. I suppose that it begins or does not begin in the cradle. Although I have felt compelled to write things down since I was five years old, I doubt that my daughter ever will, for she is a singularly blessed and accepting child, delighted with life exactly as life presents itself to her, unafraid to go to sleep and unafraid to wake up. Keepers of private notebooks are a different breed altogether, lonely and resistant rearrangers of things, anxious malcontents, children afflicted apparently at birth with some presentiment of loss.

My first notebook was a Big Five tablet, given to me by my mother with the sensible suggestion that I stop whining and learn to amuse myself by writing down my thoughts. She returned the tablet to me a few years ago; the first entry is an account of a woman who believed herself to be freezing to death in the Arctic night, only to find, when day broke, that she had stumbled onto the Sahara Desert, where she would die of the heat before lunch. I have no idea what turn of a five-year-old's mind could have prompted so insistently "ironic" and exotic a story, but it does reveal a certain predilection for the extreme which has dogged me into adult life; perhaps if I were analytically inclined I would find it a truer story than any I might have told about Donald Johnson's birthday party or the day my cousin Brenda put Kitty Litter in the Aquarium.

So the point of my keeping a notebook has never been, nor is it now, to have an accurate factual record of what I have been doing or thinking. That would be a different impulse entirely, an instinct for reality which I sometimes envy but do not possess. At no point have I ever been able successfully to keep a diary; my approach to daily life ranges from the grossly negligent to the merely absent, and on those few occasions when I have tried dutifully to record a day's events, boredom has so overcome me that the results are mysterious at best. What is this business about "shopping, typing piece, dinner with E, depressed"? Shopping for what? Typing what piece? Who is E? Was this "E" depressed, or was I depressed? Who cares?

In fact I have abandoned altogether that kind of pointless entry; instead I tell what some would call lies. "That's simply not true," the members of my family frequently tell me when they come up against my memory of a shared event. "The party was *not* for you, the spider was *not* a black widow, *it wasn't that way at all.*" Very likely they are right, for not only have I always had trouble distinguishing between what happened and what merely might have happened, but I remain unconvinced that the distinction, for my purposes, matters. The cracked crab that I recall having for lunch the day my father came home from Detroit in 1945 must certainly be embroidery, worked into the day's pattern to lend verisimilitude; I was ten years old and would not now remember the cracked crab. The day's events did not turn on cracked crab. And yet it is precisely that fictitious crab that makes me see the afternoon all over again, a home movie run all too often, the father bearing gifts, the child weeping, an exercise in family love and guilt. Or that is what it was to me. Similarly, perhaps it never did snow that August in Vermont; perhaps there never were flurries in the night wind, and maybe no one else felt the ground hardening and summer already dead even as we pretended to bask in it, but that was how it felt to me, and it might as well have snowed, could have snowed, did snow.

*How it felt to me:* that is getting closer to the truth about a notebook. I sometimes delude myself about why I keep a notebook, imagine that some thrifty virtue derives from preserving everything observed. See enough and write it down, I tell myself, and then some morning when the world seems drained of wonder, some day when I am only going through the motions of doing what I am supposed to do, which is write—on that bankrupt morning I will simply open my notebook and there it will all be, a forgotten account with accumulated interest, paid passage back to the world out there: dialogue overheard in hotels and elevators and at the hat-check counter in Pavillon (one middle-aged man shows his hat check to another and says, "That's my old football number"); impressions of Bettina Aptheker and Benjamin Sonnenberg and Teddy ("Mr. Acapulco") Stauffer; careful *aperçus* about tennis bums and failed fashion models and Greek shipping heiresses, one of whom taught me a significant lesson (a lesson I could have learned from F. Scott Fitzgerald, but perhaps we all must meet the very rich for ourselves) by asking, when I arrived to interview her in her orchid-filled sitting room on the second day of a paralyzing New York blizzard, whether it was snowing outside.

I imagine, in other words, that the notebook is about other people. But of course it is not. I have no real business with what one stranger said to another at the hat-check counter in Pavillon; in fact I suspect that the line

"That's my old football number" touched not my own imagination at all, but merely some memory of something once read, probably "The Eighty-Yard Run." Nor is my concern with a woman in a dirty crepe-de-Chine wrapper in a Wilmington bar. My stake is always, of course, in the unmentioned girl in the plaid silk dress. *Remember what it was to be me:* that is always the point.

It is a difficult point to admit. We are brought up in the ethic that others, any others, all others, are by definition more interesting than ourselves; taught to be diffident, just this side of self-effacing. ("You're the least important person in the room and don't forget it," Jessica Mitford's governess would hiss in her ear on the advent of any social occasion; I copied that into my notebook because it is only recently that I have been able to enter a room without hearing some such phrase in my inner ear.) Only the very young and the very old may recount their dreams at breakfast, dwell upon self, interrupt with memories of beach picnics and favorite Liberty lawn dresses and the rainbow trout in a creek near Colorado Springs. The rest of us are expected, rightly, to affect absorption in other people's favorite dresses, other people's trout.

And so we do. But our notebooks give us away, for however dutifully we record what we see around us, the common denominator of all we see is always, transparently, shamelessly, the implacable "I." We are not talking here about the kind of notebook that is patently for public consumption, a structural conceit for binding together a series of graceful *pensées;* we are talking about something private, about bits of the mind's string too short to use, an indiscriminate and erratic assemblage with meaning only for its maker.

And sometimes even the maker has difficulty with the meaning. There does not seem to be, for example, any point in my knowing for the rest of my life that, during 1964, 720 tons of soot fell on every square mile of New York City, yet there it is in my notebook, labeled "FACT." Nor do I really need to remember that Ambrose Bierce liked to spell Leland Stanford's name "£eland $tanford" or that "smart women almost always wear black in Cuba," a fashion hint without much potential for practical application. And does not the relevance of these notes seem marginal at best?:

> In the basement museum of the Inyo County Courthouse in Independence, California, sign pinned to a mandarin coat: "This MANDARIN COAT was often worn by Mrs. Minnie S. Brooks when giving lectures on her TEAPOT COLLECTION."

Redhead getting out of car in front of Beverly Wilshire Hotel, chinchilla stole, Vuitton bags with tags reading:

MRS LOU FOX

HOTEL SAHARA

VEGAS

Well, perhaps not entirely marginal. As a matter of fact, Mrs. Minnie S. Brooks and her MANDARIN COAT pull me back into my own childhood, for although I never knew Mrs. Brooks and did not visit Inyo County until I was thirty, I grew up in just such a world, in houses cluttered with Indian relics and bits of gold ore and ambergris and the souvenirs my Aunt Mercy Farnsworth brought back from the Orient. It is a long way from that world to Mrs. Lou Fox's world, where we all live now, and is it not just as well to remember that? Might not Mrs. Minnie S. Brooks help me to remember what I am? Might not Mrs. Lou Fox help me to remember what I am not?

But sometimes the point is harder to discern. What exactly did I have in mind when I noted down that it cost the father of someone I know $650 a month to light the place on the Hudson in which he lived before the Crash? What use was I planning to make of this line by Jimmy Hoffa: "I may have my faults, but being wrong ain't one of them"? And although I think it interesting to know where the girls who travel with the Syndicate have their hair done when they find themselves on the West Coast, will I ever make suitable use of it? Might I not be better off just passing it on to John O'Hara? What is a recipe for sauerkraut doing in my notebook? What kind of magpie keeps this notebook? *"He was born the night the Titanic went down."* That seems a nice enough line, and I even recall who said it, but is it not really a better line in life than it could ever be in fiction?

But of course that is exactly it: not that I should ever use the line, but that I should remember the woman who said it and the afternoon I heard it. We were on her terrace by the sea, and we were finishing the wine left from lunch, trying to get what sun there was, a California winter sun. The woman whose husband was born the night the *Titanic* went down wanted to rent her house, wanted to go back to her children in Paris. I remember wishing that I could afford the house, which cost $1,000 a month. "Someday you will," she said lazily. "Someday it all comes." There in the sun on her terrace it seemed easy to believe in someday, but later I had a low-grade afternoon hangover and ran over a black snake on the way to the supermarket and was flooded with inexplicable fear when I heard the checkout clerk explaining to the man ahead of me why she was finally divorcing her husband. "He left me no choice," she said over and over as she punched the register. "He has a little seven-month-old baby by her, he left me no choice." I would like to believe that my dread then was for the human condition, but of course it was for me, because I wanted a baby and did not then have one and because I wanted to own the house that cost $1,000 a month to rent and because I had a hangover.

It all comes back. Perhaps it is difficult to see the value in having one's self back in that kind of mood, but I do see it; I think we are well advised to keep on nodding terms with the people we used to be, whether we find them attractive company or not. Otherwise they turn up unannounced and surprise us, come hammering on the mind's door at 4 A.M. of a bad night and demand to know who deserted them, who betrayed them, who is going to make amends. We forget all too soon the things we thought we could never forget. We forget the loves and the betrayals alike, forget what we whispered and what we screamed, forget who we were. I have already lost touch with a couple of people I used to be; one of them, a seventeen-year-old, presents little threat, although it would be of some interest to me to know again what it feels like to sit on a river levee drinking vodka-and-orange-juice and listening to Les Paul and Mary Ford and their echoes sing "How High the Moon" on the car radio. (You see I still have the scenes, but I no longer perceive myself among those present, no longer could even improvise the dialogue.) The other one, a twenty-three-year-old, bothers me more. She was always a good deal of trouble, and I suspect she will reappear when I least want to see her, skirts too long, shy to the point of aggravation, always the injured party, full of recriminations and little hurts and stories I do not want to hear again, at once saddening me and angering me with her vulnerability and ignorance, an apparition all the more insistent for being so long banished.

It is a good idea, then, to keep in touch, and I suppose that keeping in touch is what notebooks are all about. And we are all on our own when it comes to keeping those lines open to ourselves: your notebook will never help me, nor mine you. "*So what's new in the whiskey business?*" What could that possibly mean to you? To me it means a blonde in a Pucci bathing suit sitting with a couple of fat men by the pool at the Beverly Hills Hotel. Another man approaches, and they all regard one another in silence for a while. "So what's new in the whiskey business?" one of the fat men finally says by way of welcome, and the blonde stands up, arches one foot and dips it in the pool, looking all the while at the cabaña where Baby Pignatari is talking on the telephone. That is all there is to that, except that several years later I saw the blonde coming out of Saks Fifth Avenue in New York with her California complexion and a voluminous mink coat. In the harsh wind that day she looked old and irrevocably tired to me, and even the skins in the mink coat were not worked the way they were doing them that year, not the way she would have wanted them done, and there is the point of the story. For a while after that I did not like to look in the mirror, and my eyes would skim the newspapers and pick out only the deaths, the cancer victims, the premature coronaries, the suicides, and I stopped riding the Lexington Avenue IRT because I noticed for the first time that all the strangers I had seen for years—the man with the seeing-eye dog, the spinster who read the classified pages every day, the fat girl who always got off with me at Grand Central—looked older than they once had.

It all comes back. Even that recipe for sauerkraut: even that brings it back. I was on Fire Island when I first made that sauerkraut, and it was raining, and we drank a lot of bourbon and ate the sauerkraut and went to bed at ten, and I listened to the rain and the Atlantic and felt safe. I made the sauerkraut again last night and it did not make me feel any safer, but that is, as they say, another story.

I. **Suggestions for Discussion:**
   1. Explain Didion's statement that "keeping in touch is what notebooks are all about."
   2. Discuss her use of selected details, comparison and contrast, and other rhetorical devices to bring her subject into focus.
   3. Discuss what Didion means when she writes that our notebooks give us away. To whom?

II. **Suggestions for Writing:**
   1. Keep a journal or notebook in which you record the events or thoughts of each day.
   2. Write an essay in which you interweave excerpts from your journal or diary with commentary on your entries.

---

# ANNIE DILLARD

## A Field of Silence

---

Annie Dillard (1945–       ) is a poet and essayist now living in the Pacific Northwest. She won the Pulitzer Prize in 1974 for her first

book of prose, *Pilgrim at Tinker Creek.* A contributor to *Harper's*
and *Atlantic Monthly,* she published *Holy the Firm* in 1977.

In the essay that follows, she describes in vivid detail the sights
and sounds she encountered while walking in a field on a farm on
an island in Puget Sound.

---

There is a place called "the farm" where I lived once, in a time that was
very lonely. Fortunately I was unconscious of my loneliness then, and felt it
only deeply, bewildered, in the half-bright way that a puppy feels pain.

I loved the place, and still do. It was an ordinary farm, a calf-raising,
haymaking farm, and very beautiful. Its flat, messy pastures ran along one
side of the central portion of a quarter-mile road in the central part of an
island, an island in Puget Sound, so that from the high end of the road you
could look west toward the Pacific, to the Sound and its hundred islands, and
from the other end—and from the farm—you could see east to the water between you and the mainland, and beyond it the mainland's mountains slicked
smooth with snow.

I liked the clutter about the place, the way everything blossomed or
seeded or rusted; I liked the hundred half-finished projects, the smells, and
the way the animals always broke loose. It is calming to herd animals. Often
a regular rodeo breaks out—two people and a clever cow can kill a morning—
but still, it is calming. You laugh for a while, exhausted, and silence is restored; the beasts are back in their pastures, the fences not fixed but disguised as if they were fixed, ensuring the animals' temporary resignation: and
a great calm descends, a lack of urgency, a sense of having to invent something to do until the next time you must run and chase cattle.

The farm seemed eternal in the crude way the earth does—extending,
that is, a very long time. The farm was as old as earth, always there, as old as
the island, the Platonic form of "farm," of human society itself and at large,
a piece of land eaten and replenished a billion summers, a piece of land
worked on, lived on, grown over, plowed under, and stitched again and again,
with fingers or with leaves, in and out and into human life's thin weave. I
lived there once.

I lived there once and I have seen, from behind the barn, the long road-
side pastures heaped with silence. Behind the rooster, suddenly, I saw the
silence heaped on the fields like trays. That day the green hayfields supported
silence evenly sown; the fields bent just so under the even pressure of silence,
bearing it, even, palming it aloft: cleared fields, part of a land, a planet, they
did not buckle beneath the heel of silence, nor split up scattered to bits, but

instead lay secret, disguised as time and matter as though that were nothing, ordinary—disguised as fields like those which bear the silence only because they are spread, and the silence spreads over them, great in size.

I do not want, I think, ever to see such a sight again. That there is loneliness here I had granted, in the abstract—but not, I thought, inside the light of God's presence, inside his sanction, and signed by his name.

I lived alone in the farmhouse and rented; the owners, Angus and Lynn, in their twenties, lived in another building just over the yard. I had been reading and restless for two or three days. It was morning. I had just read at breakfast an Updike story, "Packed Dirt, Churchgoing, A Dying Cat, A Traded Car," which moved me. I heard our own farmyard rooster and two or three roosters across the street screeching. I quit the house, hoping at heart to see Lynn or Angus, but immediately to watch our rooster as he crowed.

It was Saturday morning late in the summer, in early September, clear-aired and still. I climbed the barnyard fence between the poultry and the pastures; I watched the red rooster, and the rooster, reptilian, kept one alert and alien eye on me. He pulled his extravagant neck to its maximum length, hauled himself high on his legs, stretched his beak as if he were gagging, screamed, and blinked. It was a ruckus. The din came from everywhere, and only the most rigorous application of reason could persuade me that it proceeded in its entirety from this lone and maniac bird.

After a pause, the roosters across the street would start, answering the proclamation, or cranking out another round, arrhythmically, interrupting. In the same way there is no pattern nor sense to the massed stridulations of cicadas; their skipped beats, enjambments, and failed alterations jangle your spirits, as though each of those thousand insects, each with identical feelings, were stubbornly deaf to the others, and loudly alone.

I shifted along the fence to see if Lynn or Angus was coming or going. To the rooster I said nothing, but only stared. And he stared at me: we were both careful to keep the wooden fence slat from our line of sight, so that his profiled eye and my two eyes could meet. From time to time I looked beyond the pastures to learn if anyone might be seen on the road.

When I was turned away in this manner, the silence gathered and struck me. It bashed me broadside from nowhere, as if I'd been hit by a plank. It dropped from the heavens above me like yard goods; ten acres of fallen, invisible sky choked the fields. The pastures on either side of the road turned green in a surrealistic fashion, monstrous, impeccable, as if they were holding their breath. The roosters stopped. All the things of the world—the fields and the fencing, the road, a parked orange truck—were stricken and self-conscious. A world pressed down on their surfaces, a world battered just within their surfaces, and that real world, so near to emerging, had got stuck.

There was only silence. It was the silence of matter caught in the act and embarrassed. There were no cells moving, and yet there were cells. I could see the shape of the land, how it lay holding silence. Its poise and its stillness were unendurable, like the ring of the silence you hear in your skull when you're little and notice you're living, the ring which resumes later in life when you're sick.

There were flies buzzing over the dirt by the henhouse, moving in circles and buzzing, black dreams in chips off the one long dream, the dream of the regular world. But the silent fields were the real world, eternity's outpost in time, whose look I remembered but never like this, this God-blasted, paralyzed day. I felt myself tall and vertical, in a blue shirt, self-conscious, and wishing to die. I heard the flies again; I looked at the rooster who was frozen looking at me.

Then at last I heard whistling, human whistling far on the air, and I was not able to bear it. I looked around, heartbroken; only at the big yellow Charolais farm far up the road was there motion—a woman, I think, dressed in pink, and pushing a wheelbarrow easily over the grass. It must have been she who was whistling and heaping on top of the silence those hollow notes of song. But the slow sound of the music—the beautiful sound of the music ringing the air like a stone bell—was isolate and detached. The notes spread into the general air and became the weightier part of silence, silence's last straw. The distant woman and her wheelbarrow were flat and detached, like mechanized and pink-painted properties for a stage. I stood in pieces, afraid I was unable to move. Something had unhinged the world. The houses and roadsides and pastures were buckling under the silence. Then a Labrador, black, loped up the distant driveway, fluid and cartoonlike, toward the pink woman. I 'had to try to turn away. Holiness is a force, and like the others can be resisted. It was given, but I didn't want to see it, God or no God. It was as if God had said, "I am here, but not as you have known me. This is the look of silence, and of loneliness unendurable: it too has always been mine, and now will be yours." I was not ready for a life of sorrow, sorrow deriving from knowledge I could just as well stop at the gate.

I turned away, willful, and the whole show vanished. The realness of things disassembled. The whistling became ordinary, familiar; the air above the fields released its pressure and the fields lay hooded as before. I myself could act. Looking to the rooster I whistled to him myself, softly, and some hens appeared at the chicken house window, greeted the day, and fluttered down.

Several months later, walking past the farm on the way to a volleyball game, I remarked to a friend, by way of information, "There are angels in those fields." Angels! That silence so grave and so stricken, that choked and unbearable green! I have rarely been so surprised at something I've said. Angels! What are angels? I had never thought of angels, in any way at all.

From that time I began to think of angels. I considered that sights such as I had seen of the silence must have been shared by the people who said they saw angels. I began to review the thing I had seen that morning. My impression now of those fields is of thousands of spirits—spirits trapped, perhaps, by my refusal to call them more fully, or by the paralysis of my own spirit at that time—thousands of spirits, angels in fact, almost discernible to the eye, and whirling. If pressed I would say they were three or four feet from the ground. Only their motion was clear (clockwise, if you insist); that, and their beauty unspeakable.

There are angels in those fields, and I presume, in all fields, and everywhere else. I would go to the lions for this conviction, to witness this fact. What all this means about perception, or language, or angels, or my own sanity, I have no idea.

## I. Suggestions for Discussion:
1. Describe what Dillard sees and hears on the farm.
2. Discuss her use of poetic imagery. Point out similes and metaphors, for example, that strike you as particularly effective.
3. Why does she believe there are angels in those fields? Is she speaking literally or figuratively?
4. Compare her ability to depict nature with that of John Ruskin in "Of the Open Sky," p. 488.

## II. Suggestions for Writing:
1. Recall a scene, either natural or social, to which you reacted strongly and write about it.
2. As clearly and vividly as possible, describe a natural setting you have observed.

---

# JOHN DONNE

## Meditation XVII

---

John Donne (1571-1631) was an English cleric who served as dean of St. Paul's from 1621 until 1631. A great metaphysical poet, he wrote elegies, epistles, and satires known for their wit, erudition, subtlety, and passion.

Donne's famous mediation reminds his readers that "no man is an island, entire of itself" and urges them to learn from the tribulations of others to turn to God, "who is our only security."

---

*Nunc lento sonitu dicunt, morieris.*

Now this bell tolling softly for another, says to me, Thou must die.

Perchance he for whom this bell tolls may be so ill as that he knows not it tolls for him; and perchance I may think myself so much better than I am, as that they who are about me and see my state may have caused it to toll for me, and I know not that. The church is catholic, universal, so are all her actions; all that she does belongs to all. When she baptizes a child, that action concerns me; for that child is thereby connected to that body which is my head too, and ingrafted into that body whereof I am a member. And when she buries a man, that action concerns me: all mankind is of one author and is one volume; when one man dies, one chapter is not torn out of the book, but translated into a better language; and every chapter must be so translated. God employs several translators; some pieces are translated by age, some by sickness, some by war, some by justice; but God's hand is in every translation, and his hand shall bind up all our scattered leaves again for that library where every book shall lie open to one another. As therefore the bell that rings to a sermon calls not upon the preacher only, but upon the congregation to come, so this bell calls us all; but how much more me, who am brought so near the door by this sickness. There was a contention as far as a suit (in which piety and dignity, religion and estimation, were mingled) which of the religious orders should ring to prayers first in the morning; and it was determined that they should ring first that rose earliest. If we understand aright the dignity of this bell that tolls for our evening prayer, we would be glad to make it ours by rising early, in that application, that it might be ours as well as his whose indeed it is. The bell doth toll for him that thinks it doth; and though it intermit again, yet from that minute that that occasion wrought upon him, he is united to God. Who casts not up his eye to the sun when it rises? but who takes off his eye from a comet when that breaks out? Who bends not his ear to any bell which upon any occasion rings? but who can remove it from that bell which is passing a piece of himself out of this world? No man is an island, entire of itself; every man is a piece of the continent, a part of the main. If a clod be washed away by the sea, Europe is the less, as well as if a promontory were, as well as if a manor of thy friend's or of thine own were. Any man's death diminishes me because I am involved in mankind, and therefore never send to know for whom the bell tolls; it tolls for thee. Neither can we call this a begging of misery or a borrowing of misery, as though we were not miserable enough of ourselves but must fetch in more from the next house, in taking upon us the misery of our neighbors. Truly it were an excusable covetousness if we did; for affliction is a treasure, and scarce any man hath enough of it. No man hath affliction enough that is not matured and ripened by it and made fit for God by that affliction. If a man carry treasure in bullion, or in a wedge of gold, and have none coined into current money, his treasure will not defray him as he travels. Tribulation is treasure in the nature of it, but it is not current money in the use of it, except we get nearer and nearer our home, heaven, by it. Another man may be sick too, and sick to death, and this affliction may lie in his bowels as gold in a mine and be of no use to him; but this bell that tells me of his affliction digs out and applies that gold to me, if by this consideration of another's danger I take mine own into contemplation and so secure myself by making my recourse to my God, who is our only security.

## I. Suggestions for Discussion:

1. What illustrations does Donne use to stress the commonality of human experience?
2. Discuss the effectiveness of Donne's use of direct address.
3. Comment on the effectiveness of the metaphors Donne uses in this meditation.

## II. Suggestions for Writing:

1. Write and deliver a brief sermon or meditation on the brotherhood of humanity under the fatherhood of God. Pick specific Biblical and other references to enrich your presentation.
2. Write an essay exploring Donne's assertion that no person is an island, entire of itself.

---

# W. E. B. DUBOIS

## From The Souls of Black Folk

---

William Edward Burghardt DuBois (1868-1963) was a major black novelist and historian. For more than twenty years he edited the NAACP journal, *Crisis. The Souls of Black Folk,* published in 1903, is a significant statement about the issues of race in America.

In this selection, DuBois eloquently argues that the years since the Emancipation Proclamation have not brought to the American black "the freedom of life and limb, the freedom to work and think, the freedom to love and aspire." He calls for work, culture, and liberty for black Americans.

---

*O water, voice of my heart, crying in the sand,*
  *All night long crying with a mournful cry,*
*As I lie and listen, and cannot understand*
    *The voice of my heart in my side or the voice*
      *of the sea,*
    *O water, crying for rest, is it I, is it I?*
    *All night long the water is crying to me.*

*Unresting water, there shall never be rest*
  *Till the last moon droop and the last tide fail,*
*And the fire of the end begin to burn in the west;–*
    *And the heart shall be weary and wonder and cry*
      *like the sea,*
    *All life long crying without avail,*
    *As the water all night long is crying to me.*

                                           Arthur Symons[1]

Between me and the other world there is ever an unasked question: unasked by some through feelings of delicacy; by others through the difficulty of rightly framing it. All, nevertheless, flutter round it. They approach me in a half-hesitant sort of way, eye me curiously or compassionately, and then, instead of saying directly, How does it feel to be a problem? they say, I know an excellent colored man in my town; or, I fought at Mechanicsville; or, Do not these Southern outrages make your blood boil? At these I smile, or am interested, or reduce the boiling to a simmer, as the occasion may require. To the real question, How does it feel to be a problem? I answer seldom a word.

And yet, being a problem is a strange experience,—peculiar even for one who has never been anything else, save perhaps in babyhood and in Europe. It is in the early days of rollicking boyhood that the revelation first bursts upon one, all in a day, as it were. I remember well when the shadow swept

---

[1] Arthur Symons (1865–1945), English poet and literary critic.

across me. I was a little thing, away up in the hills of New England, where the dark Housatonic winds between Hoosac and Taghkanic to the sea. In a wee wooden schoolhouse, something put it into the boys' and girls' heads to buy gorgeous visiting-cards—ten cents a package—and exchange. The exchange was merry, till one girl, a tall newcomer, refused my card,—refused it peremptorily, with a glance. Then it dawned upon me with a certain suddenness that I was different from the others; or like, mayhap, in heart and life and longing, but shut out from their world by a vast veil. I had thereafter no desire to tear down that veil, to creep through; I held all beyond it in common contempt, and lived above it in a region of blue sky and great wandering shadows. That sky was bluest when I could beat my mates at examination-time, or beat them at a foot-race, or even beat their stringy heads. Alas, with the years all this fine contempt began to fade; for the worlds I longed for, and all their dazzling opportunities, were theirs, not mine. But they should not keep these prizes, I said; some, all, I would wrest from them. Just how I would do it I could never decide: by reading law, by healing the sick, by telling the wonderful tales that swam in my head,—some way. With other black boys the strife was not so fiercely sunny: their youth shrunk into tasteless sycophancy, or into silent hatred of the pale world about them and mocking distrust of everything white; or wasted itself in a bitter cry. Why did God make me an outcast and a stranger in mine own house? The shades of the prison-house closed round about us all: walls strait and stubborn to the whitest, but relentlessly narrow, tall, and unscalable to sons of night who must plod darkly on in resignation, or beat unavailing palms against the stone, or steadily, half hopelessly, watch the streak of blue above.

After the Egyptian and Indian, the Greek and Roman, the Teuton and Mongolian, the Negro is a sort of seventh son, born with a veil, and gifted with second-sight in this American world,—a world which yields him no true self-consciousness, but only lets him see himself through the revelation of the other world. It is a peculiar sensation, this double-consciousness, this sense of always looking at one's self through the eyes of others, of measuring one's soul by the tape of a world that looks on in amused contempt and pity. One ever feels his twoness,—an American, a Negro; two souls, two thoughts, two unreconciled strivings; two warring ideals in one dark body, whose dogged strength alone keeps it from being torn asunder.

The history of the American Negro is the history of this strife,—this longing to attain self-conscious manhood, to merge his double self into a better and truer self. In this merging he wishes neither of the older selves to be lost. He would not Africanize America, for America has too much to teach the world and Africa. He would not bleach his Negro soul in a flood of white

Americanism, for he knows that Negro blood has a message for the world. He simply wishes to make it possible for a man to be both a Negro and an American, without being cursed and spit upon by his fellows, without having the doors of Opportunity closed roughly in his face.

This, then, is the end of the striving; to be a co-worker in the kingdom of culture, to escape both death and isolation, to husband and use his best powers and his latent genius. These powers of body and mind have in the past been strangely wasted, dispersed, or forgotten. The shadow of a mighty Negro past flits through the tale of Ethiopia the Shadowy and of Egypt the Sphinx. Throughout history, the powers of single black men flash here and there like falling stars, and die sometimes before the world has rightly gauged their brightness. Here in America, in the few days since Emancipation, the black man's turning hither and thither in hesitant and doubtful striving has often made his very strength to lose effectiveness, to seem like absence of power, like weakness. And yet it is not weakness,—it is the contradiction of double aims. The double-aimed struggle of the black artisan—on the one hand to escape white contempt for a nation of mere hewers of wood and drawers of water, and on the other hand to plough and nail and dig for a poverty-stricken horde—could only result in making him a poor craftsman, for he had but half a heart in either cause. By the poverty and ignorance of his people, the Negro minister or doctor was tempted toward quackery and demagogy; and by the criticism of the other world, toward ideals that made him ashamed of his lowly tasks. The would-be black *savant* was confronted by the paradox that the knowledge his people needed was a twice-told tale to his white neighbors, while the knowledge which would teach the white world was Greek to his own flesh and blood. The innate love of harmony and beauty that set the ruder souls of his people a-dancing and a-singing raised but confusion and doubt in the soul of the black artist; for the beauty revealed to him was the soul-beauty of a race which his larger audience despised, and he could not articulate the message of another people. This waste of double aims, this seeking to satisfy two unreconciled ideals, has wrought sad havoc with the courage and faith and deeds of ten thousand thousand people,—has sent them often wooing false gods and invoking false means of salvation, and at times has even seemed about to make them ashamed of themselves.

Away back in the days of bondage they thought to see in one divine event the end of all doubt and disappointment; few men ever worshipped Freedom with half such unquestioning faith as did the American Negro for two centuries. To him, so far as he thought and dreamed, slavery was indeed the sum of all villainies, the cause of all sorrow, the root of all prejudice; Emancipation was the key to a promised land of sweeter beauty than ever

stretched before the eyes of wearied Israelites. In song and exhortation
swelled one refrain—Liberty; in his tears and curses the God he implored had
Freedom in his right hand. At last it came,—suddenly, fearfully, like a dream.
With one wild carnival of blood and passion came the message in his own
plaintive cadences:—

> "Shout, O children!
> Shout, you're free!
> For God has bought your liberty!"

Years have passed away since then,—ten, twenty, forty; forty years of
national life, forty years of renewal and development, and yet the swarthy
spectre sits in its accustomed seat at the Nation's feast. In vain do we cry to
this our vastest social problem:—

> "Take any shape but that, and my firm nerves
> Shall never tremble!"

The Nation has not yet found peace from its sins; the freed man has not yet
found in freedom his promised land. Whatever of good may have come in
these years of change, the shadow of a deep disappointment rests upon the
Negro people,—a disappointment all the more bitter because the unattained
ideal was unbounded save by the simple ignorance of a lowly people.

The first decade was merely a prolongation of the vain search for freedom, the boon that seemed ever barely to elude their grasp,—like a tantalizing
will-o'-the-wisp, maddening and misleading the headless host. The holocaust
of war, the terrors of the Ku-Klux Klan, the lies of carpet-baggers, the disorganization of industry, and the contradictory advice of friends and foes,
left the bewildered serf with no new watchword beyond the old cry for
freedom. As the time flew, however, he began to grasp a new idea. The ideal
of liberty demanded for its attainment powerful means, and these the Fifteenth Amendment gave him. The ballot, which before he had looked upon
as a visible sign of freedom, he now regarded as the chief means of gaining
and perfecting the liberty with which war had partially endowed him. And
why not? Had not votes made war and emancipated millions? Had not votes
enfranchised the freedmen? Was anything impossible to a power that had
done all this? A million black men started with renewed zeal to vote themselves into the kingdom. So the decade flew away, the revolution of 1876
came, and left the half-free serf weary, wondering but still inspired. Slowly
but steadily, in the following years, a new vision began gradually to replace
the dream of political power,—a powerful movement, the rise of another

ideal to guide the unguided, another pillar of fire by night after a clouded day. It was the ideal of "book-learning"; the curiosity, born of compulsory ignorance, to know and test the power of the cabalistic letters of the white man, the longing to know. Here at last seemed to have been discovered the mountain path to Canaan; longer than the highway of Emancipation and law, steep and rugged, but straight, leading to heights high enough to over-look life.

Up the new path the advance guard toiled, slowly, heavily, doggedly; only those who have watched and guided the faltering feet, the misty minds, the dull understandings, of the dark pupils of these schools know how faith-fully, how piteously, this people strove to learn. It was weary work. The cold statistician wrote down the inches of progress here and there, noted also where here and there a foot had slipped or some one had fallen. To the tired climbers, the horizon was ever dark, the mists were often cold, the Canaan was always dim and far away. If, however, the vistas disclosed as yet no goal, no resting-place, little but flattery and criticism, the journey at least gave leisure for reflection and self-examination; it changed the child of Emancipa-tion to the youth with dawning self-consciousness, self-realization, self-respect. In those sombre forests of his striving his own soul rose before him, and he saw himself,—darkly as through a veil; and yet he saw in himself some faint revelation of his power, of his mission. He began to have a dim feeling that, to attain his place in the world, he must be himself, and not another. For the first time he sought to analyze the burden he bore upon his back, that deadweight of social degradation partially masked behind a half-named Negro problem. He felt his poverty; without a cent, without a home, without land, tools, or savings, he had entered into competition with rich, landed, skilled neighbors. To be a poor man is hard, but to be a poor race in a land of dollars is the very bottom of hardships. He felt the weight of his ignorance,— not simply of letters, but of life, of business, of the humanities; the accumu-lated sloth and shirking and awkwardness of decades and centuries shackled his hands and feet. Nor was his burden all poverty and ignorance. The red stain of bastardy, which two centuries of systemic legal defilement of Negro women had stamped upon his race, meant not only the loss of ancient Afri-can chastity, but also the hereditary weight of a mass of corruption from white adulterers, threatening almost the obliteration of the Negro home.

A people thus handicapped ought not to be asked to race with the world, but rather allowed to give all its time and thought to its own social problems. But alas! while sociologists gleefully count his bastards and his prostitutes, the very soul of the toiling, sweating black man is darkened by the shadow of a vast despair. Men call the shadow prejudice, and learnedly explain it as the natural defense of culture against barbarism, learning against ignorance, purity against crime, the "higher" against the "lower" races. To which the Negro cries Amen! and swears that to so much of this strange prejudice as is founded on just homage to civilization, culture, righteousness, and progress, he humbly bows and meekly does obeisance. But before that nameless prejudice that leaps beyond all this he stands helpless, dismayed, and well-nigh speechless; before that personal disrespect and mockery, the ridicule and systematic humiliation, the distortion of fact and wanton license of fancy, the cynical ignoring of the better and the boisterous welcoming of the worse, the all-pervading desire to inculcate disdain for everything black, from Toussaint to the devil,—before this there rises a sickening despair that would disarm and discourage any nation save that black host to whom "discouragement" is an unwritten word.

But the facing of so vast a prejudice could not but bring the inevitable self-questioning, self-disparagement, and lowering of ideals which ever accompany repression and breed in an atmosphere of contempt and hate. Whispering and portents came borne upon the four winds: Lo! we are diseased and dying, cried the dark hosts; we cannot write, our voting is vain; what need of education, since we must always cook and serve? And the Nation echoed and enforced this self-criticism, saying: Be content to be servants, and nothing more; what need of higher culture for half-men? Away with the black man's ballot, by force or fraud,—and behold the suicide of a race! Nevertheless, out of the evil came something of good,—the more careful adjustment of education to real life, the clearer perception of the Negroes' social responsibilities, and the sobering realization of the meaning of progress.

So dawned the time of *Sturm und Drang:* storm and stress to-day rocks our little boat on the mad waters of the world-sea; there is within and without the sound of conflict, the burning of body and rending of soul; inspiration strives with doubt, and faith with vain questionings. The bright ideals of the past,—physical freedom, political power, the training of brains and the training of hands,—all these in turn have waxed and waned, until even the last grows dim and overcast. Are they all wrong,—all false? No. not that, but each alone was over-simple and incomplete,—the dreams of a credulous race, childhood, or the fond imaginings of the other world which does not know and does not want to know our power. To be really true, all these ideals must be melted and welded into one. The training of the schools we need to-day more than ever,—the training of deft hands, quick eyes and ears, and above all the broader, deeper, higher culture of gifted minds and pure hearts. The power of the ballot we need in sheer self-defence,—else what shall save us from a second slavery? Freedom, too, the long-sought, we still seek,—the freedom of life and limb, the freedom to work and think, the freedom to love and aspire. Work, culture, liberty,—all these we need, not singly but to-gether, not successively but together, each growing and aiding each, and all striving toward that vaster ideal that swims before the Negro people, the ideal of human brotherhood, gained through the unifying ideal of Race; the ideal of fostering and developing the traits and talents of the Negro, not in opposition to or contempt for other races, but rather in large conformity to the greater ideals of the American Republic, in order that some day on American soil two world-races may give each to each those characteristics both so sadly lack. We the darker ones come even now not altogether empty-handed: there are to-day no truer exponents of the pure human spirit of the Declaration of Independence than the American Negroes; there is no true American music but the wild sweet melodies of the Negro slave; the American fairy tales and folk-lore are Indian and African; and, all in all, we black men seem the sole oasis of simple faith and reverence in a dusty desert of dollars and smartness. Will America be poorer if she replace her brutal dyspeptic blundering with light-hearted but determined Negro humility? or her coarse and cruel wit with loving jovial good-humor? or her vulgar music with the soul of Sorrow Songs?

Merely a concrete test of the underlying principles of the great republic is the Negro Problem, and the spiritual striving of the freedmen's sons is the travail of souls whose burden is almost beyond the measure of their strength, but who bear it in the name of an historic race, in the name of this the land of their fathers' fathers, and in the name of human opportunity.

I. **Suggestions for Discussion**:
   1. In what sense does DuBois mean that he is a problem? Define what he calls the "Negro Problem."
   2. Discuss the rhetorical devices he uses to strengthen his arguments for black rights.
   3. Compare his arguments and prose style with those of Dr. Martin Luther King in "Letter from Birmingham Jail," p. 293.

II. **Suggestions for Writing**:
   1. In a letter to DuBois, discuss areas of concern to him in which black Americans have made significant gains.
   2. Compare the tone and style of DuBois's essay with those of James Baldwin's *New York Times* column, p. 51.

# LOREN EISELEY

## The Illusion of the Two Cultures

Loren Eiseley (1907–1977) was an anthropologist and academic administrator at the University of Pennsylvania. His publications include *Darwin's Century* (1958), for which he won the National Phi Beta Kappa Science Award, *The Mind as Nature* (1962), *Francis Bacon and the Modern Dilemma* (1962), *The Unexpected Universe* (1969), and *The Invisible Pyramid* (1970).

In the following essay, Eiseley argues that scientists must use human insights and understandings in order to solve the problems of the world in our age of power. Creation in science, he writes, demands a high level of imaginative insight and intuitive perception.

Not long ago an English scientist, Sir Eric Ashby, remarked that "To train young people in the dialectic between orthodoxy and dissent is the unique contribution which universities make to society." I am sure that Sir Eric meant by this remark that nowhere but in universities are the young given the opportunity to absorb past tradition and at the same time to experience the impact of new ideas—in the sense of a constant dialogue between past and present—lived in every hour of the students' existence. This dialogue, ideally, should lead to a great winnowing and sifting of experience and to a heightened consciousness of self which, in turn, should lead on to greater sensitivity and perception on the part of the individual.

Our lives are the creation of memory and the accompanying power to extend ourselves outward into ideas and relive them. The finest intellect is that which employs an invisible web of gossamer running into the past as well as across the minds of living men, and which constantly responds to the vibrations transmitted through these tenuous lines of sympathy. It would be contrary to fact, however, to assume that our universities always perform this unique function of which Sir Eric speaks, with either grace or perfection; in fact our investment in man, it has been justly remarked, is deteriorating even as the financial investment in science grows.

Over thirty years ago, George Santayana[1] had already sensed this trend.

[1] George Santayana (1863–1952), the Spanish-born American philosopher and poet, is

He commented, in a now forgotten essay, that one of the strangest consequences of modern science was that as the visible wealth of nature was more
and more transferred and abstracted, the mind seemed to lose courage and
to become ashamed of its own fertility. "The hard-pressed natural man will
not indulge his imagination," continued Santayana, "unless it poses for truth;
and being half-aware of this imposition, he is more troubled at the thought of
being deceived than at the fact of being mechanized or being bored; and he
would wish to escape imagination altogether."

"Man would wish to escape imagination altogether." I repeat that last
phrase, for it defines a peculiar aberration of the human mind found on both
sides of that bipolar division between the humanities and the sciences, which
C. P. Snow has popularized under the title of the two cultures.[2] The idea is
not solely a product of this age. It was already emerging with the science of
the seventeenth century; one finds it in Bacon. One finds the fear of it faintly
foreshadowed in Thoreau. Thomas Huxley lent it weight when he referred
contemptuously to the "caterwauling of poets."

Ironically, professional scientists berated the early evolutionists such as
Lamarck and Chambers for overindulgence in the imagination. Almost eighty
years ago John Burroughs observed that some of the animus once directed by
science toward dogmatic theology seemed in his day increasingly to be vented
upon the literary naturalist. In the early 1900's a quarrel over "nature faking"
raised a confused din in America and aroused W. H. Hudson to some dry and
pungent comment upon the failure to distinguish the purposes of science
from those of literature. I know of at least one scholar who, venturing to
develop some personal ideas in an essay for the layman, was characterized by
a reviewer in a leading professional journal as a worthless writer, although, as
it chanced, the work under discussion had received several awards in literature, one of them international in scope. More recently, some scholars not
indifferent to humanistic values have exhorted poets to leave their personal
songs in order to portray the beauty and symmetry of molecular structures.

Now some very fine verse has been written on scientific subjects, but, I
fear, very little under the dictate of scientists as such. Rather there is evident
here, precisely that restriction of imagination against which Santayana in-
veighed; namely, an attempt to constrain literature itself to the delineation of

---

the first in a series of well-known Western thinkers and writers whom Eiseley cites to
help make his case.

[2]C. P. Snow (1905-1980), the British scientist and novelist, published a monograph
called *The Two Cultures* (1959) which argued that science is a culture separate from
the traditional literary, humanistic, religious culture and that the culture of science
is more relevant to the needs of modern society.

objective or empiric truth, and to dismiss the whole domain of value, which after all constitutes the very nature of man, as without significance and beneath contempt.

Unconsciously, the human realm is denied in favor of the world of pure technics. Man, the tool user, grows convinced that he is himself only useful as a tool, that fertility except in the use of the scientific imagination is wasteful and without purpose, even, in some indefinable way, sinful. I was reading J. R. R. Tolkien's great symbolic trilogy, *The Fellowship of the Ring,* a few months ago, when a young scientist of my acquaintance paused and looked over my shoulder. After a little casual interchange the man departed leaving an accusing remark hovering in the air between us. "I wouldn't waste my time with a man who writes fairy stories." He might as well have added, "or with a man who reads them."

As I went back to my book I wondered vaguely in what leafless landscape one grew up without Hans Christian Andersen, or Dunsany, or even Jules Verne. There lingered about the young man's words a puritanism which seemed the more remarkable because, as nearly as I could discover, it was unmotivated by any sectarian religiosity unless a total dedication to science brings to some minds a similar authoritarian desire to shackle the human imagination. After all, it is this impossible, fertile world of our imagination which gave birth to liberty in the midst of oppression, and which persists in seeking until what is sought is seen. Against such invisible and fearful powers, there can be found in all ages and in all institutions—even the institutions of professional learning—the humorless man with the sneer, or if the sneer does not suffice, then the torch, for the bright unperishing letters of the human dream.

One can contrast this recalcitrant attitude with an 1890 reminiscence from that great Egyptologist, Sir Flinders Petrie, which steals over into the realm of pure literature. It was written, in unconscious symbolism, from a tomb:

> I here live, and do not scramble to fit myself to the requirements of other. In a narrow tomb, with the figure of Néfermaat standing on each side of me—as he has stood through all that we know as human history—I have just room for my bed, and a row of good reading in which I can take pleasure after dinner. Behind me is that Great Peace, the Desert. It is an entity—a power—just as much as the sea is. No wonder men fled to it from the turmoil of the ancient world.

It may now reasonably be asked why one who has similarly, if less dramatically, spent his life among the stones and broken shards of the remote past should be writing here about matters involving literature and science. It was while considering this with humility and trepidation that my eye fell upon a stone in my office. I am sure that professional journalists must recall times when an approaching deadline has keyed all their senses and led them to glance wildly around in the hope that something might leap out at them from the most prosaic surroundings. At all events my eyes fell upon this stone.

Now the stone antedated anything that the historians would call art; it had been shaped many hundreds of thousands of years ago by men whose faces would frighten us if they sat among us today. Out of old habit, since I like the feel of worked flint, I picked it up and hefted it as I groped for words over this difficult matter of the growing rift between science and art. Certainly the stone was of no help to me; it was a utilitarian thing which had cracked marrow bones, if not heads, in the remote dim morning of the human species. It was nothing if not practical. It was, in fact, an extremely early example of the empirical tradition which has led on to modern science.

The mind which had shaped this artifact knew its precise purpose. It had found out by experimental observation, that the stone was tougher, sharper, more enduring than the hand which wielded it. The creature's mind had solved the question of the best form of the implement and how it could be manipulated most effectively. In its day and time this hand ax was as grand an intellectual achievement as a rocket.

As a scientist my admiration went out to that unidentified workman. How he must have labored to understand the forces involved in the fracturing of flint, and all that involved practical survival in his world. My uncalloused twentieth-century hand caressed the yellow stone lovingly. It was then that I made a remarkable discovery.

## Art in Stone

In the mind of this gross-featured, early exponent of the practical approach to nature—the technician, the no-nonsense practitioner of survival—two forces had met and merged. There had not been room in his short and desperate life for the delicate and supercilious separation of the arts from the sciences. There did not exist then the refined distinctions set up between the scholarly percipience of reality and what has sometimes been called the vaporings of the artistic imagination.

As I clasped and unclasped the stone, running my fingers down its edges, I began to perceive the ghostly emanations from a long-vanished mind, the kind of mind which, once having shaped an object of any sort, leaves an individual trace behind it which speaks to others across the barriers of time and language. It was not the practical experimental aspect of this mind that startled me, but rather that the fellow had wasted time.

In an incalculably brutish and dangerous world he had both shaped an instrument of practical application and then, with a virtuoso's elegance, proceeded to embellish his product. He had not been content to produce a plain, utilitarian implement. In some wistful, inarticulate way, in the grip of the dim aesthetic feelings which are one of the marks of man—or perhaps I should say, some men—this archaic creature had lingered over his handiwork.

One could still feel him crouching among the stones on a long-vanished river bar, turning the thing over in his hands, feeling its polished surface, striking, here and there, just one more blow that no longer had usefulness as its criterion. He had, like myself, enjoyed the texture of the stone. With skills lost to me, he had gone on flaking the implement with an eye to beauty until it had become a kind of rough jewel, equivalent in its day, to the carved and gold inlaid pommel of the iron dagger placed in Tutankhamen's tomb.

All the later history of man contains these impractical exertions expended upon a great diversity of objects, and, with literacy, breaking even into printed dreams. Today's secular disruption between the creative aspect of art and that of science is a barbarism that would have brought lifted eyebrows in a Cro-Magnon cave. It is a product of high technical specialization, the deliberate blunting of wonder, and the equally deliberate suppression of a phase of our humanity in the name of an authoritarian institution: science, which has taken on, in our time, curious puritanical overtones. Many scientists seem unaware of the historical reasons for this development, or the fact that the creative aspect of art is not so remote from that of science as may seem, at first glance, to be the case.

I am not so foolish as to categorize individual scholars or scientists. I am, however, about to remark on the nature of science as an institution. Like all such structures it is apt to reveal certain behavioral rigidities and conformities which increase with age. It is no longer the domain of the amateur, though some of its greatest discoverers could be so defined. It is now a professional body, and with professionalism there tends to emerge a greater emphasis upon a coherent system of regulations. The deviant is more sharply treated, and the young tend to imitate their successful elders. In short, an "Establishment"—a trade union—has appeared.

Similar tendencies can be observed among those of the humanities concerned with the professional analysis and interpretation of the works of the creative artist. Here too, a similar rigidity and exclusiveness make their appearance. It is not that in the case of both the sciences and the humanities standards are out of place. What I am briefly cautioning against is that too frequently they afford an excuse for stifling original thought, or constricting much latent creativity within traditional molds.

Such molds are always useful to the mediocre conformist who instinctively castigates and rejects what he cannot imitate. Tradition, the continuity of learning, are, it is true, enormously important to the learned disciplines. What we must realize as scientists is that the particular institution we inhabit has its own irrational accretions and authoritarian dogmas which can be as unpleasant as some of those encountered in sectarian circles—particularly so since they are frequently unconsciously held and surrounded by an impenetrable wall of self-righteousness brought about because science is regarded as totally empiric and open-minded by tradition.

## Professionalism

This type of professionalism, as I shall label it, in order to distinguish it from what is best in both the sciences and humanities, is characterized by two assumptions: that the accretions of fact are cumulative and lead to progress, whereas the insights of art are, at best, singular, and lead nowhere, or, when introduced into the realm of science, produce obscurity and confusion. The convenient label "mystic" is, in our day, readily applied to men who pause for simple wonder, or who encounter along the borders of the known, that "awful power" which Wordsworth characterized as the human imagination. It can, he says, rise suddenly from the mind's abyss and enwrap the solitary traveler like a mist.

We do not like mists in this era, and the word *imagination* is less and less used. We like, instead, a clear road, and we abhor solitary traveling. Indeed one of our great scientific historians remarked not long ago that the literary naturalist was obsolescent if not completely outmoded. I suppose he meant that with our penetration into the biophysical realm, life, like matter, would become increasingly represented by abstract symbols. To many it must appear that the more we can dissect life into its elements, the closer we are getting to its ultimate resolution. While I have some reservations on this score, they are not important. Rather, I should like to look at the symbols which in the one case, denote science and, in the other constitute those vaporings and cloud wraiths that are the abomination, so it is said, of the true scientist, but are the delight of the poet and literary artist.

## Creation in Science

Creation in science demands a high level of imaginative insight and intuitive perception. I believe no one would deny this, even though it exists in varying degrees, just as it does, similarly, among writers, musicians, or artists. The scientist's achievement, however, is quantitatively transmissible. From a single point his discovery is verifiable by other men who may then, on the basis of corresponding data, accept the innovation and elaborate upon it in the cumulative fashion which is one of the great triumphs of science.

Artistic creation, on the other hand, is unique. It cannot be twice discovered as, say, natural selection was discovered. It may be imitated stylistically, in a genre, a school, but, save for a few items of technique, it is not cumulative. A successful work of art may set up reverberations and is, in this, just as transmissible as science, but there is a qualitative character about it. Each reverberation in another mind is unique. As the French novelist François Mauriac has remarked, each great novel is a separate and distinct world operating under its own laws with a flora and fauna totally its own. There is communication, or the work is a failure, but the communication releases our own visions, touches some highly personal chord in our own experience.

The symbols used by the great artist are a key releasing our humanity from the solitary tower of the self. "Man," says Lewis Mumford, "is first and foremost the self-fabricating animal." I will merely add that the artist plays an enormous role in this act of self-creation. It is he who touches the hidden strings of pity, who searches our hearts, who makes us sensitive to beauty, who asks questions about fate and destiny. Such questions, though they lurk always around the corners of the external universe which is the peculiar province of science, the rigors of the scientific method do not enable us to pursue directly.

And yet I wonder.

It is surely possible to observe that it is the successful analogy or symbol which frequently allows the scientist to leap from a generalization in one field of thought to a triumphant achievement in another. For example, Progressionism in a spiritual sense later became the model contributing to the discovery of organic evolution. Such analogies genuinely resemble the figures and enchantments of great literature, whose meanings similarly can never be totally grasped because of their endless power to ramify in the individual mind.

John Donne, in the seventeenth century, gave powerful expression to a feeling applicable as much to science as to literature when he said devoutly of certain Biblical passages: "the literall sense is always to be preserved; but the literall sense is not alwayes to be discerned; for the literall sense is not alwayes that which the very letter and grammar of the place presents."—A figurative sense, he argues cogently, can sometimes be the most "literall intention of the Holy Ghost."

It is here that the scientist and artist sometimes meet in uneasy opposition, or at least along lines of tension. The scientist's attitude is sometimes, I suspect, that embodied in Samuel Johnson's remark that, wherever there is mystery, roguery is not far off.

Yet surely it was not roguery when Sir Charles Lyell glimpsed in a few fossil prints of raindrops the persistence of the world's natural forces through the incredible, mysterious aeons of geologic time. The fossils were a symbol of a vast hitherto unglimpsed order. They are, in Donne's sense, both literal and symbolic. As fossils they merely denote evidence of rain in a past era. Figuratively they are more. To the perceptive intelligence they afford the hint of lengthened natural order, just as the eyes of ancient trilobites tell us similarly of the unchanging laws of light. Equally, the educated mind may discern in a scratched pebble the retreating shadow of vast ages of ice and gloom. In Donne's archaic phraseology these objects would bespeak the principal intention of the Divine Being, that is, of order beyond our power to grasp.

Such images drawn from the world of science are every bit as powerful as great literary symbolism and equally as demanding upon the individual imagination of the scientist who would fully grasp the extension of meaning which is involved. It is, in fact, one and the same creative act in both domains.

Indeed evolution itself has become such a figurative symbol, as has also the hypothesis of the expanding universe. The laboratory worker may think of these concepts in a totally empirical fashion as subject to proof or disproof by the experimental method. Like Freud's doctrine of the subconscious, however, such ideas frequently escape from the professional scientist into the public domain. There they may undergo further individual transformation and embellishment. Whether the scholar approves or not, such hypotheses are now as free to evolve as the creations of art in the mind of the individual. All the resulting enrichment and confusion will bear about it something suggestive of the world of artistic endeavor.

## Figurative Insights

As figurative insights into the nature of things, such embracing conceptions may become grotesquely distorted or glow with added philosophical wisdom. As in the case of the trilobite eye or the fossil raindrop, there lurks behind the visible evidence vast shadows no longer quite of that world which we term natural. Like the words in Donne's Bible enormous implications have transcended the literal expression of the thought. Reality itself has been superseded by a greater reality. As Donne himself asserted, "The substance of the truth is in the great images which lie behind."

It is because these two types of creation—the artistic and the scientific— have sprung from the same being and have their points of contact even in division, that I have the temerity to assert that, in a sense, the two cultures are an illusion, that they are a product of unreasoning fear, professionalism, and misunderstanding. Because of the emphasis upon science in our society, much has been said about the necessity of educating the layman and even the professional student of the humanities upon the ways and the achievements of science. I admit that a barrier exists, but I am also concerned to express the view that there persists in the domain of science itself, an occasional marked intolerance of those of its own membership who venture to pursue the way of letters. As I have previously remarked, this intolerance can the more successfully clothe itself in seeming objectivity because of the supposed open nature of the scientific society. It is not remarkable that this trait is sometimes more manifest in the younger and less secure disciplines.

There was a time, not too many centuries ago, when to be active in scientific investigation was to invite suspicion. Thus it may be that there now lingers among us, even in the triumph of the experimental method, a kind of vague fear of that other artistic world of deep emotion, of strange symbols, lest it seize upon us or distort the hard-won objectivity of our thinking—lest it corrupt, in other words, that crystalline and icy objectivity which, in our scientific guise, we erect as a model of conduct. This model, incidentally, if pursued to its absurd conclusion, would lead to a world in which the computer would determine all aspects of our existence; one in which the bomb would be as welcome as the discoveries of the physician.

Happily, the very great in science, or even those unique scientist-artists such as Leonardo, who foreran the emergence of science as an institution, have been singularly free from this folly. Darwin decried it even as he recognized that he had paid a certain price in concentrated specialization for his achievement. Einstein, it is well known, retained a simple sense of wonder; Newton felt like a child playing with pretty shells on a beach. All show a deep humility and an emotional hunger which is the prerogative of the artist. It is with the lesser men, with the institutionalization of method, with the appearance of dogma and mapped-out territories that an unpleasant suggestion of fenced preserves begins to dominate the university atmosphere.

As a scientist, I can say that I have observed it in my own and others' specialties. I have had occasion, also to observe its effects in the humanities. It is not science *per se;* it is, instead, in both regions of thought, the narrow professionalism which is also plainly evident in the trade union. There can be small men in science just as there are small men in government, or business. In fact it is one of the disadvantages of big science, just as it is of big government, that the availability of huge sums attracts a swarm of elbowing and contentious men to whom great dreams are less than protected hunting preserves.

The sociology of science deserves at least equal consideration with the biographies of the great scientists, for powerful and changing forces are at work upon science, the institution, as contrasted with science as a dream and an ideal of the individual. Like other aspects of society, it is a construct of men, and is subject, like other social structures, to human pressures and inescapable distortions.

Let me give you an illustration. Even in learned journals, clashes occasionally occur between those who would regard biology as a separate and distinct domain of inquiry and the reductionists who, by contrast, perceive in the living organism only a vaster and more random chemistry. Understandably, the concern of the reductionists is with the immediate. Thomas Hobbes was expressing a similar point of view when he castigated poets as "working on mean minds with words and distinctions that of themselves signifie nothing, but betray (by their obscurity) that there walketh . . . another kingdome, as it were a kingdome of fayries in the dark." I myself have been similarly criticized for speaking of a nature "beyond the nature that we know."

## Semantic Confusion

Yet consider for a moment this dark, impossible realm of Fayrie. Man is not totally compounded of the nature we profess to understand. He contains, instead, a lurking unknown future, just as the man-apes of the Pliocene contained in embryo the future that surrounds us now. The world of human culture itself was an unpredictable fairy world until, in some Pre-Ice-Age meadow, the first meaningful sounds in all the world broke through the jungle babble of the past, the nature, until that moment, "known."

It is fascinating to observe that, in the very dawn of science, Bacon, the spokesman for the empirical approach to nature, shared with Shakespeare, the poet, a recognition of the creativeness which adds to nature, and which emerges from nature as "an art which nature makes." Neither the great scholar nor the great poet had renounced the kingdome of Fayrie. They had realized what Bergson was later to express so effectively, that life inserts a vast "indetermination into matter." It is, in a sense, an intrusion from a realm which can never be completely subject to prophetic analysis by science. The novelties of evolution emerge; they cannot be predicted. They haunt, until their arrival, a world of unimaginable possibilities behind the living screen of events, as these last exist to the observer confined to a single point on the time scale.

Oddly enough, much of the confusion that surrounded my phrase, "a nature beyond the nature that we know," resolves itself into pure semantics. I might have pointed out what must be obvious even to the most dedicated scientific mind that the nature which we know has been many times reinterpreted in human thinking, and that the hard, substantial matter of the nineteenth century has already vanished into a dark, bodiless void, a web of "events" in space-time. This is a realm, I venture to assert, as weird as any we have tried, in the past, to exorcise by the brave use of seeming solid words. Yet some minds exhibit an almost instinctive hostility toward the mere attempt to wonder, or to ask what lies below that microcosmic world out of which emerge the particles which compose our bodies, and which now take on this wraithlike quality.

Is there something here we fear to face, except when clothed in safely sterilized professional speech? Have we grown reluctant in this age of power to admit mystery and beauty into our thoughts, or to learn where power ceases? I referred a few moments ago to one of our own forebears on a gravel bar, thumbing a pebble. If, after the ages of building and destroying, if after the measuring of light-years, and the powers probed at the atom's heart, if after the last iron is rust-eaten and the last glass lies shattered in the streets, a man, some savage, some remnant of what once we were, pauses on his way to the tribal drinking place and feels rising from within his soul the inexplicable mist of terror and beauty that is evoked from old ruins—even the ruins of the greatest city in the world—then, I say, all will still be well with man.

## The Stone of Power

And if that savage can pluck a stone from the gravel because it shone like crystal when the water rushed over it, and hold it against the sunset, he will be as we were in the beginning, whole—as we were when we were children, before we began to split the knowledge from the dream. All talk of the two cultures is an illusion; it is the pebble which tells man's story. Upon it is written man's two faces, the artistic and the practical. They are expressed upon one stone over which a hand once closed, no less firm because the mind behind it was submerged in light and shadow and deep wonder.

Today we hold a stone, the heavy stone of power. We must perceive beyond it, however, by the aid of the artistic imagination, those humane insights and understandings which alone can lighten our burden and enable us to shape ourselves, rather than the stone, into the forms which great art has anticipated.

### I. Suggestions for Discussion:
1. What is Eiseley's attitude toward the activity of organized scientific research?
2. What is his attitude toward the scientist who says, "I wouldn't waste my time with a man who writes fairy stories"?
3. Discuss the effectiveness of his comparison of the stone-age ax with the modern rocket.

### II. Suggestions for Writing:
1. Using Eiseley's ideas as a starting point, discuss the dangers inherent in the triumph of the scientific attitude.
2. Compare and contrast Eiseley's thoughts about artistic and scientific creation with Thomas DeQuincey's observations about the "Literature of Power and the Literature of Knowledge," p. 120.

---

# RALPH WALDO EMERSON

## The American Scholar

---

Ralph Waldo Emerson (1803–1882) was an American essayist, orator, philosopher, and poet who lectured and wrote on literature, history, and human culture. He published *Nature* in 1836, *Essays* in 1841 and 1844, and a collection of *Poems* in 1847. John Dewey called Emerson "the philosopher of democracy."

*The American Scholar,* which follows, was delivered at the Phi Beta Kappa exercise at Harvard on August 31, 1837. In his powerful and controversial address, Emerson used all of his sophisticated rhetorical skills to urge America to assert its intellectual and cultural independence from Europe.

---

## AN ORATION

Delivered Before the Phi Beta Kappa Society,
at Cambridge, August 31, 1837

MR. PRESIDENT, AND GENTLEMEN,

I greet you on the re-commencement of our literary year. Our anniversary is one of hope, and, perhaps, not enough of labor. We do not meet for games of strength or skill, for the recitation of histories, tragedies and odes, like the ancient Greeks; for parliaments of love and poesy, like the Troubadours; nor for the advancement of science, like our contemporaries in the British and European capitals. Thus far, our holiday has been simply a friendly sign of the survival of the love of letters amongst a people too busy to give to letters any more. As such, it is precious as the sign of an indestructible instinct. Perhaps the time is already come, when it ought to be, and will be something else; when the sluggard intellect of this continent will look from under its iron lids and fill the postponed expectation of the world with something better than the exertions of mechanical skill. Our day of dependence, our long apprenticeship to the learning of other lands, draws to a close. The millions that around us are rushing into life, cannot always be fed on the sere remains of foreign harvests. Events, actions arise, that must be sung, that will sing themselves. Who can doubt that poetry will revive and lead in a new age, as the star in the constellation Harp which now flames in our zenith, astronomers announce, shall one day be the pole-star for a thousand years?

In the light of this hope, I accept the topic which not only usage, but the nature of our association, seem to prescribe to this day,—the AMERICAN SCHOLAR. Year by year, we come up hither to read one more chapter of his biography. Let us inquire what light new days and events have thrown on his character, his duties and his hopes.

It is one of those fables, which out of an unknown antiquity, convey an unlooked-for wisdom, that the gods, in the beginning, divided Man into men, that he might be more helpful to himself; just as the hand was divided into fingers, the better to answer its end.

The old fable covers a doctrine ever new and sublime; that there is One Man,—present to all particular men only partially, or through one faculty;

and that you must take the whole society to find the whole man. Man is not a farmer, or a professor, or an engineer, but he is all. Man is priest, and scholar, and statesman, and producer, and soldier. In the *divided* or social state, these functions are parcelled out to individuals, each of whom aims to do his stint of the joint work, whilst each other performs his. The fable implies that the individual to possess himself, must sometimes return from his own labor to embrace all the other laborers. But unfortunately, this original unit, this fountain of power, has been so distributed to multitudes, has been so minutely subdivided and peddled out, that it is spilled into drops, and cannot be gathered. The state of society is one in which the members have suffered amputation from the trunk, and strut about so many walking monsters,—a good finger, a neck, a stomach, an elbow, but never a man.

Man is thus metamorphosed into a thing, into many things. The planter, who is Man sent out into the field to gather food, is seldom cheered by any idea of the true dignity of his ministry. He sees his bushel and his cart, and nothing beyond, and sinks into the farmer, instead of Man on the farm. The tradesman scarcely ever gives an ideal worth to his work, but is ridden by the routine of his craft, and the soul is subject to dollars. The priest becomes a form; the attorney, a statute-book; the mechanic, a machine; the sailor, a rope of a ship.

In this distribution of functions, the scholar is the delegated intellect. In the right state, he is, *Man Thinking.* In the degenerate state, when the victim of society, he tends to become a mere thinker, or, still worse, the parrot of other men's thinking.

In this view of him, as Man Thinking, the whole theory of his office is contained. Him nature solicits, with all her placid, all her monitory pictures. Him the past instructs. Him the future invites. Is not, indeed, every man a student, and do not all things exist for the student's behoof? And, finally, is not the true scholar the only true master? But, as the old oracle said, "All things have two handles. Beware of the wrong one." In life, too often, the scholar errs with mankind and forfeits his privilege. Let us see him in his school, and consider him in reference to the main influences he receives.

I. The first in time and the first in importance of the influences upon the mind is that of nature. Every day, the sun; and, after sunset, night and her stars. Ever the winds blow; ever the grass grows. Every day, men and women, conversing, beholding and beholden. The scholar must needs stand wistful and admiring before this great spectacle. He must settle its value in his mind. What is nature to him? There is never a beginning, there is never an end to the inexplicable continuity of this web of God, but always circular power returning into itself. Therein it resembles his own spirit, whose beginning, whose ending he never can find—so entire, so boundless. Far, too, as her splendors shine, system on system shooting like rays, upward, downward, without centre, without circumference,—in the mass and in the particle nature hastens to render account of herself to the mind. Classification begins. To the young mind, every thing is individual, stands by itself. By and by, it finds how to join two things, and see in them one nature; then three, then three thousand; and so, tyrannized over by its own unifying instinct, it goes on tying things together, diminishing anomalies, discovering roots running under ground, whereby contrary and remote things cohere, and flower out from one stem. It presently learns, that, since the dawn of history, there has been a constant accumulation and classifying of facts. But what is classification but the perceiving that these objects are not chaotic, and are nor foreign, but have a law which is also a law of the human mind? The astronomer discovers that geometry, a pure abstraction of the human mind, is the measure of planetary motion. The chemist finds proportions and intelligible method throughout matter: and science is nothing but the finding of analogy, identity in the most remote parts. The ambitious soul sits down before each refractory fact; one after another, reduces all strange constitutions, all new powers, to their class and their law, and goes on forever to animate the last fibre of organization, the outskirts of nature, by insight.

Thus to him, to this school-boy under the bending dome of day, is suggested, that he and it proceed from one root; one is leaf and one is flower; relation, sympathy, stirring in every vein. And what is that Root? Is not that the soul of his soul?—A thought too bold—a dream too wild. Yet when this spiritual light shall have revealed the law of more earthly natures,—when he has learned to worship the soul, and to see that the natural philosophy that now is, is only the first gropings of its gigantic hand, he shall look forward to an ever expanding knowledge as to a becoming creator. He shall see that nature is the opposite of the soul, answering to it part for part. One is seal, and one is print. Its beauty is the beauty of his own mind. Its laws are the laws of his own mind. Nature then becomes to him the measure of his attainments. So much of nature as he is ignorant of, so much of his own mind does he not yet possess. And, in fine, the ancient precept, "Know thyself," and the modern precept, "Study nature," become at last one maxim.

II. The next great influence into the spirit of the scholar, is, the mind of the Past,—in whatever form, whether of literature, of art, of institutions, that mind is inscribed. Books are the best type of the influence of the past, and perhaps we shall get at the truth—learn the amount of this influence more conveniently—by considering their value alone.

The theory of books is noble. The scholar of the first age received into him the world around; brooded there on; gave it the new arrangement of his own mind, and uttered it again. It came into him—life; it went out from him—truth. It came to him—short-lived actions; it went out from him—immortal thoughts. It came to him—business; it went from him—poetry. It was—dead fact; now, it is quick thought. It can stand, and it can go. It now endures, it now flies, it now inspires. Precisely in proportion to the depth of mind from which it issued, so high does it soar, so long does it sing.

Or, I might say, it depends on how far the process had gone, of transmuting life into truth. In proportion to the completeness of the distillation, so will the purity and imperishableness of the product be. But none is quite perfect. As no air-pump can by any means make a perfect vacuum, so neither can any artist entirely exclude the conventional, the local, the perishable from his book, or write a book of pure thought that shall be as efficient, in all respects, to a remote posterity, as to contemporaries, or rather to the second age. Each age, it is found, must write its own books; or rather, each generation for the next succeeding. The books of an older period will not fit this.

Yet hence arises a grave mischief. The sacredness which attaches to the act of creation,—the act of thought,—is instantly transferred to the record. The poet chanting, was felt to be a divine man. Henceforth the chant is divine also. The writer was a just and wise spirit. Henceforward it is settled, the book is perfect; as love of the hero corrupts into worship of his statue. Instantly, the book becomes noxious. The guide is a tyrant. We sought a brother, and lo, a governor. The sluggish and perverted mind of the multitude, always slow to open to the incursions of Reason, having once so opened, having once received this book, stands upon it, and makes an outcry, if it is disparaged. Colleges are built on it. Books are written on it by thinkers, not by Man Thinking; by men of talent, that is, who start wrong, who set out from accepted dogmas, not from their own sight of principles. Meek young men grow up in libraries, believing it their duty to accept the views which Cicero, which Locke, which Bacon have given, forgetful that Cicero, Locke and Bacon[1] were only young men in libraries when they wrote these books.

Hence, instead of Man Thinking, we have the bookworm. Hence, the book-learned class, who value books, as such; not as related to nature and the human constitution, but as making a sort of Third Estate with the world

---

[1] Students of the day regularly read such authors as Marcus Tullius Cicero (106–43 B.C.), the Roman orator and philosopher, John Locke (1632–1704), the English philosopher, and Francis Bacon (1561–1626), the English philosopher who founded the inductive method of science.

and the soul. Hence, the restorers of readings, the emendators, the biblio-maniacs of all degrees.

This is bad; this is worse than it seems. Books are the best of things, well used; abused, among the worst. What is the right use? What is the one end which all means go to effect? They are for nothing but to inspire. I had better never see a book than to be warped by its attraction clean out of my own orbit, and made a satellite instead of a system. The one thing in the world of value, is, the active soul,—the soul, free, sovereign, active. This every man is entitled to; this every man contains within him, although in almost all men, obstructed, and as yet unborn. The soul active sees absolute truth; and utters truth, or creates. In this action, it is genius; not the privilege of here and there a favorite, but the sound estate of every man. In its essence, it is progressive. The book, the college, the school of art, the institution of any kind, stop with some past utterance of genius. This is good, say they,—let us hold by this. They pin me down. They look backward and not forward. But genius always looks forward. The eyes of man are set in his forehead, not in his hindhead. Man hopes. Genius creates. To create,—to create,—is the proof of a divine presence. Whatever talents may be, if the man create not, the pure efflux of the Deity is not his:—cinders and smoke, there may be, but not yet flame. There are creative manners, there are creative actions, and creative words; manners, actions, words, that is, indicative of no custom or authority, but springing spontaneous from the mind's own sense of good and fair.

On the other part, instead of being its own seer, let it receive always from another mind its truth, though it were in torrents of light, without periods of solitude, inquest and self-recovery, and a fatal disservice is done. Genius is always sufficiently the enemy of genius by over-influence. The literature of every nation bear me witness. The English dramatic poets have Shakespearized now for two hundred years.

Undoubtedly there is a right way of reading,—so it be sternly subordinated. Man Thinking must not be subdued by his instruments. Books are for the scholar's idle times. When he can read God directly, the hour is too precious to be wasted in other men's transcripts of their readings. But when the intervals of darkness come, as come they must,—when the soul seeth not, when the sun is hid, and the stars withdraw their shining,—we repair to the lamps which were kindled by their ray to guide our steps to the East again, where the dawn is. We hear that we may speak. The Arabian proverb says, "A fig tree looking on a fig tree, becometh fruitful."

It is remarkable, the character of the pleasure we derive from the best books. They impress us ever with the conviction that one nature wrote and

the same reads. We read the verses of one of the great English poets, of
Chaucer, of Marvell, of Dryden, with the most modern joy,—with a pleasure,
I mean, which is in great part caused by the abstraction of all *time* from their
verses. There is some awe mixed with the joy of our surprise, when this poet,
who lived in some past world, two or three hundred years ago, says that
which lies close to my own soul, that which I also had wellnigh thought and
said. But for the evidence thence afforded to the philosophical doctrine of
the identity of all minds, we should suppose some preestablished harmony,
some foresight of souls that were to be, and some preparation of stores for
their future wants, like the fact observed in insects, who lay up food before
death for the young grub they shall never see.

I would not be hurried by any love of system, by any exaggeration of
instincts, to underrate the Book. We all know, that as the human body can
be nourished on any food, though it were boiled grass and the broth of shoes,
so the human mind can be fed by any knowledge. And great and heroic men
have existed, who had almost no other information than by the printed page.
I only would say, that it needs a strong head to bear that diet. One must be
an inventor to read well. As the proverb says, "He that would bring home the
wealth of the Indies, must carry out the wealth of the Indies." There is then
creative reading, as well as creative writing. When the mind is braced by labor
and invention, the page of whatever book we read becomes luminous with
manifold allusion. Every sentence is doubly significant, and the sense of our
author is as broad as the world. We then see, what is always true, that as the
seer's hour of vision is short and rare among heavy days and months, so is its
record, perchance, the least part of his volume. The discerning will read in his
Plato or Shakspeare, only that least part,—only the authentic utterances of
the oracle,—and all the rest he rejects, were it never so many times Plato's and
Shakspeare's.

Of course, there is a portion of reading quite indispensable to a wise
man. History and exact science he must learn by laborious reading. Colleges,
in like manner, have their indispensable office,—to teach elements. But they
can only highly serve us, when they aim not to drill, but to create; when they
gather from far every ray of various genius to their hospitable halls, and, by
the concentrated fires, set the hearts of their youth on flame. Thought and
knowledge are natures in which apparatus and pretension avail nothing.
Gowns, and pecuniary foundations, though of towns of gold, can never coun-
tervail the least sentence or syllable of wit. Forget this, and our American
colleges will recede in their public importance whilst they grow richer every
year.

III. There goes in the world a notion that the scholar should be a re-
cluse, a valetudinarian,—as unfit for any handiwork or public labor, as a pen-
knife for an axe. The so-called "practical men" sneer at speculative men, as
if, because they speculate or *see,* they could do nothing. I have heard it said
that the clergy,—who are always more universally than any other class, the
scholars of their day,—are addressed as women: that the rough, spontaneous
conversation of men they do not hear, but only a mincing and diluted speech.
They are often virtually disfranchised; and, indeed, there are advocates for
their celibacy. As far as this is true of the studious classes, it is not just and
wise. Action is with the scholar subordinate, but it is essential. Without it,
he is not yet man. Without it, thought can never ripen into truth. Whilst the
world hangs before the eye as a cloud of beauty, we cannot even see its
beauty. Inaction is cowardice, but there can be no scholar without the heroic
mind. The preamble of thought, the transition through which it passes from
the unconscious to the conscious, is action. Only so much do I know, as I
have lived. Instantly we know whose words are loaded with life, and whose
not.

The world,—this shadow of the soul, or *other me,* lies wide around. Its
attractions are the keys which unlock my thoughts and make me acquainted
with myself. I run eagerly into this resounding tumult. I grasp the hands of
those next me, and take my place in the ring to suffer and to work, taught by
an instinct that so shall the dumb abyss be vocal with speech. I pierce its
order; I dissipate its fear; I dispose of it within the circuit of my expanding
life. So much only of life as I know by experience, so much of the wilderness
have I vanquished and planted, or so far have I extended my being, my
dominion. I do not see how any man can afford, for the sake of his nerves
and his nap, to spare any action in which he can partake. It is pearls and
rubies to his discourse. Drudgery, calamity, exasperation, want, are in-
structers in eloquence and wisdom. The true scholar grudges every opportunity of action past by, as a loss of power.

It is the raw material out of which the intellect moulds her splendid
products. A strange process too, this, by which experience is converted into
thought, as a mulberry leaf is converted into satin. The manufacture goes
forward at all hours.

The actions and events of our childhood and youth are now matters of
calmest observation. They lie like fair pictures in the air. Not so with our
recent actions,—with the business which we now have in hand. On this we
are quite unable to speculate. Our affections as yet circulate through it. We
no more feel or know it, then we feel the feet, or the hand, or the brain of

our body. The new deed is yet a part of life,—remains for a time immersed in our unconscious life. In some contemplative hour, it detaches itself from the life like a ripe fruit, to become a thought of the mind. Instantly, it is raised, transfigured; the corruptible has put on incorruption. Always now it is an object of beauty, however base its origin and neighborhood. Observe, too, the impossibility of antedating this act. In its grub state, it cannot fly, it cannot shine,—it is a dull grub. But suddenly, without observation, the self-same thing unfurls beautiful wings, and is an angel of wisdom. So is there no fact, no event, in our private history, which shall not, sooner or later, lose its adhesive inert form, and astonish us by soaring from our body into the empyrean. Cradle and infancy, school and playground, the fear of boys, and dogs, and ferules, the love of little maids and berries, and many another fact that once filled the whole sky, are gone already; friend and relative, profession and party, town and country, nation and world, must also soar and sing.

Of course, he who has put forth his total strength in fit actions, has the richest return of wisdom. I will not shut myself out of this globe of action and transplant an oak into a flower pot, there to hunger and pine; nor trust the revenue of some single faculty, and exhaust one vein of thought, much like those Savoyards, who, getting their livelihood by carving shepherds, shepherdesses, and smoking Dutchmen, for all Europe, went out one day to the mountain to find stock, and discovered that they had whittled up the last of their pine trees. Authors we have in numbers, who have written out their vein, and who, moved by a commendable prudence, sail for Greece or Palestine, follow the trapper into the prairie, or ramble round Algiers to replenish their merchantable stock.

If it were only for a vocabulary the scholar would be covetous of action. Life is our dictionary. Years are well spent in country labors; in town—in the insight into trades and manufactures; in frank intercourse with many men and women; in science; in art; to the one end of mastering in all their facts a language, by which to illustrate and embody our perceptions. I learn immediately from any speaker how much he has already lived, through the poverty or the splendor of his speech. Life lies behind us as the quarry from whence we get tiles and copestones for the masonry of to-day. This is the way to learn grammar. Colleges and books only copy the language which the field and the work-yard made.

But the final value of action, like that of books, and better than books, is, that it is a resource. That great principle of Undulation in nature, that shows itself in the inspiring and expiring of the breath; in desire and satiety; in the ebb and flow of the sea, in day and night, in heat and cold, and as yet more deeply ingrained in every atom and every fluid, is known to us under the name of Polarity,—these "fits of easy transmission and reflection," as Newton[2] called them, are the law of nature because they are the law of spirit.

The mind now thinks; now acts; and each fit reproduces the other. When the artist has exhausted his materials, when the fancy no longer paints, when thoughts are no longer apprehended, and books are a weariness,—he has always the resource *to live*. Character is higher than intellect. Thinking is the function. Living is the functionary. The stream retreats to its source. A great soul will be strong to live, as well as strong to think. Does he lack organ or medium to impart his truths? He can still fall back on this elemental force of living them. This is a total act. Thinking is a partial act. Let the grandeur of justice shine in his affairs. Let the beauty of affection cheer his lowly roof. Those "far from fame" who dwell and act with him, will feel the force of his constitution in the doings and passages of the day better than it can be measured by any public and designed display. Time shall teach him that the scholar loses no hour which the man lives. Herein he unfolds the sacred germ of his instinct, screened from influence. What is lost in seemliness is gained in strength. Not out of those on whom systems of education have exhausted their culture, comes the helpful giant to destroy the old or to build the new, but out of unhandselled[3] savage nature, out of terrible Druids and Berserkers, come at last Alfred[4] and Shakspeare.

I hear therefore with joy whatever is beginning to be said of the dignity and necessity of labor to every citizen. There is virtue yet in the hoe and the spade, for learned as well as for unlearned hands. And labor is every where welcome; always we are invited to work; only be this limitation observed, that a man shall not for the sake of wider activity sacrifice any opinion to the popular judgments and modes of action.

I have now spoken of the education of the scholar by nature, by books, and by action. It remains to say somewhat of his duties.

They are such as become Man Thinking. They may all be comprised in self-trust. The office of the scholar is to cheer, to raise, and to guide men by showing them facts amidst appearances. He plies the slow, unhonored, and unpaid task of observation. Flamsteed and Herschel,[5] in their glazed observatories, may catalogue the stars with the praise of all men, and, the results

---

[2] Sir Isaac Newton (1642–1727) was an English mathematician and astronomer.
[3] Unfurnished.
[4] Druids (ancient pagan Celtic priests) and Berserkers (savage warriors of Norse mythology) give way to figures like King Alfred (849–899), the greatest of the Saxon kings.
[5] John Flamstead (1646–1719) and Sir F.W. Herschel (1738–1822) were noted English astronomers.

being splendid and useful, honor is sure. But he, in his private observatory, cataloguing obscure and nebulous stars of the human mind, which as yet no man has thought of as such,—watching days and months, sometimes, for a few facts; correcting still his old records;—must relinquish display and immediate fame. In the long period of his preparation, he must betray often an ignorance and shiftlessness in popular arts, incurring the disdain of the able who shoulder him aside. Long he must stammer in his speech; often forego the living for the dead. Worse yet, he must accept—how often! poverty and solitude. For the ease and pleasure of treading the old road, accepting the fashions, the education, the religion of society, he takes the cross of making his own, and, of course, the self-accusation, the faint heart, the frequent uncertainty and loss of time which are the nettles and tangling vines in the way of the self-relying and self-directed; and the state of virtual hostility in which he seems to stand to society, and especially to educated society. For all this loss and scorn, what offset? He is to find consolation in exercising the highest functions of human nature. He is one who raises himself from private considerations, and breathes and lives on public and illustrious thoughts. He is the world's eye. He is the world's heart. He is to resist the vulgar prosperity that retrogrades ever to barbarism, by preserving and communicating heroic sentiments, noble biographies, melodious verse, and the conclusions of history. Whatsoever oracles the human heart in all emergencies, in all solemn hours has uttered as its commentary on the world of actions,—these he shall receive and impart. And whatsoever new verdict Reason from her inviolable seat pronounces on the passing men and events of to-day,—this he shall hear and promulgate.

These being his functions, it becomes him to feel all confidence in himself, and to defer never to the popular cry. He and he only knows the world. The world of any moment is the merest appearance. Some great decorum, some fetish of a government, some ephemeral trade, or war, or man, is cried up by half mankind and cried down by the other half, as if all depended on this particular up or down. The odds are that the whole question is not worth the poorest thought which the scholar has lost in listening to the controversy. Let him not quit his belief that a popgun is a popgun, though the ancient and honorable of the earth affirm it to be the crack of doom. In silence, in steadiness, in severe abstraction, let him hold himself; add observation to observation, patient of neglect, patient of reproach; and bide his own time,—happy enough if he can satisfy himself alone that this day he has seen something truly. Success treads on every right step. For the instinct is sure that prompts him to tell his brother what he thinks. He then learns that in going down into the secrets of his own mind, he has descended into the secrets of all minds. He learns that he who has mastered any law in his private thoughts, is master to that extent of all men whose language he speaks, and of all into whose language his own can be translated. The poet in utter solitude remembering his spontaneous thoughts and recording them, is found to have recorded that which men in crowded cities find true for them also. The orator distrusts at first the fitness of his frank confessions,—his want of knowledge of the persons he addresses,—until he finds that he is the complement of his hearers;—that they drink his words because he fulfils for them their own nature; the deeper he dives into his privatest secretest presentiment,—to his wonder he finds, this is the most acceptable, most public, and universally true. The people delight in it; the better part of every man feels, This is my music: this is myself.

In self-trust, all the virtues are comprehended. Free should the scholar be,—free and brave. Free even to the definition of freedom, "without any hindrance that does not arise out of his own constitution." Brave; for fear is a thing which a scholar by his very function puts behind him. Fear always springs from ignorance. It is a shame to him if his tranquillity, amid dangerous times, arise from the presumption that like children and women, his is a protected class; or if he seek a temporary peace by the diversion of his thoughts from politics or vexed questions, hiding his head like an ostrich in the flowering bushes, peeping into microscopes, and turning rhymes, as a boy whistles to keep his courage up. So is the danger a danger still: so is the fear worse. Manlike let him turn and face it. Let him look into its eye and search its nature, inspect its origin,—see the whelping of this lion,—which lies no great way back; he will then find in himself a perfect comprehension of its nature and extent; he will have made his hands meet on the other side, and can henceforth defy it, and pass on superior. The world is his who can see through its pretension. What deafness, what stone-blind custom, what overgrown error you behold, is there only by sufferance,—by your sufferance. See it to be a lie, and you have already dealt it its mortal blow.

Yes, we are the cowed,—we the trustless. It is a mischievous notion that we are come late into nature; that the world was finished a long time ago. As the world was plastic and fluid in the hands of God, so it is ever to so much of his attributes as we bring to it. To ignorance and sin, it is flint. They adapt themselves to it as they may; but in proportion as a man has anything in him divine, the firmament flows before him, and takes his signet and form. Not he is great who can alter matter, but he who can alter my state of mind. They are the kings of the world who give the color of their present thought to all nature and all art, and persuade men by the cheerful serenity of their carrying the matter, that this thing which they do, is the apple which the ages

have desired to pluck, now at last ripe, and inviting nations to the harvest.
The great man makes the great thing. Wherever Macdonald sits, there is the
head of the table. Linnaeus makes botany the most alluring of studies and
wins it from the farmer and the herb-woman. Davy, chemistry: and Cuvier,
fossils.[6] The day is always his, who works in it with serenity and great aims.
The unstable estimates of men crowd to him whose mind is filled with a
truth, as the heaped waves of the Atlantic follow the moon.

For this self-trust, the reason is deeper than can be fathomed,—darker
than can be enlightened. I might not carry with me the feeling of my audience in stating my own belief. But I have already shown the ground of my
hope, in adverting to the doctrine that man is one. I believe man has been
wronged: he has wronged himself. He has almost lost the light that can lead
him back to his prerogatives. Men are become of no account. Men in history,
men in the world of to-day are bugs, are spawn, and are called "the mass"
and "the herd." In a century, in a millennium, one or two men; that is to
say—one or two approximations to the right state of every man. All the rest
behold in the hero or the poet their own green and crude being—ripened; yes,
and are content to be less, so *that* may attain to its full stature. What a
testimony—full of grandeur, full of pity, is borne to the demands of his own
nature, by the poor clansman, the poor partisan, who rejoices in the glory of
his chief. The poor and the low find some amends to their immense moral
capacity, for their acquiescence in a political and social inferiority. They are
content to be brushed like flies from the path of a great person, so that
justice shall be done by him to that common nature which it is the dearest
desire of all to see enlarged and glorified. They sun themselves in the great
man's light, and feel it to be their own element. They cast the dignity of man
from their downtrod selves upon the shoulders of a hero, and will perish to
add one drop of blood to make that great heart beat, those giant sinews
combat and conquer. He lives for us, and we live in him.

Men such as they are, very naturally seek money or power; and power
because it is as good as money,—the "spoils," so called, "of office." And why
not? for they aspire to the highest, and this, in their sleep-walking, they
dream is highest. Wake them, and they shall quit the false good and leap to
the true, and leave governments to clerks and desks. This revolution is to be
wrought by the gradual domestication of the idea of Culture. The main enterprise of the world for splendor, for extent, is the upbuilding of a man. Here
are the materials strown along the ground. The private life of one man shall
be a more illustrious monarchy,—more formidable to its enemy, more sweet

[6]Emerson mentioned eminent biologists, chemists, and paleontologists of the time.

and serene in its influence to its friend, than any kingdom in history. For a man, rightly viewed, comprehendeth the particular natures of all men. Each philosopher, each bard, each actor, has only done for me, as by a delegate, what one day I can do for myself. The books which once we valued more than the apple of the eye, we have quite exhausted. What is that but saying that we have come up with the point of view which the universal mind took through the eyes of that one scribe; we have been that man, and have passed on. First, one; then, another; we drain all cisterns, and waxing greater by all these supplies, we crave a better and more abundant food. The man has never lived that can feed us ever. The human mind cannot be enshrined in a person who shall set a barrier on any one side to this unbounded, unboundable empire. It is one central fire which flaming now out of the lips of Etna, lightens the capes of Sicily; and now out of the throat of Vesuvius, illuminates the towers and vineyards of Naples. It is one light which beams out of a thousand stars. It is one soul which animates all men.

But I have dwelt perhaps tediously upon this abstraction of the Scholar. I ought not to delay longer to add what I have to say, of nearer reference to the time and to this country.

Historically, there is thought to be a difference in the ideas which predominate over successive epochs, and there are data for marking the genius of the Classic, of the Romantic, and now of the Reflective or Philosophical age. With the views I have intimated of the oneness or the identity of the mind through all individuals, I do not much dwell on these differences. In fact, I believe each individual passes through all three. The boy is a Greek; the youth, romantic; the adult, reflective. I deny not, however, that a revolution in the leading idea may be distinctly enough traced.

Our age is bewailed as the age of Introversion. Must that needs be evil? We, it seems, are critical. We are embarrassed with second thoughts. We cannot enjoy any thing for hankering to know whereof the pleasure consists. We are lined with eyes. We see with our feet. The time is infected with Hamlet's unhappiness,—

"Sicklied o'er with the pale cast of thought."

Is it so bad then? Sight is the last thing to be pitied. Would we be blind? Do we fear lest we should outsee nature and God, and drink truth dry? I look upon the discontent of the literary class as a mere announcement of the fact that they find themselves not in the state of mind of their fathers, and regret the coming state as untried; as a boy dreads the water before he has learned that he can swim. If there is any period one would desire to be born in,—is it not the age of Revolution; when the old and the new stand side by side, and admit of being compared; when the energies of all men are searched by fear and by hope; when the historic glories of the old, can be compensated by the rich possibilities of the new era? This time, like all times, is a very good one, if we but know what to do with it.

I read with joy some of the auspicious signs of the coming days as they glimmer already through poetry and art, through philosophy and science, through church and state.

One of these signs is the fact that the same movement which effected the elevation of what was called the lowest class in the state, assumed in literature a very marked and as benign an aspect. Instead of the sublime and beautiful, the near, the low, the common, was explored and poetized. That which had been negligently trodden under foot by those who were harnessing and provisioning themselves for long journeys into far countries, is suddenly found to be richer than all foreign parts. The literature of the poor, the feelings of the child, the philosophy of the street, the meaning of household life, are the topics of the time. It is a great stride. It is a sign—is it not? of new vigor, when the extremities are made active, when currents of warm life run into the hands and the feet. I ask not for the great, the remote, the romantic; what is doing in Italy or Arabia; what is Greek art, or Provencal Minstrelsy; I embrace the common, I explore and sit at the feet of the familiar, the low. Give me insight into to-day, and you may have the antique and future worlds. What would we really know the meaning of? The meal in the firkin; the milk in the pan; the ballad in the street; the news of the boat; the glance of the eye; the form and the gait of the body;—show me the ultimate reason of these matters;—show me the sublime presence of the highest spiritual cause lurking, as always it does lurk, in these suburbs and extremities of nature; let me see every trifle bristling with the polarity that ranges it instantly on an eternal law; and the shop, the plough, and the ledger, referred to the like cause by which light undulates and poets sing;—and the world lies no longer a dull miscellany and lumber room, but has form and order; there is no trifle; there is no puzzle; but one design unites and animates the farthest pinnacle and the lowest trench.

This idea has inspired the genius of Goldsmith, Burns, Cowper, and, in a newer time, of Goethe, Wordsworth, and Carlyle. This idea they have differently followed and with various success. In contrast with their writing, the style of Pope, of Johnson, of Gibbon, looks cold and pedantic. This writing is blood-warm. Man is surprised to find that things near are not less beautiful and wondrous than things remote. The near explains the far. The drop is a

small ocean. A man is related to all nature. This perception of the worth of
the vulgar, is fruitful in discoveries. Goethe, in this very thing the most
modern of the moderns, has shown us, as none ever did, the genius of the
ancients.

There is one man of genius who has done much for this philosophy of
life, whose literary value has never yet been rightly estimated;—I mean
Emanuel Swedenborg. The most imaginative of men, yet writing with the
precision of a mathematician, he endeavored to engraft a purely philosophical
Ethics on the popular Christianity of his time. Such an attempt, of course,
must have difficulty which no genius could surmount. But he saw and showed
the connexion between nature and the affections of the soul. He pierced the
emblematic or spiritual character of the visible, audible, tangible world.
Especially did his shade-loving muse hover over and interpret the lower parts
of nature; he showed the mysterious bond that allies moral evil to the foul
material forms, and has given in epical parables a theory of insanity, of beasts,
of unclean and fearful things.

Another sign of our times, also marked by an analogous political movement is, the new importance given to the single person. Every thing that tends
to insulate the individual,—to surround him with barriers of natural respect,
so that each man shall feel the world is his, and man shall treat with man as
a sovereign state with a sovereign state;—tends to true union as well as greatness. "I learned," said the melancholy Pestalozzi,[7] "that no man in God's
wide earth is either willing or able to help any other man." Help must come
from the bosom alone. The scholar is that man who must take up into himself
all the ability of the time, all the contributions of the past, all the hopes of
the future. He must be an university of knowledges. If there be one lesson
more than another which should pierce his ear, it is, The world is nothing,
the man is all; in yourself is the law of all nature, and you know not yet how
a globule of sap ascends; in yourself slumbers the whole of Reason; it is for
you to know all, it is for you to dare all. Mr. President and Gentlemen, this
confidence in the unsearched might of man, belongs by all motives, by all
prophecy, by all preparation, to the American Scholar. We have listened too
long to the courtly muses of Europe. The spirit of the American freeman is
already suspected to be timid, imitative, tame. Public and private avarice
make the air we breathe thick and fat. The scholar is decent, indolent, complaisant. See already the tragic consequence. The mind of his country, taught

---

[7] Johann Henrich Pestalozzi (1746–1827) was a Swiss educational reformer who influenced Emerson.

to aim at low objects, eats upon itself. There is no work for any but the decorous and the complaisant. Young men of the fairest promise, who begin life upon our shores, inflated by the mountain winds, shined upon by all the stars of God, find the earth below not in unison with these,—but are hindered from action by the disgust which the principles on which business is managed inspire, and turn drudges, or die of disgust,—some of them suicides. What is the remedy? They did not yet see, and thousands of young men as hopeful now crowding to the barriers for the career, do not yet see, that if the single man plant himself indomitably on his instincts, and there abide, the huge world will come round to him. Patience—patience;—with the shades of all the good and great for company; and for solace, the perspective of your own infinite life; and for work, the study and the communication of principles, the making those instincts prevalent, the conversion of the world. Is it not the chief disgrace in the world, not to be an unit;—not to be reckoned one character;—not to yield that peculiar fruit which each man was created to bear, but to be reckoned in the gross, in the hundred, or the thousand, of the party, the section, to which we belong; and our opinion predicted geographically, as the north, or the south. Not so, brothers and friends,—please God, ours shall not be so. We will walk on our own feet; we will work with our own hands; we will speak our own minds. The study of letters shall be no longer a name for pity, for doubt, and for sensual indulgence. The dread of man and the love of man shall be a wall of defence and a wreath of joy around all. A nation of men will for the first time exist, because each believes himself inspired by the Divine Soul which also inspires all men.

I. **Suggestions for Discussion**:
   1. What does Emerson mean by "Man Thinking"? How does "Man Thinking" gain and exhibit self-trust?
   2. Summarize Emerson's discussion of the education of the scholar by nature, by books, and by action.
   3. Discuss Emerson's interest in "the familiar, the low" and in "the single person."

II. **Suggestions for Writing**:
   1. Write an essay arguing that American intellectuals have indeed asserted their cultural and intellectual independence from European culture, as Emerson called for more than a hundred years ago.
   2. Prepare and present a speech in which you outline your hopes and aspirations for American intellectuals in the 1980s.

# WILLIAM FAULKNER

## Nobel Prize Award Speech

William Faulkner (1897-1962) spent most of his life in Oxford, Mississippi. The history and legends of the South and of his own family were the material from which he shaped such novels as *Sartoris* (1929), *The Sound and the Fury* (1929), and *As I Lay Dying* (1930). He was awarded the Nobel Prize for Literature in 1949.

Faulkner's brief Nobel Prize Award Speech is an eloquent tribute to humanity's ability to endure and prevail.

I feel that this award was not made to me as a man but to my work—a life's work in the agony and sweat of the human spirit, not for glory and least of all for profit, but to create out of the materials of the human spirit something which did not exist before. So this award is only mine in trust. It will not be difficult to find a dedication for the money part of it commensurate with the purpose and significance of its origin. But I would like to do the same with the acclaim too, by using this moment as a pinnacle from which I might be listened to by the young men and women already dedicated to the same anguish and travail, among whom is already that one who will some day stand here where I am standing.

Our tragedy today is a general and universal physical fear so long sustained by now that we can even bear it. There are no longer problems of the spirit. There is only the question: When will I be blown up? Because of this, the young man or woman writing today has forgotten the problems of the human heart in conflict with itself which alone can make good writing because only that is worth writing about, worth the agony and the sweat.

He must learn them again. He must teach himself that the basest of all things is to be afraid; and, teaching himself that, forget it forever, leaving no room in his workshop for anything but the old verities and truths of the heart, the old universal truths lacking which any story is ephemeral and doomed—love and honor and pity and pride and compassion and sacrifice. Until he does so, he labors under a curse. He writes not of love but of lust, of defeats in which nobody loses anything of value, of victories without hope and, worst of all, without pity or compassion. His griefs grieve on no universal bones leaving no scars. He writes not of the heart but of the glands.

Until he relearns these things, he will write as though he stood alone and watched the end of man. I decline to accept the end of man. It is easy enough to say that man is immortal simply because he will endure; that when the last ding-dong of doom has clanged and faded from the last worthless rock hanging tideless in the last red and dying evening, that even then there will still be one more sound: that of his puny inexhaustible voice, still talking. I refuse to accept this. I believe that man will not merely endure: he will prevail. He is immortal, not because he alone among creatures has an inexhaustible voice but because he has a soul, a spirit capable of compassion and sacrifice and endurance. The poet's, the writer's, duty is to write about these things. It is his privilege to help man endure by lifting his heart, by reminding him of the courage and honor and hope and pride and compassion and pity and sacrifice which have been the glory of his past. The poet's voice need not merely be the record of man, it can be one of the props, the pillars to help him endure and prevail.

## I. Suggestions for Discussions:

1. To what extent do humans still live in a state of "general and universal physical fear"?
2. Discuss Faulkner's optimistic statement about the human ability to "endure and prevail." Do you agree? Explain.
3. Compare Faulkner's brief address with Abraham Lincoln's "Second Inaugural Address," p. 314.

## II. Suggestions for Writing:

1. Prepare and deliver a short speech accepting an important prize for achievement in one of the arts.
2. Write an essay expressing your views about humanity's ability to survive in the next hundred years. What dangers and threats must human beings overcome?

# HENRY FIELDING

## The Education of English Youth

Henry Fielding (1707–1754) was an essayist, novelist, and playwright in eighteenth-century England. He is most frequently remembered for his novels, which include *The Adventures of Joseph Andrews* (1742), *Tom Jones* (1749), and *Amelia* (1751).

French remarks on ill-breeding lead Fielding, in the following essay from *The Covent-Garden Journal,* to call for a better education for both young English men and women.

No. 56.                                                Saturday, July 25, 1752.

*Hoc fonte derivata.*   Horace
*These are the sources.*

At the conclusion of my last paper, I asserted that the summary of good breeding was no other than that comprehensive and exalted rule, which the greatest Authority hath told us is the sum total of all religion and all morality.

Here, however, my readers will be pleased to observe that the subject matter of good breeding being only what is called behaviour, it is this only to which we are to apply it on the present occasion. Perhaps therefore we shall be better understood, if we vary the word, and read it thus: *Behave unto all men, as you would they should behave unto you.*

This will most certainly oblige us to treat all mankind with the utmost civility and respect, there being nothing which we desire more than to be treated so by them. This will most effectually restrain the indulgence of all those violent and inordinate desires, which, as we have endeavoured to show, are the true seeds of humour in the human mind: the growth of which good breeding will be sure to obstruct; or will at least so overtop and shadow, that they shall not appear. The ambitious, the covetous, the proud, the vain, the angry, the debauchee, the glutton, are all lost in the character of the well-bred man; or, if nature should now and then venture to peep forth, she withdraws in an instant, and doth not show enough of herself to become ridiculous.

Now humour arises from the very opposite behaviour, from throwing the reins on the neck of our favourite passion, and giving it a full scope and indulgence. The ingenious Abbé, whom I quoted in my former paper, paints this admirably in the characters of ill-breeding, which he mentions as the first scene of the ridiculous. "Ill breeding (*l'Impolitesse*), says he, is not a single defect, it is the result of many. It is sometimes a gross ignorance of decorum, or a stupid indolence, which prevents us from giving to others what is due to them. It is a peevish malignity which inclines us to oppose the inclinations of those with whom we converse. It is the consequence of a foolish vanity, which hath no complaisance for any other person; the effect of a proud and whimsical humour, which soars above all the rules of civility; or, lastly, it is produced by a melancholy turn of mind, which pampers itself (*qui trouve du Ragoût*) with a rude and disobliging behaviour."

Having thus shown, I think very clearly, that good breeding is, and must be, the very bane of the ridiculous, that is to say, of all humorous characters; it will perhaps be no difficult task to discover why this character hath been in a singular manner attributed to this nation.

For this I shall assign two reasons only, as these seem to me abundantly satisfactory, and adequate to the purpose.

The first is that method so general in this kingdom of giving no education to the youth of both sexes; I say general only, for it is not without some few exceptions.

Much the greater part of our lads of fashion return from school at fifteen or sixteen, very little wiser, and not at all the better, for having been sent thither. Part of these return to the place from whence they came, their fathers' country seats; where racing, cock-fighting, hunting, and other rural sports, with smoking, drinking, and party become their pursuit, and form the whole business and amusement of their future lives. The other part escape to town, in the diversions, fashion, follies and vices of which they are immediately initiated. In this academy some finish their studies, while others by their wiser parents are sent abroad to add the knowledge of the diversions, fashions, follies, and vices of all Europe, to that of those of their own country.

Hence then we are to derive two great general characters of humour, which are the clown and the coxcomb, and both of these will be almost infinitely diversified according to the different passions and natural dispositions of each individual; and according to their different walks in life. Great will be the difference, for instance, whether the country gentleman be a Whig or a Tory; whether he prefers women, drink, or dogs; so will it be whether the town spark be allotted to serve his country as a politician, a courtier, a soldier, a sailor, or possibly a churchman (for by draughts from this academy, all these offices are supplied); or lastly, whether his ambition shall be contented with no other appellation than merely that of a beau.

Some of our lads, however, are destined to a further progress in learning; these are not only confined longer to the labours of a school, but are sent thence to the university. Here, if they please, they may read on; and if they please, they may (as most of them do) let it alone, and betake themselves as their fancy leads, to the imitation of their elder brothers either in town or country.

This is a matter which I shall handle very tenderly, as I am clearly of an opinion that an university education is much the best we have; for here at least there is some restraint laid on the inclinations of our youth. The sportsman, the gamester, and the sot, cannot give such a loose to their extravagance, as if they were at home and under no manner of government; nor can our spark who is disposed to the town pleasures find either gaming-houses or play-houses, nor half the taverns or bawdy-houses which are ready to receive him in Covent-Garden.

So far, however, I hope I may say without offense, that, among all the schools at the universities, there is none where the science of good-breeding is taught; no lectures like the excellent lessons on the ridiculous, which I have quoted above, and which I do most earnestly recommend to all my young readers. Hence the learned professions produce such excellent characters of humour; and the rudeness of physicians, lawyers, and parsons, however dignified or distinguished, affords such pleasant stories to divert private companies, and sometimes the public.

I come now to the beautiful part of the creation, who, in the sense I here use the word, I am assured can hardly (for the most part) be said to have any education.

As to the counterpart of my country squire, the country gentlewoman, I apprehend, that, except in the article of the dancing-master, and perhaps in that of being barely able to read and write, there is very little difference between the education of many a squire's daughter, and that of his dairymaid, who is most likely her principal companion; nay, the little difference which there is, is, I am afraid, not in the favour of the former; who, by being constantly flattered with her beauty and her wealth, is made the vainest and most selfconceited thing alive, at the same time that such care is taken to instil into her the principles of bashfulness and timidity, that she becomes ashamed and afraid of she knows not what.

If by any chance this poor creature drops afterwards, as it were, into the world, how absurd must be her behaviour! If a man looks at her, she is confounded; and if he speaks to her, she is frightened out of her wits. She acts, in short, as if she thought the whole sex was engaged in a conspiracy to possess themselves of her person and fortune.

This poor girl, it is true, however she may appear to her own sex, especially if she is handsome, is rather an object of compassion than of just ridicule; but what shall we say when time or marriage have carried off all this bashfulness and fear, and when ignorance, awkwardness, and rusticity, are embellished with the same degree, though perhaps not the same kind of affectation, which are to be found in a court. Here sure is a plentiful source of all that various humour which we find in the character of a country gentlewoman.

All this, I apprehend, will be readily allowed; but to deny good-breeding to the town lady, may be the more dangerous attempt. Here, besides the professors of reading, writing, and dancing, the French and Italian masters, the music master, and of modern times, the whist master, all concur in forming this character. The manners master alone, I am afraid is omitted. And what is the consequence? not only bashfulness and fear are entirely subdued, but modesty and discretion are taken off at the same time. So far from running away from, she runs after, the men; and instead of blushing when a modest man looks at her, or speaks to her, she can bear, without any such emotion, to stare an impudent fellow in the face, and sometimes to utter what, if he be not very impudent indeed, may put him to the blush.—Hence all those agreeable ingredients which form the humour of a rampant woman of—the town.

I cannot quit this part of my subject, in which I have been obliged to deal a little more freely than I am inclined with the loveliest part of the creation, without preserving my own character of good-breeding, by saying that this last excess is by much the most rare; and that every individual among my female readers, either is already, or may be, when she pleases, an example of a contrary behaviour.

The second general reason why humour so much abounds in this nation, seems to me to arise from the great number of people, who are daily raised by trade to the rank of gentry, without having had any education at all; or, to use no improper phrase, without having served an apprenticeship to this calling. But I have dwelt so long on the other branch, that I have no room at present to animadvert on this; nor is it indeed necessary I should, since most readers with the hints I have already given them, will easily suggest to themselves a great number of humorous characters with which the public have been furnished this way. I shall conclude by wishing, that this excellent source of humour may still continue to flow among us, since, though it may make us a little laughed at, it will be sure to make us the envy of all the nations of Europe.

**I. Suggestions for Discussion:**
1. Discuss Fielding's contrast between good breeding and ill breeding.
2. Describe the defects in the education of young English men and women Fielding identifies.
3. Compare Fielding's views on educating women with those expressed by Daniel Defoe in "An Academy for Women," p. 112.

**II. Suggestions for Writing:**
1. Compare and contrast Fielding's picture of the country squire and country gentlewoman with Samuel Butler's depiction of a bumpkin, p. 73.
2. Write an essay describing a situation in which you have been uncomfortable in the role you have had to play.

---

# E. M. FORSTER

## Art for Art's Sake

from *Two Cheers for Democracy*

---

Edward Morgan Forster (1879–1970) was a British novelist and critic whose best-known novels include *Howard's End* (1910) and *A Passage to India* (1924). His criticism appears in such works as *Aspects of the Novel* (1927), *Abinger Harvest* (1936), and *Two Cheers for Democracy* (1949), from which the following selection is taken.

In this essay, Forster asks his readers to consider his notion that a work of art is a self-contained entity, with a life of its own imposed on it by its creator. He contrasts order in a work of art with political and social order and with changing ideas about the heavens and the earth.

---

I believe in art for art's sake. It is an unfashionable belief, and some of my statements must be of the nature of an apology. Sixty years ago I should have faced you with more confidence. A writer or a speaker who chose "Art for Art's Sake" for his theme sixty years ago could be sure of being in the swim, and could feel so confident of success that he sometimes dressed himself in aesthetic costumes suitable to the occasion—in an embroidered dressing-gown, perhaps, or a blue velvet suit with a Lord Fauntleroy collar; or a toga, or a kimono, and carried a poppy or a lily or a long peacock's feather in his mediaeval hand. Times have changed. Not thus can I present either myself or my theme to-day. My aim rather is to ask you quietly to reconsider for a few minutes a phrase which has been much misused and much abused, but which has, I believe, great importance for us—has, indeed, eternal importance.

Now we can easily dismiss those peacock's feathers and other affectations—they are but trifles—but I want also to dismiss a more dangerous heresy, namely the silly idea that only art matters, an idea which has somehow got mixed up with the idea of art for art's sake, and has helped to discredit it. Many things besides art, matter. It is merely one of the things that matter, and high though the claims are that I make for it, I want to keep them in proportion. No one can spend his or her life entirely in the creation or the appreciation of masterpieces. Man lives, and ought to live, in a complex world, full of conflicting claims, and if we simplified them down into the aesthetic he would be sterilised. Art for art's sake does not mean that only art matters and I would also like to rule out such phrases as, "The Life of Art," "Living for Art," and "Art's High Mission." They confuse and mislead.

What does the phrase mean? Instead of generalising, let us take a specific instance—Shakespeare's *Macbeth,* for example, and pronounce the words, *"Macbeth for Macbeth's sake."* What does that mean? Well, the play has several aspects—it is educational, it teaches us something about legendary Scotland, something about Jacobean England, and a good deal about human nature and its perils. We can study its origins, and study and enjoy its dramatic technique and the music of its diction. All that is true. But *Macbeth* is furthermore a world of its own, created by Shakespeare and existing in virtue of its own poetry. It is in this aspect *Macbeth for Macbeth's* sake, and that is what I intend by the phrase "art for art's sake." A work of art—whatever else it may be—is a self-contained entity, with a life of its own imposed on it by its creator. It has internal order. It may have external form. That is how we recognise it.

Take for another example that picture of Seurat's which I saw two years ago in Chicago—"*La Grande Jatte.*" Here again there is much to study and to enjoy: the pointillism, the charming face of the seated girl, the nineteenth-century Parisian Sunday sunlight, the sense of motion in immobility. But here again there is something more; "*La Grande Jatte*" forms a world of its own, created by Seurat and existing by virtue of its own poetry: "*La Grande Jatte*" *pour* "*La Grande Jatte*": *l'art pour l'art.* Like *Macbeth* it has internal order and internal life.

It is to the conception of order that I would now turn. This is important to my argument, and I want to make a digression, and glance at order in daily life, before I come to order in art.

In the world of daily life, the world which we perforce inhabit, there is much talk about order, particularly from statesmen and politicians. They tend, however, to confuse order with orders, just as they confuse creation with regulations. Order, I suggest, is something evolved from within, not something imposed from without; it is an internal stability, a vital harmony, and in the social and political category it has never existed except for the convenience of historians. Viewed realistically, the past is really a series of *dis*-orders, succeeding one another by discoverable laws, no doubt, and certainly marked by an increasing growth of human interference, but disorders all the same. So that, speaking as a writer, what I hope for to-day is a disorder which will be more favourable to artists than is the present one, and which will provide them with fuller inspirations and better material conditions. It will not last—nothing lasts—but there have been some advantageous disorders in the past—for instance, in ancient Athens, in Renaissance Italy, eighteenth-century France, periods in China and Persia—and we may do something to accelerate the next one. But let us not again fix our hearts where true joys are not to be found. We were promised a new order after the first world war through the League of Nations. It did not come, nor have I faith in present promises, by whomsoever endorsed. The implacable offensive of Science forbids. We cannot reach social and political stability for the reason that we continue to make scientific discoveries and to apply them, and thus to destroy the arrangements which were based on more elementary discoveries. If Science would discover rather than apply—if, in other words, men were more interested in knowledge than in power—mankind would be in a far safer position, the stability statesmen talk about would be a possibility, there could be a new order based on vital harmony, and the earthly millennium might approach. But Science shows no signs of doing this: she gave us the internal combustion engine, and before we had digested and assimilated it with terrible pains into our social system, she harnessed the atom, and destroyed any new order that seemed to be evolving. How can man get into harmony with his surroundings when he is constantly altering them? The future of our race is, in this direction, more unpleasant than we care to admit, and it has sometimes seemed to me that its best chance lies through apathy, uninventiveness, and inertia. Universal exhaustion might promote that Change of Heart which is at present so briskly recommended from a thousand pulpits. Universal exhaustion would certainly be a new experience. The human race has never undergone it, and is still too perky to admit that it may be coming and might result in a sprouting of new growth through the decay.

I must not pursue these speculations any further—they lead me too far from my terms of reference and maybe from yours. But I do want to emphasize that order in daily life and in history, order in the social and political category, is unattainable under our present psychology.

Where is it attainable? Not in the astronomical category, where it was for many years enthroned. The heavens and the earth have become terribly alike since Einstein. No longer can we find a reassuring contrast to chaos in the night sky and look up with George Meredith to the stars, the army of unalterable law, or listen for the music of the spheres. Order is not there. In the entire universe there seem to be only two possibilities for it. The first of them—which again lies outside my terms of reference—is the divine order, the mystic harmony, which according to all religions is available for those who can contemplate it. We much admit its possibility, on the evidence of the adepts, and we must believe them when they say that it is attained, if attainable, by prayer. "O thou who changest not, abide with me," said one of its poets. " *Ordina questo amor, o tu che m'ami,*" said another: "Set love in order thou who lovest me." The existence of a divine order, though it cannot be tested, has never been disproved.

The second possibility for order lies in the aesthetic category, which is my subject here: the order which an artist can create in his own work, and to that we must now return. A work of art, we are all agreed, is a unique product. But why? It is unique not because it is clever or noble or beautiful or enlightened or original or sincere or idealistic or useful or educational—it may embody any of those qualities—but because it is the only material object in the universe which may possess internal harmony. All the others have been pressed into shape from outside, and when their mould is removed they collapse. The work of art stands up by itself, and nothing else does. It achieves something which has often been promised by society, but always delusively. Ancient Athens made a mess—but the *Antigone* stands up. Renaissance Rome made a mess—but the ceiling of the Sistine got painted. James I made a mess— but there was *Macbeth*. Louis XIV—but there was *Phedre*. Art for art's sake? I should just think so, and more so than ever at the present time. It is the one orderly product which our muddling race has produced. It is the cry of a thousand sentinels, the echo from a thousand labyrinths; it is the lighthouse which cannot be hidden: *c'est le meilleur temoignage que nous puissions donner de notre dignite.*[1] *Antigone* for *Antigone's* sake, *Macbeth* for *Macbeth's,* "La Grande Jatte" pour "La Grande Jatte."

If this line of argument is correct, it follows that the artist will tend to

---

[1] It is the best witness that we can give for our dignity.

be an outsider in the society to which he has been born, and that the nine-teenth century conception of him as a Bohemian was not inaccurate. The conception erred in three particulars: it postulated an economic system where art could be a full-time job, it introduced the fallacy that only art matters, and it over-stressed idiosyncracy and waywardness—the peacock-feather aspect—rather than order. But it is a truer conception than the one which prevails in official circles on my side of the Atlantic—I don't know about yours: the conception which treats the artist as if he were a particularly bright government advertiser and encourages him to be friendly and matey with his fellow citizens, and not to give himself airs.

Estimable is mateyness, and the man who achieves it gives many a pleas-ant little drink to himself and to others. But it has no traceable connection with the creative impulse, and probably acts as an inhibition on it. The artist who is seduced by mateyness may stop himself from doing the one thing which he, and he alone, can do—the making of something out of words or sounds or paint or clay or marble or steel or film which has internal harmony and presents order to a permanently disarranged planet. This seems worth doing, even at the risk of being called uppish by journalists. I have in mind an article which was published some years ago in the London *Times,* an article called "The Eclipse of the Highbrow," in which the "Average Man" was exalted, and all contemporary literature was censured if it did not toe the line, the precise position of the line being naturally known to the writer of the article. Sir Kenneth Clark, who was at that time director of our National Gallery, commented on this pernicious doctrine in a letter which cannot be too often quoted. "The poet and the artist," wrote Clark, "are important pre-cisely because they are not average men; because in sensibility, intelligence, and power of invention they far exceed the average." These memorable words, and particularly the words "power of invention," are the Bohemian's passport. Furnished with it, he slinks about society, saluted now by a brick-bat and now by a penny, and accepting either of them with equanimity. He does not consider too anxiously what his relations with society may be, for he is aware of something more important than that—namely the invitation to invent, to create order, and he believes he will be better placed for doing this if he attempts detachment. So round and round he slouches, with his hat pulled over his eyes, and maybe with a louse in his beard, and—if he really wants one—with a peacock's feather in his hand.

If our present society should disintegrate—and who dare prophesy that it won't?—this old-fashioned and demode figure will become clearer: the Bohemian, the outsider, the parasite, the rat—one of those figures which have at present no function either in a warring or a peaceful world. It may not be dignified to be a rat, but many of the ships are sinking, which is not dignified either—the officials did not build them properly. Myself, I would sooner be a swimming rat than a sinking ship—at all events I can look around me for a little longer—and I remember how one of us, a rat with particularly bright eyes called Shelley, squeaked out, "Poets are the unacknowledged legislators of the world," before he vanished into the waters of the Mediterranean.

What laws did Shelley propose to pass? None. The legislation of the artist is never formulated at the time, though it is sometimes discerned by future generations. He legislates through creating. And he creates through his sensitiveness and his power to impose form. Without form the sensitiveness vanishes. And form is as important to-day, when the human race is trying to ride the whirlwind, as it ever was in those less agitating days of the past, when the earth seemed solid and the stars fixed, and the discoveries of science were made slowly, slowly. Form is not tradition. It alters from generation to generation. Artists always seek a new technique, and will continue to do so as long as their work excites them. But form of some kind is imperative. It is the surface crust of the internal harmony, it is the outward evidence of order.

My remarks about society may have seemed too pessimistic, but I believe that society can only represent a fragment of the human spirit, and that another fragment can only get expressed through art. And I wanted to take this opportunity, this vantage ground, to assert not only the existence of art, but its pertinacity. Looking back into the past, it seems to me that that is all there has ever been: vantage grounds for discussion and creation, little vantage grounds in the changing chaos, where bubbles have been blown and webs spun, and the desire to create order has found temporary gratification, and the sentinels have managed to utter their challenges, and the huntsmen, though lost individually, have heard each other's calls through the impenetrable wood, and the lighthouses have never ceased sweeping the thankless seas. In this pertinacity there seems to me, as I grow older, something more and more profound, something which does in fact concern people who do not care about art at all.

In conclusion, let me summarise the various categories that have laid claim to the possession of Order.

(1) The social and political category. Claim disallowed on the evidence of history and of our own experience. If man altered psychologically, order here might be attainable: not otherwise.

(2) The astronomical category. Claim allowed up to the present century, but now disallowed on the evidence of the physicists.

(3) The religious category. Claim allowed on the evidence of the mystics.

(4) The aesthetic category. Claim allowed on the evidence of various works
of art, and on the evidence of our own creative impulses, however weak
these may be or however imperfectly they may function. Works of art,
in my opinion, are the only objects in the material universe to possess
internal order, and that is why, though I don't believe that only art matters, I do believe in Art for Art's Sake.

## I. Suggestions for Discussion:
1. Explain what Forster means by the phrase "*Macbeth* for *Macbeth*'s
   sake."
2. Discuss Forster's comparisons of the order of art and order in life.
3. Discuss his use of specific allusions and examples to strengthen his
   argument.

## II. Suggestions for Writing:
1. Give your own opinions about the various categories Forster identifies
   as having laid claim to the possession of order.
2. Write an essay in which you agree or disagree with Forster's belief that
   works of art are the only objects in the material universe to possess
   internal order. Use specific references whenever possible.
3. Compare Forster's views about art with those expressed by Walter
   Pater, p. 463.

---

# BENJAMIN FRANKLIN

## On Literary Style

---

Benjamin Franklin (1706-1790) was a great American inventor,
journalist, and statesman. A successful printer, he played a major
role in the founding of the United States. The maxims and pro-
verbs in *Poor Richard's Almanac* (1733-58) display his characteristic good humor and common sense.

Franklin, writing in *The Pennsylvania Gazette,* identifies ways by
which an author can please his readers and critics. His specific
advice is as appropriate today as it was in 1733.

---

To the Printer of the *Gazette*.

There are few Men, of Capacity for making any considerable Figure in Life, who have not frequent Occasion to communicate their Thoughts to others in *Writing;* if not sometimes publickly as Authors, yet continually in the Management of their private Affairs, both of Business and Friendship: and since, when ill-express'd, the most proper Sentiments and justest Reasoning lose much of their native Force and Beauty, it seems to me that there is scarce any Accomplishment more necessary to a Man of Sense, than that of *Writing well* in his Mother Tongue: But as most other polite Acquirements, make a greater Appearance in a Man's Character, this however useful, is generally neglected or forgotten.

I believe there is no better Means of learning to write well, than this of attempting to entertain the Publick now and then in one of your Papers. When the Writer conceals himself, he has the Advantage of hearing the Censure both of Friends and Enemies, express'd with more Impartiality. And since, in some degree, it concerns the Credit of the Province, that such Things as are printed be performed tolerably well, mutual Improvement seems to be the Duty of all Lovers of Writing: I shall therefore frankly request those of others in Return.

I have thought in general, that whoever would write so as not to displease good Judges, should have particular Regard to these three Things, viz. That his Performance be *smooth, clear,* and *short:* For the contrary Qualities are apt to offend, either the Ear, the Understanding, or the Patience.

'Tis an Observation of Dr. Swift,[1] that modern Writers injure the Smoothness of our Tongue, by omitting Vowels wherever it is possible, and joining the harshest Consonants together with only an Apostrophe between; thus for *judged,* in it self not the smoothest of Words, they say *judg'd;* for *disturbed, disturb'd,* etc. It may be added to this, says another, that by changing *eth* into *s,* they have shortned one Syllable in a multitude of Words, and have thereby encreased, not only the *Hissing,* too offensive before, but also the great Number of Monosyllables, of which, without great Difficulty, a smooth Sentence cannot be composed. The Smoothness of a Period is also often Hurt by Parentheses, and therefore the best Writers endeavour to avoid them.

To write *clearly,* not only the most expressive, but the plainest Words should be chosen. In this, as well as in every other Particular requisite to Clearness, Dr. Tillotson[2] is an excellent Example. The Fondness of some

---

[1] Jonathan Swift (1667–1745) was a great Irish satirist.
[2] John Tillotson (1630–1694) was much admired for his prose style.

Writers for such Words as carry with them an Air of Learning, renders them unintelligible to more than half their Countrymen. If a Man would that his Writings have an Effect on the Generality of Readers, he had better imitate that Gentleman, who would use no Word in his Works that was not well understood by his Cook-maid.

A too frequent Use of Phrases ought likewise to be avoided by him that would write clearly. They trouble the Language, not only rendring it extreamly difficult to Foreigners, but make the Meaning obscure to a great number of English Readers. Phrases, like learned Words, are seldom used without Affectation; when, with all true Judges, the simplest Stile is the most beautiful.

But supposing the most proper Words and Expressions chosen, the Performance may yet be weak and obscure, if it has not *Method*. If a Writer would *persuade*, he should proceed gradually from Things already allow'd, to those from which Assent is yet with-held, and make their Connection manifest. If he would *inform*, he must advance regularly from Things known to things unknown, distinctly without Confusion, and the lower he begins the better. It is a common Fault in Writers, to allow their Readers too much Knowledge: They begin with that which should be the Middle, and skipping backwards and forwards, 'tis impossible for any one but he who is perfect in the Subject before, to understand their Work, and such an one has no Occasion to read it. Perhaps a Habit of using good Method, cannot be better acquired, than by learning a little Geometry or Algebra.

*Amplification,* or the Art of saying Little in Much, should only be allowed to Speakers. If they preach, a Discourse of considerable Length is expected from them, upon every Subject they undertake, and perhaps they are not stock'd with naked Thoughts sufficient to furnish it out. If they plead in the Courts, it is of Use to speak abundance, tho' they reason little; for the Ignorant in a Jury, can scarcely believe it possible that a Man can talk so much and so long without being in the Right. Let them have the Liberty then, of repeating the same Sentences in other Words; let them put an Adjective to every Substantive, and double every Substantive with a Synonima; for this is more agreeable than hauking, spitting, taking Snuff, or any other Means of concealing Hesitation. Let them multiply Definitions, Comparisons, Similitudes and Examples. Permit them to make a Detail of Causes and Effects, enumerate all the Consequences, and express one Half by Metaphor and Circumlocution: Nay, allow the Preacher to tell us whatever a Thing is negatively, before he begins to tell us what it is affirmatively; and suffer him to divide and subdivide as far as *Two and fiftiethly.* All this is not intolerable while it is not written. But when a Discourse is to be bound down upon

Paper, and subjected to the calm leisurely Examination of nice Judgment, everything that is needless gives Offense; and therefore should be retrenched, that does not directly conduce to the End design'd. Had this been always done, many large and tiresome Folio's would have shrunk into Pamphlets, and many a Pamphlet into a single Period. However, tho' a multitude of Words obscure the Sense, and 'tis necessary to abridge a verbose Author in order to understand him; yet a Writer should take especial Care on the other Hand, that his Brevity doth not hurt his Perspicuity.

After all, if the Author does not intend his Piece for general Reading, he must exactly suit his Stile and Manner to the particular Taste of those he proposes for his Readers. Every one observes, the different Ways of Writing and Expression used by the different Sects of Religion; and can readily enough pronounce, that it is improper to use some of these Stiles in common, or to use the common Stile, when we address some of these Sects in particular.

To conclude, I shall venture to lay it down as a Maxim, *That no Piece can properly be called good, and well written, which is void of any Tendency to benefit the Reader, either by improving his Virtue or his Knowledge.* This Principle every Writer would do well to have in View, whenever he undertakes to write. All Performances done for meer Ostentation of Parts, are really contemptible; and withal far more subject to the Severity of Criticism, than those more meanly written, wherein the Author appears to have aimed at the Good of others. For when 'tis visible to every one, that a Man writes to show his Wit only, all his Expressions are sifted, and his Sense examined, in the nicest and most ill-natur'd manner; and every one is glad of an Opportunity to mortify him. But, what a vast Destruction would there be of Books, if they were to be saved or condemned on a Tryal by this Rule!

Besides, Pieces meerly humorous, are of all Sorts the hardest to succeed in. If they are not natural, they are stark naught; and there can be no real Humour in an Affectation of Humour.

Perhaps it may be said, that an ill Man is able to write an ill Thing well; that is, having an ill Design, and considering who are to be his Readers, he may use the properest Stile and Arguments to attain his Point. In this Sense, that is best wrote, which is best adapted to the Purpose of the Writer.

I am apprehensive, dear Readers, lest in this Piece, I should be guilty of every Fault I condemn, and deficient in every Thing I recommend; so much easier it is to offer Rules than to practise them. I am sure, however, of this, that I am Your very sincere Friend and Servant.

## I. Suggestions for Discussion:

1. Explain Franklin's advice that writers be smooth, clear, and short. Is his advice still sound? Explain.

2. What does Franklin mean by amplification?
3. Discuss the examples Franklin uses to make his points. Substitute examples from contemporary usage whenever appropriate.

**II.  Suggestions for Writing:**

1. Write an essay in which you give your reasons for agreeing or disagreeing with Franklin's maxim that good writing must improve either a reader's virtue or knowledge. Be sure to define your terms.
2. Compare Franklin's advice to writers to that of his contemporary, Dr. Samuel Johnson, p. 277.

---

# MARGARET FULLER

## From *Woman in the Nineteenth Century*

---

Margaret Fuller (1810–1850), friend to Emerson and Thoreau, was a transcendentalist who advocated women's rights. Her most important work is *Woman in the Nineteenth Century* (1845), from which the present selection is taken. On her return to America after a European tour, she drowned in a shipwreck off Fire Island.

In her highly rhetorical style, she argues that as the principle of liberty is better understood and more nobly interpreted, a broader protest will be made in behalf of women's rights. She asks that every path be laid open to women as freely as to men.

---

A better comment could not be made on what is required to perfect Man, and place him in that superior position for which he was designed, than by the interpretation of Bacon[1] upon the legends of the Siren coast. "When the wise Ulysses passed," says he, "he caused his mariners to stop their ears with wax, knowing there was in them no power to resist the lure of that voluptuous song. But he, the much experienced man, who wished to be experienced in all, and use all to the service of wisdom, desired to hear the song that he might understand its meaning. Yet, distrusting his own power to be firm in his better purpose, he caused himself to be bound to the mast, that he

---

[1] Francis Bacon (1561–1626) was an English philosopher and essayist.

might be kept secure against his own weakness. But Orpheus passed unfet-
tered, so absorbed in singing hymns to the gods that he could not even hear
those sounds of degrading enchantment."

Meanwhile not a few believe, and men themselves have expressed the
opinion, that the time is come when Eurydice is to call for an Orpheus rather
than Orpheus for Eurydice; that the idea of Man, however imperfectly
brought out, has been far more so than that of Woman; that she, the other
half of the same thought, the other chamber of the heart of life, needs now
take her turn in the full pulsation, and that improvement in the daughters will
best aid in the reformation of the sons of this age.

It should be remarked that as the principle of liberty is better understood, and more nobly interpreted, a broader protest is made in behalf of
Woman. As men become aware that few men have had a fair chance, they are
inclined to say that no women have had a fair chance. The French Revolution, that strangely disguised angel, bore witness in favor of Woman, but
interpreted her claims no less ignorantly than those of Man. Its idea of happiness did not rise beyond outward enjoyment, unobstructed by the tyranny of
others. The title it gave was *citoyen, citoyenne* [citizen] ; and it is not unim-
portant to Woman that even this species of quality was awarded her. Before,
she could be condemned to perish on the scaffold for treason, not as a citizen
but as a subject. The right with which this title then invested a human being
was that of bloodshed and license. The Goddess of Liberty was impure. As we
read the poem addressed to her not long since by Beranger,[2] we can scarcely
refrain from tears as painful as the tears of blood that flowed when "such
crimes were committed in her name." Yes! Man, born to purify and animate
the unintelligent and the cold, can in his madness degrade and pollute no less
the fair and the chaste. Yet truth was prophesied in the ravings of that
hideous fever caused by long ignorance and abuse. Europe is conning a valued
lesson from the bloodstained page. The same tendencies further unfolded will
bear good fruit in this country.

Yet by men in this country, as by the Jews when Moses was leading
them to the promised land, everything has been done that inherited depravity
could do to hinder the promise of Heaven from its fulfillment. The cross, here
as elsewhere, has been planted only to be blasphemed by cruelty and fraud.
The name of the Prince of Peace has been profaned by all kinds of injustice
toward the Gentile whom he said he came to save. But I need not speak of
what has been done toward the Red Man, the Black Man. Those deeds are the
scoff of the world; and they have been accompanied by such pious words that

---

[2] Pierre Jean De Beranger (1780–1857) was a French poet.

the gentlest would not dare to intercede with, "Father, forgive them, for they know not what they do."

Here as elsewhere the gain of creation consists always in the growth of individual minds, which live and aspire as flowers bloom and birds sing in the midst of morasses; and in the continual development of that thought, the thought of human destiny, which is given to eternity adequately to express, and which ages of failure only seemingly impede. Only seemingly; and whatever seems to the contrary, this country is as surely destined to elucidate a great moral law as Europe was to promote the mental culture of Man.

Though the national independence be blurred by the servility of individuals; though freedom and equality have been proclaimed only to leave room for a monstrous display of slavedealing and slavekeeping; though the free American so often feels himself free, like the Roman, only to pamper his appetites and his indolence through the misery of his fellow-beings; still it is not in vain that the verbal statement has been made, "All men are born free and equal." There it stands, a golden certainty wherewith to encourage the good, to shame the bad. The New World may be called clearly to perceive that it incurs the utmost penalty if it reject or oppress the sorrowful brother. And if men are deaf, the angels hear. But men cannot be deaf. It is inevitable that an external freedom, an independence of the encroachments of other men such as has been achieved for the nation, should be so also for every member of it. That which has once been clearly conceived in the intelligence cannot fail sooner or later to be acted out.

We sicken no less at the pomp than the strife of words. We feel that never were lungs so puffed with the wind of declamation on moral and religious subjects as now. We are tempted to implore these "word-heroes," these word-Catos,[3] word-Christs, to beware of cant above all things; to remember that hypocrisy is the most hopeless as well as the meanest of crimes, and that those must surely be polluted by it who do not reserve a part of their morality and religion for private use. Landor[4] says that he cannot have a great deal of mind who cannot afford to let the larger part of it lie fallow; and what is true of genius is not less so of virtue. The tongue is a valuable member, but should appropriate but a small part of the vital juices that are needful all over the body. We feel that the mind may "grow black and rancid in the smoke" even "of altars." We start up from the harangue to go into our closet and shut the door. There inquires the spirit, "Is this rhetoric the bloom of healthy blood, or a false pigment artfully laid on?" And yet again we know

[3] censors
[4] Walter Savage Landor (1775–1864) was an English poet.

where is so much smoke, must be some fire; with so much talk about virtue and freedom, must be mingled some desire for them; that it cannot be in vain that such have become the common topics of conversation among men rather than schemes for tyranny and plunder, that the very newspapers see it best to proclaim themselves "Pilgrims," "Puritans," "Heralds of Holiness." The king that maintains so costly a retinue cannot be a mere boast or Barabbas fiction. We have waited here long in the dust, we are tired and hungry, but the triumphal procession must appear at last.

Of all its banners, none has been more steadily upheld, and under none have more valor and willingness for real sacrifices been shown, than that of the champions of the enslaved African. And this band it is which, partly from a natural following out of principles, partly because many women have been prominent in that cause, makes just now the warmest appeal in behalf of Woman.

Though there has been a growing liberality on this subject, yet society at large is not so prepared for the demands of this party, but that its members are and will be for some time coldly regarded as the Jacobins of their day.

"Is it not enough," cries the irritated trader, "that you have done all you could to break up the national union and thus destroy the prosperity of our country, but now you must be trying to break up family union, to take my wife away from the cradle and the kitchen-hearth to vote at polls and preach from a pulpit? Of course, if she does such things, she cannot attend to those of her own sphere. She is happy enough as she is. She has more leisure than I have—every means of improvement, every indulgence."

"Have you asked her whether she was satisfied with these *indulgences*?"

"No, but I know she is. She is too amiable to desire what would make me unhappy, and too judicious to wish to step beyond the sphere of her sex. I will never consent to have our peace disturbed by any such discussions."

" 'Consent—you?' It is not consent from you that is in question—it is assent from your wife."

"Am not I the head of my house?"

"You are not the head of your wife. God has given her a mind of her own."

"I am the head, and she the heart."

"God grant you play true to one another, then! I suppose I am to be grateful that you did not say she was only the hand. If the head represses no natural pulse of the heart, there can be no question as to your giving your consent. Both will be of one accord, and there needs but to present any question to get a full and true answer. There is no need of precaution, of indulgence, or consent. But our doubt is whether the heart *does* consent with the head, or only obeys its decrees with a passiveness that precludes the exercise of its natural powers, or a repugnance that turns sweet qualities to bitter, or a doubt that lays waste the fair occasions of life. It is to ascertain the truth that we propose some liberating measures."

Thus vaguely are these questions proposed and discussed at present. But their being proposed at all implies much thought and suggests more. Many women are considering within themselves what they need that they have not, and what they can have if they find they need it. Many men are considering whether women are capable of being and having more than they are and have, *and* whether, if so, it will be best to consent to improvement in their condition.

This morning, I open the Boston *Daily Mail,* and find in its "poet's corner" a translation of Schiller's "Dignity of Woman."[5] In the advertisement of a book on America, I see in the table of contents this sequence, "Republican Institutions. American Slavery. American Ladies."

I open the *Deutsche Schnellpost,* published in New York, and find at the head of a column, *Juden-und Frauen-emanzipation in Ungarn* ("Emancipation of Jews and Women in Hungary").

The past year has seen action in the Rhode Island legislature to secure married women rights over their own property, where men showed that a very little examination of the subject could teach them much; an article in the *Democratic Review* on the same subject more largely considered, written by a woman impelled, it is said, by glaring wrong to a distinguished friend, having shown the defects in the existing laws and the state of opinion from which they spring; and an answer from the revered old man, J. Q. Adams, in some respects the Phocion of his time,[6] to an address made him by some ladies. To this last I shall again advert in another place.

These symptoms of the times have come under my view quite accidentally: one who seeks may each month or week collect more.

The numerous party, whose opinions are already labeled and adjusted too much to their mind to admit of any new light, strive by lectures on some model woman of bridelike beauty and gentleness, by writing and lending little treatises intended to mark out with precision the limits of Woman's sphere and Woman's mission, to prevent other than the rightful shepherd from climbing the wall, or the flock from using any chance to go astray.

Without enrolling ourselves at once on either side, let us look upon the

---

[5] Johann Christolph Friedrich von Schiller (1795–1805) was a German poet and dramatist.
[6] President John Quincy Adams (1767–1848) is compared to Phocion (c. 402–317 B.C.), an Athenian general and statesman.

subject from the best point of view which today offers; no better, it is to be feared, than a high house-top. A high hilltop or at least a cathedralspire would be desirable.

It may well be an Anti-Slavery party that pleads for Woman, if we consider merely that she does not hold property on equal terms with men; so that if a husband dies without making a will, the wife, instead of taking at once his place as head of the family, inherits only a part of his fortune, often brought him by herself, as if she were a child or ward only, not an equal partner.

We will not speak of the innumerable instances in which profligate and idle men live upon the earnings of industrious wives; or if the wives leave them and take with them the children to perform the double duty of mother and father, follow from place to place and threaten to rob them of the children, if deprived of the rights of a husband as they call them, planting themselves in their poor lodgings, frightening them into paying tribute by taking from them the children, running into debt at the expense of these otherwise so overtasked helots. Such instances count up by scores within my own memory. I have seen the husband who had stained himself by a long course of low vice, till his wife was wearied from her heroic forgiveness by finding that his treachery made it useless, and that if she would provide bread for herself and her children, she must be separate from his ill fame—I have known this man come to install himself in the chamber of a woman who loathed him, and say she should never take food without his company. I have known these men steal their children, whom they knew they had no means to maintain, take them into dissolute company, expose them to bodily danger, to frighten the poor woman to whom, it seems, the fact that she alone had borne the pangs of their birth and nourished their infancy does not give an equal right to them. I do believe that this mode of kidnapping—and it is frequent enough in all classes of society—will be by the next age viewed as it is by Heaven now, and that the man who avails himself of the shelter of men's laws to steal from a mother her own children, or arrogate any superior right in them, save that of superior virtue, will bear the stigma he deserves in common with him who steals grown men from their motherland, their hopes, and their homes.

I said we will not speak of this now; yet I *have* spoken, for the subject makes me feel too much. I could give instances that would startle the most vulgar and callous; but I will not, for the public opinion of their own sex is already against such men, and where cases of extreme tyranny are made known, there is private action in the wife's favor. But she ought not to need this, nor, I think, can she long. Men must soon see that as on their own ground Woman is the weaker party, she ought to have legal protection which would make such oppression impossible. But I would not deal with "atrocious instances" except in the way of illustration, neither demand from men a partial redress in some one matter, but go to the root of the whole. If principles could be established, particulars would adjust themselves aright. Ascertain the true destiny of Woman; give her legitimate hopes, and a standard within herself; marriage and all other relations would by degrees be harmonized with these.

But to return to the historical progress of this matter. Knowing that there exists in the minds of men a tone of feeling toward women as toward slaves, such as is expressed in the common phrase, "Tell that to women and children"; that the infinite soul can only work through them in already ascertained limits; that the gift of reason, Man's highest prerogative, is allotted to them in much lower degree; that they must be kept from mischief and melancholy by being constantly engaged in active labor, which is to be furnished and directed by those better able to think, &c., &c.—we need not multiply instances, for who can review the experience of last week without recalling words which imply, whether in jest or earnest, these views or views like these—knowing this, can we wonder that many reformers think that measures are not likely to be taken in behalf of women, unless their wishes could be publicly represented by women?

"That can never be necessary," cry the other side. "All men are privately influenced by women; each has his wife, sister, or female friends, and is too much biased by these relations to fail of representing their interests; and if this is not enough, let them propose and enforce their wishes with the pen. The beauty of home would be destroyed, the delicacy of the sex be violated, the dignity of halls of legislation degraded by an attempt to introduce them there. Such duties are inconsistent with those of a mother"; and then we have ludicrous pictures of ladies in hysterics at the polls, and senate chambers filled with cradles.

But if in reply we admit as truth that Woman seems destined by nature rather for the inner circle, we must add that the arrangements of civilized life have not been as yet such as to secure it to her. Her circle, if the duller, is not the quieter. If kept from "excitement," she is not from drudgery. Not only the Indian squaw carries the burdens of the camp, but the favorites of Louis XIV accompany him in his journeys, and the washerwoman stands at her tub and carries home her work at all seasons and in all states of health. Those who think the physical circumstances of Woman would make a part in the affairs of national government unsuitable are by no means those who think it impossible for Negresses to endure field work even during pregnancy, or for seamstresses to go through their killing labors.

As to the use of the pen, there was quite as much opposition to Woman's possessing herself of that help to free agency as there is now to her seizing on the rostrum or the desk; and she is likely to draw, from a permission to plead her cause that way, opposite inferences to what might be wished by those who now grant it.

As to the possibility of her filling with grace and dignity any such position, we should think those who had seen the great actresses and heard the Quaker preachers of modern times would not doubt that Woman can express publicly the fullness of thought and creation without losing any of the peculiar beauty of her sex. What can pollute and tarnish is to act thus from any motive except that something needs to be said or done. Woman could take part in the processions, the songs, the dances of old religion; no one fancied her delicacy was impaired by appearing in public for such a cause.

As to her home, she is not likely to leave it more than she now does for balls, theaters, meetings for promoting missions, revival meetings, and others to which she flies in hope of an animation for her existence commensurate with what she sees enjoyed by men. Governors of ladies' fairs are no less engrossed by such a charge than the governor of a state by his; presidents of Washingtonian societies no less away from home than presidents of conventions. If men look straitly to it, they will find that unless their lives are domestic, those of the women will not be. A house is no home unless it contains food and fire for the mind as well as for the body. The female Greek of our day is as much in the street as the male to cry, "What news?" We doubt not it was the same in Athens of old. The woman, shut out from the marketplace, made up for it at the religious festivals. For human beings are not so constituted that they can live without expansion. If they do not get it in one way, they must in another perish.

As to men's representing women fairly at present, while we hear from men who owe to their wives not only all that is comfortable or graceful but all that is wise in the arrangement of their lives the frequent remark, "You cannot reason with a woman"—when from those of delicacy, nobleness, and poetic culture falls the contemptuous phrase "women and children," and that in no light sally of the hour, but in works intended to give a permanent statement of the best experiences—when not one man in the million, shall I say? no, not in the hundred million, can rise above the belief that Woman was made *for Man*—when such traits as these are daily forced upon the attention, can we feel that Man will always do justice to the interests of Woman? Can we think that he takes a sufficiently discerning and religious view of her office and destiny *ever* to do her justice, except when prompted by sentiment—accidentally or transiently, that is, for the sentiment will vary according to the relations in which he is placed? The lover, the poet, the artist are likely to view her nobly. The father and the philosopher have some chance of liberality; the man of the world, the legislator for expediency none.

Under these circumstances, without attaching importance in themselves to the changes demanded by the champions of Woman, we hail them as signs of the times. We would have every arbitrary barrier thrown down. We would have every path laid open to Woman as freely as to Man. Were this done and slight temporary fermentation allowed to subside, we should see crystallizations more pure and of more various beauty. We believe the divine energy would pervade nature to a degree unknown in the history of former ages, and that no discordant collision but a ravishing harmony of the spheres would ensue.

Yet then and only then will mankind be ripe for this, when inward and outward freedom for Woman as much as for Man shall be acknowledged as a *right,* not yielded as a concession. As the friend of the Negro assumes that one man cannot by right hold another in bondage, so should the friend of Woman assume that Man cannot by right lay even well-meant restrictions on Woman. If the Negro be a soul, if the woman be a soul, appareled in flesh, to one Master only are they accountable. There is but one law for souls, and if there is to be an interpreter of it, he must come not as man or son of man, but as son of God.

Were thought and feeling once so far elevated that Man should esteem himself the brother and friend, but nowise the lord and tutor, of Woman— were he really bound with her in equal worship—arrangements as to function and employment would be of no consequence. What Woman needs is not as a woman to act or rule, but as a nature to grow, as an intellect to discern, as a soul to live freely and unimpeded to unfold such powers as were given her when we left our common home. If fewer talents were given her, yet if allowed the free and full employment of these, so that she may render back to the giver his own with usury, she will not complain; nay, I dare to say she will bless and rejoice in her earthly birthplace, her earthly lot. Let us consider what obstructions impede this good era, and what signs give reason to hope that it draws near.

I was talking on this subject with Miranda, a woman, who, if any in the world could, might speak without heat and bitterness of the position of her sex. Her father was a man who cherished no sentimental reverence for Woman, but a firm belief in the equality of the sexes. She was his eldest child, and came to him at an age when he needed a companion. From the time she could speak and go alone, he addressed her not as a plaything but as a living mind. Among the few verses he ever wrote was a copy addressed to this child, when the first locks were cut from her head; and the reverence expressed on this occasion for that cherished head, he never belied. It was to him the temple of immortal intellect. He respected his child, however, too much to be an indulgent parent. He called on her for clear judgment, for courage, for honor and fidelity; in short, for such virtues as he knew. In so far as he possessed the keys to the wonders of this universe, he allowed free use of them to her, and by the incentive of a high expectation he forbade, so far as possible, that she should let the privilege lie idle.

Thus this child was early led to feel herself a child of the spirit. She took her place easily not only in the world of organized being, but in the world of mind. A dignified sense of self-dependence was given as all her portion, and she found it a sure anchor. Herself securely anchored, her relations with others were established with equal security. She was fortunate in a total absence of those charms which might have drawn to her bewildering flatteries, and in a strong electric nature which repelled those who did not belong to her and attracted those who did. With men and women her relations were noble—affectionate without passion, intellectual without coldness. The world was free to her, and she lived freely in it. Outward adversity came and inward conflict, but that faith and self-respect had early been awakened which must always lead at last to an outward serenity and an inward peace.

Of Miranda I had always thought as an example, that the restraints upon the sex were insuperable only to those who think them so, or who noisily strive to break them. She had taken a course of her own, and no man stood in her way. Many of her acts had been unusual, but excited no uproar. Few helped but none checked her; and the many men who knew her mind and her life showed to her confidence as to a brother, gentleness as to a sister. And not only refined, but very coarse men approved and aided one in whom they saw resolution and clearness of design. Her mind was often the leading one, always effective.

When I talked with her upon these matters and had said very much what I have written, she smilingly replied: "And yet we must admit that I have been fortunate, and this should not be. My good father's early trust gave the first bias, and the rest followed of course. It is true that I have had less outward aid in after years than most women; but that is of little consequence. Religion was early awakened in my soul—a sense that what the soul is capable to ask it must attain, and that though I might be aided and instructed by others, I must depend on myself as the only constant friend. This self-dependence, which was honored in me, is deprecated as a fault in most women. They are taught to learn their rule from without, not to unfold it from within.

"This is the fault of Man, who is still vain, and wishes to be more important to Woman than by right he should be."

"Men have not shown this disposition toward you," I said.

"No, because the position I early was enabled to take was one of self-reliance. And were all women as sure of their wants as I was, the result would be the same. But they are so overloaded with precepts by guardians who think that nothing is so much to be dreaded for a woman as originality of thought or character, that their minds are impeded by doubts till they lose their chance of fair, free proportions. The difficulty is to get them to the point from which they shall naturally develop self-respect and learn self-help.

"Once I thought that men would help to forward this state of things more than I do now. I saw so many of them wretched in the connections they had formed in weakness and vanity. They seemed so glad to esteem women whenever they could.

"'The soft arms of affection,' said one of the most discerning spirits, 'will not suffice for me, unless on them I see the steel bracelets of strength.'

"But early I perceived that men never in any extreme of despair wished to be women. On the contrary, they were ever ready to taunt one another at any sign of weakness with,

Art thou not like the women, who—

"The passage ends various ways, according to the occasion and rhetoric of the speaker. When they admired any woman, they were inclined to speak of her as 'above her sex.' Silently I observed this, and feared it argued a rooted skepticism which for ages had been fastening on the heart and which only an age of miracles could eradicate. Ever I have been treated with great sincerity; and I look upon it as a signal instance of this, that an intimate friend of the other sex said in a fervent moment that I 'deserved in some star to be a man.' He was much surprised when I disclosed my view of my position and hopes, when I declared my faith that the feminine side, the side of love, of beauty, of holiness, was now to have its full chance, and that if either were better, it was better now to be a woman; for even the slightest achievement of good was furthering an especial work of our time. He smiled incredulously. 'She makes the best she can of it,' thought he. 'Let Jews believe the pride of Jewry, but I am of the better sort, and know better.'

"Another used as highest praise in speaking of a character in literature, the words 'a manly woman.'

"So in the noble passage of Ben Jonson:

> I meant the day-star should not brighter ride,
>     Nor shed like influence from its lucent seat;
> I meant she should be courteous, facile, sweet,
>     Free from that solemn vice of greatness, pride;
> I meant each softest virtue there should meet,
>     Fit in that softer bosom to abide,
> Only a learned and a *manly* soul
> I purposed her, that should with even powers
> The rock, the spindle, and the shears control
> Of destiny, and spin her own free hours."

"Methinks," said I, "you are too fastidious in objecting to this. Jonson in using the word 'manly' only meant to heighten the picture of this, the true, the intelligent fate with one of the deeper colors."

"And yet," said she, "so invariable is the use of this word when a heroic quality is to be described, and I feel so sure that persistence and courage are the most womanly no less than the most manly qualities, that I would exchange these words for others of a larger sense, at the risk of marring the fine tissue of the verse. Read, 'A heavenward and instructed soul,' and I should be satisfied. Let it not be said, wherever there is energy or creative genius, 'She has a masculine mind.' "

I. **Suggestions for Discussion**:
   1. Discuss Fuller's use of dialogue to help make her argument.
   2. What part does the story of Miranda play in the argument? To what extent is Miranda intended to be a model for other women?
   3. Compare Fuller's arguments and illustrations with those of Germaine Greer in "The Stereotype," p. 215.

II. **Suggestions for Writing**:
   1. Write a letter to Fuller pointing out the gains women have made since her day. Identify, too, major goals still to be achieved.
   2. Compare and contrast Fuller's arguments with those of Shirley Chisholm in "Women and Their Liberation," p. 83.

# VICKI GOLDBERG

## The Undressed Man

Vicki Goldberg is a contributing editor of *American Photographer* whose essays also appear in *Saturday Review.*

A new artistic interest in the nude male leads her to review the history of male nudity in western art in the following essay and to discuss current attitudes toward sexuality and the nude male form.

The mind teems with naked women from the history of art—Ingres, Renoir, Matisse—but it pauses a moment to recall male nudes more recent than antiquity. Which merely indicates how limited the mind can be. For centuries the male nude dominated painting and sculpture. Artists and patrons considered him the chief glory of art; only in the 19th century did he become an embarrassment. From the Renaissance onward, the naked hero had a distinct public function. He could be admired in church, playing the martyred saint, or in the public square, where the Florentines voted to place Michelangelo's *David.* By the 20th century, public appreciation of the nude male's heroism, classicism, virtue, and symbolism had evaporated as humanism declined, and the naked male went into eclipse. A scant 10 or more years ago he staged an undramatic comeback. Today the form, still tentative and threatening, has regained a crumb of attention.

But no more than a crumb. When Margaret Walters's *The Nude Male: A New Perspective* (Paddington Press) was published in England, it was widely reviewed in the press and discussed on radio; when published here, radio kept mum and only one major paper touched it. Not until 1978 would a gallery, the Pfeifer Gallery in New York, hang an historical selection of photographs of the male nude.

The struggle to erase the blush from the male body has run up against a major obstacle: the public. The year 1979 gallops along, but in the psyche, 1850 still walks with solemn gait. Marcuse Pfeifer, assembling her photography show, was advised several times that the idea was more than a little perverse. To a man, the critics found the show hard to deal with. Gene Thornton of the *New York Times* felt there was "something disconcerting about the sight of a man's naked body being presented primarily as a sex object." Ben Lifson of the *Village Voice* thought most looked like pin-up shots. Both apparently expressed a widespread fear of passivity, femininity, homosexuality. *New York* magazine's John Ashbery commented that "Nude women seem to be in their natural state; men, for some reason, merely look undressed"—a resounding thump for the *status quo,* which assumes that women's bodies are made primarily for men's contemplation. Lifson's review added that "a man's body doesn't lend itself to abstraction like a woman's." This remark is nonsense. The marble Greek male nudes of the sixth century B.C. are magnificently abstracted.

The male nude today does present a challenge to traditional aesthetics by adding two new elements—sex and realism. Historically, male nudity was almost never exclusively a sexual matter. In Greece and Rome it stood for, among other things, kinship to the gods. Roman emperors, such as Hadrian, had themselves immortalized in a state of godly undress. (Their wives did not.) In the Renaissance and for several centuries afterward, male nudity signified classical aspirations, often combined with Christian morality, as when the Holy Roman Emperor Charles V was portrayed in bronze as naked Virtue. The conceit of nude heroism lasted long enough to inspire a mighty nude Napoleon, a Beethoven, and Rodin's planned naked monuments to Victor Hugo and Balzac. Michelangelo had set the standard; from his day to the early 19th century, the male nude was considered nobler than the female.

Artists in the 1960s and 70s have changed the tapes again. Eunice Golden paints erections, Alice Neel puts John Perreault into the languid posture of an odalisque, Anita Steckel pokes fun at the phallus, which sprouts wings or impulsively flashes out across staid school portraits. The contemporary nude is often deliberately impolite. Peter Hujar photographs a young man masturbating, and Jacqueline Livingston, a young boy. Kenneth Clark never prepared us for this.

Nor for the realism of photographs. Art in its endless idealization long kept men young, slim, and scraped clean of body hair, and made the penis tidy and sweet and pale. Photography will not oblige. It is bad enough that there is no comfortable setting to put a male nude into today, so that painters tend to shift them about in studios and photographers to corner them implausibly in factories. We are also forced to confront their hairy reality.

Sex and reality sneaked into the male nude picture without much warning. John H. Gagnon, Professor of Sociology at the State University of New York at Stony Brook, remarked in an interview that this century's campaign to liberate sexuality was for a long time a literary affair. There were no censored paintings to be considered by the Supreme Court partly because artists were not violently flouting accepted priorities. The literary revolution that broke down barriers in books and life was inspired by heterosexual men like Lawrence and Joyce whose preference for female bodies was perfectly clear even when their prose was not. The printed page became unabashedly libertine, but the visual image, which is harder for the poor psyche to defend against, clung to the established lubricity: Matisse's available, expressionless houris, Modigliani's juicy and vulnerable sirens. The passive female nude has long been a staple on the shopping list of the male consumer of art.

A raised consciousness would like to rewrite that scenario. Women (and some men) artists are seeking a new validity and a newly viable form for the male nude. Explicitness is one gambit, anonymity another—many photographers focus on torsos or fragments of the headless body. Since tradition has handed down almost no artistic conventions for depicting naked male sexuality, the up-to-date nude sometimes looks uneasily like a female nude transposed and sometimes simply looks uneasy. In the past, women did not limn the male nude; the current situation embarrassingly disrupts the male monopoly on voyeurism. Earlier centuries forbade women to draw naked men; since men were the traditional, and in the European academies the only, models, this stricture kept many women out of the profession. Michelangelo's Libyan Sibyl on the Sistine ceiling is based on a study of the male nude to which he added a breast or two. The model in the 18th-century French academy was male and a civil servant at that, with no fixed retirement age, a distinct drawback if the fellow was long-lived and the painter wished to paint Cupid. The great female nudes of the past were generally recruited out on the street or from a man's bed.

Today, although accomplished painters like Jillian Denby and Martha Edelheit can turn the male nude into art, and Lucas Samaras can distort his own body on Polaroid into the semblance of a dream, the male nude is essentially homeless. There is neither reverence nor fondness for it, nor even much public acceptance.

Women's frank appreciation, however, might be rearranging matters; it would be splendid, and ironic, if women were the ones to restore men's sense of the beauty and dignity of their bodies. But art without allies cannot mold an attitude. Michelangelo's conviction that the soul was expressed through the body and Jacques-Louis David's belief in the inherent nobility of the classic form were shared by their viewing public. Joy in the body's grace must exist in the culture, as it did in Greece, in order to be sanctified in art. To reinstate the male nude as an important art form would require a return to some consensus that it was precious, or connoted virtue, godliness, or at least

Christian shame. Otherwise we shall have to achieve some measure of familiarity and comfort with the lineaments of desire. Barring that, the male nude
will remain half-private, slightly awkward, an art form cast loose from its
traditions and in search of some niche to call home.

**I. Suggestions for Discussion:**
  1. What place has male nudity had in European art?
  2. Why has there been resistance to male nudity since the nineteenth
     century? Are the examples Goldberg cites good ones?
  3. What attitudes will be necessary to reinstate the male nude as an im-
     portant art form? What role might feminists play?
**II. Suggestions for Writing:**
  1. Argue for or against the inclusion of frontal nudes of men and women
     in a campus art show.
  2. Write a review of an exhibition or of an art book that includes nude
     figures.

---

## OLIVER GOLDSMITH

### Adventures of a Strolling Player

---

Oliver Goldsmith (1728–1774) was born in Ireland but practiced
medicine in England. He made his literary reputation as an occasional essayist, a novelist (*The Vicar of Wakefield,* published in
1762), poet (*The Deserted Village,* published in 1770), and
dramatist (*She Stoops to Conquer,* played in 1773).

Goldsmith, writing in the *British Magazine* in 1760, narrates the
story of a good-natured vagabond who recounts his adventures
as an itinerant actor in return for a good dinner and several
tankards of ale.

---

I am fond of amusement in whatever company it is to be found; and
wit, though dressed in rags, is ever pleasing to me. I went some days ago to
take a walk in St. James's Park, about the hour in which company leave it to
go to dinner. There were but few in the walks, and those who stayed seemed

by their looks rather more willing to forget that they had an appetite than gain one. I sat down on one of the benches, at the other end of which was seated a man in very shabby clothes.

We continued to groan, to hem, and to cough, as usual upon such occasions; and at last ventured upon conversation. "I beg pardon, Sir," cried I, "but I think I have seen you before; your face is familiar to me." "Yes, Sir," replied he, "I have a good familiar face, as my friends tell me. I am as well known in every town in England as the dromedary, or live crocodile. You must understand, Sir, that I have been these sixteen years Merry Andrew [clown] to a puppet-show; last Bartholomew Fair my master and I quarrelled, beat each other, and parted; he to sell his puppets to the pincushion-makers in Rosemary-lane, and I to starve in St. James's Park."

"I am sorry, Sir, that a person of your appearance should labour under any difficulties."—"O Sir," returned he, "my appearance is very much at your service; but, though I cannot boast of eating much, yet there are few that are merrier: if I had twenty thousand a year I should be very merry; and, thank the Fates, though not worth a groat, I am very merry still. If I have three pence in my pocket, I never refuse to be my three halfpence; and if I have no money, I never scorn to be treated by any that are kind enough to pay my reckoning. What think you, Sir, of a steak and a tankard? You shall treat me now; and I will treat you again when I find you in the Park in love with eating, and without money to pay for a dinner."

As I never refuse a small expense for the sake of a merry companion, we instantly adjourned to a neighbouring alehouse, and in a few moments had a frothing tankard and a smoking steak spread on the table before us. It is impossible to express how much the sight of such good cheer improved my companion's vivacity. "I like this dinner, Sir," says he, "for three reasons: first, because I am naturally fond of beef; second, because I am hungry; and, thirdly and lastly, because I get it for nothing: no meat eats so sweet as that for which we do not pay."

He therefore now fell to, and his appetite seemed to correspond with his inclination. After dinner was over, he observed that the steak was tough; "and yet, Sir," returns he, "bad as it was, it seemed a rump-steak to me. O the delights of poverty and a good appetite! We beggars are the very foundlings of nature: the rich she treats like an arrant step-mother; they are pleased with nothing; cut a steak from what part you will, and it is insupportably tough; dress it up with pickles, and even pickles cannot procure them an appetite. But the whole creation is filled with good things for the beggar; Calvert's butt out-tastes Champagne, and Sedgeley's home-brewed excels Tokay. Joy, joy, my blood, though our estates lie no where, we have fortunes wherever we go. If an inundation sweeps away half the grounds of Cornwall, I am content; I have no lands there: if the stocks sink, that gives me no uneasiness; I am no Jew." The fellow's vivacity, joined to his poverty, I own, raised my curiosity to know something of his life and circumstances; and I entreated that he would indulge my desire. "That I will, Sir," said he, "and welcome; only let us drink to prevent our sleeping; let us have another tankard while we are awake; let us have another tankard; for, ah, how charming a tankard looks when full!

"You must know, then, that I am very well descended; my ancestors have made some noise in the world; for my mother cried oysters, and my father beat a drum: I am told we have even had some trumpeters in our family. Many a nobleman cannot show so respectful a genealogy: but that is neither here nor there. As I was their only child, my father designed to breed me up to his own employment, which was that of a drummer to a puppet-show. Thus the whole employment of my younger years was that of interpreter to Punch and King Solomon in all his glory. But though my father was very fond of instructing me in beating all the marches and points of war, I made no very great progress, because I naturally had no ear for music; so at the age of fifteen I went and listed for a soldier. As I had ever hated beating a drum so I soon found that I disliked carrying a musket also; neither the one trade nor the other were to my taste, for I was by nature fond of being a gentleman: besides, I was obliged to obey my captain; he has his will, I have mine, and you have yours: now I very reasonably concluded, that it was much more comfortable for a man to obey his own will than another's.

"The life of a soldier soon therefore gave me the spleen; I asked leave to quit the service; but as I was tall and strong, my captain thanked me for my kind intention, and said, because he had a regard for me, we should not part. I wrote to my father a very dismal penitent letter, and desired that he would raise money to pay for my discharge; but the good man was as fond of drinking as I was (Sir, my service to you), and those who are fond of drinking never pay for other people's discharges: in short, he never answered my letter. What could be done? If I have not money, said I to myself, to pay for my discharge I must find an equivalent some other way: and that must be by running away. I deserted, and that answered my purpose every bit as well as if I had bought my discharge.

"Well, I was now fairly rid of my military employment; I sold my soldier's clothes, bought worse, and, in order not to be overtaken, took the most unfrequented roads possible. One evening as I was entering a village, I perceived a man, whom I afterwards found to be the curate of the parish, thrown from his horse in a miry road, and almost smothered in the mud. He desired my assistance; I gave it, and drew him out with some difficulty. He thanked me for my trouble, and was going off; but I followed him home, for I loved always to have a man thank me at his own door. The curate asked an hundred questions; as whose son I was; from whence I came; and whether I would be faithful? I answered him greatly to his satisfaction; and gave myself one of the best characters in the world for sobriety (Sir, I have the honour of drinking your health), discretion, and fidelity. To make a long story short, he wanted a servant, and hired me. With him I lived but two months; we did not much like each other; I was fond of eating, and he gave me but little to eat; I loved a pretty girl, and the old woman, my fellow-servant, was ill-natured, and ugly. As they endeavoured to starve me between them, I made a pious resolution to prevent their committing murder: I stole the eggs as soon as they were laid; I emptied every unfinished bottle that I could lay my hands on; whatever eatable came in my way was sure to disappear: in short, they found I would not do; so I was discharged one morning, and paid three shillings and sixpence for two months wages.

"While my money was getting ready, I employed myself in making preparations for my departure; two hens were hatching in an out-house, I went and habitually took the eggs, and not to separate the parents from the children I lodged hens and all in my knapsack. After this piece of frugality, I returned to receive my money, and with my knapsack on my back, and a staff in my hand, I bade adieu with tears in my eyes to my old benefactor. I had not got far from the house when I heard behind me the cry of Stop thief! but this only increased my dispatch: it would have been foolish to stop, as I knew the voice could not be levelled at me. But hold, I think I passed those two months at the curate's without drinking; come, the times are dry, and may this be my poison if ever I spent two more pious stupid months in all my life!

"Well, after travelling some days, whom should I light upon, but a company of strolling players. The moment I saw them at a distance my heart warmed to them; I had a sort of natural love for everything of the vagabond order: they were employed in settling their baggage, which had been overturned in a narrow way; I offered my assistance, which they accepted, and we soon became so well acquainted that they took me as a servant. This was a paradise to me; they sung, danced, drank, eat, and travelled, all at the same time. By the blood of the Mirabels, I thought I had never lived till then; I grew as merry as a grig, and laughed at every word that was spoken. They liked me as much as I liked them; I was a very good figure, as you see; and, though I was poor, I was not modest.

"I love a straggling life above all things in the world; sometimes good, sometimes bad; to be warm to-day, and cold to-morrow; to eat when one can get it, and drink when (the tankard is out) it stands before me. We arrived that evening at Tenderden, and took a large room at the Greyhound; where we resolved to exhibit Romeo and Juliet, with the funeral procession, the grave and the garden scene. Romeo was to be performed by a gentleman from Theatre-Royal in Drury-lane; Juliet by a lady who had never appeared on any stage before; and I was to snuff the candles: all excellent in our way. We had figures enough, but the difficulty was to dress them. The same coat that served Romeo, turned with the blue lining outwards, served for his friend Mercutio: a large piece of crape sufficed at once for Juliet's petticoat and pall: a pestle and mortar from a neighbouring apothecary's answered all the purposes of a bell; and our landlord's own family, wrapped in white sheets, served to fill up the procession. In short, there were but three figures among us that might be said to be dressed with any propriety: I mean the nurse, the starved apothecary, and myself. Our performance gave universal satisfaction: the whole audience were enchanted with our powers, and Tenderden is a town of taste.

"There is one rule by which a strolling player may be ever secure of success; that is, in our theatrical way of expressing it, to make a great deal of the character. To speak and act as in common life, is not playing, nor is it what people come to see: natural speaking, like sweet wine, runs glibly over the palate, and scarce leaves any taste behind it; but being high in a part resembles vinegar, which grates upon the taste, and one feels it while he is drinking. To please in town or country, the way is to cry, wring, cringe into attitudes, mark the emphasis, slap the pockets, and labour like one in the falling sickness: that is the way to work for applause; that is the way to gain it.

"As we received much reputation for our skill on this first exhibition, it was but natural for me to ascribe part of the success to myself; I snuffed the candles, and let me tell you, that without a candle-snuffer, the piece would lose half its embellishments. In this manner we continued a fortnight, and drew tolerable houses; but the evening before our intended departure, we gave out our very best piece, in which all our strength was to be exerted. We had great expectations from this, and even doubled our prices, when behold one of the principal actors fell ill of a violent fever. This was a stroke like thunder to our little company: they were resolved to go in a body, to scold the man for falling sick at so inconvenient a time, and that too of a disorder that threatened to be expensive; I seized the moment, and offered to act the part myself in his stead. The case was desperate: they accepted my offer; and I accordingly sat down with the part in my hand and a tankard

before me (Sir, your health), and studied the character, which was to be rehearsed the next day, and played soon after.

"I found my memory excessively helped by drinking: I learned my part
with astonishing rapidity, and bade adieu to snuffing candles ever after. I
found that nature had designed me for more noble employments, and I was
resolved to take her when in the humour. We got together in order to re-
hearse; and I informed my companions, masters now no longer, of the surprising change I felt within me. Let the sick man, said I, be under no uneasiness to get well again; I'll fill his place to universal satisfaction; he may even
die if he thinks proper; I'll engage that he shall never be missed. I rehearsed
before them, strutted, ranted, and received applause. They soon gave out that
a new actor of eminence was to appear, and immediately all the genteel places
were bespoke. Before I ascended the stage, however, I concluded within myself, that as I brought money to the house, I ought to have my share in the
profits. Gentlemen, said I addressing our company, I don't pretend to direct
you; far be it from me to treat you with so much ingratitude: you have published my name in the bills with the utmost good-nature; and as affairs stand,
cannot act without me; so, gentlemen, to show you my gratitude, I expect to
be paid for my acting as much as any of you, otherwise I declare off; I'll
brandish my snuffers, and clip candles as usual. This was a very disagreeable
proposal, but they found that it was impossible to refuse it, it was irresistible, it was adamant: they consented, and I went on in King Bajazet;[1] my
frowning brows, bound with a stocking stuffed into a turban, while on my
captived arms I brandished a jack-chain. Nature seemed to have fitted me for
the part; I was tall, and had a loud voice; my very entrance excited universal
applause; I looked round on the audience with a smile, and made a most low
and graceful bow, for that is the rule among us. As it was a very passionate
part, I invigorated my spirits with three full glasses (the tankard is almost out)
of brandy. By Alla! it is almost inconceivable how I went through it; Tamerlane was but a fool to me; though he was sometimes loud enough too, yet I
was still louder than he: but then, besides, I had attitudes in abundance: in
general I kept my arms folded up thus, upon the pit of my stomach; it is
the way at Drury-lane, and has always a fine effect. The tankard would sink
to the bottom before I could get through the whole of my merits: in short,
I came off like a prodigy; and such was my success, that I could ravish the
laurels even from a sirloin of beef. The principal gentlemen and ladies of the
town came to me, after the play was over, to compliment me upon my suc-

---

[1] The oriental emperor in Nicholas Rowe's play, *Tamerlane* (1723).

cess; one praised my voice, another my person: Upon my word, says the 'squire's lady, he will make one of the finest actors in Europe; I say it, and I think I am something of a judge.—Praise in the beginning is agreeable enough, and we receive it as a favour; but when it comes in great quantities, we regard it only as a debt, which nothing but our merit could extort: instead of thanking them, I internally applauded myself. We were desired to give our piece a second time; we obeyed, and I was applauded even more than before.

"At last we left the town, in order to be at a horse-race at some distance from thence. I shall never think of Tenderden without tears of gratitude and respect. The ladies and gentlemen there, take my word for it, are very good judges of plays and actors. Come, let us drink their healths, if you please, Sir. We quitted the town, I say; and there was a wide difference between my coming in and going out: I entered the town a candle-snuffer, and I quitted it an hero!—Such is the world; little to-day, and great tomorrow. I could say a great deal more upon that subject; something truly sublime upon the ups and downs of fortune; but it would give us both the spleen, and so I shall pass it over.

"The races were ended before we arrived at the next town, which was no small disappointment to our company; however, we were resolved to take all we could get. I played capital characters there too, and came off with my usual brilliancy. I sincerely believe I should have been the first actor of Europe had my growing merit been properly cultivated; but there came an unkindly frost which nipped me in the bud, and levelled me once more down to the common standard of humanity. I played Sir Harry Wildair;[2] all the country ladies were charmed: if I but drew out my snuff-box, the whole house was in a roar of rapture; when I exercised my cudgel, I thought they would have fallen into convulsions.

"There was here a lady who had received an education of nine months in London; and this gave her pretensions to taste, which rendered her the indisputable mistress of the ceremonies wherever she came. She was informed of my merits; everybody praised me; yet she refused at first going to see me perform: she could not conceive, she said, anything but stuff from a stroller; talked something in praise of Garrick, and amazed the ladies with her skill in enunciations, tones, and cadences; she was at last, however, prevailed upon to go; and it was privately intimated to me what a judge was to be present at my next exhibition: however, no way intimidated, I came on in Sir Harry, one hand stuck in my breeches, and the other in my bosom, as usual at Drury-lane; but instead of looking at me, I perceived the whole audience had

[2] In George Farquhar's *Trip to the Jubilee* (1701).

their eyes turned upon the lady who had been nine months in London; from
her they expected the decision which was to secure the general's truncheon in
my hand, or sink me down into a theatrical letter-carrier. I opened my snuff-
box, took snuff; the lady was solemn, and so were the rest: I broke my cudgel
on alderman Smuggler's back; still gloomy, melancholy all, the lady groaned
and shrugged her shoulders: I attempted by laughing myself, to excite at least
a smile; but the devil a cheek could I perceive wrinkled into sympathy: I
found it would not do: all my good-humour now became forced; my laughter
was converted into hysteric grinning; and while I pretended spirits, my eye
showed the agony of my heart: in short, the lady came with an intention
to be displeased and displeased she was; my fame expired; I am here and—(the
tankard is no more!)."

I. **Suggestions for Discussion:**
   1. Describe the setting in which Goldsmith's story unfolds. What details
      help animate the scene?
   2. Why was the story teller attracted to the life of a strolling player?
   3. How sincere and honest an account of his life do you think the actor
      gives? What evidence can you cite?
II. **Suggestions for Writing:**
   1. Narrate another adventure which the strolling player might have told
      in return for another tankard of ale.
   2. Describe one of your own experiences on stage. Were you suited for the
      role you played? Did you play the part well? Were you well received?

---

# GERMAINE GREER

## The Stereotype

### from *The Female Eunuch*

---

Germaine Greer (1939–    ) is an Australian-born writer and
educator, best known for her advocacy of women's rights and as
the author of *The Female Eunuch* (1971). Her latest book is *The
Obstacle Race* (1979), a study of female artists.

In this popular essay from *The Female Eunuch,* Greer describes
and deplores the female stereotype as the emblem of spending
ability, the most effective seller of the world's goods, and as the
ultimate sexual object whose essential quality is castratedness.

---

In that mysterious dimension where the body meets the soul the stereotype is born and has her being. She is more body than soul, more soul than
mind. To her belongs all that is beautiful, even the very word beauty itself.
All that exists, exists to beautify her. The sun shines only to burnish her skin
and gild her hair; the wind blows only to whip up the color in her cheeks;

> Taught from infancy that beauty is woman's sceptre, the mind
> shapes itself to the body, and roaming round its gilt cage, only
> seeks to adorn its prison.
>
> Mary Wollstonecraft, *A Vindication of the Rights of Woman,* 1792, p. 90.

the sea strives to bathe her; flowers die gladly so that her skin may luxuriate
in their essence. She is the crown of creation, the masterpiece. The depths of
the sea are ransacked for pearl and coral to deck her; the bowels of the earth
are laid open that she might wear gold, sapphires, diamonds and rubies. Baby
seals are battered with staves, unborn lambs ripped from their mothers'
wombs, millions of moles, muskrats, squirrels, minks, ermines, foxes, beavers,
chinchillas, ocelots, lynxes, and other small and lovely creatures die untimely
deaths that she might have furs. Egrets, ostriches and peacocks, butterflies
and beetles yield her their plumage. Men risk their lives hunting leopards for
her coats, and crocodiles for her handbags and shoes. Millions of silkworms
offer her their yellow labors; even the seamstresses roll seams and whip lace
by hand, so that she might be clad in the best that money can buy.

The men of our civilization have stripped themselves of the fineries of
the earth so that they might work more freely to plunder the universe for
treasures to deck my lady in. New raw materials, new processes, new machines are all brought into her service. My lady must therefore be the chief
spender as well as the chief symbol of spending ability and monetary success.
While her mate toils in his factory, she totters about the smartest streets and
plushiest hotels with his fortune upon her back and bosom, fingers and wrists,
continuing that essential expenditure in his house which is her frame and her
setting, enjoying that silken idleness which is the necessary condition of maintaining her mate's prestige and her qualification to demonstrate it. Once upon
a time only the aristocratic lady could lay claim to the title of crown of crea-

tion: only her hands were white enough, her feet tiny enough, her waist narrow enough, her hair long and golden enough; but every well-to-do burgher's wife set herself up to ape my lady and to follow fashion, until my lady was forced to set herself out like a gilded doll overlaid with monstrous rubies and pearls like pigeons' eggs. Nowadays the Queen of England still considers it part of her royal female role to sport as much of the family jewelry as she can manage at any one time on all public occasions, although the male monarchs have escaped such showcase duty, which develops exclusively upon their wives.

At the same time as woman was becoming the showcase for wealth and caste, while men were slipping into relative anonymity and "handsome is as handsome does," she was emerging as the central emblem of western art. For the Greeks the male and female body had beauty of a human, not necessarily a sexual, kind; indeed they may have marginally favored the young male form as the most powerful and perfectly proportioned. Likewise the Romans showed no bias towards the depiction of femininity in their predominantly monumental art. In the Renaissance the female form began to predominate, not only as the mother in the predominate emblem of *madonna col bambino,* but as an aesthetic study in herself. At first naked female forms took their chances in crowd scenes or diptychs of Adam and Eve, but gradually Venus claims ascendancy, Mary Magdalene ceases to be wizened and emaciated, and becomes nubile and ecstatic, portraits of anonymous young women, chosen only for their prettiness, begin to appear, are gradually disrobed, and renamed Flora or Primavera. Painters begin to paint their own wives and mistresses and royal consorts as voluptuous beauties, divesting them of their clothes if desirable, but not of their jewelry. Susanna keeps her bracelets on in the bath, and Hélène Fourment keeps ahold of her fur as well!

What happened to women in painting happened to her in poetry as well. Her beauty was celebrated in terms of the riches which clustered around her: her hair was gold wires, her brow ivory, her lips ruby, her teeth gates of pearl, her breasts alabaster veined with lapis lazuli, her eyes as black as jet. The fragility of her loveliness was emphasized by the inevitable comparisons with the rose, and she was urged to employ her beauty in love-making before it withered on the stem. She was for consumption; other sorts of imagery spoke of her in terms of cherries and cream, lips as sweet as honey and skin white as milk, breasts like cream uncrudded, hard as apples. Some celebrations yearned over her finery as well, her lawn more transparent than morning mist, her lace as delicate as gossamer, the baubles that she toyed with and the favors that she gave. Even now we find the thriller hero describing his classy dames' elegant suits, cheeky hats, well-chosen accessories and footwear; the imagery no longer dwells on jewels and flowers but the consumer emphasis is the same. The mousy secretary blossoms into the feminine stereotype when she reddens her lips, lets down her hair, and puts on something frilly.

Nowadays women are not expected, unless they are Paola di Liegi or Jackie Onassis, and then only on gala occasions, to appear with a king's ransom deployed upon their bodies, but they are required to look expensive, fashionable, well-groomed, and not to be seen in the same dress twice. If the duty of the few may have become less onerous, it has also become the duty of the many. The stereotype marshals an army of servants. She is supplied with cosmetics, underwear, foundation garments, stockings, wigs, postiches and hairdressing as well as her outer garments, her jewels and furs. The effect is to be built up layer by layer, and it is expensive. Splendor has given way to fit, line and cut. The spirit of competition must be kept up, as more and more women struggle towards the top drawer, so that the fashion industry can rely upon an expanding market. Poorer women fake it, ape it, pick up on the fashions a season too late, use crude effects, mistaking the line, the sheen, the gloss of the high-class article for a garish simulacrum. The business is so complex that it must be handled by an expert. The paragons of the stereotype must be dressed, coifed and painted by the experts and the style-setters, although they may be encouraged to give heart to the housewives studying their lives in pulp magazines by claiming a lifelong fidelity to their own hair and soap and water. The boast is more usually discouraging than otherwise, unfortunately.

As long as she is young and personable, every woman may cherish the dream that she may leap up the social ladder and dim the sheen of luxury by sheer natural loveliness; the few examples of such a feat are kept before the eye of the public. Fired with hope, optimism and ambition, young women study the latest forms of the stereotype, set out in *Vogue, Nova, Queen* and other glossies, where the mannequins stare from among the advertisements for fabulous real estate, furs and jewels. Nowadays the uniformity of the year's fashions is severely affected by the emergence of the pert female designers who direct their appeal to the working girl, emphasizing variety, comfort, and simple, striking effects. There is no longer a single face of the year: even Twiggy has had to withdraw into marketing and rationed personal appearances, while the Shrimp works mostly in New York. Nevertheless the stereotype is still supreme. She has simply allowed herself a little more variation.

The stereotype is the Eternal Feminine. She is the Sexual Object sought by all men, and by all women. She is of neither sex, for she has herself no sex at all. Her value is solely attested by the demand she excites in others. All she must contribute is her existence. She need achieve nothing, for she is the reward of achievement. She need never give positive evidence of her moral character because virtue is assumed from her loveliness, and her passivity. If any man who has no right to her be found with her she will not be punished, for she is morally neuter. The matter is solely one of male rivalry. Innocently she may drive men to madness and war. The more trouble she can cause, the more her stocks go up, for possession of her means more the more demand she excites. Nobody wants a girl whose beauty is imperceptible to all but him; and so men welcome the stereotype because it directs their taste

> The myth of the strong black woman is the other side of the coin of the myth of the beautiful dumb blonde. The white man turned the white woman into a weak-minded, weak-bodied, delicate freak, a sexpot, and placed her on a pedestal; he turned the black woman into a strong self-reliant Amazon and deposited her in his kitchen. . . . The white man turned himself into the Omnipotent Administrator and established himself in the Front Office.
>
> Eldridge Cleaver, "The Allegory of the Black Eunuchs," *Soul on Ice*, 1968, p. 162

into the most commonly recognized areas of value, although they may protest because some aspects of it do not tally with their fetishes. There is scope in the stereotype's variety for most fetishes. The leg man may follow miniskirts, the tit man can encourage see-through blouses and plunging necklines, although the man who likes fat women may feel constrained to enjoy them in secret. There are stringent limits to the variations on the stereotype, for nothing must interfere with her function as sex object. She may wear leather, as long as she cannot actually handle a motorbike: she may wear rubber, but it ought not to indicate that she is an expert diver or waterskier. If she wears athletic clothes the purpose is to underline her unathleticism. She may sit astride a horse, looking soft and curvy, but she must not crouch over its neck with her rump in the air.

Because she is the emblem of spending ability and the chief spender, she is also the most effective seller of this world's goods. Every survey ever held has shown that the image of an attractive woman is the most effective advertising gimmick. She may sit astride the mudguard of a new car, or step into it ablaze with jewels; she may lie at a man's feet stroking his new socks; she may hold the petrol pump in a challenging pose, or dance through woodland glades in slow motion in all the glory of a new shampoo; whatever she does her image sells. The gynolatry of our civilization is written large upon its face, upon hoardings, cinema screens, television, newspapers, magazines, tins, packets, cartons, bottles, all consecrated to the reigning deity, the female fetish. Her dominion must not be thought to entail the rule of women, for she is not a woman. Her glossy lips and mat complexion, her unfocused eyes and flawless fingers, her extraordinary hair all floating and shining, curling and gleaming, reveal the inhuman triumph of cosmetics, lighting, focusing and printing, cropping and composition. She sleeps unruffled, her lips red and juicy and closed, her eyes as crisp and black as if new painted, and her false lashes immaculately curled. Even when she washes her face with a new and creamier toilet soap her expression is as tranquil and vacant and her paint as flawless as ever. If ever she should appear tousled and troubled, her features are miraculously smoothed to their proper veneer by a new washing powder or a bouillon cube. For she is a doll: weeping, pouting or smiling, running or reclining, she is a doll. She is an idol, formed of the concatenation of lines and masses, signifying the lineaments of satisfied impotence.

Her essential quality is castratedness. She absolutely must be young, her

She was created to be the toy of man, his rattle, and it must jingle in his ears whenever, dismissing reason, he chooses to be amused.

Mary Wollstonecraft, *A Vindication of the Rights of Woman*, 1792, p. 66

body hairless, her flesh buoyant, and *she must not have a sexual organ.* No musculature must distort the smoothness of the lines of her body, although she may be painfully slender or warmly cuddly. Her expression must betray no hint of humor, curiosity or intelligence, although it may signify hauteur to an extent that is actually absurd, or smoldering lust, very feebly signified by drooping eyes and a sullen mouth (for the stereotype's lust equals irrational submission), or, most commonly, vivacity and idiot happiness. Seeing that the world despoils itself for this creature's benefit, she must be happy; the entire structure would topple if she were not. So the image of woman appears plastered on every surface imaginable, smiling interminably. An apple pie evokes a glance of tender beatitude, a washing machine causes hilarity, a cheap box of chocolates brings forth meltingly joyous gratitude, a Coke is the cause of a rictus of unutterable brilliance, even a new stick-on bandage is saluted by a smirk of satisfaction. A real woman licks her lips and opens her mouth and flashes her teeth when photographers appear: *she* must arrive at the premiere of her husband's film in a paroxysm of delight, or his success might be murmured about. The occupational hazard of being a Playboy Bunny is the aching facial muscles brought on by the obligatory smiles.

So what is the beef? Maybe I couldn't make it. Maybe I don't have a pretty smile, good teeth, nice tits, long legs, a cheeky arse, a sexy voice. Maybe I don't know how to handle men and increase my market value, so that the rewards due to the feminine will accrue to me. Then again, maybe I'm sick of the masquerade. I'm sick of pretending eternal youth. I'm sick of belying my own intelligence, my own will, my own sex. I'm sick of peering at the world through false eyelashes, so everything I see is mixed with a shadow of bought hairs; I'm sick of weighting my head with a dead mane, unable to move my neck freely, terrified of rain, of wind, of dancing too vigorously in case I sweat into my lacquered curls. I'm sick of the Powder Room. I'm sick of pretending that some fatuous male's self-important pronouncements are the objects of my undivided attention. I'm sick of going to films and plays when someone else wants to, and sick of having no opinions of my own about either. I'm sick of being a transvestite. I refuse to be a female impersonator. I am a woman, not a castrate.

> Discretion is the better part of Valerie
> though all of her is nice
> lips as warm as strawberries
> eyes as cold as ice
> the very best of everything
> only will suffice
> not for her potatoes
> and puddings made of rice
>
> Roger McGough, *Discretion*

April Ashley was born male. All the information supplied by genes, chromosomes, internal and external sexual organs added up to the same thing. April was a man. But he longed to be a woman. He longed for the stereotype, not to embrace, but to be. He wanted soft fabrics, jewels, furs, makeup, the love and protection of men. So he was impotent. He couldn't fancy women at all, although he did not particularly welcome homosexual addresses. He did not think of himself as a pervert, or even as a transvestite, but as a woman cruelly transmogrified into manhood. He tried to die, became a female impersonator, but eventually found a doctor in Casablanca who came up with a more acceptable alternative. He was to be castrated, and his penis used as the lining of a surgically constructed cleft, which would be a vagina. He would be infertile, but that has never affected the attribution of feminity. April returned to England, resplendent. Massive hormone treatment had eradicated his beard, and formed tiny breasts: he had grown his hair and bought feminine clothes during the time he had worked as an impersonator. He became a model, and began to illustrate the feminine stereotype as he was perfectly qualified to do, for he was elegant, voluptuous, beautifully groomed, and in love with his own image. On an ill-fated day he married the heir to a peerage, the Hon. Arthur Corbett, acting out the highest achievement of the feminine dream, and went to live with him in a villa in Marbella. The marriage was never consummated. April's incompetence as a woman is what we must expect from a castrate, but it is not so very different after all from the impotence of feminine women, who submit to sex without desire, with only the infantile pleasure of cuddling and affection, which is their favorite reward. As long as the feminine stereotype remains the definition of the female sex, April Ashley is a woman, regardless of the legal decision ensuing from her divorce. She is as much a casualty of the polarity of the sexes as we all are. Disgraced, unsexed April Ashley is our sister and our symbol.

> To what end is the laying out of the embroidered Hair, embared Breasts; Vermilion Cheeks, alluring looks, Fashion gates, and artful Countenances, effeminate intangling and insnaring Gestures, their Curls and Purls of proclaiming Petulancies, boulstered and laid out with such example and authority in these our days, as with Allowance and beseeming Conveniency?
>
> Doth the world wax barren through decrease of Generations, and become, like the Earth, less fruitful heretofore? Doth the Blood lose his Heat or do the Sunbeams become waterish and less fervent, than formerly they have been, that men should be thus inflamed and persuaded on to lust?

Alex. Niccholes, *A Discourse of Marriage and Wiving*, 1615, pp. 143–52

## I. Suggestions for Discussion:

1. What does Greer mean by the stereotype? How does she develop and support her extended definition?
2. Explain her claim that the essential quality of the stereotype is castratedness.
3. Why does Greer introduce April Ashley at the conclusion of her essay? What rhetorical purpose is served by the introduction of this unusual allusion?

## II. Suggestions for Writing:

1. Collect and describe examples from the media which support Greer's claim that the female stereotype is the most effective seller of this world's goods.
2. Using your own experience and observation, write an essay on stereotypes.
3. Compare Greer's observations on the stereotype with those of Marya Mannes in "Television Advertising: The Splitting Image," p. 353.

---

# WILLIAM HAZLITT

### From *On Familiar Style*

---

William Hazlitt (1778–1830) was an English essayist who wrote abundantly for various periodicals. Among his best-known works are *Characters of Shakespeare's Plays* (1817–1818), *English Comic Writers* (1819), and *Table Talk, or Original Essays on Men and Manners* (1821–1822).

In his own essay, Hazlitt demonstrates the qualities of the familiar style of writing he advocates.

---

It is not easy to write a familiar style. Many people mistake a familiar for a vulgar style, and suppose that to write without affectation is to write at random. On the contrary, there is nothing that requires more precision, and, if I may so say, purity of expression, than the style I am speaking of. It utterly rejects not only all unmeaning pomp, but all low, cant phrases, and loose, unconnected, *slipshod* allusions. It is not to take the first word that offers, but the best word in common use; it is not to throw words together in any combination we please, but to follow and avail ourselves of the true idiom of the language. To write a genuine familiar or truly English style, is to write as any one would speak in common conversation, who had a thorough command and choice of words, or who could discourse with ease, force, and perspicuity, setting aside all pedantic and oratorical flourishes. Or to give another illustration, to write naturally is the same thing in regard to common conversation, as to read naturally is in regard to common speech. It does not follow that it is an easy thing to give the true accent and inflection to the words you utter, because you do not attempt to rise above the level of ordinary life and colloquial speaking. You do not assume indeed the solemnity of the pulpit, or the tone of stage-declamation: neither are you at liberty to gabble on at a venture, without emphasis or discretion, or to resort to vulgar dialect or clownish pronunciation. You must steer a middle course. You are tied down to a given and appropriate articulation, which is determined by the habitual associations between sense and sound, and which you can only hit by entering into the author's meaning, as you must find the proper words and style to express yourself by fixing your thoughts on the subject you have to write about. Any one may mouth out a passage with a theatrical cadence, or get upon stilts to tell his thoughts: but to write or speak with propriety and simplicity is a more difficult task. Thus it is easy to affect a pompous style, to use a word twice as big as the thing you want to express: it is not so easy to pitch upon the very word that exactly fits it. Out of eight or ten words equally common, equally intelligible, with nearly equal pretensions, it is a matter of some nicety and discrimination to pick out the very one, the preferableness of which is scarcely perceptible, but decisive. The reason why I object to Dr. Johnson's[1] style is, that there is no discrimination, no selection, no variety in it. He uses none but "tall, opaque words," taken from the "first row of the rubric":—words with the greatest number of syllables, or Latin phrases with merely English terminations. If a fine style depended on this sort of arbitrary pretension, it would be fair to judge of an author's elegance by the measurement of his words, and the substitution of foreign circumlocutions (with no precise associations) for the mother-tongue. How simple it is to be dignified without ease, to be pompous without meaning! Surely, it is but a mechanical rule for avoiding what is low to be always pedantic and affected. It is clear you cannot use a vulgar English word, if you never use a common English word at all. A fine tact is shown in adhering to those which are perfectly common, and yet never falling into any expressions which are debased by disgusting circumstances, or which owe their signification and point to technical or professional allusions. A truly natural or familiar style can never be quaint or vulgar, for this reason, that it is of universal force and applicability, and that quaintness and vulgarity arise out of the immediate connection of certain words with coarse and disagreeable, or with confined ideas. The last form what we understand by *cant* or *slang* phrases.— To give an example of what is not very clear in the general statement. I

---

[1] Dr. Samuel Johnson (1709–1784) was an English poet, essayist, critic, and lexicographer.

should say that the phrase *To cut with a knife,* or *To cut a piece of wood,* is perfectly free from vulgarity, because it is perfectly common: but to *cut an acquaintance* is not quite unexceptionable, because it is not perfectly common or intelligible, and has hardly yet escaped out of the limits of slang phraseology. I should hardly therefore use the word in this sense without putting it in italics as a license of expression, to be received *cum grano salis.*[2] All provincial or bye-phrases come under the same mark of reprobation—all such as the writer transfers to the page from his fireside or a particular *coterie,* or that he invents for his own sole use and convenience. I conceive that words are like money, not the worse for being common, but that it is the stamp of custom alone that gives them circulation or value. I am fastidious in this respect, and would almost as soon coin the currency of the realm as counterfeit the King's English. I never invented or gave a new and unauthorized meaning to any word but one single one (the term *impersonal* applied to feelings) and that was in an abstruse metaphysical discussion to express a very difficult distinction. I have been (I know) loudly accused of revelling in vulgarisms and broken English. I cannot speak to that point: but so far I plead guilty to the determined use of acknowledged idioms and common elliptical expressions. I am not sure that the critics in question know the one from the other, that is, can distinguish any medium between formal pedantry and the most barbarous solecism. As an author, I endeavor to employ plain words and popular modes of construction, as were I a chapman and dealer, I should common weights and measures.

The proper force of words lies not in the words themselves, but in their application. A word may be a fine-sounding word, of an unusual length, and very imposing from its learning and novelty, and yet in the connection in which it is introduced, may be quite pointless and irrelevant. It is not pomp or pretension, but the adaptation of the expression to the idea that clenches a writer's meaning:—as it is not the size or glossiness of the materials, but their being fitted each to its place, that gives strength to the arch; or as the pegs and nails are as necessary to the support of the building as the larger timbers, and more so than the mere showy, unsubstantial ornaments. I hate anything that occupies more space than it is worth. I hate to see a load of band-boxes go along the street, and I hate to see a parcel of big words without any thing in them. A person who does not deliberately dispose of all his thoughts alike in cumbrous draperies and flimsy disguises, may strike out twenty varieties of familiar everyday language, each coming somewhat nearer to the feeling he wants to convey, and at last not hit upon that particular

---

[2]With a grain of salt.

and only one, which may be said to be identical with the exact impression in his mind. This would seem to show that Mr. Cobbett is hardly right in saying that the first word that occurs is always the best. It may be a very good one; and yet a better may present itself on reflection or from time to time. It should be suggested naturally, however, and spontaneously, from a fresh and lively conception of the subject. We seldom succeed by trying at improvement, or by merely substituting one word for another that we are not satisfied with, as we cannot recollect the name of a place or person by merely plaguing ourselves about it. We wander farther from the point by persisting in a wrong scent; but it starts up accidentally in the memory when we least expect it, by touching some link in the chain of previous association.

There are those who hoard up and make a cautious display of nothing but rich and rare phraseology;—ancient medals, obscure coins, and Spanish pieces of eight. They are very curious to inspect; but I myself would neither offer nor take them in the course of exchange. A sprinkling of archaisms is not amiss; but a tissue of obsolete expressions is more fit *for keep than wear.* I do not say I would not use any phrase that had been brought into fashion before the middle or the end of the last century; but I should be shy of using any that had not been employed by any approved author during the whole of that time. Words, like clothes, get old-fashioned, or mean and ridiculous, when they have been for some time laid aside. Mr. Lamb[3] is the only imitator of old English style I can read with pleasure; and he is so thoroughly imbued with the spirit of his authors that the idea of imitation is almost done away. There is an inward unction, a marrowy vein both in the thought and feeling, an intuition, deep and lively, of his subject, that carries off any quaintness or awkwardness arising from an antiquated style and dress. The matter is completely his own, though the manner is assumed. Perhaps his ideas are altogether so marked and individual, as to require their point and pungency to be neutralized by the affectation of a singular but traditional form of conveyance. Tricked out in the prevailing costume, they would probably seem more startling and out of the way. The old English authors, Burton, Fuller, Coryate, Sir Thomas Browne, are a kind of mediators between us and the more eccentric and whimsical modern, reconciling us to his peculiarities. I do not, however, know how far this is the case or not, till he condescends to write like one of us. I must confess that what I like best of his papers under the signature of Elia (still I do not presume, amidst such excellence, to decide

---

[3]Charles Lamb (1775–1834), English essayist, published collections of miscellaneous essays called *Essays of Elia* in 1823 and 1833.

on what is most excellent) is the account of *Mrs. Battle's Opinion on Whist,* which is also the most free from obsolete allusions and turns of expression—

A well of native English undefiled.

To those acquainted with his admired prototypes, these Essays of the ingenious and highly gifted author have the same sort of charm and relish, that Erasmus's *Colloquies* or a fine piece of modern Latin have to the classical scholar. Certainly, I do not know any borrowed pencil that has more power or felicity of execution than the one of which I have here been speaking.

It is as easy to write a gaudy style without ideas, as it is to spread a pallet of showy colors, or to smear in a flaunting transparency. "What do you read?"—"Words, words, words."—"What is the matter?"—"*Nothing,*" it might be answered. The florid style is the reverse of the familiar. The last is employed as an unvarnished medium to convey ideas; the first is resorted to as a spangled veil to conceal the want of them.

I. **Suggestions for Discussion**:
 1. What does Hazlitt mean by steering "a middle course"? Be specific.
 2. Summarize Hazlitt's advice on how to write a familiar style. Does he follow his own advice?
 3. After reading Charles Lamb's "A Dissertation Upon Roast Pig," p. 308, comment on Hazlitt's critique of Lamb's style.

II. **Suggestions for Writing**:
 1. Discuss the extent to which Hazlitt's advice is applicable to all the writing you do in college. Are there necessary exceptions? Explain.
 2. Compare Hazlitt's observations on good writing with those of Benjamin Franklin in "On Literary Style," p. 189 or of George Orwell in "Politics and the English Language," p. 437.

---

# ALDOUS HUXLEY

## Madness, Badness, Sadness

---

Aldous Huxley (1894-1963) was born in England and educated at Oxford University. He is the author of many novels, including

*Point Counter Point* (1928) and *Brave New World* (1932). He also wrote essays, short stories, poetry, and plays. *The Doors of Perception* (1954) describes his experiences with hallucinogenic drugs.

In the following essay, Huxley documents in terrifying detail the record of Western man's treatment of the mentally ill.

---

Goering and Hitler displayed an almost maudlin concern for the welfare of animals; Stalin's favorite work of art was a celluloid musical about Old Vienna, called *The Great Waltz*. And it is not only dictators who divide their thoughts and feelings into unconnected, logic-tight compartments; the whole world lives in a state of chronic and almost systematic inconsistency. Every society is a case of multiple personality and modulates, without a qualm, without even being aware of what it is up to, from Jekyll to Hyde, from the scientist to the magician, from the hardheaded man of affairs to the village idiot. Ours, for example, is the age of unlimited violence; but it is also the age of the welfare state, of bird sanctuaries, of progressive education, of a growing concern for the old, the physically handicapped, the mentally sick. We build orphanages, and at the same time we stockpile the bombs that will be dropped on orphanages. "A foolish consistency," says Emerson, "is the hobgoblin of little minds, adored by little statesmen, philosophers and divines." In that case, we must be very great indeed.

That all, or even most, human beings will ever be consistently humane seems very unlikely. We must be content with the smaller mercies of unemployment benefits and school lunches in the midst and in spite of an armament race. We must console ourselves with the thought that our inky darks are relieved by quite a number of lights.

Between Los Angeles and Long Beach, California, there stands a mental hospital which admirably illustrates our blessed inconsistency. Bomber plants and guided-missile laboratories surround it on every side, but have not succeeded in obliterating this oasis of organized and instructed benevolence. With their wide lawns, their tree-lined walks, their scattering of nondescript buildings, the hospital grounds look like the campus of an unpretentious college. The inmates, unfortunately, could never be mistaken for undergraduates and co-eds. The mind is its own place, and their gait, their posture, the distressed or remotely preoccupied expression of their faces reveal them as the inhabitants of dark worlds, full of confusion, fertile in private terrors. But at least nothing is being done in this green oasis among the jets and the rockets to deepen the confusion or intensify the terrors. On the contrary, much good will and intelligence, much knowledge and skill are going into a concerted effort to transform their isolated, purgatorial universes into something happier and more accessible.

Not long ago a psychiatrist friend took me with him to this oasis. Walking through one of the Disturbed Wards, I found myself suddenly remembering the first occasion on which I had visited a mental hospital. The place was Kashmir, the time more than thirty years ago, and the hospital was actually no hospital, but that part of the local prison which was used for the confinement of maniacs. Naked, unkempt, horribly unwashed, these unfortunates were shut up in cages. Not the spacious enclosures reserved, in zoos, for gibbons and orangutans, but filthy little pens, in which a couple of steps in any direction would bring their occupants to the confining bars. Kashmir is remote, "uncivilized," non-Christian. But let us be in no hurry to flatter ourselves. The horrors I witnessed there, among the Himalayas, were of exactly the same kind as the horrors which my grandfather and his contemporaries could see in any asylum in civilized and Christian England, France or Germany, in civilized and Christian America. Of the many dark and hideous pages of our history, few are more shameful than the record of Western man's treatment of the mentally ill. The story has been told at length in Doctor Gregory Zilboorg's *History of Medical Psychology* and there are whole libraries of books dealing with special periods and particular aspects of the long martyrdom of the insane.

The tormentors of the insane have been drawn, in the main, from two professions—the medical and the clerical. To which shall we award the palm? Have clergymen been responsible for more gratuitous suffering than doctors? Or have doctors made up for a certain lack of intensity in their brand of torture (after all, they never went so far as to burn anyone alive for being mad) by its longer duration and the greater number of the victims to whom it was applied? It is a nice point. To prevent hard feelings, let us divide the prize equally between the contenders.

So far as the mentally sick are concerned, Western history has had only two golden ages. The first lasted from about fifty years before the birth of Christ into the second century of our era; the second began, very hesitantly, in the early years of the nineteenth century and is still continuing. During these golden ages the mentally sick, or at least the more fortunate of them in the more civilized parts of the classical and modern world, were treated with a measure of common decency, as though they were unfortunate human beings. During the intervening centuries they were either ignored, or else systematically tormented, first (on the highest theological grounds) by the clergy, later (for the soundest of medical reasons) by the doctors.

Let us ask ourselves a question. If I had lived in the eighteenth century, and if I had been afflicted by some mental illness, what would have happened to me?

What happened to you in those days depended, first of all, on the financial situation of your family. People with money either locked up their insane relatives in some remote corner of the family mansion, or banished them, with a staff of attendants, to an isolated cottage in the country, or else boarded them out, at considerable expense, in a private madhouse run for profit by a doctor or, under medical supervision, by some glorified jailer. Lunatics confined in the attics (like Mr. Rochester's wife in *Jane Eyre*) or in a country cottage were spared the rigors of medical treatment, which could only be administered in an institution staffed by brawny attendants and equipped with the instruments of coercion. Those who were sent to such an institution were first stripped naked. Mad people were generally kept in a state of partial or complete nudity. Nakedness solved the problem of soiled clothes and contributed, in what was felt to be a most salutary way, to the patient's sense of degradation and inferiority. After being stripped, the patient was shaved, so as to prepare him or her for that part of the treatment which consisted in rubbing various salves into the scalp with a view to soothing or stimulating the brain. Then he or she was taken to a cell, tied down to the bed and locked in for the night. If the patient struggled and screamed, that was a sign of mania; if he reacted with silent resignation, he was obviously suffering from some form of melancholy. In either case he needed treatment and, duly, next morning the treatment was commenced. In the medical literature of the time it was referred to as "Reducing the Patient by Physic." Over a period of eight or ten weeks the victim was repeatedly bled, at least one pound of blood being taken on each occasion. Once a week, or if the doctor thought it advisable at shorter intervals, he or she was given an emetic—a "Brisk Vomit" as our ancestors, with their admirable command of English, liked to call it. The favorite Brisk Vomit was a concoction of the roots of black hellebore. Hellebore had been used in the treatment of the insane since the time of Melampus, a legendary soothsayer, first mentioned by Homer. Taken internally, the toxicologists tell us, hellebore "occasions ringing in the ears, vertigo, stupor, thirst, with a feeling of suffocation, swelling of the tongue and fauces, emesis and catharsis, slowing of the pulse and finally collapse and death from cardiac paralysis. Inspection after death reveals much inflammation of the stomach and intestines, more especially the rectum."

The doses prescribed by the old psychiatrists were too small to be fatal, but quite large enough to produce a dangerous syndrome, known in medical circles as "helleborism." Every administration of the drug resulted in an iatrogenic (doctor-induced) disease of the most distressing and painful kind. One Brisk Vomit was more than enough; there were no volunteers for a second dose. All the later administrations of hellebore had to be forcible. After five or six bouts of helleborism, the time was ripe for purgatives. Senna, rhubarb, sulphur, colocynth, antimony, aloes—blended into Black Draughts or worked up into enormous boluses, these violent cathartics were forced, day after day, down the patient's throat. At the end of the two-month course of bloodlettings, vomits and purges, most psychotics were "reduced by physic" to a point where they were in no condition to give trouble. These reductions were repeated every spring during the patient's incarceration and in the meantime he was kept on a low diet, deficient in proteins, vitamins and even calories. It is a testimony to the amazing toughness of the human species that many psychotics survived under this treatment for decades. Indeed, they did more than survive; in spite of chronic undernourishment and periodical reductions by physic, some of them still found the strength to be violent. The answer to violence was mechanical restraint and corporal punishment. "I have seen," wrote Dorothea Dix in 1848, "more than nine thousand idiots, epileptics and insane in the United States, destitute of appropriate care and protection, bound with galling chains, bowed beneath fetters and heavy iron balls attached to drag chains, lacerated with ropes, scourged with rods and terrified beneath storms of execration and cruel blows." The armamentarium of an English asylum of the Early Victorian period comprised "straitwaistcoats, handcuffs, leg locks, various coarse devices of leather and iron, including gags and horrible screws to force open the mouths of patients who were unwilling or even unable to take food." In the Lancaster Asylum good old-fashioned chains had been ingeniously combined with the very latest in plumbing. In 1840 its two Restraint Rooms were fitted up with "rows of stalled seats serving the double purpose of a water closet and an ordinary seat. The patients were secured, by hand locks to the upper portion of the stalls and by leg locks to the lower portion." The Lancaster lunatics were relatively well off. The toilets to which they were chained guaranteed a certain cleanliness and the newly installed heating system, of which the asylum was justly proud, preserved them from the long-drawn torture-by-freezing, which was the lot, each winter, of the overwhelming majority of mentally sick paupers. For while the private madhouses provided a few of the rudimentary creature comforts, the public asylums and workhouses, in which the psychotic "Objects of Charity" were confined, were simply dungeons. (In official documents the phrase, "Objects of Charity" is abbreviated, and the insane poor are regularly referred to as "Objects.") "I have seen them naked," wrote Esquirol of the Objects in French asylums, "and protected only by straw from the damp, cold pavement on which they were lying." And here is William Tuke's account of what he saw in the lunatic ward of an English workhouse in 1811: "The poor women were absolutely without any clothes. The weather was intensely cold, and the evening previous to our visit the thermometer had been sixteen degrees below freezing. One of these forlorn Objects lay buried under a miserable covering of straw, without a blanket or even a horsecloth to defend her from the cold." The feet of chained lunatics often became frostbitten. From frostbite to gangrene was a short step, and from gangrene through amputation to death was only a little longer.

Lunatics were not merely confined. Attempts were even made to cure them. The procedures by which patients were reduced to physical exhaustion were also supposed to restore them to sanity. Psychoses were thought to be due to an imbalance between the four humors of the body, together with a local excess or deficiency of the vital and animal spirits. The bloodlettings, the vomits and the purges were intended to rid the viscera and the circulatory system of peccant humors, and at the same time to relieve the pressure of the animal spirits upon the brain. Physical treatment was supplemented by psychological treatment. This last was based upon the universally accepted principle that the most effective cure for insanity is terror. Boerhaave, the most influential medical teacher of the first half of the eighteenth century, instructed his pupils "to throw the Patient into the Sea, and to keep him under for as long as he can possibly bear without being stifled." In the intervals between duckings the mentally sick were to be kept in constant fear by the threat of punishment. The simplest and handiest form of punishment is beating, and beating, in consequence, was regularly resorted to. During his psychotic episodes even George III was beaten—with the permission, of course, of his Privy Council and both Houses of Parliament. But beating "was only one form, and that the slightest, of cruelty toward the insane." (I quote the words of the great French reformer, Doctor Pinel.) "The inventions to give pain were truly marvelous." Thus an eminent German doctor had devised a therapeutic punishment, which consisted in tying a rope about the patient's middle, hoisting him to a great height and then lowering him very rapidly, so that he should have the sensation of falling, into a dark cellar, "which was to be all the better if it could be stocked with serpents." A very similar torture is minutely described by the Marquis de Sade, the heroine of whose novel, *Justine,* is punished for being virtuous (among many other ways) by being dangled halfway down a shaft opening into a cavern full of rats and corpses,

while her tormentor of the moment keeps threatening, from above, to cut the
rope. That this fiendish notion should have occurred not only to the most
famous psychotic of the period, but also to one of its leading psychiatrists,
throws a revealing light on our ancestors' attitude toward the mentally sick.
In relation to these predestined victims sadistic behavior was right and proper,
so much so that it could be publicly avowed and rationalized in terms of cur-
ent scientific theories.

So much for what would have happened to me, if I had become
mentally sick in the eighteenth, or even the first half of the nineteenth,
century. If I had lived in the sixteenth century, my fate might have been even
worse. For in the sixteenth century most of the symptoms of mental illness
were regarded as supernatural in origin. For example, the pathological refusal
or inability to speak was held to be a sure sign of diabolic possession. Mutism
was frequently punished by the infliction of torture and death at the stake.
Dumb devils are mentioned in the Gospels; but the evangelists made no mention of another hysterical symptom, localized insensibility to pain. Unfortunately for the mentally ill, the Early Fathers noticed this curious phenomenon. For them, the insensitive spots on the body of a mentally sick person
were "the Devil's stigmata," the marks with which Satan branded his human
cattle. In the sixteenth century anyone suspected of witchcraft would be
systematically pricked with an awl or bodkin. If an insensitive spot were
found, it was clear that the victim was allied with the devil and must therefore be tortured and burned alive. Again, some mentally sick persons hear
voices, see visions of sinister figures, have phantasies of omnipotence or
alternatively of persecution, believe themselves to be capable of flying, of
being subject to metamorphosis into animals. In the sixteenth century these common symptoms of mental derangement were treated as so
many statements of objective fact, so many confessions, explicit or implicit,
of collaboration with the Enemy. But, obviously, anyone who collaborated
with the Devil had to be tortured and burned alive. And what about the
neurotics, particularly the female neurotics, who suffer from sexual illusions.
"All witchcraft," proclaim the learned clerical authors of the *Malleus Male-
ficarum,* the standard textbook for sixteenth-century inquisitors and magistrates, "all witchcraft comes from carnal lust, which in women is insatiable."
From this it followed that any disturbed woman, whose sexual daydreams
were more than ordinarily vivid, was having relations with an Incubus. But an
Incubus is a devil. Therefore she too must be tortured and burned alive.

Doctor Johann Weier, who has been called the Father of Psychiatry,
had the humanity, courage and common sense to assail the theories and
hellish practices of the Catholic theologians and magistrates, and the no-less-

ferocious Protestant witch-hunters of his time. But the majority even of well-educated men approved the crimes and follies of the Church. For having ventured to treat the witches' confessions as symptoms of mental illness, Weier was regarded as a diabolical fellow traveler, even a full-blown sorcerer. That he was not arrested, tortured and burned was due to the fact that he was the personal physician of a ruling prince. Weier died in his bed; but his book was placed on the Index, and the persecution of the mentally ill continued, unabated, for another century. How many witches were tortured and burned during the sixteenth century is not exactly known. The total number is variously estimated at anything from one hundred thousand to several millions. Many of the victims were perfectly sane adherents of the old fertility cult which still lingered on in every part of Europe. Of the rest, some were persons incriminated by informers, some the unhappy victims of a mental illness. "If we took the whole of the population of our present-day hospitals for mental diseases," writes Dr. Zilboorg, "and if we sorted out the cases of dementia praecox, some of the senile psychoses, some of those afflicted with general paralysis, and some of the so-called involution melancholies, we should see that Bodin (the great French jurist, who denounced Dr. Weier as a sorcerer and heretic) would not have hesitated to plead for their death at the stake, so similar and characteristic are their trends to those he describes. It is truly striking that the ideational contents of the mental diseases of four hundred years ago are so similar to those of today."

In the second half of the seventeenth century the mentally sick ceased to be the prey of the clergy and the theologically minded lawyers, and were left instead to the tender mercies of the doctors. The crimes and follies committed in the name of Galen were, as we have seen, almost as monstrous as those committed at an earlier period in the name of God. Improvement came at last in the closing years of the eighteenth century, and was due to the efforts of a few nonconforming individuals, some of them doctors, others outside the pale of medicine. These nonconformists did their work in the teeth of official indifference, sometimes of active official resistance. As corporations, neither the Church nor the medical profession ever initiated any reform in the treatment of the mentally sick. Obscure priests and nuns had often cared for the insane with kindness and understanding; but the theological bigwigs thought of mental illness in terms of diabolic possession, heresy and apostasy. It was the same with the medical bigwigs. Strait jackets, Brisk Vomits and systematic terrorism remained the official medical policy until well into the nineteenth century. It was only tardily and reluctantly that the bigwigs accepted the reforms initiated by heroic nonconformists, and officially changed their old, bad tune.

Reform began almost simultaneously on either side of the Channel. In England a Quaker merchant, William Tuke, set up the York Retreat, a hospital for the mentally sick, in which restraint was never used and the psychological treatment was aimed, not at frightening the patients, but at bringing them back from their isolation by persuading them to work, play, eat, talk and worship together. In France the pioneer in reform was Doctor Philippe Pinel, who was appointed to the direction of the Bicêtre Asylum in Paris at the height of the French Revolution. Many of the patients were kept permanently chained in unlighted cells. Pinel asked permission of the revolutionary government to set them free. It was refused. Liberty, Equality and Fraternity were not for lunatics. Pinel insisted, and at last permission was grudgingly given. The account of what followed is touching in the extreme. "The first man on whom the experiment was tried was an English captain, whose history no one knew, as he had been in chains for forty years. He was thought to be one of the most furious among them. His keepers approached him with caution, as he had in a fit of fury killed one of them on the spot with a blow from his manacles. He was chained more rigorously than any of the others. Pinel entered his cell unattended and calmly said to him, 'Captain, I will order your chains to be taken off and give you liberty to walk in the court, if you will promise me to behave well and injure no one.' 'Yes, I promise,' said the maniac. 'But you are laughing at me. . . .' His chains were removed and the keepers retired, leaving the door of his cell open. He raised himself many times from the seat, but fell again on it; for he had been in a sitting posture so long that he had lost the use of his legs. In a quarter of an hour he succeeded in maintaining his balance and with tottering steps came to the door of his dark cell. His first look was at the sky, and he exclaimed, 'How beautiful, how beautiful!' During the rest of the day he was constantly in motion, uttering exclamations of delight. In the evening he returned of his own accord to his cell and slept tranquilly."

In Europe the pioneer work of Tuke and Pinel was continued by Conolly, Esquirol and a growing number of their followers in every country. In America, the standard bearer of reform was a heroic woman, Dorothea Dix. By the middle of the century many of the worst abominations of the old regime were things of the past. The mentally ill began to be treated as unfortunate human beings, not as Objects. It was an immense advance; but it was not yet enough. Reform had produced institutional care, but still no adequate treatment. For most nineteenth-century doctors, things were more real than thoughts and the study of matter seemed more scientific than the study of mind. The dream of Victorian medicine was, in Zilboorg's phrase, to develop a psychiatry that should be completely independent of psychology. Hence the widespread and passionate rejection of the procedures lumped under the names of Animal Magnetism and Hypnotism. In France, Charcot, Liébault and Bernheim achieved remarkable results with hypnosis; but the intellectually respectable psychiatrists of Europe and America turned their backs on this merely psychological treatment of mental illness and concentrated instead on the more "objective," the more "scientific" methods of surgery.

It had all happened before, of course. Cutting holes in the skull was an immemorially ancient form of psychiatry. So was castration, as a cure for epilepsy. Continuing this grand old tradition, the Victorian doctors removed the ovaries of their hysterical patients and treated neurosis in young girls by the gruesome operation known to ethnologists as "female circumcision." In the early years of the present century Metchnikoff was briefly a prophet, and autointoxication was all the rage in medical circles. Along with practically every other disease, neuroses were supposed to be due to intestinal stasis. No intestine, no stasis—what could be more logical? The lucky neurotics who could afford a major operation went to hospital, had their colons cut out and the end of their small intestines stitched to the stump. Those who recovered found themselves with yet another reason for being neurotic: they had to hurry to the bathroom six or eight times a day. Intestinal stasis went out with the hobble skirt, and the new vogue was focal infection. According to the surgical psychiatrists, people were neurotic not because of conflicts in their unconscious mind, but because of inflammation in their tonsils or abscesses at the roots of their teeth. The dentists, the nose-and-throat men set to work with a will. Toothless and tonsilectomized, the neurotics, needless to say, went on behaving just as neurotically as ever. Focal infections followed intestinal stasis into oblivion, and the surgical psychiatrists now prefer to make a direct assault upon the brain. The current fashion is shock treatment or, on great occasions, prefrontal lobotomy. Meanwhile the pharmacologists have not been idle. The barbiturates, hailed not so long ago as panaceas, have given place to Chlorpromazine, Reserpine, Frenquel and Miltown. Insofar as they facilitate the specifically psychological treatment of mental disorders, these tranquilizers may prove to be extremely valuable. Even as symptom stoppers they have their uses.

The green oasis among the jets and the rockets is crammed to overflowing. So are all the other mental hospitals of the Western world. Technological and economic progress seems to have been accompanied by psychological regress. The incidence of neuroses and psychoses is apparently on the increase. Still larger hospitals, yet kinder treatment of patients, more psychiatrists and better pills—we need them all and need them urgently. But they will not solve our problem. In this field prevention is incomparably more important than cure; for cure merely returns the patient to an environment which begets mental illness. But how is prevention to be achieved? That is the sixty-four-billion-dollar question.

### I. Suggestions for Discussion:
1. Describe the treatment of the mentally ill in the eighteenth century. Are Huxley's illustrations and examples well chosen? Explain.
2. How did the Church view the mentally ill in the sixteenth century?
3. Compare and contrast Huxley's descriptions of conditions for the mentally ill with Jessica Mitford's description of conditions for women prisoners in "Women in Cages," p. 399.

### II. Suggestions for Writing:
1. Write an essay explaining your views on how to reduce mental illness in our society.
2. Read and write about one of the prominent reformers in the treatment of mentally ill mentioned by Huxley.

---

# THOMAS HENRY HUXLEY

## A Liberal Education; and Where to Find It

### from *Science and Education*

---

Thomas Henry Huxley (1825–1895) was an English philosophical and religious thinker. He coined the word "agnostic" to express his own philosophical attitudes.

In the following long, discursive, clearly written essay, which was originally presented as a speech in 1868 and later published in *Science and Education,* Huxley reviews the school and university curriculum in Victorian England and finds it woefully inadequate. He then proposes in detail the essentials of a modern liberal education. Note, particularly, the famous passage on life as a game of chess.

---

The business which the South London Working Men's College has undertaken is a great work; indeed, I might say, that Education, with which that college proposes to grapple, is the greatest work of all those which lie ready to a man's hand just at present.

And, at length, this fact is becoming generally recognised. You cannot go anywhere without hearing a buzz of more or less confused and contra-dictory talk on this subject—nor can you fail to notice that, in one point at any rate, there is a very decided advance upon like discussions in former days. Nobody outside the agricultural interest now dares to say that education is a bad thing. If any representative of the once large and powerful party, which, in former days, proclaimed this opinion, still exists in the semi-fossil state, he keeps his thoughts to himself. In fact, there is a chorus of voices, almost distressing in their harmony, raised in favour of the doctrine that education is the great panacea for human troubles, and that, if the country is not shortly to go to the dogs, everybody must be educated.

The politicians tell us, 'You must educate the masses because they are going to be masters.' The clergy join in the cry for education, for they affirm that the people are drifting away from church and chapel into the broadest infidelity. The manufacturers and the capitalists swell the chorus lustily. They declare that ignorance makes bad workmen; that England will soon be unable to turn out cotton goods, or steam engines, cheaper than other people; and then, Ichabod! Ichabod! the glory will be departed from us. And a few voices are lifted up in favour of the doctrine that the masses should be educated because they are men and women with unlimited capacities of being, doing, and suffering, and that it is as true now, as it ever was, that the people perish for lack of knowledge.

These members of the minority, with whom I confess I have a good deal of sympathy, are doubtful whether any of the other reasons urged in favour of the education of the people are of much value—whether, indeed, some of them are based upon either wise or noble grounds of action. They question if it be wise to tell people that you will do for them, out of fear of their power, what you have left undone, so long as your only motive was compassion for their weakness and their sorrows. And, if ignorance of every-thing which is needful a ruler should know is likely to do so much harm in the governing classes of the future, why is it, they ask reasonably enough, that such ignorance in the governing classes of the past has not been viewed with equal horror?

Compare the average artisan and the average country squire, and it may be doubted if you will find a pin to choose between the two in point of ignorance, class feeling, or prejudice. It is true that the ignorance is of a different sort—that the class feeling is in favour of a different class—and that the prejudice has a distinct savour of wrong-headedness in each case—but it is questionable if the one is either a bit better, or a bit worse, than the other. The old protectionist theory is the doctrine of trades unions as applied by the squires, and the modern trades unionism is the doctrine of the squires applied by the artisans. Why should we be worse off under one *régime* than under the other?

Again, this sceptical minority asks the clergy to think whether it is really want of education which keeps the masses away from their ministrations—whether the most completely educated men are not as open to reproach on this score as the workmen; and whether, perchance, this may not indicate that it is not education which lies at the bottom of the matter?

Once more, these people, whom there is no pleasing, venture to doubt whether the glory which rests upon being able to undersell all the rest of the world, is a very safe kind of glory—whether we may not purchase it too dear; especially if we allow education, which ought to be directed to the making of men, to be diverted into a process of manufacturing human tools, wonderfully adroit in the exercise of some technical industry, but good for nothing else.

And, finally, these people inquire whether it is the masses alone who need a reformed and improved education. They ask whether the richest of our public schools[1] might not well be made to supply knowledge, as well as gentlemanly habits, a strong class feeling, and eminent proficiency in cricket. They seem to think that the noble foundations of our old universities are hardly fulfilling their functions in their present posture of half-clerical seminaries, half racecourses, where men are trained to win a senior wranglership, or a double-first,[2] as horses are trained to win a cup, with as little reference to the needs of after-life in the case of a man as in that of the racer. And, while as zealous for education as the rest, they affirm that, if the education of the richer classes were such as to fit them to be the leaders and the governors of the poorer; and, if the education of the poorer classes were such as to enable them to appreciate really wise guidance and good governance, the politicians need not fear mob-law, nor the clergy lament their want of flocks, nor the capitalists prognosticate the annihilation of the prosperity of the country.

Such is the diversity of opinion upon the why and the wherefore of education. And my hearers will be prepared to expect that the practical recommendations which are put forward are not less discordant. There is a

---

[1] "Public schools," in England mean private schools like Rugby and Eton.
[2] Highest honors in mathematics or in both mathematics and classics.

loud cry for compulsory education. We English, in spite of constant experience to the contrary, preserve a touching faith in the efficacy of acts of Parliament; and I believe we should have compulsory education in the courses of next session, if there were the least probability that half a dozen leading statesmen of different parties would agree what that education should be.

Some hold that education without theology is worse than none. Others maintain, quite as strongly, that education with theology is in the same predicament. But this is certain, that those who hold the first opinion can by no means agree what theology should be taught; and that those who maintain the second are in a small minority.

At any rate 'make people learn to read, write, and cipher,' say a great many; and the advice is undoubtedly sensible as far as it goes. But, as has happened to me in former days, those who, in despair of getting anything better, advocate this measure, are met with the objection that it is very like making a child practise the use of a knife, fork, and spoon, without giving it a particle of meat. I really don't know what reply is to be made to such an objection.

But it would be unprofitable to spend more time in disentangling, or rather in showing up the knots in, the ravelled skeins of our neighbours. Much more to the purpose is it to ask if we possess any clue of our own which may guide us among these entanglements. And by way of a beginning, let us ask ourselves—What is education? Above all things, what is our ideal of a thoroughly liberal education?—of that education which, if we could begin life again, we would give ourselves—of that education which, if we could mould the fates to our own will, we would give our children? Well, I know not what may be your conceptions upon this matter, but I will tell you mine, and I hope I shall find that our views are not very discrepant.

Suppose it were perfectly certain that the life and fortune of every one of us would, one day or other, depend upon his winning or losing a game of chess. Don't you think that we should all consider it to be a primary duty to learn at least the names and the moves of the pieces; to have a notion of a gambit[3] and a keen eye for all the means of giving and getting out of check? Do you not think that we should look with a disapprobation amounting to scorn, upon the father who allowed his son, or the state which allowed its members, to grow up without knowing a pawn from a knight?

Yet it is a very plain and elementary truth, that the life, the fortune, and the happiness of every one of us, and, more or less, of those who are connected with us, do depend upon our knowing something of the rules of a game infinitely more difficult and complicated than chess. It is a game which

[3] An opening play in chess.

has been played for untold ages, every man and woman of us being one of the two players in a game of his or her own. The chessboard is the world, the pieces are the phenomena of the universe, the rules of the game are what we call the laws of Nature. The player on the other side is hidden from us. We know that his play is always fair, just, and patient. But also we know, to our cost, that he never overlooks a mistake, or makes the smallest allowance for ignorance. To the man who plays well, the highest stakes are paid, with that sort of overflowing generosity with which the strong shows delight in strength. And one who plays ill is checkmated—without haste, but without remorse.

My metaphor will remind some of you of the famous picture in which Retzsch[4] has depicted Satan playing at chess with man for his soul. Substitute for the mocking fiend in that picture a calm, strong angel who is playing for love, as we say, and would rather lose than win—and I should accept it as an image of human life.

Well, what I mean by Education is learning the rules of this mighty game. In other words, education is the instruction of the intellect in the laws of Nature, under which name I include not merely things and their forces, but men and their ways; and the fashioning of the affections and of the will into an earnest and loving desire to move in harmony with those laws. For me, education means neither more nor less than this. Anything which professes to call itself education must be tried by this standard, and if it fails to stand the test, I will not call it education, whatever may be the force of authority, or of numbers, upon the other side.

It is important to remember that, in strictness, there is no such thing as an uneducated man. Take an extreme case. Suppose that an adult man, in the full vigour of his faculties, could be suddenly placed in the world, as Adam is said to have been, and then left to do as he best might. How long would he be left uneducated? Not five minutes. Nature would begin to teach him, through the eye, the ear, the touch, the properties of objects. Pain and pleasure would be at his elbow telling him to do this and avoid that; and by slow degrees the man would receive an education which, if narrow, would be thorough, real, and adequate to his circumstances, though there would be no extras and very few accomplishments.

And if to this solitary man entered a second Adam or, better still, an Eve, a new and greater world, that of social and moral phenomena, would be revealed. Joys and woes, compared with which all others might seem but faint shadows, would spring from the new relations. Happiness and sorrow would take the place of the coarser monitors, pleasure and pain; but conduct

---

[4] Friedrich August Moritz Retzsch (1779-1856) was a German artist.

would still be shaped by the observation of the natural consequences of actions; or, in other words, by the laws of the nature of man.

To every one of us the world was once as fresh and new as to Adam. And then, long before we were susceptible of any other mode of instruction, Nature took us in hand, and every minute of waking life brought its educational influence, shaping our actions into rough accordance with Nature's laws, so that we might not be ended untimely by too gross disobedience. Nor should I speak of this process of education as past for any one, be he as old as he may. For every man the world is as fresh as it was at the first day, and as full of untold novelties for him who has the eyes to see them. And Nature is still continuing her patient education of us in that great university, the universe, of which we are all members—Nature having no Test-Acts.

Those who take honours in Nature's university, who learn the laws which govern men and things and obey them, are the really great and successful men in this world. The great mass of mankind are the 'Poll,'[5] who pick up just enough to get through without much discredit. Those who won't learn at all are plucked; and then you can't come up again. Nature's pluck means extermination.

Thus the question of compulsory education is settled so far as Nature is concerned. Her bill on that question was framed and passed long ago. But, like all compulsory legislation, that of Nature is harsh and wasteful in its operation. Ignorance is visited as sharply as wilful disobedience—incapacity meets with the same punishment as crime. Nature's discipline is not even a word and a blow, and the blow first; but the blow without the word. It is left to you to find out why your ears are boxed.

The object of what we commonly call education—that education in which man intervenes and which I shall distinguish as artificial education—is to make good these defects in Nature's methods; to prepare the child to receive Nature's education, neither incapably nor ignorantly, nor with wilful disobedience; and to understand the preliminary symptoms of her pleasure, without waiting for the box on the ear. In short, all artificial education ought to be an anticipation of natural education. And a liberal education is an artificial education which has not only prepared a man to escape the great evils of disobedience to natural laws, but has trained him to appreciate and to seize upon the rewards, which Nature scatters with as free a hand as her penalties.

That man, I think, has had a liberal education who has been so trained in youth that his body is the ready servant of his will, and does with ease and

[5] The mass of students.

pleasure all the work that, as a mechanism, it is capable of; whose intellect is a clear, cold, logic engine, with all its parts of equal strength, and in smooth working order; ready, like a steam engine, to be turned to any kind of work, and spin the gossamers as well as forge the anchors of the mind; whose mind is stored with a knowledge of the great and fundamental truths of Nature and of the laws of her operations; one who, no stunted ascetic, is full of life and fire, but whose passions are trained to come to heel by a vigorous will, the servant of a tender conscience; who has learned to love all beauty, whether of Nature or of art, to hate all vileness, and to respect others as himself.

Such an one and no other, I conceive, has had a liberal education; for he is, as completely as a man can be, in harmony with Nature. He will make the best of her, and she of him. They will get on together rarely; she as his ever beneficent mother; he as her mouthpiece, her conscious self, her minister and interpreter.

Where is such an education as this to be had? Where is there any approximation to it? Has any one tried to found such an education? Looking over the length and breadth of these islands, I am afraid that all these questions must receive a negative answer. Consider our primary schools and what is taught in them. A child learns:—

1. To read, write, and cipher, more or less well; but in a very large proportion of cases not so well as to take pleasure in reading, or to be able to write the commonest letter properly.

2. A quantity of dogmatic theology, of which the child, nine times out of ten, understands next to nothing.

3. Mixed up with this, so as to seem to stand or fall with it, a few of the broadest and simplest principles of morality. This, to my mind, is much as if a man of science should make the story of the fall of the apple in Newton's garden an integral part of the doctrine of gravitation, and teach it as of equal authority with the law of the inverse squares.

4. A good deal of Jewish history and Syrian geography, and, perhaps, a little something about English history and the geography of the child's own country. But I doubt if there is a primary school in England in which hangs a map of the hundred in which the village lies, so that the children may be practically taught by it what a map means.

5. A certain amount of regularity, attentive obedience, respect for others: obtained by fear, if the master be incompetent or foolish; by love and reverence, if he be wise.

So far as this school course embraces a training in the theory and practice of obedience to the moral laws of Nature, I gladly admit, not only that it contains a valuable educational element, but that, so far, it deals with the most valuable and important part of all education. Yet, contrast what is done in this direction with what might be done; with the time given to matters of comparatively no importance; with the absence of any attention to things of the highest moment; and one is tempted to think of Falstaff's bill and 'the halfpenny worth of bread to all that quantity of sack.'

Let us consider what a child thus 'educated' knows, and what it does not know. Begin with the most important topic of all—morality, as the guide of conduct. The child knows well enough that some acts meet with approbation and some with disapprobation. But it has never heard that there lies in the nature of things a reason for every moral law, as cogent and as well defined as that which underlies every physical law; that stealing and lying are just as certain to be followed by evil consequences, as putting your hand in the fire, or jumping out of a garret window. Again, though the scholar may have been made acquainted, in dogmatic fashion, with the broad laws of morality, he has had no training in the application of those laws to the difficult problems which result from the complex conditions of modern civilisation. Would it not be very hard to expect any one to solve a problem in conic sections who had merely been taught the axioms and definitions of mathematical science?

A workman has to bear hard labour, and perhaps privation, while he sees others rolling in wealth, and feeding their dogs with what would keep his children from starvation. Would it not be well to have helped that man to calm the natural promptings of discontent by showing him, in his youth, the necessary connexion of the moral law which prohibits stealing with the stability of society—by proving to him, once for all, that it is better for his own people, better for himself, better for future generations, that he should starve than steal? If you have no foundation of knowledge, or habit of thought, to work upon, what chance have you of persuading a hungry man that a capitalist is not a thief 'with a circumbendibus?'[6] And if he honestly believes that, of what avail is it to quote the commandment against stealing, when he proposes to make the capitalist disgorge?

Again, the child learns absolutely nothing of the history or the political organisation of his own country. His general impression is, that everything of much importance happened a very long while ago; and that the Queen and the gentlefolks govern the country much after the fashion of King David and the elders and nobles of Israel—his sole models. Will you give a man with this much information a vote? In easy times he sells it for a pot of beer. Why

[6] A thief by any other name.

should he not? It is of about as much use to him as a chignon, and he knows as much what to do with it, for any other purpose. In bad times, on the contrary, he applies his simple theory of government, and believes that his rulers are the cause of his sufferings—a belief which sometimes bears remarkable practical fruits.

Least of all, does the child gather from this primary 'education' of ours a conception of the laws of the physical world, or of the relations of cause and effect therein. And this is the more to be lamented, as the poor are especially exposed to physical evils, and are more interested in removing them than any other class of the community. If any one is concerned in knowing the ordinary laws of mechanics one would think it is the hand-labourer, whose daily toil lies among levers and pulleys; or among the other implements of artisan work. And if any one is interested in the laws of health, it is the poor workman, whose strength is wasted by ill-prepared food, whose health is sapped by bad ventilation and bad drainage, and half whose children are massacred by disorders which might be prevented. Not only does our present primary education carefully abstain from hinting to the workman that some of his greatest evils are traceable to mere physical agencies, which could be removed by energy, patience, and frugality; but it does worse—it renders him, so far as it can, deaf to those who could help him, and tries to substitute an Oriental submission to what is falsely declared to be the will of God, for his natural tendency to strive after a better condition.

What wonder then, if very recently, an appeal has been made to statistics for the profoundly foolish purpose of showing that education is of no good—that it diminishes neither misery, nor crime, among the masses of mankind? I reply, why should the thing which has been called education do either the one or the other? If I am a knave or a fool, teaching me to read and write won't make me less of either one or the other—unless somebody shows me how to put my reading and writing to wise and good purposes.

Suppose any one were to argue that medicine is of no use, because it could be proved statistically, that the percentage of deaths was just the same, among people who had been taught how to open a medicine chest, and among those who did not so much as know the key by sight. The argument is absurd; but it is not more preposterous than that against which I am contending. The only medicine for suffering, crime, and all the other woes of mankind, is wisdom. Teach a man to read and write, and you have put into his hands the great keys of the wisdom box. But it is quite another matter whether he ever opens the box or not. And he is as likely to poison as to cure himself, if, without guidance, he swallows the first drug that comes to hand. In these times a man may as well be purblind, as unable to read—lame, as unable to write. But I protest that, if I thought the alternative were a necessary one, I would rather that the children of the poor should grow up ignorant of both these mighty arts, than that they should remain ignorant of that knowledge to which these arts are means.

It may be said that all these animadversions may apply to primary schools, but that the higher schools, at any rate, must be allowed to give a liberal education. In fact, they professedly sacrifice everything else to this object.

Let us inquire into this matter. What do the higher schools, those to which the great middle class of the country sends its children, teach, over and above the instruction given in the primary schools? There is a little more reading and writing of English. But, for all that, every one knows that it is a rare thing to find a boy of the middle or upper classes who can read aloud decently, or who can put his thoughts on paper in clear and grammatical (to say nothing of good or elegant) language. The 'ciphering' of the lower schools expands into elementary mathematics in the higher; into arithmetic, with a little algebra, a little Euclid.[7] But I doubt if one boy in five hundred has ever heard the explanation of a rule of arithmetic, or knows his Euclid otherwise than by rote.

Of theology, the middle class schoolboy gets rather less than poorer children, less absolutely and less relatively, because there are so many other claims upon his attention. I venture to say that, in the great majority of cases, his ideas on this subject when he leaves school are of the most shadowy and vague description, and associated with painful impressions of the weary hours spent in learning collects and catechism by heart.

Modern geography, modern history, modern literature; the English language, as a language; the whole circle of the sciences, physical, moral, and social, are even more completely ignored in the higher than in the lower schools. Up till within a few years back, a boy might have passed through any one of the great public schools with the greatest distinction and credit, and might never so much as have heard of one of the subjects I have just mentioned. He might never have heard that the earth goes round the sun; that England underwent a great revolution in 1688, and France another in 1789; that there once lived certain notable men called Chaucer, Shakespeare, Milton, Voltaire, Goethe, Schiller. The first might be a German and the last an Englishman for anything he could tell you to the contrary. And as for science, the only idea the word would suggest to his mind would be dexterity in boxing.

I have said that this was the state of things a few years back, for the sake of the few righteous who are to be found among the educational cities

---

[7]Euclid (323–283 B.C.) wrote the first systematic geometry.

of the plain. But I would not have you too sanguine about the result, if you sound the minds of the existing generation of public schoolboys, on such topics as those I have mentioned.

Now let us pause to consider this wonderful state of affairs; for the time will come when Englishmen will quote it as the stock example of the stolid stupidity of their ancestors in the nineteenth century. The most thoroughly commercial people, the greatest voluntary wanderers and colonists the world has ever seen, are precisely the middle classes of this country. If there be a people which has been busy making history on the great scale for the last three hundred years—and the most profoundly interesting history—history which, if it happened to be that of Greece or Rome, we should study with avidity—it is the English. If there be a people which, during the same period, has developed a remarkable literature, it is our own. If there be a nation whose prosperity depends absolutely and wholly upon their mastery over the forces of Nature, upon their intelligent apprehension of, and obedience to, the laws of the creation and distribution of wealth, and of the stable equilibrium of the forces of society, it is precisely this nation. And yet this is what these wonderful people tell their sons:—'At the cost of from one to two thousand pounds of our hard earned money, we devote twelve of the most precious years of your lives to school. There you shall toil, or be supposed to toil; but there you shall not learn one single thing of all those you will most want to know, directly you leave school and enter upon the practical business of life. You will in all probability go into business, but you shall not know where, or how, any article of commerce is produced, or the difference between an export or an import, or the meaning of the word "capital." You will very likely settle in a colony, but you shall not know whether Tasmania is part of New South Wales, or *vice versa.*

'Very probably you may become a manufacturer, but you shall not be provided with the means of understanding the working of one of your own steam-engines, or the nature of the raw products you employ; and, when you are asked to buy a patent, you shall not have the slightest means of judging whether the inventor is an imposter who is contravening the elementary principles of science, or a man who will make you as rich as Croesus.

'You will very likely get into the House of Commons. You will have to take your share in making laws which may prove a blessing or a curse to millions of men. But you shall not hear one word respecting the political organisation of your country; the meaning of the controversy between free traders and protectionists shall never have been mentioned to you; you shall not so much as know that there are such things as economical laws.

'The mental power which will be of most importance in your daily life will be the power of seeing things as they are without regard to authority; and

of drawing accurate general conclusions from particular facts. But at school
and at college you shall know of no source of truth but authority; nor exercise your reasoning faculty upon anything but deduction from that which is
laid down by authority.

'You will have to weary your soul with work, and many a time eat your
bread in sorrow and in bitterness, and you shall not have learned to take
refuge in the great source of pleasure without alloy, the serene resting place
for worn human nature,—the world of art.'

Said I not rightly that we are a wonderful people? I am quite prepared
to allow, that education entirely devoted to these omitted subjects might not
be a completely liberal education. But is an education which ignores them all,
a liberal education? Nay, is it too much to say that the education which
should embrace these subjects and no others, would be a real education,
though an incomplete one; while an education which omits them is really not
an education at all, but a more or less useful course of intellectual gymnastics?

For what does the middle-class school put in the place of all these
things which are left out? It substitutes what is usually comprised under the
compendious title of the 'classics'—that is to say, the languages, the literature,
and the history of the ancient Greeks and Romans, and the geography of so
much of the world as was known to these two great nations of antiquity.
Now, do not expect me to depreciate the earnest and enlightened pursuit of
classical learning. I have not the least desire to speak ill of such occupations,
nor any sympathy with those who run them down. On the contrary, if my
opportunities had lain in that direction, there is no investigation into which
I could have thrown myself with greater delight than that of antiquity.

What science can present greater attractions than philology? How can a
lover of literary excellence fail to rejoice in the ancient masterpieces? And
with what consistency could I, whose business lies so much in the attempt to
decipher the past, and to build up intelligible forms out of the scattered fragments of long-extinct beings, fail to take a sympathetic, though an unlearned,
interest in the labours of a Niebuhr, a Gibbon, or a Grote?[8] Classical history
is a great section of the palaeontology of man; and I have the same double
respect for it as for other kinds of palaeontology—that is to say, a respect for
the facts which it establishes as for all facts, and a still greater respect for it
as a preparation for the discovery of a law of progress.

But if the classics were taught as they might be taught—if boys and

[8] Barthold Georg Niebuhr (1776–1831), Edward Gibbon (1737–1794), and George Grote
(1794–1871) were well-known historians.

girls were instructed in Greek and Latin, not merely as languages, but as illustrations of philological science; if a vivid picture of life on the shores of the Mediterranean, two thousand years ago, were imprinted on the minds of scholars; if ancient history were taught, not as a weary series of feuds and fights, but traced to its causes in such men placed under such conditions; if, lastly, the study of the classical books were followed in such a manner as to impress boys with their beauties, and with the grand simplicity of their statement of the everlasting problems of human life, instead of with their verbal and grammatical peculiarities; I still think it as little proper that they should form the basis of a liberal education for our contemporaries, as I should think it fitting to make that sort of palaeontology with which I am familiar, the back-bone of modern education.

It is wonderful how close a parallel to classical training could be made out of that palæontology to which I refer. In the first place I could get up an osteological primer so arid, so pedantic in its terminology, so altogether distasteful to the youthful mind, as to beat the recent famous production of the head-masters out of the field in all these excellences. Next, I could exercise my boys upon easy fossils, and bring out all their powers of memory and all their ingenuity in the application of my osteogrammatical rules to the interpretation, or construing, of those fragments. To those who had reached the higher classes, I might supply odd bones to be built up into animals, giving great honour and reward to him who succeeded in fabricating monsters most entirely in accordance with the rules. That would answer to verse-making and easy-writing in the dead languages.

To be sure, if a great comparative anatomist were to look at these fabrications he might shake his head, or laugh. But what then? Would such a catastrophe destroy the parallel. What think you would Cicero, or Horace, say to the production of the best sixth form[9] going? And would not Terence[10] stop his ears and run out if he could be present at an English performance of his own plays? Would Hamlet, in the mouths of a set of French actors, who should insist on pronouncing English after the fashion of their own tongue, be more hideously ridiculous?

But it will be said that I am forgetting the beauty, and the human interest, which appertain to classical studies. To this I reply that it is only a very strong man who can appreciate the charms of a landscape, as he is toiling up a steep hill, along a bad road. What with short-windedness, stones, ruts, and a

[9] Senior class.
[10] Publius Terentius Afer (185–159 B.C.) wrote Latin comedies.

pervading sense of the wisdom of rest and be thankful, most of us have little enough sense of the beautiful under these circumstances. The ordinary schoolboy is precisely in this case. He finds Parnassus uncommonly steep, and there is no chance of his having much time or inclination to look about him till he gets to the top. And nine times out of ten he does not get to the top.

But if this be a fair picture of the results of classical teaching at its best—and I gather from those who have authority to speak on such matters that it is so—what is to be said of classical teaching at its worst, or in other words, of the classics of our ordinary middle-class schools? I will tell you. It means getting up endless forms and rules by heart. It means turning Latin and Greek into English, for the mere sake of being able to do it, and without the smallest regard to the worth, or worthlessness, of the author read. It means the learning of innumerable, not always decent, fables in such a shape that the meaning they once had is dried up into utter trash; and the only impression left upon a boy's mind is, that the people who believed such things must have been the greatest idiots the world ever saw. And it means, finally, that after a dozen years spent at this kind of work, the sufferer shall be incompe-tent to interpret a passage in an author he has not already got up; that he shall loathe the sight of a Greek or Latin book; and that he shall never open, or think of, a classical writer again, until, wonderful to relate, he insists upon submitting his sons to the same process.

These be your gods, O Israel! For the sake of this net result (and re-spectability) the British father denies his children all the knowledge they might turn to account in life, not merely for the achievement of vulgar suc-cess, but for guidance in the great crises of human existence. This is the stone he offers to those whom he is bound by the strongest and tenderest ties to feed with bread.

If primary and secondary education are in this unsatisfactory state, what is to be said to the universities? This is an awful subject, and one I almost fear to touch with my unhallowed hands; but I can tell you what those say who have authority to speak.

The Rector of Lincoln College, in his lately published, valuable 'Sug-gestions for Academical Organization with especial reference to Oxford,' tells us (p. 127):—

'The colleges were, in their origin, endowments, not for the ele-ments of a general liberal education, but for the prolonged study of special and professional faculties by men of riper age. The universities embraced both these objects. The colleges, while they incidentally aided in elementary education, were specially devoted to the highest learning. . . .

'This was the theory of the middle-age university and the design of collegiate foundations in their origin. Time and circumstances have brought about a total change. The colleges no longer promote the researches of science, or direct professional study. Here and there college walls may shelter an occasional student, but not in larger proportions than may be found in private life. Elementary teaching of youths under twenty is now the only function performed by the university, and almost the only object of college endowments. Colleges were homes for the lifestudy of the highest and most abstruse parts of knowledge. They have become boarding schools in which the elements of the learned languages are taught to youths.'

If Mr. Pattison's high position, and his obvious love and respect for his university, be insufficient to convince the outside world that language so severe is yet no more than just, the authority of the Commissioners who reported on the University of Oxford in 1850 is open to no challenge. Yet they write:—

'It is generally acknowledged that both Oxford and the country at large suffer greatly from the absence of a body of learned men devoting their lives to the cultivation of science, and to the direction of academical education.

'The fact that so few books of profound research emanate from the University of Oxford, materially impairs its character as a seat of learning, and consequently its hold on the respect of the nation.'

Cambridge can claim no exemption from the reproaches addressed to Oxford. And thus there seems no escape from the admission that what we fondly call our great seats of learning are simply 'boarding schools' for bigger boys; that learned men are not more numerous in them than out of them; that the advancement of knowledge is not the object of fellows of colleges; that, in the philosophic calm and meditative stillness of their greenswarded courts, philosophy does not thrive, and meditation bears few fruits.

It is my great good fortune to reckon amongst my friends resident members of both universities, who are men of learning and research, zealous cultivators of science, keeping before their minds a noble ideal of a university, and doing their best to make that ideal a reality; and, to me, they would necessarily typify the universities, did not the authoritative statements I have quoted compel me to believe that they are exceptional, and not representative men. Indeed, upon calm consideration, several circumstances lead me to think that the Rector of Lincoln College and the Commissioners cannot be far wrong.

I believe there can be no doubt that the foreigner who should wish to become acquainted with the scientific, or the literary, activity of modern England, would simply lose his time and his pains if he visited our universities with that object.

And, as for works of profound research on any subject, and, above all, in that classical lore for which universities profess to sacrifice almost everything else, why, a third-rate, poverty-stricken German university turns out more produce of that kind in one year, than our vast and wealthy foundations elaborate in ten.

Ask the man who is investigating any question, profoundly and thoroughly—be it historical, philosophical, philological, physical, literary, or theological; who is trying to make himself master of any abstract subject (except, perhaps, political economy and geology, both of which are intensely Anglican sciences) whether he is not compelled to read half a dozen times as many German, as English, books? And whether, of these English books, more than one in ten is the work of a fellow of a college, or a professor of an English university?

Is this from any lack of power in the English as compared with the German mind? The countrymen of Grote and of Mill, of Faraday, of Robert Brown, of Lyell,[11] and of Darwin, to go no further back than the contemporaries of men of middle age, can afford to smile at such a suggestion. England can show now, as she has been able to show in every generation since civilisation spread over the West, individual men who hold their own against the world, and keep alive the old tradition of her intellectual eminence.

But, in the majority of cases, these men are what they are in virtue of their native intellectual force, and of a strength of character which will not recognise impediments. They are not trained in the courts of the Temple of Science, but storm the walls of that edifice in all sorts of irregular ways, and with much loss of time and power, in order to obtain their legitimate positions.

Our universities not only do not encourage such men; do not offer them positions, in which it should be their highest duty to do, thoroughly, that which they are most capable of doing; but, as far as possible, university training shuts out of the minds of those among them, who are subjected to it, the prospect that there is anything in the world for which they are specially fitted. Imagine the success of the attempt to still the intellectual hunger of any of the men I have mentioned, by putting before him, as the object of existence, the successful mimicry of the measure of a Greek song, or the roll of

---

[11] Michael Faraday (1791–1867), Robert Brown (1773–1858), Sir Charles Lyell (1795–1875), and Charles Darwin (1809–1882) were famous scientists.

Ciceronian prose! Imagine how much success would be likely to attend the attempt to persuade such men, that the education which leads to perfection in such elegancies is alone to be called culture; while the facts of history, the process of thought, the conditions of moral and social existence, and the laws of physical nature, are left to be dealt with as they may, by outside barbarians!

It is not thus that the German universities, from being beneath notice a century ago, have become what they are now—the most intensely cultivated and the most productive intellectual corporations the world has ever seen.

The student who repairs to them sees in the list of classes and of professors a fair picture of the world of knowledge. Whatever he needs to know there is some one ready to teach him, some one competent to discipline him in the way of learning; whatever his special bent, let him but be able and diligent, and in due time he shall find distinction and a career. Among his professors, he sees men whose names are known and revered throughout the civilised world; and their living example infects him with a noble ambition, and a love for the spirit of work.

The Germans dominate the intellectual world by virtue of the same simple secret as that which made Napoleon the master of old Europe. They have declared *la carrière ouverte aux talents*,[12] and every Bursch[13] marches with a professor's gown in his knapsack. Let him become a great scholar, or man of science, and ministers will compete for his services. In Germany, they do not leave the chance of his holding the office he would render illustrious to the tender mercies of a hot canvass, and the final wisdom of a mob of country parsons.

In short, in Germany, the universities are exactly what the Rector of Lincoln and the Commissioners tell us the English universities are not; that is to say, corporations 'of learned men devoting their lives to the cultivation of science, and the direction of academical education.' They are not 'boarding schools for youths,' nor clerical seminaries; but institutions for the higher culture of men, in which the theological faculty is of no more importance, or prominence, than the rest; and which are truly 'universities," since they strive to represent and embody the totality of human knowledge, and to find room for all forms of intellectual activity.

May zealous and clear-headed reformers like Mr. Pattison succeed in their noble endeavours to shape our universities towards some such ideal as

[12] The career open to the talents.
[13] German student.

this, without losing what is valuable and distinctive in their social tone! But until they have succeeded, a liberal education will be no more obtainable in our Oxford and Cambridge Universities than in our public schools.

If I am justified in my conception of the ideal of a liberal education; and if what I have said about the existing educational institutions of the country is also true, it is clear that the two have no sort of relation to one another; that the best of our schools and the most complete of our university trainings give but a narrow, one-sided, and essentially illiberal education—while the worst give what is really next to no education at all. The South London Working-Men's College could not copy any of these institutions if it would. I am bold enough to express the conviction that it ought not if it could.

For what is wanted is the reality and not the mere name of a liberal education; and this College must steadily set before itself the ambition to be able to give that education sooner or later. At present we are but beginning, sharpening our educational tools, as it were, and, except a modicum of physical science, we are not able to offer much more than is to be found in an ordinary school.

Moral and social science—one of the greatest and most fruitful of our future classes, I hope—at present lacks only one thing in our programme, and that is a teacher. A considerable want, no doubt; but it must be recollected that it is much better to want a teacher than to want the desire to learn.

Further, we need what, for want of a better name, I must call Physical Geography. What I mean is that which the Germans call *'Erdkunde.'*[14] It is a description of the earth, of its place and relation to other bodies; of its general structure, and of its great features—winds, tides, mountains, rains, plains; of the chief forms of the vegetable and animal worlds, of the varieties of man. It is the peg upon which the greatest quantity of useful and entertaining scientific information can be suspended.

Literature is not upon the College programme; but I hope some day to see it there. For literature is the greatest of all sources of refined pleasure, and one of the great uses of a liberal education is to enable us to enjoy that pleasure. There is scope enough for the purposes of liberal education in the study of the rich treasures of our own language alone. All that is needed is direction, and the cultivation of a refined taste by attention to sound criticism. But there is no reason why French and German should not be mastered sufficiently to read what is worth reading in those languages, with pleasure and with profit.

[14] Earth-knowledge.

And finally, by-and-by, we must have History; treated not as a succession of battles and dynasties; not as a series of biographies; not as evidence that Providence has always been on the side of either Whigs or Tories; but as the development of man in times past, and in other conditions than our own.

But, as it is one of the principles of our College to be self-supporting, the public must lead, and we must follow, in these matters. If my hearers take to heart what I have said about liberal education, they will desire these things, and I doubt not we shall be able to supply them. But we must wait till the demand is made.

### I. Suggestions for Discussion:

1. How does Huxley define education? A liberal education?
2. What faults does he find with the three levels of schooling in England he analyzes. How detailed are these analyses?
3. What course of study does he recommend for a liberal education? Do you agree? Explain.

### II. Suggestions for Writing:

1. Write an essay outlining the elements of a liberal education for a man or woman in the 1980s. How might your recommendations differ from Huxley's?
2. Compare and contrast Huxley's views on university education with John Henry Newman's in "What Is a University," p. 421.

---

# ADA LOUISE HUXTABLE

## The Queens That Ruled Seas and Set Styles

---

Ada Louise Huxtable was assistant curator of architecture and design at the Museum of Modern Art in New York from 1946 until 1950. Since 1963 she has written on architecture for the *New York Times.* Her books include *Classic New York* (1964) and *Will They Ever Finish Bruckner Boulevard?* (1970).

A museum exhibition in New York leads her to analyze the ocean liner's status as one of the unique design objects of the twentieth century.

---

Of the great design triumvirate that represented "modernism" to the poets and prophets of the first part of the 20th century—the ocean liner, the train and the plane—two are already obsolete. The trans-Atlantic liner and the transcontinental train have become objects of extreme nostalgia; the ocean liner is, in effect, extinct. And yet it was to these three icons of movement, change and speed that architects like Le Corbusier and critics like Sheldon Cheney fashioned hymns of praise. They became the symbols of freedom and mobility that the century craved.

At the same time, the ocean liner was the last gasp of an age of leisure and elegance, soon to be sacrificed to the speed and efficiency of air travel. It was a glorious anachronism, and those who experienced it have glorious memories of a special mix of conviviality, adventure, grand luxe, ocean air and haute cuisine that started with champagne midnight sailings. The mid-ocean suspension of time and reality is an experience unique in the history of travel and hedonism.

In retrospect, it becomes clear that the ocean liner was one of the unique design objects of the 20th century. It is that significant aspect of its history that is being celebrated in an exhibition called "The Ocean Liner: Speed, Style, Symbol," that will open on Jan. 22 at the Cooper-Hewitt Museum, 2 East 91st Street, and run through April 6, under the direction of Richard B. Oliver, curator of Contemporary Architecture and Design.

Symbol and style are never far apart. In the heyday of the big ships in the 1920's and 30's, the future was very much in fashion. The ocean liner was a supersymbol of a sleek new world, a mechanical marvel that could be nicely romanticized into a rich Art Deco setting for Old World pleasures. It was the synthesis of Art and Industry and Escoffier.

Before long, the suave spirit of those shipboard salons invaded everything from Hollywood movies to department store furnishings. The railings and decks of Le Corbusier's seminal Savoy House, the steel tubing, indirect lighting and extraordinary mix of exotic wood veneers, lacquers, marbles, plastic and aluminum called "modernistic" at the time, became the universal standard of chic. Much was owed to what became known as le style paquebot.

The Cooper-Hewitt show is a thoughtful analysis of the design aspects of the ocean liner, which are divided into three areas: the technological developments of the hull, superstructure and propulsion systems responsible for speed and size; the complex, innovative planning required to accommodate passengers, crew, services and machinery; and the style and decoration of the interiors, meant to provide not only comfort and luxury but an exceptional image and ambiance.

Mr. Oliver's catalogue is wonderfully informative, and the prints, photographs and artifacts in the show are an endless delight. For more expansive reading, there are two splendid books, John Maxtone-Graham's "The Only Way to Cross" (Macmillan, 1972), and "The Sway of the Grand Saloon" (Delacorte, 1971), John Malcolm Brinnin's "social history of the North Atlantic." For Mr. Oliver's purposes, the story of the great liners starts in 1892 with the Lucania, which, he tells us, "set new standards for technological advance and decorative opulence."

He traces the technology from compound steam engine to steam turbine engine, notes the changes from wood to steel and aluminum and describes radical revisions in hull and superstructure design. The race, of course, was in size and speed.

The liners' public rooms grew constantly in number and splendor. To the Dining Saloons, Smoking Rooms and Ladies' Parlors were added Veranda Cafes, Observation Cocktail Lounges and Pompeian Swimming Pools. At first, the style was elaborately eclectic. A ship was meant to be a floating grand hotel with a familiar, land-based image. The Aquitania of 1914 had a Louis XVI Dining Saloon and Main Staircase, an Adam Drawing Room, a Jacobean Grille Room and a Swimming Pool decorated with replicas of Egyptian ornaments in the British Museum.

The Italian Line Ships were carved and gilded versions of ponderous palazzi. The Cunard Line had working fireplaces. The German-built Amerika reproduced the restaurant of the Ritz-Carlton in London. The United States Line used frescoes of Indians and mounted moose heads. All had potted palms, and tassels and fringes trembled and swayed with the engines and the sea.

There was a superb understanding of the psychology of design for social purposes in such features as the Grand Staircases, which were catalysts for circulation and show. Balconied approaches to the first-class dining rooms offered unparalleled grand entrances. An architectural gem of a domed and decorated Grand Stair distinguished the Paris in 1921, and a triple-decker masterpiece of wood-veneered, Deco-railed, flying balconies debouched into a Grand Salon on the Ile de France in 1927. (Later design descendants were bowdlerized versions in Miami Beach hotels.)

The Ile de France was the acknowledged turning point of le style paquebot, described by John Maxtone-Graham as the "great divide from which point on decorators reached forward rather than back." Consortiums of artists were pressed into service by competing lines for the new style in the 1930's. The Queen Mary mounted more than 50 varieties of exotic wood veneers on flannel—to reduce creaking. The Normandie's Dining Salon, with two-story, sculptured Lalique glass panels, stretched literally for blocks.

There was only one standard—the superlative. In the realm of the sybaritic, the French always seemed to do it best. Until its very last days, the liner France was considered the finest French restaurant in the world. The vin ordinaire was free, the cellars were a hushed treasury of rare vintages, and the chefs leaped to anticipate the most epicurean demand.

In the 1950's, in a regrettable excess of modernity, the last great ships of the United States and Italian Lines stressed an overabundance of linoleum and aluminum. The economics, the pace and the clientele all changed. The glory that was Cunard and the grandeur that was the Compagnie Générale Transatlantique were sold for scrap or demoted to a tourist attraction. It was the end of the voyage. A great era, and a great style, died in corporate decisions made far from the sea.

**I. Suggestions for Discussion:**
1. Explain Huxtable's assertion that the ocean liner was the last gasp of an age of leisure and elegance.
2. What influence did ocean-liner decor have on modern fashion? Be specific.
3. Discuss Huxtable's use of details to support her observations. Does she provide a sufficient number of examples to make her points? Are the details she provides well chosen and specific?

**II. Suggestions for Writing:**
1. Describe a ship on which you have sailed.
2. Huxtable uses a museum show as a springboard for a general discussion of the influence of ocean liners on fashion. Use a gallery or museum exhibit you have seen as the basis for a more general discussion of prevailing interests or tastes on your campus or in your town.

---

# WASHINGTON IRVING

## The Author's Account of Himself

from *The Sketch-Book of Geoffrey Crayon, Gent.*

---

Washington Irving (1783–1859) is generally considered to have been the first American man of letters to have been internationally celebrated. His *Sketch-Book of Geoffrey Crayon, Gent.* (1820)

included his famous stories, *Rip van Winkle* and *The Legend of Sleepy Hollow.*

In the following "Account" taken from *The Sketch-Book,* Irving creates a persona to narrate sketches and stories in the volume. The "author" briefly recounts his travels in America and in Europe.

---

I am of this mind with Homer, that as the snaile that crept out of her shel was turned eftsoons into a toad, and thereby was forced to make a stoole to sit on; so the traveller that stragleth from his owne country is in a short time transformed into so monstrous a shape, that he is faine to alter his mansion with his manners, and to live where he can, not where he would.        *-Lyly's EUPHUES.*

I was always fond of visiting new scenes, and observing strange characters and manners. Even when a mere child I began my travels, and made many tours of discovery into foreign parts and unknown regions of my native city, to the frequent alarm of my parents, and the emolument of the town-crier. As I grew into boyhood, I extended the range of my observations. My holiday afternoons were spent in rambles about the surrounding country. I made myself familiar with all its places famous in history or fable. I knew every spot where a murder or robbery had been committed, or a ghost seen. I visited the neighboring villages, and added greatly to my stock of knowledge, by noting their habits and customs, and conversing with their sages and great men. I even journeyed one long summer's day to the summit of the most distant hill, whence I stretched my eye over many a mile of terra incognita, and was astonished to find how vast a globe I inhabited.

This rambling propensity strengthened with my years. Books of voyages and travels became my passion, and in devouring their contents, I neglected the regular exercises of the school. How wistfully would I wander about the pier-heads in fine weather, and watch the parting ships, bound to distant climes—with what longing eyes would I gaze after their lessening sails, and waft myself in imagination to the ends of the earth!

Further reading and thinking, though they brought this vague inclination into more reasonable bounds, only served to make it more decided. I visited various parts of my own country; and had I been merely a lover of fine scenery, I should have felt little desire to seek elsewhere its gratification, for on no country have the charms of nature been more prodigally lavished. Her mighty lakes, like oceans of liquid silver; her mountains, with their bright aerial tints; her valleys, teeming with wild fertility; her tremendous cataracts, thundering in their solitudes; her boundless plains, waving with spontaneous verdure; her broad deep rivers, rolling in solemn silence to the ocean; her trackless forests, where vegetation puts forth all its magnificence; her skies, kindling with the magic of summer clouds and glorious sunshine; no, never need an American look beyond his own country for the sublime and beautiful of natural scenery.

But Europe held forth the charms of storied and poetical association. There were to be seen the masterpieces of art, the refinements of highly-cultivated society, the quaint peculiarities of ancient and local custom. My native country was full of youthful promise: Europe was rich in the accumulated treasures of age. Her very ruins told the history of times gone by, and every mouldering stone was a chronicle. I longed to wander over the scenes of renowned achievement—to tread, as it were, in the footsteps of antiquity—to loiter about the ruined castle—to meditate on the falling tower—to escape, in short, from the commonplace realities of the present, and lose myself among the shadowy grandeurs of the past.

I had, beside all this, an earnest desire to see the great men of the earth. We have, it is true, our great men in America: not a city but has an ample share of them. I have mingled among them in my time, and been almost withered by the shade into which they cast me; for there is nothing so baleful to a small man as the shade of a great one, particularly the great man of a city. But I was anxious to see the great men of Europe; for I had read in the works of various philosophers, that all animals degenerated in America, and man among the number. A great man of Europe, thought I, must therefore be as superior to a great man of America, as a peak of the Alps to a highland of the Hudson; and in this idea I was confirmed, by observing the comparative importance and swelling magnitude of many English travellers among us, who, I was assured, were very little people in their own country. I will visit this land of wonders, thought I, and see the gigantic race from which I am degenerated.

It has been either my good or evil lot to have my roving passion gratified. I have wandered through different countries, and witnessed many of the shifting scenes of life. I cannot say that I have studied them with the eye of a philosopher; but rather with the sauntering gaze with which humble lovers of the picturesque stroll from the window of one print-shop to another; caught sometimes by the delineations of beauty, sometimes by the distortions of caricature, and sometimes by the loveliness of landscape. As it is the fashion for modern tourists to travel pencil in hand, and bring home their port-folios filled with sketches, I am disposed to get up a few for the entertainment of my friends. When, however, I look over the hints and memorandums I have taken down for the purpose, my heart almost fails me at finding how my idle humor has led me aside from the great objects studied by every regular traveller who would make a book. I fear I shall give equal disappointment with an unlucky landscape painter, who had travelled on the continent, but, following the bent of his vagrant inclination, had sketched in nooks, and corners, and by-places. His sketch-book was accordingly crowded with cottages, and landscapes, and obscure ruins; but he had neglected to paint St. Peter's, or the Coliseum; the cascade of Terni, or the bay of Naples; and had not a single glacier or volcano in his whole collection.

I. **Suggestions for Discussion:**
    1. Discuss the persona established by Irving. Is the first-person narrative an effective way of introducing the character? Explain.
    2. Discuss Irving's use of comparison and contrast in his descriptions of Europe and America.
    3. In what sense does Irving feel that Europe is the country of the past?
II. **Suggestions for Writing:**
    1. Write in detail about a place you have visited. Compare and contrast it with your home town.
    2. Compare and contrast the impressions places in the United States and in some other country you visited had on you.

---

# JANE JACOBS

## The Uses of Sidewalks: Contact

from *The Death and Life of Great American Cities*

---

Jane Jacobs (1916–      ) served as associate editor of *Architectural Forum* from 1952 until 1962. She has written about the urban environment in such books as *The Economy of Cities* (1969) and *The Death and Life of Great American Cities* (1961), from which the following chapter is taken.

In this long selection, she demonstrates through illustration, description, and discussion the importance of sidewalk contact in building and maintaining a neighborhood. Neighborhood stores and specialized sidewalk characters, for example, play important roles in knitting together a stable community.

---

Reformers have long observed city people loitering on busy corners, hanging around in candy stores and bars and drinking soda pop on stoops, and have passed a judgment, the gist of which is: "This is deplorable! If these people had decent homes and a more private or bosky outdoor place, they wouldn't be on the street!"

This judgment represents a profound misunderstanding of cities. It makes no more sense than to drop in at a testimonial banquet in a hotel and conclude that if these people had wives who could cook, they would give their parties at home.

The point of both the testimonial banquet and the social life of city sidewalks is precisely that they are public. They bring together people who do not know each other in an intimate, private social fashion and in most cases do not care to know each other in that fashion.

Nobody can keep open house in a great city. Nobody wants to. And yet if interesting, useful and significant contacts among the people of cities are confined to acquaintanceships suitable for private life, the city becomes stultified. Cities are full of people with whom, from your viewpoint, or mine, or any other individual's, a certain degree of contact is useful or enjoyable; but you do not want them in your hair. And they do not want you in theirs either.

In speaking about city sidewalk safety, I mentioned how necessary it is that there should be, in the brains behind the eyes on the street, an almost unconscious assumption of general street support when the chips are down—when a citizen has to choose, for instance, whether he will take responsibility, or abdicate it, in combating barbarism or protecting strangers. There is a short word for this assumption of support: trust. The trust of a city street is formed over time from many, many little public sidewalk contacts. It grows out of people stopping by at the bar for a beer, getting advice from the grocer and giving advice to the newsstand man, comparing opinions with other customers at the bakery and nodding hello to the two boys drinking pop on the stoop, eying the girls while waiting to be called for dinner, admonishing the children, hearing about a job from the hardware man and borrowing a dollar from the druggist, admiring the new babies and sympathizing over the way a coat faded. Customs vary: in some neighborhoods people compare notes on their dogs; in others they compare notes on their landlords.

Most of it is ostensibly utterly trivial but the sum is not trivial at all. The sum of such casual, public contact at a local level—most of it fortuitous, most of it associated with errands, all of it metered by the person concerned and not thrust upon him by anyone—is a feeling for the public identity of people, a web of public respect and trust, and a resource in time of personal or neighborhood need. The absence of this trust is a disaster to a city street. Its cultivation cannot be institutionalized. And above all, *it implies no private commitments.*

I have seen a striking difference between presence and absence of casual public trust on two sides of the same wide street in East Harlem, composed of residents of roughly the same incomes and same races. On the old-city side, which was full of public places and the sidewalk loitering so deplored by Utopian minders of other people's leisure, the children were being kept well in hand. On the project side of the street across the way, the children, who had a fire hydrant open beside their play area, were behaving destructively, drenching the open windows of houses with water, squirting it on adults who ignorantly walked on the project side of the street, throwing it into the windows of cars as they went by. Nobody dared to stop them. These were anonymous children, and the identities behind them were an unknown. What if you scolded or stopped them? Who would back you up over there in the blind-eyed Turf? Would you get, instead, revenge? Better to keep out of it. Impersonal city streets make anonymous people, and this is not a matter of esthetic quality nor of a mystical emotional effect in architectural scale. It is a matter of what kinds of tangible enterprises sidewalks have, and therefore of how people use the sidewalks in practical, everyday life.

The casual public sidewalk life of cities ties directly into other types of public life, of which I shall mention one as illustrative, although there is no end to their variety.

Formal types of local city organizations are frequently assumed by planners and even by some social workers to grow in direct, common-sense fashion out of announcements of meetings, the presence of meeting rooms, and the existence of problems of obvious public concern. Perhaps they grow so in suburbs and towns. They do not grow so in cities.

Formal public organizations in cities require an informal public life underlying them, mediating between them and the privacy of the people of the city. We catch a hint of what happens by contrasting, again, a city area possessing a public sidewalk life with a city area lacking it, as told about in the report of a settlement-house social researcher who was studying problems relating to public schools in a section of New York City:

Mr. W—— [principal of an elementary school] was questioned on the effect of J—— Houses on the school, and the uprooting of the community around the school. He felt that there had been many effects and of these most were negative. He mentioned that the project had torn out numerous institutions for socializing. The present atmosphere of the project was in no way similar to the gaiety of the streets before the project was built. He noted that in general there seemed fewer people on the streets because there were fewer places for people to gather. He also contended that before the projects were built the Parents Association had been very strong, and now there were only very few active members.

Mr. W—— was wrong in one respect. There were not fewer places (or at any rate there was not less space) for people to gather in the project, if we count places deliberately planned for constructive socializing. Of course there were no bars, no candy stores, no hole-in-the-wall *bodegas,* no restaurants in the project. But the project under discussion was equipped with a model complement of meeting rooms, craft, art and game rooms, outdoor benches, malls, etc., enough to gladden the heart of even the Garden City advocates.

Why are such places dead and useless without the most determined efforts and expense to inveigle users—and then to maintain control over the users? What services do the public sidewalk and its enterprises fulfill that these planned gathering places do not? And why? How does an informal public sidewalk life bolster a more formal, organizational public life?

To understand such problems—to understand why drinking pop on the stoop differs from drinking pop in the game room, and why getting advice from the grocer or the bartender differs from getting advice from either your next-door neighbor or from an institutional lady who may be hand-in-glove with an institutional landlord—we must look into the matter of city privacy.

Privacy is precious in cities. It is indispensable. Perhaps it is precious and indispensable everywhere, but most places you cannot get it. In small settlements everyone knows your affairs. In the city everyone does not—only those you choose to tell will know much about you. This is one of the attributes of cities that is precious to most city people, whether their incomes are high or their incomes are low, whether they are white or colored, whether they are old inhabitants or new, and it is a gift of great-city life deeply cherished and jealously guarded.

Architectural and planning literature deals with privacy in terms of windows, overlooks, sight lines. The idea is that if no one from outside can peek into where you live—behold, privacy. This is simple-minded. Window privacy is the easiest commodity in the world to get. You just pull down the shades or adjust the blinds. The privacy of keeping one's personal affairs to those selected to know them, and the privacy of having reasonable control over who shall make inroads on your time and when, are rare commodities in most of this world, however, and they have nothing to do with the orientation of windows.

Anthropologist Elena Padilla, author of *Up from Puerto Rico,* describing Puerto Rican life in a poor and squalid district of New York, tells how much people know about each other—who is to be trusted and who not, who is defiant of the law and who upholds it, who is competent and well informed and who is inept and ignorant—and how these things are known from the public life of the sidewalk and its associated enterprises. These are matters of public character. But she also tells how select are those permitted to drop into the kitchen for a cup of coffee, how strong are the ties, and how limited the number of a person's genuine confidants, those who share in a person's private life and private affairs. She tells how it is not considered dignified for everyone to know one's affairs. Nor is it considered dignified to snoop on others beyond the face presented in public. It does violence to a person's privacy and rights. In this, the people she describes are essentially the same as the people of the mixed, Americanized city street on which I live, and essentially the same as the people who live in high-income apartments or fine town houses, too.

A good city street neighborhood achieves a marvel of balance between its people's determination to have essential privacy and their simultaneous wishes for differing degrees of contact, enjoyment or help from the people around. This balance is largely made up of small, sensitively managed details, practiced and accepted so casually that they are normally taken for granted.

Perhaps I can best explain this subtle but all-important balance in terms of the stores where people leave keys for their friends, a common custom in New York. In our family, for example, when a friend wants to use our place while we are away for a weekend or everyone happens to be out during the day, or a visitor for whom we do not wish to wait up is spending the night, we tell such a friend that he can pick up the key at the delicatessen across the street. Joe Cornacchia, who keeps the delicatessen, usually has a dozen or so keys at a time for handing out like this. He has a special drawer for them.

Now why do I, and many others, select Joe as a logical custodian for keys? Because we trust him, first, to be a responsible custodian, but equally important because we know that he combines a feeling of good will with a feeling of no personal responsibility about our private affairs. Joe considers it no concern of his whom we choose to permit in our places and why.

Around on the other side of our block, people leave their keys at a Spanish grocery. On the other side of Joe's block, people leave them at the candy store. Down a block they leave them at the coffee shop, and a few hundred feet around the corner from that, in a barber shop. Around one corner from two fashionable blocks of town houses and apartments in the Upper East Side, people leave their keys in a butcher shop and a bookshop; around another corner they leave them in a cleaner's and a drug store. In unfashionable East Harlem keys are left with at least one florist, in bakeries, in luncheonettes, in Spanish and Italian groceries.

The point, wherever they are left, is not the kind of ostensible service that the enterprise offers, but the kind of proprietor it has.

A service like this cannot be formalized. Identifications . . . questions . . . insurance against mishaps. The all-essential line between public service and privacy would be transgressed by institutionalization. Nobody in his right mind would leave his key in such a place. The service must be given as a favor by someone with an unshakable understanding of the difference between a person's key and a person's private life, or it cannot be given at all.

Or consider the line drawn by Mr. Jaffe at the candy store around our corner—a line so well understood by his customers and by other storekeepers too that they can spend their whole lives in its presence and never think about it consciously. One ordinary morning last winter, Mr. Jaffe, whose formal business name is Bernie, and his wife, whose formal business name is Ann, supervised the small children crossing at the corner on the way to P.S. 41, as Bernie always does because he sees the need; lent an umbrella to one customer and a dollar to another; took custody of two keys; took in some packages for people in the next building who were away; lectured two youngsters who asked for cigarettes; gave street directions; took custody of a watch to give the repair man across the street when he opened later; gave out information on the range of rents in the neighborhood to an apartment seeker; listened to a tale of domestic difficulty and offered reassurance; told some rowdies they could not come in unless they behaved and then defined (and got) good behavior; provided an incidental forum for half a dozen conversations among customers who dropped in for oddments; set aside certain newly arrived papers and magazines for regular customers who would depend on getting them; advised a mother who came for a birthday present not to get the ship-model kit because another child going to the same birthday party was giving that; and got a back copy (this was for me) of the previous day's newspaper out of the deliverer's surplus returns when he came by.

After considering this multiplicity of extra-merchandising services I asked Bernie, "Do you ever introduce your customers to each other?"

He looked startled at the idea, even dismayed. "No," he said thoughtfully. "That would just not be advisable. Sometimes, if I know two customers who are in at the same time have an interest in common, I bring up the subject in conversation and let them carry it on from there if they want to. But oh no, I wouldn't introduce them."

When I told this to an acquaintance in a suburb, she promptly assumed that Mr. Jaffe felt that to make an introduction would be to step above his social class. Not at all. In our neighborhood, storekeepers like the Jaffees enjoy an excellent social status, that of businessmen. In income they are apt to be the peers of the general run of customers and in independence they are the superiors. Their advice, as men or women of common sense and experience, is sought and respected. They are well known as individuals, rather than unknown as class symbols. No; this is that almost unconsciously enforced, well-balanced line showing, the line between the city public world and the world of privacy.

This line can be maintained, without awkwardness to anyone, because of the great plenty of opportunities for public contact in the enterprises along the sidewalks, or on the sidewalks themselves as people move to and fro or deliberately loiter when they feel like it, and also because of the presence of many public hosts, so to speak, proprietors of meeting places like Bernie's where one is free either to hang around or dash in and out, no strings attached.

Under this system, it is possible in a city street neighborhood to know all kinds of people without unwelcome entanglements, without boredom, necessity for excuses, explanations, fears of giving offense, embarrassments respecting impositions or commitments, and all such paraphernalia of obligations which can accompany less limited relationships. It is possible to be on excellent sidewalk terms with people who are very different from oneself, and even, as time passes, on familiar public terms with them. Such relationships can, and do, endure for many years, for decades; they could never have formed without that line, much less endured. They form precisely because they are by-the-way to people's normal public sorties.

"Togetherness" is a fittingly nauseating name for an old ideal in planning theory. This ideal is that if anything is shared among people, much should be shared. "Togetherness," apparently a spiritual resource of the new suburbs, works destructively in cities. The requirement that much shall be shared drives city people apart.

When an area of a city lacks a sidewalk life, the people of the place must enlarge their private lives if they are to have anything approaching equivalent contact with their neighbors. They must settle for some form of "togetherness," in which more is shared with one another than in the life of the sidewalks, or else they must settle for lack of contact. Inevitably the outcome is one or the other; it has to be; and either has distressing results.

In the case of the first outcome, where people do share much, they become exceedingly choosy as to who their neighbors are, or with whom they associate at all. They have to become so. A friend of mine, Penny Kostritsky, is unwittingly and unwillingly in this fix on a street in Baltimore. Her street of nothing but residences, embedded in an area of almost nothing but residences, has been experimentally equipped with a charming sidewalk park. The sidewalk has been widened and attractively paved, wheeled traffic discouraged from the narrow street roadbed, trees and flowers planted, and a piece of play sculpture is to go in. All these are splendid ideas so far as they go.

However, there are no stores. The mothers from nearby blocks who bring small children here, and come here to find some contact with others themselves, perforce go into the houses of acquaintances along the street to warm up in winter, to make telephone calls, to take their children in emergencies to the bathroom. Their hostesses offer them coffee, for there is no other place to get coffee, and naturally considerable social life of this kind has arisen around the park. Much is shared.

Mrs. Kostritsky, who lives in one of the conveniently located houses, and who has two small children, is in the thick of this narrow and accidental social life. "I have lost the advantage of living in the city," she says, "Without getting the advantages of living in the suburbs." Still more distressing, when mothers of different income or color or educational background bring their children to the street park, they and their children are rudely and pointedly ostracized. They fit awkwardly into the suburbanlike sharing of private lives that has grown in default of city sidewalk life. The park lacks benches purposely; the "togetherness" people ruled them out because they might be interpreted as an invitation to people who cannot fit in.

"If only we had a couple of stores on the street," Mrs. Kostritsky laments. "If only there were a grocery store or a drug store or a snack joint. Then the telephone calls and the warming up and the gathering could be done naturally in public, and then people would act more decent to each other because everybody would have a right to be here."

Much the same thing that happens in this sidewalk park without a city public life happens sometimes in middle-class projects and colonies, such as

Chatham Village in Pittsburgh for example, a famous model of Garden City planning.

The houses here are grouped in colonies around shared interior lawns and play yards, and the whole development is equipped with other devices for close sharing, such as a residents' club which holds parties, dances, reunions, has ladies' activities like bridge and sewing parties, and holds dances and parties for the children. There is no public life here, in any city sense. There are differing degrees of extended private life.

Chatham Village's success as a "model" neighborhood where much is shared has required that the residents be similar to one another in their standards, interests and backgrounds. In the main they are middle-class professionals and their families.* It has also required that residents set themselves distinctly apart from the different people in the surrounding city; these are in the main also middle class, but lower middle class, and this is too different for the degree of chumminess that neighborliness in Chatham Village entails.

The inevitable insularity (and homogeneity) of Chatham Village has practical consequences. As one illustration, the junior high school serving the area has problems, as all schools do. Chatham Village is large enough to dominate the elementary school to which its children go, and therefore to work at helping solve this school's problems. To deal with the junior high, however, Chatham Village's people must cooperate with entirely different neighborhoods. But there is no public acquaintanceship, no foundation of casual public trust, no cross-connections with the necessary people—and no practice or ease in applying the most ordinary techniques of city public life at lowly levels. Feeling helpless, as indeed they are, some Chatham Village families move away when their children reach junior high age; others contrive to send them to private high schools. Ironically, just such neighborhood islands as Chatham Village are encouraged in orthodox planning on the specific grounds that cities need the talents and stabilizing influence of the middle class. Presumably these qualities are to seep out by osmosis.

People who do not fit happily into such colonies eventually get out, and in time managements become sophisticated in knowing who among applicants will fit in. Along with basic similarities of standards, values and backgrounds, the arrangement seems to demand a formidable amount of forbearance and tact.

---

*One representative court, for example, contains as this is written four lawyers, two doctors, two engineers, a dentist, a salesman, a banker, a railroad executive, a planning executive.

City residential planning that depends, for contact among neighbors, on personal sharing of this sort, and that cultivates it, often does work well socially, if rather narrowly, *for self-selected upper-middle-class people.* It solves easy problems for an easy kind of population. So far as I have been able to discover, it fails to work, however, even on its own terms, *with any other kind of population.*

The more common outcome in cities, where people are faced with the choice of sharing much or nothing, is nothing. In city areas that lack a natural and casual public life, it is common for residents to isolate themselves from each other to a fantastic degree. If mere contact with your neighbors threatens to entangle you in their private lives, or entangle them in yours, and if you cannot be so careful who your neighbors are as self-selected upper-middle-class people can be, the logical solution is absolutely to avoid friendliness or casual offers of help. Better to stay thoroughly distant. As a practical result, the ordinary public jobs—like keeping children in hand—for which people must take a little personal initiative, or those for which they must band together in limited common purposes, go undone. The abysses this opens up can be almost unbelievable.

For example, in one New York City project which is designed—like all orthodox residential city planning—for sharing much or nothing, a remarkably outgoing woman prided herself that she had become acquainted, by making a deliberate effort, with the mothers of every one of the ninety families in her building. She called on them. She buttonholed them at the door or in the hall. She struck up conversations if she sat beside them on a bench.

It so happened that her eight-year-old son, one day, got stuck in the elevator and was left there without help for more than two hours, although he screamed, cried and pounded. The next day the mother expressed her dismay to one of her ninety acquaintances. "Oh, was that *your* son?" said the other woman. "I didn't know whose boy he was. If I had realized he was *your* son I would have helped him."

This woman, who had not behaved in any such insanely calloused fashion on her old public street—to which she constantly returned, by the way, for public life—was afraid of a possible entanglement that might not be kept easily on a public plane.

Dozens of illustrations of this defense can be found wherever the choice is sharing much or nothing. A thorough and detailed report by Ellen Lurie, a social worker in East Harlem, on life in a low-income project there, has this to say:

It is . . . extremely important to recognize that for considerably complicated reasons, many adults either don't want to become involved in any friendship-relationships at all with their neighbors, or, if they do succumb to the need for some form of society, they strictly limit themselves to one or two friends, and no more. Over and over again, wives repeated their husband's warning:

"I'm not to get too friendly with anyone. My husband doesn't believe in it."

"People are too gossipy and they could get us in a lot of trouble."

"It's best to mind your own business."

One woman, Mrs. Abraham, always goes out the back door of the building because she doesn't want to interfere with the people standing around in the front. Another man, Mr. Colan . . . won't let his wife make any friends in the project, because he doesn't trust the people here. They have four children, ranging from 8 years to 14, but they are not allowed downstairs alone, because the parents are afraid someone will hurt them.* What happens then is that all sorts of barriers to insure self-protection are being constructed by many families. To protect their children from a neighborhood they aren't sure of, they keep them upstairs in the apartment. To protect themselves, they make few, if any, friends. Some are afraid that friends will become angry or envious and make up a story to report to management, causing them great trouble. If the husband gets a bonus (which he decides not to report) and the wife buys new curtains, the visiting friends will see and might tell the management, who, in turn, investigates and issues a rent increase. Suspicion and fear of trouble often outweigh any need for neighborly advice and help. For these families the sense of privacy has already been extensively violated. The deepest secrets, all the family skeletons, are well known not only to management but often to other public agencies, such as the Welfare Department. To preserve any last remnants of privacy, they choose to avoid close relationships with others. This same phenomenon may be found to a much lesser degree in non-planned slum housing, for there too it is often necessary for other reasons to build up these forms of self-protection. But, it is surely true that this withdrawing from the society of others is much more extensive in planned housing. Even in England, this suspicion of the neighbors and the ensuing aloofness was found in studies of planned towns. Perhaps this pattern is nothing more than an elaborate group mechanism to protect and preserve inner dignity in the face of so many outside pressures to conform.

*This is very common in public projects in New York.

Along with nothingness, considerable "togetherness" can be found in such places, however. Mrs. Lurie reports on this type of relationship:

Often two women from two different buildings will meet in the laundry room, recognize each other; although they may never have spoken a single word to each other back on 99th Street, suddenly here they become "best friends." If one of these two already has a friend or two in her own building, the other is likely to be drawn into that circle and begins to make her friend-ships, not with women on her floor, but rather on her friend's floor.

These friendships do not go into an ever-widening circle. There are certain definite well-traveled paths in the project, and after a while no new people are met.

Mrs. Lurie, who works at community organization in East Harlem, with remarkable success, has looked into the history of many past attempts at project tenant organization. She has told me that "togetherness," itself, is one of the factors that make this kind of organization so difficult. "These projects are not lacking in natural leaders," she says. "They contain people with real ability, wonderful people many of them, but the typical sequence is that in the course of organization leaders have found each other, gotten all involved in each others' social lives, and have ended up talking to nobody but each other. They have not found their followers. Everything tends to de-generate into ineffective cliques, as a natural course. There is no normal public life. Just the mechanics of people learning what is going on is so diffi-cult. It all makes the simplest social gain extra hard for these people."

Residents of unplanned city residential areas that lack neighborhood commerce and sidewalk life seem sometimes to follow the same course as residents of public projects when faced with the choice of sharing much or nothing. Thus researchers hunting the secrets of the social structure in a dull gray-area district of Detroit came to the unexpected conclusion there was no social structure.

The social structure of sidewalk life hangs partly on what can be called self-appointed public characters. A public character is anyone who is in fre-quent contact with a wide circle of people and who is sufficiently interested to make himself a public character. A public character need have no special talents or wisdom to fulfill his function—although he often does. He just needs to be present, and there need to be enough of his counterparts. His main qualification is that he *is* public, that he talks to lots of different people. In this way, news travels that is of sidewalk interest.

Most public sidewalk characters are steadily stationed in public places. They are storekeepers or barkeepers or the like. These are the basic public characters. All other public characters of city sidewalks depend on them—if only indirectly because of the presence of sidewalk routes to such enterprises and their proprietors.

Settlement-house workers and pastors, two more formalized kinds of public characters, typically depend on the street grapevine news systems that have their ganglia in the stores. The director of a settlement of New York's Lower East Side, as an example, makes a regular round of stores. He learns from the cleaner who does his suits about the presence of dope pushers in the neighborhood. He learns from the grocer that the Dragons are working up to something and need attention. He learns from the candy store that two girls are agitating the Sportsmen toward a rumble. One of his most important information spots is an unused breadbox on Rivington Street. That is, it is not used for bread. It stands outside a grocery and is used for sitting on and lounging beside, between the settlement house, a candy store and a pool parlor. A message spoken there for any teen-ager within many blocks will reach his ears unerringly and surprisingly quickly, and the opposite flow along the grapevine similarly brings news quickly in to the breadbox.

Blake Hobbs, the head of the Union Settlement music school in East Harlem, notes that when he gets a first student from one block of the old busy street neighborhoods, he rapidly gets at least three or four more and sometimes almost every child on the block. But when he gets a child from the nearby projects—perhaps through the public school or a playground conversation he has initiated—he almost never gets another as a direct sequence. Word does not move around where public characters and sidewalk life are lacking.

Besides the anchored public characters of the sidewalk, and the well-recognized roving public characters, there are apt to be various more specialized public characters on a city sidewalk. In a curious way, some of these help establish an identity not only for themselves but for others. Describing the everyday life of a retired tenor at such sidewalk establishments as the restaurant and the *bocce* court, a San Francisco news story notes, "It is said of Meloni that because of his intensity, his dramatic manner and his lifelong interest in music, he transmits a feeling of vicarious importance to his many friends." Precisely.

One need not have either the artistry or the personality of such a man to become a specialized sidewalk character—but only a pertinent specialty of some sort. It is easy. I am a specialized public character of sorts along our street, owing of course to the fundamental presence of the basic, anchored

public characters. The way I became one started with the fact that Greenwich
Village, where I live, was waging an interminable and horrendous battle to
save its main park from being bisected by a highway. During the course of
battle I undertook, at the behest of a committee organizer away over on the
other side of Greenwich Village, to deposit in stores on a few blocks of our
street supplies of petition cards protesting the proposed roadway. Customers
would sign the cards while in the stores, and from time to time I would make
my pickups.* As a result of engaging in this messenger work, I have since become automatically the sidewalk public character on petition strategy. Before
long, for instance, Mr. Fox at the liquor store was consulting me, as he
wrapped up my bottle, on how we could get the city to remove a long abandoned and dangerous eyesore, a closed-up comfort station near his corner. If I
would undertake to compose the petitions and find the effective way of presenting them to City Hall, he proposed, he and his partners would undertake
to have them printed, circulated and picked up. Soon the stores round about
had comfort station removal petitions. Our street by now has many public
experts on petition tactics, including the children.

Not only do public characters spread the news and learn the news at
retail, so to speak. They connect with each other and thus spread word
wholesale, in effect.

A sidewalk life, so far as I can observe, arises out of no mysterious
qualities or talents for it in this or that type of population. It arises only
when the concrete, tangible facilities it requires are present. These happen to
be the same facilities, in the same abundance and ubiquity, that are required
for cultivating sidewalk safety. If they are absent, public sidewalk contacts
are absent too.

The well-off have many ways of assuaging needs for which poorer
people may depend much on sidewalk life—from hearing of jobs to being
recognized by the headwaiter. But nevertheless, many of the rich or near-rich
in cities appear to appreciate sidewalk life as much as anybody. At any rate,
they pay enormous rents to move into areas with an exuberant and varied
sidewalk life. They actually crowd out the middle class and the poor in lively
areas like Yorkville or Greenwich Village in New York, or Telegraph Hill
just off the North Beach streets of San Francisco. They capriciously desert,
after only a few decades of fashion at most, the monotonous streets of "quiet
residential areas" and leave them to the less fortunate. Talk to residents of

*This, by the way, is an efficient device, accomplishing with a fraction of the effort what
would be a mountainous task door to door. It also makes more public conversation and
opinion than door-to-door visits.

Georgetown in the District of Columbia and by the second or third sentence at least you will begin to hear rhapsodies about the charming restaurants, "more good restaurants than in all the rest of the city put together," the uniqueness and friendliness of the stores, the pleasures of running into people when doing errands at the next corner—and nothing but pride over the fact that Georgetown has become a specialty shopping district for its whole metropolitan area. The city area, rich or poor or in between, harmed by an interesting sidewalk life and plentiful sidewalk contacts has yet to be found.

Efficiency of public sidewalk characters declines drastically if too much burden is put upon them. A store, for example, can reach a turnover in its contacts, or potential contacts, which is so large and so superficial that it is socially useless. An example of this can be seen at the candy and newspaper store owned by the housing cooperative of Corlears Hook on New York's Lower East Side. This planned project store replaces perhaps forty superficially similar stores which were wiped out (without compensation to their proprietors) on that project site and the adjoining sites. The place is a mill. Its clerks are so busy making change and screaming ineffectual imprecations at rowdies that they never hear anything except "I want that." This, or utter disinterest, is the usual atmosphere where shopping center planning or repressive zoning artificially contrives commercial monopolies for city neighborhoods. A store like this would fail economically if it had competition. Meantime, although monopoly insures the financial success planned for it, it fails the city socially.

Sidewalk public contact and sidewalk public safety, taken together, bear directly on our country's most serious social problem—segregation and racial discrimination.

I do not mean to imply that a city's planning and design, or its types of streets and street life, can automatically overcome segregation and discrimination. Too many other kinds of effort are also required to right these injustices.

But I do mean to say that to build and to rebuild big cities whose sidewalks are unsafe and whose people must settle for sharing much or nothing, *can* make it *much harder* for American cities to overcome discrimination no matter how much effort is expended.

Considering the amount of prejudice and fear that accompany discrimination and bolster it, overcoming residential discrimination is just that much harder if people feel unsafe on their sidewalks anyway. Overcoming residential discrimination comes hard where people have no means of keeping a civilized public life on a basically dignified public footing, and their private lives on a private footing.

To be sure, token model housing integration schemes here and there can be achieved in city areas handicapped by danger and by lack of public life—achieved by applying great effort and settling for abnormal (abnormal for cities) choosiness among new neighbors. This is an evasion of the size of the task and its urgency.

The tolerance, the room for great differences among neighbors—differences that often go far deeper than differences in color—which are possible and normal in intensely urban life, but which are so foreign to suburbs and pseudosuburbs, are possible and normal only when streets of great cities have built-in equipment allowing strangers to dwell in peace together on civilized but essentially dignified and reserved terms.

Lowly, unpurposeful and random as they may appear, sidewalk contacts are the small change from which a city's wealth of public life may grow.

Los Angeles is an extreme example of a metropolis with little public life, depending mainly instead on contacts of a more private social nature.

On one plane, for instance, an acquaintance there comments that although she has lived in the city for ten years and knows it contains Mexicans, she has never laid eyes on a Mexican or an item of Mexican culture, much less ever exchanged any words with a Mexican.

On another plane, Orson Welles has written that Hollywood is the only theatrical center in the world that has failed to develop a theatrical bistro.

And on still another plane, one of Los Angeles' most powerful businessmen comes upon a blank in public relationships which would be inconceivable in other cities of this size. This businessman, volunteering that the city is "culturally behind," as he put it, told me that he for one was at work to remedy this. He was heading a committee to raise funds for a first-rate art museum. Later in our conversation, after he had told me about the businessmen's club life of Los Angeles, a life with which he is involved as one of its leaders, I asked him how or where Hollywood people gathered in corresponding fashion. He was unable to answer this. He then added that he knew no one at all connected with the film industry, nor did he know anyone who did have such acquaintanceship. "I know that must sound strange," he reflected. "We are glad to have the film industry here, but those connected with it are just not people one would know socially."

Here again is "togetherness" or nothing. Consider this man's handicap in his attempts to get a metropolitan art museum established. He has no way of reaching with any ease, practice or trust some of his committee's potentially best prospects.

In its upper economic, political and cultural echelons, Los Angeles operates according to the same provincial premises of social insularity as the street with the sidewalk park in Baltimore or as Chatham Village in Pittsburgh. Such a metropolis lacks means for bringing together necessary ideas, necessary enthusiasms, necessary money. Los Angeles is embarked on a strange experiment: trying to run not just projects, not just gray areas, but a whole metropolis, by dint of "togetherness" or nothing. I think this is an inevitable outcome for great cities whose people lack city public life in ordinary living and working.

I. **Suggestions for Discussion:**
1. How does sidewalk use promote contact in an urban area? Why is such contact desirable?
2. What does Jacobs mean by city privacy?
3. Discuss the effectiveness of her use of illustrations and examples in her analysis of the uses of sidewalks.

II. **Suggestions for Writing:**
1. Write an essay analyzing other uses of sidewalks in cities. You may wish to read more from her book, *The Death and Life of Great American Cities.*
2. Describe the street life you observe on any block in your college or home town.

# SAMUEL JOHNSON

## Rambler 4—On Fiction

Dr. Samuel Johnson (1709-1784), the great eighteenth century English man of letters, was known for his essays, poetry, criticism, and editorial projects. "The Vanity of Human Wishes," his finest poem, appeared in 1749. From 1750-1752 he wrote essays for the *Rambler,* a periodical. His famous *Dictionary* appeared in 1755, followed by his novel, *Rasselas, Prince of Abyssinia* (1759), and his monumental *Lives of the Poets* (1779-1781).

A growing reading public in England was increasingly attracted to fiction at the time that Dr. Johnson published the following essay in the *Rambler.* In typically long, Latinate sentences, he explains

why authors of fiction must maintain high moral standards in
their works.

---

No. 4.                                                    Saturday, March 31, 1750
       *Simul et jucunda et idonea dicere vitae.*        *Horace*

And join both profit and delight in one.        *—Creech.*

The works of fiction, with which the present generation seems more
particularly delighted, are such as exhibit life in its true state, diversified only
by accidents that daily happen in the world, and influenced by passions and
qualities which are really to be found in conversing with mankind.

This kind of writing may be termed, not improperly, the comedy of
romance, and is to be conducted nearly by the rules of comic poetry. Its
province is to bring about natural events by easy means, and to keep up curiosity without the help of wonder: it is therefore precluded from the machines
and expedients of the heroic romance, and can neither employ giants to
snatch away a lady from the nuptial rites, nor rites, nor knights to bring her
back from captivity; it can neither bewilder its personages in deserts, nor
lodge them in imaginary castles.

I remember a remark made by Scaliger upon Pontanus, that all his
writings are filled with the same images; and that if you take from him his
lilies and his roses, his satyrs and his dryads, he will have nothing left that
can be called poetry. In like manner, almost all the fictions of the last age
will vanish, if you deprive them of a hermit and a wood, a battle and a
shipwreck.

Why this wild strain of imagination found reception so long in polite
and learned ages, it is not easy to conceive; but we cannot wonder that while
readers could be procured, the authors were willing to continue it; for when a
man had by practice gained some fluency of language, he had no further care
than to retire to his closet, let loose his invention, and heat his mind with
incredibilities; a book was thus produced without fear of criticism, without
the toil of study, without knowledge of nature, or acquaintance with life.

The task of our present writers is very different; it requires, together
with that learning which is to be gained from books, that experience which
can never be attained by solitary diligence, but must arise from general converse and accurate observation of the living world. Their performances have,
as Horace expresses it, "*plus oneris quantum veniae minus,*" little indulgence,
and therefore more difficulty. They are engaged in portraits of which every

one knows the original, and can detect any deviation from exactness of re-semblance. Other writings are safe, except from the malice of learning, but these are in danger from every common reader; as the slipper ill executed was censured by a shoemaker who happened to stop in his way at the Venus of Apelles.

By the fear of not being approved as just copiers of human manners, is not the most important concern that an author of this sort ought to have before him. These books are written chiefly to the young, the ignorant, and the idle, to whom they serve as lectures of conduct, and introductions into life. They are the entertainment of minds unfurnished with ideas, and there-fore easily susceptible of impressions; not fixed by principles, and therefore easily following the current of fancy; not informed by experience, and con-sequently open to every false suggestion and partial account.

That the highest degree of reverence should be paid to youth, and that nothing indecent should be suffered to approach their eyes or ears, are pre-cepts extorted by sense and virtue from an ancient writer, by no means eminent for chastity of thought. The same kind, though not the same de-gree, of caution, is required in everything which is laid before them, to secure them from unjust prejudices, perverse opinions, and incongruous combina-tions of images.

In the romances formerly written, every transaction and sentiment was so remote from all that passes among men, that the reader was in very little danger of making any applications to himself; the virtues and crimes were equally beyond his sphere of activity; and he amused himself with heroes and with traitors, deliverers and persecutors, as with beings of another species, whose actions were regulated upon motives of their own, and who had neither faults nor excellencies in common with himself.

But when an adventurer is levelled with the rest of the world, and acts in such scenes of the universal drama, as may be the lot of any other man, young spectators fix their eyes upon him with closer attention, and hope, by observing his behaviour and success, to regulate their own practices, when they shall be engaged in the like part.

For this reason these familiar histories may perhaps be made of greater use than the solemnities of professed morality, and convey the knowledge of vice and virtue with more efficacy than axioms and definitions. But if the power of example is so great as to take possession of the memory by a kind of violence, and produce effects almost without the intervention of the will, care ought to be taken, that, when the choice is unrestrained, the best ex-amples only should be exhibited; and that which is likely to operate so strongly, should not be mischievous or uncertain in its effects.

The chief advantage which these fictions have over real life is, that their authors are at liberty, though not to invent, yet to select objects, and to cull from the mass of mankind, those individuals upon which the attention ought most to be employed; as a diamond, though it cannot be made, may be polished by art, and placed in such situation, as to display that lustre which before was buried among common stones.

It is justly considered as the greatest excellency of art, to imitate nature; but it is necessary to distinguish those parts of nature which are most proper for imitation: greater care is still required in representing life, which is so often discoloured by passion, or deformed by wickedness. If the world be promiscuously described, I cannot see of what use it can be to read the account; or why it may not be as safe to turn the eye immediately upon mankind as upon a mirror which shows all that presents itself without discrimination.

It is therefore not a sufficient vindication of a character, that it is drawn as it appears; for many characters ought never to be drawn: nor of a narrative, that the train of events is agreeable to observation and experience; for that observation which is called knowledge of the world will be found much more frequently to make men cunning than good. The purpose of these writings is surely not only to show mankind, but to provide that they may be seen hereafter with less hazard; to teach the means of avoiding the snares which are laid by TREACHERY for INNOCENCE, without infusing any wish for that superiority with which the betrayer flatters his vanity; to give the power of counteracting fraud, without the temptation to practice it; to initiate youth by mock encounters in the art of necessary defense, and to increase prudence without impairing virtue.

Many writers, for the sake of following nature, so mingle good and bad qualities in their principal personages, that they are both equally conspicuous; and as we accompany them through their adventures with delight, and are led by degrees to interest ourselves in their favour, we lose the abhorrence of their faults, because they do not hinder our pleasure, or perhaps regard them with some kindness, for being united with so much merit.

There have been men indeed splendidly wicked, whose endowments threw a brightness on their crimes, and whom scarce any villainy made perfectly detestable, because they never could be wholly divested of their excellencies; but such have been in all ages the great corrupters of the world, and their resemblance ought no more to be preserved, than the art of murdering without pain.

Some have advanced, without due attention to the consequence of this notion, that certain virtues have their correspondent faults, and therefore that to exhibit either apart is to deviate from probability. Thus men are observed by Swift to be "grateful in the same degree as they are resentful." This principle, with others of the same kind, supposes man to act from a brute impulse, and pursue a certain degree of inclination, without any choice of the object; for, otherwise, though it should be allowed that gratitude and resentment arise from the same constitution of the passions, it follows not that they will be equally indulged when reason is consulted; yet, unless that consequence be admitted, this sagacious maxim becomes an empty sound, without any relation to practice or to life.

Nor is it evident that even the first motions to these effects are always in the same proportion. For pride, which produces quickness of resentment, will obstruct gratitude, by unwillingness to admit that inferiority which obligation implies; and it is very unlikely that he who cannot think he receives a favour, will acknowledge or repay it.

It is of the utmost importance to mankind that positions of this tendency should be laid open and confuted; for while men consider good and evil as springing from the same root, they will spare the one for the sake of the other, and in judging, if not of others at least of themselves, will be apt to estimate their virtues by their vices. To this fatal error all those will contribute who confound the colours of right and wrong, and, instead of helping to settle their boundaries, mix them with so much art, that no common mind is able to disunite them.

In narratives where historical veracity has no place, I cannot discover why there should not be exhibited the most perfect idea of virtue; of virtue not angelical, nor above probability—for what we cannot credit, we shall never imitate—but the highest and purest that humanity can reach, which, exercised in such trials as the various revolutions of things shall bring upon it, may, by conquering some calamities, and enduring others, teach us what we may hope, and what we can perform. Vice, for vice is necessary to be shown, should always disgust; nor should the graces of gaiety, nor the dignity of courage, be so united with it, as to reconcile it to the mind, Wherever it appears, it should raise hatred by the malignity of its practices, and contempt by the meanness of its stratagems: for while it is supported by either parts or spirit, it will be seldom heartily abhorred. The Roman tyrant was content to be hated, if he was but feared; and there are thousands of the readers of romances willing to be thought wicked, if they may be allowed to be wits. It is therefore to be steadily inculcated, that virtue is the highest proof of understanding, and the only solid basis of greatness; and that vice is the natural consequence of narrow thoughts; that it begins in mistake, and ends in ignominy.

I. **Suggestions for Discussion**:
  1. What does Dr. Johnson mean by the comedy of romance?
  2. Discuss his belief that an author of fiction has a responsibility to celebrate virtue and to condemn vice.
  3. Comment on his elaborate sentence structure and rich vocabulary.
II. **Suggestions for Writing**:
  1. Write an essay agreeing or disagreeing with Dr. Johnson's notion that many characters in fiction ought never to be drawn.
  2. State your opinion about the appropriateness of any kind of censorship of books, magazines, films, or television programs. Is there ever a time when censorship is appropriate? Do parents have an obligation to keep certain kinds of materials away from young children? Consider such questions in your response.

---

# ALFRED KAZIN

## Epilogue 1945

### from *Starting Out in the Thirties*

---

Alfred Kazin (1915–      ), American essayist and critic, has written such important books as *On Native Grounds* (1942), *A Walker in the City* (1951), and *Starting Out in the Thirties* (1962). More than seventy of his critical essays were published in *Contemporaries* (1962). His latest work, *New York Jew* (1978), surveys the New York literary and intellectual scene.

In only four paragraphs in the conclusion to *Starting Out in the Thirties,* Kazin paints indelible pictures of two moments five years apart in movie theaters in New York and London. Note his use of comparison and contrast.

---

One day in the fall of 1940, when the United States had begun to rearm on a great scale, I sat in a newsreel theater on Broadway looking at lines of tanks and heavy guns lumbering heavily, busily, cheerfully out of the factories like new automobiles, and knew that the depression was over. The depression ended only with the war, and the war created a new age of unique and boundless technical power that was to make the lean and angry Thirties seem the end of the old dog-eat-dog society and not the beginning of a new.

It was the war that launched us on our present confidence and power—and the war, in the form of permanent rearmament, goes on and on, incidentally protecting us from another period of mass unemployment and social hysteria. Probably nothing so disruptive of the social order will again be allowed to spread. The war was the first payment on the more accomplished society in which we are now living. It was a sacrifice to progress.

One day in the spring of 1945, when the war against Hitler was almost won, I sat in a newsreel theater in Piccadilly looking at the first films of newly liberated Belsen. On the screen, sticks in black-and-white prison garb leaned on a wire, staring dreamily at the camera; other sticks shuffled about, or sat vaguely on the ground, next to an enormous pile of bodies, piled up like cordwood, from which protruded legs, arms, heads. A few guards were collected sullenly in a corner, and for a moment a British Army bulldozer was shown digging an enormous hole in the ground. Then the sticks would come back on the screen, hanging on the wire, looking at us.

It was unbearable. People coughed in embarrassment, and in embarrassment many laughed.

## I. Suggestions for Discussion:
1. Discuss Kazin's use of details to make his point in this brief selection.
2. How much does the effectiveness of the selection depend on comparison and contrast? Explain.

## II. Suggestions for Writing:
1. Illustrate a point by comparing and contrasting two situations or experiences.
2. Describe the reactions of an audience to a particularly moving or disturbing film that you have seen.

---

# HELEN KELLER

## Three Days to See

---

Helen Keller (1880-1968) learned to communicate despite an early childhood illness that left her blind and deaf. Her inspiring story is told in her two books, *The Story of My Life* (1902) and

*The World I Live In* (1908), and on the stage and screen in *The Miracle Worker.*

In the following moving essay, she describes the things she would most want to see if she were given the use of her eyes for just three days.

---

All of us have read thrilling stories in which the hero had only a limited and specified time to live. Sometimes it was as long as a year; sometimes as short as twenty-four hours. But always we were interested in discovering just how the doomed man chose to spend his last days or his last hours. I speak, of course, of free men who have a choice, not condemned criminals whose sphere of activities is strictly delimited.

Such stories set us thinking, wondering what we should do under similar circumstances. What events, what experiences, what associations should we crowd into those last hours as mortal beings? What happiness should we find in reviewing the past, what regrets?

Sometimes I have thought it would be an excellent rule to live each day as if we should die tomorrow. Such an attitude would emphasize sharply the values of life. We should live each day with a gentleness, a vigor, and a keenness of appreciation which are often lost when time stretches before us in the constant panorama of more days and months and years to come. There are those, of course, who would adopt the epicurean motto of "Eat, drink, and be merry," but most people would be chastened by the certainty of impending death.

In stories, the doomed hero is usually saved at the last minute by some stroke of fortune, but almost always his sense of values is changed. He becomes more appreciative of the meaning of life and its permanent spiritual values. It has often been noted that those who live, or have lived, in the shadow of death bring a mellow sweetness to everything they do.

Most of us, however, take life for granted. We know that one day we must die, but usually we picture that day as far in the future. When we are in buoyant health, death is all but unimaginable. We seldom think of it. The days stretch out in an endless vista. So we go about our petty tasks, hardly aware of our listless attitude toward life.

The same lethargy, I am afraid, characterizes the use of all our faculties and senses. Only the deaf appreciate hearing, only the blind realize the manifold blessings that lie in sight. Particularly does this observation apply to those who have lost sight and hearing in adult life. But those who have never suffered impairment of sight or hearing seldom make the fullest use of these blessed faculties. Their eyes and ears take in all sights and sounds hazily, without concentration and with little appreciation. It is the same old story of not being grateful for what we have until we lose it, of not being conscious of health until we are ill.

I have often thought it would be a blessing if each human being were stricken blind and deaf for a few days at some time during his early adult life. Darkness would make him more appreciative of sight: silence would teach him the joys of sound.

Now and then I have tested my seeing friends to discover what they see. Recently I was visited by a very good friend who had just returned from a long walk in the woods, and I asked her what she had observed. "Nothing in particular," she replied. I might have been incredulous had I not been accustomed to such responses, for long ago I became convinced that the seeing see little.

How was it possible, I asked myself, to walk for an hour through the woods and see nothing worthy of note? I who cannot see find hundreds of things to interest me through mere touch. I feel the delicate symmetry of a leaf. I pass my hands lovingly about the smooth skin of a silver birch, or the rough shaggy bark of a pine. In spring I touch the branches of trees hopefully in search of a bud, the first sign of awakening Nature after her winter's sleep. I feel the delightful, velvety texture of a flower, and discover its remarkable convolutions, and something of the miracle of Nature is revealed to me. Occasionally, if I am fortunate, I place my hand gently on a small tree and feel the happy quiver of a bird in full song. I am delighted to have the cool waters of a brook rush through my open fingers. To me a lush carpet of pine needles or spongy grass is more welcome than the most luxurious Persian rug. To me the pageant of seasons is a thrilling and unending drama, the action of which streams through my finger tips.

At times my heart cries out with longing to see all these things. If I can get so much pleasure from mere touch, how much more beauty must be revealed by sight. Yet, those who have eyes apparently see little. The panorama of color and action which fills the world is taken for granted. It is human, perhaps, to appreciate little that which we have and to long for that which we have not, but it is a great pity that in the world of light the gift of sight is used only as a mere convenience rather than as a means of adding fullness to life.

If I were the president of a university I should establish a compulsory course in "How to Use Your Eyes." The professor would try to show his pupils how they could add joy to their lives by really seeing what passes unnoticed before them. He would try to awake their dormant and sluggish faculties.

Perhaps I can best illustrate by imagining what I should most like to see if I were given the use of my eyes, say, for just three days. And while I am imagining, suppose you, too, set your mind to work on the problem of how you would use your own eyes if you had only three more days to see. If with the oncoming darkness of the third night you knew that the sun would never rise for you again, how would you spend those three precious intervening days? What would you most want to let your gaze rest upon?

I, naturally, should want most to see the things which have become dear to me through my years of darkness. You, too, would want to let your eyes rest long on the things that have become dear to you so that you could take the memory of them with you into the night that loomed before you.

If, by some miracle I were granted three seeing days, to be followed by a relapse into darkness, I should divide the period into three parts.

On the first day, I should want to see the people whose kindness and gentleness have made my life worth living. First I should like to gaze long upon the face of my dear teacher, Mrs. Anne Sullivan Macy, who came to me when I was a child and opened the outer world to me. I should want not merely to see the outline of her face, so that I could cherish it in my memory, but to study that face and find in it the living evidence of the sympathetic tenderness and patience with which she accomplished the difficult task of my education. I should like to see in her eyes that strength of character which has enabled her to stand firm in the face of difficulties, and that compassion for all humanity which she has revealed to me so often.

I do not know what it is to see into the heart of a friend through that "window of the soul," the eye. I can only "see" through my finger tips the outline of a face. I can detect laughter, sorrow, and many other obvious emotions. I know my friends from the feel of their faces. But I cannot really picture their personalities by touch. I know their personalities, of course, through other means, through the thoughts they express to me, through whatever of their actions are revealed to me. But I am denied that deeper understanding of them which I am sure would come through sight of them, through watching their reactions to various expressed thoughts and circumstances, through noting the immediate and fleeting reactions of their eyes and countenance.

Friends who are near to me I know well, because through the months and years they reveal themselves to me in all their phases; but of casual friends I have only an incomplete impression, an impression gained from a handclasp, from spoken words which I take from their lips with my finger tips, or which they tap into the palm of my hand.

How much easier, how much more satisfying it is for you who can see to grasp quickly the essential qualities of another person by watching the subtleties of expression, the quiver of a muscle, the flutter of a hand. But does it ever occur to you to use your sight to see into the inner nature of a friend or acquaintance? Do not most of you seeing people grasp casually the outward features of a face and let it go at that?

For instance, can you describe accurately the faces of five good friends? Some of you can, but many cannot. As an experiment, I have questioned husbands of long standing about the color of their wives' eyes, and often they express embarrassed confusion and admit they do not know. And, incidentally, it is a chronic complaint of wives that their husbands do not notice new dresses, new hats, and changes in household arrangements.

The eyes of seeing persons soon become accustomed to the routine of their surroundings, and they actually see only the startling and spectacular. But even in viewing the most spectacular sights the eyes are lazy. Court records reveal every day how inaccurately "eye-witnesses" see. A given event will be "seen" in several different ways by as many witnesses. Some see more than others, but few see everything that is within the range of their vision.

Oh, the things that I should see if I had the power of sight for just three days!

The first day would be a busy one. I should call to me all my dear friends and look long into their faces, imprinting upon my mind the outward evidences of the beauty that is within them. I should let my eyes rest, too, on the face of a baby, so that I could catch a vision of the eager, innocent beauty which precedes the individual's consciousness of the conflicts which life develops.

And I should like to look into the loyal, trusting eyes of my dogs—the grave, canny little Scottie, Darkie, and the stalwart, understanding Great Dane, Helga, whose warm, tender, and playful friendships are so comforting to me.

On that busy first day I should also view the small simple things of my home. I want to see the warm colors in the rugs under my feet, the pictures on the walls, the intimate trifles that transform a house into home. My eyes would rest respectfully on the books in raised type which I have read, but they would be more eagerly interested in the printed books which seeing people can read, for during the long night of my life the books I have read and those which have been read to me have built themselves into a great shining lighthouse, revealing to me the deepest channels of human life and the human spirit.

In the afternoon of that first seeing day, I should take a long walk in the woods and intoxicate my eyes on the beauties of the world of Nature, trying desperately to absorb in a few hours the vast splendor which is constantly unfolding itself to those who can see. On the way home from my woodland jaunt my path would lie near a farm so that I might see the patient horses plowing in the field (perhaps I should see only a tractor!) and the serene content of men living close to the soil. And I should pray for the glory of a colorful sunset.

When dusk had fallen, I should experience the double delight of being able to see by artificial light, which the genius of man has created to extend the power of his sight when Nature decrees darkness.

In the night of that first day of sight, I should not be able to sleep, so full would be my mind of the memories of the day.

The next day—the second day of sight—I should arise with the dawn and see the thrilling miracle by which night is transformed into day. I should behold with awe the magnificent panorama of light with which the sun awakens the sleeping earth.

This day I should devote to a hasty glimpse of the world, past and present. I should want to see the pageant of man's progress, the kaleidoscope of the ages. How can so much be compressed into one day? Through the museums, of course. Often I have visited the New York Museum of Natural History to touch with my hands many of the objects there exhibited, but I have longed to see with my eyes the condensed history of the earth and its inhabitants displayed there—animals and the races of men pictured in their native environment; gigantic carcasses of dinosaurs and mastodons which roamed the earth long before man appeared, with his tiny stature and powerful brain, to conquer the animal kingdom; realistic presentations of the processes of evolution in animals, in man, and in the implements which man has used to fashion for himself a secure home on this planet; and a thousand and one other aspects of natural history.

I wonder how many readers of this article have viewed this panorama of the face of living things as pictured in that inspiring museum. Many, of course, have not had the opportunity, but I am sure that many who have had the opportunity have not made use of it. There, indeed, is a place to use your eyes. You who see can spend many fruitful days there, but I, with my imaginary three days of sight, could only take a hasty glimpse, and pass on.

My next stop would be the Metropolitan Museum of Art, for just as the Museum of Natural History reveals the material aspects of the world, so does the Metropolitan show the myriad facets of the human spirit. Throughout the history of humanity the urge to artistic expression has been almost as powerful as the urge for food, shelter, and procreation. And here, in the vast chambers of the Metropolitan Museum, is unfolded before me the spirit of Egypt, Greece, and Rome, as expressed in their art. I know well through my hands the sculptured gods and goddesses of the ancient Nile-land. I have felt copies of Parthenon friezes, and I have sensed the rhythmic beauty of charging Athenian warriors. Apollos and Venuses and the Winged Victory of Samothrace are friends of my finger tips. The gnarled, bearded features of Homer are dear to me, for he, too, knew blindness.

My hands have lingered upon the living marble of Roman sculpture as well as that of later generations. I have passed my hands over a plaster cast of Michelangelo's inspiring and heroic Moses; I have sensed the power of Rodin; I have been awed by the devoted spirit of Gothic wood carving. These arts which can be touched have meaning for me, but even they were meant to be seen rather than felt, and I can only guess at the beauty which remains hidden from me. I can admire the simple lines of a Greek vase, but its figured decorations are lost to me.

So on this, my second day of sight, I should try to probe into the soul of man through his art. The things I knew through touch I should now see. More splendid still, the whole magnificent world of painting would be opened to me, from the Italian Primitives, with their serene religious devotion, to the Moderns, with their feverish visions. I should look deep into the canvases of Raphael, Leonardo da Vinci, Titian, Rembrandt. I should want to feast my eyes upon the warm colors of Vernonese, study the mysteries of El Greco, catch a new vision of Nature from Corot. Oh, there is so much rich meaning and beauty in the art of the ages for you who have eyes to see!

Upon my short visit to this temple of art I should not be able to review a fraction of that great world of art which is open to you. I should be able to get only a superficial impression. Artists tell me that for a deep and true appreciation of art one must educate the eye. One must learn through experience to weigh the merits of line, of composition, of form and color. If I had eyes, how happily would I embark upon so fascinating a study! Yet I am told that, to many of you who have eyes to see, the world of art is a dark night, unexplored and unilluminated.

It would be with extreme reluctance that I should leave the Metropolitan Museum, which contains the key to beauty—a beauty so neglected. Seeing persons, however, do not need a Metropolitan to find this key to beauty. The same key lies waiting in smaller museums, and in books on the shelves of even small libraries. But naturally, in my limited time of imaginary sight, I should choose the place where the key unlocks the greatest treasures in the shortest time.

The evening of my second day of sight I should spend at a theater or at the movies. Even now I often attend theatrical performances of all sorts, but the action of the play must be spelled into my hand by a companion. But how I should like to see with my own eyes the fascinating figure of Hamlet, or the gusty Falstaff amid colorful Elizabethan trappings! How I should like to follow each movement of the graceful Hamlet, each strut of the hearty Falstaff! And since I could see only one play, I should be confronted by a many-horned dilemma, for there are scores of plays I should want to see. You who have eyes can see any you like. How many of you, I wonder, when you gaze at a play, a movie, or any spectacle, realize and give thanks for the miracle of sight which enables you to enjoy its color, grace, and movement?

I cannot enjoy the beauty of rhythmic movement except in a sphere restricted to the touch of my hands. I can vision only dimly the grace of a Pavlova, although I know something of the delight of rhythm, for often I can sense the beat of music as it vibrates through the floor. I can well imagine that cadenced motion must be one of the most pleasing sights in the world. I have been able to gather something of this by tracing with my fingers the lines in sculptured marble; if this static grace can be so lovely, how much more acute must be the thrill of seeing grace in motion.

One of my dearest memories is of the time when Joseph Jefferson allowed me to touch his face and hands as he went through some of the gestures and speeches of his beloved Rip Van Winkle. I was able to catch thus a meager glimpse of the world of drama, and I shall never forget the delight of that moment. But, oh, how much I must miss, and how much pleasure you seeing ones can derive from watching and hearing the interplay of speech and movement in the unfolding of a dramatic performance! If I could see only one play, I should know how to picture in my mind the action of a hundred plays which I have read or had transferred to me through the medium of the manual alphabet.

So, through the evening of my second imaginary day of sight, the great figures of dramatic literature would crowd sleep from my eyes.

The following morning, I should again greet the dawn, anxious to discover new delights, for I am sure that, for those who have eyes which really see, the dawn of each day must be a perpetually new revelation of beauty.

This, according to the terms of my imagined miracle, is to be my third and last day of sight. I shall have no time to waste in regrets or longings; there is too much to see. The first day I devoted to my friends, animate and inanimate. The second revealed to me the history of man and Nature. Today I shall spend in the workaday world of the present, amid the haunts of men going about the business of life. And where can one find so many activities and conditions of men as in New York? So the city becomes my destination.

I start from my home in the quiet little suburb of Forest Hills, Long Island. Here, surrounded by green lawns, trees, and flowers, are neat little houses, happy with the voices and movements of wives and children, havens of peaceful rest for men who toil in the city. I drive across the lacy structure of steel which spans the East River, and I get a new and startling vision of the power and ingenuity of the mind of man. Busy boats chug and scurry about the river—racy speed boats, stolid, snorting tugs. If I had long days of sight ahead, I should spend many of them watching the delightful activity upon the river.

I look ahead, and before me rise the fantastic towers of New York, a city that seems to have stepped from the pages of a fairy story. What an awe-inspiring sight, these glittering spires, these vast banks of stone and steel—structures such as the gods might build for themselves! This animated picture is a part of the lives of millions of people every day. How many, I wonder, give it so much as a second glance? Very few, I fear. Their eyes are blind to this magnificent sight because it is so familiar to them.

I hurry to the top of one of those gigantic structures, the Empire State Building, for there, a short time ago, I "saw" the city below through the eyes of my secretary. I am anxious to compare my fancy with reality. I am sure I should not be disappointed in the panorama spread out before me, for to me it would be a vision of another world.

Now I begin my rounds of the city. First, I stand at a busy corner, merely looking at people, trying by sight of them to understand something of their lives. I see smiles, and I am happy. I see serious determination, and I am proud. I see suffering, and I am compassionate.

I stroll down Fifth Avenue. I throw my eyes out of focus so that I see no particular object but only a seething kaleidoscope of color. I am certain that the colors of women's dresses moving in a throng must be a gorgeous spectacle of which I should never tire. But perhaps if I had sight I should be like most other women—too interested in styles and the cut of individual dresses to give much attention to the splendor of color in the mass. And I am convinced, too, that I should become an inveterate window shopper, for it must be a delight to the eye to view the myriad articles of beauty on display.

From Fifth Avenue I make a tour of the city—to Park Avenue, to the slums, to factories, to parks where children play. I take a stay-at-home trip abroad by visiting the foreign quarters. Always my eyes are open wide to all the sights of both happiness and misery so that I may probe deep and add to my understanding of how people work and live. My heart is full of the images of people and things. My eye passes lightly over no single trifle; it strives to touch and hold closely each thing its gaze rests upon. Some sights are pleasant, filling the heart with happiness; but some are miserably pathetic. To these latter I do not shut my eyes, for they, too, are part of life. To close the eye on them is to close the heart and mind.

My third day of sight is drawing to an end. Perhaps there are many serious pursuits to which I should devote the few remaining hours, but I am afraid that on the evening of that last day I should again run away to the theater, to a hilariously funny play, so that I might appreciate the overtones of comedy in the human spirit.

At midnight my temporary respite from blindness would cease, and permanent night would close in on me again. Naturally in those three short days I should not have seen all I wanted to see. Only when darkness had again descended upon me should I realize how much I had left unseen. But my mind would be so crowded with glorious memories that I should have little time for regrets. Thereafter the touch of every object would bring a flowing memory of how that object looked.

Perhaps this short outline of how I should spend three days of sight does not agree with the program you would set for yourself if you knew that you were about to be stricken blind. I am, however, sure that if you actually faced that fate your eyes would open to things you had never seen before, storing up memories for the long night ahead. You would use your eyes as never before. Everything you saw would become dear to you. Your eyes would touch and embrace every object that came within your range of vision. Then, at last, you would really see, and a new world of beauty would open itself before you.

I who am blind can give one hint to those who see—one admonition to those who would make full use of the gift of sight: Use your eyes as if tomorrow you would be stricken blind. And the same method can be applied to the other senses. Hear the music of voices, the song of a bird, the mighty strains of an orchestra, as if you would be stricken deaf tomorrow. Touch each object you want to touch as if tomorrow your tactile sense would fail. Smell the perfume of flowers, taste with relish each morsel, as if tomorrow you could never smell and taste again. Make the most of every sense; glory in all the facets of pleasure and beauty which the world reveals to you through the several means of contact with Nature provides. But of all the senses, I am sure that sight must be the most delightful.

I. **Suggestions for Discussion:**
   1. What is the central point or thesis of Keller's essay? Where and how is it stated?
   2. How does Helen Keller indicate that she would use her three days of sight? Would you use the time in the same way? Explain.

   3. Discuss her use of figurative language to illustrate her choices.
**II. Suggestions for Writing:**
   1. Describe in detail a close friend or relative.
   2. Write an essay indicating which of the five senses you would be willing
      to give up if you had to make the choice.

---

# MARTIN LUTHER KING, JR.

## Letter from Birmingham Jail

### from *Why We Can't Wait*

---

Martin Luther King, Jr. (1929–1968), a Baptist minister and president of the Southern Leadership Conference, was awarded the Nobel Peace Prize in 1964 for his leadership in the American civil rights movement. He was the author of *Stride Toward Freedom* (1958), *Strength to Love* (1963), and *Why We Can't Wait* (1964), in which the following essay appeared.

King drafted the following letter while in jail in Birmingham, Alabama. Using references from the Bible and from Western history, he offers a persuasive argument for black civil disobedience.

---

April 16, 1963

*My Dear Fellow Clergymen:*

    While confined here in the Birmingham city jail, I came across your recent statement calling my present activities "unwise and untimely." Seldom do I pause to answer criticism of my work and ideas. If I sought to answer all the criticisms that cross my desk, my secretaries would have little time for anything other than such correspondence in the course of the day, and I

AUTHOR'S NOTE: This response to a published statement by eight fellow clergymen from Alabama (Bishop C. C. J. Carpenter, Bishop Joseph A. Durick, Rabbi Hilton L. Grafman, Bishop Paul Hardin, Bishop Holan B. Harmon, the Reverend George M. Murray, the Reverend Edward V. Ramage and the Reverend Earl Stallings) was composed under somewhat constricting circumstances. Begun on the margins of the newspaper in which the statement appeared while I was in jail, the letter was continued on scraps of writing paper supplied by a friendly Negro trusty, and concluded on a pad my attorneys were eventually permitted to leave me. Although the text remains in substance unaltered, I have indulged in the author's prerogative of polishing it for publication.

would have no time for constructive work. But since I feel that you are men of genuine good will and that your criticisms are sincerely set forth, I want to try to answer your statement in what I hope will be patient and reasonable terms.

I think I should indicate why I am here in Birmingham, since you have been influenced by the view which argues against "outsiders coming in." I have the honor of serving as president of the Southern Christian Leadership Conference, an organization operating in every southern state, with head-quarters in Atlanta, Georgia. We have some eighty-five affiliated organizations across the South, and one of them is the Alabama Christian Movement for Human Rights. Frequently we share staff, educational and financial resources with our affiliates. Several months ago the affiliate here in Birmingham asked us to be on call to engage in a nonviolent direct-action program if such were deemed necessary. We readily consented, and when the hour came we lived up to our promise. So I, along with several members of my staff, am here because I was invited here. I am here because I have organizational ties here.

But more basically, I am in Birmingham because injustice is here. Just as the prophets of the eighth century B.C. left their villages and carried their "thus saith the Lord" far beyond the boundaries of their home towns, and just as the Apostle Paul left his village of Tarsus and carried the gospel of Jesus Christ to the far corners of the Greco-Roman world, so am I compelled to carry the gospel of freedom beyond my own home town. Like Paul, I must constantly respond to the Macedonian call for aid.

Moreover, I am cognizant of the interrelatedness of all communities and states. I cannot sit idly by in Atlanta and not be concerned about what happens in Birmingham. Injustice anywhere is a threat to justice everywhere. We are caught in an inescapable network of mutuality, tied in a single garment of destiny. Whatever affects one directly, affects all indirectly. Never again can we afford to live with the narrow, provincial "outside agitator" idea. Anyone who lives inside the United States can never be considered an outsider any-where within its bounds.

You deplore the demonstrations taking place in Birmingham. But your statement, I am sorry to say, fails to express a similar concern for the conditions that brought about the demonstrations. I am sure that none of you would want to rest content with the superficial kind of social analysis that deals merely with effects and does not grapple with underlying causes. It is unfortunate that demonstrations are taking place in Birmingham, but it is even more unfortunate that the city's white power structure left the Negro community with no alternative.

In any nonviolent campaign there are four basic steps: collection of the facts to determine whether injustices exist; negotiation; self-purification; and direct action. We have gone through all these steps in Birmingham. There can be no gainsaying the fact that racial injustice engulfs this community. Birmingham is probably the most thoroughly segregated city in the United States. Its ugly record of brutality is widely known. Negroes have experienced grossly unjust treatment in the courts. There have been more unsolved bombings of Negro homes and churches in Birmingham than in any other city in the nation. These are the hard brutal facts of the case. On the basis of these conditions, Negro leaders sought to negotiate with the city fathers. But the latter consistently refused to engage in good-faith negotiation.

Then, last September, came the opportunity to talk with leaders of Birmingham's economic community. In the course of the negotiations, certain promises were made by the merchants—for example, to remove the stores' humiliating racial signs. On the basis of these promises, the Reverend Fred Shuttlesworth and the leaders of the Alabama Christian Movement for Human Rights agreed to a moratorium on all demonstrations. As the weeks and months went by, we realized that we were the victims of a broken promise. A few signs, briefly removed, returned; the others remained.

As in so many past experiences, our hopes had been blasted, and the shadow of deep disappointment settled upon us. We had no alternative except to prepare for direct action, whereby we would present our very bodies as a means of laying our case before the conscience of the local and the national community. Mindful of the difficulties involved, we decided to undertake a process of self-purification. We began a series of workshops on nonviolence, and we repeatedly asked ourselves: "Are you able to accept blows without retaliating?" "Are you able to endure the ordeal of jail?" We decided to schedule our direct-action program for the Easter season, realizing that except for Christmas, this is the main shopping period of the year. Knowing that a strong economic-withdrawal program would be the by-product of direct action, we felt that this would be the best time to bring pressure to bear on the merchants for the needed change.

Then it occurred to us that Birmingham's mayoralty election was coming up in March, and we speedily decided to postpone action until after election day. When we discovered that the Commissioner of Public Safety, Eugene "Bull" Connor, had piled up enough votes to be in the run-off, we decided again to postpone action until the day after the run-off so that the demonstrations could not be used to cloud the issues. Like many others, we waited to see Mr. Connor defeated, and to this end we endured postponement after postponement. Having aided in this community need, we felt that our direct-action program could be delayed no longer.

You may well ask: "Why direct action? Why sit-ins, marches and so forth? Isn't negotiation a better path?" You are quite right in calling for negotiation. Indeed, this is the very purpose of direct action. Nonviolent direct action seeks to create such a crisis and foster such a tension that a community which has constantly refused to negotiate is forced to confront the issue. It seeks so to dramatize the issue that it can no longer be ignored. My citing the creation of tension as part of the work of the nonviolent-resister may sound rather shocking. But I must confess that I am not afraid of the word "tension." I have earnestly opposed violent tension, but there is a type of constructive nonviolent tension which is necessary for growth. Just as Socrates felt that it was necessary to create a tension in the mind so that individuals could rise from the bondage of myths and half-truths to the un-fettered realm of creative analysis and objective appraisal, so must we see the need for nonviolent gadflies to create the kind of tension in society that will help men rise from the dark depths of prejudice and racism to the majestic heights of understanding and brotherhood.

The purpose of our direct-action program is to create a situation so crisis-packed that it will inevitably open the door to negotiation. I therefore concur with you in your call for negotiation. Too long has our beloved South-land been bogged down in a tragic effort to live in monologue rather than dialogue.

One of the basic points in your statement is that the action that I and my associates have taken in Birmingham is untimely. Some have asked: "Why didn't you give the new city administration time to act?" The only answer that I can give to this query is that the new Birmingham administration must be prodded about as much as the outgoing one, before it will act. We are sadly mistaken if we feel that the election of Albert Boutwell as mayor will bring the millennium to Birmingham. While Mr. Boutwell is a much more gentle person than Mr. Connor, they are both segregationists, dedicated to maintenance of the status quo. I have hope that Mr. Boutwell will be reason-able enough to see the futility of massive resistance to desegregation. But he will not see this without pressure from devotees of civil rights. My friends, I must say to you that we have not made a single gain in civil rights without determined legal and nonviolent pressure. Lamentably, it is an historical fact that privileged groups seldom give up their privileges voluntarily. Individuals may see the moral light and voluntarily give up their unjust posture; but, as Reinhold Niebuhr has reminded us, groups tend to be more immoral than individuals.

We know through painful experience that freedom is never voluntarily given by the oppressor; it must be demanded by the oppressed. Frankly, I have yet to engage in a direct-action campaign that was "well timed" in the view of those who have not suffered unduly from the disease of segregation. For years now I have heard the word "Wait!" It rings in the ear of every Negro with piercing familiarity. This "Wait" has almost always meant "Never." We must come to see, with one of our distinguished jurists, that "justice too long delayed is justice denied."

We have waited for more than 340 years for our constitutional and Godgiven rights. The nations of Asia and Africa are moving with jetlike speed toward gaining political independence, but we still creep at horse-and-buggy pace toward gaining a cup of coffee at a lunch counter. Perhaps it is easy for those who have never felt the stinging darts of segregation to say, "Wait." But when you have seen vicious mobs lynch your mothers and fathers at will and drown your sisters and brothers at whim; when you have seen hate-filled policemen curse, kick and even kill your black brothers and sisters; when you see the vast majority of your twenty million Negro brothers smothering in an airtight cage of poverty in the midst of an affluent society; when you suddenly find your tongue twisted and your speech stammering as you seek to explain to your six-year-old daughter why she can't go to the public amusement park that has just been advertised on television, and see tears welling up in her eyes when she is told that Funtown is closed to colored children, and see ominous clouds of inferiority beginning to form in her little mental sky, and see her beginning to distort her personality by developing an unconscious bitterness toward white people; when you have to concoct an answer for a five-year-old son who is asking: "Daddy, why do white people treat colored people so mean?"; when you take a cross-country drive and find it necessary to sleep night after night in the uncomfortable corners of your automobile because no motel will accept you; when you are humiliated day in and day out by nagging signs reading "white" and "colored"; when your first name becomes "nigger," your middle name becomes "boy" (however old you are) and your last name becomes "John," and your wife and mother are never given the respected title "Mrs."; when you are harried by day and haunted by night by the fact that you are a Negro, living constantly at tiptoe stance, never quite knowing what to expect next, and are plagued with inner fears and outer resentments; when you are forever fighting a degenerating sense of "nobodiness"—then you will understand why we find it difficult to wait. There comes a time when the cup of endurance runs over, and men are no longer willing to be plunged into the abyss of despair. I hope, sirs, you can understand our legitimate and unavoidable impatience.

You express a great deal of anxiety over our willingness to break laws. This is certainly a legitimate concern. Since we so diligently urge people to obey the Supreme Court's decision of 1954 outlawing segregation in the public schools, at first glance it may seem rather paradoxical for us consciously to break laws. One may well ask: "How can you advocate breaking some laws and obeying others?" The answer lies in the fact that there are two types of laws: just and unjust. I would be the first to advocate obeying just laws. One has not only a legal but a moral responsibility to obey just laws. Conversely, one has a moral responsibility to disobey unjust laws. I would agree with St. Augustine that "an unjust law is no law at all."

Now, what is the difference between the two? How does one determine whether a law is just or unjust? A just law is a man-made code that squares with the moral law or the law of God. An unjust law is a code that is out of harmony with the moral law. To put it in the terms of St. Thomas Aquinas: An unjust law is a human law that is not rooted in eternal law and natural law. Any law that uplifts human personality is just. Any law that degrades human personality is unjust. All segregation statutes are unjust because segregation distorts the soul aand damages the personality. It gives the segregator a false sense of superiority and the segregated a false sense of inferiority. Segregation, to use the terminology of the Jewish philosopher Martin Buber, substitutes an "I-it" relationship for an "I-thou" relationship and ends up relegating persons to the status of things. Hence segregation is not only politically, economically and sociologically unsound, it is morally wrong and sinful. Paul Tillich has said that sin is separation. Is not segregation an existential expression of man's tragic separation, his awful estrangement, his terrible sinfulness. Thus it is that I can urge men to obey the 1954 decision of the Supreme Court, for it is morally right; and I can urge them to disobey segregation ordinances, for they are morally wrong.

Let us consider a more concrete example of just and unjust laws. An unjust law is a code that a numerical or power majority group compels a minority group to obey but does not make binding on itself. This is *difference* made legal. By the same token, a just law is a code that a majority compels a minority to follow and that it is willing to follow itself. This is *sameness* made legal.

Let me give another explanation. A law is unjust if it is inflicted on a minority that, as a result of being denied the right to vote, had no part in enacting or devising the law. Who can say that the legislature of Alabama which set up that state's segregation laws was democratically elected? Throughout Alabama all sorts of devious methods are used to prevent Negroes from becoming registered voters, and there are some counties in which even though Negroes constitute a majority of the population, not a single Negro is registered. Can any law enacted under such circumstances be considered democratically structured?

Sometimes a law is just on its face and unjust in its application. For instance, I have been arrested on a charge of parading without a permit. Now, there is nothing wrong in having an ordinance which requires a permit for a parade. But such an ordinance becomes unjust when it is used to maintain segregation and to deny citizens the First-Amendment privilege of peaceful assembly and protest.

I hope you are able to see the distinction I am trying to point out. In no sense do I advocate evading or defying the law, as would the rabid segregationist. That would lead to anarchy. One who breaks an unjust law must do so openly, lovingly, and with a willingness to accept the penalty. I submit that an individual who breaks a law that conscience tells him is unjust, and who willingly accepts the penalty of imprisonment in order to arouse the conscience of the community over its injustice, is in reality expressing the highest respect for law.

Of course, there is nothing new about this kind of civil disobedience. It was evidenced sublimely in the refusal of Shadrach, Meshach and Abednego to obey the laws of Nebuchadnezzar, on the ground that a higher moral law was at stake. It was practiced superbly by the early Christians, who were willing to face hungry lions and the excruciating pain of chopping blocks rather than submit to certain unjust laws of the Roman Empire. To a degree, academic freedom is a reality today because Socrates practiced civil disobedience. In our own nation, the Boston Tea Party represented a massive act of civil disobedience.

We should never forget that everything Adolf Hitler did in Germany was "legal" and everything the Hungarian freedom fighters did in Hungary was "illegal." It was "illegal" to aid and comfort a Jew in Hitler's Germany. Even so, I am sure that, had I lived in Germany at the time, I would have aided and comforted my Jewish brothers. If today I lived in a Communist country where certain principles dear to the Christian faith are suppressed, I would openly advocate disobeying that country's anti-religious laws.

I must make two honest confessions to you, my Christian and Jewish brothers. First, I must confess that over the past few years I have been gravely disappointed with the white moderate. I have almost reached the regrettable conclusion that the Negro's great stumbling block in his stride toward freedom is not the White Citizen's Counciler or the Ku Klux Klanner, but the white moderate, who is more devoted to "order" than to justice; who prefers a negative peace which is the absence of tension to a positive peace which is the presence of justice; who constantly says: "I agree with you in the goal you seek, but I cannot agree with your methods of direct action"; who paternalistically believes he can set the timetable for another man's freedom; who lives by a mythical concept of time and who constantly advises the

Negro to wait for a "more convenient season." Shallow understanding from people of good will is more frustrating than absolute misunderstanding from people of ill will. Lukewarm acceptance is much more bewildering than outright rejection.

I had hoped that the white moderate would understand that law and order exist for the purpose of establishing justice and that when they fail in this purpose they become the dangerously structured dams that block the flow of social progress. I had hoped that the white moderate would understand that the present tension in the South is a necessary phase of the transition from an obnoxious negative peace, in which the Negro passively accepted his unjust plight, to a substantive and positive peace, in which all men will respect the dignity and worth of human personality. Actually, we who engage in nonviolent direct action are not the creators of tension. We merely bring to the surface the hidden tension that is already alive. We bring it out in the open, where it can be seen and dealt with. Like a boil that can never be cured so long as it is covered up but must be opened with all its ugliness to the natural medicines of air and light, injustice must be exposed, with all the tension its exposure creates, to the light of human conscience and the air of national opinion before it can be cured.

In your statement you assert that our actions, even though peaceful, must be condemned because they precipitate violence. But is this a logical assertion? Isn't this like condemning a robbed man because his possession of money precipitated the evil act of robbery? Isn't this like condemning Socrates because his unswerving commitment to truth and his philosophical inquiries precipitated the act by the misguided populace in which they made him drink hemlock? Isn't this like condemning Jesus because his unique God-consciousness and never-ceasing devotion to God's will precipitated the evil act of crucifixion? We must come to see that, as the federal courts have consistently affirmed, it is wrong to urge an individual to cease his efforts to gain his basic constitutional rights because the quest may precipitate violence. Society must protect the robbed and punish the robber.

I had also hoped that the white moderate would reject the myth concerning time in relation to the struggle for freedom. I have just received a letter from a white brother in Texas. He writes: "All Christians know that the colored people will receive equal rights eventually, but it is possible that you are in too great a religious hurry. It has taken Christianity almost two thousand years to accomplish what it has. The teachings of Christ take time to come to earth." Such an attitude stems from a tragic misconception of time, from the strangely irrational notion that there is something in the very flow of time that will inevitably cure all ills. Actually, time itself is neutral;

it can be used either destructively or constructively. More and more I feel that the people of ill will have used time much more effectively than have the people of good will. We will have to repent in this generation not merely for the hateful words and actions of the bad people but for the appalling silence of the good people. Human progress never rolls in on wheels of inevitability; it comes through the tireless efforts of men willing to be co-workers with God, and without this hard work, time itself becomes an ally of the forces of social stagnation. We must use time creatively, in the knowledge that the time is always ripe to do right. Now is the time to make real the promise of democracy and transform our pending national elegy into a creative psalm of brotherhood. Now is the time to lift our national policy from the quicksand of racial injustice to the solid rock of human dignity.

You speak of our activity in Birmingham as extreme. At first I was rather disappointed that fellow clergymen would see my nonviolent efforts as those of an extremist. I began thinking about the fact that I stand in the middle of two opposing forces in the Negro community. One is a force of complacency, made up in part of Negroes who, as a result of long years of oppression, are so drained of self-respect and a sense of "somebodiness" that they have adjusted to segregation; and in part of a few middle-class Negroes who, because of a degree of academic and economic security and because in some ways they profit by segregation, have become insensitive to the problems of the masses. The other force is one of bitterness and hatred, and it comes perilously close to advocating violence. It is expressed in the various black nationalist groups that are springing up across the nation, the largest and best-known being Elijah Muhammad's Muslim movement. Nourished by the Negro's frustration over the continued existence of racial discrimination, this movement is made up of people who have lost faith in America, who have absolutely repudiated Christianity, and who have concluded that the white man is an incorrigible "devil."

I have tried to stand between these two forces, saying that we need emulate neither the "do-nothingism" of the complacent nor the hatred and despair of the black nationalist. For there is the more excellent way of love and nonviolent protest. I am grateful to God that, through the influence of the Negro church, the way of nonviolence became an integral part of our struggle.

If this philosophy had not emerged, by now many streets of the South would, I am convinced, be flowing with blood. And I am further convinced that if our white brothers dismiss as "rabble-rousers" and "outside agitators" those of us who employ nonviolent direct action, and if they refuse to support our non-violent efforts, millions of Negroes will, out of frustration and despair, seek solace and security in black-nationalist ideologies—a development that would inevitably lead to a frightening racial nightmare.

Oppressed people cannot remain oppressed forever. The yearning for freedom eventually manifests itself, and that is what has happened to the American Negro. Something within has reminded him of his birthright of freedom, and something without has reminded him that it can be gained. Consciously or unconsciously, he has been caught up by the *Zeitgeist,* and with his black brothers of Africa and his brown and yellow brothers of Asia, South America and the Caribbean, the United States Negro is moving with a sense of great urgency toward the promised land of racial justice. If one recognizes this vital urge that has engulfed the Negro community, one should readily understand why public demonstrations are taking place. The Negro has many pent-up resentments and latent frustrations, and he must release them. So let him march; let him make prayer pilgrimages to the city hall; let him go on freedom rides—and try to understand why he must do so. If his repressed emotions are not released in nonviolent ways, they will seek expression through violence; this is not a threat but a fact of history. So I have not said to my people: "Get rid of your discontent." Rather, I have tried to say that this normal and healthy discontent can be channeled into the creative outlet of nonviolent direct action. And now this approach is being termed extremist.

But though I was initially disappointed at being categorized as an extremist, as I continued to think about the matter I gradually gained a measure of satisfaction from the label. Was not Jesus an extremist for love: "Love your enemies, bless them that curse you, do good to them that hate you, and pray for them which despitefully use you, and persecute you." Was not Amos an extremist for justice: "Let justice roll down like waters and righteousness like an ever-flowing stream." Was not Paul an extremist for the Christian gospel: "I bear in my body the marks of the Lord Jesus." Was not Martin Luther an extremist: "Here I stand; I cannot do otherwise, so help me God." And John Bunyan: "I will stay in jail to the end of my days before I make a butchery of my conscience." And Abraham Lincoln: "This nation cannot survive half slave and half free." And Thomas Jefferson: "We hold these truths to be self-evident, that all men are created equal. . . ." So the question is not whether we will be extremists, but what kind of extremists we will be. Will we be extremists for hate or for love? Will we be extremists for the preservation of injustice or for the extension of justice? In that dramatic scene on Calvary's hill three men were crucified. We must never forget that all three were crucified for the same crime—the crime of extremism. Two were extremists for immorality, and thus fell below their environment. The other, Jesus Christ, was an extremist for love, truth and goodness, and thereby rose above his environment. Perhaps the South, the nation and the world are in dire need of creative extremists.

I had hoped that the white moderate would see this need. Perhaps I was too optimistic; perhaps I expected too much. I suppose I should have realized that few members of the oppressor race can understand the deep groans and passionate yearnings of the oppressed race, and still fewer have the vision to see that injustice must be rooted out by strong, persistent and determined action. I am thankful, however, that some of our white brothers in the South have grasped the meaning of this social revolution and committed themselves to it. They are still all too few in quantity, but they are big in quality. Some—such as Ralph McGill, Lillian Smith, Harry Golden, James McBride Dabbs, Ann Braden and Sarah Patton Boyle—have written about our struggle in eloquent and prophetic terms. Others have marched with us down nameless streets of the South. They have languished in filthy, roach-infested jails, suffering the abuse and brutality of policemen who view them as "dirty nigger-lovers." Unlike so many of their moderate brothers and sisters, they have recognized the urgency of the moment and sensed the need for powerful "action" antidotes to combat the disease of segregation.

Let me take note of my other major disappointment. I have been so greatly disappointed with the white church and its leadership. Of course, there are some notable exceptions. I am not unmindful of the fact that each of you has taken some significant stands on this issue. I commend you, Reverend Stallings, for your Christian stand on this past Sunday, in welcoming Negroes to your worship service on a nonsegregated basis. I commend the Catholic leaders of this state for integrating Spring Hill College several years ago.

But despite these notable exceptions, I must honestly reiterate that I have been disappointed with the church. I do not say this as one of those negative critics who can always find something wrong with the church. I say this as a minister of the gospel, who loves the church; who was nurtured in its bosom; who has been sustained by its spiritual blessings and who will remain true to it as long as the cord of life shall lengthen.

When I was suddenly catapulted into the leadership of the bus protest in Montgomery, Alabama, a few years ago, I felt we would be supported by the white church. I felt that the white ministers, priests and rabbis of the South would be among our strongest allies. Instead, some have been outright opponents, refusing to understand the freedom movement and misrepresenting its leaders; all too many others have been more cautious than courageous and have remained silent behind the anesthetizing security of stained-glass windows.

In spite of my shattered dreams, I came to Birmingham with the hope that the white religious leadership of this community would see the justice of our cause and, with deep moral concern, would serve as the channel through which our just grievances could reach the power structure. I had hoped that each of you would understand. But again I have been disappointed.

I have heard numerous southern religious leaders admonish their worshipers to comply with a desegregation decision because it is the law, but I have longed to hear white ministers declare: "Follow this decree because integration is morally right and because the Negro is your brother." In the midst of blatant injustices inflicted upon the Negro, I have watched white churchmen stand on the sideline and mouth pious irrelevancies and sanctimonious trivialities. In the midst of a mighty struggle to rid our nation of racial and economic injustice, I have heard many ministers say: "Those are social issues, with which the gospel has no real concern." And I have watched many churches commit themselves to a completely other-worldly religion which makes a strange, un-Biblical distinction between body and soul, between the sacred and the secular.

I have traveled the length and breadth of Alabama, Mississippi and all the other southern states. On sweltering summer days and crisp autumn mornings I have looked at the South's beautiful churches with their lofty spires pointing heavenward. I have beheld the impressive outlines of her massive religious-education buildings. Over and over I have found myself asking: "What kind of people worship here? Who is their God? Where were their voices when the lips of Governor Barnett dripped with words of interposition and nullification? Where were they when Governor Wallace gave a clarion call for defiance and hatred? Where were their voices of support when bruised and weary Negro men and women decided to rise from the dark dungeons of complacency to the bright hills of creative protest?"

Yes, these questions are still in my mind. In deep disappointment I have wept over the laxity of the church. But be assured that my tears have been tears of love. There can be no deep disappointment where there is not deep love. Yes, I love the church. How could I do otherwise? I am in the rather unique position of being the son, the grandson and the great-grandson of preachers. Yes, I see the church as the body of Christ. But, oh! How we have blemished and scarred that body through social neglect and through fear of being nonconformists.

There was a time when the church was very powerful—in the time when the early Christians rejoiced at being deemed worthy to suffer for what they believed. In those days the church was not merely a thermometer that recorded the ideas and principles of popular opinion; it was a thermostat that transformed the mores of society. Whenever the early Christians entered a

town, the people in power became disturbed and immediately sought to convict the Christians for being "disturbers of the peace" and "outside agitators." But the Christians pressed on, in the conviction that they were "a
colony of heaven," called to obey God rather than man. Small in number,
they were big in commitment. They were too God-intoxicated to be "astro-
nomically intimidated." By their effort and example they brought an end to
such ancient evils as infanticide and gladiatorial contests.

Things are different now. So often the contemporary church is a weak,
ineffectual voice with an uncertain sound. So often it is an archdefender of
the status quo. Far from being disturbed by the presence of the church, the
power structure of the average community is consoled by the church's silent—
and often even vocal—sanction of things as they are.

But the judgment of God is upon the church as never before. If today's
church does not recapture the sacrificial spirit of the early church, it will lose
its authenticity, forfeit the loyalty of millions, and be dismissed as an irrelevant social club with no meaning for the twentieth century. Every day I
meet young people whose disappointment with the church has turned into
outright disgust.

Perhaps I have once again been too optimistic. Is organized religion too
inextricably bound to the status quo to save our nation and the world? Perhaps I must turn my faith to the inner spiritual church, the church within the
church, as the true *ekklesia* and the hope of the world. But again I am thankful to God that some noble souls from the ranks of organized religion have
broken loose from the paralyzing chains of conformity and joined us as active
partners in the struggle for freedom. They have left their secure congregations
and walked the streets of Albany, Georgia, with us. They have gone down the
highways of the South on tortuous rides for freedom. Yes, they have gone to
jail with us. Some have been dismissed from their churches, have lost the
support of their bishops and fellow ministers. But they have acted in the faith
that right defeated is stronger than evil triumphant. Their witness has been
the spiritual salt that has preserved the true meaning of the gospel in these
troubled times. They have carved a tunnel of hope through the dark mountain of disappointment.

I hope the church as a whole will meet the challenge of this decisive
hour. But even if the church does not come to the aid of justice, I have no
despair about the future. I have no fear about the outcome of our struggle
in Birmingham, even if our motives are at present misunderstood. We will
reach the goal of freedom in Birmingham and all over the nation, because
the goal of America is freedom. Abused and scorned though we may be,
our destiny is tied up with America's destiny. Before the pilgrims landed at

Plymouth, we were here. Before the pen of Jefferson etched the majestic words of the Declaration of Independence across the pages of history, we were here. For more than two centuries our forebears labored in this country without wages; they made cotton king; they built the homes of their masters while suffering gross injustice and shameful humiliation—and yet out of a bottomless vitality they continued to thrive and develop. If the inexpressible cruelties of slavery could not stop us, the opposition we now face will surely fail. We will win our freedom because the sacred heritage of our nation and the eternal will of God are embodied in our echoing demands.

Before closing I feel impelled to mention one other point in your state-ment that has troubled me profoundly. You warmly commended the Birming-ham police force for keeping "order" and "preventing violence." I doubt that you would have so warmly commended the police force if you had seen its dogs sinking their teeth into unarmed, nonviolent Negroes. I doubt that you would so quickly commend the policemen if you were to observe their ugly and inhumane treatment of Negroes here in the city jail; if you were to watch them push and curse old Negro women and young Negro girls; if you were to see them slap and kick old Negro men and young boys; if you were to observe them as they did on two occasions, refuse to give us food because we wanted to sing our grace together. I cannot join you in your praise of the Birmingham police department.

It is true that the police have exercised a degree of discipline in handling the demonstrators. In this sense they have conducted themselves rather "non-violently" in public. But for what purpose? To preserve the evil system of segregation. Over the past few years I have consistently preached that non-violence demands that the means we use must be as pure as the ends we seek. I have tried to make clear that it is wrong to use immoral means to attain moral ends. But now I must affirm that it is just as wrong, or perhaps even more so, to use moral means to preserve immoral ends. Perhaps Mr. Connor and his policemen have been rather nonviolent in public, as was Chief Pritchett in Albany, Georgia, but they have used the moral means of nonviolence to maintain the immoral end of racial injustice. As T. S. Eliot has said: "The last temptation is the greatest treason: To do the right deed for the wrong reason."

I wish you had commended the Negro sit-inners and demonstrators of Birmingham for their sublime courage, their willingness to suffer and their amazing discipline in the midst of great provocation. One day the South will recognize its real heroes. They will be the James Merediths, with the noble sense of purpose that enables them to face jeering and hostile mobs, and with the agonizing loneliness that characterizes the life of the pioneer. They will be old, oppressed, battered Negro women, symbolized in a seventy-two-year-old woman in Montgomery, Alabama, who rose up with a sense of dignity and with her people decided not to ride segregated buses, and who responded with ungrammatical profundity to one who inquired about her weariness: "My feet is tired, but my soul is at rest." They will be the young high school and college students, the young ministers of the gospel and a host of their elders, courageously and nonviolently sitting in at lunch counters and willingly going to jail for conscience' sake. One day the South will know that when these disinherited children of God sat down at lunch counters, they were in reality standing up for what is best in the American dream and for the most sacred values in our Judaeo-Christian heritage, thereby bringing our nation back to those great wells of democracy which were dug deep by the founding fathers in their formulation of the Constitution and the Declaration of Independence.

Never before have I written so long a letter. I'm afraid it is much too long to take your precious time. I can assure you that it would have been much shorter if I had been writing from a comfortable desk, but what else can one do when he is alone in a narrow jail cell, other than write long letters, think long thoughts and pray long prayers?

If I have said anything in this letter that overstates the truth and indicates an unreasonable impatience, I beg you to forgive me. If I have said anything that understates the truth and indicates my having a patience that allows me to settle for anything less than brotherhood, I beg God to forgive me.

I hope this letter finds you strong in the faith. I also hope that circumstances will soon make it possible for me to meet each of you, not as an integrationist or a civil-rights leader but as a fellow clergyman and a Christian brother. Let us all hope that the dark clouds of racial prejudice will soon pass away and the deep fog of misunderstanding will be lifted from our fear-drenched communities, and in some not too distant tomorrow the radiant stars of love and brotherhood will shine over our great nation with all their scintillating beauty.

Yours for the cause of Peace and Brotherhood,<br>
*Martin Luther King, Jr.*

## I. Suggestions for Discussion:

1. What is the difference between a just and an unjust law, according to Dr. King? Do you agree? Explain.
2. Discuss the various audiences for this letter.

3. Discuss Dr. King's disappointment with white moderates and with the white church and its leadership.

II. **Suggestions for Writing**:

1. Write a vigorous, well-documented letter defending an unpopular position you espouse.

2. Compare the tone of Dr. King's letter with that of James Baldwin's *New York Times* column, p. 51.

---

# CHARLES LAMB

## A Dissertation Upon Roast Pig

---

Charles Lamb (1775–1834), the English critic, essayist, and poet, was a friend of Coleridge, Keats, and Wordsworth. With his invalid sister, he published *Tales from Shakespeare* in 1807. While a regular contributor to the *London Magazine* (1820–1823), he published the well-known essay which follows.

Lamb begins the charming essay with an illustrative narrative which whimsically explains how human beings began to eat cooked flesh. He then describes the delights of eating roast pork.

---

Mankind, says a Chinese manuscript, which my friend M. was obliging enough to read and explain to me, for the first seventy thousand ages ate their meat raw, clawing or biting it from the living animal, just as they do in Abyssinia to this day. This period is not obscurely hinted at by their great Confucius in the second chapter of his Mundane Mutations, where he designates a kind of golden age by the term Chofang, literally the Cooks' Holiday. The manuscript goes on to say, that the art of roasting, or rather broiling (which I take to be the elder brother) was accidentally discovered in the manner following. The swine-herd, Ho-ti, having gone out into the woods one morning, as his manner was, to collect mast for his hogs, left his cottage in the care of his eldest son Bo-bo, a great lubberly boy, who being fond of playing with fire, as younkers of his age commonly are, let some sparks escape into a bundle of straw, which kindling quickly, spread the conflagration over every part of their poor mansion, till it was reduced to ashes. Together with the cottage (a sorry antediluvian make-shift of a building, you may think it), what was of much more importance, a fine litter of new-farrowed pigs, no less than nine in number, perished. China pigs have been esteemed a luxury all over the East, from the remotest periods that we read of. Bo-bo was in the utmost consternation, as you may think, not so much for the sake of the tenement, which his father and he could easily build up again with a few dry branches, and the labor of an hour or two, at any time, as for the loss of the pigs. While he was thinking what he should say to his father, and wringing his hands over the smoking remnants of one of those untimely sufferers, an odor assailed his nostrils, unlike any scent which he had before experienced. What could it proceed from?—not from the burnt cottage—he had smelt that smell before—indeed this was by no means the first accident of the kind which had occurred through the negligence of this unlucky young fire-brand. Much less did it resemble that of any known herb, weed, or flower. A premonitory moistening at the same time overflowed his nether lip. He knew not what to think. He next stooped down to feel the pig, if there were any signs of life in it. He burnt his fingers, and to cool them he applied them in his booby fashion to his mouth. Some of the crumbs of the scorched skin had come away with his fingers, and for the first time in his life (in the world's life indeed, for before him no man had known it) he tasted—*crackling*! Again he felt and fumbled at the pig. It did not burn him so much now, still he licked his fingers from a sort of habit. The truth at length broke into his slow understanding, that it was the pig that smelt so, and the pig that tasted so delicious; and surrendering himself up to the new-born pleasure, he fell to tearing up whole handfuls of the scorched skin with the flesh next it, and was cramming it down his throat in his beastly fashion, when his sire entered amid the smoking rafters, armed with retributory cudgel, and finding how affairs stood, began to rain blows upon the young rogue's shoulders, as thick as hailstones, which Bo-bo heeded not any more than if they had been flies. The tickling pleasure, which he experienced in his lower regions, had rendered him quite callous to any inconveniences he might feel in those remote quarters. His father might lay on, but he could not beat him from his pig, till he had fairly made an end of it, when, becoming a little more sensible of his situation, something like the following dialogue ensued.

"You graceless whelp, what have you got there devouring? Is it not enough that you have burnt me down three houses with your dog's tricks, and be hanged to you! but you must be eating fire, and I know not what—what have you got there, I say?"

"O father, the pig, the pig! do come and taste how nice the burnt pig eats."

The ears of Ho-ti tingled with horror. He cursed his son, and he cursed himself that ever he should beget a son that should eat burnt pig.

Bo-bo, whose scent was wonderfully sharpened since morning, soon raked out another pig, and fairly rending it asunder, thrust the lesser half by main force into the fists of Ho-ti, still shouting out, "Eat, eat, eat the burnt pig, father, only taste—O Lord!"—with such-like barbarous ejaculations, cramming all the while as if he would choke.

Ho-ti trembled every joint while he grasped the abominable thing, wavering whether he should not put his son to death for an unnatural young monster, when the crackling scorching his fingers, as it had done his son's, and applying the same remedy to them, he in his turn tasted some of its flavor, which, make what sour mouths he would for a pretense, proved not altogether displeasing to him. In conclusion (for the manuscript here is a little tedious), both father and son fairly set down to the mess, and never left off till they had dispatched all that remained of the litter.

Bo-bo was strictly enjoined not to let the secret escape, for the neighbors would certainly have stoned them for a couple of abominable wretches, who could think of improving upon the good meat which God had sent them. Nevertheless, strange stories got about. It was observed that Ho-ti's cottage was burnt down now more frequently than ever. Nothing but fires from this time forward. Some would break out in broad day, others in the night-time. As often as the sow farrowed, so sure was the house of Ho-ti to be in a blaze; and Ho-ti himself, which was the more remarkable, instead of chastising his son, seemed to grow more indulgent to him than ever. At length they were watched, the terrible mystery discovered, and father and son summoned to take their trial at Pekin, then an inconsiderable assize town. Evidence was given, the obnoxious food itself produced in court, and verdict about to be pronounced, when the foreman of the jury begged that some of the burnt pig, of which the culprits stood accused, might be handed into the box. He handled it, and they all handled it; and burning their fingers, as Bo-bo and his father had done before them, and nature prompting to each of them the same remedy, against the face of all the facts, and the clearest charge which judge had ever given—to the surprise of the whole court, townsfolk, strangers, reporters, and all present—without leaving the box, or any manner of consultation whatever, they brought in a simultaneous verdict of Not Guilty.

The judge, who was a shrewd fellow, winked at the manifest iniquity of the decision: and when the court was dismissed, went privily and bought up all the pigs that could be had for love or money. In a few days his lordship's town-house was observed to be on fire. The thing took wing, and now there was nothing to be seen but fire in every direction. Fuel and pigs grew enormously dear all over the district. The insurance-offices one and all shut up shop. People built slighter and slighter every day, until it was feared that the very science of architecture would in no long time be lost to the world. Thus this custom of firing houses continued, till in process of time, says my manuscript, a sage arose, like our Locke, who made a discovery that the flesh of swine, or indeed of any other animal, might be cooked (*burnt,* as they called it) without the necessity of consuming a whole house to dress it. Then first began the rude form of a girdiron. Roasting by the string or spit came in a century or two later, I forget in whose dynasty. By such slow degrees, concludes the manuscript, do the most useful, and seemingly the most obvious, arts make their way among mankind——

Without placing too implicit faith in the account above given, it must be agreed that if a worthy pretext for so dangerous an experiment as setting houses on fire (especially in these days) could be assigned in favor of any culinary object, that pretext and excuse might be found in Roast Pig.

Of all the delicacies in the whole *mundus edibilis,*[1] I will maintain it to be the most delicate—*princeps obsoniorum.*

I speak not of your grown porkers—things between pig and pork—those hobbydehoys—but a young and tender suckling—under a moon old—guiltless as yet of the sty—with no original speck of the *amor immunditae,* the hereditary failing of the first parent, yet manifest—his voice as yet not broken, but something between a childish treble and a grumble—the mild forerunner or *praeludium* of a grunt.

*He must be roasted.* I am not ignorant that our ancestors ate them seethed, or boiled—but what a sacrifice to the exterior tegument!

There is no flavor comparable, I will contend, to that of the crisp, tawny, well-watched, not over-roasted, *crackling,* as it is well called—the very teeth are invited to their share of the pleasure at this banquet in overcoming the coy, brittle resistance—with the adhesive oleaginous—O call it not fat! but an indefinable sweetness growing up to it—the tender blossoming of fat—fat cropped in the bud—taken in the shoot—in the first innocence—the cream and quintessence of the child—pig's yet pure food—the lean, no lean, but a kind of animal manna—or, rather, fat and lean (if it must be so) so blended and running into each other, that both together make but one ambrosian result or common substance.

Behold him, while he is "doing"—it seemeth rather a refreshing warmth, than a scorching heat, that he is so passive to. How equably he twirleth round

---

[1] World of food. The next two Latin phrases mean "foremost of delicacies" and "love of filth."

the string!—Now he is just done. To see the extreme sensibility of that tender age! he hath wept out his pretty eyes—radiant jellies—shooting stars.—

See him in the dish, his second cradle, how meek he lieth!—wouldst thou have had this innocent grow up to the grossness and indocility which too often accompany maturer swinehood? Ten to one he would have proved a glutton, a sloven, an obstinate, disagreeable animal—wallowing in all manner of filthy conversation—from these sins he is happily snatched away——

> Ere sin could blight or sorrow fade,
> Death came with timely care—

his memory is odoriferous—no clown curseth, while his stomach half rejecteth, the rank bacon—no coal-heaver bolteth him in reeking sausages—he hath a fair sepulchre in the grateful stomach of the judicious epicure—and for such a tomb might be content to die.

He is the best of sapors. Pine-apple is great. She is indeed almost too transcendent—a delight, if not sinful, yet so like to sinning that really a tender-conscienced person would do well to pause—too ravishing for mortal taste, she woundeth and excoriateth the lips that approach her—like lovers' kisses, she biteth—she is a pleasure bordering on pain from the fierceness and insanity of her relish—but she stoppeth at the palate—she meddleth not with the appetite—and the coarsest hunger might barter her consistently for a mutton-chop.

Pig—let me speak his praise—is no less provocative of the appetite, than he is satisfactory to the criticalness of the censorious palate. The strong man may batten on him, and the weakling refuseth not his mild juices.

Unlike to mankind's mixed characters, a bundle of virtues and vices, inexplicably intertwisted, and not to be unravelled without hazard, he is—good throughout. No part of him is better or worse than another. He helpeth, as far as his little means extend, all around. He is the least envious of banquets. He is all neighbors' fare.

I am one of those, who freely and ungrudgingly impart a share of the good things of this life which fall to their lot (few as mine are in this kind) to a friend. I protest I take as great an interest in my friend's pleasures, his relishes, and proper satisfactions, as in mine own. "Presents," I often say, "endear Absents." Hares, pheasants, partridges, snipes, barndoor chickens (those "tame villatic fowl"), capons, plovers, brawn, barrels of oysters, I dispense as freely as I receive them. I love to taste them, as it were, upon the tongue of my friend. But a stop must be put somewhere. One would not, like Lear, "give everything." I make my stand upon pig. Methinks it is an ingratitude to the Giver of all good flavors to extra-domiciliate, or send out of the house slightingly (under pretext of friendship, or I know not what) a blessing so particularly adapted, predestined, I may say, to my individual palate—It argues an insensibility.

I remember a touch of conscience in this kind at school. My good old aunt, who never parted from me at the end of a holiday without stuffing a sweetmeat, or some nice thing into my pocket, had dismissed me one evening with a smoking plum-cake, fresh from the oven. In my way to school (it was over London Bridge) a gray-headed old beggar saluted me (I have no doubt, at this time of day, that he was a counterfeit). I had no pence to console him with, and in the vanity of self-denial and the very coxcombry of charity, schoolboy-like, I made him a present of—the whole cake! I walked on a little, buoyed up, as one is on such occasions, with a sweet soothing of self-satisfaction; but before I had got to the end of the bridge, my better feelings returned, and I burst into tears, thinking how ungrateful I had been to my good aunt, to go and give her good gift away to a stranger that I had never seen before, and who might be a bad man for aught I knew; and then I thought of the pleasure my aunt would be taking in thinking that I—I myself, and not another—would eat her nice cake—and what should I say to her the next time I saw her—how naughty I was to part with her pretty present!—and the odor of that spicy cake came back upon my recollection, and the pleasure and the curiosity I had taken in seeing her make it, and her joy when she sent it to the oven, and how disappointed she would feel that I had never had a bit of it in my mouth at last—and I blamed my impertinent spirit of alms-giving, and out-of-place hypocrisy of goodness; and above all I wished never to see the face again of that insidious, good-for-nothing, old gray imposter.

Our ancestors were nice in their method of sacrificing these tender victims. We read of pigs whipt to death with something of a shock, as we hear of any other obsolete custom. The age of discipline is gone by, or it would be curious to inquire (in a philosophical light merely) what effect this process might have toward intenerating and dulcifying a substance, naturally so mild and dulcet as the flesh of young pigs. It looks like refining a violet. Yet we should be cautious, while we condemn the inhumanity, how we censure the wisdom of the practice. It might impart a gusto.—

I remember an hypothesis, argued upon by the young students, when I was at St. Omer's, and maintained with much learning and pleasantry on both sides, "Whether, supposing that the flavor of a pig who obtained his death by whipping (*per flagellationem extremam*) superadded a pleasure upon the palate of a man more intense than any possible suffering we can conceive in the animal, is man justified in using that method of putting the animal to death?" I forget the decision.

His sauce should be considered. Decidedly, a few bread crumbs, done up with his liver and brains, a dash of mild sage. But banish, dear Mr. Cook, I beseech you, the whole onion tribe. Barbecue your whole hogs to your palate, steep them in shalots, stuff them out with plantations of the rank and guilty garlic; you cannot poison them or make them stronger than they are—but consider, he is a weakling—a flower.

I. **Suggestions for Discussion:**
   1. Discuss the sources of Lamb's humor. A dissertation, for example, ordinarily means an elaborate and learned discourse on an intellectually important subject. Is Lamb's title here appropriate?
   2. Note and discuss Lamb's use of archaic or antiquated words and phrases.
   3. Discuss Lamb's use of hyperbole or exaggeration. Be specific.

II. **Suggestions for Writing:**
   1. Using his essay as a model, write an imaginary history and sensory description of a favorite food.
   2. Give a colorful recipe, as though you were writing a food column for a magazine like *Gourmet* or *Sunset.*

---

# ABRAHAM LINCOLN

## Second Inaugural Address

---

Abraham Lincoln (1809–1865) was the sixteenth President of the United States. The "Second Inaugural Address" was delivered only six weeks before his assassination in Ford's Theatre in Washington, D.C. on April 14, 1865.

Briefly and powerfully, President Lincoln called upon the nation "to finish the work we are in; to bind up the nation's wounds." The balanced, rhetorical conclusion is justly famous.

---

FELLOW COUNTRYMEN:

At this second appearing to take the oath of the presidential office, there is less occasion for an extended address than there was at the first. Then a statement, somewhat in detail, of course to be pursued, seemed fitting and proper. Now, at the expiration of four years, during which public declarations have been constantly called forth on every point and phase of the great contest which still absorbs the attention and engrosses the energies of the nation, little that is new could be presented. The progress of our arms, upon which all else chiefly depends, is as well known to the public as to myself; and it is, I trust, reasonably satisfactory and encouraging to all. With high hope for the future, no prediction in regard to it is ventured.

On the occasion corresponding to this four years ago, all thoughts were anxiously directed to an impending civil war. All dreaded it—all sought to avert it. While the inaugural address was being delivered from this place, devoted altogether to saving the Union without war, insurgent agents were in the city seeking to destroy it without war—seeking to dissolve the Union, and divide effects, by negotiation. Both parties deprecated war; but one of them would make war rather than let the nation survive; and the other would accept war rather than let it perish. And the war came.

One-eighth of the whole population were colored slaves, not distributed generally over the Union, but localized in the Southern part of it. These slaves constituted a peculiar and powerful interest. All knew that this interest was, somehow, the cause of the war. To strengthen, perpetuate, and extend this interest was the object for which the insurgents would rend the Union, even by war; while the government claimed no right to do more than to restrict the territorial enlargement of it.

Neither party expected for the war the magnitude or the duration which it has already attained. Neither anticipated that the cause of the conflict might cease with, or even before, the conflict itself should cease. Each looked for an easier triumph, and a result less fundamental and astounding. Both read the same Bible, and pray to the same God; and each invokes his aid against the other. It may seem strange that any men should dare to ask a just God's assistance in wringing their bread from the sweat of other men's faces; but let us judge not, that we be not judged. The prayers of both could not be answered—that of neither has been answered fully.

The Almighty has his own purposes. "Woe unto the world because of offences! for it must needs be that offences come; but woe to that man by whom the offence cometh." If we shall suppose that American slavery is one of those offences which, in the providence of God, must needs come, but which, having continued through his appointed time, he now wills to remove, and that he gives to both North and South this terrible war, as the woe due to those by whom the offence came, shall we discern therein any departure from those divine attributes which the believers in a living God always ascribe to him? Fondly do we hope—fervently do we pray—that this mighty scourge of war may speedily pass away. Yet, if God wills that it continue until all the wealth piled by the bondsman's two hundred and fifty years of unrequited toil shall be sunk, and until every drop of blood drawn with the lash shall be paid by another drawn with the sword, as was said three thousand years ago, so still it must be said, "The judgments of the Lord are true and righteous altogether."

With malice toward none; with charity for all: with firmness in the right, as God gives us to see the right, let us strive on to finish the work we are in; to bind up the nation's wounds; to care for him who shall have borne the battle, and for his widow, and his orphan—to do all which may achieve and cherish a just and lasting peace among ourselves, and with all nations.

I. **Suggestions for Discussion:**
1. Discuss Lincoln's use of rhetorical devices to give dignity and stature to his remarks.
2. Discuss whether or not such a brief address is appropriate for such an important occasion. Consider Benjamin Franklin's comments in "On Literary Style," p. 189.
3. Compare the eloquent brevity of Lincoln's address with William Faulkner's "Nobel Prize Award Speech," p. 177.

II. **Suggestions for Writing:**
1. Write and deliver an address arguing for national unity and purpose in the 1980s.
2. Write a newspaper account of Lincoln's "Second Inaugural Address." Write an editorial response to the address.

---

## JACK LONDON

### What Life Means to Me

---

Jack London (1876–1916), the American novelist and short-story writer, drew upon his extensive travels to the Klondike and to the South Seas in such works as *The Call of the Wild* (1903) and *South Sea Tales* (1911). He developed social themes in other works like *The Iron Heel* (1907).

In the autobiographical essay which follows, London traces his work experience as a member of the working class, his aspiration *to rise into the world of affluence and accomplishment, and his disillusionment with the materialism he encounters there. Vivid details bring the characters he describes to life.*

---

I was born in the working-class. Early I discovered enthusiasm, ambition, and ideals; and to satisfy these became the problem of my child-life. My environment was crude and rough and raw. I had no outlook, but an uplook rather. My place in society was at the bottom. Here life offered nothing but sordidness and wretchedness, both of the flesh and the spirit; for here flesh and spirit were alike starved and tormented.

Above me towered the collosal edifice of society, and to my mind the only way out was up. Into this edifice I early resolved to climb. Up above, men wore black clothes and boiled shirts, and women dressed in beautiful gowns. Also, there were good things to eat, and there was plenty to eat. This much for the flesh. Then there were the things of the spirit. Up above me, I knew, were unselfishnesses of the spirit, clean and noble thinking, keen intellectual living. I knew all this because I read "Seaside Library" novels, in which, with the exception of the villains and adventuresses, all men and women thought beautiful thoughts, spoke a beautiful tongue, and performed glorious deeds. In short, as I accepted the rising of the sun, I accepted that up above me was all that was fine and noble and gracious, all that gave decency and dignity to life, all that made life worth living and that remunerated one for his travail and misery.

But it is not particularly easy for one to climb up out of the working-class—especially if he is handicapped by the possession of ideals and illusions. I lived on a ranch in California, and I was hard put to find the ladder whereby to climb. I early inquired the rate of interest on invested money, and worried my child's brain into an understanding of the virtues and excellencies of that remarkable invention of man, compound interest. Further, I ascertained the current rates of wages for workers of all ages, and the cost of living. From all this data I concluded that if I began immediately and worked and saved until I was fifty years of age, I could then stop working and enter into participation in a fair portion of the delights and goodnesses that would then be open to me higher up in society. Of course, I resolutely determined not to marry, while I quite forgot to consider at all that great rock of disaster in the working-class world—sickness.

But the life that was in me demanded more than a meagre existence of scraping and scrimping. Also, at ten years of age, I became a newsboy on the streets of a city, and found myself with a changed uplook. All about me were still the same sordidness and wretchedness, and up above me was still the same paradise waiting to be gained; but the ladder whereby to climb was a different one. It was now the ladder of business. Why save my earnings and invest in government bonds, when, by buying two newspapers for five cents, with a turn of the wrist I could sell them for ten cents and double my capital? The business ladder was the ladder for me, and I had a vision of myself becoming a baldheaded and successful merchant prince.

Alas for visions! When I was sixteen I had already earned the title of "prince." But this title was given me by a gang of cut-throats and thieves, by whom I was called "The Prince of the Oyster Pirates." And at that time I had climbed the first rung of the business ladder. I was a capitalist. I owned a boat and a complete oyster-pirating outfit. I had begun to exploit my fellow-creatures. I had a crew of one man. As captain and owner I took two-thirds of the spoils, and gave the crew one-third, though the crew worked just as hard as I did and risked just as much his life and liberty.

This one rung was the height I climbed up the business ladder. One night I went on a raid amongst the Chinese fishermen. Ropes and nets were worth dollars and cents. It was robbery, I grant, but it was precisely the spirit of capitalism. The capitalist takes away the possessions of his fellow-creatures by means of a rebate, or of a betrayal of trust, or by the purchase of senators and supreme-court judges. I was merely crude. That was the only difference. I used a gun.

But my crew that night was one of those inefficients against whom the capitalist is wont to fulminate, because, forsooth, such inefficients increase expenses and reduce dividends. My crew did both. What of his carelessness: he set fire to the big mainsail and totally destroyed it. There weren't any dividends that night, and the Chinese fishermen were richer by the nets and ropes we did not get. I was bankrupt, unable just then to pay sixty-five dollars for a new mainsail. I left my boat at anchor and went off on a bay-pirate boat on a raid up the Sacramento River. While away on this trip, another gang of bay pirates raided my boat. They stole everything, even the anchors; and later on, when I recovered the drifting hulk, I sold it for twenty dollars. I had slipped back the one rung I had climbed, and never again did I attempt the business ladder.

From then on I was mercilessly exploited by other capitalists. I had the muscle, and they made money out of it while I made but a very indifferent living out of it. I was a sailor before the mast, a longshoreman, a roustabout; I worked in canneries, and factories, and laundries; I mowed lawns, and cleaned carpets, and washed windows. And I never got the full product of my toil. I looked at the daughter of the cannery owner, in her carriage, and knew that it was my muscle, in part, that helped drag along that carriage on its rubber tires. I looked at the son of the factory owner, going to college, and knew that it was my muscle that helped, in part, to pay for the wine and good fellowship he enjoyed.

But I did not resent this. It was all in the game. They were the strong. Very well, I was strong. I would carve my way to a place amongst them and make money out of the muscles of other men. I was not afraid of work. I loved hard work. I would pitch in and work harder than ever and eventually become a pillar of society.

And just then, as luck would have it, I found an employer that was of the same mind. I was willing to work, and he was more than willing that I should work. I thought I was learning a trade. In reality, I had displaced two men. I thought he was making an electrician out of me; as a matter of fact, he was making fifty dollars per month out of me. The two men I had displaced had received forty dollars each per month; I was doing the work of both for thirty dollars per month.

This employer worked me nearly to death. A man may love oysters, but too many oysters will disincline him toward that particular diet. And so with me. Too much work sickened me. I did not wish ever to see work again. I fled from work. I became a tramp, begging my way from door to door, wandering over the United States and sweating bloody sweats in slums and prisons.

I had been born in the working-class, and I was now, at the age of eighteen, beneath the point at which I had started. I was down in the cellar of society, down in the subterranean depths of misery about which it is neither nice nor proper to speak. I was in the pit, the abyss, the human cess-pool, the shambles and charnel-house of our civilization. This is the part of the edifice of society that society chooses to ignore. Lack of space compels me here to ignore it, and I shall say only that the things I there saw gave me a terrible scare.

I was scared into thinking. I saw the naked simplicities of the complicated civilization in which I lived. Life was a matter of food and shelter. In order to get food and shelter men sold things. The merchant sold shoes, the politician sold his manhood, and the representative of the people, with exceptions, of course, sold his trust; while nearly all sold their honor. Women, too, whether on the street or in the holy bond of wedlock, were prone to sell their flesh. All things were commodities, all people bought and sold. The one commodity that labor had to sell was muscle. The honor of labor had no price in the market-place. Labor had muscle, and muscle alone, to sell.

But there was a difference, a vital difference. Shoes and trust and honor had a way of renewing themselves. They were imperishable stocks. Muscle, on the other hand, did not renew. As the shoe merchant sold shoes, he continued to replenish his stock. But there was no way of replenishing the laborer's stock of muscle. The more he sold of his muscle, the less of it remained to him. It was his one commodity, and each day his stock of it diminished. In the end, if he did not die before, he sold out and put up his shutters. He was a muscle bankrupt, and nothing remained to him but to go down into the cellar of society and perish miserably.

I learned, further, that brain was likewise a commodity. It, too, was different from muscle. A brain seller was only at his prime when he was fifty or sixty years old, and his wares were fetching higher prices than ever. But a laborer was worked out or broken down at forty-five or fifty. I had been in the cellar of society, and I did not like the place as a habitation. The pipes and drains were unsanitary, and the air was bad to breathe. If I could not live on the parlor floor of society, I could, at any rate, have a try at the attic. It was true, the diet there was slim, but the air at least was pure. So I resolved to sell no more muscle, and to become a vender of brains.

Then began a frantic pursuit of knowledge. I returned to California and opened the books. While thus equipping myself to become a brain merchant, it was inevitable that I should delve into sociology. There I found, in a certain class of books, scientifically formulated, the simple sociological concepts I had already worked out for myself. Other and greater minds, before I was born, had worked out all that I had thought and a vast deal more. I discovered that I was a socialist.

The socialists were revolutionists, inasmuch as they struggled to overthrow the society of the present, and out of the material to build the society of the future. I, too, was a socialist and a revolutionist. I joined the groups of working-class and intellectual revolutionists, and for the first time came into intellectual living. Here I found keen-flashing intellects and brilliant wits; for here I met strong and alert-brained, withal horny-handed, members of the working-class; unfrocked preachers too wide in their Christianity for any congregation of Mammon-worshippers; professors broken on the wheel of university subservience to the ruling class and flung out because they were quick with knowledge which they strove to apply to the affairs of mankind.

Here I found, also, warm faith in the human, glowing idealism, sweetnesses of unselfishness, renunciation, and martyrdom—all the splendid, stinging things of the spirit. Here life was clean, noble, and alive. Here life rehabilitated itself, became wonderful and glorious; and I was glad to be alive. I was in touch with great souls who exalted flesh and spirit over dollars and cents, and to whom the thin wail of the starved slum child meant more than all the pomp and circumstance of commercial expansion and world empire. All about me were nobleness of purpose and heroism of effort, and my days and nights were sunshine and starshine, all fire and dew, with before my eyes, ever burning and blazing, the Holy Grail, Christ's own Grail, the warm human, long-suffering and maltreated, but to be rescued and saved at the last.

And I, poor foolish I, deemed all this to be a mere foretaste of the delights of living I should find higher above me in society. I had lost many illusions since the day I read "Seaside Library" novels on the California ranch. I was destined to lose many of the illusions I still retained.

As a brain merchant I was a success. Society opened its portals to me. I entered right in on the parlor floor, and my disillusionment proceeded rapidly. I sat down to dinner with the masters of society, and with the wives and daughters of the masters of society. The women were gowned beautifully, I admit; but to my naïve surprise I discovered that they were of the same clay as all the rest of the women I had known down below in the cellar. "The colonel's lady and Judy O'Grady were sisters under their skins"—and gowns.

It was not this, however, so much as their materialism, that shocked me. It is true, these beautifully gowned, beautiful women prattled sweet little ideals and dear little moralities; but in spite of their prattle the dominant key of the life they lived was materialistic. And they were so sentimentally selfish! They assisted in all kinds of sweet little charities, and informed one of the fact, while all the time the food they ate and the beautiful clothes they wore were bought out of dividends stained with the blood of child labor, and sweated labor, and of prostitution itself. When I mentioned such facts, expecting in my innocence that these sisters of Judy O'Grady would at once strip off their blood-dyed silks and jewels, they became excited and angry, and read me preachments about the lack of thrift, the drink, and the innate depravity that caused all the misery in society's cellar. When I mentioned that I couldn't quite see that it was the lack of thrift, the intemperance, and the depravity of a half-starved child of six that made it work twelve hours every night in a Southern cotton mill, these sisters of Judy O'Grady attacked my private life and called me an "agitator"—as though that, forsooth, settled the argument.

Nor did I fare better with the masters themselves. I had expected to find men who were clean, noble, and alive, whose ideals were clean, noble, and alive. I went about amongst the men who sat in the high places—the preachers, the politicians, the business men, the professors, and the editors. I ate meat with them, drank wine with them, automobiled with them, and studied them. It is true, I found many that were clean and noble; but with rare exceptions, they were not *alive*. I do verily believe I could count the exceptions on the fingers of my two hands. Where they were not alive with rottenness, quick with unclean life, they were merely the unburied dead—clean and noble, like well-preserved mummies, but not alive. In this connection I may especially mention the professors I met, the men who live up to that decadent university ideal, "the passionless pursuit of passionless intelligence."

I met men who invoked the name of the Prince of Peace in their diatribes against war, and who put rifles in the hands of Pinkertons with which to shoot down strikers in their own factories. I met men incoherent with indignation at the brutality of prize-fighting, and who, at the same time, were parties to the adulteration of food that killed each year more babies than even red-handed Herod had killed.

I talked in hotels and clubs and homes and Pullmans and steamer-chairs with captains of industry, and marvelled at how little travelled they were in the realm of intellect. On the other hand, I discovered that their intellect, in the business sense, was abnormally developed. Also, I discovered that their morality, where business was concerned, was nil.

This delicate, aristocratic-featured gentleman, was a dummy director and a tool of corporations that secretly robbed widows and orphans. This gentleman, who collected fine editions and was an especial patron of literature, paid blackmail to a heavy-jowled, black-browed boss of a municipal machine. This editor, who published patent medicine advertisements and did not dare print the truth in his paper about said patent medicines for fear of losing the advertising, called me a scoundrelly demagogue because I told him that his political economy was antiquated and that his biology was contemporaneous with Pliny.

This senator was the tool and the slave, the little puppet of a gross, uneducated machine boss; so was this governor and this supreme court judge; and all three rode on railroad passes. This man, talking soberly and earnestly about the beauties of idealism and the goodness of God, had just betrayed his comrades in a business deal. This man, a pillar of the church and heavy contributor to foreign missions, worked his shop girls ten hours a day on a starvation wage and thereby directly encouraged prostitution. This man, who endowed chairs in universities, perjured himself in courts of law over a matter of dollars and cents. And this railroad magnate broke his word as a gentleman and a Christian when he granted a secret rebate to one of two captains of industry locked together in a struggle to the death.

It was the same everywhere, crime and betrayal, betrayal and crime—

men who were alive, but who were neither clean nor noble, men who were clean and noble but who were not alive. Then there was a great, hopeless mass, neither noble nor alive, but merely clean. It did not sin positively nor deliberately; but it did sin passively and ignorantly by acquiescing in the current immorality and profiting by it. Had it been noble and alive it would not have been ignorant, and it would have refused to share in the profits of betrayal and crime.

I discovered that I did not like to live on the parlor floor of society. Intellectually I was bored. Morally and spiritually I was sickened. I remembered my intellectuals and idealists, my unfrocked preachers, broken professors, and clean-minded, class-conscious workingmen. I remembered my days and nights of sunshine and starshine, where life was all a wild sweet wonder, a spiritual paradise of unselfish adventure and ethical romance. And I saw before me, ever blazing and burning the Holy Grail.

So I went back to the working-class, in which I had been born and where I belonged. I care no longer to climb. The imposing edifice of society above my head holds no delights for me. It is the foundation of the edifice that interests me. There I am content to labor, crowbar in hand, shoulder to shoulder with intellectuals, idealists, and class-conscious workingmen, getting a solid pry now and again and setting the whole edifice rocking. Some day, when we get a few more hands and crowbars to work, we'll topple it over, along with all its rotten life and unburied dead, its monstrous selfishness and sodden materialism. Then we'll cleanse the cellar and build a new habitation for mankind, in which there will be no parlor floor, in which all the rooms will be bright and airy, and where the air that is breathed will be clean, noble, and alive.

Such is my outlook. I look forward to a time when man shall progress upon something worthier and higher than his stomach, when there will be a finer incentive to impel men to action than the incentive of today, which is the incentive of the stomach. I retain my belief in the nobility and excellence of the human. I believe that spiritual sweetness and unselfishness will conquer the gross gluttony of today. And last of all, my faith is in the working-class. As some Frenchman has said, "The stairway of time is ever echoing with the wooden shoe going up, the polished boot descending."

## I. Suggestions for Discussion:

1. To what extent is London's metaphor of "the colossal edifice of society" still appropriate in America today?

2. What bored and sickened London with the "parlor floor of society"?

3. Discuss London's ultimate faith in the working class. Do his earlier experiences seem to justify that faith? Explain.

II. **Suggestions for Writing:**

1. Write an essay in which you recall an illusion you formerly had and describe the events that destroyed the illusion.

2. Describe one or more work experiences in which you were, like London, "mercilessly exploited."

---

## THOMAS MACAULAY

## The Execution of Monmouth

from *The History of England*

---

Thomas Babington Macaulay (1800-1859) was an English politician, statesman, and historian. For his service to England, he was raised to the peerage with the title of Baron Macaulay of Rothley, and in 1860 honored with burial in Westminster Abbey. *The History of England,* from which the following selection is taken, was published in five volumes from 1849 to 1861.

Macaulay paints a grisly picture of the death of James Scott, Duke of Monmouth, the illegitimate son of Charles II, who had led an unsuccessful rebellion against King James II of England in 1685. The executioner, Macaulay tells his readers, struck with the axe, "again and again, but still the neck was not severed, and the body continued to move." Macaulay's narrative is unusually rich in descriptive details.

---

. . . It was ten o'clock. The coach of the Lieutenant of the Tower was ready. Monmouth requested his spiritual advisers to accompany him to the place of execution; and they consented: but they told him that, in their judgement, he was about to die in a perilous state of mind, and that, if they attended him, it would be their duty to exhort him to the last. As he passed along the ranks of the guards he saluted them with a smile, and mounted the scaffold with a firm tread. Tower Hill was covered up to the chimney tops with an innumerable multitude of gazers, who, in awful silence, broken only by sighs and the noise of weeping, listened for the last accents of the darling of the people. 'I shall say little,' he began. 'I come here, not to speak, but to die. I die a Protestant of the Church of England.' The Bishops interrupted him, and told him that, unless he acknowledged resistance to be sinful, he was no member of their church. He went on to speak of his Henrietta.[1] She was, he said, a young lady of virtue and honour. He loved her to the last, and he could not die without giving utterance to his feelings. The Bishops again interfered, and begged him not to use such language. Some altercation followed. The divines have been accused of dealing harshly with the dying man. But they appear to have only discharged what, in their view, was a sacred duty. Monmouth knew their principles, and, if he wished to avoid their importunity, should have dispensed with their attendance. Their general arguments against resistance had no effect on him. But when they reminded him of the ruin which he had brought on his brave and loving followers, of the blood which had been shed, of the souls which had been sent unprepared to the great account, he was touched, and said, in a softened voice, 'I do own that I am sorry that it ever happened.' They prayed with him long and fervently; and he joined in their petitions till they invoked a blessing on the King. He remained silent. 'Sir,' said one of the Bishops, 'do you not pray for the King with us?' Monmouth paused some time, and after an internal struggle, exclaimed 'Amen.' But it was in vain that the prelates implored him to address to the soldiers and to the people a few words on the duty of obedience to the government. 'I will make no speeches,' he exclaimed. 'Only ten words, my Lord.' He turned away, called his servant, and put into the man's hand a toothpick case, the last token of ill-starred love. 'Give it,' he said, 'to that person.' He then accosted John Ketch the executioner, a wretch who had butchered many brave and noble victims, and whose name has, during a century and a half, been vulgarly given to all who have succeeded him in his odious office. 'Here,' said the Duke, 'are six guineas for you. Do not hack me as you did my Lord Russell. I have heard that you struck him three or four times. My servant will give you some more gold if you do the work well.' He then undressed, felt the edge of the axe, expressed some fear that it was not sharp enough, and laid his head on the block. The divines in the meantime continued to ejaculate with great energy; 'God accept your repentence! God accept your imperfect repentance!'

The hangman addressed himself to his office. But he had been disconcerted by what the Duke had said. The first blow inflicted only a slight wound. The Duke struggled, rose from the block, and looked reproachfully at

[1] Henrietta Maria, Baroness Wentworth (1657–1686) was Monmouth's mistress.

the executioner. The head sank down once more. The stroke was repeated again and again; but still the neck was not severed, and the body continued to move. Yells of rage and horror rose from the crowd. Ketch flung down the axe with a curse. 'I cannot do it,' he said; 'my heart fails me.' 'Take up the axe, man,' cried the sheriff. 'Fling him over the rails,' roared the mob. At length the axe was taken up. Two more blows extinguished the last remains of life; but a knife was used to separate the head from the shoulders. The crowd was wrought up to such an ecstasy of rage that the executioner was in danger of being torn in pieces, and was conveyed away under a strong guard.

In the meantime many handkerchiefs were dipped in the Duke's blood; for, by a large part of the multitude he was regarded as a martyr who had died for the Protestant religion. The head and body were placed in a coffin covered with black velvet, and were laid privately under the communion table of St. Peter's Chapel in the Tower. Within four years the pavement of the chancel was again disturbed, and hard by the remains of Monmouth were laid the remains of Jeffreys.[2] In truth there is no sadder spot on the earth than that little cemetery. Death is there associated, not, as in Westminster Abbey and Saint Paul's, with genius and virtue, with public veneration and with imperishable renown; not, as in our humblest churches and churchyards, with everything that is most endearing in social and domestic charities; but with whatever is darkest in human nature and in human destiny, with the savage triumph of implacable enemies, with the inconstancy, the ingratitude, the cowardice of friends, with all the miseries of fallen greatness and of blighted fame. Thither have been carried, through successive ages, by the rude hands of jailers, without one mourner following, the bleeding relics of men who had been the captains of armies, the leaders of parties, the oracles of senates, and the ornaments of courts. Thither was borne, before the window where Jane Grey was praying, the mangled corpse of Guilford Dudley. Edward Seymour, Duke of Somerset, and Protector of the realm, reposes there by the brother whom he murdered. There has mouldered away the headless trunk of John Fisher, Bishop of Rochester and Cardinal of Saint Vitalis, a man worthy to have lived in a better age, and to have died in a better cause. There are laid John Dudley, Duke of Northumberland, Lord High Admiral, and Thomas Cromwell, Earl of Essex, Lord High Treasurer. There, too, is another Essex, on whom nature and fortune had lavished all their bounties in vain, and whom valour, grace, genius, royal favour, popular

---

[2] George, first Baron Jeffreys of Wem (1648–1689) was known as the hanging judge. Macaulay mentions several men and women who were confined, executed, and buried in the Tower of London.

applause, conducted to an early and ignominious doom. Not far off sleep two chiefs of the great house of Howard—Thomas, fourth Duke of Norfolk, and Philip, eleventh Earl of Arundel. Here and there, among the thick graves of unquiet and aspiring statesmen, lie more delicate sufferers; Margaret of Salisbury, the last of the proud name of Plantagenet, and those two fair Queens who perished by the jealous rage of Henry. Such was the dust with which the dust of Monmouth mingled. . . .

I. **Suggestions for Discussion:**
1. What is Macaulay's attitude toward his subject? Is he sympathetic or detached? Discuss.
2. Discuss his use of striking details to give vitality to the scene he depicts.
3. Compare Macaulay's narrative with Carlyle's narrative of the death of Louis XVI in *The French Revolution,* p. 75.

II. **Suggestions for Writing:**
1. Describe, in graphic terms, a public event you have witnessed.
2. State and defend your position on capital punishment.
3. Write a newspaper account of the death of Monmouth.

---

# NICCOLO MACHIAVELLI

## The Morals of the Prince

---

Niccolò Machiavelli (1469-1527) was a Florentine statesman and political theorist. His most famous work, *The Prince,* written in 1513, is a treatise on statecraft by an astute observer of the contemporary Italian political scene. The work was known in England as early as 1602 but was not published in an English translation until 1640.

The selection that follows is taken from Chapters 15–18 of *The Prince.* Machiavelli explains that a ruler should always *appear* merciful, trustworthy, humane, religious, and honest. In order to maintain his rule and serve the state well, however, the ruler must be ready to exercise his power as fully and ruthlessly as necessary.

---

## On Things for Which Men, and Particularly Princes,
## Are Praised or Blamed

We now have left to consider what should be the manners and attitudes of a prince toward his subjects and his friends. As I know that many have written on this subject I feel that I may be held presumptuous in what I have to say, if in my comments I do not follow the lines laid down by others. Since, however, it has been my intention to write something which may be of use to the understanding reader, it has seemed wiser to me to follow the real truth of the matter rather than what we imagine it to be. For imagination has created many principalities and republics that have never been seen or known to have any real existence, for how we live is so different from how we ought to live that he who studies what ought to be done rather than what is done will learn the way to his downfall rather than to his preservation. A man striving in every way to be good will meet his ruin among the great number who are not good. Hence it is necessary for a prince, if he wishes to remain in power, to learn how not to be good and to use his knowledge or refrain from using it as he may need.

Putting aside then the things imagined as pertaining to a prince and considering those that really do, I will say that all men, and particularly princes because of their prominence, when comment is made of them, are noted as having some characteristics deserving either praise or blame. One is accounted liberal, another stingy, to use a Tuscan term—for in our speech avaricious (*avaro*) is applied to such as are desirous of acquiring by rapine whereas stingy (*misero*) is the term used for those who are reluctant to part with their own—one is considered bountiful, another rapacious; one cruel, another tender-hearted; one false to his word, another trustworthy; one effeminate and pusillanimous, another wild and spirited; one humane, another haughty; one lascivious, another chaste; one a man of integrity and another sly; one tough and another pliant; one serious and another frivolous; one religious and another skeptical, and so on. Everyone will agree, I know, that it would be a most praiseworthy thing if all the qualities accounted as good in the above enumeration were found in a Prince. But since they cannot be so possessed nor observed because of human conditions which do not allow of it, what is necessary for the prince is to be prudent enough to escape the infamy of such vices as would result in the loss of his state; as for the others which would not have that effect, he must guard himself from them as far as possible but if he cannot, he may overlook them as being of less importance. Further, he should have no concern about incurring the infamy of such vices without which the preservation of his state would be difficult.

For, if the matter be well considered, it will be seen that some habits which appear virtuous, if adopted would signify ruin, and others that seem vices lead to security and the well-being of a prince.

## Generosity and Meanness

To begin then with the first characteristic set forth above, I will say that it would be well always to be considered generous, yet generosity used in such a way as not to bring you honor does you harm, for if it is practiced virtuously and as it is meant to be practiced it will not be publicly known and you will not lose the name of being just the opposite of generous. Hence to preserve the reputation of being generous among your friends you must not neglect any kind of lavish display, yet a prince of this sort will consume all his property in such gestures and, if he wishes to preserve his reputation for generosity, he will be forced to levy heavy taxes on his subjects and turn to fiscal measures and do everything possible to get money. Thus he will begin to be regarded with hatred by his subjects and should he become poor he will be held in scant esteem; having by his prodigality given offense to many and rewarded only a few, he will suffer at the first hint of adversity, and the first danger will be critical for him. Yet when he realizes this and tries to reform he will immediately get the name of being a miser. So a prince, as he is unable to adopt the virtue of generosity without danger to himself, must, if he is a wise man, accept with indifference the name of miser. For with the passage of time he will be regarded as increasingly generous when it is seen that, by virtue of his parsimony, his income suffices for him to defend himself in wartime and undertake his enterprises without heavily taxing his people. For in that way he practices generosity towards all from whom he refrains from taking money, who are many, and stinginess only toward those from whom he withholds gifts, who are few.

In our times we have seen great things accomplished only by such as have had the name of misers; all others have come to naught. Pope Julius made use of his reputation for generosity to make himself Pope but later, in order to carry on his war against the King of France, he made no effort to maintain it; and he has waged a great number of wars without having had recourse to heavy taxation because his persistent parsimony has made up for the extra expenses. The present King of Spain, had he had any reputation for generosity, would never have carried through to victory so many enterprises.

A prince then, if he wishes not to rob his subjects but to be able to defend himself and not to become poor and despised nor to be obliged to become rapacious, must consider it a matter of small importance to incur the name of miser, for this is one of the vices which keep him on this throne. Some may say Caesar through generosity won his way to the purple, and others either through being generous or being accounted so have risen to the highest ranks. But I will answer by pointing out that either you are already a prince or you are on the way to becoming one and in the first case generosity is harmful while in the second it is very necessary to be considered open-handed. Caesar was seeking to arrive at the domination of Rome but if he had survived after reaching his goal and had not moderated his lavishness he would certainly have destroyed the empire.

It might also be objected that there have been many princes, accomplishing great things with their armies, who have been acclaimed for their generosity. To which I would answer that the prince either spends his own (or his subjects') money or that of others; in the first case he must be very sparing but in the second he should overlook no aspect of open-handedness. So the prince who leads his armies and lives on looting and extortion and booty, thus handling the wealth of others, must indeed have this quality of generosity for otherwise his soldiers will not follow him. You can be very free with wealth not belonging to yourself or your subjects, in the fashion of Cyrus, Caesar, or Alexander, for spending what belongs to others rather enhances your reputation than detracts from it; it is only spending your own wealth that is dangerous. There is nothing that consumes itself as does prodigality; even as you practice it you lose the faculty of practicing it and either you become poor and despicable or, in order to escape poverty, rapacious and unpopular. And among the things a prince must guard against is precisely the danger of becoming an object either of contempt or of hatred. Generosity leads you to both these evils, wherefore it is wiser to accept the name of miserly, since the reproach it brings is without hatred, than to seek a reputation for generosity and thus perforce acquire the name of rapacious, which breeds hatred as well as infamy.

## Cruelty and Clemency and Whether It Is Better to Be Loved or Feared

Now to continue with the list of characteristics. It should be the desire of every prince to be considered merciful and not cruel, yet he should take care not to make poor use of his clemency. Cesare Borgia was regarded as cruel, yet his cruelty reorganized Romagna and united it in peace and loyalty. Indeed, if we reflect, we shall see that this man was more merciful than the Florentines who, to avoid the charge of cruelty, allowed Pistoia to be destroyed. A prince should care nothing for the accusation of cruelty so long as he keeps his subjects united and loyal; by making a very few examples he can be more truly merciful than those who through too much tender-heartedness allow disorders to arise whence come killings and rapine. For these offend an entire community, while the few executions ordered by the prince affect only a few individuals. For a new prince above all it is impossible not to earn a reputation for cruelty since new states are full of dangers. Virgil indeed has Dido apologize for the inhumanity of her rule because it is new, in the words:

> Res dura et regni novitas me talia cogunt
> Moliri et late fines custode tueri.
> . . . my cruel fate
> And doubts attending an unsettled state
> Force me to guard my coast from foreign foes.

Nevertheless a prince should not be too ready to listen to tale-bearers nor to act on suspicion, nor should he allow himself to be easily frightened. He should proceed with a mixture of prudence and humanity in such a way as not to be made incautious by over-confidence nor yet intolerable by excessive mistrust.

Here the question arises; whether it is better to be loved than feared or feared than loved. The answer is that it would be desirable to be both but, since that is difficult, it is much safer to be feared than to be loved, if one must choose. For on men in general this observation may be made: they are ungrateful, fickle, and deceitful, eager to avoid dangers, and avid for gain, and while you are useful to them they are all with you, offering you their blood, their property, their lives, and their sons so long as danger is remote, as we noted above, but when it approaches they turn on you. Any prince, trusting only in their words and having no other preparations made, will fall to his ruin, for friendships that are bought at a price and not by greatness and nobility of soul are paid for indeed, but they are not owned and cannot be called upon in time of need. Men have less hesitation in offending a man who is loved than one who is feared, for love is held by a bond of obligation which, as men are wicked, is broken whenever personal advantage suggests it, but fear is accompanied by the dread of punishment which never relaxes.

Yet a prince should make himself feared in such a way that, if he does not thereby merit love, at least he may escape odium, for being feared and not hated may well go together. And indeed the prince may attain this end if he but respect the property and the women of his subjects and citizens. And if it should become necessary to seek the death of someone, he should find a proper justification and a public cause, and above all he should keep his hands off another's property, for men forget more readily the death of their father than the loss of their patrimony. Besides, pretexts for seizing property are never lacking, and when a prince begins to live by means of rapine he will always find some excuse for plundering others, and conversely pretexts for execution are rarer and are more quickly exhausted.

A prince at the head of his armies and with vast number of soldiers under his command should give not the slightest heed if he is esteemed cruel, for without such a reputation he will not be able to keep his army united and ready for action. Among the marvelous things told of Hannibal is that, having a vast army under his command made up of all kinds and races of men and waging war far from his own country, he never allowed any dissension to arise either as between the troops and their leaders or among the troops themselves, and this both in times of good fortune and bad. This could only have come about through his most inhuman cruelty which, taken in conjunction with his great valor, kept him always an object of respect and terror in the eyes of his soldiers. And without the cruelty his other characteristics would not have achieved this effect. Thoughtless writers have admired his actions and at the same time deplored the cruelty which was the basis of them. As evidence of the truth of our statement that his other virtues would have been insufficient let us examine the case of Scipio, an extraordinary leader not only in his own day but for all recorded history. His army in Spain revolted and for no other reason than because of his kind-heartedness, which had allowed more license to his soldiery than military discipline properly permits. His policy was attacked in the Senate by Fabius Maximus, who called him a corrupter of the Roman arms. When the Locrians had been mishandled by one of his lieutenants, his easy-going nature prevented him from avenging them or disciplining his officer, and it was apropos of this incident that one of the senators remarked, wishing to find an excuse for him, that there were many men who knew better how to avoid error themselves than to correct it in others. This characteristic of Scipio would have clouded his fame and glory had he continued in authority, but as he lived under the government of the Senate, its harmful aspect was hidden and it reflected credit on him.

Hence, on the subject of being loved or feared I will conclude that since love depends on the subjects, but the prince has it in his own hands to create fear, a wise prince will rely on what is his own, remembering at the same time that he must avoid arousing hatred, as we have said.

## In What Manner Princes Should Keep Their Word

How laudable it is for a prince to keep his word and govern his actions by integrity rather than trickery will be understood by all. Nonetheless we have in our times seen great things accomplished by many princes who have thought little of keeping their promises and have known the art of mystifying the minds of men. Such princes have won out over those whose actions were based on fidelity to their word.

It must be understood that there are two ways of fighting, one with laws and the other with arms. The first is the way of men, the second is the style of beasts, but since very often the first does not suffice it is necessary to turn to the second. Therefore a prince must know how to play the beast as well as the man. This lesson was taught allegorically by the ancient writers who related that Achilles and many other princes were brought up by Chiron the Centaur, who took them under his discipline. The clear significance of this half-man and half-beast preceptorship is that a prince must know how to use either of these two natures and that one without the other has no enduring strength. Now since the prince must make use of the characteristics of beasts he should choose those of the fox and the lion, though the lion cannot defend himself against snares and the fox is helpless against wolves. One must be a fox in avoiding traps and a lion in frightening wolves. Such as choose simply the role of a lion do not rightly understand the matter. Hence a wise leader cannot and should not keep his word when keeping it is not to his advantage or when the reasons that made him give it are no longer valid. If men were good, this would not be a good precept, but since they are wicked and will not keep faith with you, you are not bound to keep faith with them.

A prince has never lacked legitimate reasons to justify his breach of faith. We could give countless recent examples and show how any number of peace treaties or promises have been broken and rendered meaningless by the faithlessness of princes, and how success has fallen to the one who best knows how to counterfeit the fox. But it is necessary to know how to disguise this nature well and how to pretend and dissemble. Men are so simple and so ready to follow the needs of the moment that the deceiver will always find some one to deceive. Of recent examples I should mention one. Alexander VI did nothing but deceive and never thought of anything else and always found some occasion for it. Never was there a man more convincing in his asseverations nor more willing to offer the most solemn oaths nor less likely to observe them. Yet his deceptions were always successful for he was an expert in this field.

So a prince need not have all the aforementioned good qualities, but it is most essential that he appear to have them. Indeed, I should go so far as to say that having them and always practising them is harmful, while seeming to have them is useful. It is good to appear clement, trustworthy, humane, religious, and honest, and also to be so, but always with the mind so disposed that, when the occasion arises not to be so, you can become the opposite. It must be understood that a prince and particularly a new prince cannot practise all the virtues for which men are accounted good, for the necessity of preserving the state often compels him to take actions which are opposed to loyalty, charity, humanity, and religion. Hence he must have a spirit ready to adapt itself as the varying winds of fortune command him. As I have said, so far as he is able, a prince should stick to the path of good but, if the necessity arises, he should know how to follow evil.

A prince must take great care that no word ever passes his lips that is not full of the above mentioned five good qualities, and he must seem to all who see and hear him a model of piety, loyalty, integrity, humanity, and religion. Nothing is more necessary than to seem to possess this last quality, for men in general judge more by the eye than the hand, as all can see but few can feel. Everyone sees what you seem to be, few experience what you really are and these few do not dare to set themselves up against the opinion of the majority supported by the majesty of the state. In the actions of all men and especially princes, where there is no court of appeal, the end is all that counts. Let a prince then concern himself with the acquisition or the maintenance of a state; the means employed will always be considered honorable and praised by all, for the mass of mankind is always swayed by appearances and by the outcome of an enterprise. And in the world there is only the mass, for the few find their place only when the majority has no base of support.

## I. Suggestions for Discussion:

1. How does Machiavelli contrast generosity with miserliness? cruelty with clemency?
2. Discuss the effectiveness of his illustrations and examples in supporting his argument.
3. Observe the careful organization of his essay. Note how he moves from a general discussion to a discussion of particular traits and then returns to a summary discussion of the proper attributes of a prince.

## II. Suggestions for Writing:

1. Write an essay in which you support or attack the kind of rules Machiavelli describes.
2. Write an essay arguing whether or not Machiavelli offers good advice to American politicians.

# JAMES MADISON

## The Federalist 10—On Factions

James Madison (1751–1836), fourth president of the United States, joined with Alexander Hamilton and John Jay to write a series of essays to persuade the people of New York to ratify the United States Constitution in 1788.

The *Federalist* Number 10, which first appeared on November 22, 1787, in *The Daily Advertiser,* displays Madison's clarity, shrewdness, practical good sense, and ability to organize an argument.

*To the People of the State of New York:*

Among the numerous advantages promised by a well-constructed Union, none deserves to be more accurately developed than its tendency to break and control the violence of faction. The friend of popular governments never finds himself so much alarmed for their character and fate, as when he contemplates their propensity to this dangerous vice. He will not fail, therefore, to set a due value on any plan which, without violating the principles to which he is attached, provides a proper cure for it. The instability, injustice, and confusion introduced into the public councils, have, in truth, been the mortal diseases under which popular governments have everywhere perished; as they continue to be the favorite and fruitful topics from which the adversaries to liberty derive their most specious declamations. The valuable improvements made by the American constitutions on the popular models, both ancient and modern, cannot certainly be too much admired; but it would be an unwarrantable partiality, to contend that they have as effectually obviated the danger on this side, as was wished and expected. Complaints are everywhere heard from our most considerate and virtuous citizens, equally the friends of public and private faith, and of public and personal liberty, that our governments are too unstable, that the public good is disregarded in the conflicts of rival parties, and that measures are too often decided, not according to the rules of justice and the rights of the minor party, but by the superior force of an interested and overbearing majority. However anxiously we may wish that these complaints had no foundation, the evidence of known facts will not permit us to deny that they are in some degree true. It will be found, indeed, on a candid review of our situation, that some of the distresses under which we labor have been erroneously charged on the operation of our governments; but it will be found, at the same time, that other causes will not alone account for many of our heaviest misfortunes; and, particularly, for that prevailing and increasing distrust of public engagements, and alarm for private rights, which are echoed from one end of the continent to the other. These must be chiefly, if not wholly, effects of the unsteadiness and injustice with which a factious spirit has tainted our public administrations.

By a faction, I understand a number of citizens, whether amounting to a majority or minority of the whole, who are united and actuated by some common impulse of passion, or of interest, adverse to the rights of other citizens, or to the permanent and aggregate interests of the community.

There are two methods of curing the mischiefs of faction: the one, by removing its causes; the other, by controlling its effects.

There are again two methods of removing the causes of faction: the one, by destroying the liberty which is essential to its existence; the other, by giving to every citizen the same opinions, the same passions, and the same interests.

It could never be more truly said than of the first remedy, that it was worse than the disease. Liberty is to faction what air is to fire, an aliment without which it instantly expires. But it could not be less folly to abolish liberty, which is essential to political life, because it nourishes faction, than it would be to wish the annihilation of air, which is essential to animal life, because it imparts to fire its destructive agency.

The second expedient is as impracticable as the first would be unwise. As long as the reason of man continues fallible, and he is at liberty to exercise it, different opinions will be formed. As long as the connection subsists between his reason and his self-love, his opinions and his passions will have a reciprocal influence on each other; and the former will be objects to which the latter will attach themselves. The diversity in the faculties of men, from which the rights of property originate, is not less an insuperable obstacle to a uniformity of interests. The protection of these faculties is the first object of government. From the protection of different and unequal faculties of acquiring property, the possession of different degrees and kinds of property immediately results; and from the influence of these on the sentiments and views of the respective proprietors ensues a division of the society into different interests and parties.

The latent causes of faction are thus sown in the nature of man; and we see them everywhere brought into different degrees of activity, according to

the different circumstances of civil society. A zeal for different opinions concerning religion, concerning government, and many other points, as well of
speculation as of practice; an attachment to different leaders ambitiously
contending for pre-eminence and power; or to persons of other descriptions
whose fortunes have been interesting to the human passions, have, in turn,
divided mankind into parties, inflamed them with mutual animosity, and
rendered them much more disposed to vex and oppress each other than to
co-operate for their common good. So strong is this propensity of mankind
to fall into mutual animosities, that where no substantial occasion presents
itself, the most frivolous and fanciful distinctions have been sufficient to
kindle their unfriendly passions and excite their most violent conflicts. But
the most common and durable source of factions has been the various and
unequal distribution of property. Those who hold and those who are without
property have ever formed distinct interests in society. Those who are creditors, and those who are debtors, fall under a like discrimination. A landed
interest, a manufacturing interest, a mercantile interest, a moneyed interest, with many lesser interests, grow up of necessity in civilized nations, and
divide them into different classes, actuated by different sentiments and views.
The regulation of these various and interfering interests forms the principal
task of modern legislation, and involves the spirit of party and faction in the
necessary and ordinary operations of the government.

    No man is allowed to be a judge in his own cause, because his interest
would certainly bias his judgment, and, not improbably, corrupt his integrity.
With equal, nay with greater reason, a body of men are unfit to be both
judges and parties at the same time; yet what are many of the most important
acts of legislation, but so many judicial determinations, not indeed concerning the rights of single persons, but concerning the rights of large bodies of
citizens? And what are the different classes of legislators but advocates and
parties to the causes which they determine? Is a law proposed concerning
private debts? It is a question to which the creditors are parties on one side
and the debtors on the other. Justice ought to hold the balance between
them. Yet the parties are, and must be, themselves the judges; and the most
numerous party, or, in other words, the most powerful faction must be expected to prevail. Shall domestic manufactures be encouraged, and in what
degree, by restrictions on foreign manufactures? are questions which would
be differently decided by the landed and the manufacturing classes, and
probably by neither with a sole regard to justice and the public good. The
apportionment of taxes on the various descriptions of property is an act
which seems to require the most exact impartiality; yet there is, perhaps, no
legislative act in which greater opportunity and temptation are given to a

predominant party to trample on the rules of justice. Every shilling with which they overburden the inferior number, is a shilling saved to their own pockets.

It is in vain to say that enlightened statesmen will be able to adjust these clashing interests, and render them all subservient to the public good. Enlightened statesmen will not always be at the helm. Nor, in many cases, can such an adjustment be made at all without taking into view indirect and remote considerations, which will rarely prevail over the immediate interest which one party may find in disregarding the rights of another or the good of the whole.

The inference to which we are brought is, that the *causes* of faction cannot be removed, and that relief is only to be sought in the means of controlling its *effects*.

If a faction consists of less than a majority, relief is supplied by the republican principle, which enables the majority to defeat its sinister views by regular vote. It may clog the administration, it may convulse the society; but it will be unable to execute and mask its violence under the forms of the Constitution. When a majority is included in a faction, the form of popular government, on the other hand, enables it to sacrifice to its ruling passion or interest both the public good and the rights of other citizens. To secure the public good and private rights against the danger of such a faction, and at the same time to preserve the spirit and the form of popular government, is then the great object to which our inquiries are directed. Let me add that it is the great desideratum by which this form of government can be rescued from the opprobrium under which it has so long labored, and be recommended to the esteem and adoption of mankind.

By what means is this object attainable? Evidently by one of two only. Either the existence of the same passion or interest in a majority at the same time must be prevented, or the majority, having such coexistent passion or interest, must be rendered, by their number and local situation, unable to concert and carry into effect schemes of oppression. If the impulse and the opportunity be suffered to coincide, we well know that neither moral nor religious motives can be relied on as an adequate control. They are not found to be such on the injustice and violence of individuals, and lose their efficacy in proportion to the number combined together, that is, in proportion as their efficacy becomes needful.

From this view of the subject it may be concluded that a pure democracy, by which I mean a society consisting of a small number of citizens, who assemble and administer the government in person, can admit of no cure for the mischiefs of faction. A common passion or interest will, in almost every case, be felt by a majority of the whole; a communication and concert result from the form of government itself; and there is nothing to check the inducements to sacrifice the weaker party or an obnoxious individual. Hence it is that such democracies have ever been spectacles of turbulence and contention; have ever been found incompatible with personal security or the rights of property; and have in general been as short in their lives as they have been violent in their deaths. Theoretic politicians, who have patronized this species of government, have erroneously supposed that by reducing mankind to a perfect equality in their political rights, they would, at the same time, be perfectly equalized and assimilated in their possessions, their opinions, and their passions.

A republic, by which I mean a government in which the scheme of representation takes place, opens a different prospect, and promises the cure for which we are seeking. Let us examine the points in which it varies from pure democracy, and we shall comprehend both the nature of the cure and the efficacy which it must derive from the Union.

The two great points of difference between a democracy and a republic are: first, the delegation of the government, in the latter, to a small number of citizens elected by the rest; secondly, the greater number of citizens, and greater sphere of country, over which the latter may be extended.

The effect of the first difference is, on the one hand, to refine and enlarge the public views, by passing them through the medium of a chosen body of citizens, whose wisdom may best discern the true interest of their country, and whose patriotism and love of justice will be least likely to sacrifice it to temporary or partial considerations. Under such a regulation, it may well happen that the public voice, pronounced by the representatives of the people, will be more consonant to the public good than if pronounced by the people themselves, convened for the purpose. On the other hand, the effect may be inverted. Men of factious tempers, of local prejudices, or of sinister designs, may, by intrigue, by corruption, or by other means, first obtain the suffrages, and then betray the interests, of the people. The question resulting is, whether small or extensive republics are more favorable to the election of proper guardians of the public weal; and it is clearly decided in favor of the latter by two obvious considerations:

In the first place, it is to be remarked that, however small the republic may be, the representatives must be raised to a certain number, in order to guard against the cabals of a few; and that, however large it may be, they must be limited to a certain number, in order to guard against the confusion of a multitude. Hence, the number of representatives in the two cases not being in proportion to that of the two constituents, and being proportionally

greater in the small republic, it follows that, if the proportion of fit characters be not less in the large than in the small republic, the former will present
a greater option, and consequently a greater probability of a fit choice.

In the next place, as each representative will be chosen by a greater
number of citizens in the large than in the small republic, it will be more
difficult for unworthy candidates to practise with success the vicious arts by
which elections are too often carried; and the suffrages of the people being
more free, will be more likely to centre in men who possess the most attractive merit and the most diffusive and established characters.

It must be confessed that in this, as in most other cases, there is a mean,
on both sides of which inconveniences will be found to lie. By enlarging
too much the number of electors, you render the representatives too little
acquainted with all their local circumstances and lesser interests; as by reducing it too much, you render him unduly attached to these, and too little fit
to comprehend and pursue great and national objects. The federal Constitution forms a happy combination in this respect; the great and aggregate interests being referred to the national, the local and particular to the State
legislatures.

The other point of difference is, the greater number of citizens and extent of territory which may be brought within the compass of republican
than of democratic government; and it is this circumstance principally which
renders factious combinations less to be dreaded in the former than in the
latter. The smaller the society, the fewer probably will be the distinct parties
and interests composing it; the fewer the distinct parties and interests, the
more frequently will a majority be found of the same party; and the smaller
the number of individuals composing a majority, and the smaller the compass
within which they are placed, the more easily will they concert and execute
their plans of oppression. Extend the sphere, and you take in a greater variety
of parties and interests; you make it less probable that a majority of the
smaller the compass within which they are placed, the more easily will they
concert and execute their plans of oppression. Extend the sphere, and you
take in a greater variety of parties and interests; you make it less probable
that a majority of the whole will have a common motive to invade the rights
of other citizens; or if such a common motive exists, it will be more difficult
for all who feel it to discover their own strength, and to act in unison with
each other. Besides other impediments, it may be remarked that, where there
is a consciousness of unjust or dishonorable purposes, communication is always checked by distrust in proportion to the number whose concurrence
is necessary.

Hence, it clearly appears, that the same advantage which a republic has over a democracy, in controlling the effects of faction, is enjoyed by a large over a small republic,—is enjoyed by the Union over the States composing it. Does the advantage consist in the substitution of representatives whose enlightened views and virtuous sentiments render them superior to local prejudices and to schemes of injustice? It will not be denied that the representation of the Union will be most likely to possess these requisite endowments. Does it consist in the greater security afforded by a greater variety of parties, against the event of any one party being able to outnumber and oppress the rest? In an equal degree does the increased variety of parties comprised within the Union, increase this security. Does it, in fine, consist in the greater obstacles opposed to the concert and accomplishment of the secret wishes of an unjust and interested majority? Here, again, the extent of the Union gives it the most palpable advantage.

The influence of factious leaders may kindle a flame within their particular States, but will be unable to spread a general conflagration through the other States. A religious sect may degenerate into a political faction in a part of the Confederacy; but the variety of sects dispersed over the entire face of it must secure the national councils against any danger from that source. A rage for paper money, for an abolition of debts, for an equal division of property, or for any other improper or wicked project, will be less apt to pervade the whole body of the Union than a particular member of it; in the same proportion as such a malady is more likely to taint a particular country or district, than an entire State.

In the extent and proper structure of the Union, therefore, we behold a republican remedy for the disease most incident to republican government. And according to the degree of pleasure and pride we feel in being republicans, ought to be our zeal in cherishing the spirit and supporting the character of Federalists.

PUBLIUS

I. **Suggestions for Discussion**:
1. How does Madison define a faction?
2. Discuss the two methods he proposes for "curing the mischiefs of faction."
3. What two great points of difference between a democracy and a republic does he analyze?

II. **Suggestions for Writing**:
1. Write a critical review of Madison's logical, carefully-argued essay.
2. Defend your position on a controversial political issue in a carefully-organized, logically-developed essay.

# NORMAN MAILER

## Who Finally Would Do the Dishes?

### from *The Prisoner of Sex*

Norman Mailer (1923–    ), the American novelist, short-story writer, and critic, grew up in Brooklyn and was educated at Harvard, where he wrote many short stories. Among his many books are *The Naked and the Dead* (1948), *The Deer Park* (1955), *An American Dream* (1965), *Of a Fire on the Moon* (1969), and *The Prisoner of Sex* (1971), from which the following selection is taken. His latest work, *The Executioner's Song: A True Life Novel,* published in 1979, was awarded a Pulitzer Prize.

Examining a marriage contract leads Mailer to reminisce about his own life and, finally, to argue for women's rights. His prose in this piece is, as usual, self-conscious, rich, and full of allusion.

Still he had not answered the question with which he began. Who finally would do the dishes? And in his reading through an Agreement drawn between husband and wife where every piece of housework was divided, and duty-shifts to baby-sit were divided, and weekends where the man worked to compensate the wife for chores of weekday transportation. Shopping was balanced, cooking was split, so was the transportation of children. It was a crystal of a contract bound to serve as model for many another, and began on this high and fundamental premise:

> We reject the notion that the work which brings in more money is more valuable. The ability to earn more money is already a privilege which must not be compounded by enabling the larger earner to buy out his/her duties and put the burden on the one who earns less, or on someone hired from outside.
>
> We believe that each member of the family has an equal right to his/her own time, work, value, choices. As long as all duties are performed, each person may use his/her extra time any way he/she chooses. If he/she wants to use it making money, fine. If he/she wants to spend it with spouse, fine. If not, fine.

As parents we believe we must share all responsibility for taking care of our children and home—not only the work, but the responsibility. At least during the first year of this agreement, *sharing responsibility* shall mean:

1. Dividing the *jobs* (see "Job Breakdown" below); and
2. Dividing the *time* (see "Schedule" below) for which each parent is responsible.

There were details which stung:

10. Cleaning: Husband does all the house-cleaning, in exchange for wife's extra childcare (3:00 to 6:30 daily) and sick care.
11. Laundry: Wife does most home laundry. Husband does all dry cleaning delivery and pick up. Wife strips beds, husband remakes them.

No, he would not be married to such a woman. If he were obliged to have a roommate, he would pick a man. The question had been answered. He could love a woman and she might even sprain her back before a hundred sinks of dishes in a month, but he would not be happy to help her if his work should suffer, no, not unless her work was as valuable as his own. But he was complacent with the importance of respecting his work—what an agony for a man if work were meaningless: then all such rights were lost before a woman. So it was another corollary of Liberation that as technique reduced labor to activities which were often absurd, like punching the buttons on an automatic machine, so did the housework of women take on magnitude, for their work was directed at least to a basic end. And thinking of that Marriage Agreement which was nearly the equal of a legal code, he was reminded of his old campain for mayor when Breslin and himself had called for New York City to become the fifty-first state and had preached Power to the Neighborhoods and offered the idea that a modern man would do well to live in a small society of his own choosing, in a legally constituted village within the city, or a corporate zone, in a traditional religious park or a revolutionary commune—the value would be to discover which of one's social ideas were able to work. For nothing was more difficult to learn in the modern world. Of course, it had been a scheme with all the profound naïveté of assuming that people voted as an expression of their desire when he had yet to learn the electorate obtained satisfaction by venting their hate. Still he wondered if it was not likely that the politics of government and property would yet begin to alter into the politics of sex. Perhaps he had been living with the subject

too closely, but he saw no major reason why one could not await a world—
assuming there would be a world—where people would found their politics
on the fundamental demands they would make of sex. So might there yet be
towns within the city which were homosexual, and whole blocks legally
organized for married couples who thought the orgy was ground for the progressive action of the day. And there would be mournful areas of the city
deserted on Sunday, all suitable for the mood of masturbators who liked the
open air and the street, perhaps even pseudo-Victorian quarters where
brothels could again be found. There could be city turfs steaming with the
nuances of bisexuals living on top of bisexuals, and funky tracts for old-
fashioned lovers where the man was the rock of the home; there would always be horizons blocked by housing projects vast as the legislation which
had gone into the division of household duties between women and men.
There would be every kind of world in the city, but their laws would be
founded on sex. It was, he supposed, the rationalized end of that violence
which had once existed between men and women as the crossed potential of
their love, violence which was part perhaps of the force to achieve and the
force to scourge, it had been that violence which entered into all the irra-
tionality of love, "the rooting out of the old bodily shame" of which Lawrence had spoke, and the rooting out of the fear in women that they were
more violent than their men, and would betray them, or destroy them in the
transcendence of sex; yes, the play of violence had been the drama of love
between a man and a woman, for too little, and they were friends never to
be gripped by any attraction which could send them far; too much, and they
were ruined, or love was ruined, or they must degenerate to bully and victim,
become no better than a transmission belt to bring in the violence and injustice of the world outside, bring it in to poison the cowardice of their
home. But the violence of lovers was on its way to disappear in all the other
deaths of the primitive which one could anticipate as the human became the
human unit—human violence would go to some place outside (like the smog)
where it could return to kill them by slow degree—and equally. But he had
made his determination on beginning his piece that he would not write of sex
and violence too long, for that would oblige him to end in the unnatural
position of explaining what he had attempted in other work. So he would
step aside by remarking that a look at sex and violence was the proper ground
of a novel and he would rather try it there. And content himself now with
one last look at his remark that "the prime responsibility of a woman probably is to be on earth long enough to find the best mate for herself, and conceive children who will improve the species." Was it too late now to suggest

that in the search for the best mate was concealed the bravery of a woman, and to find the best mate, whatever ugly or brutal or tyrannical or unbalanced or heart-searing son of misery he might appear, his values nonetheless, mysterious fellow of values, would inevitably present themselves in those twenty-three chromosomes able to cut through fashion, tradition, and class.

There is a famous study of neurotics which shows that patients who received psychoanalysis had an improvement rate of 44 percent; psychotherapy was more effective—a rate of 64 percent; and 72 percent was the unhappiest improvement, for that was the rate of cure of patients who had never been treated at all. The Eysenck study it is called, and later studies confirm its results. It was, the prisoner decided, a way of telling us that the taste in the mouth of explaining too much is the seating of the next disease. One cannot improve the human condition through comfort and security, or through generalized sympathy and support—it is possible the untreated patients got better because the violence of their neurosis was not drained. The cure of the human was in his leap.

But now he could comprehend why woman bridled at the thought she must "find the best mate for herself and . . . improve the species." How full of death was the idea if one looked at any scheme which brought people who were fundamentally unattracted to each other down marriage aisles, their qualifications superb, their qualities neuter. So he was grateful to a writer who wrote a book. *The Lady,* published in 1910, Emily James Putnam, first dean of Barnard. She was a writer with a whip of the loveliest wit. He would give the last quotation to her for she had given the hint of a way.

Apart from the crude economic question, the things that most women mean when they speak of "happiness," that is, love and children and the little republic of the home, depend upon the favour of men, and the qualities that win this favour are not in general those that are most useful for other purposes. A girl should not be too intelligent or too good or too highly differentiated in any direction. Like a ready-made garment she should be designed to fit the average man. She should have "just about as much religion as my William likes." The age-long operation of this rule, by which the least strongly individualised women are the most likely to have a chance to transmit their qualities, has given it the air of a natural law.

It was finally obvious. Women must have their rights to a life which would allow them to look for a mate. And there would be no free search until they were liberated. So let woman be what she would, and what she could. Let her cohabit on elephants if she had to, and fuck with Borzoi hounds, let her bed with eight pricks and a whistle, yes, give her freedom and let her burn it, or blow it, or build it to triumph or collapse. Let her conceive her children, and kill them in the womb if she thought they did not have it, let her travel to the moon, write the great American novel, and allow her husband to send her off to work with her lunch pail and a cigar; she could kiss the cooze of forty-one Rockettes in Macy's store window; she could legislate, incarcerate, and wear a uniform; she could die of every male disease, and years of burden was the first, for she might learn that women worked at onerous duties and men worked for egos which were worse than onerous and often insane. So women could have the right to die of men's diseases, yes, and might try to live with men's egos in their own skull case and he would cheer them on their way—would he? Yes, he thought that perhaps they may as well do what they desired if the anger of the centuries was having its say. Finally, he would agree with everything they asked but to quit the womb, for finally a day had to come when women shattered the pearl of their love for pristine and feminine will and found the man, yes that man in the million who could become the point of the seed which would give an egg back to nature, and let the woman return with a babe who came from the root of God's desire to go all the way, wherever was that way. And who was there to know that God was not the greatest lover of them all? The idiocy was to assume the oyster and the clam knew more than the trees and the grass. (Unless dear God was black and half-Jewish and a woman, and small and mean as mother-wit. We will never know until we take the trip. And so saying realized he had been able to end a portentous piece in the soft sweet flesh of parentheses.)

I. **Suggestions for Discussion**:
   1. How does Mailer finally resolve the question he poses in the opening lines of the essay?
   2. How does Mailer relate his mayoral campaign in New York to women's liberation?
   3. What importance does Mailer give to the woman's role in the preservation of the species?

II. **Suggestions for Writing**:
   1. Compare and contrast Mailer's views on women with those expressed by Germaine Greer in "The Stereotype," p. 215 or Dorothy Sayers in "Are Women Human?", p. 504.
   2. Write a marriage contract with which you could live happily.

# MARYA MANNES

## How Do You Know It's Good?

Marya Mannes (1904–     ), the American journalist and novelist, has written frequently and shrewdly about American customs and about the arts and media. Her works include an autobiographical volume, *Out of My Times* (1971) and *Last Rights* (1973), about dying with dignity.

In the following essay, she deplores the abandonment of standardards of judgment in modern art, music, poetry, and theater. She argues that her readers have a responsibility to exercise critical judgment and to search for purpose and craftsmanship in the arts.

Suppose there were no critics to tell us how to react to a picture, a play, or a new composition of music. Suppose we wandered innocent as the dawn into an art exhibition of unsigned paintings. By what standards, by what values would we decide whether they were good or bad, talented or untalented, successes or failures? How can we ever know that what we think is right?

For the last fifteen or twenty years the fashion in criticism or appreciation of the arts has been to deny the existence of any valid criteria and to make the words "good" or "bad" irrelevant, immaterial, and inapplicable. There is no such thing, we are told, as a set of standards, first acquired through experience and knowledge and later imposed on the subject under discussion. This has been a popular approach, for it relieves the critic of the responsibility of judgment and the public of the necessity of knowledge. It pleases those resentful of disciplines, it flatters the empty-minded by calling them open-minded, it comforts the confused. Under the banner of democracy and the kind of equality which our forefathers did *not* mean, it says, in effect, "Who are you to tell us what is good or bad?" This is the same cry used so long and so effectively by the producers of mass media who insist that it is the public, not they, who decides what it wants to hear and see, and that for a critic to say that *this* program is bad and *this* program is good is purely a reflection of personal taste. Nobody recently has expressed this

philosophy more succinctly than Dr. Frank Stanton, the highly intelligent
president of CBS television. At a hearing before the Federal Communications
Commission, this phrase escaped him under questioning: "One man's medi-
ocrity is another man's good program."

There is no better way of saying "No values are absolute." There is
another important aspect to this philosophy of *laissez faire:* It is the fear, in
all observers of all forms of art, of guessing wrong. This fear is well come by,
for who has not heard of the contemporary outcries against artists who later
were called great? Every age has its arbiters who do not grow with their times,
who cannot tell evolution from revolution or the difference between frivolous
faddism, amateurish experimentation, and profound and necessary change.
Who wants to be caught *flagrante delicto* with an error of judgment as serious
as this? It is far safer, and certainly easier, to look at a picture or a play or a
poem and to say "This is hard to understand, but it may be good," or simply
to welcome it as a new form. The word "new"—in our country especially—has
magical connotations. What is new must be good; what is old is probably
bad, and if a critic can describe the new in language that nobody can understand, he's safer still. If he has mastered the art of saying nothing with exquisite complexity, nobody can quote him later as saying anything.

But all these, I maintain, are forms of abdication from the responsibility of judgment. In creating, the artist commits himself; in appreciating,
you have a commitment of your own. For after all, it is the audience which
makes the arts. A climate of appreciation is essential to its flowering, and the
higher the expectations of the public, the better the performance of the
artist. Conversely, only a public ill-served by its critics could have accepted as
art and literature so much in these last years that has been neither. If anything goes, everything goes; and at the bottom of the junkpile lie the dis-
carded standards too.

But what are these standards? How do you get them? How do you
know they're the right ones? How can you make a clear pattern out of so
many intangibles, including that greatest one, the very private I?

Well for one thing, it's fairly obvious that the more you read and see
and hear, the more equipped you'll be to practice that art of association
which is at the basis of all understanding and judgment. The more you live
and the more you look, the more aware you are of a consistent pattern—as
universal as the stars, as the tides, as breathing, as night and day—underlying
everything. I would call this pattern and this rhythm an order. Not order—*an*
order. Within it exists an incredible diversity of forms. Without it lies chaos.
I would further call this order—this incredible diversity held within one pat-

tern—health. And I would call chaos—the wild cells of destruction—sickness. It is in the end up to you to distinguish between the diversity that is health and the chaos that is sickness, and you can't do this without a process of association that can link a bar of Mozart with the corner of a Vermeer painting, or a Stravinsky score with a Picasso abstraction; or that can relate an aggressive act with a Franz Kline painting and a fit of coughing with a John Cage composition.

There is no accident in the fact that certain expressions of art live for all time and that others die with the moment, and although you may not always define the reasons, you can ask the questions. What does an artist say that is timeless; how does he say it? How much is fashion, how much is merely reflection? Why is Sir Walter Scott so hard to read now, and Jane Austen not? Why is baroque right for one age and too effulgent for another?

Can a standard of craftsmanship apply to art of all ages, or does each have its own, and different, definitions? You may have been aware, inadvertently, that craftsmanship has become a dirty word these years because, again, it implies standard—something done well or done badly. The result of this convenient avoidance is a plenitude of actors who can't project their voices, singers who can't phrase their songs, poets who can't communicate emotion, and writers who have no vocabulary—not to speak of painters who can't draw. The dogma now is that craftsmanship gets in the way of expression. You can do better if you don't know *how* you do it, let alone *what* you're doing.

I think it is time you helped reverse this trend by trying to rediscover craft: the command of the chosen instrument, whether it is a brush, a word, or a voice. When you begin to detect the difference between freedom and sloppiness, between serious experimentation and ego-therapy, between skill and slickness, between strength and violence, you are on your way to separating the sheep from the goats, a form of segregation denied us for quite a while. All you need to restore it is a small bundle of standards and a Geiger counter that detects fraud, and we might begin our tour of the arts in an area where both are urgently needed: contemporary painting.

I don't know what's worse: to have to look at acres of bad art to find the little good, or to read what the critics say about it all. In no other field of expression has so much double-talk flourished, so much confusion prevailed, and so much nonsense been circulated: further evidence of the close interdependence between the arts and the critical climate they inhabit. It will be my pleasure to share with you some of this double-talk so typical of our times.

Item one: preface for a catalogue of an abstract painter:

"Time-bound meditation experiencing a life; sincere with plastic piety at the threshold of hallowed arcana; a striving for pure ideation giving shape to inner drive; formalized patterns where neural balances reach a fiction." End of quote. Know what this artist paints like now?

Item two: a review in the *Art News:*

". . . a weird and disparate assortment of material, but the monstrosity which bloomed into his most recent cancer of aggregations is present in some form everywhere. . . ." Then, later, "A gluttony of things and processes terminated by a glorious constipation."

Item three, same magazine, review of an artist who welds automobile fragments into abstract shapes:

"Each fragment . . . is made an extreme of human exasperation, torn at and fought all the way, and has its rightness of form as if by accident. *Any technique that requires order or discipline would just be the human ego.* No, these must be egoless, uncontrolled, undesigned and different enough to give you a bang—fifty miles an hour around a telephone pole. . . ."

"Any technique that requires order or discipline would just be the human ego." What does he mean—"just be"? What are they really talking about? Is this journalism? Is it criticism? Or is it that other convenient abdication from standards of performance and judgment practiced by so many artists and critics that they, like certain writers who deal only in sickness and depravity, "reflect the chaos about them..? Again, whose chaos? Whose depravity?

I had always thought that the prime function of art was to create order *out* of chaos—again, not the order of neatness or rigidity or convention or artifice, but the order of clarity by which one will and one vision could draw the essential truth out of apparent confusion. I still do. It is not enough to use parts of a car to convey the brutality of the machine. This is a slavishly representative, and just as easy, as arranging dried flowers under glass to convey nature.

Speaking of which, i.e., the use of real materials (burlap, old gloves, bottletops) in lieu of pigment, this is what one critic had to say about an exhibition of Assemblage at the Museum of Modern Art last year:

"Spotted throughout the show are indisputable works of art, accounting for a quarter or even half of the total display. But the remainder are works of non-art, anti-art, and art substitutes that are the aesthetic counterparts of the social deficiencies that land people in the clink on charges of vagrancy. These aesthetic bankrupts . . . have no legitimate ideological roof over their heads and not the price of a square intellectual meal, much less a spiritual sandwich, in their pockets."

I quote these words of John Canaday of *The New York Times* as an example of the kind of criticism which puts responsibility to an intelligent public above popularity with an intellectual coterie. Canaday has the courage to say what he thinks and the capacity to say it clearly: two qualities notably absent from his profession.

Next to art, I would say that appreciation and evaluation in the field of music is the most difficult. For it is rarely possible to judge a new composition at one hearing only. What seems confusing or fragmented at first might well become clear and organic a third time. Or it might not. The only salvation here for the listener is, again, an instinct born of experience and association which allows him to separate intent from accident, design from experimentation, and pretense from conviction. Much of contemporary music is, like its sister art, merely a reflection of the composer's own fragmentation: an absorption in self and symbols at the expense of communication with others. The artist, in short, says to the public: If you don't understand this, it's because you're dumb. I maintain that you are not. You may have to go part way or even halfway to meet the artist, but if you must go the whole way, it's his fault, not yours. Hold fast to that. And remember it too when you read new poetry, that estranged sister of music.

"A multitude of causes, unknown to former times, are now acting with a combined force to blunt the discriminating powers of the mind, and, unfitting it for all voluntary exertion, to reduce it to a state of almost savage torpor. The most effective of these causes are the great national events which are daily taking place and the increasing accumulation of men in cities, where the uniformity of their occupations produces a craving for extraordinary incident, which the rapid communication of intelligence hourly gratifies. To this tendency of life and manners, the literature and theatrical exhibitions of the country have conformed themselves."

This startingly applicable comment was written in the year 1800 by William Wordsworth in the preface to his "Lyrical Ballads"; and it has been cited by Edwin Muir in his recently published book, *The Estate of Poetry*. Muir states that poetry's effective range and influence have diminished alarmingly in the modern world. He believes in the inherent and indestructible qualities of the human mind and the great and permanent objects that act upon it, and suggests that the audience will increase when "poetry loses what obscurity is left in it by attempting greater themes, for great themes have to be stated clearly." If you keep that firmly in mind and resist, in Muir's words, "the vast dissemination of secondary objects that isolate us from the natural world," you have gone a long way toward equipping yourself for the examination of any work of art.

When you come to theatre, in this extremely hasty tour of the arts, you can approach it on two different levels. You can bring to it anticipation and innocence, giving yourself up, as it were, to the life on the stage and reacting to it emotionally, if the play is good, or listlessly, if the play is boring; a part of the audience organism that expresses its favor by silence or laughter and its disfavor by coughing and rustling. Or you can bring to it certain critical faculties that may heighten, rather than diminish, your enjoyment.

You can ask yourselves whether the actors are truly in their parts or merely projecting themselves; whether the scenery helps or hurts the mood; whether the playwright is honest with himself, the characters, and you. Somewhere along the line you can learn to distinguish between the true creative act and the false arbitrary gesture; between fresh observation and stale cliché; between the avant-garde play that is pretentious drivel and the avant-garde play that finds new ways to say old truths.

Purpose and craftsmanship—end and means—these are the keys to your judgment in all the arts. What is this painter trying to say when he slashed a broad band of black across a white canvas and lets the edges dribble down? Is it a statement of violence? Is it a self-portrait? If it is *one* of these, has he made you believe it? Or is this a gesture of the ego or a form of therapy? If it shocks you, what does it shock you into?

And what of this tight little painting of bright flowers in a vase? Is the painter saying anything new about flowers? Is it different from a million other canvases of flowers? Has it any life, any meaning, beyond its statement? Is there any pleasure in its forms or texture? The question is not whether a thing is abstract or representational, whether it is "modern" or conventional. The question, inexorably, is whether it is good. And this is a decision which only you, on the basis of instinct, experience, and association, can make for yourself. It takes independence and courage. It involves, moreover, the risk of wrong decision and the humility, after the passage of time, of recognizing it as such. As we grow and change and learn, our attitudes can change too, and what we once thought obscure or "difficult" can later emerge as coherent and illuminating. Entrenched prejudices, obdurate opinions are as sterile as no opinions at all.

Yet standards there are, timeless as the universe itself. And when you have committed yourself to them, you have acquired a passport to that elusive but immutable realm of truth. Keep it with you in the forest of bewilderment. And never be afraid to speak up.

I. **Suggestions for Discussion:**
  1. What evidence does Mannes offer that standards in the arts have been abandoned?
  2. Discuss the effect of the many rhetorical questions in her essay. Do her questions succeed in drawing the reader's attention to her subject? Do they help to hold the reader's interest? Discuss.
  3. How does Mannes propose that you develop an independent judgment?
II. **Suggestions for Writing:**
  1. Write a review of a play, film, or exhibit in which you state clearly the critical standards you are employing.
  2. Write a critique of several reviews of a play, film, or exhibit. Discuss whether or not the reviewers have applied common standards.

---

## MARYA MANNES

## Television Advertising: The Splitting Image

---

Using many specific examples in the essay that follows, Marya Mannes analyzes the faults in commercial television advertising. She discusses the effects of commercials that demean both men and women, and calls for sponsors to exercise accuracy and restraint and to enlarge public consciousness and human stature.

---

A bride who looks scarcely fourteen whispers, "Oh, Mom, I'm so *happy!*" while a doting family adjust her gown and veil and a male voice croons softly, "A woman is a harder thing to be than a man. She has more feelings to feel." The mitigation of these excesses, it appears, is a feminine deodorant called Secret, which allows our bride to approach the altar with security as well as emotion.

Eddie Albert, a successful actor turned pitchman, bestows his attention on a lady with two suitcases, which prompt him to ask her whether she has been on a journey, "No," she says, or words to that effect, as she opens the suitcases. "My two boys bring back their soiled clothes every weekend from college for me to wash." And she goes into the familiar litany of grease, chocolate, mud, coffee, and fruit-juice stains, which presumably record the life of the average American male from two to fifty. Mr. Albert compliments her on this happy device to bring her boys home every week and hands her a box of Biz, because "Biz *is* better."

Two women with stony faces meet cart to cart in a supermarket as one takes a jar of peanut butter off a shelf. When the other asks her in a voice of nitric acid why she takes that brand, the first snaps, "Because I'm choosy for my family!" The two then break into delighted smiles as Number Two makes Number One taste Jif for "mothers who are choosy."

If you have not come across these dramatic interludes, it is because you are not home during the day and do not watch daytime television. It also means that your intestinal tract is spared from severe assaults, your credibility unstrained. Or, for that matter, you may look at commercials like these every day and manage either to ignore them or find nothing—given the fact of advertising—wrong with them. In that case, you are either so brainwashed or so innocent that you remain unaware of what this daily infusion may have done and is doing to an entire people as the long-accepted adjunct of free enterprise and support of "free" television.

"Given the fact" and "long-accepted" are the key words here. Only socialists, communists, idealists (or the BBC) fail to realize that a mass television system cannot exist without the support of sponsors, that the massive cost of maintaining it as a free service cannot be met without the massive income from selling products. You have only to read of the unending struggle to provide financial support for public, noncommercial television for further evidence.

Besides, aren't commercials in the public interest? Don't they help you choose what to buy? Don't they provide needed breaks from programing? Aren't many of them brilliantly done, and some of them funny? And now, with the new sexual freedom, all those gorgeous chicks with their shining hair and gleaming smiles? And if you didn't have commercials taking up a good part of each hour, how on earth would you find enough program material to fill the endless space/time void?

Tick off the yesses and what have you left? You have, I venture to submit, these intangible but possibly high costs: the diminution of human worth, the infusion and hardening of social attitudes no longer valid or desirable, pervasive discontent, and psychic fragmentation.

Should anyone wonder why deception is not an included detriment, I suggest that our public is so conditioned to promotion as a way of life, whether in art or politics or products, that elements of exaggeration or distortion are taken for granted. Nobody really believes that a certain shampoo will get a certain swain, or that an unclogged sinus can make a man a swinger. People are merely prepared to hope it will.

But the diminution of human worth is much more subtle and just as pervasive. In the guise of what they consider comedy, the producers of television commercials have created a loathsome gallery of men and women patterned, presumably, on Mr. and Mrs. America. Women liberationists have a major target in the commercial image of woman flashed hourly and daily to the vast majority. There are, indeed, only four kinds of females in this relentless sales procession: the gorgeous teen-age swinger with bouncing locks; the young mother teaching her baby girl the right soap for skin care; the middle-aged housewife with a voice like a power saw; and the old lady with dentures and irregularity. All these women, to be sure, exist. But between the swinging sex object and the constipated granny there are millions of females never shown in commercials. These are—married or single—intelligent, sensitive women who bring charm to their homes, who work at jobs as well as lend grace to their marriage, who support themselves, who have talents or hobbies or commitments, or who are skilled at their professions.

To my knowledge, as a frequent if reluctant observer, I know of only one woman on a commercial who has a job; a comic plumber pushing Comet. Funny, heh? Think of a dame with a plunger.

With this one representative of our labor force, which is well over thirty million women, we are left with nothing but the full-time housewife in all her whining glory: obsessed with whiter wash, moister cakes, shinier floors, cleaner children, softer diapers, and greaseless fried chicken. In the rare instances when these ladies are not in the kitchen, at the washing machine, or waiting on hubby, they are buying beauty shops (fantasy, see?) to take home so that their hair will have more body. Or out at the supermarket being choosy.

If they were attractive in their obsessions, they might be bearable. But they are not. They are pushy, loud-mouthed, stupid, and—of all things now—bereft of sexuality. Presumably, the argument in the tenets of advertising is that once a woman marries she changes overnight from plaything to floor-waxer.

To be fair, men make an equivalent transition in commercials. The swinging male with the mod hair and the beautiful chick turns inevitably into the paunchy slob who chokes on his wife's cake. You will notice, however, that the voice urging the viewer to buy the product is nearly always male: gentle, wise, helpful, seductive. And the visible presence telling the housewife how to get shinier floors and whiter wash and lovelier hair is almost invariably a man: the Svengali in modern dress, the Trilby[1] (if only she were!), his willing object.

---

[1] In George Du Maurier's novel, *Trilby* (1894), Svengali causes Trilby to become a famous singer, but she loses her voice after his death.

Woman, in short, is consumer first and human being fourth. A wife and mother who stays home all day buys a lot more than a woman who lives alone or who—married or single—has a job. The young girl hell-bent on marriage is the next most susceptible consumer. It is entirely understandable, then, that the potential buyers of detergents, foods, polishes, toothpastes, pills, and housewares are the housewives, and that the sex object spends most of *her* money on cosmetics, hair lotions, soaps, mouthwashes, and soft drinks.

Here we come, of course, to the youngest class of consumers, the swinging teen-agers so beloved by advertisers keen on telling them (and us) that they've "got a lot to live, and Pepsi's got a lot to give." This affords a chance to show a squirming, leaping, jiggling group of beautiful kids having a very loud high on rock and—of all things—soda pop. One of commercial TV's most dubious achievements, in fact, is the reinforcement of the self-adulation characteristic of the young as a group.

As for the aging female citizen, the less shown of her the better. She is useful for ailments, but since she buys very little of anything, not having a husband or any children to feed or house to keep, nor—of course—sex appeal to burnish, society and commercials have little place for her. The same is true, to be sure, of older men, who are handy for Bosses with Bad Breath or Doctors with Remedies. Yet, on the whole, men hold up better than women at any age—in life or on television. Lines on their faces are marks of distinction, while on women they are signatures of decay.

There is no question, in any case, that television commercials (and many of the entertainment programs, notably the soap serials that are part of the selling package) reinforce, like an insistent drill, the assumption that a woman's only valid function is that of wife, mother, and servant of men: the inevitable sequel to her earlier function as sex object and swinger.

At a time when more and more women are at long last learning to reject these assumptions as archaic and demeaning, and to grow into individual human beings with a wide option of lives to live, the sellers of the nation are bent upon reinforcing the ancient pattern. They know only too well that by beaming their message to the Consumer Queen they can justify her existence as the housebound Mrs. America: dumber than dumb, whiter than white.

The conditioning starts very early: with the girl child who wants the skin Ivory soap has reputedly given her mother, with the nine-year-old who brings back a cake of Camay instead of the male deodorant her father wanted. (When she confesses that she bought it so she could be "feminine," her father hugs her, and, with the voice of a child-molester, whispers, "My little girl is growing up on me, huh.") And then, before long, comes the teen-aged bride who "has feelings to feel." It is the little boys who dream of wings, in an airplane commercial; who grow up (with fewer cavities) into the doers. Their little sisters turn into Cosmopolitan girls, who in turn become housewives furious that their neighbors' wash is cleaner than theirs.

There is good reason to suspect that this manic obsession with cleanliness, fostered, quite naturally, by the giant soap and detergent interests, may bear some responsibility for the cultivated sloppiness of so many of the young in their clothing as well as in their chosen hideouts. The compulsive housewife who spends more time washing and vacuuming and polishing her possessions than communicating to, or stimulating her children creates a kind of sterility that the young would instinctively reject. The impeccably tidy home, the impeccably tidy lawn are—in a very real sense—unnatural and confining. Yet the commercials confront us with broods of happy children, some of whom—believe it or not—notice the new fresh smell their clean, white sweatshirts exhale thanks to Mom's new "softener."

Some major advertisers, for that matter, can even cast a benign eye on the population explosion. In another Biz commercial, the genial Eddie Albert surveys with surprise a long row of dirty clothes heaped before him by a young matron. She answers his natural query by telling him gaily they are the products of her brood of eleven "with one more to come!" she adds as the twelfth turns up. "That's great!" says Mr. Albert, curdling the soul of Planned Parenthood and the future of this planet.

Who are, one cannot help but ask, the writers who manage to combine the sale of products with the selling-out of human dreams and dignity? Who people this cosmos of commercials with dolts and fools and shrews and narcissists? Who know so much about quirks and mannerisms and ailments and so little about life? So much about presumed wants and so little about crying needs?

Can women advertisers so demean their own sex? Or are there no women in positions of decision high enough to see that their real selves stand up? Do they not know, these extremely clever creators of commercials, what they could do for their audience even while they exploit and entertain them? How they could raise the levels of manners and attitudes while they sell their wares? Or do they really share the worm's-eye view of mass communication that sees, and addresses, only the lowest common denominator?

It can be argued that commercials are taken too seriously, that their function is merely to amuse, engage, and sell, and that they do this brilliantly. If that were all to this wheedling of millions, well and good. But it is not. There are two more fallouts from this chronic sales explosion that cannot be measured but that at least can be expected. One has to do with the continual celebration of youth at the expense of maturity. In commercials only the young have access to beauty, sex, and joy in life. What do older women feel, day after day, when love is the exclusive possession of a teen-age girl with a bobbing mantle of hair? What older man would not covet her in restless impotence?

The constant reminder of what is inaccessible must inevitably produce a subterranean but real discontent, just as the continual sight of things and places beyond reach has eaten deeply into the ghetto soul. If we are constantly presented with what we are not or cannot have, the dislocation deepens, contentment vanishes, and frustration reigns. Even for the substantially secure, there is always a better thing, a better way, to buy. That none of these things makes a better life may be consciously acknowledged, but still the desire lodges in the spirit, nagging and pulling.

This kind of fragmentation works in potent ways above and beyond the mere fact of program interruption, which is much of the time more of a blessing than a curse, especially in those rare instances when the commercial is deft and funny: the soft and subtle sell. Its overall curse, due to the large number of commercials in each hour, is that it reduces the attention span of a people already so conditioned to constant change and distraction that they cannot tolerate continuity in print or on the air.

Specifically, commercial interruption is most damaging during that 10 per cent of programing (a charitable estimate) most important to the mind and spirit of a people: news and public affairs, and drama. To many (and among these are network news producers), commercials have no place or business during the vital process of informing the public. There is something obscene about a newscaster pausing to introduce a deodorant or shampoo commercial between an airplane crash and a body count. It is more than an interruption; it tends to reduce news to a form of running entertainment, to smudge the edges of reality by treating death or disaster or diplomacy on the same level as household appliances or a new gasoline.

The answer to this would presumably be to lump the commercials before and after the news or public affairs broadcasts—an answer unpalatable, needless to say, to the sponsors who support them.

The same is doubly true of that most unprofitable sector of television, the original play. Essential to any creative composition, whether drama, music or dance, are mood and continuity, both inseparable from form and meaning. They are shattered by the periodic intrusion of commercials, which have become intolerable to the serious artists who have deserted commercial television in droves because the system allows them no real freedom or autonomy. The selling comes first, the creation must accommodate itself.

It is the rare and admirable sponsor who restricts or fashions his commercials so as to provide a minimum of intrusion or damaging inappropriateness.

If all these assumptions and imponderables are true, as many suspect, what is the answer or alleviation?

One is in the course of difficult emergence: the establishment of a public television system sufficiently funded so that it can give a maximum number of people an alternate diet of pleasure, enlightenment, and stimulation free from commercial fragmentation. So far, for lack of funds to buy talent and equipment, this effort has been in terms of public attention a distinctly minor operation. Even if public television should greatly increase its scope and impact, it cannot in the nature of things and through long public conditioning equal the impact and reach the size of audience now tuned to commercial television.

Enormous amounts of time, money, and talent go into commercials. Technically they are often brilliant and innovative, the product not only of the new skills and devices but of imaginative minds. A few of them are both funny and endearing. Who, for instance, will forget the miserable young man with the appalling cold, or the kids taught to use—as an initiation into manhood—a fork instead of a spoon with a certain spaghetti? Among the enlightened sponsors, moreover, are some who manage to combine an image of their corporation and their products with accuracy and restraint.

What has to happen to mass medium advertisers as a whole, and especially on TV, is a totally new approach to their function not only as sellers but as social influencers. They have the same obligation as the broadcast medium itself: not only to entertain but to reflect, not only to reflect but to enlarge public consciousness and human stature.

This may be a tall order, but it is a vital one at a time when Americans have ceased to know who they are and where they are going, and when all the multiple forces acting upon them are daily diminishing their sense of their own value and purpose in life, when social upheaval and social fragmentation have destroyed old patterns, and when survival depends on new ones.

If we continue to see ourselves as the advertisers see us, we have no place to go. Nor, I might add, has commercial broadcasting itself.

### I. Suggestions for Discussion:

1. Evaluate the pros and cons of television advertising listed by Mannes.
2. Discuss the effectiveness of the illustrations and examples she uses to support her argument. Notice how she moves frrom particular examples of television advertising to general observations.

3. What suggestions does she offer for the improvement of commercial broadcasting? Are they reasonable? Are they likely to be adopted? Are her suggestions sufficiently developed to be convincing to you?

II. **Suggestions for Writing:**
1. Keep a television log for a week and analyze the ways in which advertisers are currently portraying husbands and wives.
2. Write the script for a television commercial that is humorous and imaginative but at the same time an honest portrayal of a relationship between a man and a woman.

---

## MARY McCARTHY

### Names

from *Memories of a Catholic Girlhood*

---

Mary McCarthy (1912-    ), American novelist, short-story writer, and essayist, is known for her biting satire. Among her many books are *The Company She Keeps* (1942), *The Oasis* (1949), *The Groves of Academe* (1952), *Memories of a Catholic Girlhood* (1957), and *The Group* (1963). Her latest novel, *Cannibals and Missionaries,* appeared in 1979.

In the following essay, taken from *Memories of a Catholic Girlhood,* she describes her life as a young girl in a Catholic convent boarding school and recounts an embarrassing incident that influenced her life there. Using many details, she discusses the names and characters of the girls with whom she lived.

---

Anna Lyons, Mary Louise Lyons, Mary von Phul, Emilie von Phul, Eugenia McLellan, Marjorie McPhail, Marie-Louise L'Abbé, Mary Danz, Julia Dodge, Mary Fordyce Blake, Janet Preston—these were the names (I can still tell them over like a rosary) of some of the older girls in the convent: the Virtues and Graces. The virtuous ones wore wide blue or green moire good-conduct ribbons, bandoleer-style, across their blue serge uniforms; the beautiful ones wore rouge and powder or at least were reputed to do so. Our class, the eighth grade, wore pink ribbons (I never got one myself) and had names like Patricia ("Pat") Sullivan, Eileen Donohoe, and Joan Kane. We were inelegant even in this respect; the best name we could show, among us, was Phyllis ("Phil") Chatham, who boasted that her father's name, Ralph, was pronounced "Rafe" as in England.

Names had a great importance for us in the convent, and foreign names, French, German, or plain English (which, to us, were foreign, because of their Protestant sound), bloomed like prize roses among a collection of spuds. Irish names were too common in the school to have any prestige either as surnames (Gallagher, Sheehan, Finn, Sullivan, McCarthy) or as Christian names (Kathleen, Eileen). Anything exotic had value: an "olive" complexion, for example. The pet girl of the convent was a fragile Jewish girl named Susie Lowenstein, who had pale red-gold hair and an exquisite retroussé nose, which, if we had had it, might have been called "pug." We liked her name too and the name of a child in the primary grades: Abbie Stuart Baillargeon. My favorite name, on the whole, though, was Emilie von Phul (pronounced "Pool"); her oldest sister, recently graduated, was called Celeste. Another name that appealed to me was Genevieve Albers, Saint Genevieve being the patron saint of Paris who turned back Attila from the gates of the city.

All these names reflected the still-pioneer character of the Pacific Northwest. I had never heard their like in the parochial school in Minneapolis, where "foreign" extraction, in any case, was something to be ashamed of, the whole drive being toward Americanization of first name and surname alike. The exceptions to this were the Irish, who could vaunt such names as Catherine O'Dea and the name of my second cousin, Mary Catherine Anne Rose Violet McCarthy, while an unfortunate German boy named Manfred was made to suffer for his. But that was Minneapolis. In Seattle, and especially in the convent of the Ladies of the Sacred Heart, foreign names suggested not immigration but emigration—distinguished exile. Minneapolis was a granary; Seattle was a port, which had attracted a veritable Foreign Legion of adventurers—soldiers of fortune, younger sons, gamblers, traders, drawn by the fortunes to be made in virgin timber and shipping and by the Alaska Gold Rush. Wars and revolutions had sent the defeated out to Puget Sound, to start a new life; the latest had been the Russian Revolution, which had shipped us, via Harbin, a Russian colony, complete with restaurant, on Queen Anne Hill. The English names in the convent, when they did not testify to direct English origin, as in the case of "Rafe" Chatham, had come to us from the South and represented a kind of internal exile; such girls as Mary Fordyce Blake and Mary McQueen Street (a class ahead of me; her sister was named Francesca) bore their double-barreled first names like titles of aristocracy from the ante-bellum South. Not all our girls, by any means, were Catholic; some of the very prettiest ones—Julia Dodge and Janet Preston, if I remember rightly—were Protestants. The nuns had taught us to behave with special courtesy to these strangers in our midst, and the whole effect was of some superior hostel for refugees of all the lost causes of the past hundred years. Money could not count for much in such an atmosphere; the fathers and grandfathers of many of our "best" girls were ruined men.

Names, often, were freakish in the Pacific Northwest, particularly girls' names. In the Episcopal boarding school I went to later, in Tacoma, there was a girl called De Vere Utter, and there was a girl called Rocena and another called Hermonie. Was Rocena a mistake for Rowena and Hermonie for Hermione? And was Vere, as we called her, Lady Clara Vere de Vere? Probably. You do not hear names like those often, in any case, east of the Cascade Mountains; they belong to the frontier, where books and libraries were few and memory seems to have been oral, as in the time of Homer.

Names have more significance for Catholics than they do for other people; Christian names are chosen for the spiritual qualities of the saints they are taken from; Protestants used to name their children out of the Old Testament and now they name them out of novels and plays, whose heroes and heroines are perhaps the new patron saints of a secular age. But with Catholics it is different. The saint a child is named for is supposed to serve, literally, as a model or pattern to imitate; your name is your fortune and it tells you what you are or must be. Catholic children ponder their names for a mystic meaning, like birthstones; my own, I learned, besides belonging to the Virgin and Saint Mary of Egypt, originally meant "bitter" or "star of the sea." My second name, Thérèse, could dedicate me either to Saint Theresa or to the saint called the Little Flower, Soeur Thérèse of Lisieux, on whom God was supposed to have descended in the form of a shower of roses. At Confirmation, I had added a third name (for Catholics then rename themselves, as most nuns do, yet another time, when they take orders); on the advice of a nun, I had taken "Clementina," after Saint Clement, an early pope—a step I soon regretted on account of "My Darling Clementine" and her number nine shoes. By the time I was in the convent, I would no longer tell anyone what my Confirmation name was. The name I had nearly picked was "Agnes," after a little Roman virgin martyr, always shown with a lamb, because of her purity. But Agnes would have been just as bad, I recognized in Forest Ridge Convent—not only because of the possibility of "Aggie," but because it was subtly, indefinably *wrong* in itself. Agnes would have made me look like an ass.

The fear of appearing ridiculous first entered my life, as a governing motive, during my second year in the convent. Up to then, a desire for prominence had decided many of my actions and, in fact, still persisted. But in the eighth grade, I became aware of mockery and perceived that I could not seek prominence without attracting laughter. Other people could, but I couldn't. This laughter was proceeding, not from my classmates, but from the girls of the class just above me, in particular from two boon companions. Elinor Heffernan and Mary Harty, a clownish pair—oddly assorted in size and shape, as teams of clowns generally are, one short, plump, and baby-faced, the other tall, lean, and owlish—who entertained the high-school department by calling attention to the oddities of the younger girls. Nearly every school has such a pair of satirists, whose marks are generally low and who are tolerated just because of their laziness and non-conformity; one of them (in this case, Mary Harty, the plump one) usually appears to be half asleep. Because of their low standing, their indifference to appearances, the sad state of their uniforms, their clowning is taken to be harmless, which, on the whole, it is, their object being not to wound but to divert; such girls are bored in school. We in the eighth grade sat directly in front of the two wits in study hall, so that they had us under close observation; yet at first I was not afraid of them, wanting, if anything, to identify myself with their laughter, to be initiated into the joke. One of their specialties was giving people nicknames, and it was considered an honor to be the first in the eighth grade to be let in by Elinor and Mary on their latest invention. This often happened to me; they would tell me, on the playground, and I would tell the others. As their intermediary, I felt myself almost their friend and it did not occur to me that I might be next on their list.

I had achieved prominence not long before by publicly losing my faith and regaining it at the end of a retreat. I believe Elinor and Mary questioned me about this on the playground, during recess, and listened with serious, respectful faces while I told them about my conversations with the Jesuits. Those serious faces ought to have been an omen, but if the two girls used what I had revealed to make fun of me, it must have been behind my back. I never heard any more of it, and yet just at this time I began to feel something, like a cold breath on the nape of my neck, that made me wonder whether the new position I had won for myself in the convent was as secure as I imagined. I would turn around in study hall and find the two girls looking at me with speculation in their eyes.

It was just at this time, too, that I found myself in a perfectly absurd situation, a very private one, which made me live, from month to month, in horror of discovery. I had waked up one morning, in my convent room, to find a few small spots of blood on my sheet; I had somehow scratched a trifling cut on one of my legs and opened it during the night. I wondered what to do about this, for the nuns were fussy about bedmaking, as they were about our white collars and cuffs, and if we had an inspection those spots might count against me. It was best, I decided, to ask the nun on dormitory duty, tall, stout Mother Slattery, for a clean bottom sheet, even though she might scold me for having scratched my leg in my sleep and order me to cut my toenails. You never know what you might be blamed for. But Mother Slattery, when she bustled in to look at the sheet, did not scold me at all; indeed, she hardly seemed to be listening as I explained to her about the cut. She told me to sit down: she would be back in a minute. "You can be excused from athletics today," she added, closing the door. As I waited, I considered this remark, which seemed to me strangely munificent, in view of the unimportance of the cut. In a moment, she returned, but without the sheet. Instead, she produced out of her big pocket a sort of cloth girdle and a peculiar flannel object which I first took to be a bandage, and I began to protest that I did not need or want a bandage; all I needed was a bottom sheet. "The sheet can wait," said Mother Slattery, succinctly, handing me two large safety pins. It was the pins that abruptly enlightened me; I saw Mother Slattery's mistake, even as she was instructing me as to how this flannel article, which I now understood to be a sanitary napkin, was to be put on.

"Oh, no, Mother," I said, feeling somewhat embarrassed. "You don't understand. It's just a little cut, on my leg." But Mother, again, was not listening; she appeared to have grown deaf, as the nuns had a habit of doing when what you were saying did not fit in with their ideas. And now that I knew what was in her mind, I was conscious of a funny constraint; I did not feel it proper to name a natural process, in so many words, to a nun. It was like trying not to think of their going to the bathroom or trying not to see the straggling irongray hair coming out of their coifs (the common notion that they shaved their heads was false). On the whole, it seemed better just to show her my cut. But when I offered to do so and unfastened my black stocking, she only glanced at my leg, cursorily. "That's only a scratch, dear," she said. "Now hurry up and put this on or you'll be late for chapel. Have you any pain?" "No, no, Mother!" I cried. "You don't understand!" "Yes, yes, I understand," she replied soothingly, "and you will too, a little later. Mother Superior will tell you about it some time during the morning. There's nothing to be afraid of. You have become a woman."

"I know all about that," I persisted. "Mother, please listen. I just cut my leg. On the athletic field. Yesterday afternoon." But the more excited I grew, the more soothing, and yet firm, Mother Slattery became. There seemed to be nothing for it but to give up and do as I was bid. I was in the grip of a higher authority, which almost had the power to persuade me that it was right and I was wrong. But of course I was not wrong; that would have been too good to be true. While Mother Slattery waited, just outside my door, I miserably donned the equipment she had given me, for there was no place to hide it, on account of drawer inspection. She led me down the hall to where there was a chute and explained how I was to dispose of the flannel thing, by dropping it down the chute into the laundry. (The convent arrangements were very old-fashioned, dating back, no doubt, to the days of Louis Philippe.)

The Mother Superior, Madame MacIllvra, was a sensible woman, and all through my early morning classes, I was on pins and needles, chafing for the promised interview with her which I trusted would clear things up. *"Ma Mère,"* I would begin, "Mother Slattery thinks . . ." Then I would tell her about the cut and the athletic field. But precisely the same impasse confronted me when I was summoned to her office at recess-time. *I* talked about my cut, and *she* talked about becoming a woman. It was rather like a round, in which she was singing "Scotland's burning, Scotland's burning," and I was singing "Pour on water, pour on water." Neither of us could hear the other, or, rather, I could hear her, but she could not hear me. Owing to our different positions in the convent she was free to interrupt me, whereas I was expected to remain silent until she had finished speaking. When I kept breaking in, she hushed me, gently, and took me on her lap. Exactly like Mother Slattery, she attributed all my references to the cut to a blind fear of this new, unexpected reality that had supposedly entered my life. Many young girls, she reassured me, were frightened if they had not been prepared. "And you, Mary, have lost your dear mother, who could have made this easier for you." Rocked on Madame MacIllvra's lap, I felt paralysis overtake me and I lay, mutely listening, against her bosom, my face being tickled by her white, starched, fluted wimple, while she explained to me how babies were born, all of which I had heard before.

There was no use fighting the convent. I had to pretend to have become a woman, just as, not long before, I had had to pretend to get my faith back—for the sake of peace. This pretense was decidedly awkward. For fear of being found out by the lay sisters downstairs in the laundry (no doubt an imaginary contingency, but the convent was so very thorough), I reopened the cut on my leg, so as to draw a little blood to stain the napkins, which were issued me regularly, not only on this occasion, but every twenty-eight days thereafter. Eventually, I abandoned this bloodletting, for fear of lockjaw, and trusted to fate. Yet I was in awful dread of detection; my only hope, as I saw it, was either to be released from the convent or to become a woman in reality, which might take a year at least, since I was only twelve. Getting out of athletics once a month was not sufficient compensation for the farce I was going through. It was not my fault; they had forced me into it; nevertheless, it was I who would look silly—worse than silly; half mad—if the truth ever came to light.

I was burdened with this guilt and shame when the nickname finally found me out. "Found me out," in a general sense, for no one ever did learn the particular secret I bore about with me, pinned to the linen band. "We've got a name for you," Elinor and Mary called out to me, one day on the playground. "What is it?" I asked half hoping, half fearing, since not all their sobriquets were unfavorable. "Cye," they answered, looking at each other and laughing. "Si?" I repeated, supposing that it was based on Simple Simon. Did they regard me as a hick? "C.Y.E.," they elucidated, spelling it out in chorus. "The letters stand for something. Can you guess?" I could not and I cannot now. The closest I could come to it in the convent was "Clean Your Ears." Perhaps that was it, though in later life I have wondered whether it did not stand, simply, for "Clever Young Egg" or "Champion Young Eccentric." But in the convent I was certain that it stood for something horrible, something even worse than dirty ears (as far as I knew, my ears were clean), something I could never guess because it represented some aspect of myself that the world could see and I couldn't, like a sign pinned on my back. Everyone in the convent must have known what the letters stood for, but no one would tell me. Elinor and Mary had made them promise. It was like halitosis; not even my best friend, my deskmate, Louise, would tell me, no matter how much I pleaded. Yet everyone assured me that it was "very good," that is, very apt. And it made everyone laugh.

This name reduced all my pretensions and solidified my sense of *wrongness.* Just as I felt I was beginning to belong to the convent, it turned me into an outsider, since I was the only pupil who was not in the know. I liked the convent, but it did not like me, as people say of certain foods that disagree with them. By this, I do not mean that I was actively unpopular, either with the pupils or with the nuns. The Mother Superior cried when I left and predicted that I would be a novelist, which surprised me. And I had finally made friends; even Emilie von Phul smiled upon me softly out of her bright blue eyes from the far end of the study hall. It was just that I did not fit into the convent pattern; the simplest thing I did, like asking for a clean sheet, entrapped me in consequences that I never could have predicted. I was not bad; I did not consciously break the rules; and yet I could never, not even for a week, get a pink ribbon, and this was something I could not understand, because I was trying as hard as I could. It was the same case as with the hated name; the nuns, evidently, saw something about me that was invisible to me.

The oddest part was all that pretending. There I was, a walking mass of lies, pretending to be a Catholic and going to confession while really I had lost my faith, and pretending to have monthly periods by cutting myself with nail scissors; yet all this had come about without my volition and even contrary to it. But the basest pretense I was driven to was the acceptance of the nickname. Yet what else could I do? In the convent, I could not live it down. To all those girls, I had become "Cye McCarthy." That was who I was. That was how I had to identify myself when telephoning my friends during vacations to ask them to the movies: "Hello, this is Cye." I loathed myself when I said it, and yet I succumbed to the name totally, making myself over into a sort of hearty to go with it—the kind of girl I hated. "Cye" was my new patron saint. This false personality stuck to me, like the name, when I entered public high school, the next fall, as a freshman, having finally persuaded my grandparents to take me out of the convent, although they could never get to the bottom of my reasons, since, as I admitted, the nuns were kind, and I had made many nice new friends. What I wanted was a fresh start, a chance to begin life over again, but the first thing I heard in the corridors of the public high school was that name called out to me, like the warmest of welcomes: "Hi, there, Si!" That was the way they thought it was spelled. But this time I was resolute. After the first weeks, I dropped the hearties who called me "Si" and I never heard it again. I got my own name back and sloughed off Clementina and even Therese—the names that did not seem to me any more to be mine but to have been imposed on my by others. And I preferred to think that Mary meant "bitter" rather than "star of the sea."

## I. Suggestions for Discussion:

1. Why were names of great importance in the convent school?
2. Discuss the effectiveness of the many vivid illustrations and examples McCarthy uses throughout the essay. What other rhetorical devices does she employ?
3. Compare her use of illustrative narration in both this essay and "Settling the Colonel's Hash," p. 368.

## II. Suggestions for Writing:

1. Write an essay listing and discussing the unusual nicknames of some of your friends and acquaintances. How were the names acquired? Did they last or change or disappear in time? Were your friends happy with the nicknames?
2. Recall an embarrassing incident in your own school experience and write an essay recounting it and analyzing your reactions and responses.

# MARY McCARTHY

## Settling the Colonel's Hash

"Settling the Colonel's Hash" is an essay about how to write and how to read a short story. Mary McCarthy uses a chance encounter with an anti-Semitic colonel as a springboard for a discussion of the ways in which writers discover meaning in their fiction. The essay uses illustrative narrative and allusions to literary works to help make its point.

Seven years ago, when I taught in a progressive college, I had a pretty girl student in one of my classes who wanted to be a short-story writer. She was not studying writing with me, but she knew that I sometimes wrote short stories, and one day, breathless and glowing, she came up to me in the hall, to tell me that she had just written a story that her writing teacher, a Mr. Converse, was terribly excited about. "He thinks it's wonderful," she said, "and he's going to help me fix it up for publication."

I asked what the story was about; the girl was a rather simple being who loved clothes and dates. Her answer had a deprecating tone. It was just about a girl (herself) and some sailors she had met on the train. But then her face, which had looked perturbed for a moment, gladdened.

"Mr. Converse is going over it with me and we're going to put in the symbols."

Another girl in the same college, when asked by us in her sophomore orals why she read novels (one of the pseudo-profound questions that ought never to be put) answered in a defensive flurry: "Well, *of course* I don't read them to find out what happens to the hero."

At the time, I thought these notions were peculiar to progressive education: it was old-fashioned or regressive to read a novel to find out what happens to the hero or to have a mere experience empty of symbolic pointers. But I now discover that this attitude is quite general, and that readers and students all over the country are in a state of apprehension, lest they read a book or story literally and miss the presence of a symbol. And like everything

This was given first as a talk at the Breadloaf School of English, in Middlebury, Vermont. (McCarthy's note).

in America, this search for meanings has become a socially competitive enterprise; the best reader is the one who detects the most symbols in a given
stretch of prose. And the benighted reader who fails to find any symbols
humbly assents when they are pointed out to him; he accepts his mortification.

I had no idea how far this process had gone until last spring, when I
began to get responses to a story I had published in *Harper's*. I say "story"
because that was what it was called by *Harper's*. I myself would not know
quite what to call it; it was a piece of reporting or a fragment of autobiography—an account of my meeting with an anti-Semitic army colonel. It began
in the club car of a train going to St. Louis; I was wearing an apple-green
shirtwaist and a dark-green skirt and pink earrings; we got into an argument
about the Jews. The colonel was a rather dapper, flashy kind of Irish-American
with a worldly blue eye; he took me, he said, for a sculptress, which made me
feel, to my horror, that I looked Bohemian and therefore rather suspect. He
was full of the usual profound clichés that anti-Semites air, like original epi-
grams, about the Jews: that he could tell a Jew, that they were different from
other people, that you couldn't trust them in business, that some of his best
friends were Jews, that he distinguished between a Jew and a kike, and finally
that, of course, he didn't agree with Hitler: Hitler went too far, the Jews were
human beings.

All the time we talked, and I defended the Jews, he was trying to get
my angle, as he called it; he thought it was abnormal for anybody who wasn't
Jewish not to feel as he did. As a matter of fact, I have a Jewish grandmother,
but I decided to keep this news to myself: I did not want the colonel to think
that I had any interested reason for speaking on behalf of the Jews, that is,
that I was prejudiced. In the end, though, I got my comeuppance. Just as we
were parting, the colonel asked me my married name, which is Broadwater,
and the whole mystery was cleared up for him, instantly; he supposed I was
married to a Jew and that the name was spelled B-r-o-d-w-a-t-e-r. I did not try
to enlighten him; I let him think what he wanted; in a certain sense, he was
right; he had unearthed my Jewish grandmother or her equivalent. There
were a few details that I must mention to make the next part clear: in my car,
there were two nuns, whom I talked to as a distraction from the colonel and
the moral problems he raised. He and I finally had lunch together in the St.
Louis railroad station, where we continued the discussion. It was a very hot
day. I had a sandwich; he had roast-beef hash. We both had an old-fashioned.

The whole point of this "story" was that it really happened; it is written in the first person; I speak of myself in my own name, McCarthy; at the
end, I mention my husband's name, Broadwater. When I was thinking about

writing the story, I decided not to treat it fictionally; the chief interest, I felt, lay in the fact that it happened, in real life, last summer, to the writer herself, who was a good deal at fault in the incident. I wanted to embarrass myself and, if possible, the reader too.

Yet, strangely enough, many of my readers preferred to think of this account as fiction. I still meet people who ask me, confidentially, "That story of yours about the colonel—was it really true?" It seemed to them perfectly natural that I would write a fabrication, in which I figured under my own name, and sign it, though in my eyes this would be like perjuring yourself in court or forging checks. Shortly after the "story" was published, I got a kindly letter from a man in Mexico, in which he criticized the menu from an artistic point of view: he thought salads would be better for hot weather and it would be more in character for the narrator-heroine to have a Martini. I did not answer the letter, though I was moved to, because I had the sense that he would not understand the distinction between what *ought* to happen and what *did* happen.

Then in April I got another letter, from an English teacher in a small college in the Middle West, that reduced me to despair. I am going to cite it at length.

"My students in freshman English chose to analyze your story, 'Artists in Uniform,' from the March issue of *Harper's*. For a week I heard oral discussions on it and then the students wrote critical analyses. In so far as it is possible, I stayed out of their discussions, encouraging them to read the story closely with your intentions as a guide to their understanding. Although some of them insisted that the story has no other level than the realistic one, most of them decided it has symbolic overtones.

"The question is: how closely do you want the symbols labeled? They wrestled with the nuns, the author's two shades of green with pink accents, with the 'materialistic godlessness' of the colonel. . . . A surprising number wanted exact symbols; for example, they searched for the significance of the colonel's eating hash and the author eating a sandwich. . . . From my standpoint, the story was an entirely satisfactory springboard for understanding the various shades of prejudice, for seeing how much of the artist goes into his painting. If it is any satisfaction to you, our campus was alive with discussions about 'Artists in Uniform.' We liked the story and we thought it amazing that an author could succeed in making readers dislike the author— for a purpose, of course!"

I probably should have answered this letter, but I did not. The gulf seemed to me too wide. I could not applaud the backward students who insisted that the story has no other level than the realistic one without giving offense to the teacher, who was evidently a well-meaning person. But I shall try now to address a reply, not to this teacher and her unfortunate class, but to a whole school of misunderstanding. There were no symbols in this story; there was no deeper level. The nuns were in the story because they were on the train; the contrasting greens were the dress I happened to be wearing; the colonel had hash because he had hash; materialistic godlessness meant just what it means when a priest thunders it from the pulpit—the phrase, for the first time, had meaning for me as I watched and listened to the colonel.

But to clarify the misunderstanding, one must go a little further and try to see what a literary symbol is. Now in one sense, the colonel's hash and my sandwich can be regarded as symbols; that is, they typify the colonel's food tastes and mine. (The man in Mexico had different food tastes which he wished to interpose into our reality.) The hash and the sandwich might even be said to show something very obvious about our characters and bringing-up, or about our sexes; I was a woman, he was a man. And though on another day I might have ordered hash myself, that day I did not, because the colonel and I, in our disagreement, were polarizing each other.

The hash and the sandwich, then, could be regarded as symbols of our disagreement, almost conscious symbols. And underneath our discussion of the Jews, there was a thin sexual current running, as there always is in such random encounters or pickups (for they have a strong suggestion of the illicit). The fact that I ordered something conventionally feminine and he ordered something conventionally masculine represented, no doubt, our awareness of a sexual possibility; even though I was not attracted to the colonel, nor he to me, the circumstances of our meeting made us define ourselves as a woman and a man.

The sandwich and the hash were our provisional, *ad hoc* symbols of ourselves. But in this sense all human actions are symbolic because they represent the person who does them. If the colonel had ordered a fruit salad with whipped cream, this too would have represented him in some way; given his other traits, it would have pointed to a complexity in his character that the hash did not suggest.

In the same way, the contrasting greens of my dress were a symbol of my taste in clothes and hence representative of me—all too representative, I suddenly saw, in the club car, when I got an "artistic" image of myself flashed back at me from the men's eyes. I had no wish to stylize myself as an artist, that is, to parade about as a symbol of flamboyant unconventionality, but apparently I had done so unwittingly when I picked those colors off a rack, under the impression that they suited me or "expressed my personality" as salesladies say.

My dress, then, was a symbol of the perplexity I found myself in with the colonel; I did not want to be categorized as a member of a peculiar minority—an artist or a Jew; but brute fate and the colonel kept resolutely cramming me into both those uncomfortable pigeonholes. I wished to be regarded as ordinary or rather as universal, to be anybody and therefore everybody (that is, in one sense, I wanted to be on the colonel's side, majestically above minorities), but every time the colonel looked at my dress and me in it with my pink earrings I shrank to minority status and felt the dress in the heat shriveling me, like the shirt of Nessus the centaur that consumed Hercules.

But this is not what the students meant when they wanted the symbols "labeled." They were searching for a more recondite significance than that afforded by the trite symbolism of ordinary life, in which a dress is a social badge. They supposed that I was engaging in literary or artificial symbolism, which would lead the reader out of the confines of reality into the vast fairy tale of myth, in which the color green would have an emblematic meaning (or did the two greens signify for them what the teacher calls "shades" of prejudice), and the colonel's hash, I imagine, would be some sort of Eucharistic mincemeat.

Apparently, the presence of the nuns assured them there were overtones of theology; it did not occur to them (a) that the nuns were there because pairs of nuns are a standardized feature of summer Pullman travel, like crying babies, and perspiring businessmen in the club car, and (b) that if I thought the nuns worth mentioning, it was also because of something very simple and directly relevant: the nuns and the colonel and I all had something in common—we had all at one time been Catholics—and I was seeking common ground with the colonel, from which to turn and attack his position.

In any account of reality, even a televised one, which comes closest to being a literal transcript or replay, some details are left out as irrelevant (though nothing is really irrelevant). The details that are not eliminated have to stand as symbols of the whole, like stenographic signs, and of course there is an art of selection, even in a newspaper account: the writer, if he has any ability, is looking for the revealing detail that will sum up the picture for the reader in a flash of recognition.

But the art of abridgment and condensation, which is familiar to anybody who tries to relate an anecdote, or give a direction—the art of natural symbolism, which is at the basis of speech and all representation—has at bottom a centripetal intention. It hovers over an object, an event, or series of events and tries to declare what it is. Analogy (that is, comparison to other objects) is inevitably one of its methods. "The weather was soupy," i.e., like soup. "He wedged his way in," i.e., he had to enter, thin edge first, as a wedge enters, and so on. All this is obvious. But these metaphorical aids to communication are a far cry from literary symbolism, as taught in the schools and practiced by certain fashionable writers. Literary symbolism is centrifugal and flees from the object, the event, into the incorporeal distance, where concepts are taken for substance and floating ideas and archetypes assume a hieratic authority.

In this dream-forest, symbols become arbitrary; all counters are interchangeable; anything can stand for anything else. The colonel's hash can be a Eucharist or a cannibal feast or the banquet of Atreus, or all three, so long as the actual dish set before the actual man is disparaged. What is depressing about this insistent symbolization is the fact that while it claims to lead to the infinite, it quickly reaches very finite limits—there are only so many myths on record, and once you have got through Bulfinch, the Scandinavian, and the Indian, there is not much left. And if all stories reduce themselves to myth and symbol, qualitative differences vanish, and there is only a single, monotonous story.

American fiction of the symbolist school demonstrates this mournful truth, without precisely intending to. A few years ago, when the mode was at its height, chic novels and stories fell into three classes: those which had a Greek myth for their framework, which the reader was supposed to detect, like finding the faces in the clouds in old newspaper puzzle contests; those which had symbolic modern figures, dwarfs, hermaphrodites, and cripples, illustrating maiming and loneliness; and those which contained symbolic animals, cougars, wild cats, and monkeys. One young novelist, a product of the Princeton school of symbolism, had all three elements going at once, like the ringmaster of a three-ring circus, with the freaks, the animals, and the statues.

The quest for symbolic referents had as its object, of course, the deepening of the writer's subject and the reader's awareness. But the result was paradoxical. At the very moment when American writing was penetrated by the symbolic urge, it ceased to be able to create symbols of its own. Babbitt,[1] I suppose, was the last important symbol to be created by an American writer; he gave his name to a type that henceforth would be recognizable to

---

[1] The principal character in Sinclair Lewis's novel, *Babbitt* (1922), is the classic burlesque of the average American businessman. McCarthy mentions other characters in well-known American and European literature.

everybody. He passed into the language. The same thing could be said, perhaps, though to a lesser degree, of Caldwell's Tobacco Road, Eliot's Prufrock, and possibly of Faulkner's Snopeses. The discovery of new symbols is not the only function of a writer, but the writer who cares about this must be fascinated by reality itself, as a butterfly collector is fascinated by the glimpse of a new specimen. Such a specimen was Mme. Bovary or M. Homais or M. de Charlus or Jupien; these specimens were precious to their discoverers, not because they repeated an age-old pattern but because their markings were new. Once the specimen has been described, the public instantly spots other examples of the kind, and the world seems suddenly full of Babbitts and Charlus, where none had been noted before.

A different matter was Joyce's Mr. Bloom.[2] Mr. Bloom can be called a symbol of eternal recurrence—the wandering Jew, Ulysses the voyager—but he is a symbol thickly incarnate, fleshed out in a Dublin advertising canvasser. He is not like Ulysses or vaguely suggestive of Ulysses; he is Ulysses, circa 1905. Joyce evidently believed in a cyclical theory of history, in which everything repeated itself; he also subscribed in youth to the doctrine that declares that the Host, a piece of bread, is also God's body and blood. How it can be both things at the same time, transubstantially, is a mystery, and Mr. Bloom is just such a mystery: Ulysses in the visible appearance of a Dublin advertising canvasser.

Mr. Bloom is not a symbol of Ulysses, but Ulysses-Bloom together, one and indivisible, symbolize or rather demonstrate eternal recurrence. I hope I make myself clear. The point is transubstantiation: Bloom and Ulysses are transfused into each other and neither reality is diminished. Both realities are locked together, like the protons and neutrons of an atom. *Finnegans Wake* is a still more ambitious attempt to create a fusion, this time a myriad fusion, and to exemplify the mystery of how a thing can be itself and at the same time be something else. The world is many and it is also one.

But the clarity and tension of Joyce's thought brought him closer in a way to the strictness of allegory than to the diffuse practices of latter-day symbolists. In Joyce, the equivalences and analogies are very sharp and distinct, as in a pun, and the real world is almost querulously audible, like the voices of the washerwomen on the Liffey that come into Earwicker's dream. But this is not true of Joyce's imitators or of the imitators of his imitators, for whom reality is only a shadowy pretext for the introduction of a whole *corps de ballet* of dancing symbols in mythic draperies and animal skins.

---

[2] The leading character in *Ulysses* by James Joyce, the Irish novelist (1882–1941), who also wrote *Finnegans Wake*.

Let me make a distinction. There are some great writers, like Joyce or Melville, who have consciously introduced symbolic elements into their work; and there are great writers who have written fables or allegories. In both cases, the writer makes it quite clear to the reader how he is to be read; only an idiot would take *Pilgrim's Progress* for a realistic story, and even a young boy, reading *Moby Dick,* realizes that there is something more than whale-fishing here, though be may not be able to name what it is. But the great body of fiction contains only what I have called natural symbolism, in which selected events represent or typify a problem, a kind of society or psychology, a philosophical theory, in the same way that they do in real life. What happens to the hero becomes of the highest importance. This symbolism needs no abstruse interpretation, and abstruse interpretation will only lead the reader away from the reality that the writer is trying to press on his attention.

I shall give an example or two of what I mean by natural symbolism and I shall begin with a rather florid one: Henry James' *The Golden Bowl.*[3] This is the story of a rich American girl who collects European objects. One of these objects is a husband, Prince Amerigo, who proves to be unfaithful. Early in the story, there is a visit to an antique shop in which the Prince picks out a gold bowl for his fiancée and finds, to his annoyance, that it is cracked. It is not hard to see that the cracked bowl is a symbol, both of the Prince himself, who is a valuable antique but a little flawed, morally, and also of the marriage, which represents an act of acquisition or purchase on the part of the heroine and her father. If the reader should fail to notice the analogy, James calls his attention to it in the title.

I myself would not regard this symbol as necessary to this particular history; it seems to me, rather, an ornament of the kind that was fashionable in the architecture and interior decoration of the period, like stylized sheaves of corn or palms on the facade of a house. Nevertheless, it is handsome and has an obvious appropriateness to the theme. It introduces the reader into the Gilded Age attitudes of the novel. I think there is also a scriptural echo in the title that conveys the idea of punishment. But having seen and felt the weight of meaning that James put into this symbol, one must not be tempted to press further and look at the bowl as a female sex symbol, a chalice, a Holy Grail, and so on; a book is not a pious excuse for reciting a litany of associations.

My second example is from Tolstoy's *Anna Karenina.*[4] Toward the be-

---

[3] Henry James (1843–1916), the American novelist, published *The Golden Bowl* in 1904.
[4] Count Leo Tolstoy (1824–1910), the Russian novelist, published *Anna Karenina* (1875–1876) and *War and Peace* (1865–1872).

ginning of the novel, Anna meets the man who will be her lover, Vronsky, on the Moscow-St. Petersburg express; as they meet, there has been an accident; a workman has been killed by the train. This is the beginning of Anna's doom, which is completed when she throws herself under a train and is killed; and the last we see of Vronsky is in a train, with a toothache; he is off to the wars. The train is necessary to the plot of the novel, and I believe it is also symbolic, both of the iron forces of material progress that Tolstoy hated so and that played a part in Anna's moral destruction, and also of those iron laws of necessity and consequence that govern human action when it remains on the sensual level.

One can read the whole novel, however, without being conscious that the train is a symbol; we do not have to "interpret" to feel the import of doom and loneliness in the train's whistle—the same import we ourselves can feel when we hear a train whistle blow in the country, even today. Tolstoy was a deeper artist than James, and we cannot be sure that the train was a conscious device with him. The appropriateness to Anna's history may have been only a *felt* appropriateness; everything in Tolstoy has such a supreme naturalness that one shrinks from attributing contrivance to him, as if it were a sort of fraud. Yet he worked very hard on his novels—I forget how many times Countess Tolstoy copied out *War and Peace* by hand.

The impression one gets from his diaries is that he wrote by ear; he speaks repeatedly, even as an old man, of having to start a story over again because he has the wrong tone, and I suspect that he did not think of the train as a symbol but that it sounded "right" to him, because it was, in that day, an almost fearsome emblem of ruthless and impersonal force, not only to a writer of genius but to the poorest peasant in the fields. And in Tolstoy's case I think it would be impossible, even for the most fanciful critic, to extricate the train from the novel and try to make it say something that the novel itself does not say directly. Every detail in Tolstoy has an almost cruel and viselike meaningfulness and truth to itself that make it tautological to talk of symbolism; he was a moralist and to him the tiniest action, even the curiosities of physical appearance, Vronsky's bald spot, the small white hands of Prince Andrei, told a moral tale.

It is now considered very old-fashioned and tasteless to speak of an author's "philosophy of life" as something that can be harvested from his work. Actually, most of the great authors did have a "philosophy of life" which they were eager to communicate to the public; this was one of their motives for writing. And to disentangle a moral philosophy from a work that evidently contains one is far less damaging to the author's purpose and the integrity of his art than to violate his imagery by symbol-hunting, as though reading a novel were a sort of paper-chase.

The images of a novel or a story belong, as it were, to a family, very closely knit and inseparable from each other; the parent "idea" of a story or a novel generates events and images all bearing a strong family resemblance. And to understand a story or a novel, you must look for the parent "idea," which is usually in plain view, if you read quite carefully and literally what the author says.

I will go back, for a moment, to my own story, to show how this can be done. Clearly, it is about the Jewish question, for that is what the people are talking about. It also seems to be about artists, since the title is "Artists in Uniform." Then there must be some relation between artists and Jews. What is it? They are both minorities that other people claim to be able to recognize by their appearance. But artists and Jews do not care for this categorization; they want to be universal, that is, like everybody else. They do not want to wear their destiny as a badge, as the soldier wears his uniform. But this aim is really hopeless, for life has formed them as Jews or artists, in a way that immediately betrays them to the majority they are trying to melt into. In my conversation with the colonel, I was endeavoring to play a double game. I was trying to force him into a minority by treating anti-Semitism as an aberration, which, in fact, I believe it is. On his side, the colonel resisted this attempt and tried to show that anti-Semitism was normal, and he was normal, while I was the queer one. He declined to be categorized as anti-Semite; he regarded himself as an independent thinker, who by a happy chance thought the same as everybody else.

I imagined I had a card up my sleeve; I had guessed that the colonel was Irish (i.e., that he belonged to a minority) and presumed that he was a Catholic. I did not see how he could possibly guess that I, with my Irish name and Irish appearance, had a Jewish grandmother in the background. Therefore when I found I had not convinced him by reasoning, I played my last card; I told him that the Church, his Church, forbade anti-Semitism. I went even further; I implied that God forbade it, though I had no right to do this, since I did not believe in God, but was only using Him as a whip to crack over the colonel, to make him feel humble and inferior, a raw Irish Catholic lad under discipline. But the colonel, it turned out, did not believe in God, either, and I lost. And since, in a sense, I had been cheating all along in this game we were playing, I had to concede the colonel a sort of moral victory in the end; I let him think that my husband was Jewish and that that "explained" every-thing satisfactorily.

Now there are a number of morals or meanings in this little tale, start-ing with the simple one: don't talk to strangers on a train. The chief moral or meaning (what I learned, in other words from this experience) was that you cannot be a universal unless you accept the fact that you are a singular, that is, a Jew or an artist or what-have-you. What the colonel and I were discussing, and at the same time illustrating and enacting, was the definition of a human being. I was trying to be something better than a human being; I was trying to be the voice of pure reason; and pride went before a fall. The colonel, without trying, was being something worse than a human being, and somehow we found ourselves on the same plane—facing each other, like mutually repellent twins. Or, put in another way: it is dangerous to be drawn into discussions of the Jews with anti-Semites: you delude yourself that you are spreading light, but you are really sinking into muck; if you endeavor to be dispassionate, you are really claiming for yourself a privileged position, a little mountain top, from which you look down, impartially, on both the Jews and the colonel.

Anti-Semitism is a horrible disease from which nobody is immune, and it has a kind of evil fascination that makes an enlightened person draw near the source of infection, supposedly, in a scientific spirit, but really to sniff the vapors and dally with the possibility. The enlightened person who lunches with the colonel in order, as she tells herself, to improve him, is cheating herself, having her cake and eating it. This attempted cheat, on my part, was related to the question of the artist and the green dress; I wanted to be an artist but not to pay the price of looking like one, just as I was willing to have Jewish blood but not willing to show it, where it would cost me something—the loss of superiority in an argument.

These meanings are all there, quite patent, to anyone who consents to look *into* the story. There were *in* the experience itself, waiting to be found and considered. I did not perceive them all at the time the experience was happening; otherwise, it would not have taken place, in all probability—I should have given the colonel a wide berth. But when I went back over the experience, in order to write it, I came upon these meanings, protruding at me, as it were, from the details of the occasion. I put in the green dress and my mortification over it because they were part of the truth, just as it had occurred, but I did not see how they were related to the general question of anti-Semitism and my grandmother until they *showed* me their relation in the course of writing.

Every short story, at least for me, is a little act of discovery. A cluster of details presents itself to my scrutiny, like a mystery that I will understand in the course of writing or sometimes not fully until afterward, when, if I have been honest and listened to these details carefully, I will find that they are connected and that there is a coherent pattern. This pattern is *in* experience itself; you do not impose it from the outside and if you try to, you will find that the story is taking the wrong tack, dribbling away from you into artificiality or inconsequence. A story that you do not learn something from while you are writing it, that does not illuminate something for you, is dead, finished before you started it. The "idea" of a story is implicit in it, on the one hand; on the other hand, it is always ahead of the writer, like a form dimly discerned in the distance; he is working *toward* the "idea."

It can sometimes happen that you begin a story thinking that you know the "idea" of it and find, when you are finished, that you have said something quite different and utterly unexpected to you. Most writers have been haunted all their lives by the "idea" of a story or a novel that they think they want to write and see very clearly: Tolstoy always wanted to write a novel about the Decembrists and instead, almost against his will, wrote *War and Peace;* Henry James thought he wanted to write a novel about Napoleon. Probably these ideas for novels were too set in their creators' minds to inspire creative discovery.

In any work that is truly creative, I believe the writer cannot be omniscient in advance about the effects that he proposes to produce. The suspense in a novel is not only in the reader, but in the novelist himself, who is intensely curious too about what will happen to the hero. Jane Austen may know in a general way that Emma will marry Mr. Knightley in the end (the reader knows this too, as a matter of fact); the suspense for the author lies in the how, in the twists and turns of circumstance, waiting but as yet unknown, that will bring the consummation about. Hence, I would say to the student of writing that outlines, patterns, arrangements of symbols may have a certain usefulness at the outset for some kinds of minds, but in the end they will have to be scrapped. If the story does not contradict the outline, overrun the pattern, break the symbols, like an insurrection against authority, it is surely a still birth. The natural symbolism of reality has more messages to communicate than the dry Morse code of the disengaged mind.

The tree of life, said Hegel, is greener than the tree of thought; I have quoted this before but I cannot forbear from citing it again in this context. This is not an incitement to mindlessness or an endorsement of realism in the short story (there are several kinds of reality, including interior reality); it means only that the writer must be, first of all, a listener and observer, who can pay attention to reality, like an obedient pupil, and who is willing, always, to be surprised by the messages reality is sending through to him. And if he gets the messages correctly he will not have to go back and put in the symbols; he will find that the symbols are there, staring at him significantly from the commonplace.

I. **Suggestions for Discussion**:
   1. Explain McCarthy's title. Is the essay really about her encounter with an anti-Semitic colonel? If not, what is her principal topic?
   2. How does she contrast natural symbolism and literary symbolism?
   3. What advice does she offer to writers of fiction.
   4. Compare her discussion of her short story with Eudora Welty's discussion in "The Point of the Story," p. 573.

II. **Suggestions for Writing**:
   1. McCarthy's essay was first presented as a speech at the Breadloaf School of English in Middlebury, Vermont. Prepare and deliver a speech about an incident of prejudice you have encountered. Tell how you handled the situation.
   2. Write a critical analysis of a short story, keeping in mind McCarthy's admonition against symbol hunting.

---

## CARSON McCULLERS

### Loneliness . . . An American Malady

from *The Mortgaged Heart*

---

Carson McCullers (1917–1967), the American novelist and short-story writer, used the South as a setting for her peculiarly intense stories and novels. Her published works include *The Heart Is a Lonely Hunter* (1940), *Reflections in a Golden Eye* (1941), *The Member of the Wedding* (1946), *The Ballad of the Sad Cafe* (1951), and *Clock Without Hands* (1961).

In this brief essay, she explores ways in which Americans seek to overcome loneliness. She emphasizes the individual's need to belong to something larger and more powerful than the weak, lonely self.

---

This city, New York—consider the people in it, the eight million of us. An English friend of mine, when asked why he lived in New York City, said that he liked it here because he could be so alone. While it was my friend's desire to be alone, the aloneness of many Americans who live in cities is an involuntary and fearful thing. It has been said that loneliness is the great American malady. What is the nature of this loneliness? It would seem essentially to be a quest for identity.

To the spectator, the amateur philosopher, no motive among the complex ricochets of our desires and rejections seems stronger or more enduring than the will of the individual to claim his identity and belong. From infancy to death, the human being is obsessed by these dual motives. During our first weeks of life, the question of identity shares urgency with the need for milk. The baby reaches for his toes, then explores the bars of his crib; again and again he compares the difference between his own body and the objects around him, and in the wavering, infant eyes there comes a pristine wonder.

Consciousness of self is the first abstract problem that the human being solves. Indeed, it is this self-consciousness that removes us from lower animals. This primitive grasp of identity develops with constantly shifting emphasis through all our years. Perhaps maturity is simply the history of those mutations that reveal to the individual the relation between himself and the world in which he finds himself.

After the first establishment of identity there comes the imperative need to lose this new-found sense of separateness and to belong to something larger and more powerful than the weak, lonely self. The sense of moral isolation is intolerable to us.

In *The Member of the Wedding* the lovely 12-year-old girl, Frankie Addams, articulates this universal need: "The trouble with me is that for a long time I have just been an *I* person. All people belong to a *We* except me. Not to belong to a *We* makes you too lonesome."

Love is the bridge that leads from the *I* sense to the *We,* and there is a paradox about personal love. Love of another individual opens a new relation between the personality and the world. The lover responds in a new way to nature and may even write poetry. Love is affirmation; it motivates the *yes* responses and the sense of wider communication. Love casts out fear, and in the security of this togetherness we find contentment, courage. We no longer fear the age-old haunting questions: "Who am I?" "Why am I?" "Where am I going?"—and having cast out fear, we can be honest and charitable.

For fear is a primary source of evil. And when the question "Who am I?" recurs and is unanswered, then fear and frustration project a negative attitude. The bewildered soul can answer only: "Since I do not understand 'Who I am,' I only know what I am *not*." The corollary of this emotional incertitude is snobbism, intolerance and racial hate. The xenophobic individual can only reject and destroy, as the xenophobic nation inevitably makes war.

The loneliness of Americans does not have its source in xenophobia; as a nation we are an outgoing people, reaching always for immediate contacts, further experience. But we tend to seek out things as individuals, alone. The European, secure in his family ties and rigid class loyalties, knows little of the moral loneliness that is native to us Americans. While the European artists tend to form groups or aesthetic schools, the American artist is the eternal maverick—not only from society in the way of all creative minds, but within the orbit of his own art.

Thoreau took to the woods to seek the ultimate meaning of his life. His creed was simplicity and his *modus vivendi* the deliberate stripping of external life to the Spartan necessities in order that his inward life could freely flourish. His objective, as he put it, was to back the world into a corner. And in that way did he discover "What a man thinks of himself, that is is which determines, or rather indicates, his fate."

On the other hand, Thomas Wolfe turned to the city, and in his wanderings around New York he continued his frenetic and lifelong search for the lost brother, the magic door. He too backed the world into a corner, and as he passed among the city's millions, returning their stares, he experienced "That silent meeting [that] is the summary of all the meetings of men's lives."

Whether in the pastoral joys of country life or in the labyrinthine city, we Americans are always seeking. We wander, question. But the answer waits in each separate heart—the answer of our own identity and the way by which we can master loneliness and feel that at last we belong.

I.  **Suggestions for Discussion:**
   1. Explain McCullers's distinction between the *I* and the *We.*
   2. What contrasts does she make between Americans and Europeans? Do you think they are valid? Explain.
   3. Read Thoreau, p. 530, and discuss whether or not you think McCullers has presented his views accurately and sympathetically.

II. **Suggestions for Writing:**
   1. Write an essay explaining and amplifying her notion that fear is a primary source of evil.
   2. Write an essay arguing that country life is or is not more conducive to the development of a sense of self than city life.

# PHYLLIS McGINLEY

## Are Children People?

Phillis McGinley (1905–1978), an American poet, essayist, and author of children's books, was awarded the Pulitzer Prize for her poetry in 1961. Her published work includes *Sixpence in Her Shoes* (1960), from which the following selection is taken.

In this charming essay, she uses anecdotes and illustrations from her personal experience and the rhetorical devices of comparison and contrast to explore the strange, wonderful world of children and their relationships with adults.

The problem of how to live with children isn't as new as you might think. Centuries before the advent of Dr. Spock or the PTA, philosophers debated the juvenile question, not always with compassion. There's a quotation from one of the antique sages floating around in what passes for my mind which, for pure cynicism, could set a Montaigne or a Mort Sahl back on his heels.

"Why," asks a disciple, "are we so devoted to our grandchildren?"

And the graybeard answers, "Because it is easy to love the enemies of one's enemies."

Philosopher he may have been but I doubt his parental certification. Any parent with a spark of natural feeling knows that children aren't our enemies. On the other hand, if we're sensible we are aware that they aren't really our friends, either. How can they be, when they belong to a totally different race?

Children admittedly are human beings, equipped with such human paraphernalia as appetites, whims, intelligence, and even hearts, but any resemblance between them and people is purely coincidental. The two nations, child and grown-up, don't behave alike or think alike or even see with the same eyes.

Take that matter of seeing, for example. An adult looks in the mirror and notices what? A familiar face, a figure currently overweight, maybe, but well-known and resignedly accepted; two arms, two legs, an entity. A child can stare into the looking glass for minutes at a time and see only the bone buttons on a snowsuit or a pair of red shoes.

Shoes, in fact, are the first personal belongings a child really looks at in an objective sense. There they are to adore—visible, shiny, round-toed ornamental extensions of himself. He can observe them in that mirror or he can look down from his small height to admire them. They are real to him, unlike his eyes or his elbows. That is why, for a child, getting a pair of new shoes is like having a birthday. When my daughters were little they invariably took just-acquired slippers to bed with them for a few nights, the way they'd take a cuddle toy or smuggle in a puppy.

Do people sleep with their shoes? Of course not. Nor do they lift them up reverently to be fondled, a gesture children offer even to perfect strangers in department stores. I used to think that a child's life was lived from new shoe to new shoe, as an adult lives for love or payday or a vacation.

Children, though, aren't consistent about their fetish. By the time they have learned to tie their own laces, they have lapsed into an opposite phase. They start to discard shoes entirely. Boys, being natural reactionaries, cling longer than girls to their first loves, but girls begin the discalced stage at twelve or thirteen—and it goes on interminably. Their closets may bulge with footwear, with everything from dubious sneakers to wisps of silver kid, while most of the time the girls themselves go unshod. I am in error, too, when I speak of shoes as reposing in closets. They don't. They lie abandoned under sofas, upside down beside the television set, rain-drenched on verandas. Guests in formal drawing rooms are confronted by them and climbers on stairways imperiled. When the phase ends, I can't tell you, but I think only with premature senescence.

My younger daughter, then a withered crone of almost twenty, once held the odd distinction of being the only girl on record to get her foot stabbed by a rusty nail at a Yale prom. She was, of course, doing the Twist barefoot, but even so the accident seems unlikely. You can't convince me it could happen to an adult.

No, children don't look at things in the same light as people. Nor do they hear with our ears, either. Ask a child a question and he has an invariable answer: "What?" (Though now and then he alters it to "Why?")

Or send one on a household errand and you will know that he—or she— is incapable of taking in a simple adult remark. I once asked an otherwise normal little girl to bring me the scissors from the kitchen drawer, and she returned, after a mysterious absence of fifteen minutes, lugging the extension hose out of the garage. Yet the young can hear brownies baking in the oven two blocks away from home or the faintest whisper of parents attempting to tell each other secrets behind closed doors.

They can also understand the language of babies, the most esoteric on earth. Our younger child babbled steadily from the age of nine months on, although not for a long while in an intelligible tongue. Yet her sister, two years older, could translate for us every time.

"That lady's bracelet—Patsy wishes she could have it," the interpreter would tell me; and I had the wit hastily to lift my visitor's arm out of danger.

Or I would be instructed, "She'd like to pat the kitten now."

We used occasionally to regret their sibling fluency of communication. Once we entertained at Sunday dinner a portrait painter known rather widely for his frequent and publicized love affairs. He quite looked the part, too, being so tall and lean and rakish, with such a predatory moustache and so formidable a smile, that my husband suggested it was a case of art imitating nature.

The two small girls had never met him, and when the baby saw him for the first time she turned tail and fled upstairs.

The older, a gracious four, came back into the living room after a short consultation, to apologize for her sister's behavior. "You see," she told him winningly, "Patsy thinks you're a wolf."

It was impossible to explain that they had somehow confused the moustache and the smile with a description of Little Red Riding Hood's arch foe and were not referring to his private life. We let it pass. I often thought, however, that it was a pity the older girl's pentecostal gifts did not outlast kindergarten. She would have been a great help to the United Nations.

Young mothers have to study such talents and revise their methods of child rearing accordingly. To attempt to treat the young like grown-ups is always a mistake.

Do people, at least those outside of institutions, drop lighted matches into wastebaskets just to see what will happen? Do they tramp through puddles on purpose? Or prefer hot dogs or jelly-and-mashed-banana sandwiches to lobster Thermidor? Or, far from gagging on the abysmal inanities of *Raggedy Ann*, beg to have it read to them every evening for three months?

Indeed, the reading habits alone of the younger generation mark them off from their betters. What does an adult do when he feels like having a go at a detective story or the evening paper?' Why, he picks out a convenient chair or props himself up on his pillows, arranges the light correctly for good vision, turns down the radio, and reaches for a cigarette or a piece of chocolate fudge.

Children, however, when the literary urge seizes them, take their comic books to the darkest corner of the room or else put their heads under the bedcovers. Nor do they sit *down* to read. They wander. They lie on the floor with their legs draped over the coffee table, or, alternatively, they sit on the coffee table and put the book on the floor. Or else they lean against the refrigerator, usually with the refrigerator door wide open. Sometimes I have seen them retire to closets.

Children in comfortable positions are uncomfortable—just as they are miserable if they can't also have the phonograph, the radio, the television and sometimes the telephone awake and lively while they pore on *The Monster of Kalliwan* or *The Jungle Book.*

But then, children don't walk like people, either, sensibly, staidly, in a definite direction. I am not sure they ever acquire our grown-up gaits. They canter, they bounce, they slither, slide, crawl, leap into the air, saunter, stand on their heads, swing from branch to branch, limp like cripples, or trot like ostriches. But I seldom recall seeing a child just plain walk. They can, however, dawdle. The longest period of recorded time is that interval between telling children to undress for bed and the ultimate moment when they have brushed their teeth, said their prayers, eaten a piece of bread and catsup, brushed their teeth all over again, asked four times for another glass of milk, checked the safety of their water pistols or their tropical fish, remembered there was something vital they had to confide to you, which they have forgotten by the time you reach their side, switched from a panda to a giraffe and back to the panda for the night's sleeping companion, begged to have the light left on in the hall, and finally, being satisfied that your screaming voice is in working order, fallen angelically into slumber.

Apprentice parents are warned to disregard at least nine-tenths of all such requests as pure subterfuge but to remember that maybe one of the ten is right and reasonable, like the night-light or the value of a panda when one is in a panda mood.

Not that reason weighs much with children. It is the great mistake we make with a child, to think progeny operate by our logic. The reasoning of children, although it is often subtle, differs from an adult's. At base there is usually a core of sanity, but one must disentangle what the lispers mean from what they say.

"I believe in Santa Claus," a daughter told me years ago, when she was five or six. "And I believe in the Easter Rabbit, too. But I just can't believe in Shirley Temple."

Until I worked out a solution for this enigmatic statement, I feared for the girl's mind. Then I realized that she had been watching the twenty-one-inch screen. After all, if you are six years old and see a grown-up Shirley Temple acting as mistress of ceremonies for a TV special one evening and the next day observe her, dimpled and brief-skirted, in an old movie, you are apt to find the transformation hard to credit.

I managed to unravel that utterance, but I never did pierce through to the heart of a gnomic pronouncement made by a young friend of hers. He meandered into the backyard one summer day when the whole family was preparing for a funeral. Our garden is thickly clustered with memorials to defunct wildlife, and on this particular afternoon we were intent on burying another robin.

John looked at the hole.

"What are you doing?" he asked, as if it weren't perfectly apparent to the most uninformed.

"Why, John," said my husband, "I'm digging a grave."

John considered the matter a while. Then he inquired again, with all the solemnity of David Susskind querying a senator, "Why don't you make it a double-decker?"

Not even Echo answered that one, but I kept my sense of proportion and went on with the ceremonies. You need a sense of proportion when dealing with children, as you also need a sense of humor. Yet you must never expect the very young to have a sense of humor of their own. Children are acutely risible, stirred to laughter by dozens of human mishaps, preferably fatal. They can understand the points of jokes, too, so long as the joke is not on them. Their egos are too new, they have not existed long enough in the world to have learned to laugh at themselves. What they love most in the way of humor are riddles, elementary puns, nonsense, and catastrophe. An elderly fat lady slipping on the ice in real life or a man in a movie falling from a fifteen-foot ladder equally transports them. They laugh at fistfights, clowns, people kissing each other, and buildings blowing up. They don't, however, enjoy seeing their parents in difficulties. Parents, they feel, were put on earth solely for their protection, and they cannot bear to have the fortress endangered.

Their peace of mind, their safety, rests on grown-up authority; and it is that childish reliance which invalidates the worth of reasoning too much with them. The longer I lived in a house with children, the less importance I put on cooperatively threshing out matters of conduct or explaining to them our theories of discipline. If I had it to do over again I wouldn't reason with them at all until they arrived at an *age* of reason—approximately twenty-one. I would give them rules to follow. I would try to be just, and I would try even harder to be strict. I would do no arguing. Children, in their hearts, like laws.

Authority implies an ordered world, which is what they—and, in the long run, most of the human race—yearn to inhabit. In law there is freedom. Be too permissive and they feel lost and alone. Children are forced to live very rapidly in order to live at all. They are given only a few years in which to learn hundreds of thousands of things about life and the planet and themselves. They haven't time to spend analyzing the logic behind every command or taboo, and they resent being pulled away by it from their proper business of discovery.

When our younger and more conversational daughter turned twelve, we found she was monopolizing the family telephone. She would reach home after school at 3:14 and at 3:15 the instrument would begin to shrill, its peal endless till bedtime. For once we had the good sense neither to scold nor to expostulate. We merely told her she could make and receive calls only between five and six o'clock in the afternoon. For the rest of the day, the telephone was ours. We expected tears. We were braced for hysterics. What we got was a calm acceptance of a Rule. Indeed, we found out later, she boasted about the prohibition—it made her feel both sheltered and popular.

But, then, children are seldom resentful, which is another difference between them and people. They hold grudges no better than a lapdog. They are too inexperienced to expect favors from the world. What happens to them happens to them, like an illness; and if it is not too extravagantly unfair, they forget about it. Parents learn that a child's angry glare or floods of tears after a punishment or a scolding may send the grown-up away feeling like a despotic brute; but that half an hour later, with adult feelings still in tatters, the child is likely as not to come flying into the room, fling both carefree arms about the beastly grown-up's neck, and shout, "I love you," into her ear.

The ability to forget a sorrow is childhood's most enchanting feature. It can also be exasperating to the pitch of frenzy. Little girls return from school with their hearts broken in two by a friend's treachery or a teacher's injustice. They sob through the afternoon, refuse dinner, and go to sleep on tear-soaked pillows. Novice mothers do not sleep at all, only lie awake with the shared burden for a nightlong companion. Experienced ones know better. They realize that if you come down in the morning to renew your solacing, you will meet—what? Refreshed, whole-hearted offspring who can't under*stand* what you're talking about. Beware of making childhood's griefs your own. They are no more lasting than soap bubbles.

I find myself hoaxed to this day by the recuperative powers of the young, even when they top me by an inch and know all about modern art.

More than once I have been called long distance from a college in New England to hear news of impending disaster.

"It's exam time and I'm down with this horrible cold," croaks the sufferer, coughing dramatically. "Can you rush me that prescription of Dr. Murphy's? I don't trust our infirmary."

Envisioning flu, pneumonia, wasting fever, and a lily maid dead before her time, I harry the doctor into scribbling his famous remedy and send it by wire. Then after worrying myself into dyspepsia, I call two days later to find out the worst. An unfogged voice answers me blithely.

"What cold?" it inquires.

Ephemeral tragedies, crises that evaporate overnight are almost certain to coincide with adolescence. Gird yourselves for them. Adolescence is a disease more virulent than measles and difficult to outgrow as an allergy. At its onset parents are bewildered like the victim. They can only stand by with patience, flexibility, and plenty of food in the larder. It's amazing how consoling is a batch of cookies in an emergency. If it doesn't comfort the child, at least it helps the baker. I stopped in at a neighbor's house the other day and found her busily putting the frosting on a coconut cake.

"It's for Steven," she told me. "His pet skunk just died, and I didn't know what else to do for him."

Food helps more than understanding. Adolescence doesn't really want to be understood. It prefers to live privately in some stone tower of its own building, lonely and unassailable. To understand is to violate. This is the age—at least for girls—of hidden diaries, locked drawers, unshared secrets. It's a trying time for all concerned. The only solace is that they do outgrow it. But the flaw there is that eventually they outgrow being children too, becoming expatriates of their own tribe.

For, impossible as it seems when one first contemplates diapers and croup, then tantrums, homework, scouting, dancing class, and finally the terrible dilemmas of the teens, childhood does come inexorably to an end. Children turn into people. They speak rationally if aloofly, lecture you on manners, condescend to teach you about eclectic criticism, and incline to get married. And there you are, left with all that learning you have so painfully accumulated in twenty-odd years and with no more progeny on whom to lavish it.

Small wonder we love our grandchildren. The old sage recognized the effect but not the cause. Enemies of our enemies indeed! They are our immortality. It is they who will inherit our wisdom, our experience, our ingenuity.

Except, of course, that the grandchildren's parents will listen benevolently (are they not courteous adults?) and not profit by a word we tell them. They must learn for themselves how to speak in another language and with an alien race.

I. **Suggestions for Discussion**:
1. Discuss the effectiveness of McGinley's opening anecdote.
2. What examples does she give to support her observation that the reasoning of children, although it is often subtle, differs from an adult's?
3. Discuss her statement that children, in their hearts, like laws. Does she offer a sufficiently convincing argument? To what extent do your own experiences and observations support or contradict her statement?

II. **Suggestions for Writing**:
1. Analyze the rules by which you lived as a child. Would you impose those same rules on your own children? Explain. What changes would you make?
2. Use several anecdotes about the behavior of children whom you know to make a generalization about their attitudes, interests, or beliefs.

---

## MARGARET MEAD

### From *Popping the Question to Popping the Pill*

---

Margaret Mead (1901–1978), the distinguished American cultural anthropologist, is the author of many books, including *Coming of Age in Samoa* (1928), *Growing Up in New Guinea* (1930), *Male and Female* (1949), and *Culture and Commitment* (1970). As in the essay that follows, she often addressed herself to problems and changes in American society.

In the very first sentence of her essay, Margaret Mead states her topic: the major changes in attitude toward courtship and marriage among middle-class Americans. Using analysis, comparison, and contrast, she examines past and contemporary attitudes and practices.

---

There have been major changes in attitudes toward courtship and marriage among those middle-class, educated Americans who are celebrated in the media and who are style setters for American life. Courtship was once a regular part of American life; it was a long period, sometimes lasting for many years, and also a tentative one, during which a future husband or wife could still turn back but during which their relationship became more and more exclusive and socially recognized. Courtship both preceded the announcement of an engagement and followed the announcement, although a broken engagement was so serious that it could be expected to throw the girl into a depression from which she might never recover.

There were definite rules governing the courtship period, from the "bundling" permitted in early New England days, when young couples slept side by side with all their clothes on, to strict etiquette that prescribed what sort of gifts a man might give his fiancée in circles where expensive presents were customary. Gifts had to be either immediately consumable, like candy or flowers, or indestructible, like diamonds—which could be given back, their value unimpaired, if there was a rift in the relationship. Objects that could be damaged by use, like gloves and furs, were forbidden. A gentleman might call for a lady in a cab or in his own equipage, but it was regarded as inappropriate for him to pay for her train fare if they went on a journey.

How much chaperoning was necessary, and how much privacy the courting couple was allowed, was a matter of varying local custom. Long walks home through country lanes after church and sitting up in the parlor after their elders had retired for the night may have been permitted, but the bride was expected to be a virgin at marriage. The procedure for breaking off an engagement, which included the return of letters and photographs, was a symbolic way of stating that an unconsummated relationship could still be erased from social memory.

The wedding day was the highest point in a girl's life—a day to which she looked forward all her unmarried days and to which she looked back for the rest of her life. The splendor of her wedding, the elegance of dress and veil, the cutting of the cake, the departure amid a shower of rice and confetti, gave her an accolade of which no subsequent event could completely rob her. Today people over 50 years of age still treat their daughter's wedding this way, prominently displaying the photographs of the occasion. Until very recently, all brides' books prescribed exactly the same ritual they had prescribed 50 years before. The etiquette governing wedding presents—gifts that were or were not appropriate, the bride's maiden initials on her linen—was also specified. For the bridegroom the wedding represented the end of his free, bachelor days, and the bachelor dinner the night before the wedding symbolized this loss of freedom. A woman who did not marry—even if she had the alibi of a fiancé who had been killed in war or had abilities and charm and money of her own—was always at a social disadvantage, while an eligible bachelor was sought after by hostess after hostess.

Courtship ended at the altar, as the bride waited anxiously for the bridegroom who might not appear or might have forgotten the ring. Suppliant gallantry was replaced overnight by a reversal of roles, the wife now becoming the one who read her husband's every frown with anxiety lest she displease him.

This set of rituals established a rhythm between the future husband and wife and between the two sets of parents who would later become co-grandparents. It was an opportunity for mistakes to be corrected; and if the parents could not be won over, there was, as a last resort, elopement, in which the young couple proclaimed their desperate attraction to each other by flouting parental blessing. Each part of the system could be tested out for a marriage that was expected to last for life. We have very different ways today.

Since World War I, changes in relationships between the sexes have been occurring with bewildering speed. The automobile presented a challenge to chaperonage that American adults met by default. From then on, except in ceremonial and symbolic ways, chaperonage disappeared, and a style of premarital relationship was set up in which the onus was put on the girl to refuse inappropriate requests, while each young man declared his suitability by asking for favors that he did not expect to receive. The disappearance of chaperonage was facilitated by the greater freedom of middle-aged women, who began to envy their daughters' freedom, which they had never had. Social forms went through a whole series of rapid changes: The dance with formal partners and programs gave way to occasions in which mothers, or daughters, invited many more young men than girls, and the popular girl hardly circled the dance floor twice in the same man's arms. Dating replaced courtship—not as a prelude to anything but rather as a way of demonstrating popularity. Long engagements became increasingly unfashionable, and a series of more tentative commitments became more popular. As college education became the norm for millions of young people, "pinning" became a common stage before engagement. The ring was likely to appear just before the wedding day. And during the 1950's more and more brides got married while pregnant—but they still wore the long white veil, which was a symbol of virginity.

In this conservative, security-minded decade love became less important than marriage, and lovers almost disappeared from parks and riverbanks as young people threatened each other: "Either you marry me now, or I'll marry someone else." Courtship and dating were embraced by young people in lower grades in school, until children totally unready for sex were enmeshed by the rituals of pairing off. Marriage became a necessity for every-one, for boys as well as for girls: Mothers worried if their sons preferred electronic equipment or chess to girls and pushed their daughters relentlessly into marriage. Divorce became more and more prevalent, and people who felt their marriages were failing began to worry about whether they ought to get a divorce, divorce becoming a duty to an unfulfilled husband or to children exposed to an unhappy marriage. Remarriage was expected, until finally, with men dying earlier than women, there were no men left to marry. The United States became the most married country in the world. Children, your own or adopted, were just as essential, and the suburban life-style—each nuclear family isolated in its own home, with several children, a station wagon and a country-club membership—became the admired life-style, dis-played in magazines for the whole world to see.

By the early sixties there were signs of change. We discovered we were running out of educated labor, and under the heading of self-fulfillment educated married women were being tempted back into the labor market. Young people began to advocate frankness and honesty, rebelling against the extreme hypocrisy of the 1950s, when religious and educational institutions alike connived to produce pregnancies that would lead to marriage. Love as an absorbing feeling for another person was rediscovered as marriage as a goal for every girl and boy receded into the background.

A series of worldwide political and ecological events facilitated these changes. Freedom for women accompanied agitation for freedom for blacks, for other minorities, for the Third World, for youth, for gay people. Zero-population growth became a goal, and it was no longer unfashionable to admit one did not plan to have children, or perhaps even to marry. The marriage age rose a little, the number of children fell a little. The enjoyment of pornography and use of obscenity became the self-imposed obligation of the emancipated women. Affirmative action catapulted many unprepared women into executive positions. Men, weary of the large families of the '50s, began to desert them; young mothers, frightened by the prospect of being deserted, pulled up stakes and left their suburban split-levels to try to make it in the cities. "Arrangements," or public cohabitation of young people with approval and support from their families, college deans and employers, became common.

By the early 1970s the doomsters were proclaiming that the family was dead. There were over 8,000,000 single-parent households, most of them headed by poorly paid women. There were endless discussions of "open mar-riages," "group marriages," communes in which the children were children of the group, and open discussion of previously taboo subjects, including an emphasis on female sexuality. Yet most Americans continued to live as they always had, with girls still hoping for a permanent marriage and viewing "arrangements" as stepping-stones to marriage. The much-publicized behavior of small but conspicuous groups filtered through the layers of society, so that the freedoms claimed by college youth were being claimed five years later by blue-collar youth; "swinging" (mate swapping) as a pastime of a bored upper-middle-class filtered down.

Perhaps the most striking change of all is that courtship is no longer a prelude to consummation. In many levels of contemporary society, sex relations require no prelude at all; the courtship that exists today tends to occur between a casual sex encounter and a later attempt by either the man or the woman to turn it into a permanent relationship. Courtship is also seen as an act in which either sex can take the lead. Women are felt to have an alternative to marriage, as once they had in the Middle Ages, when convent life was the choice of a large part of the population. Weddings are less conventional, although new conventions, like reading from Kahlil Gibran's *The Prophet,* spread very quickly. There is also a growing rebellion against the kind of town planning and housing that isolate young couples from the help of older people and friends that they need.

But the family is not dead. It is going through stormy times, and millions of children are paying the penalty of current disorganization, experimentation and discontent. In the process, the adults who should never marry are sorting themselves out. Marriage and parenthood are being viewed as a vocation rather than as the duty of every human being. As we seek more human forms of existence, the next question may well be how to protect our young people from a premature, pervasive insistence upon precocious sexuality, sexuality that contains neither love nor delight.

The birthrate is going up a little; women are having just as many babies as before, but having them later. The rights of fathers are being discovered and placed beside the rights of mothers. Exploitive and commercialized abortion mills are being questioned, and the Pill is proving less a panacea than was hoped. In a world troubled by economic and political instability, unemployment, highjacking, kidnapping and bombs, the preoccupation with private decisions is shifting to concern about the whole of humankind.

Active concern for the world permits either celibacy *or* marriage, but continuous preoccupation with sex leaves no time for anything else. As we used to say in the '20s, promiscuity, like free verse, is lacking in structure.

## I. Suggestions for Discussion:

1. Discuss the accuracy and rhetorical effectiveness of the topic sentence that begins Mead's essay.
2. What evidence does she offer that changes in relationships between the

sexes have been occurring with bewildering speed since World War I?
Are her examples and illustrations well-chosen?

3. What current trends does she find most notable? Do you agree? What
   other trends have you observed?

## II. Suggestions for Writing:

1. Compare and contrast your own dating patterns with those of your
   parents or other older family members or friends.
2. Write an essay stating your opinion about the dangers of a premature,
   pervasive insistence upon precocious sexuality.

---

# H. L. MENCKEN

## The Author at Work

---

Henry Louis Mencken (1880–1956), American journalist, critic,
and philologist, edited *The Smart Set* and *The American Mercury.*
In addition to his autobiography, he published six volumes of
*Prejudices* and the three-volume *The American Language* (1919,
1936).

As in this brief essay from *Prejudices* (1926), Mencken was forever puncturing balloons. In typically dry, satiric fashion, he de-
bunks the literary profession, accusing authors of yearning to
make money and to make a noise. In the process, he does not
spare other professions.

---

If authors could work in large, well-ventilated factories, like cigar-
makers or garment-workers, with plenty of their mates about and a flow of
lively professional gossip to entertain them, their labor would be immensely
lighter. But it is essential to their craft that they perform its tedious and
vexatious operations *a cappella,* and so the horrors of loneliness are added
to stenosis and their other professional infirmities. An author at work is con-
tinuously and inescapably in the presence of himself. There is nothing to divert and soothe him. Every time a vagrant regret or sorrow assails him, it has
him instantly by the ear, and every time a wandering ache runs down his leg
it shakes him like the bite of a tiger. I have yet to meet an author who was
not a hypochondriac. Saving only medical men, who are always ill and in

fear of death, the literati are perhaps the most lavish consumers of pills and philtres in this world, and the most assiduous customers of surgeons. I can scarcely think of one, known to me personally, who is not constantly dosing himself with medicines, or regularly resorting to the knife.

It must be obvious that other men, even among the intelligentsia, are not beset so cruelly. A judge on the bench, entertaining a ringing in the ears, can do his work quite as well as if he heard only the voluptuous rhetoric of the lawyers. A clergyman, carrying on his mummery, is not appreciably crippled by a sour stomach: what he says has been said before, and only scoundrels question it. And a surgeon, plying his exhilarating art and mystery, suffers no professional damage from the wild thought that the attending nurse is more sightly than his wife. But I defy anyone to write a competent sonnet with a ringing in his ears, or to compose sound criticism with a sour stomach, or to do a plausible love scene with a head full of private amorous fancies. These things are sheer impossibilities. The poor literatus encounters them and their like every time he enters his work-room and spits on his hands. The moment the door bangs he begins a depressing, losing struggle with his body and his mind.

Why then, do rational men and women engage in so barbarous and exhausting a vocation—for there are relatively intelligent and enlightened authors, remember, just as there are relatively honest politicians, and even bishops. What keeps them from deserting it for trades that are less onerous, and, in the eyes of their fellow creatures, more respectable? One reason, I believe, is that an author, like any other so-called artist, is a man in whom the normal vanity of all men is so vastly exaggerated that he finds it a sheer impossibility to hold it in. His overpowering impulse is to gyrate before his fellow men, flapping his wings and emitting defiant yells. This being forbidden by the police of all civilized countries, he takes it out by putting his yells on paper. Such is the thing called self-expression.

In the confidences of the literati, of course, it is always depicted as something much more mellow and virtuous. Either they argue that they are moved by a yearning to spread the enlightenment and save the world, or they allege that what steams them and makes them leap is a passion for beauty. Both theories are quickly disposed of by an appeal to the facts. The stuff written by nine authors out of ten, it must be plain at a glance, has as little to do with spreading the enlightenment as the state papers of the late Chester A. Arthur.[1] And there is no more beauty in it, and no more sign of a feeling of beauty, than you will find in the décor of a night-club. The impulse to

[1] The twenty-first president of the United States (1881–1885).

create beauty, indeed, is rather rare in literary men, and almost completely absent from the younger ones. If it shows itself at all, it comes as a sort of afterthought. Far ahead of it comes the yearning to make money. And after the yearning to make money comes the yearning to make a noise. The impulse to create beauty lingers far behind. Authors, as a class, are extraordinarily insensitive to it, and the fact reveals itself in their customary (and often incredibly extensive) ignorance of the other arts. I'd have a hard job naming six American novelists who could be depended upon to recognize a fugue without prompting, or six poets who could give a rational account of the difference between a Gothic cathedral and a Standard Oil filling-station.

The thing goes even further. Most novelists, in my experience, know nothing of poetry, and very few poets have any feeling for the beauties of prose. As for the dramatists, three-fourths of them are unaware that such things as prose and poetry exist at all. It pains me to set down such inconvenient and blushful facts. If they ought to be concealed, then blame my babbling upon scientific passion. That passion, today, has me by the ear.

## I. Suggestions for Discussion:
1. What serious observations does Mencken make in this satiric sketch about authors?
2. Analyze his use of irony. Cite specific examples.
3. Does he choose his comparisons because they are apt, humorous, or outrageous? Examine his motivation.

## II. Suggestions for Writing:
1. Write an ironic sketch about any of the professions he mentions.
2. Compare Mencken's attitude toward the commercialism of authors with Marya Mannes's attitude toward television advertisers, p. 353.

---

# H. L. MENCKEN

## The Incomparable Buzz-Saw

---

In this brief essay from the *Smart Set* (1919), H. L. Mencken examines relationships between men and women in his typically laconic, sardonic fashion.

The allurement that women hold out to men is precisely the allurement that Cape Hatteras holds out to sailors: they are enormously dangerous and hence enormously fascinating. To the average man, doomed to some banal drudgery all his life long, they offer the only grand hazard that he ever encounters. Take them away and his existence would be as flat and secure as that of a moo-cow. Even to the unusual man, the adventurous man, the imaginative and romantic man, they offer the adventure of adventures. Civilization tends to dilute and cheapen all other hazards. Even war has been largely reduced to caution and calculation; already, indeed, it employs almost as many press-agents, letter-openers and generals as soldiers. But the duel of sex continues to be fought in the Berserker manner. Whoso approaches women still faces the immemorial dangers. Civilization has not made them a bit more safe than they were in Solomon's time; they are still inordinately menacing, and hence inordinately provocative, and hence inordinately charming.

The most disgusting cad in the world is the man who, on grounds of decorum and morality, avoids the game of love. He is one who puts his own ease and security above the most laudable of philanthropies. Women have a hard time of it in this world. They are oppressed by man-made laws, man-made social customs, masculine egoism, the delusion of masculine superiority. Their one comfort is the assurance that, even though it may be impossible to prevail against man it is always possible to enslave and torture a man. This feeling is fostered when one makes love to them. One need not be a great beau, a seductive catch, to do it effectively. Any man is better than none. To shrink from giving so much happiness at such small expense, to evade the business on the ground that it has hazards—this is the act of a puling and tacky fellow.

## I. Suggestions for Discussion:

1. Discuss Mencken's observations about the duel of the sexes.
2. To what extent can Mencken be charged with male chauvinism in this brief essay?
3. Compare Mencken's irony in this selection with that of "The Author at Work," p. 395.

## II. Suggestions for Writing:

1. Write an essay responding to Mencken's observations about women.
2. Write an essay indicating how Germaine Greer (p. 215) or Shirley Chisholm (p. 83) might respond to Mencken's essay.

# JESSICA MITFORD

## Women in Cages

### from *Kind and Usual Punishment*

Jessica Mitford (1917–      ), the American essayist and journalist, is a distinguished social critic. Her exposé of the business of
dying, *The American Way of Death,* was published in 1963. Her
critique of the American prison system, *Kind and Usual Punishment,* from which the following selection is taken, appeared in
1973. She has also published an autobiography, *Daughters and
Rebels* (1960).

As part of a workshop on crime and corrections, Jessica Mitford
spent a day and a night as a prisoner in the District of Columbia
Women's Detention Center. Her essay vividly describes that
frightening, demoralizing experience.

. . . The Women's Detention Center is a gloomy pile of masonry at the
edge of the ghetto, formerly used by the police department as a temporary
lock-up for people taken into custody. Since 1966 it has been used for detention of women awaiting trial and as a reformatory for sentenced women.
Once inside, we were taken in charge by several women guards, symbolically
clanking real keys.

The first step for the newly arrested is called "Reception," although it
was unlike any reception I have ever attended. The handcuffs now dispensed
with, we were assembled in a large room; our handbags emptied on a counter
and the contents catalogued, we were photographed and fingerprinted.
Ordered to strip, we were searched for narcotics: "Bend over, spread cheeks."
Our heads were examined for lice. From a bin of prison dresses in brightly
patterned cottons with unfinished hem and sleeves we chose for approximate
fit. (I learned later that these bizarre garments were ordered by Mr. Kenneth
Hardy, director of D.C. Corrections, a benign administrator who told me he
thought they would restore "a sense of individuality" to women formerly
required to wear prison gray.) Cigarettes, lipsticks, paperback books were
scrutinized for contraband and then returned to us.

From the recesses of the building we heard a disturbing muffled, rhythmic wail. Was it the sound of mechanical equipment, an air-conditioner gone slightly out of kilter? I asked a guard. "Oh, that's just Viola, she's in Adjustment for her nerves."

"It doesn't seem to be doing her nerves much good."

"Her trouble is she's mental, always bothering the other inmates. So we keep her in Adjustment."

## Waiting for Trial

Living quarters at the Detention Center are on two floors, each accommodating some 45 women. About half the women confined there have not been convicted of any crime. Their sole offense: inability to make bail, for which they are imprisoned, often for months on end, waiting for their cases to come to trial. (A recent census report reveals that 52 percent of the nation's jail population are "confined for reasons other than being convicted of a crime," or, to put it more bluntly, because they are too poor to pay the bail bond broker.) Unlike most jails, where the "presumed innocent" are herded in with the guilty, the Detention Center segregates those awaiting trial from the convicted offenders.

We were placed with the latter group. Our fellow-inmates were mostly "misdemeanants" serving sentences of less than one year (three months is the average term here), but there were also women sentenced for felonies—robbery, murder, aggravated assault—awaiting transfer to a federal women's penitentiary. More than 90 percent of both inmates and staff of this prison are black, as is 71 percent of the general population of the District. A ghetto within a ghetto.

Our domicile was a short and narrow corridor on one side of which are the cells, at the far end a dining room with television set. Women were standing in desultory knots in the corridor, sitting in their cells, or watching TV. The overall impression: a combination of college dorm (silly jokes, putdowns, occasional manifestations of friendliness), lunatic asylum (underlying sense of desolate futility), a scene from *The Threepenny Opera* (graffiti on the walls: "Welcome to the Whores' Paradise!"). I was struck by the number of little-girl faces, kids who except for their funny-looking clothes could be part of a high-school class, and by one or two sad, vacant old faces. The median age here is twenty-five.

## A Cell with Della

As we entered, our names were called out, we were handed sheets and led to our assigned cells, tiny cubicles with two beds, a dresser, and a clothesline for hanging coats and dresses (the prison, like most, is fearfully overcrowded and now holds more than twice its intended capacity). My cellmate was a pleasant-faced black women in her early thirties, named Della. She welcomed me like a good hostess, helped my make my bed, and apologized for the stale, dead smell compounded of people, food, and disinfectant that pervaded our quarters: "We used to have at least some breeze, but they've cut off the air. There's a new rule against opening the corridor window because they claim the inmates were letting down rope to haul up contraband brought by their boyfriends. Now, does that make any sense? With the officers watching you like a hawk every minute of the day and night?"

From Della I learned that, as I had suspected, we had been let off lightly at "Reception." The usual routine, she told me, includes a vaginal examination as part of the search for contraband and a Lysol spraying of the head. She had found the experience horrifying, totally degrading. Furthermore some of the guards "get their kicks" from scaring the neophyte inmate by horrendous hints of what to expect from the bulldaggers" (prison slang for lesbians). Is there actually much homosexuality, I asked? A certain amount, but not as much as the administration seems to think. "They are really hipped on the subject," she said. "They have bed checks all hours of the night, they come around flashing their bright lights, it's hard to get any sleep."

Della had been in the section for unsentenced prisoners for nine weeks waiting for her trial. In all that time she never saw her court-appointed lawyer, and her letters to him were unanswered. She met him for the first and only time in court on the day of her trial, where he advised her to plead guilty: "But he never asked me anything about my case, said he didn't want to hear. Said if we tried to fight it, the judge would be hard on me. But I don't see how he could have been any harder—six months for one count of soliciting!"

We wandered out into the crowded corridor to join the others. Because of the visitors, Della told me, everyone was on good behavior: "We *scrubbed* this place, girl!" And clean, though dreary, it certainly was.

Our group was there to learn, so we started asking questions. The Maryland legislator inquired about recreation facilities. "Re-cre-ation!" an inmate hooted derisively. "Come here, girls, I'll show you." She led us to one of the barred windows, through which we could barely descry a small concrete quadrangle entirely hemmed in by the building. On fine days, she explained, the entire population is sometimes taken down there for an hour or so if the correctional officers have time. Vocational training programs? "There's eight old broken-down typewriters somewhere in the building. I don't know if anybody ever uses them, though. Or you can go down to group therapy, but who wants it? A bunch of us bullshitting about our deprived lives?"

## Punishment for Laughter

We had been told the authorities had arranged for the visitors to sample various aspects of prison life, that some would spend the night in sickbay, others would be brought before a disciplinary committee, accused of breaking the rules. To fortify myself against the latter eventuality I asked for a copy of the prison rule book. "No inmate shall engage in loud or boisterous talk, laughter, whistling or other vocal expression," it said in part. "Talking is permitted at all times except in church and in school, but talking must be conducted in a normal voice except on the recreation fields." One of the prisoners, a vivacious young black woman, confided to me that she was due to be disciplined that day for laughing too loud but had been reprieved because of our visit: "It's a dumb thing anyway to be punished for laughing. When you come to think of it, sometimes it's sort of a release to laugh out loud."

As in hospitals, food is served at unexpected times. At four thirty we went into the dining room to collect our trays of dinner. The food wasn't bad, but like most institutional cooking it was dull and starchy with a touch of wilted green. We ate tuna casserole, Jell-O, a choice of weak coffee or a puce-colored synthetic fruit drink. One of the few white prisoners came and sat beside me, a romantic-looking blonde in her early twenties; she reminded me vaguely of prison movies I had seen. Convicted of possession of heroin, she described her first days in the Detention Center as absolute torture: "You come down cold-turkey, they're not equipped here to treat addicts." She proved to be a discriminating connoisseur of the nation's prisons, and twinkled quite merrily as she rated them for me, one-star, two-star, as in a motel guide. "This joint's by no means the worst, but it's not the best, either." Her goal is to be admitted into one of the treatment centers for narcotics addicts, but so far she has been blocked because they are all full up. She has no idea when, or if, there will ever be an opening for her. What does she do all day? "I work some in the kitchen, just to keep from going crazy. There *isn't* anything to do here." Housekeeping jobs, she explained, are available on our floor but not for the unsentenced women on the floor below: "In some ways they're punished worse than we are, although they haven't even been found guilty of anything." Pay ranges from $5 a month to a top of $13, the higher rate being awarded on the basis of performance and "attitude"; there is no compensation for working part of a month.

## To Disciplinary Committee

"Jessica . . . Mitford . . . to the third . . . floor." The voice over the intercom was tinny and disembodied. I started to the door of our corridor and was at once intercepted by a correctional officer. "No, no, you can't go down by yourself," she said, shocked, and, siezing my arm, led me to the elevator. "You're wanted by the disciplinary committee," she said severely. Lock, double-lock all the way, from our fourth-floor abode to the elevator and down. A third-floor guard took over and led me to the small office where I was to be tried.

My prosecutors, jury, and judges (for the disciplinary committee incorporates all three functions) were the prison psychologist and two correctional officers. They were trying to look suitably stern, to make it all as "real" as possible. One of the officers read off the charges: "At 17.05 hours, Officer Smith opened the door to your cell and found you locked in a passionate embrace with Maureen [the reporter from the Washington *Post*]. As you know, this is an extremely serious offense. What have you to say?"

What, indeed. I could of course deny all (insist she wasn't my type?), but, mindful of my assignment for the ACLU, I decided to go another route. What if I challenged the whole legality of this "trial"? I took a deep breath.

## Prison Rules vs. Prison Crimes

"First, I should like to draw your attention to the prison rule book." (The trio seemed surprised; the rule book, it seems, is not generally available to prisoners.) "I see you have infractions broken down into two categories: *crimes* such as assault, theft, possession of narcotics, and failure to obey *rules*—wasting food, vulgar conversation, not making one's bed. Homosexual acts between inmates are listed here as a crime. Before I plead guilty or not guilty to the charge, I should like to see a copy of the statute under which homosexuality between consenting females is a crime. I don't believe it is a crime in any jurisdiction. I'm already in here for one crime. If you find me guilty of another, it will go very hard with me when my case comes before the parole board."

My inquisitors exchanged uncertain looks. "It's not a *statute,* it's a rule," said one.

"But as you've listed it as a *crime,* I want a lawyer to represent me. I want to cross-examine the officer who accused me, and to call witnesses who'll verify that I was in the dining room watching TV at 17.05 hours."

Nonplussed, the chief correctional officer said she thought they should send for Mrs. Patricia Taylor, the director of the Detention Center. This was done, and I repeated my request.

"Jessica, you must realize we're only trying to help you," said Mrs. Taylor.

"Well, thanks a lot. But I should still like to assert my right to the same procedural safeguards that should apply to any citizen accused of crime."

"You don't understand, Jessica, you are in an institution now, you're an inmate, you haven't a right to a trial. *We'll* decide who's telling the truth. Now, if Officer Smith hadn't seen that, why would she say she had?"

"But I say she's lying, I'm not guilty and I want a chance to prove it. Why don't you bring her down here so I can question her, and clear myself?"

"Jessica, do you realize what would happen to discipline if we permitted the inmates to cross-examine the officers?"

We went over this a few times; I had made my point, but since it was only a charade (and I knew Maureen was waiting for her turn before the disciplinary committee) I soon gave up, and was duly sentenced to "ten days in Adjustment."

What if the situation had been real, I kept thinking? Instead of making this well-reasoned little speech about my constitutional rights I would have been shouting furiously, perhaps in tears. And instead of listening and answering calmly, would not my captors have responded in kind—put me down as a troublemaker or psycho for asserting my rights, and treated me accordingly? Now I was beginning to "feel." The governessy young criminology student would be proud of me!

## To Adjustment

Accompanied by the chief correctional officer, who firmly gripped my arm (did she think I might try to escape?), I traversed several corridors and those eerie wails gradually came closer. The officer in charge of Adjustment took me over. Here the stripping of individuality is turned up a notch. I am given a gray cotton shift in place of the patterned dress from the bin. Bra, shoes, cigarettes, wristwatch, wedding ring, paperback books are confiscated. To her chagrin, the officer discovers that all eight solitary cells are occupied (which means that about one in ten of the inmates is locked up there). I will have to double up with a thief who was put in Adjustment for beating up other women. Not a terribly reassuring thought. The door giving onto the corridor of solitary cells is immensely thick, opened by my keeper with several huge keys. Now we hear the screams full force—not just from Viola, they seem to be coming from several cells. "*Let me out*!" "*I want out*!" Women are moaning, shrieking, pounding with their fists against their doors. This is "Adjustment"? To what are they being adjusted?

"You have company," the officer announces tersely to my cellmate, and she double-locks the door behind us. Mindful of my companion's alleged infraction I flash her a conciliatory smile, but she is pleased to see me, makes me welcome, we sit on the bed (sole furnishing except for an open toilet that flushes only from the outside) and talk.

The Thief's Tale was well larded with fantasy, or so it seemed to me. A tall, attractive black woman about thirty years old, she was essentially "state-raised": orphaned at the age of eight, in and out of trouble, in and out of juvenile detention (but mostly in) until her middle twenties. "I tried to go straight for a spell, but I don't really dig it. On welfare, with two little kids to raise—what kind of life is that?" She turned to pickpocketing, a discipline in which she had received much theoretical instruction during her many years in reformatories. "The best place is near the Americana Hotel in New York, that's where lots of businessmen hang out." She told me she could clear upward of $500 on a good night and that once she netted $14,000 from the wallet of an unsuspecting passerby. Yet, in view of her expanding needs, she found it slow going: "My boyfriend and I wanted to start a nightclub in Atlantic City, we figured on $100,000 to open it. So I told him leave it to me, I'd raise it." The quickest way, she decided, was to travel around the country from motel to motel cashing bad checks in amounts of $500 to $1,000. She had got up to $40,000 of the needed capital when the feds caught up with her.

## 17-Year-Old Screams

Our corridor had all but quieted down after the guard left. Now the screams started up again, coming apparently from the cell directly opposite ours, a terrible outcry of rage and misery, shrieks and obscenities interspersed with deep, racking sobs. We peered through the tiny grill in our door and could dimly see movement behind the opposite grill, hands clawing, head wildly shaking. My cellmate shouted soothing words across the corridor: "Now, honey, hush up, won't you? If you be a good girl and stop all that noise, I'll speak to Mrs. Taylor, and I'll see that she lets you out of there. If I say to let you out, she'll do it."

"Who is she?" I asked.

"She's a juvenile, she's down here because she's too young to go up-stairs."

"*Too young*?" How old is she?"

"Seventeen."

Of course I didn't believe a word of it. Just another of her delusions, I thought, like the $14,000 wallet, the obliging motel managers who cash $1,000 checks for strangers, her role as confidante and adviser to Mrs. Taylor.

Soon—in an hour and a half, to be exact—my "ten days" were up. For further clarification I sought out Mrs. Taylor, a highly qualified black ad-ministrator with a long background in social work and Corrections. No longer an "inmate," I was formally ushered into her office, where we discussed what I had heard and seen that day.

## Prostitution and Narcotics

First, as to the general prison scene, what are the women here being punished for? The great majority, about 85 percent, are in for a combination of prostitution and narcotics (as one inmate had told me, "They go together like salt and pepper; once you're hooked on the stuff, you have to hustle to support your habit"). Does Mrs. Taylor think prostitution is a crime? No, she believes many women are driven to it by circumstances outside their control. What about drug addiction? That's not a crime either, it's a sickness and should be treated as such.

Checking Mrs. Taylor's opinions against those of others in authority, from correctional officers to Mr. Kenneth Hardy, director of the department, I found unanimity on these points. *None* believed that prostitution and drug addiction are "crimes." Thus the patently crazy situation in which the keepers themselves, up and down the line, believe their mandate to imprison these women rests on a fundamentally unsound premise. But, they all point out, they are merely doing the job required of them by the courts, the legis-lature, the public: "We don't choose the inmates, we have to take whoever the judges send us."

In our discussion of the Adjustment setup, this sense of total irrational-ity deepened.

The case of Viola: she is a diagnosed schizophrenic, Mrs. Taylor explained. Because of a recent court decision, she cannot be transferred to a mental institution without a sanity hearing; but the courts are so clogged with cases that no date for such a hearing has been set. How long will she stay locked away in Adjustment? Nobody knows.

The screaming girl across the corridor? My cellmate was right after all, she really *is* only seventeen, she really *is* there because she is too young to go upstairs—in solitary because of a mistake of the Juvenile Court. Finding that she was incorrigible in the children's prison, the judge sentenced her to Women's Detention. But the law says that juvenile offenders may not mix with the adult prison population, so she was put in Adjustment. At first she was allowed "privileges"—mail, books, cigarettes. After several days of total solitude she set her mattress on fire (perhaps, Mrs. Taylor surmised, "to draw attention to herself?"). Consequently she is now considered a "disciplinary case" and all privileges have been withdrawn. How long will she have to stay there? For about three months, until she turns eighteen.

## Risk of Insanity?

"Aren't you afraid she'll go completely insane by that time?"

"Well . . . there is that danger . . ."

Why, I wanted to know, is the inmate who is being punished for some infraction denied books, newspapers, games—*anything* that might make solitary confinement more tolerable?

"The idea is to remove her completely from the environment. You heard those women screaming in there. If we'd kept you in there for twenty-four hours, you would have been screaming, too."

"Then—is that your purpose, to destroy my self-control, to reduce me to a helpless, howling infant?"

"That's a risk we have to take," said Mrs. Taylor with a faint smile.

What of homosexuality, recognized by everyone in Corrections as an inevitable consequence of long-term segregation of the sexes? Having driven them to it, why punish for it? "Love affairs" between women inmates, born out of loneliness, longing for human affection, lack of male companionship—does Mrs. Taylor consider this sort of behavior criminal? "No, but if permitted it might lead to jealousy and fights. Besides, I am responsible for their morals while they are in here." *Their* morals? Yet Mrs. Taylor had something there, I thought. Is this not the essence of women's prisons, the punishment of unchaste, unwomanly behavior, a grotesque bow to long-outmoded nineteenth-century notions of feminine morality?

## No Training or Education

There is, Mrs. Taylor regretfully conceded, barely even the pretense of a useful trade or educational program for the women, most of whom she expects to see back again in her custody shortly after they are let out. They exit and reenter as through a revolving door, three quarters of those who are in now have been here before. Chances of getting a decent job when they leave, slim enough for ghetto women in any circumstances, are almost nonexistent for those with prison records, so inevitably they turn to their old ways when released.

This, then, is an American women's prison of the 1970's—and "not the worst," as my dinner companion said. A life of planned, unrelieved inactivity and boredom . . . no overt brutality but plenty of random, largely unintentional cruelty . . . a pervasive sense of helplessness and frustration engulfing not only the inmates but their keepers, themselves prisoners trapped in the weird complex of paradoxes that is the prison world.

I. **Suggestions for Discussion:**
   1. What illustrations best support Mitford's conclusions that prison life is boring, cruel, and frustrating?
   2. What rhetorical function does her extensive use of dialogue and conversation have in her essay?
   3. What responses does Mitford succeed in awakening in you as a reader? Explain how she arouses your responses.

II. **Suggestions for Writing:**
   1. Write an essay urging prison reform. Draw on Mitford's essay and on other reading to document conditions that need to be changed.
   2. Prepare and deliver a speech in which you welcome prisoners to a detention center and lay out rules for their behavior.

---

## MONTAIGNE

### It Is Folly to Measure the True and False by Our Own Capacity

---

Michel Eyquem de Montaigne (1533-1592) is often called the father of the essay. A French intellectual who served as mayor of

Bordeaux for two terms (1581-1585), he published the first two books of his *Essais* in 1580 and an enlarged edition with a third book in 1588. The *Essais* were first translated into English in 1603.

Montaigne's rationality is readily apparent in this plea for open-mindedness. He uses quotations and allusions to buttress his case for not disdaining what we do not fully comprehend.

---

Perhaps it is not without reason that we attribute facility in belief and conviction to simplicity and ignorance; for it seems to me I once learned that belief was a sort of impression made on our mind, and that the softer and less resistant the mind, the easier it was to imprint something on it. *As the scale of the balance must necessarily sink under the weight placed upon it, so must the mind yield to evident things.* [Cicero] The more a mind is empty and without counterpoise, the more easily it gives beneath the weight of the first persuasive argument. That is why children, common people, women, and sick people are most subject to being led by the ears. But then, on the other hand, it is foolish presumption to go around disdaining and condemning as false whatever does not seem likely to us; which is a common vice in those who think they have more than normal ability. I used to do so once; and if I heard of returning spirits, prognostications of future events, enchantments, sorcery, or some other story that I could not swallow,

> *Dreams, witches, miracles, magic alarms,*
> *Nocturnal specters, and Thessalian charms,*
>
> > [Horace]

I felt compassion for the poor people who were taken in by these follies. And now I think that I was at least as much to be pitied myself. Not that experience has since shown me anything surpassing my first beliefs, and that through no fault of my curiosity; but reason has taught me that to condemn a thing thus, dogmatically, as false and impossible, is to assume the distinction of knowing the bounds and limits of God's will and of the power of our mother Nature; and that there is no more notable folly in the world than to measure these things by our capacity and competence. If we call prodigies or miracles whatever our reason cannot reach, how many of these appear continually before our eyes! Let us consider through what clouds and how gropingly we are led to the knowledge of most of the things that are right in

our hands; assuredly we shall find that it is rather familiarity than knowledge
that takes away their strangeness,

>     *But no one now, so tired of seeing are our eyes,*
>     *Deigns to look up at the bright temples of the skies,*
>                                                     [Lucretius]

and that if those things were presented to us for the first time, we should find
them as incredible, or more so, than any others.

>     *If they were here for the first time for men to see,*
>     *If they were set before us unexpectedly,*
>     *Nothing more marvelous than these things could be told,*
>     *Nothing more unbelievable for men of old.*
>                                                     [Lucretius]

He who had never seen a river thought that the first one he came across
was the ocean. And the things that are the greatest within our knowledge we
judge to be the utmost that nature can do in that category.

>     *A fair-sized stream seems vast to one who until then*
>     *Has never seen a greater; so with trees, with men.*
>     *In every field each man regards as vast in size*
>     *The greatest objects that have come before his eyes.*
>                                                     [Lucretius]

> *The mind becomes accustomed to things by the habitual sight of*
> *them, nor wonders nor inquires about the reasons for the things*
> *it sees all the time.*                             [Cicero]

The novelty of things incites us more than their greatness to seek
their causes.

We must judge with more reverence the infinite power of nature, and
with more consciousness of our ignorance and weakness. How many things of
slight probability there are, testified by trustworthy people, which, if we cannot be convinced of them, we should at least leave in suspense! For to condemn them as impossible is to pretend, with rash presumption, to know the
limits of possibility. If people rightly understood the difference between the
impossible and the unusual, and between what is contrary to the orderly
course of nature and what is contrary to the common opinion of men, not

believing rashly nor disbelieving easily, they would observe the rule of "nothing too much," enjoined by Chilo.

When we find in Froissart that the Count de Foix, in Béarn, learned of the defeat of King John of Castile at Juberoth the day after it happened, we can laugh at it; and also at the story our annals tell, that Pope Honorius performed public funeral rites for King Philip Augustus and commanded them to be performed throughout Italy on the very day he died at Mantes. For the authority of these witnesses is perhaps not high enough to keep us in hand. But then, if Plutarch, after several examples that he cites from antiquity, says that he knows with certain knowledge that in the time of Domitian, the news of the battle lost by Antonius in Germany was published in Rome, several days' journey from there, and dispersed throughout the whole world, on the same day it was lost; and if Caesar maintains that it has often happened that the report has preceded the event—shall we say that these simple men let themselves be hoaxed like the common herd, because they were not clear-sighted like ourselves? Is there anything more delicate, clearer and more alert than Pliny's judgment, when he sees fit to bring it into play, or anything farther from inanity? Leaving aside the excellence of his knowledge, which I count for less, in which of these qualities do we surpass him? However, there is no schoolboy so young but he will convict him of falsehood, and want to give him a lesson on the progress of Nature's works.

When we read in Bouchet about the miracles done by the relics of Saint Hilary, let it go: his credit is not great enough to take away our right to contradict him. But to condemn wholesale all similar stories seems to me a singular impudence. The great Saint Augustine testifies that he saw a blind child restored to sight upon the relics of Saint Gervaise and Saint Protasius at Milan; a woman at Carthage cured of a cancer by the sign of the cross that a newly baptized woman made over her; Hesperius, a close friend of his, cast out the spirits that infested his house, with a little earth from the sepulcher of our Lord, and a paralytic promptly cured by this earth, later, when it had been carried to church; a woman in a procession, having touched Saint Stephen's shrine with a bouquet, and rubbed her eyes with this bouquet, recover her long-lost sight; and several other miracles at which he says he himself was present. Of what shall we accuse both him and two holy bishops, Aurelius and Maximinus, whom he calls upon as his witnesses? Shall it be of ignorance, simplicity, and credulity, or of knavery and imposture? Is there any man in our time so impudent that he thinks himself comparable to them, either in virtue and piety, or in learning, judgment, and ability? *Who, though they brought forth no proof, might crush me by their mere authority.* [Cicero]

It is dangerous and presumptuous, besides the absurd temerity that it implies, to disdain what we do not comprehend. For after you have established, according to your fine understanding, the limits of truth and falsehood, and it turns out that you must necessarily believe things even stranger than those you deny, you are obliged from then on to abandon them. Now, what seems to me to bring as much disorder into our consciences as anything, is this partial surrender of their beliefs by Catholics. It seems to them that they are being very moderate and understanding when they yield to their opponents some of the articles in dispute. But, besides the fact that they do not see what an advantage it is to a man charging you for you to begin to give ground and withdraw, and how much that encourages him to pursue his point, those articles which they select as the most trivial are sometimes very important. Either we must submit completely to the authority of our ecclesiastical government, or do without it completely. It is not for us to decide what portion of obedience we owe it.

Moreover, I can say this for having tried it, having in other days exercised this freedom of personal choice and selection, regarding with negligence certain points in the observances of our Church which seemed more pointless or strange than others; coming to tell learned men about them, I found that these things have a massive and very solid foundation, and that it is only stupidity and ignorance that makes us receive them with less reverence than the rest. Why do we not remember how much contradiction we sense even in our own judgment, how many things were articles of faith to us yesterday, which are fables to us today? Vainglory and curiosity are the two scourges of our soul. The latter leads us to thrust our noses into everything, and the former forbids us to leave anything unresolved and undecided.

I. **Suggestions for Discussion:**
   1. How does Montaigne use allusions to historical figures to strengthen his argument?
   2. What does his extensive use of illustrative quotations contribute to his essay?
   3. Pick out and discuss the validity of his aphorisms.
II. **Suggestions for Writing:**
   1. Write an essay describing the process by which you came to believe something you formerly thought untrue.
   2. Write an essay discussing a controversial national issue on which you have kept an open mind because of conflicting claims.

# MONTAIGNE

## Of Idleness

In the following brief autobiographical note, Montaigne reflects upon the fact that an idle mind needs focus and occupation.

Just as we see that fallow land, if rich and fertile, teems with a hundred thousand wild and useless weeds, and that to set it to work we must subject it and sow it with certain seeds for our service; and as we see that women, all alone, produce shapeless masses and lumps of flesh, but that to create a good and natural offspring they must be made fertile with a different kind of seed; so it is with minds. Unless you keep them busy with some definite subject that will bridle and control them, they will throw themselves in disorder hither and yon in the vague field of imagination.

> *As when the light of waters in an urn,*
> *Trembling, reflects the sun or moon, in turn*
> *It flickers round the room, and darts its rays*
> *Aloft, and on the panelled ceiling plays.*
>
> [Virgil]

And there is no mad or idle fancy that they will not bring forth in this agitation:

> *They form vain visions, like a sick man's dreams.*
>
> [Horace]

The soul that has no fixed goal loses itself; for, as they say, to be everywhere is to be nowhere:

> *He who dwells everywhere, Maximus, nowhere dwells.*
>
> [Martial]

Lately when I retired to my home, determined so far as possible to bother about nothing except spending the little life I have left in rest and privacy, it seemed to me I could do my mind no greater favor than to let it entertain itself in idleness and stay and settle in itself, which I hoped it might do more easily now, having become heavier and more mature with time. But I find—

> *Ever idle hours breed wandering thoughts*
>
> [Lucan]

—that, on the contrary, like a runaway horse, it gives itself a hundred times more trouble than it took for others, and gives birth to so many chimeras and fantastic monsters, one after another, without order or purpose, that in order to contemplate their strangeness and foolishness at my pleasure, I have begun to put them in writing, hoping in time to make even my mind ashamed of them.

### I. Suggestions for Discussion:
1. Compare Montaigne's use of quotations in this brief, personal essay with their use in "It Is Folly," p. 408. Do these quotations advance his argument or merely illustrate his points? Discuss.
2. Discuss the tone of his essay. Which of the following words might be used to describe his tone: arrogant, concerned, didactic, friendly, personal, sarcastic? What other words come to your mind?
3. What does Montaigne hope to accomplish by writing down his thoughts?

### II. Suggestions for Writing:
1. Write a brief essay on either the pleasures or the dangers of idleness.
2. Describe how you handle idleness in your own life.

---

## SIR THOMAS MORE

### On Slaves

#### from *Utopia*

---

Sir Thomas More (1478-1535), Lord Chancellor of England under Henry VIII, was executed for high treason. The great humanist wrote his *Utopia* in Latin in 1516.

In the following selection from *Utopia,* More illustrates the quality
of life in Utopia by describing the treatment of slaves, marriage
customs, attitudes toward the mentally ill, the legal and adminis-
trative system, and the management of international affairs.

---

For slaves they do not have men captured in war (unless they fought
the war themselves), nor the children of slaves, nor anyone who could be
bought as a slave in another country. Instead they have any of their own
citizens who have been reduced to slavery for some offense, or the inhabitants of foreign cities who have been condemned to death for some crime
they have committed. This latter class is by far the more common. For they
take away many of these, sometimes for a small price, more often for nothing, just by asking for them. They keep this kind of slave not merely in constant labor, but also in chains. Their own people they treat more severely:
they think they are the more hopeless and deserving of the harsher punishment, because after such an excellent training to virtue they still could not be
restrained from crime.

There is another class of slaves, composed of poor overworked drudges
from another country, who have deliberately chosen to be slaves in Utopia.
These are decently treated, and handled with not much less kindness than
Utopians, except that they have a little more work imposed on them as they
are used to it. It does not often happen that one wishes to leave, but if he
does, they do not hold him against his will, nor do they send him away
empty-handed.

As I have said, they treat the sick with great kindness and leave nothing
undone to restore their health, whether it is by drugs or by dieting. If anyone
is suffering from an incurable disease, they console him by sitting with him,
talking to him and supplying all the comforts they can. But if a disease is not
merely beyond treatment, but also a constant source of pain and agony, the
priests and magistrates remind him that he is not up to all the tasks of life,
is troublesome to others and a burden to himself, and is now outliving his
own death. Then they advise him not to resolve to feed that pestilence and
sickness any longer, nor to hesitate to die, since life is a torment to him. They
bid him to take good hope and release himself from that bitter life, as if from
a prison or torture rack, or at least give his permission for others to remove
him. They tell him that since he is going to put an end not to pleasure but to
punishment, he would be well advised to do it; and since in that matter he is
going to take the advice of priests, the interpreters of God, his action will also

be pious and holy. Those who are persuaded by this either end their own lives by abstinence from food, or else are released from it while they are asleep, without any sensation of death. But they never remove anyone against his will, nor are they any the less considerate to him. It is considered honorable to yield to persuasion and die like this. But they think a man unworthy of burial or cremation who commits suicide without having a reason approved of by the priests and Senate. Instead, in great disgrace, he is flung unburied into some bog.

A woman does not marry before she is eighteen years old, and a man not until he is four years older than that. If a man or woman is found guilty of secret lust before marriage, the offender is severely punished and both are forbidden to marry forever, unless the President pardons them and forgives their offense. But also the head of the household and his wife in whose home the shameful act was committed are held in great disgrace, on the grounds that they were remiss in their duty. The reason for the severe punishment of this crime is the realization that very few people would join in married love, in which they saw they had to spend all their lives with one person and endure all the consequent inconvenience, if they were not carefully restrained from random sexual relations.

Moreover, in choosing partners, they seriously and rigidly observe a ritual that to us seemed quite absurd and ridiculous. A respectable and honored matron shows the woman (whether she is a maiden or a widow) to her suitor in complete nakedness. And in turn some trustworthy man shows the suitor naked to the girl. When we were laughing at this custom as being a silly one and were finding fault with it, the Utopians expressed their surprise at the amazing stupidity of all other nations. For, they said, in a matter involving a trifling sum of money, like buying a horse, other people are so careful that they refuse to buy the horse, however uncovered he may be, if the saddle and harness are not taken off, in case there is a sore hidden under those coverings. But in choosing a wife (a matter which will bring pleasure or revulsion for the rest of one's life) they are so careless that, while the rest of her body is concealed by clothes, they judge the whole woman from a space of a few inches (for only her face is visible) and then marry her—not without a great danger of a bad match if anything offends their taste afterward. For not all men are wise enough to regard character only, and in the marriages of such wise men bodily endowments make a useful addition to the spiritual virtues. Naturally so fond a deformity can lie concealed under those clothes that it can quite alienate the mind from one's wife, when it is no longer possible he be bodily separated from her. If such a deformity should happen to come about after marriage, then each man must bear his lot. But there ought to be legal provision to prevent anyone from being caught by such guile before marriage. The Utopians had to be all the more cautious on this, as they are the only people in that world who are content with one wife, and marriage is not often dissolved for them except by death, unless the reason is adultery or some unendurable fault of character. If either husband or wife is afflicted in this way, the Senate gives permission to him or her to find another partner. The other partner forever lives a single life, in disgrace. But they in no way tolerate a man to divorce his wife, if she is blameless, just because some physical misfortune strikes her. For they think it cruel to abandon anyone in his hour of greater need, and believe that it will also breed great distrust in old age, which both brings sickness and is a sickness itself. But it sometimes happens that the characters of husband and wife are quite irreconcilable, and they both discover others with whom they hope they can live more pleasantly. So they separate by mutual consent and contract new marriages. But this cannot be done without the permission of the Senate, which allows divorces only after its members and their wives have carefully examined the case. It is not easy even then, as they know that a ready hope of new marriage is most disadvantageous for strengthening the love of husband and wife.

Adulterers are punished with the severest slavery. If both offenders were married, the injured parties, if they wish, may gain a divorce and marry each other. Otherwise they may marry anyone they want. But if the injured party remains in love with so ill-deserving a partner, he is not forbidden to enjoy his right of marriage, as long as he is willing to follow the convicted partner in his hard labor. It sometimes happens that the repentance of the one and the constant kindness of the other move the President to compassion and gain them freedom once more. But if such a person falls back into his criminal ways, he is put to death.

For other crimes there is no fixed punishment regulated by any law, but the Senate judges the severity or mildness of the offense and decides upon an appropriate punishment. Husbands chastise their wives and parents their children, unless they have committed so terrible a crime that its public punishment is beneficial to morality. But usually the most serious crimes are punished with slavery. For they think this just as unpleasant for the criminals and more profitable for the state than if they hurried to execute the guilty and do away with them immediately. For their work brings more profit than their death, and by their example they can deter others from similar offenses for a longer time. But if in this treatment they rebel and fight against authority, then they are slaughtered like wild beasts that no prison or chain can confine. Yet if they are patient, not absolutely all hope is taken away. If after being subdued by long misfortune they clearly show enough repentance to demonstrate that their sin is more displeasing to them than their punishment, then sometimes by the President's prerogative, sometimes by the vote of the people, their slavery is mitigated or altogether remitted. To have tried to commit adultery is no less dangerous than to have succeeded. For in the case of every crime, they judge a fixed and clearly aimed attempt to be the equivalent of the deed itself. Nor do they think it ought to be in his favor that he did not go all the way, since it was not his doing that he failed.

They take great delight in fools. Although it is considered shameful to do them any harm, yet it is permissible to get pleasure from their foolishness. For they think that this is very good for the fools themselves. If anyone is so stern and severe that he cannot laugh at any word or action of theirs, to his safekeeping they refuse to entrust a fool. For they are afraid that a man who finds no use and no amusement in a fool (and this is a fool's only advantage) will not look after him with sufficient kindness.

To mock a man who is deformed or crippled is considered disgusting and disgraceful, not to the man mocked, but to the mocker. For he stupidly reproaches as a failing something that the man could not possibly avoid. They think a person lazy and slothful who does not look after his natural beauty; but with them it is disgraceful arrogance to seek help from paint. For they know by experience how little husbands are attracted by their wives' beauty as compared with integrity and humility of character. For althouth some men are won by physical beauty alone, no one's affection is kept except by virtue and obedience.

They do not merely deter people from crimes by punishment; they also set up rewards to incite them to virtue. And so they put up statues in the marketplace to distinguished men and those who have been great benefactors to the state. This is done as a memorial to their benefactions, and also so that the glory of their ancestors may serve their descendants as a spur and incitement to virtue. Anyone who canvasses for an office is debarred from all promotion. They live together in love, as no magistrate is haughty or terrifying. They are called "fathers" and so do they act. Those who wish may pay them respect, as is only right, but this is not demanded of men against their will. Not even the President himself is distinguished by his clothing or by a crown. His only distinctive mark is a small sheaf of corn which he carries, just as the Bishop's is a wax candle carried before him.

They have very few laws, as people so trained do not need many. The chief criticism they bring against other people is that an infinite number of books of laws and commentaries is not enough. The Utopians think it most unjust that any men should be bound by laws that are either too numerous to

read or too obscure for anyone to understand. Moreover, they exclude absolutely all lawyers since these plead cases with cunning and slyly dispute the
laws. For they think it useful that each man should plead his own case and
repeat to the judge what he would have told his counsel. In this way there
will be less doubt and the truth can be elicited more easily, since the speaker
has not been taught any deceit by his lawyer, and the judge can shrewdly
weigh up each point and help simpler minds against the false accusations of
the cunning. It is hard for this procedure to be observed in other countries
amid such a mass of tangled laws. But in Utopia every man has a good knowledge of law. For, as I have said, the laws are very few, and they think that the
bluntest interpretation is the best. All laws, they say, are passed with the sole
reason of reminding each man of his duty; therefore a more subtle interpretation reminds fewer people, as only few can follow it; whereas a more
straightforward and simple meaning of the laws is open to everyone. Otherwise, as far as the common people are concerned (and they are the most
numerous and most in need of being reminded), you might just as well pass
no law at all as pass one and then interpret it in a sense that no one could
possibly discover except by a very keen mind and much debate. For the blunt
judgment of the common man could never discover such an interpretation,
nor does he have enough time, with his days spent in working for his living.

These virtues of the Utopians have incited their neighbors, who are free
and under their own control (for the Utopians long ago freed many of them
from tyranny), to take their magistrates from them, some every year, others
for a period of five years. After they have completed their term of office,
they escort them back with glory and honor, and take back fresh ones with
them to their country. Now, these nations take an excellent and healthy care
of their states. Since the safety or destruction of a state depends on the
character of its magistrates, they could have made no wiser choice than men
who are strangers in the land and could not be deflected from honesty by any
bribe (since it would shortly be useless to them when they returned to their
own country), nor influenced by favor or hatred toward anyone. If ever these
two evils of bias and greed settle on the law courts, they immediately destroy
all justice, the strongest sinew of the state. The Utopians call the people who
fetch magistrates from them "allies," and the others to whom they have given
aid they call "friends."

Other nations are in the habit of making treaties all the time, then
breaking them and renewing them. But the Utopians make none at all. For
what is the purpose of a treaty? they say. It is as if nature does not put
enough love between man and man. If a man scorns nature, do you think he
would care about words? They are led to this opinion particularly because in

that part of the world the treaties and pacts of princes are not observed very faithfully. For in Europe, and especially those parts controlled by the faith and religion of Christ, the majesty of treaties is everywhere holy and unbreakable. This is partly because of the justice and goodness of the princes, partly because of the reverence and fear felt for the popes, who most religiously perform whatever they undertake and bid all other princes keep exactly to their promises, while those who seek to evade them they coerce with the severity of their pontifical censure. For they quite rightly think it most disgraceful if there is no faith in the treaties of men who are called by the special name of "faithful."

But in that new world, as far separated from us by the equator as by their way of life and character, there is no confidence in treaties. The more numerous and sacred are the rites tying the knot, the more quickly it is undone. They easily find some verbal quibble, and occasionally formulate treaties deliberately in ambiguous language, so that they can never be bound by firm ties without having some loophole for wriggling out of the treaty and their good faith at the same time. If they found that this cunning, or rather this fraud and deceit, had played a part in an agreement between private individuals, they would look angry and shout "Sacrilege! They deserve the gallows!" while all the time they pride themselves on having given the same advice to their princes. This makes all justice seem either a lowly and humble virtue, far below princely eminence, or else capable of two divisions: The one befits the common people, going on foot and crawling along the ground, unable to leap over barriers, restricted with many fetters. The other is the virtue of princes, more august than the popular kind and much freer, which is allowed to do anything it wants.

As I said, I think that the reason why the Utopians make no treaties lies in the character of the princes there who keep their treaties so badly. Perhaps they would change their opinion if they lived here. However, they think that even if they are scrupulously observed, yet it was bad that the habit of making treaties started in the first place. This is the reason why nations think themselves born enemies and adversaries, just as if there were no natural bond uniting two peoples separated merely by a hill or a stream. Consequently such people think it right to plot the other's destruction if no treaties stand in the way. Even when they have entered upon a treaty they imagine that no friendship has been formed, rather that they still have freedom to plunder as far as the treaty has not been carefully worded and contains no sufficiently precise clause to ban this. But the Utopians are of the contrary opinion, that no one must be considered an enemy who has done no harm, that the fellowship of nature acts as a treaty, and that a better and more powerful bond

exists between men from kindness than from treaties, that is to say, from the
spirit rather than from words.

### I. Suggestions for Discussion:
1. Discuss whether or not you would want to live in More's Utopia.
2. Discuss the issues of human rights and justice raised by this selection from *Utopia*.
3. Compare and contrast the harshness of More's Utopia with our own society.

### II. Suggestions for Writing:
1. Describe one or more aspects of an ideal society which you create.
2. Write an essay attacking one or more of the practices described by More. Present your alternatives.

---

# JOHN HENRY NEWMAN

## What Is a University?

from *The Rise and Progress of Universities*

---

John Henry Newman (1801-1890), an Englishman who became
a Roman Catholic in 1845, was ordained a priest, appointed
rector of the new Catholic University of Dublin in 1854, and
created a cardinal in 1879. His *Apologia Pro Vita Sua* (1864) is
his moving and eloquent spiritual history.

Newman's long, difficult essay, first published in 1854, and later
collected in *The Rise and Progress of Universities,* is an extended
definition of a university. He uses comparison and contrast to
relate his notion of a university to the world of society, to the
British Parliament, to professional scientific meetings, and to the
vitality of great metropolitan centers.

---

If I were asked to describe as briefly and popularly as I could, what a
University was, I should draw my answer from its ancient designation of a
*Studium Generale,* or 'School of University Learning.' This description im-

plies the assemblage of strangers from all parts in one spot;—*from all parts;* else, how will you find professors and students for every department of knowledge? and *in one spot;* else, how can there be any school at all? Accordingly, in its simple and rudimental form, it is a school of knowledge of every kind, consisting of teachers and learners from every quarter. Many things are requisite to complete and satisfy the idea embodied in this description; but such as this a University seems to be in its essence, a place for the communication and circulation of thought, by means of personal intercourse, through a wide extent of country.

There is nothing far-fetched or unreasonable in the idea thus presented to us; and if this be a University, then a University does but contemplate a necessity of our nature, and is but one specimen in a particular medium, out of many which might be adduced in others, of a provision for that necessity. Mutual education, in a large sense of the word, is one of the great and incessant occupations of human society, carried on partly with set purpose, and partly not. One generation forms another; and the existing generation is ever acting and reacting upon itself in the persons of its individual members. Now, in this process, books, I need scarcely say, that is, the *litera scripta,*[1] are one special instrument. It is true; and emphatically so in this age. Considering the prodigious powers of the press, and how they are developed at this time in the never-intermitting issue of periodicals, tracts, pamphlets, works in series, and light literature, we must allow there never was a time which promised fairer for dispensing with every other means of information and instruction. What can we want more, you will say, for the intellectual education of the whole man, and for every man, than so exuberant and diversified and persistent a promulgation of all kinds of knowledge? Why, you will ask, need we go up to knowledge, when knowledge comes down to us? The Sibyl wrote her prophecies upon the leaves of the forest, and wasted them; but here such careless profusion might be prudently indulged, for it can be afforded without loss, in consequence of the almost fabulous fecundity of the instrument which these latter ages have invented. We have sermons in stones, and books in the running brooks; works larger and more comprehensive than those which have gained for ancients an immortality, issue forth every morning, and are projected onwards to the ends of the earth at the rate of hundreds of miles a day. Our seats are strewed, our pavements are powdered, with swarms of little tracts; and the very bricks of our city walls preach wisdom, by informing us by their placards where we can at once cheaply purchase it.

I allow all this, and much more; such certainly is our popular education,

---

[1] The written word.

and its effects are remarkable. Nevertheless, after all, even in this age, whenever men are really serious about getting what, in the language of trade, is called 'a good article,' when they aim at something precise, something refined, something really luminous, something really large, something choice, they go to another market; they avail themselves, in some shape or other, of the rival method, the ancient method, of oral instruction, of present communication between man and man, of teachers instead of learning, of the personal influence of a master, and the humble initiation of a disciple, and, in consequence, of great centres of pilgrimage and throng, which such a method of education necessarily involves. This, I think, will be found to hold good in all those departments or aspects of society, which possess an interest sufficient to bind men together, or to constitute what is called 'a world.' It holds in the political world, and in the high world, and in the religious world; and it holds also in the literary and scientific world.

If the actions of men may be taken as any test of their convictions, then we have reason for saying this, viz.: that the province and the inestimable benefit of the *litera scripta* is that of being a record of truth, and an authority of appeal, and an instrument of teaching in the hands of a teacher; but that, if we wish to become exact and fully furnished in any branch of knowledge which is diversified and complicated, we must consult the living man and listen to his living voice. I am not bound to investigate the cause of this, and anything I may say will, I am conscious, be short of its full analysis;—perhaps we may suggest, that no books can get through the number of minute questions which it is possible to ask on any extended subject, or can hit upon the very difficulties which are severally felt by each reader in succession. Or again, that no book can convey the special spirit and delicate peculiarities of its subject with that rapidity and certainty which attend on the sympathy of mind with mind, through the eyes, the look, the accent, and the manner, in casual expressions thrown off at the moment, and the unstudied turns of familiar conversation. But I am already dwelling too long on what is but an incidental portion of my main subject. Whatever be the cause, the fact is undeniable. The general principles of any study you may learn by books at home; but the detail, the colour, the tone, the air, the life which makes it live in us, you must catch all these from those in whom it lives already. You must imitate the student in French or German, who is not content with his grammar, but goes to Paris or Dresden: you must take example from the young artist, who aspires to visit the great Masters in Florence and in Rome. Till we have discovered some intellectual daguerreotype, which takes off the course of thought, and the form, lineaments, and features of truth, as completely and minutely, as the optical instrument reproduces the sensible object, we must come to the teachers of wisdom to learn wisdom, we must repair to the fountain, and drink there. Portions of it may go from thence to the ends of the earth by means of books; but the fulness is in one place alone. It is in such assemblages and congregations of intellect that books themselves, the masterpieces of human genius, are written, or at least originated.

The principle on which I have been insisting is so obvious, and instances in point are so ready, that I should think it tiresome to proceed with the subject, except that one or two illustrations may serve to explain my own language about it, which may not have done justice to the doctrine which it has been intended to enforce.

For instance, the polished manners and high-bred bearing which are so difficult of attainment, and so strictly personal when attained,—which are so much admired in society, from society are acquired. All that goes to constitute a gentleman,—the carriage, gait, address, gestures, voice; the ease, the self-possession, the courtesy, the power of conversing, the talent of not offending; the lofty principle, the delicacy of thought, the happiness of expression, the taste and propriety, the generosity and forbearance, the candour and consideration, the openness of hand;—these qualities, some of them come by nature, some of them may be found in any rank, some of them are a direct precept of Christianity; but the full assemblage of them, bound up in the unity of an individual character, do we expect they can be learned from books? are they not necessarily acquired, where they are to be found, in high society? The very nature of the case leads us to say so; you cannot fence without an antagonist, nor challenge all comers in disputation before you have supported a thesis; and in like manner, it stands to reason, you cannot learn to converse till you have the world to converse with; you cannot unlearn your natural bashfulness, or awkwardness, or stiffness, or other besetting deformity, till you serve your time in some school of manners. Well, and is it not so in matter of fact? The metropolis, the court, the great houses of the land, are the centres to which at stated times the country comes up, as to shrines of refinement and good taste; and then in due time the country goes back again home, enriched with a portion of the social accomplishments, which those very visits serve to call out and heighten in the gracious dispensers of them. We are unable to conceive how the 'gentlemanlike' can otherwise be maintained; and maintained in this way it is.

And now a second instance: and here, too, I am going to speak without personal experience of the subject I am introducing. I admit I have not been in Parliament, any more than I have figured in the *beau monde;*[2] yet I cannot

2 World of fashion.

but think that statesmanship, as well as high breeding, is learned, not by books, but in certain centres of education. If it be not presumption to say so, Parliament puts a clever man *au courant*[3] with politics and affairs of state in a way surprising to himself. A member of the Legislature, if tolerably observant, begins to see things with new eyes, even though his views undergo no change. Words have a meaning now, and ideas a reality, such as they had not before. He hears a vast deal in public speeches and private conversation, which is never put into print. The bearings of measures and events, the action of parties, and the persons of friends and enemies, are brought out to the man who is in the midst of them with a distinctness, which the most diligent perusal of newspapers will fail to impart to them. It is access to the fountainheads of political wisdom and experience, it is daily intercourse, of one kind or another, with the multitude who go up to them, it is familiarity with business, it is access to the contributions of fact and opinion thrown together by many witnesses from many quarters, which does this for him. However, I need not account for a fact, to which it is sufficient to appeal; that the Houses of Parliament and the atmosphere around them are a sort of University of politics.

As regards the world of science, we find a remarkable instance of the principle which I am illustrating, in the periodical meetings for its advance, which have arisen in the course of the last twenty years, such as the British Association.[4] Such gatherings would to many persons appear at first sight simply preposterous. Above all subjects of study, Science is conveyed, is propagated, by books, or by private teaching; experiments and investigations are conducted in silence; discoveries are made in solitude. What have philosophers to do with festive celebrities, and panegyrical solemnities with mathematical and physical truth? Yet on a closer attention to the subject, it is found that not even scientific thought can dispense with the suggestions, the instruction, the stimulus, the sympathy, the intercourse with mankind on a large scale, which such meetings secure. A fine time of year is chosen, when days are long, skies are bright, the earth smiles, and all nature rejoices; a city or town is taken by turns, of ancient name or modern opulence, where buildings are spacious and hospitality hearty. The novelty of place and circumstance, the excitement of strange, or the refreshment of well-known faces, the majesty of rank or of genius, the amiable charities of men pleased both with themselves and with each other; the elevated spirits, the circulation of thought, the curiosity; the morning sections, the outdoor exercise, the well-furnished, well-earned board, the not ungraceful hilarity, the evening circle;

[3] Well-informed.
[4] The British Association for the Advancement of Science held its first meeting in 1831.

the brilliant lecture, the discussions or collisions or guesses of great men one with another, the narratives of scientific processes, of hopes, disappointments, conflicts, and successes, the splendid eulogistic orations; these and the like constituents of the annual celebration are considered to do something real and substantial for the advance of knowledge which can be done in no other way. Of course they can but be occasional; they answer to the annual Act or Commencement, or Commemoration, of a University, not to its ordinary condition; but they are of a University nature; and I can well believe in their utility. They issue in the promotion of a certain living and, as it were, bodily communication of knowledge from one to another, of a general interchange of ideas, and a comparison and adjustment of science with science, of an enlargement of mind, intellectual and social, of an ardent love of the particular study, which may be chosen by each individual, and a noble devotion to its interests.

Such meetings, I repeat, are but periodical, and only partially represent the idea of a University. The bustle and whirl which are their usual concomitants, are in ill keeping with the order and gravity of earnest intellectual education. We desiderate means of instruction which involve no interruption of our ordinary habits; nor need we seek it long, for the natural course of things brings it about, while we debate over it. In every great country, the metropolis itself becomes a sort of necessary University, whether we will or not. As the chief city is the seat of the court, of high society, of politics, and of law, so as a matter of course is it the seat of letters also; and at this time, for a long term of years, London and Paris are in fact and in operation Universities, though in Paris its famous University is no more, and in London a University scarcely exists except as a board of administration. The newspapers, magazines, reviews, journals, and periodicals of all kinds, the publishing trade, the libraries, museums, and academies there found, the learned and scientific societies, necessarily invest it with the functions of a University; and that atmosphere of intellect, which in a former age hung over Oxford or Bologna or Salamanca, has, with the change of times, moved away to the centre of civil government. Thither come up youths from all parts of the country, the students of law, medicine, and the fine arts, and the *employés* and *attachés* of literature. There they live, as chance determines; and they are satisfied with their temporary home, for they find in it all that was promised to them there. They have not come in vain, as far as their own object in coming is concerned. They have not learned any particular religion, but they have learned their own particular profession well. They have, moreover, become acquainted with the habits, manners, and opinions of their place of sojourn, and done their part in maintaining the tradition of them. We cannot then be without virtual Universities; a metropolis is such: the simple question is, whether the education sought and given should be based on principle, formed upon rule, directed to the highest ends, or left to the random succession of masters and schools, one after another, with a melancholy waste of thought and an extreme hazard of truth.

Religious teaching itself affords us an illustration of our subject to a certain point. It does not, indeed, seat itself merely in centres of the world; this is impossible from the nature of the case. It is intended for the many, not the few; its subject-matter is truth necessary for us, not truth recondite and rare; but it concurs in the principle of a University so far as this, that its great instrument, or rather organ, has ever been that which nature prescribes in all education, the personal presence of a teacher, or, in theological language, Oral Tradition. It is the living voice, the breathing form, the expressive countenance, which preaches, which catechises. Truth, a subtle, invisible, manifold spirit, is poured into the mind of the scholar by his eyes and ears, through his affections, imagination, and reason; it is poured into his mind and is sealed up there in perpetuity, by propounding and repeating it, by questioning and requestioning, by correcting and explaining, by progressing and then recurring to first principles, by all those ways which are implied in the word 'catechising.' In the first ages, it was a work of long time; months, sometimes years, were devoted to the arduous task of disabusing the mind of the incipient Christian of its pagan errors, and of moulding it upon the Christian faith. The Scriptures, indeed, were at hand for the study of those who could avail themselves of them; but St. Irenaeus does not hesitate to speak of whole races, who had been converted to Christianity, without being able to read them. To be unable to read or write was in those times no evidence of want of learning: the hermits of the deserts were, in this sense of the word, illiterate; yet the great St. Anthony, though he knew not letters, was a match in disputation for the learned philosophers who came to try him. Didymus again, the great Alexandrian theologian, was blind. The ancient discipline, called the *Disciplina Arcani*,[5] involved the same principle. The more sacred doctrines of Revelation were not committed to books but passed on by successive tradition. The teaching on the Blessed Trinity and the Eucharist appears to have been so handed down for some hundred years; and when at length reduced to writing, it has filled many folios, yet has not been exhausted.

[5] St. Iraneus was a Greek Father of the Church in the Second century. St. Anthony (250–350), the first Christian monk, founded a monastic order. Didymus (309?–394) was head of the school at Alexandria. The Disciplina Arcani was "The Discipline of the Secret."

But I have said more than enough in illustration; I end as I began;—a University is a place of concourse, whither students come from every quarter for every kind of knowledge. You cannot have the best of every kind every.-where; you must go to some great city or emporium for it. There you have all the choicest productions of nature and art all together, which you find each in its own separate place elsewhere. All the riches of the land, and of the earth, are carried up thither; there are the best markets, and there the best workmen. It is the centre of trade, the supreme court of fashion, the umpire of rival talents, and the standard of things rare and precious. It is the place for seeing galleries of first-rate pictures, and for hearing wonderful voices and performers of transcendent skill. It is the place for great preachers, great orators, great nobles, great statesmen. In the nature of things, greatness and unity go together; excellence implies a centre. And such, for the third or fourth time, is a University; I hope I do not weary out the reader by repeating it. It is the place to which a thousand schools make contributions; in which the intellect may safely range and speculate, sure to find its equal in some antagonist activity, and its judge in the tribunal of truth. It is a place where inquiry is pushed forward, and discoveries verified and perfected, and rash-ness rendered innocuous, and error exposed, by the collision of mind with mind, and knowledge with knowledge. It is the place where the professor becomes eloquent, and is a missionary and a preacher, displaying his science in its most complete and most winning form, pouring it forth with the zeal of enthusiasm, and lighting up his own love of it in the breasts of his hearers. It is the place where the catechist makes good his ground as he goes, treading in the truth day by day into the ready memory, and wedging and tightening it into the expanding reason. It is a place which wins the admiration of the young by its celebrity, kindles the affections of the middle-aged by its beauty, and rivets the fidelity of the old by its associations. It is a seat of wis-dom, a light of the world, a minister of the faith, an Alma Mater of the rising generation. It is this and a great deal more, and demands a somewhat better head and hand than mine to describe it well.

Such is a University in its idea and in its purpose; such in good measure has it before now been in fact. Shall it ever be again? We are going forward in the strength of the Cross, under the patronage of the Blessed Virgin, in the name of St. Patrick, to attempt it.

### I. Suggestions for Discussion:
1. Discuss Newman's definition of a university.
2. Newman's extended definition of a university is built, in part, on a

series of comparisons with other parts of English and European society. Discuss the relationships he establishes in each case.
3. Discuss his use of figurative language for rhetorical effect, particularly in the concluding paragraphs of his essay.

II. **Suggestions for Writing**:
1. Write an essay measuring your own college or university against the standards proposed by Newman.
2. Compare and contrast Newman's ideas about a university with those of T. H. Huxley in "A Liberal Education," p. 237, or Matthew Arnold in "The Duties of a Professor," p. 33.

---

# JOYCE CAROL OATES

## New Heaven and New Earth

---

Joyce Carol Oates (1938–      ), the highly acclaimed American novelist and short-story writer, won the O'Henry Prize Story award in 1967-1968. Among her many novels are *With Shuddering Fall* (1964), *Expensive People* (1968), *Them* (1969), and *Unholy Loves* (1979).

She uses the rhetorical device of identification in the following essay to bring her subject, the next phase of human experience, into sharper focus by exploring what that phase might be, how it will differ from the past and present, and how society will move toward it. The essay is filled with literary and cultural allusions.

---

In spite of current free-roaming terrors in this country, it is really not the case that we are approaching some apocalyptic close. Both those who seem to be awaiting it with excitement and dread and those who are trying heroically to comprehend it in terms of recent American history are mistaking a crisis of transition for a violent end. Even Charles Reich's much maligned and much misinterpreted *The Greening of America,* which was the first systematic attempt to indicate the direction we are surely moving in, focuses much too narrowly upon a single decade in a single nation and, in

spite of its occasional stunning accuracy, is a curiously American product—
that is, it imagines all of history as running up into and somehow culminating
in the United States. Consider Reich's last two sentences:

> . . For one almost convinced that it was necessary to
> accept ugliness and evil, that it was necessary to be a miser of
> dreams, it is an invitation to cry or laugh. For one who thought
> the world was irretrievably encased in metal and plastic and
> sterile stone, it seems a veritable greening of America.

Compare that with the following passage from Teilhard de Chardin's[1]
*The Phenomenon of Man,* a less historical-nationalistic vision:

> In every domain, when anything exceeds a certain measure-
> ment, it suddenly changes its aspect, condition or nature. The
> curve doubles back, the surface contracts to a point, the solid
> disintegrates, the liquid boils, the germ cell divides, intuition
> suddenly bursts on the piled up facts. . . . Critical points have
> been reached, rungs on the ladder, involving a change of state—
> jumps of all sorts *in the course* of development.

Or consider these lines from D. H. Lawrence's[2] poem "Nullus," in
which he is speaking of the private "self" that is Lawrence but also of the
epoch in which this self exists:

> There are said to be creative pauses,
> pauses that are as good as death, empty and dead as death itself.
> And in these awful pauses the evolutionary change takes place.

What appears to be a breaking-down of civilization may well be simply
the breaking-up of old forms by life itself (not an eruption of madness or
self-destruction), a process that is entirely natural and inevitable. Perhaps we
are in the tumultuous but exciting close of a centuries-old kind of consciousness—a few of us like theologians of the medieval church encountering the
unstoppable energy of the Renaissance. What we must avoid is the paranoia
of history's "true believers," who have always misinterpreted a natural,
evolutionary transformation of consciousness as being the violent conclusion
of all of history.

---

[1] Pierre Teilhard de Chardin (1881–1955) was a French Jesuit priest, geologist, philosopher, and theologian.
[2] David Herbert Lawrence (1885–1930), the great English novelist, published his collected poems in 1928.

The God-centered, God-directed world of the Middle Ages was transformed into the complex era we call the Renaissance, but the transition was
as terrifying as it was inevitable, if the innumerable prophecies of doom that
were made at the time are any accurate indication. Shakespeare's most disturbing tragedies—*King Lear* and *Troilus and Cressida*—reflect that communal
anxiety, as do the various expressions of anxiety over the "New Science"
later in the seventeenth century. When we look back into history, we are
amazed, not at the distance that separates one century from another, but at
their closeness, the almost poetic intimacy.

As I see it, the United States is the first nation—though so complex and
unclassifiable an entity almost resists definition as a single unit—to suffer/
enjoy the death throes of the Renaissance. How could it be otherwise, since
our nation is sensitive, energetic, swarming with life, and, beyond any other
developed nation in the world, the most obsessed with its own history and its
own destiny? Approaching a kind of manic stage, in which suppressed voices
are at last being heard, in which *no extreme viewpoint is any longer "extreme,"* the United States is preparing itself for a transformation of "being"
similar to that experienced by individuals as they approach the end of one
segment of their lives and must rapidly, and perhaps desperately, sum up
everything that has gone before.

It is easy to misread the immediate crises, to be frightened by the spontaneous eruptions into consciousness of disparate groups (blacks, women,
youth, "the backlash of the middle class"); it is possible to overlook how the
collective voices of many of our best poets and writers serve to dramatize
and exorcise current American nightmares. Though some of our most brilliant
creative artists are obsessed with disintegration and with the isolated ego, it is
clear by now that they are all, with varying degrees of terror, saying the same
thing—that we are helpless, unconnected with any social or cultural unit,
unable to direct the flow of history, that we cannot effectively communicate.
The effect is almost that of a single voice, as if a communal psychoanalytic
process were taking place. But there does come a time in an individual
writer's experience when he realizes, perhaps against his will, that his voice is
one of many, his fiction one of many fictions, and that all serious fictions are
half-conscious dramatizations of what is going on in the world.

Here is a simple test to indicate whether you are ready for the new
vision of man or whether you will fear and resist it: Imagine you are high in
the air, looking down on a crowded street scene from a height so great that
you cannot make out individual faces but can see only shapes, scurrying figures rather like insects. Your imagination projects you suddenly down into
that mass. You respond with what emotion—dread or joy?

In many of us the Renaissance ideal is still powerful, its voice tyrannical. It declares: *I* will, *I* want, *I* demand, *I* think, *I* am. This voice tells us that
we are not quite omnipotent but must act as if we were, pushing out into a
world of other people or of nature that will necessarily resist us, that will try
to destroy us, and that we must conquer. *I will exist* has meant only *I will
impose my will on others.* To that end man has developed his intellect and
has extended his physical strength by any means possible because, indeed, at
one time the world did have to be conquered. The Renaissance leapt ahead
into its own necessary future, into the development and near perfection of
machines. Machines are not evil, or even "unnatural," but simply extensions
of the human brain. The designs for our machines are no less the product of
our creative imaginations than are works of art, though it might be difficult
for most people—especially artists—to acknowledge this. But a great deal that
is difficult, even outrageous, will have to be acknowledged.

If technology appears to have dehumanized civilization, that is a temporary failing or error—for the purpose of technology is the furthering of
the "human," the bringing to perfection of all the staggering potentialities in
each individual, which are nearly always lost, layered over with biological or
social or cultural crusts. Anyone who imagines that a glorious pastoral world
has been lost, through machines, identifies himself as a child of the city, perhaps a second- or third-generation child of the city. An individual who has
lived close to nature, on a farm, for instance, knows that "natural" man was
never *in* nature; he had to fight nature, at the cost of his own spontaneity
and, indeed, his humanity. It is only through the conscious control of the
"machine" (i.e., through man's brain) that man can transcend the miserable
struggle with nature, whether in the form of sudden devastating hailstorms
that annihilate an entire crop, or minute deadly bacteria in the bloodstream,
or simply the commonplace (but potentially tragic) condition of poor eyesight. It is only through the machine that man can become more human,
more spiritual. Understandably, only a handful of Americans have realized
this obvious fact, since technology seems at present to be villainous. Had our
earliest ancestors been gifted with a box of matches, their first actions would
probably have been destructive—or self-destructive. But we know how beneficial fire has been to civilization.

The Renaissance man invented and brought to near perfection the civilization of the machine. In doing this, he was simply acting out the conscious
and unconscious demand of his time—the demand that man (whether man-in-
the-world or man supposedly superior to worldly interests) master everything
about him, including his own private nature, his own "ego," redefining himself in terms of a conqueror whose territory should be as vast as his own
desire to conquer. The man who "masters" every aspect of his own being,

subduing or obliterating his own natural instincts, leaving nothing to be unknown, uninvestigated, is the ideal of our culture, whether he is an industrial-
ist or a "disinterested" scientist or a literary man. In other words, I see no
difference between the maniacal acquisitiveness of traditional American
capitalists and the meticulous, joyless, ironic manner of many scholars and
writers.

It is certainly time to stop accusing "industry" or "science" or the
"Corporate State" or "Amerika" of being inhuman or antihuman. The exaggerated and suprahuman potency attributed to machines, investing them with
the power of the long-vanquished Devil himself, is amazing. It is also rather
disheartening, if we observe the example of one of our most brilliant writers,
Norman Mailer, who argues—with all the doomed, manic intensity of a late-
medieval churchman resisting the future even when it is upon him—that the
universe can still sensibly be divided into God and Devil, that there can be an
"inorganic" product of the obviously organic mind of man. Mailer (and many
others) exemplifies the old, losing, pitiful Last Stand of the Ego, the Self-
Against-All-Others, the Conqueror, the Highest of all Protoplasms, Namer and
Begetter of all Fictions.

What will the next phase of human experience be? A simple evolution
into a higher humanism, perhaps a kind of intelligent pantheism, in which all
substance in the universe (including the substance fortunate enough to perceive it) is there by equal right.

We have come to the end of, we are satiated with, the "objective,"
valueless philosophies that have always worked to preserve a status quo, however archaic. We are tired of the old dichotomies: Sane/Insane, Normal/
Sick, Black/White, Man/Nature, Victor/Vanquished, and—above all this
Cartesian dualism—I/It. Although once absolutely necessary to get us through
the exploratory, analytical phase of our development as human beings, they
are no longer useful or pragmatic. They are no longer *true*. Far from being
locked inside our own skins, inside the "dungeons" of ourselves, we are now
able to recognize that our minds belong, quite naturally, to a collective
"mind," a mind in which we share everything that is mental, most obviously
language itself, and that the old boundary of the skin is no boundary at all
but a membrane connecting the inner and outer experiences of existence. Our
intelligence, our wit, our cleverness, our unique personalities—all are simultaneously "our own" possessions and the world's. This has always been a
mystical vision, but more and more in our time it is becoming a rational
truth. It is no longer the private possession of a Blake, a Whitman,[3] or a
Lawrence, but the public, articulate offering of a Claude Lévi-Strauss, to

[3] William Blake (1752–1827) and Walt Whitman (1819–1892) were visionary poets.

whom anthropology is "part of a cosmology" and whose humanism is one that sees everything in the universe, including man, in its own place. It is the lifelong accumulative statement of Abraham Maslow, the humanist psychologist who extended the study of psychology from the realm of the disordered into that of the normal and the "more-than-normal," including people who would once have been termed mystics and been dismissed as irrational. It is the unique, fascinating voice of Buckminster Fuller, who believes that "human minds and brains may be essential in the total design" of the universe. And it is the abrasive argument of R. D. Laing, the Freudian/post-Freudian mystic, who has denied the medical and legal distinctions between "normal" and "abnormal" and has set out not only to experience but to articulate a metaphysical "illumination" whereby self and other become joined. All these are men of genius, whose training has been rigorously scientific. That they are expressing views once considered the exclusive property of mystics proves that the old dichotomy of Reason/Intuition has vanished or is vanishing.

As with all dichotomies, it will be transcended—not argued away, not battered into silence. The energies wasted on the old debates—Are we rational? Are we 90 percent Unconscious Impulses?—will be utilized for higher and more worthy human pursuits. Instead of hiding our most amazing, mysterious, and inexplicable experiences, we will learn to articulate and share them; instead of insisting upon rigid academic or intellectual categories (for instance, that "science fiction" is different from other fiction, or less traditional than the very recent "realistic novel"), we will see how naturally they flow into one another, supporting and explaining each other. Yesterday's wildly ornate, obscure, poetic prophecies evolve into today's calm statements of fact.

The vision of a new, higher humanism or pantheism is not irrational but is a logical extension of what we now know. It may frighten some of us because it challenges the unquestioned assumptions that we have always held. But these assumptions were never *ours*. We never figured them out, never discovered them for ourselves; we inherited them from the body of knowledge created by our men of genius. Now men of genius, such as British physicist/philosopher Sir James Jeans, are saying newer, deeper things:

Today there is a wide measure of agreement, which on the physical side of science approaches almost to unanimity, that the stream of knowledge is heading toward a non-mechanical reality; the universe begins to look more like a great thought than like a great machine. Mind no longer appears as an accidental intruder into the realm of matter; we are beginning to suspect that we ought rather to hail it as the creator and governor of the realm of matter. . . .

Everywhere, suddenly, we hear the prophetic voice of Nietzsche[4] once again, saying that man must overcome himself, that he must interpret and create the universe. (Nietzsche was never understood until now, until the world caught up with him, or approached him.) In such a world, which belongs to consciousness, there can be no distracting of energies from the need to push forward, to synthesize, to converge, to make a unity out of ostensible diversity. But too facile optimism is as ultimately distracting as the repetitive nihilism and despair we have inherited from the early part of this century. An absolutely honest literature, whether fiction or nonfiction, must dramatize for us the complexities of this epoch, showing us how deeply related we are to one another, how deeply we act out, even in our apparently secret dreams, the communal crises of our world. If demons are reawakened and allowed to run loose across the landscape of suburban shopping malls and parks, it is only so that their symbolic values—wasteful terror, despair, entropy—can be recognized. If all other dichotomies are ultimately transcended, there must still be the tension between a healthy acceptance of change and a frightened, morbid resistance to change.

The death throes of the old values are everywhere around us, but they are not at all the same thing as the death throes of particular human beings. We can transform ourselves, overleap ourselves beyond even our most flamboyant estimations. A conversion is always imminent; one cannot revert back to a lower level of consciousness. The "conversion" of the I-centered personality into a higher, or transcendental, personality cannot be an artificially, externally enforced event; it must be a natural event. It is surely as natural as the upward growth of a plant—if the plant's growth is not impeded. It has nothing to do with drugs, with the occult, with a fashionable cultivation of Eastern mysticism (not at all suitable for us in the West—far too passive, too life-denying, too ascetic); it has nothing to do with political beliefs. It is not Marxist, not Communist, not Socialist, not willing to align itself with any particular ideology. If anything, it is a flowering of the democratic ideal, a community of equals, but not a community mobilized against the rest of the world, not a unity arising out of primitive paranoia.

In the Sixties and at present we hear a very discordant music. We have got to stop screaming at one another. We have got to bring into harmony the various discordant demands, voices, stages of personality. Those more ad-

---

[4] Friederich Wilhelm Nietzsche (1844–1900) affirmed the notion of the superman.

vanced must work to transform the rest, by being, themselves, models of sanity and integrity. The angriest of the ecologists must stop blaming industry for having brought to near perfection the implicit demands of society, as if anyone in our society—especially at the top—has ever behaved autonomously, unshaped by that society and its history. The optimism of *The Greening of America* seems to me a bit excessive or at least premature. There is no doubt that the future—the new consciousness—is imminent, but it may take generations to achieve it. The rapidly condensed vision, the demand for immediate gratification, is, once again, typically (and sadly) American. But, though the achievement of Reich's vision is much farther off than he seems to think, it is an inevitable one, and those of us who will probably not share personally in a transformed world can, in a way, anticipate it now, almost as if experiencing it now. If we are reasonably certain of the conclusion of a novel (especially one we have ourselves imagined), we can endure and even enjoy the intermediary chapters that move us toward that conclusion.

One of the unfortunate aspects of American intellectual life has been the nearly total divorce of academic philosophy from the issues of a fluid, psychic social reality. There are obvious reasons for this phenomenon, too complex to consider at the moment. But the book that needs to be written about the transformation of America cannot really be written by anyone lacking a thorough knowledge of where we have been and where we are right now, in terms of an intellectual development that begins and ends with the faculties of the mind. We require the meticulous genius of a Kant, a man of humility who is awakened from some epoch-induced "slumber" to synthesize vast exploratory fields of knowledge, to write the book that is the way into the future for us.

This essay, totally nonacademic in its lyric disorganization, in its bringing together of voices that, for all their differences, seem to be saying one thing, is intended only to suggest—no, really, to make a plea for—the awakening of that someone's slumber, the rejection of the positivist-linguist-"naming" asceticism that has made American philosophy so disappointing. We need a tradition similar to that in France, where the role of "philosopher" is taken naturally by men of genius who can address themselves to varied groups of people—scientists, writers, artists, and the public itself. Our highly educated and highly cultivated reading public is starved for books like *The Greening of America.* We have an amazingly fertile but somehow separate nation of writers and poets, living dreamily inside a culture but no more than symbiotically related to it. Yet these writers and poets are attempting to define that culture, to "act it out," to somehow make sense of it. The novel is the most human of all art forms—there are truths we can get nowhere else but in the novel—but now our crucial need is for something else. We need a large, generous, meticulous work that will synthesize our separate but deeply similar voices, one that will climb up out of the categories of "rational" and "irrational" to show why the consciousness of the future will feel joy, not dread, at the total rejection of the Renaissance ideal, the absorption into the psychic stream of the universe.

Lawrence asks in his strange poem "New Heaven and Earth" a question that seems to me parallel with Yeat's[5] famous question in the sonnet "Leda and the Swan." In the Yeats poem mortal woman is raped by an immortal force, and, yes, this will and must happen; this cannot be escaped. But the point is: Did she put on his knowledge *with* his power, before the terrifying contact was broken? Lawrence speaks of mysterious "green streams" that flow from the new world (our everyday world—seen with new eyes) and asks, ". . . what are they?" What are the conversions that await us?

### I. Suggestions for Discussion:
1. Discuss Oates's statement that the United States is the first nation to suffer/enjoy the death throes of the Renaissance.
2. What does she believe will be the next phase of human experience? Discuss whether or not you agree.
3. Examine her use of literary references. How do they help to support her thesis?

### II. Suggestions for Writing:
1. Write an essay stating your vision of the future of humanity.
2. From your own experience, observations, or reading, demonstrate that it is easy to misread the significance of an immediate crisis.

---

# GEORGE ORWELL

## Politics and the English Language

---

George Orwell (1903-1950) was the pen name of Eric Blair, an Englishman who served for five years as a police officer in India and later fought on the Republican side in the Spanish Civil War.

[5] William Butler Yeats (1865-1939), the Irish poet and patriot, published "Leda and the Swan" in 1928.

He is best known for two allegorical novels, *Animal Farm* (1945) and *1984* (1949). The selection that follows is taken from his collection of essays, *Shooting an Elephant and Other Essays* (1945).

In this essay, Orwell considers language as an instrument for expressing, and not for concealing or preventing, thought. He classifies various problems with contemporary usage, uses examples and metaphors to illustrate his points, and offers five rules for improving writing.

---

Most people who bother with the matter at all would admit that the English language is in a bad way, but it is generally assumed that we cannot by conscious action do anything about it. Our civilization is decadent and our language—so the argument runs—must inevitably share in the general collapse. It follows that any struggle against the abuse of language is a sentimental archaism, like preferring candles to electric light or hansom cabs to aeroplanes. Underneath this lies the half-conscious belief that language is a natural growth and not an instrument which we shape for our own purposes.

Now, it is clear that the decline of a language must ultimately have political and economic causes: it is not due simply to the bad influence of this or that individual writer. But an effect can become a cause, reinforcing the original cause and producing the same effect in an intensified form, and so on indefinitely. A man may take to drink because he feels himself to be a failure, and then fail all the more completely because he drinks. It is rather the same thing that is happening to the English language. It becomes ugly and inaccurate because our thoughts are foolish, but the slovenliness of our language makes it easier for us to have foolish thoughts. The point is that the process is reversible. Modern English, especially written English, is full of bad habits which spread by imitation and which can be avoided if one is willing to take the necessary trouble. If one gets rid of these habits one can think more clearly, and to think clearly is a necessary first step towards political regeneration: so that the fight against bad English is not frivolous and is not the exclusive concern of professional writers. I will come back to this presently, and I hope that by that time the meaning of what I have said here will have become clearer. Meanwhile, here are five specimens of the English language as it is now habitually written.

These five passages have not been picked out because they are especially bad—I could have quoted far worse if I had chosen—but because they illustrate various of the mental vices from which we now suffer. They are a little below the average, but are fairly representative samples. I number them so that I can refer back to them when necessary:

1. I am not, indeed, sure whether it is not true to say that the Milton who once seemed not unlike a seventeenth-century Shelley had not become, out of an experience ever more bitter in each year, more alien [*sic*] to the founder of that Jesuit sect which nothing could induce him to tolerate.

PROFESSOR HAROLD LASKI (Essay in *Freedom of Expression*).

2. Above all, we cannot play ducks and drakes with a native battery of idioms which prescribes such egregious collocations of vocables as the Basic *put up with* for *tolerate* or *put at a loss* for *bewilder*.

PROFESSOR LANCELOT HOGBEN (*Interglossa*).

3. On the one side we have the free personality: by definition it is not neurotic, for it has neither conflict nor dream. Its desires, such as they are, are transparent, for they are just what institutional approval keeps in the forefront of consciousness; another institutional pattern would alter their number and intensity; there is little in them that is natural, irreducible, or culturally dangerous. But *on the other side,* the social bond itself is nothing but the mutual reflection of these self-secure integrities. Recall the definition of love. Is not this the very picture of a small academic? Where is there a place in this hall of mirrors for either personality or fraternity?

ESSAY ON PSYCHOLOGY in *Politics* (New York).

4. All the "best people" from the gentlemen's clubs, and all the frantic fascist captains, united in common hatred of Socialism and bestial horror of the rising tide of the mass revolutionary movement, have turned to acts of provocation, to foul incendiarism, to medieval legends of poisoned wells, to legalize their own destruction of proletarian organizations, and rouse the agitated petty-bourgeoisie to chauvinistic fervor on behalf of the fight against the revolutionary way out of the crisis.

COMMUNIST PAMPHLET.

5. If a new spirit *is* to be infused into this old country, there is one thorny and contentious reform which must be tackled, and that is the humanization and galvanization of the B.B.C. Timidity here will bespeak canker and atrophy of the soul. The heart of Britain may be sound and of strong beat, for instance, but the British lion's roar at present is like that of Bottom in Shakespeare's *Midsummer Night's Dream*—as gentle as

any sucking dove. A virile new Britain cannot continue indefinitely to be traduced in the eyes or rather ears, of the world
by the effete languors of Langham Place, brazenly masquerading
as "standard English." When the voice of Britain is heard at nine
o'clock, better far and infinitely less ludicrous to hear aitches
honestly dropped than the present priggish, inflated, inhibited,
school-ma'amish arch braying of blameless bashful mewing
maidens!

LETTER in *Tribune.*

Each of these passages has faults of its own, but, quite apart from
avoidable ugliness, two qualities are common to all of them. The first is stale-
ness of imagery; the other is lack of precision. The writer either has a meaning
and cannot express it, or he inadvertently says something else, or he is almost
indifferent as to whether his words mean anything or not. This mixture of
vagueness and sheer incompetence is the most marked characteristic of
modern English prose, and especially of any kind of political writing. As soon
as certain topics are raised, the concrete melts into the abstract and no one
seems able to think of turns of speech that are not hackneyed: prose consists
less and less of *words* chosen for the sake of their meaning, and more and
more of *phrases* tacked together like the sections of a prefabricated henhouse. I list below, with notes and examples, various of the tricks by means
of which the work of prose-construction is habitually dodged:

## Dying Metaphors

A newly invented metaphor assists thought by evoking a visual image,
while on the other hand a metaphor which is technically "dead" (e.g. *iron
resolution*) has in effect reverted to being an ordinary word and can generally
be used without loss of vividness. But in between these two classes there is a
huge dump of worn-out metaphors which have lost all evocative power and
are merely used because they save people the trouble of inventing phrases for
themselves. Examples are: *Ring the changes on, take up the cudgels for, toe
the line, ride roughshod over, stand shoulder to shoulder with, play into the
hands of, no axe to grind, grist to the mill, fishing in troubled waters, on the
order of the day, Achilles' heel, swan song, hotbed.* Many of these are used
without knowledge of their meaning (what is a "rift," for instance?), and incompatible metaphors are frequently mixed, a sure sign that the writer is not
interested in what he is saying. Some metaphors now current have been
twisted out of their original meaning without those who use them even being

aware of the fact. For example, *toe the line* is sometimes written *tow the line.*
Another example is *the hammer and the anvil,* now always used with the
implication that the anvil gets the worst of it. In real life it is always the anvil
that breaks the hammer, never the other way about: a writer who stopped to
think what he was saying would be aware of this, and would avoid perverting
the original phrase.

## Operators or Verbal False Limbs

These save the trouble of picking out appropriate verbs and nouns, and
at the same time pad each sentence with extra syllables which give it an appearance of symmetry. Characteristic phrases are *render inoperative, militate
against, make contact with, be subjected to, give rise to, give grounds for,
have the effect of, play a leading part (role) in, make itself felt, take effect,
exhibit a tendency to, serve the purpose of, etc., etc.* The keynote is the
elimination of simple verbs. Instead of being a single word, such as *break,
stop, spoil, mend, kill,* a verb becomes *a phrase,* made up of a noun or adjective tacked on to some general-purpose verb such as *prove, serve, form, play,
render.* In addition, the passive voice is wherever possible used in preference
to the active, and noun constructions are used instead of gerunds (*by examination of* instead of *by examining*). The range of verbs is further cut down by
means of the *-ize* and *de-* formations, and the banal statements are given an
appearance of profundity by means of the *not un-* formation. Simple con-
junctions and prepositions are replaced by such phrases as *with respect to,
having regard to, the fact that, by dint of, in view of, in the interests of, on
the hypothesis that;* and the ends of sentences are saved from anticlimax by
such resounding common-places as *greatly to be desired, cannot be left out of
account, a development to be expected in the near future, deserving of serious consideration, brought to a satisfactory conclusion,* and so on and so
forth.

## Pretentious Diction

Words like *phenomenon, element, individual* (as noun), *objective, cate-
gorical, effective, virtual, basic, primary, promote, constitute, exhibit, exploit, utilize, eliminate, liquidate,* are used to dress up simple statements and
give an air of scientific impartiality to biased judgments. Adjectives like
*epoch-making, epic, historic, unforgettable, triumphant, age-old, inevitable,*

*inexorable, veritable,* are used to dignify the sordid processes of international politics, while writing that aims at glorifying war usually takes on an archaic color, its characteristic words being: *realm, throne, chariot, mailed fist, trident, sword, shield, buckler, banner, jackboot, clarion.* Foreign words and expressions such as *cul de sac, ancien régime, deus ex machina, mutatis mutandis, status quo, gleichschaltung, weltanschauung,* are used to give an air of culture and elegance. Except for the useful abbreviations *i.e., e.g.,* and *etc.,* there is no real need for any of the hundreds of foreign phrases now current in English. Bad writers, and especially scientific, political and sociological writers, are nearly always haunted by the notion that Latin or Greek words are grander than Saxon ones, and unnecessary worlds like *expedite, ameliorate, predict, extraneous, deracinated, clandestine, subaqueous* and hundreds of others constantly gain ground from their Anglo-Saxon opposite numbers.[1] The jargon peculiar to Marxist writing (*hyena, hangman, cannibal, petty bourgeois, these gentry, lacquey, flunkey, mad dog, White Guard,* etc.) consists largely of words and phrases translated from Russian, German or French; but the normal way of coining a new word is to use a Latin or Greek root with the appropriate affix and, where necessary, the *-ize* formation. It is often easier to make up words of this kind (*deregionalize, impermissible, extramarital, non-fragmentary* and so forth) than to think up the English words that will cover one's meaning. The result, in general, is an increase in slovenliness and vagueness.

## Meaningless Words

In certain kinds of writing, particularly in art criticism and literary criticism, it is normal to come across long passages which are almost completely lacking in meaning.[2] Words like *romantic, plastic, values, human, dead, sentimental, natural, vitality,* as used in art criticism, are strictly meaningless, in the sense that they not only do not point to any discoverable object, but are

---

[1] An interesting illustration of this is the way in which the English flower names which were in use till very recently are being ousted by Greek ones, *snapdragon* becoming *antirrhinum, forget-me-not* becoming *myosotis,* etc. It is hard to see any practical reason for this change of fashion: it is probably due to an instinctive turning-away from the more homely word and a vague feeling that the Greek word is scientific.

[2] Example: "Comfort's catholicity of perception and image, strangely Whitmanesque in range, almost the exact opposite in aesthetic compulsion, continues to evoke that trembling atmospheric accumulative hinting at a cruel, an inexorably serene timelessness. ... Wrey Gardiner scores by aiming at simple bull's-eyes with precision. Only they are not so simple, and through this contented sadness runs more than the surface bittersweet of resignation." (*Poetry Quarterly.*)

hardly ever expected to do so by the reader. When one critic writes, "The outstanding feature of Mr. X's work is its living quality," while another writes, "The immediately striking thing about Mr. X's work is its peculiar deadness," the reader accepts this as a simple difference of opinion. If words like *black* and *white* were involved, instead of the jargon words *dead* and *living,* he would see at once that language was being used in an improper way. Many political words are similarly abused. The word *Fascism* has now no meaning except in so far as it signifies "something not desirable." The words *democracy, socialism, freedom, patriotic, realistic, justice,* have each of them several different meanings which cannot be reconciled with one another. In the case of a word like *democracy,* not only is there no agreed definition, but the attempt to make one is resisted from all sides. It is almost universally felt that when we call a country democratic we are praising it: consequently the defenders of every kind of régime claim that it is a democracy, and fear that they might have to stop using the word if it were tied down to any one meaning. Words of this kind are often used in a consciously dishonest way. That is, the person who uses them has his own private definition, but allows his hearer to think he means something quite different. Statements like *Marshal Pétain was a true patriot, The Sovier Press is the freest in the world, The Catholic Church is opposed to persecution,* are almost always made with intent to deceive. Other words used in variable meanings, in most cases more or less dishonestly, are: *class, totalitarian, science, progressive, reactionary, bourgeois, equality.*

Now that I have made this catalogue of swindles and perversions, let me give another example of the kind of writing that they lead to. This time it must of its nature be an imaginary one. I am going to translate a passage of good English into modern English of the worst sort. Here is a well-known verse from *Ecclesiastes:*

> I returned and saw under the sun, that the race is not to the swift, nor the battle to the strong, neither yet bread to the wise, nor yet riches to men of understanding, nor yet favour to men of skill; but time and chance happeneth to them all.

Here it is in modern English:

> Objective consideration of contemporary phenomena compels the conclusion that success or failure in competitive activities exhibits no tendency to be commensurate with innate capacity, but that a considerable element of the unpredictable must invariably be taken into account.

This is a parody, but not a very gross one. Exhibit (3), above, for instance, contains several patches of the same kind of English. It will be seen that I have not made a full translation. The beginning and ending of the sentence follow the original meaning fairly closely, but in the middle the concrete illustrations—race, battle, bread—dissolve into the vague phrase "success or failure in competitive activities." This had to be so, because no modern writer of the kind I am discussing—no one capable of using phrases like "objective consideration of contemporary phenomena"—would ever tabulate his thoughts in that precise and detailed way. The whole tendency of modern prose is away from concreteness. Now analyze these two sentences a little more closely. The first contains forty-nine words but only sixty syllables, and all its words are those of everyday life. The second contains thirty-eight words of ninety syllables: eighteen of its words are from Latin roots, and one from Greek. The first sentence contains six vivid images, and only one phrase ("time and chance") that could be called vague. The second contains not a single fresh, arresting phrase, and in spite of its ninety syllables it gives only a shortened version of the meaning contained in the first. Yet without a doubt it is the second kind of sentence that is gaining ground in modern English. I do not want to exaggerate. This kind of writing is not yet universal, and outcrops of simplicity will occur here and there in the worst-written page. Still, if you or I were told to write a few lines on the uncertainty of human fortunes, we should probably come much nearer to my imaginary sentence than to the one from *Ecclesiastes*.

As I have tried to show, modern writing at its worst does not consist in picking out words for the sake of their meaning and inventing images in order to make the meaning clearer. It consists in gumming together long strips of words which have already been set in order by someone else, and making the results presentable by sheer humbug. The attraction of this way of writing is that it is easy. It is easier—even quicker, once you have the habit—to say *In my opinion it is not an unjustifiable assumption that* than to say *I think*. If you use ready-made phrases, you not only don't have to hunt about for words; you also don't have to bother with the rhythms of your sentences, since these phrases are generally so arranged as to be more or less euphonious. When you are composing in a hurry—when you are dictating to a stenographer, for instance, or making a public speech—it is natural to fall into a pretentious, Latinized style. Tags like *a consideration which we should do well to bear in mind* or *a conclusion to which all of us would readily assent* will save many a sentence from coming down with a bump. By using stale metaphors, similes and idioms, you save much mental effort, at the cost of leaving your meaning vague, not only for your reader but for yourself. This is the significance of mixed metaphors. The sole aim of a metaphor is to call up a visual image. When these images clash—as in *The Fascist octopus has sung its swan song, the jackboot is thrown into the melting pot*—it can be taken as certain that the writer is not seeing a mental image of the objects he is naming; in other words he is not really thinking. Look again at the examples I gave at the beginning of this essay. Professor Laski (1) uses five negatives in fifty-three words. One of these is superfluous, making nonsense of the whole passage, and in addition there is the slip *alien* for *akin,* making further nonsense, and several avoidable pieces of clumsiness which increase the general vagueness. Professor Hogben (2) plays ducks and drakes with a battery which is able to write prescriptions, and, while disapproving of the everyday phrase *put up with,* is unwilling to look *egregious* up in the dictionary and see what it means; (3), if one takes an uncharitable attitude towards it, is simply meaningless: probably one could work out its intended meaning by reading the whole of the article in which it occurs. In (4), the writer knows more or less what he wants to say, but an accumulation of stale phrases chokes him like tea leaves blocking a sink. In (5), words and meaning have almost parted company. People who write in this manner usually have a general emotional meaning—they dislike one thing and want to express solidarity with another—but they are not interested in the detail of what they are saying. A scrupulous writer, in every sentence that he writes, will ask himself at least four questions, thus: What am I trying to say? What words will express it? What image or idiom will make it clearer? Is this image fresh enough to have an effect? And he will probably ask himself two more: Could I put it more shortly? Have I said anything that is avoidably ugly? But you are not obliged to go to all this trouble. You can shirk it by simply throwing your mind open and letting the ready-made phrases come crowding in. They will construct your sentences for you—even think your thoughts for you, to a certain extent—and at need they will perform the important service of partially concealing your meaning even from yourself. It is at this point that the special connection between politics and the debasement of language becomes clear.

In our time it is broadly true that political writing is bad writing. Where it is not true, it will generally be found that the writer is some kind of rebel, expressing his private opinions and not a "party line." Orthodoxy, of whatever color, seems to demand a lifeless, imitative style. The political dialects to be found in pamphlets, leading articles, manifestos, White Papers and the speeches of under-secretaries do, of course, vary from party to party, but they are all alike in that one almost never finds in them a fresh, vivid, homemade turn of speech. When one watches some tired hack on the platform mechanically repeating the familiar phrases—*bestial atrocities, iron heel, bloodstained tyranny, free peoples of the world, stand shoulder to shoulder—* one often has a curious feeling that one is not watching a live human being but some kind of dummy: a feeling which suddenly becomes stronger at moments when the light catches the speaker's spectacles and turns them into blank discs which seem to have no eyes behind them. And this is not altogether fanciful. A speaker who uses that kind of phraseology has gone some distance towards turning himself into a machine. The appropriate noises are coming out of his larynx, but his brain is not involved as it would be if he were choosing his words for himself. If the speech he is making is one that he is accustomed to make over and over again, he may be almost unconscious of what he is saying, as one is when one utters the responses in church. And this reduced state of consciousness, if not indispensable, is at any rate favorable to political conformity.

In our time, political speech and writing are largely the defense of the indefensible. Things like the continuance of British rule in India, the Russian purges and deportations, the dropping of the atom bombs on Japan, can indeed be defended, but only by arguments which are too brutal for most people to face, and which do not square with the professed aims of political parties. Thus political language has to consist largely of euphemism, question-begging and sheer cloudy vagueness. Defenseless villages are bombarded from the air, the inhabitants driven out into the countryside, the cattle machine-gunned, the huts set on fire with incendiary bullets: this is called *pacification.* Millions of peasants are robbed of their farms and sent trudging along the roads with no more than they can carry: this is called *transfer of population* or *rectification of frontiers.* People are imprisoned for years without trial, or shot in the back of the neck or sent to die of scurvy in Arctic lumber camps: this is called *elimination of unreliable elements.* Such phraseology is needed if one wants to name things without calling up mental pictures of them. Consider for instance some comfortable English professor defending Russian totalitarianism. He cannot say outright, "I believe in killing off your opponents when you can get good results by doing so." Probably, therefore, he will say something like this:

> While freely conceding that the Soviet regime exhibits certain features which the humanitarian may be inclined to deplore, we must, I think, agree that a certain curtailment of the right to political opposition is an unavoidable concomitant of transitional periods, and that the rigors which the Russian people have been called upon to undergo have been amply justified in the sphere of concrete achievement.

The inflated style is itself a kind of euphemism. A mass of Latin words falls upon the facts like soft snow, blurring the outlines and covering up all the details. The great enemy of clear language is insincerity. When there is a gap between one's real and one's declared aims, one turns as it were instinctively to long words and exhausted idioms, like a cuttlefish squirting out ink. In our age there is no such thing as "keeping out of politics." All issues are political issues, and politics itself is a mass of lies, evasions, folly, hatred and schizophrenia. When the general atmosphere is bad, language must suffer. I should expect to find—this is a guess which I have not sufficient knowledge to verify—that the German, Russian and Italian languages have all deteriorated in the last ten to fifteen years, as a result of dictatorship.

But if thought corrupts language, language can also corrupt thought. A bad usage can spread by tradition and imitation, even among people who should and do know better. The debased language that I have been discussing is in some ways very convenient. Phrases like *a not unjustifiable assumption, leaves much to be desired, would serve no good purpose, a consideration which we should do well to bear in mind,* are a continuous temptation, a packet of aspirins always at one's elbow. Look back through this essay, and for certain you will find that I have again and again committed the very faults I am protesting against. By this morning's post I have received a pamphlet dealing with conditions in Germany. The author tells me that he "felt impelled" to write it. I open it at random, and here is almost the first sentence that I see: "[The Allies] have an opportunity not only of achieving a radical transformation of Germany's social and political structure in such a way as to avoid a nationalistic reaction in Germany itself, but at the same time of laying the foundations of a cooperative and unified Europe." You see, he "feels impelled" to write—feels, presumably, that he has something new to say—and yet his words, like cavalry horses answering the bugle, group themselves automatically into the familiar dreary pattern. This invasion of one's mind by ready-made phrases (*lay the foundations, achieve a radical transformation*) can only be prevented if one is constantly on guard against them, and every such phrase anaesthetizes a portion of one's brain.

I said earlier that the decadence of our language is probably curable. Those who deny this would argue, if they produced an argument at all, that language merely reflects existing social conditions, and that we cannot influence its development by any direct tinkering with words and constructions. So far as the general tone or spirit of a language goes, this may be true, but it is not true in detail. Silly words and expressions have often disappeared, not through any evolutionary process but owing to the conscious action of a minority. Two recent examples were *explore every avenue* and *leave no stone unturned,* which were killed by the jeers of a few journalists. There is a long list of flyblown metaphors which could  similarly be got rid of it if enough people would interest themselves in the job; and it should also be possible to laugh the *not un-* formation out of existence,[3] to reduce the amount of Latin and Greek in the average sentence, to drive out foreign phrases and strayed scientific words, and, in general, to make pretentiousness unfashionable. But all these are minor points. The defense of the English language implies more than this, and perhaps it is best to start by saying what it does *not* imply.

To begin with it has nothing to do with archaism, with the salvaging of obsolete words and turns of speech, or with the setting up of a "standard English" which must never be departed from. On the contrary, it is especially concerned with the scrapping of every word or idiom which has outworn its usefulness. It has nothing to do with correct grammar and syntax, which are of no importance so long as one makes one's meaning clear, or with the avoidance of Americanisms, or with having what is called a "good prose style." On the other hand it is not concerned with fake simplicity and the attempt to make written English colloquial. Nor does it even imply in every case preferring the Saxon word to the Latin one, though it does imply using the fewest and shortest words that will cover one's meaning. What is above all needed is to let the meaning choose the word, and not the other way about. In prose, the worst thing one can do with words is to surrender to them. When you think of a concrete object, you think wordlessly, and then, if you want to describe the thing you have been visualizing you probably hunt about till you find the exact words that seem to fit it. When you think of something abstract you are more inclined to use words from the start, and unless you make a conscious effort to prevent it, the existing dialect will come rushing in and do the job for you, at the expense of blurring or even changing your meaning. Probably it is better to put off using words as long as possible and get one's meaning as clear as one can through pictures or sensations. Afterwards one can choose—not simply *accept*—the phrases that will best cover the meaning, and then switch round and decide what impression one's words are likely to make on another person. This last effort of the mind cuts out all stale or mixed images, all prefabricated phrases, needless repetitions, and humbug and vagueness generally. But one can often be in doubt about the effect of a word or a phrase, and one needs rules that one can rely on when instinct fails. I think the following rules will cover most cases:

---

[3] One can cure oneself of the *not un-* formation by memorizing this sentence: *A not unblack dog was chasing a not unsmall rabbit across a not ungreen field.*

(i)    Never use a metaphor, simile or other figure of speech which you are used to seeing in print.

(ii)   Never use a long word where a short one will do.

(iii)  If it is possible to cut a word out, always cut it out.

(iv)  Never use the passive where you can use the active.

(v)   Never use a foreign phrase, a scientific word or a jargon word if you can think of an everyday English equivalent.

(vi)  Break any of these rules sooner than say anything outright barbarous.

These rules sound elementary, and so they are, but they demand a deep change of attitude in anyone who has grown used to writing in the style now fashionable. One could keep all of them and still write bad English, but one could not write the kind of stuff that I quoted in those five specimens at the beginning of this article.

I have not here been considering the literary use of language, but merely language as an instrument for expressing and not for concealing or preventing thought. Stuart Chase and others have come near to claiming that all abstract words are meaningless, and have used this as a pretext for advocating a kind of political quietism. Since you don't know what Fascism is, how can you struggle against Fascism? One need not swallow such absurdities as this, but one ought to recognize that the present political chaos is connected with the decay of language, and that one can probably bring about some improvement by starting at the verbal end. If you simplify your English, you are freed from the worst follies of orthodoxy. You cannot speak any of the necessary dialects, and when you make a stupid remark its stupidity will be obvious, even to yourself. Political language—and with variations this is true of all political parties, from Conservatives to Anarchists—is designed to make lies sound truthful and murder respectable, and to give an appearance of solidity to pure wind. One cannot change this all in a moment, but one can at least change one's own habits, and from time to time one can even, if one jeers loudly enough, send some worn-out and useless phrase—some *jackboot, Achilles' heel, hotbed, melting pot, acid test, veritable inferno* or other lump of verbal refuse—into the dustbin where it belongs.

## I. Suggestions for Discussion:

  1. In class, rewrite several of Orwell's examples of bad writing.
  2. Which of the bad habits Orwell discusses are you conscious of in your own writing?
  3. Discuss Orwell's six rules for improving writing.

**II. Suggestions for Writing:**
1. Write an essay classifying and analyzing your own list of examples of bad writing culled from current newspapers and magazines.
2. Compare and contrast Orwell's advice on writing with that of William Hazlitt in *On Familiar Style*, p. 223.

---

# THOMAS PAINE

## Thoughts on the Present State of American Affairs

### from *Common Sense*

---

Thomas Paine (1737–1809), encouraged by Benjamin Franklin, came from England to America in 1774. His *Common Sense* (1776) is generally agreed to have had more influence than any other single force on the popular decision in favor of national independence. Also a defender of the French Revolution, he published *The Rights of Man* (1791 and 1792) and, in 1793, *The Age of Reason.*

Despite his claim to "offer nothing more than simple facts, plain arguments, and common sense," Paine displays in the following selection from *Common Sense* a mastery of an inflammatory, highly rhetorical style. His essay eloquently persuades American colonists to fight for independence against the British.

---

In the following pages I offer nothing more than simple facts, plain arguments, and common sense: and have no other preliminaries to settle with the reader, than that he will divest himself of prejudice and prepossession, and suffer his reason and his feeling to determine for themselves: that he will put on, or rather that he will not put off, the true character of a man, and generously enlarge his views beyond the present day.

Volumes have been written on the subject of the struggle between England and America. Men of all ranks have embarked in the controversy, from different motives, and with various designs; but all have been ineffectual, and the period of debate is closed. Arms as the last resource decide the contest; the appeal was the choice of the King, and the continent has accepted the challenge.

It hath been reported of the late Mr. Pelham[1] (who tho' an able minister was not without his faults) that on his being attacked in the House of Commons on the score that his measures were only of a temporary kind, replied, "*they will last my time.*" Should a thought so fatal and unmanly possess the Colonies in the present contest, the name of Ancestors will be remembered by future generations with detestation.

The sun never shined on a cause of greater worth. 'Tis not the affair of a city, a county, a province, or a kingdom; but of a continent—of at least one eighth part of the habitable globe. 'Tis not the concern of a day, a year, or an age; posterity are virtually involved in the contest, and will be more or less affected even to the end of time by the proceedings now. Now is the seed-time of continental union, faith and honor. The least fracture now, will be like a name engraved with the point of a pin on the tender rind of a young oak; the wound would enlarge with the tree, and posterity read it in full grown characters.

By referring the matter from argument to arms, a new aera for politics is struck—a new method of thinking has arisen. All plans, proposals, etc. prior to the nineteenth of April, i.e. to the commencement of hostilities, are like the almanacs of last year; which though proper then, are superseded and useless now. Whatever was advanced by the advocates on either side of the question then, terminated in one and the same point, viz. a union with Great Britain; the only difference between the parties was the method of effecting it; the one proposing force, the other friendship; but it has so far happened that the first has failed, and the second has withdrawn her influence.

As much has been said of the advantages of reconciliation, which, like an agreeable dream, has passed away and left us as we were, it is but right that we should examine the contrary side of the argument, and inquire into some of the many material injuries which these colonies sustain, and always will sustain, by being connected with and dependent on Great Britain. To examine that connection and dependence, on the principles of nature and common sense, to see what we have to trust to, if separated, and what we are to expect, if dependent.

I have heard it asserted by some, that as America has flourished under her former connection with Great Britain, the same connection is necessary toward her future happiness, and will always have the same effect.—Nothing can be more fallacious than this kind of argument.—We may as well assert

[1] Henry Pelham was prime minister of England from 1744 to 1754.

that because a child has thrived upon milk, that it is never to have meat, or that the first twenty years of our lives is to become a precedent for the next twenty. But even this is admitting more than is true; for I answer roundly, that America would have flourished as much, and probably much more, had no European power taken any notice of her. The commerce by which she hath enriched herself are the necessaries of life, and will always have a market while eating is the custom of Europe.

But she has protected us, say some. That she hath engrossed us is true, and defended the continent at our expense as well as her own, is admitted, and she would have defended Turkey from the same motive, *viz.* for the sake of trade and dominion.

Alas! we have been long led away by ancient prejudices and made large sacrifices to superstition. We have boasted the protection of Great Britain, without considering, that her motive was *interest* not *attachment;* and that she did not protect us from *our enemies* on *our account,* but from her enemies on her own account, from those who had no quarrel with us on any *other account,* and who will always be our enemies on the *same account.* Let Britain waive her pretensions to the continent, or the continent throw off the dependence, and we should be at peace with France and Spain were they at war with Britain. The miseries of Hanover's last war ought to warn us against connections.

It hath lately been asserted in Parliament, that the colonies have no relation to each other but through the parent country, i.e. that Pennsylvania and the Jerseys, and so on for the rest, are sister colonies by the way of England; this is certainly a very roundabout way of proving relationship, but it is the nearest and only true way of proving enmity (or enemyship, if I may so call it). France and Spain never were, nor perhaps ever will be, our enemies as *Americans,* but as our being the *subjects of Great Britain.*

But Britain is the parent country, say some. Then the more shame upon her conduct. Even brutes do not devour their young, nor savages make war upon their families; wherefore, the assertion, if true, turns to her reproach; but it happens not to be true, or only partly so, and the phrase *parent* or *mother country* hath been jesuitically adopted by the King and his parasites, with a low papistical design of gaining an unfair bias on the credulous weakness of our minds. Europe, and not England, is the parent country of America. This new world hath been the asylum for the persecuted lovers of civil and religious liberty from *every part* of Europe. Hither have they fled, not from the tender embraces of the mother, but from the cruelty of the monster; and it is so far true of England, that the same tyranny which drove the first emigrants from home, pursues their descendants still.

In this extensive quarter of the globe, we forget the narrow limits of three hundred and sixty miles (the extent of England) and carry our friendship on a larger scale; we claim brotherhood with every European Christian, and triumph in the generosity of the sentiment.

It is pleasant to observe by what regular gradations we surmount the force of local prejudices, as we enlarge our acquaintance with the world. A man born in any town in England divided into parishes, will naturally associate most with his fellow parishioners (because their interests in many cases will be common) and distinguish him by the name of *neighbor;* if he meet him but a few miles from home, he drops the narrow idea of a street, and salutes him by the name of *townsman;* if he travel out of the county and meet him in any other, he forgets the minor divisions of street and town, and calls him *country-man, i.e. county-man;* but if in their foreign excursions they should associate in France, or any other part of *Europe,* their local remembrance would be enlarged into that of *Englishman.* And by a just parity of reasoning, all Europeans meeting in America, or any other quarter of the globe, are *countrymen;* for England, Holland, Germany, or Sweden, when compared with the whole, stand in the same places on the larger scale, which the divisions of street, town, and county do on the smaller ones; distinctions too limited for continental minds. Not one-third of the inhabitants, even of this province are of English descent. Wherefore, I reprobate the phrase of parent or mother country applied to England only, as being false, selfish, narrow and ungenerous.

But, admitting that we were all of English descent, what does it amount to? Nothing. Britain, being now an open enemy, extinguishes every other name and title: and to say that reconciliation is our duty, is truly farcical. The first king of England, of the present line (William the Conqueror) was a Frenchman, and half the peers of England are descendants from the same country; wherefore, by the same method of reasoning, England ought to be governed by France.

Much hath been said of the united strength of Britain and the colonies, that in conjunction they might bid defiance to the world: but this is mere presumption, the fate of war is uncertain, neither do the expressions mean anything, for this continent would never suffer itself to be drained of inhabitants, to support the British arms in either Asia, Africa or Europe.

Besides, what have we to do with setting the world at defiance? Our plan is commerce, and that, well attended to, will secure us the peace and friendship of all Europe; because it is the interest of all Europe to have America a *free port.* Her trade will always be a protection, and her barrenness of gold and silver secure her from invaders.

I challenge the warmest advocate of reconciliation to show a single advantage that this continent can reap, by being connected with Great Britain.
I repeat the challenge, not a single advantage is derived. Our corn will fetch
its price in any market in Europe, and our imported goods must be paid for
buy them where we will.

But the injuries and disadvantages which we sustain by that connection,
are without number; and our duty to mankind at large, as well as to ourselves,
instructs us to renounce the alliance: because, any submission to, or dependence on, Great Britain, tends directly to involve this continent in European
wars and quarrels, and set us at variance with nations who would otherwise
seek our friendship, and against whom we have neither anger nor complaint.
As Europe is our market for trade, we ought to form no partial connection
with any part of it. 'Tis the true interest of America to steer clear of European contentions, which she can never do, while by her dependence on
Britain, she is made the make-weight in the scale of British politics.

Europe is too thickly planted with kingdoms to be long at peace, and
whenever a war breaks out between England and any foreign power, the trade
of America goes to ruin, *because of her connection with Britain.* The next
war may not turn out like the last, and should it not, the advocates for reconciliation now will be wishing for separation then, because neutrality in that
case would be a safer convoy than a man of war. Everything that is right or
reasonable pleads for separation. The blood of the slain, the weeping voice of
nature cries, **'tis time to part.** Even the distance at which the Almighty hath
placed England and America is a strong and natural proof that the authority
of the one over the other, was never the design of heaven. The time likewise at which the continent was discovered, adds weight to the argument, and
the manner in which it was peopled, increases the force of it.—The Reformation was preceded by the discovery of America: as if the Almighty graciously
meant to open a sanctuary to the persecuted in future years, when home
should afford neither friendship nor safety.

The authority of Great Britain over this continent, is a form of government, which sooner or later must have an end. And a serious mind can draw
no true pleasure by looking forward, under the painful and positive conviction that what he calls "the present constitution" is merely temporary. As
parents, we can have no joy, knowing that *this government* is not sufficiently
lasting to insure anything which we may bequeath to posterity: and by a
plain method of argument, as we are running the next generation into debt,
we ought to do the work of it, otherwise we use them meanly and pitifully.
In order to discover the line of our duty rightly, we should take our children

in our hand, and fix our station a few years farther into life; that eminence will present a prospect which a few present fears and prejudices conceal from our sight.

Though I would carefully avoid giving unnecessary offense, yet I am inclined to believe, that all those who espouse the doctrine of reconciliation, may be included within the following descriptions.

Interested men, who are not to be trusted, weak men who *cannot* see, prejudiced men who *will not* see, and a certain set of moderate men who think better of the European world than it deserves; and this last class, by an ill-judged deliberation, will be the cause of more calamities to this continent than all the other three.

It is the good fortune of many to live distant from the scene of present sorrow; the evil is not sufficiently brought to *their* doors to make *them* feel the precariousness with which all American property is possessed. But let our imaginations transport us a few moments to Boston; that seat of wretchedness will teach us wisdom, and instruct us for ever to renounce a power in whom we can have no trust. The inhabitants of that unfortunate city who but a few months ago were in ease and affluence, have now no other alternative than to stay and starve, or turn out to beg. Endangered by the fire of their friends if they continue within the city, and plundered by the soldiery if they leave it, in their present situation they are prisoners without the hope of redemption, and in a general attack for their relief they would be exposed to the fury of both armies.

Men of passive tempers look somewhat lightly over the offenses of Great Britain, and, still hoping for the best, are apt to call out, *come, come, we shall be friends again for all this.* But examine the passions and feelings of mankind: bring the doctrine of reconciliation to the touchstone of nature, and then tell me whether you can hereafter love, honor, and faithfully serve the power that hath carried fire and sword into your land? If you cannot do all these, then are you only deceiving yourselves, and by your delay bringing ruin upon posterity. Your future connection with Britain, whom you can neither love nor honor, will be forced and unnatural, and being formed only on the plan of present convenience, will in a little time fall into a relapse more wretched than the first. But if you say, you can still pass the violations over, then I ask, Hath your house been burnt? Hath your property been destroyed before your face? Are your wife and children destitute of a bed to lie on, or bread to live on? Have you lost a parent or child by their hands, and yourself the ruined and wretched survivor? If you have not, then are you not a judge of those who have. But if you have, and can still shake hands with the murderers, then are you unworthy the name of husband, father, friend, or lover, and whatever may be your rank or title in life, you have the heart of a coward, and the spirit of a sycophant.

This is not inflaming or exaggerating matters, but trying them by those feelings and affections which nature justifies, and without which we should be incapable of discharging the social duties of life, or enjoying the felicities of it. I mean not to exhibit horror for the purpose of provoking revenge, but to awaken us from fatal and unmanly slumbers, that we may pursue determinately some fixed object. 'Tis not in the power of Britain or of Europe to conquer America, if she doth not conquer herself by *delay* and *timidity*. The present winter is worth an age if rightly employed, but if lost or neglected the whole continent will partake of the misfortune; and there is no punishment which that man doth not deserve, be he who, or what, or where he will, that may be the means of sacrificing a season so precious and useful.

'Tis repugnant to reason, to the universal order of things; to all examples from former ages, to suppose, that this continent can long remain subject to any external power. The most sanguine in Britain doth not think so. The utmost stretch of human wisdom cannot, at this time, compass a plan, short of separation, which can promise the continent even a year's security. Reconciliation is *now* a fallacious dream. Nature has deserted the connection, and art cannot supply her place. For, as Milton wisely expresses, "never can true reconcilement grow where wounds of deadly hate have pierced so deep."

Every quiet method for peace hath been ineffectual. Our prayers have been rejected with disdain; and hath tended to convince us that nothing flatters vanity or confirms obstinacy in kings more than repeated petitioning—and nothing hath contributed more than that very measure to make the kings of Europe absolute. Witness Denmark and Sweden. Wherefore, since nothing but blows will do, for God's sake let us come to a final separation, and not leave the next generation to be cutting throats under the violated unmeaning names of parent and child.

To say they will never attempt it again is idle and visionary; we thought so at the repeal of the Stamp Act, yet a year or two undeceived us; as well may we suppose that nations which have been once defeated will never renew the quarrel.

As to government matters, 'tis not in the power of Britain to do this continent justice: the business of it will soon be too weighty and intricate to be managed with any tolerable degree of convenience, by a power so distant from us, and so very ignorant of us; for if they cannot conquer us they cannot govern us. To be always running three or four thousand miles with a tale or a petition, waiting four or five months for an answer, which, when obtained, requires five or six more to explain it in, will in a few years be looked upon as folly and childishness.—There was a time when it was proper, and there is a proper time for it to cease.

Small islands not capable of protecting themselves, are the proper objects for government to take under their care; but there is something absurd in supposing a continent to be perpetually governed by an island. In no instance hath nature made the satellite larger than its primary planet; and as England and America, with respect to each other, reverse the common order of nature, it is evident that they belong to different systems. England to Europe: America to itself.

I am not induced by motives of pride, party or resentment to espouse the doctrine of separation and independence; I am clearly, positively, and conscientiously persuaded that 'tis the true interest of this continent to be so; that everything short of *that* is mere patchwork, that it can afford no lasting felicity—that it is leaving the sword to our children, and shrinking back at a time when a little more, a little further, would have rendered this continent the glory of the earth.

As Britain hath not manifested the least inclination towards a compromise, we may be assured that no terms can be obtained worthy the acceptance of the continent, or any ways equal to the expense of blood and treasure we have been already put to.

The object contended for, ought always to bear some just proportion to the expense. The removal of North,[2] or the whole detestable junto, is a matter unworthy the millions we have expended. A temporary stoppage of trade was an inconvenience, which would have sufficiently balanced the repeal of all the acts complained of, had such repeals been obtained; but if the whole continent must take up arms, if every man must be a soldier, 'tis scarcely worth our while to fight against a contemptible ministry only. Dearly, dearly do we pay for the repeal of the acts, if that is all we fight for; for, in a just estimation 'tis as great a folly to pay a bunker-hill price[3] for law as for land. As I have always considered the independency of this continent, as an event which sooner or later must arrive, so from the late rapid progress of the continent to maturity, the event cannot be far off. Wherefore, on the breaking out of hostilities, it was not worth the while to have disputed a matter which time would have finally redressed, unless we meant to be in earnest: otherwise it is like wasting an estate on a suit at law, to regulate the

[2] Frederick, Lord North, was then prime minister of England.
[3] Many died at the Battle of Bunker Hill in 1775.

trespasses of a tenant whose lease is just expiring. No man was a warmer wisher for a reconciliation than myself, before the fatal nineteenth of April, 1775, but the moment the event of that day was made known, I rejected the hardened, sullen-tempered Pharaoh of England forever; and disdain the wretch, that with the pretended title of **father of his people** can unfeelingly hear of their slaughter, and composedly sleep with their blood upon his soul.

But admitting that matters were now made up, what would be the event? I answer, the ruin of the continent. And that for several reasons.

*First.* The powers of governing still remaining in the hands of the King, he will have a negative over the whole legislation of this continent. And as he hath shown himself such an inveterate enemy to liberty, and discovered such a thirst for arbitrary power, is he, or is he not, a proper person to say to these colonies, *You shall make no laws but what I please*!? And is there any inhabitant of America so ignorant as not to know, that according to what is called the *present Constitution,* this continent can make no laws but what the King gives leave to; and is there any man so unwise as not to see, that (considering what has happened) he will suffer no law to be made here but such as suits his purpose? We may be as effectually enslaved by the want of laws in America, as by submitting to laws made for us in England. After matters are made up (as it is called), can there be any doubt, but the whole power of the Crown will be exerted to keep this continent as low and humble as possible? Instead of going forward we shall go backward, or be perpetually quarrelling, or ridiculously petitioning.—We are already greater than the King wishes us to be, and will he not hereafter endeavor to make us less? To bring the matter to one point, Is the power who is jealous of our prosperity, a proper power to govern us? Whoever says No, to this question, is an Independent for independency means no more than this, whether we shall make our own laws, or, whether the King, the greatest enemy this continent hath, or can have, shall tell us *"there shall be no laws but such as I like."*

But the King, you'll say, has a negative in England; the people there can make no laws without his consent. In point of right and good order, it is something very ridiculous that a youth of twenty-one (which hath often happened) shall say to several millions of people older and wiser than himself, "I forbid this or that act of yours to be law." But in this place I decline this sort of reply, tho' I will never cease to expose the absurdity of it, and only answer that England being the King's residence, and America not so, makes quite another case. The King's negative here is ten times more dangerous and fatal than it can be in England; for *there* he will scarcely refuse his consent to a bill for putting England into as strong a state of defense as possible, and in America he would never suffer such a bill to be passed.

America is only a secondary object in the system of British politics, England consults the good of *this* country no further than it answers her *own* purpose. Wherefore, her own interest leads her to suppress the growth of *ours*, in every case which doth not promote *her* advantage, or in the least interfere with it. A pretty state we should soon be in under such a second-hand government, considering what has happened! Men do not change from enemies to friends by the alteration of a name: and in order to show that reconciliation *now* is a dangerous doctrine, I affirm, *that it would be policy in the King at this time to repeal the acts, for the sake of reinstating himself in the government of the provinces;* in order that **he may accomplish by craft and subtlety, in the long run, what he cannot do by force and violence in the short one.** Reconciliation and ruin are nearly related.

*Secondly.*—That as even the best terms which we can expect to obtain can amount to no more than a temporary expedient, or a kind of government by guardianship, which can last no longer than till the colonies come of age, so the general face and state of things in the interim will be unsettled and unpromising: emigrants of property will not choose to come to a country whose form of government hangs but by a thread, and who is every day tottering on the brink of commotion and disturbance: and numbers of the present inhabitants would lay hold of the interval to dispose of their effects, and quit the continent.

But the most powerful of all arguments is, that nothing but independence, i.e. a continental form of government, can keep the peace of the continent and preserve it inviolate from civil wars. I dread the event of a reconciliation with Britain *now,* as it is more than probable that it will be followed by a revolt somewhere or other, the consequences of which may be far more fatal than all malice of Britain.

Thousands are already ruined by British barbarity (thousands more will probably suffer the same fate). Those men have other feelings than us who have nothing suffered. All they *now* possess is liberty; what they have before enjoyed is sacrificed to its service, and having nothing more to lose they disdain submission. Besides, the general temper of the colonies, towards a British government will be like that of a youth who is nearly out of his time; they will care very little about her: and a government which cannot preserve the peace is no government at all, and in that case we pay our money for nothing; and pray what is it that Britain can do, whose power will be wholly on paper, should a civil tumult break out the very day after reconciliation? I have heard some men say, many of whom I believe spoke without thinking, that they dreaded an independence, fearing that it would produce civil wars: it is but seldom that our first thoughts are truly correct, and that is the case here; for there is ten times more to dread from a patched up connection than from independence. I make the sufferer's case my own, and I protest, that were I driven from house and home, my property destroyed, and my circumstances ruined, that as a man, sensible of injuries, I could never relish the doctrine of reconciliation, or consider myself bound thereby.

The colonies have manifested such a spirit of good order and obedience to continental government, as is sufficient to make every reasonable person easy and happy on that head. No man can assign the least pretense for his fears, on any other grounds, than such as are truly childish and ridiculous, viz., that one colony will be striving for superiority over another.

Where there are no distinctions there can be no superiority; perfect equality affords no temptation. The republics of Europe are all (and we may say always) in peace. Holland and Switzerland are without wars, foreign or domestic: monarchical governments, it is true, are never long at rest: the Crown itself is a temptation to enterprising ruffians at *home;* and that degree of pride and insolence ever attendant on regal authority, swells into a rupture with foreign powers in instances where a republican government, by being formed on more natural principles, would negotiate the mistake.

If there is any true cause of fear regarding independence, it is because no plan is yet laid down. Men do not see their way out.—Wherefore, as an opening into that business I offer the following hints; at the same time modestly affirming, that I have no other opinion of them myself, than that they may be the means of giving rise to something better. Could the straggling thoughts of individuals be collected, they would frequently form materials for wise and able men to improve into useful matter.

**Let** the assemblies be annual, with a president only. The representation more equal, their business wholly domestic, and subject to the authority of a Continental Congress.

Let each colony be divided into six, eight, or ten, convenient districts, each district to send a proper number of delegates to Congress, so that each colony send at least thirty. The whole number in Congress will be at least 390. Each Congress to sit and to choose a president by the following method. When the delegates are met, let a colony be taken from the whole thirteen colonies by lot, after which let the Congress choose (by ballot) a president from out of the delegates of that province. In the next Congress, let a colony be taken by lot from twelve only, omitting that colony from which the president was taken in the former Congress, and so proceeding on till the whole thirteen shall have had their proper rotation. And in order that nothing may pass into a law but what is satisfactorily just, not less than three-fifths of the Congress to be called a majority.—He that will promote discord, under a government so equally formed as this, would have joined Lucifer in his revolt.

But as there is a peculiar delicacy from whom, or in what manner, this business must first arise, and as it seems most agreeable and consistent that it should come from some intermediate body between the governed and the governors, that is, between the Congress and the People, Let a **continental conference** be held in the following manner, and for the following purpose.

A committee of twenty-six members of Congress, *viz.* two for each colony. Two members from each house or assembly, or provincial convention; and five representatives of the People at large, to be chosen in the capital city or town of each province, for, and in behalf of the whole province, by as many qualified voters as shall think proper to attend from all parts of the province for that purpose; or, if more convenient, the representatives may be chosen in two or three of the most populous parts thereof. In this **conference**, thus assembled, will be united the two grand principles of business, *knowledge* and *power*. The members of Congress, assemblies, or conventions, by having had experience in national concerns, will be able and useful counsellors, and the whole, being impowered by the people, will have a truly legal authority.

The conferring members being met, let their business be to frame a **Continental Charter,** or Charter of the United Colonies (answering to what is called the Magna Charta of England), fixing the number and manner of choosing members of Congress, members of Assembly, with their date of sitting; and drawing the line of business and jurisdiction between them: always remembering, that our strength is continental, not provincial. Securing freedom and property to all men, and above all things, the free exercise of religion, according to the dictates of conscience, with such other matter as it is necessary for a charter to contain. Immediately after which the said conference to dissolve, and the bodies which shall be chosen conformable to the said charter, to be the legislators and governors of this continent for the time being: whose peace and happiness, may God preserve. **Amen.**

Should any body of men be hereafter delegated for this or some similar purpose, I offer them the following extracts from that wise observer on governments, **Dragonetti.**[4] "The science," says he, "of the politician consists in fixing the true point of happiness and freedom. Those men would deserve the gratitude of ages, who should discover a mode of government that contained the greatest sum of individual happiness, with the least national expense."

But where, say some, is the king of America? I'll tell you, Friend, he reigns above, and doth not make havoc of mankind like the Royal Brute of

---

[4]Giacinto Dragonetti (1738–1818) was a judge in Naples.

Great Britain. Yet that we may not appear to be defective even in earthly honors, let a day be solemnly set apart for proclaiming the Charter; let it be brought forth placed on the divine law, the Word of God; let a crown be placed thereon, by which the world may know, that so far as we approve of monarchy, that in America **the law is king**. For as in absolute governments the king is law, so in free countries the law *ought* to **be** king, and there ought to be no other. But lest any ill use should afterwards arise, let the crown at the conclusion of the ceremony be demolished, and scattered among the People whose right it is.

A government of our own is our natural right: and when a man seriously reflects on the precariousness of human affairs, he will become convinced, that it is infinitely wiser and safer, to form a Constitution of our own in a cool deliberate manner, while we have it in our power, than to trust such an interesting event to time and chance. If we omit it now, some Massanello[5] may hereafter arise, who, laying hold of popular disquietudes, may collect together the desperate and the discontented, and by assuming to themselves the powers of government, finally sweep away the liberties of the continent like a deluge. Should the government of America return again into the hands of Britain, the tottering situation of things will be a temptation for some desperate adventurer to try his fortune; and in such a case, what relief can Britain give? Ere she could hear the news, the fatal business might be done; and ourselves suffering like the wretched Britons under the oppression of the conqueror. Ye that oppose independence now, ye know not what ye do; ye are opening a door to eternal tyranny, by keeping vacant the seat of government. There are thousands and tens of thousands, who would think it glorious to expel from the continent, that barbarous and hellish power, which hath stirred up the Indians and the Negroes to destroy us; the cruelty hath a double guilt, it is dealing brutally by us, and treacherously by them.

To talk of friendship with those in whom our reason forbids us to have faith, and our affections wounded thro' a thousand pores instruct us to detest, is madness and folly. Every day wears out the little remains of kindred between us and them; and can there be any reason to hope, that as the relationship expires, the affection will increase, or that we shall agree better when we have ten times more and greater concerns to quarrel over than ever?

Ye that tell us of harmony and reconciliation, can ye restore to us the time that is past? Can ye give to prostitution its former innocence? Neither can ye reconcile Britain and America. The last cord now is broken, the people of England are presenting addresses against us. There are injuries which nature cannot forgive; she would cease to be nature if she did. As well can the lover

---

[5]Thomas Anello was a Neapolitan revolutionary leader who became king.

forgive the ravisher of his mistress, as the Continent forgive the murders of Britain. The Almighty hath implanted in us these inextinguishable feelings for good and wise purposes. They are the guardians of His image in our hearts. They distinguish us from the herd of common animals. The social compact would dissolve, and justice be extirpated from the earth, or have only a casual existence were we callous to the touches of affection. The robber and the murderer would often escape unpunished, did not the injuries which our tempers sustain, provoke us into justice.

O! ye that love mankind! Ye that dare oppose not only the tyranny but the tyrant, stand forth! Every spot of the old world is over-run with oppression. Freedom hath been hunted round the globe. Asia and Africa have long expelled her.—Europe regards her like a stranger, and England hath given her warning to depart. O receive the fugitive, and prepare in time an asylum for mankind.

I. **Suggestions for Discussion:**
   1. Contrast Paine's claims in the first paragraph with his prose style in the final two paragraphs. What rhetorical devices does he use to influence his readers?
   2. Outline Paine's principal arguments for fighting against Great Britain. Are they clearly defined in the essay? Does he support his arguments with evidence as well as with rhetoric? Explain.
   3. Discuss his plan for a Continental Conference.

II. **Suggestions for Writing:**
   1. Write an essay urging the citizens of the United States to take a strong stand on a matter of current controversy.
   2. Write a response to Paine from the point of view of a loyal British citizen living in America.

---

# WALTER PATER

## Conclusion

### to *Studies in the History of the Renaissance*

---

Walter Pater (1839–1894), the English essayist and art critic, won fame in 1873 with the publication of *Studies in the History of the Renaissance,* from which the following selection is taken. He later published a work of fiction, *Marius the Epicurean* (1885) and two critical works, *Imaginary Portraits* (1887) and *Appreciations* (1889).

Although modern readers often find his florid style excessive, Pater successfully uses comparison and contrast in this selection to help explain his belief that "to burn always with this hard, gem-like flame, to maintain this ecstasy, is success in life."

---

Δέγει που Ἡράκλειτος ὅτι πάντα χωρεῖ καὶ οὐδὲν μένει
All things give way; nothing remains

To regard all things and principles of things as inconstant modes or fashions has more and more become the tendency of modern thought. Let us begin with that which is without—our physical life. Fix upon it in one of its more exquisite intervals, the moment, for instance, of delicious recoil from the flood of water in summer heat. What is the whole physical life in that moment but a combination of natural elements to which science gives their names? But those elements, phosphorus and lime and delicate fibres, are present not in the human body alone: we detect them in places most remote from it. Our physical life is a perpetual motion of them—the passage of the blood, the waste and repairing of the lenses of the eye, the modification of the tissues of the brain under every ray of light and sound—processes which science reduces to simpler and more elementary forces. Like the elements of which we are composed, the action of these forces extends beyond us: it rusts iron and ripens corn. Far out on every side of us those elements are broadcast, driven in many currents; and birth and gesture and death and the springing of violets from the grave are but a few out of ten thousand resultant combinations. That clear, perpetual outline of face and limb is but an image of ours, under which we group them— a design in a web, the actual threads of which pass out beyond it. This at least of flame-like our life has, that it is but the concurrence, renewed from moment to moment, of forces parting sooner or later on their ways.

Or, if we begin with the inward world of thought and feeling, the whirlpool is still more rapid, the flame more eager and devouring. There it is no longer the gradual darkening of the eye, the gradual fading of colour from the wall—movements of the shore-side, where the water flows down indeed, though in apparent rest—but the race of the mid-stream, a drift of momentary acts of sight and passion and thought. At first sight experience seems to bury us under a flood of external objects, pressing upon us with a sharp and importunate reality, calling us out of ourselves in a thousand forms of action. But when reflexion begins to play upon those objects they are dissipated under its influence; the cohesive force seems suspended like some trick of magic; each object is loosed into a group of impressions—colour, odour, texture—in the mind of the observer. And if we continue to dwell in thought on this world, not of objects in the solidity with which language invests them, but of impressions, unstable, flickering, inconsistent, which burn and are extinguished with our consciousness of them, it contracts still further: the whole scope of observation is dwarfed into the narrow chamber of the individual mind. Experience, already reduced to a group of impressions, is ringed round for each one of us by that thick wall of personality through which no real voice has ever pierced on its way to us, or from us to that which we can only conjecture to be without. Every one of those impressions is the impression of the individual in his isolation, each mind keeping as a solitary prisoner its own dream of a world. Analysis goes a step farther still, and assures us that those impressions of the individual mind to which, for each one of us, experience dwindles down, are in perpetual flight; that each of them is limited by time, and that as time is infinitely divisible, each of them is infinitely divisible also; all that is actual in it being a single moment, gone while we try to apprehend it, of which it may ever be more truly said that it has ceased to be than that it is. To such a tremulous wisp constantly reforming itself on the stream, to a single sharp impression, with a sense in it, a relic more or less fleeting, of such moments gone by, what is real in our life fines itself down. It is with this movement, with the passage and dissolution of impressions, images, sensations, that analysis leaves off—that continual vanishing away, that strange, perpetual weaving and unweaving of ourselves.

*Philosophiren,* says Novalis, *ist dephlegmatisiren, vivificiren.*[1] The service of philosophy, of speculative culture, towards the human spirit, is to rouse, to startle it to a life of constant and eager observation. Every moment some form grows perfect in hand or face; some tone on the hills or the sea is choicer than the rest; some mood of passion or insight or intellectual excitement is irresistibly real and attractive to us,—for that moment only. Not the fruit of experience, but experience itself, is the end. A counted number of pulses only is given to us of a variegated, dramatic life. How may we see in them all that is to be seen in them by the finest senses? How shall we pass most swiftly from point to point, and be present always at the focus where the greatest number of vital forces unite in their purest energy?

---

[1] To philosophize is to cast off inertia, to make oneself alive.

To burn always with this hard, gemlike flame, to maintain this ecstasy, is success in life. In a sense it might even be said that our failure is to form habits: for, after all, habit is relative to a stereotyped world, and meantime it is only the roughness of the eye that makes any two persons, things, situations, seem alike. While all melts under our feet, we may well grasp at any exquisite passion, or any contribution to knowledge that seems by a lifted horizon to set the spirit free for a moment, or any stirring of the senses, strange dyes, strange colours, and curious odours, or work of the artist's hands, or the face of one's friend. Not to discriminate every moment some passionate attitude in those about us, and in the very brilliancy of their gifts some tragic dividing of forces on their ways, is, on this short day of frost and sun, to sleep before evening. With this sense of the splendour of our experience and of its awful brevity, gathering all we are into one desperate effort to see and touch, we shall hardly have time to make theories about the things we see and touch. What we have to do is to be for ever curiously testing new opinions and courting new impressions, never acquiescing in a facile orthodoxy of Comte, or of Hegel,[2] or of our own. Philosophical theories or ideas, as points of view, instruments of criticism, may help us to gather up what might otherwise pass unregarded by us. 'Philosophy is the microscope of thought.' The theory or idea or system which requires of us the sacrifice of any part of this experience, in consideration of some interest into which we cannot enter, or some abstract theory we have not identified with ourselves, or of what is only conventional, has no real claim upon us.

One of the most beautiful passages of Rousseau is that in the sixth book of the *Confessions*,[3] where he describes the awakening in him of the literary sense. An undefinable taint of death had clung always about him, and now in early manhood he believed himself smitten by mortal disease. He asked himself how he might make as much as possible of the interval that remained; and he was not biassed by anything in his previous life when he decided that it must be by intellectual excitement, which he found just then in the clear, fresh writings of Voltaire. Well! we are all *condamnés* as Victor Hugo says: we are all under sentence of death but with a sort of indefinite reprieve—*les hommes sont tous condamnés à mort avec des sursis indéfinis:*[4] we have an interval, and then our place knows us no more. Some spend this interval in listlessness, some in high passions, the wisest, at least among 'the children of this world,' in art and song. For our one chance lies in expanding

[2] August Comte (1798–1857) and George Wilhelm Friederich Hegel (1770–1813) were influential philosophers.
[3] The *Confessions* of Jean-Jacques Rousseau (1712–1778) were published after his death.
[4] Men are condemned to death with indefinite reprieves.

that interval, in getting as many pulsations as possible into the given time. Great passions may give us this quickened sense of life, ecstasy and sorrow of love, the various forms of enthusiastic activity, disinterested or otherwise, which come naturally to many of us. Only be sure it is passion—that it does yield you this fruit of a quickened, multiplied consciousness. Of such wisdom, the poetic passion, the desire of beauty, the love of art for its own sake, has most. For art comes to you proposing frankly to give nothing but the highest quality to your moments as they pass, and simply for those moments' sake.

### I. Suggestions for Discussion:
1. Characterize Pater's essay as abstract or concrete, general or specific. Explain.
2. Discuss Pater's use of analogy to explain physical and mental life.
3. Describe Pater's tone and style. Does he, for example, seem effusive or detached from his subject? Give your personal reaction to his tone and style.

### II. Suggestions for Writing:
1. Write an essay speculating on what it would mean in your own life to follow Pater's advice.
2. Compare and contrast Pater's attitude toward art with that of E. M. Forster in "Art for Art's Sake," p. 183.

---

# PLATO

## The Death of Socrates

### from *Phaedo*

---

Plato (427?–347 B.C.), the pupil of Socrates, founded the famous Academy in Athens in 388 B.C., where science, philosophy, and politics were taught for almost nine hundred years. There he composed the *Dialogues* in which Socrates figures prominently. Plato, it is said, first demonstrated that truth was a matter of knowledge rather than mere opinion.

The following selection is taken from the *Phaedo,* the last in a
series of dialogues which tell the story of the trial and death of
Socrates. Plato is at his narrative and dramatic best as he relates
the conversation Socrates is supposed to have held with Simmias,
Cebes, and Crito on the last day of his life, as he waited in his cell
for the executioner to bring him the hemlock cup of poison.

---

Such is the nature of the other world; and when the dead arrive at the
place to which the genius of each severally guides them, first of all they have
sentence passed upon them, as they have lived well and piously or not. And
those who appear to have lived neither well nor ill go to the river Acheron,
and, embarking in any vessels which they may find, are carried in them to the
lake, and there they dwell and are purified of their evil deeds, and having suffered the penalty of the wrongs which they have done to others, they are
absolved, and receive the rewards of their good deeds, each of them according
to his deserts. But those who appear to be incurable by reason of the greatness of their crimes—who have committed many and terrible deeds of sacrilege, murders foul and violent, or the like—such are hurled into Tartarus
which is their suitable destiny, and they never come out.

Those again who have committed crimes which, although great, are not
irremediable—who in a moment of anger, for example, have done some violence to a father or a mother, and have repented for the remainder of their
lives, or who have taken the life of another under the like extenuating circumstances—these are plunged into Tartarus, the pains of which they are compelled to undergo for a year, but at the end of the year the wave casts them
forth—mere homicides by way of Cocytus, parricides and matricides by
Pyriphlegethon—and they are borne to the Acherusian lake, and there they
lift up their voices and call upon the victims whom they have slain or wronged,
to have pity on them, and to be kind to them, and let them come out into the
lake. And if they prevail, then they come forth and cease from their troubles;
but if not, they are carried back again into Tartarus and from thence into the
rivers unceasingly, until they obtain mercy from those whom they have
wronged; for that is the sentence inflicted upon them by their judges.

Those too who have been pre-eminent for holiness of life are released
from this earthly prison, and go to their pure home which is above, and dwell
in the purer earth; and of these, such as have duly purified themselves with
philosophy live henceforth altogether without the body, in mansions fairer
still, which may not be described, and of which the time would fail me to tell.

Wherefore, Simmias, seeing all these things, what ought not we to do that we may obtain virtue and wisdom in this life? Fair is the prize, and the hope great!

A man of sense ought not to say, nor will I be very confident, that the description which I have given of the soul and her mansions is exactly true. But I do say that, inasmuch as the soul is shown to be immortal, he may venture to think, not improperly or unworthily, that something of the kind is true. The venture is a glorious one, and he ought to comfort himself with words like these, which is the reason why I lengthen out the tale. Wherefore, I say, let a man be of good cheer about his soul, who having cast away the pleasures and ornaments of the body as alien to him and working harm rather than good, has sought after the pleasures of knowledge; and has arrayed the soul, not in some foreign attire, but in her own proper jewels, temperance, and justice, and courage, and nobility, and truth—in these adorned she is ready to go on her journey to the world below, when her hour comes. You, Simmias and Cebes, and all other men, will depart at some time or other. Me already, as a tragic poet would say, the voice of fate calls. Soon I must drink the poison; and I think that I had better repair to the bath first, in order that the women may not have the trouble of washing my body after I am dead.

When he had done speaking, Crito said: And have you any commands for us, Socrates—anything to say about your children, or any other matter in which we can serve you?

Nothing particular, Crito, he replied: only, as I have always told you, take care of yourselves; that is a service which you may be ever rendering to me and mine and to all of us, whether you promise to do so or not. But if you have no thought for yourselves, and care not to walk according to the rule which I have prescribed for you, not now for the first time, however much you may profess or promise at the moment, it will be of no avail.

We will do our best, said Crito: And in what way shall we bury you?

In any way that you like; but you must get hold of me, and take care that I do not run away from you. Then he turned to us, and added with a smile:—I cannot make Crito believe that I am the same Socrates who has been talking and conducting the argument; he fancies that I am the other Socrates whom he will soon see a dead body—and he asks, How shall he bury me? And though I have spoken many words in the endeavour to show that when I have drunk the poison I shall leave you and go to the joys of the blessed,—these words of mine, with which I was comforting you and myself, have had, as I perceive, no effect upon Crito. And therefore I want you to be surety for me to him now, as at the trial he was surety to the judges for me: but let the promise be of another sort; for he was surety for me to the judges that I would remain, and you must be my surety to him that I shall not re-main, but go away and depart; and then he will suffer less at my death, and not be grieved when he sees my body being burned or buried. I would not have him sorrow at my hard lot, or say at the burial, Thus we lay out Socrates, or, Thus we follow him to the grave or bury him; for false words are not only evil in themselves, but they infect the soul with evil. Be of good cheer, then, my dear Crito, and say that you are burying my body only, and do with that whatever is usual, and what you think best.

When he had spoken these words, he arose and went into a chamber to bathe; Crito followed him and told us to wait. So we remained behind, talking and thinking of the subject of discourse, and also of the greatness of our sorrow; he was like a father of whom we were being bereaved, and we were about to pass the rest of our lives as orphans. When he had taken the bath his children were brought to him—(he had two young sons and an elder one); and the women of his family also came, and he talked to them and gave them a few directions in the presence of Crito; then he dismissed them and returned to us.

Now the hour of sunset was near, for a good deal of time had passed while he was within. When he came out, he sat down with us again after his bath, but not much was said. Soon the jailer, who was the servant of the Eleven, entered and stood by him, saying:—To you, Socrates, whom I know to be the noblest and gentlest and best of all who ever came to this place, I will not impute the angry feelings of other men, who rage and swear at me, when, in obedience to the authorities, I bid them drink the poison—indeed, I am sure that you will not be angry with me; for others, as you are aware, and not I, are to blame. And so fare you well, and try to bear lightly what must needs be—you know my errand. Then bursting into tears he turned away and went out.

Socrates looked at him and said: I return your good wishes, and will do as you bid. Then turning to us, he said, How charming the man is: since I have been in prison he has always been coming to see me, and at times he would talk to me, and was as good to me as could be, and now see how gener-ously he sorrows on my account. We must do as he says, Crito; and therefore let the cup be brought, if the poison is prepared: if not, let the attendant prepare some.

Yet, said Crito, the sun is still upon the hill-tops, and I know that many a one has taken the draught late, and after the announcement has been made to him, he has eaten and drunk, and enjoyed the society of his beloved; do not hurry—there is time enough.

Socrates said: Yes, Crito, and they of whom you speak are right in so acting, for they think that they will be gainers by the delay; but I am right in not following their example, for I do not think that I should gain anything by drinking the poison a little later; I should only be ridiculous in my own eyes for sparing and saving a life which is already forfeit. Please then to do as I say, and not to refuse me.

Crito made a sign to the servant, who was standing by; and he went out, and having been absent for some time, returned with the jailer carrying the cup of poison. Socrates said: You, my good friend, who are experienced in these matters, shall give me directions how I am to proceed. The man answered: You have only to walk about until your legs are heavy, and then to lie down, and the poison will act. At the same time he handed the cup to Socrates, who in the easiest and gentlest manner, without the least fear or change of colour or feature, looking at the man with all his eyes, Echecrates, as his manner was, took the cup and said: What do you say about making a libation out of this cup to any god? May I, or not? The man answered: We only prepare, Socrates, just so much as we deem enough. I understand, he said: but I may and must ask the gods to prosper my journey from this to the other world—even so—and so be it according to my prayer. Then raising the cup to his lips, quite readily and cheerfully he drank of the poison. And hitherto most of us had been able to control our sorrow; but now when we saw him drinking, and saw too that he had finished the draught, we could no longer forbear, and in spite of myself my own tears were flowing fast; so that I covered my face and wept, nor for him, but at the thought of my own calamity in having to part from such a friend. Nor was I the first; for Crito, when he found himself unable to restrain his tears, had got up, and I followed; and at that moment, Apollodorus, who had been weeping all the time, broke out in a loud and passionate cry which made cowards of us all. Socrates alone retained his calmness: What is this strange outcry? he said. I sent away the women mainly in order that they might not misbehave in this way, for I have been told that a man should die in peace. Be quiet then, and have patience. When we heard his words we were ashamed, and refrained our tears; and he walked about until, as he said, his legs began to fail, and then he lay on his back, according to the directions, and the man who gave him the poison now and then looked at his feet and legs; and after a while he pressed his foot hard, and asked him if he could feel; and he said, No; and then his leg, and so upwards and upwards, and showed us that he was cold and stiff. And he felt them himself, and said: When the poison reaches the heart, that will be the end. He was beginning to grow cold about the groin, when he uncovered his face, for he had covered himself up, and said—they were his last words—he said: Crito, I owe a cock to Asclepius; will you remember to pay the debt? The debt shall be paid, said Crito; is there anything else? There was no answer to this question; but in a minute or two a movement was heard, and the attendants uncovered him; his eyes were set, and Crito closed his eyes and mouth.

Such was the end, Echecrates, of our friend; concerning whom I may truly say, that of all the men of his time whom I have known, he was the wisest and justest and best.

I. **Suggestions for Discussion:**
1. According to Socrates, what happens after death?
2. Why does Socrates urge his friends and disciples to be of good cheer?
3. What can you tell about the character of Socrates from his words and actions?

II. **Suggestions for Writing:**
1. Write a newspaper account of the death of Socrates or an extended obituary notice for him.
2. Write a personal account of the death of a friend or family member.
3. Compare Plato's account of the death of Socrates with Thomas Carlyle's account of the death of Louis XVI in *The French Revolution*, p. 75.

---

## KATHERINE ANNE PORTER

### The Necessary Enemy

from *Collected Essays and Occasional Writings*

---

Katherine Anne Porter (1890-1980), the American short story writer and novelist, is the author of such highly respected stories as *Flowering Judas* (1930) and *Pale Horse, Pale Rider* (1939) and of a powerful novel, *Ship of Fools* (1962). The selection that follows is taken from her *Collected Essays and Occasional Writings* (1948).

In the essay, Porter analyzes the role of hate, which she defines as the necessary enemy and ally of romantic love, in marriage.

---

She is a frank, charming, fresh-hearted young woman who married for love. She and her husband are one of those gay, good-looking young pairs who ornament this modern scene rather more in profusion perhaps than ever before in our history. They are handsome, with a talent for finding their way in their world, they work at things that interest them, their tastes agree and their hopes. They intend in all good faith to spend their lives together, to have children and do well by them and each other—to be happy, in fact, which for them is the whole point of their marriage. And all in stride, keeping their wits about them. Nothing romantic, mind you; their feet are on the ground.

Unless they were this sort of person, there would be not much point to what I wish to say; for they would seem to be an example of the high-spirited, right-minded young whom the critics are always invoking to come forth and do their duty and practice all those sterling old-fashioned virtues which in every generation seem to be falling into disrepair. As for virtues, these young people are more or less on their own, like most of their kind; they get very little moral or other aid from their society; but after three years of marriage this very contemporary young woman finds herself facing the oldest and ugliest dilemma of marriage.

She is dismayed, horrified, full of guilt and forebodings because she is finding out little by little that she is capable of hating her husband, whom she loves faithfully. She can hate him at times as fiercely and mysteriously, indeed in terribly much the same way, as often she hated her parents, her brothers and sisters, whom she loves, when she was a child. Even then it had seemed to her a kind of black treacherousness in her, her private wickedness that, just the same, gave her her only private life. That was one thing her parents never knew about her, never seemed to suspect. For it was never given a name. They did and said hateful things to her and to each other as if by right, as if in them it was a kind of virtue. But when they said to her, "Control your feelings," it was never when she was amiable and obedient, only in the black times of her hate. So it was her secret, a shameful one. When they punished her, sometimes for the strangest reasons, it was, they said, only because they loved her—it was for her good. She did not believe this, but she thought herself guilty of something worse than ever they had punished her for. None of this really frightened her: the real fright came when she discovered that at times her father and mother hated each other; this was like standing on the doorsill of a familiar room and seeing in a lightning flash that the floor was gone, you were on the edge of a bottomless pit. Sometimes she felt that both of them hated her, but that passed, it was simply not a thing to be thought of, much less believed. She thought she had outgrown all this, but here it was again, an element in her own nature she could not control, or feared she could not. She would have to hide from her husband, if she could, the same spot in her feelings she had hidden from her parents, and for the same no doubt disreputable, selfish reason: she wants to keep his love.

Above all, she wants him to be absolutely confident that she loves him, for that is the real truth, no matter how unreasonable it sounds, and no matter how her own feelings betray them both at times. She depends recklessly on his love; yet while she is hating him, he might very well be hating her as much or even more, and it would serve her right. But she does not want to be served right, she wants to be loved and forgiven—that is, to be sure he would forgive her anything, if he had any notion of what she had done. But best of all she would like not to have anything in her love that should ask for forgiveness. She doesn't mean about their quarrels—they are not so bad. Her feelings are out of proportion, perhaps. She knows it is perfectly natural for people to disagree, have fits of temper, fight it out; they learn quite a lot about each other that way, and not all of it disappointing either. When it passes, her hatred seems quite unreal. It always did.

Love. We are early taught to say it. I love you. We are trained to the thought of it as if there were nothing else, or nothing else worth having without it, or nothing worth having which it could not bring with it. Love is taught, always by precept, sometimes by example. Then hate, which no one meant to teach us, comes of itself. It is true that if we say I love you, it may be received with doubt, for there are times when it is hard to believe. Say I hate you, and the one spoken to believes it instantly, once for all.

Say I love you a thousand times to that person afterward and mean it every time, and still it does not change the fact that once we said I hate you, and meant that too. It leaves a mark on that surface love had worn so smooth with its eternal caresses. Love must be learned, and learned again and again; there is no end to it. Hate needs no instruction, but waits only to be provoked . . . hate, the unspoken word, the unacknowledged presence in the house, that faint smell of brimstone among the roses, that invisible tongue-tripper, that unkempt finger in every pie, that sudden oh-so-curiously *chilling* look—could it be boredom?—on your dear one's features, making them quite ugly. Be careful: love, perfect love, is in danger.

If it is not perfect, it is not love, and if it is not love, it is bound to be hate sooner or later. This is perhaps a not too exaggerated statement of the extreme position of Romantic Love, more especially in America, where we are all brought up on it, whether we know it or not. Romantic Love is changeless, faithful, passionate, and its sole end is to render the two lovers happy. It has no obstacles save those provided by the hazards of fate (that is to say, society), and such sufferings as the lovers may cause each other are only another word for delight: exciting jealousies, thrilling uncertainties, the ritual dance of courtship within the charmed closed circle of their secret alliance; all *real* troubles come from without, they face them unitedly in perfect confidence. Marriage is not the end but only the beginning of true happiness, cloudless, changeless to the end. That the candidates for this blissful condition have never seen an example of it, nor ever knew anyone who had, makes no difference. That is the ideal and they will achieve it.

How did Romantic Love manage to get into marriage at last, where it was most certainly never intended to be? At its highest it was tragic: the love of Héloïse and Abélard. At its most graceful, it was the homage of the trouvère for his lady. In its most popular form, the adulterous strayings of solidly married couples who meant to stray for their own good reasons, but at the same time do nothing to upset the property settlements or the line of legitimacy; at its most trivial, the pretty trifling of shepherd and shepherdess.

This was generally condemned by church and state and a word of fear to honest wives whose mortal enemy it was. Love within the sober, sacred realities of marriage was a matter of personal luck, but in any case, private feelings were strictly a private affair having, at least in theory, no bearing whatever on the fixed practice of the rules of an institution never intended as a recreation ground for either sex. If the couple discharged their religious and social obligations, furnished forth a copious progeny, kept their troubles to themselves, maintained public civility and died under the same roof, even if not always on speaking terms, it was rightly regarded as a successful marriage. Apparently this testing ground was too severe for all but the stoutest spirits; it too was based on an ideal, as impossible in its way as the ideal Romantic Love. One good thing to be said for it is that society took responsibility for the conditions of marriage, and the sufferers within its bonds could always blame the system, not themselves. But Romantic Love crept into the marriage bed, very stealthily, by centuries, bringing its absurd notions about love as eternal springtime and marriage as a personal adventure meant to provide personal happiness. To a Western romantic such as I, though my views have been much modified by painful experience, it still seems to be a charming work of the human imagination, and it is a pity its central notion has been taken too literally and has hardened into a convention as cramping and enslaving as the older one. The refusal to acknowledge the evils in ourselves which therefore are implicit in any human situation is as extreme and unworkable a proposition as the doctrine of total depravity;

but somewhere between them, or maybe beyond them, there does exist a possibility for reconciliation between our desires for impossible satisfactions and the simple unalterable fact that we also desire to be unhappy and that we create our own sufferings; and out of these sufferings we salvage our fragments of happiness.

Our young woman who has been taught that an important part of her human nature is not real because it makes trouble and interferes with her peace of mind and shakes her self-love, has been very badly taught; but she has arrived at a most important stage of her re-education. She is afraid her marriage is going to fail because she has not love enough to face its difficulties; and this because at times she feels a painful hostility toward her husband, and cannot admit its reality because such an admission would damage in her own eyes her view of what love should be, an absurd view, based on her vanity of power. Her hatred is real as her love is real, but her hatred has the advantage at present because it works on a blind instinctual level, it is lawless; and her love is subjected to a code of ideal conditions, impossible by their very nature of fulfillment, which prevents its free growth and deprives it of its right to recognize its human limitations and come to grips with them. Hatred is natural in a sense that love, as she conceives it, a young person brought up in the tradition of Romantic Love, is not natural at all. Yet it did not come by hazard, it is the very imperfect expression of the need of the human imagination to create beauty and harmony out of chaos, no matter how mistaken its notion of these things may be, nor how clumsy its methods. It has conjured love out of the air, and seeks to preserve it by incantations; when she spoke a vow to love and honor her husband until death, she did a very reckless thing, for it is not possible by an act of the will to fulfill such an engagement. But it was the necessary act of faith performed in defense of a mode of feeling, the statement of honorable intention to practice as well as she is able the noble, acquired faculty of love, that very mysterious overtone to sex which is the best thing in it. Her hatred is part of it, the necessary enemy and ally.

## I. Suggestions for Discussion:
1. Explain why Porter calls hate the necessary enemy.
2. Contrast the expectations of romantic love with the realities of marriage.
3. What does Porter mean by insisting that love must be learned and learned again and again?

## II. Suggestions for Writing:
1. Using your own experiences and observations, write an account of the decline and end of a romantic relationship.

2. Discuss in an essay whether or not Porter's observations are equally applicable to husbands and wives. Consider whether or not she identifies special problems with which a woman must deal.

---

## REYNOLDS PRICE

### The Heroes of Our Times

---

Reynolds Price, the Southern novelist, short-story writer, editor, and poet, is James B. Duke Professor at Duke University. His novels include *A Long and Happy Life* (1962), *A Generous Man* (1966), and *The Surface of Earth* (1975).

In the following essay, Price attempts to define the nature of a contemporary hero and to compare and contrast current standards with those of the past. He finds our lack of substantive heroes a serious reflection on our times.

---

Our need for heroes is at least as old as our need for enemies. The earliest literary texts of western civilization were propped in powerful compulsion round the names of actual men—large, honorable, and honored in proportion: Gilgamesh, Abraham, Moses, Achilles. The compulsion and its famous results continued, with few interruptions, till a hundred years ago. Tennyson's "Ode on the Death of the Duke of Wellington" and Whitman's poems on the death of Lincoln remain, oddly, the most recent in a line of heroic monuments nearly four millennia long. Where are their successors?

Maybe the pause is not odd and is in fact a break. Where after all are our epics and tragedies?—fragmented into novels and movies, ghosts of their old life-giving forms. Tennyson himself, in contemplating the Iron Duke's corpse, predicted the end—"Mourn, for to us he seems the last." Of later poets writing in English only Auden, in his elegies for Yeats and Freud, succeeded in erecting sizable and apparently durable memorials. Where are the poems on, the distinguished portraits of, the hymns to Marie Curie, Albert Einstein, Douglas MacArthur, Pablo Picasso, Franklin and Eleanor Roosevelt, Claus von Stauffenberg? Where are the odes to the three popular heroes of the recent American past—John and Robert Kennedy and Martin Luther King, Jr.? They are plainly honored in the national imagination—millions of

chromos in millions of homes attest to that, and a grotesque hunger for news
of their survivors (no gobbet too small or rank) continues to gorge itself.
They are of course the subject of numerous memoirs, biographies, films. But
is their absence from serious imaginative art only another sign of the disas-.
trous separation of cultured life from common life; or have good writers,
painters, sculptors, and composers been sensitive and responsive for years
to a rising sound that is only now being widely heard?—*There are no present
heroes. Most dead ones were frauds.*

An answer to the first question would lead far afield (though whatever claims are made for a national "arts explosion" can be quickly re-
futed by any good artist). My answers to the second is a quick yes—artists
in droves have turned their backs on their ancient love and preservation of
heroes. Why? Because artists of all sorts, as society's most attentive observers,
began early in this century to abandon the traditional definitions of heroism
and have found no equally fertilizing substitutes. The explanations, again,
would be complex; but important among them are the growth of compassion
for the poor and powerless (traditional heroes being mostly highborn and
powerful), the backwash of revulsion after the Great War at the patent
stupidity and savagery of politicians and generals, and—crucial—the steady
spread by press, radio, and now television of intimate information.

It's the merciless flood of *information* that has made living heroes apparently so rare, if not invisible, and so perilous on their heights. The classical
world decided wisely that any human being accorded the honors and monuments of a hero must be, above all, dead. Even with their primitive apparatus
for the dissemination of news, Greeks, Romans, Jews, and early Christians
saw that today's still-breathing "hero" may easily be tomorrow's criminal or
fool. (The first hero of whom we possess anything approaching a full picture
is King David; and if—with his womanizing, his murders and family scandals—
he seems more human and interesting than Moses or Elijah, he is also pro-
portionately less inspiring of reverence and emulation.)

By contrast, Americans in the 19th and 20th centuries have often
rushed to elevate the living only to discover dark patches of fungus on the
idol's face and hands—Henry Ward Beecher, Warren Harding, Richard Nixon,
to name only three from a long roll of fallen. All subsequent would-be heroes
have suffered from the ensuing disillusion. (It's obvious but accurate to say
that President Carter and his family are unavoidably attacked by the lingering
spores of the Johnson-Nixon blight). And in the past decade the dead themselves have proved alarmingly vulnerable. Posthumous allegations of sexual
adventuring by Franklin Roosevelt, John and Robert Kennedy, and Martin
Luther King, Jr.—men who capitalized on the public desire for immaculate

family loyalty—have shaken if not toppled their shrines. In short, another human need—for unashamed praise this side idolatry—has been balked; and any parent now searching the walls of his child's room for icons of heroes is likely to find no face older than a rock star's or an athlete's, no person likely to do what he presently does throughout a lifetime.

"Alas. But ho-hum. It was always thus," you may well respond, and I'll partly concur. The cult of living heroes has always been dangerously close to adolescent crush at best and, at worst, to psychopathic craving. At the very word *hero,* a number of our minds automatically run vivid home-movies of Hitler, Mussolini, Stalin on balconies—genuine beasts borne grinning toward us on seas of faces damp with adoration. And nearer to home, most of us endured the daily televised arrival in our homes of the villainous faces of the Vietnam War—just as we continue to endure the efforts of newly skilled electronic artisans to stoke our old hungers to fever-pitch for some man or woman with no greater claim than an out-of-hand ego yearning for worship. In such a dizzying tide, surely we could relish a period of calm, admiring the admirable souls we meet in daily life but sworn off the hunt for national saviors or personal outsized templates for glamour and bravery?

I doubt we can. The need is too old, too ingrained in the kind of creature we are (slow to leave childhood and capable of love). At its purest, the need has always been our strongest lure to education; lives of great men and women *have* always reminded us we can make our lives quite literally sublime—lifted up, raised above the customary trails our nature has cut for itself through eons. And while many of us have had the early good luck to encounter and recognize heroic figures in our own homes, schools, or towns, such encounters have not often permanently satisfied the full need. The need is for figures both grand *and* distant. Why?

Partly because grandeur is best comprehended from a distance—an eye pressed to the floor of the Grand Canyon is seeing only grit. Partly because grandeur seen close often reveals beer cans, chicken bones, immortal plastic. Mainly, though, because distance itself implies a journey—time and effort, endurance and strengthening. Hometown models have a disconcerting tendency to seem too possible and to shrink as we grow. What we want are models visible on their heights and all-but-inimitable in gifts and achievements. Tennyson at Wellington's bier defined the hope—"On God and Godlike men we build our trust." Provided that our God is merciful and just, we have always profited from real demigods who lure us up. And *up* is the catch. Illusory heroes have frequently lured us *on* if not *down.* Hence the current healthy suspicion and aversion, the falling-off in attendance at old shrines, the consequent awarding of fame and awe to pathetic instant celebrities.

But a lull is a good time to look back and forward, to brace for the next wave—bound to come. What, in an age of nearly total information, can heroes be? Can they exist at all, in any form worth noting? Must we choose them blind as romantic lovers choose—and accept them at our doors like found-lings, bane or blessing? Or may we exercise study and judgment and select what is likely to serve and last? Since I'm proposing a true fool's errand—laying down law for regions where whim has always prevailed—I'll push to a rash end and answer the questions.

Heroes must be figures whom we feel to be unnaturally charged with some force we want but seem to lack—courage, craft, intelligence, stamina, beauty—and by imaginary contact with whom we experience a transfer of the force desired. Since we require that they stand at a distance and since they no longer come to us veiled in impenetrable art, we learn of their tri-umphs from a press that is equally prone to discover their faults. We're lucky, therefore, when our heroes are chosen for qualities that function more or less independently of our personal sense of morality. If we admire a priest for his charity and self-sacrifice, our admiration will be shattered by news of his intricate involvement with a ring of superior call-girls. If the same revela-tion includes the name of an idolized professional athlete, the new light may only enhance the athlete's glamour and power (Tennyson was plainly undeterred by Wellington's parallel fame as the sexual hero of a thousand boudoirs).

Hence there's profound unconscious wisdom at work in the present mass cults for athletes, actors, musicians. Since we honor them for what we perceive as *physical* skills, the honor is not so fragile as that we bestow on peacetime rulers, clergy, doctors, lawyers, all kinds of teachers (in wartime, obviously, soldiers are honored for defensive ferocity). Brilliant performing artists *are* the safest heroes. In the current state of moral tolerance, their heroism is seriously threatened only by their health, and maybe by discovery of some involvement in the cruel exploitation of children.

Ideally then, in prevailing conditions of scrutiny, our heroes should be either dead (and judged safe) or alive but revered for strengths that are rela-tively amoral, though never vicious. Such a caution isn't meant to preclude the finding of large rewarding figures almost anywhere one needs to look—commerce, science, literature, fine arts, law, the military, cookery, labor, even government. It is, however, meant to define again the original core of true heroism, its first and most nearly irresistible base—the human *body* (at its strongest, boldest, most beautiful) and the deeds that flow direct from that body, broad memorable gestures on the waiting air. Few of us are agile, graceful, picturesque, or eloquent enough to be immune to the use of models who stand today in that ancient line. And luckily there's a long line of candidates—from Leontyne Price, John Travolta, and Natalia Makarova to Johnny Weismuller, Bruce Jenner, Martha Graham and on: their recorded perfection preserved from age and failure.

Yet, however heroic in their different ways such names seem to me, I cannot hope to convey them intact into your pantheon. For if the recent hawking of celebrities (solid or weightless) has demonstrated their fragility as models, it has simultaneously proved the impossibility of arousing the degree of permanent excitement and admiration that is indispensable for the choice of heroes, by masses or individuals. Lasting and useful heroes *are* objects of love—love of all sorts: altruistic, erotic, passive, potentially destructive—and are chosen by levels of the mind beyond the reach of external persuasion. They may thus be either helpful or damaging, but not premeditated, interviewed, selected by cool personnel procedures. Their suddenness and mystery is precisely their power, their promise and threat. The best we can do, as we scan their dazzling faces and feel their strong pull, is to scan ourselves—to probe our own weaknesses, vacancies, and know which of them need filling and why. Then at least we can wait, informed and prepared, for the unconscious acts of choice and ardor.

It may in fact seem a bad time for heroes. Their old gleam, the old force they promised to lend us, seem genuinely and justly tarnished, worthy of suspicion. It also seems a bad time for love. There can be no question that it's always seemed so (world literature says very little else). Still the world has proved lovable year after year—though in shrinking enclaves of beauty, honesty, excellence, persistence. The chief surviving enclaves, now as always, are single human beings. The list of those whom we—at our own best—can love, serve, honor, and use as anchors in the riptides round us is surely no shorter than it's ever been. To say we lack heroes is to come dangerously close to saying we lack the capacity to love. It is certainly to say that we lack self-knowledge of our own predicament as incomplete creatures, capable of height.

I. **Suggestions for Discussion**:
   1. Why, according to Price, is our need for heroes so great?
   2. How has the flood of information in our society affected living heroes?
   3. What kinds of persons are most likely to become heroes today?
II. **Suggestions for Writing**:
   1. Write an essay explaining why you consider some living American to be a hero.

2. Write an essay relating Price's discussion of heroes to Barbara Tuchman's discussion of leaders in "The Missing Element: Moral Courage," p. 557.

---

## MARIO PUZO

### Meet Me Tonight in Dreamland

---

Mario Puzo (1920–      ), the novelist and author of books for juveniles, has written such best sellers as *The Godfather* (1969) and *Fools Die* (1978).

In the following essay, Puzo colorfully describes the Coney Island seaside resort of the nineteenth and early twentieth centuries. He contrasts the glories of its former days with the drabness of its present condition and offers a plan for its revitalization.

---

Ah, Coney Island, Coney Island, how beautiful you were. What a bright, glowing star in the memories of millions who as children soared up to a black sky on spinning wheels studded with cascading multicolored lights. Where could you ever find hot dogs so juicy, clams so succulent, freaks so fearsome, Cyclone rides so scary? Where were the summer breezes ever so fresh, the sand so voluptuous, the ocean so beckoning?

There was a time when every child in New York loved Coney Island, and so it breaks your heart to see what a slothful, bedraggled harridan it has become, endangered by the violence of its poor and hopeless people, as well as by the city planners who would improve it out of existence. If I were a wizard with one last magic trick in my bag, I would bring back the old Coney Island.

For nearly 100 years, Coney Island was the most famous—or notorious—seaside resort in the world. By 1890, preachers called it "Sodom by the Sea." Anthony Comstock himself descended upon it, biblical ax in hand.

The Coney Island of the turn of the century was a meeting ground for crooks, con men, and high-class call girls. When Boss Tweed escaped from prison, he was stashed in a Coney Island bordello before being put on a boat to Europe. There were illegal gambling joints, knockout-drop saloons, and runaway girls who had left the desolate farms of Kansas for the less than kindly wizards of a sinful Oz.

But it was also the fashionable summer resort for the high-society riff-raff of New York, the sports celebrities, the show-biz stars. Many of the rich had summer-vacation mansions built, and the Union League Club, the University Club, and the Jockey Club opened branches there. Huge restaurants seating 8,000 people, complete with tree-filled gardens and Sousa bands, spread along the shore. These establishments boasted the finest French cuisine, and one was so classy that it refused to serve beer but offered draft champagne. There was a glass pavilion holding 500 drinkers and a huge hotel built in the shape of an elephant that drew thousands of sightseers. (It drew thousands more for quite another purpose. In the slang of the period, when someone was "going to see the elephant," it meant he was going to get laid.)

The hot dog was invented at Coney Island, and the first sidewalk stand with built-in cooker was designed by an unknown Coney Island genius. More radical perhaps was Coney Island's invention of mass ocean bathing in America, renting bathing suits to the public at 25 cents a day (that included a dish of clams). After all, who would buy a bathing suit when you could use it only four times a year?

Brightly colored pavilions that stocked 20,000 suits were constructed. Amusement parks sprang up with towers and flag-flying battlements. Three first-class tracks made Coney Island the racing capital of America; the city fathers winked an indulgent eye at illegal gambling.

And the people poured in. The only thing Charles Dickens liked about America was Coney Island. Maxim Gorki called it marvelous. Eddie Cantor, Jimmy Durante, George Burns, and Irving Berlin told their first jokes and sang their first songs in German beer gardens by the sea. Houdini served his apprenticeship there. Marie Dressler sold tickets and popcorn. The mayor of London acclaimed Coney Island as unique in the history of civilization. In 1900, a hot Sunday drew 100,000. By 1914, the same hot Sunday enchanted a million, and over a million was commonplace until 1940. The peak was reached on July 3, 1947, when 2.5 million people appeared on the beach. After that date, Coney Island went into a sharp decline.

In its glory days, Coney Island had three great amusement parks: Steeplechase (which still exists), Luna Park (now a housing project), and Dreamland, the greatest of them all.

Dreamland was the most ambitious of all amusement parks built by the turn of the century. One million light bulbs illuminated its 375-foot tower and the fifteen acres of enclosed space for rides. It offered every wonder of a child's imagination. There were 100 animals—lions, leopards, bears, wolves, anteaters, monkeys, pumas, hyenas, and a famous elephant called "Little Hip." There was a wild man from Borneo, and Lilliputin, a village of 300 midgets. Six premature babies were exhibited in incubators, and it was Dreamland's boast that these tiny infants survived longer than those in the best hospitals. Mothers from all over Brooklyn rushed to offer their premature offspring as a tourist attraction at Coney Island.

The rides were equally grandiose. Shoot-the-Chutes, Tunnels of Love, scenic railways, the canals of Venice—complete with gondolas. There was a great ballroom built on a pier reaching out into the ocean, and on its fifteen acres were scattered white castles for food concessionaires and games. But although it cost $3.5 million—in that day a huge sum of money—to build, Dreamland, like the rest of Coney Island, was constructed with lath and cardboard.

On May 27, 1911, Dreamland went up in flames. The destruction surpassed the special effects of our most extravagant disaster movies. "Little Hip" died. Lions and tigers were roasted alive. The great tower crumbled to ashes. The white castles melted. The million electric bulbs, their colored lights consumed by dark red flames, were extinguished. Ammunition in the shooting galleries exploded and sent bullets flying. Fifty thousand rental bathing suits disintegrated in the smoke. The wild man of Borneo fled, wearing French pajamas and carrying an umbrella.

The six premature babies were saved.

The next day a million people came to Coney Island and paid 10 cents to see the ruins. For 10 cents more, the corpse of Black Prince, the greatest of all lions could also be viewed. Perhaps hundreds of people paid $5 to buy the "only" dog saved from the inferno. That fire finished Coney Island as an elegant seaside resort and gave it back to the working people of New York.

In July 1979, the carnival lights strung across the streets and over the rides near the boardwalk seem old and dim. The concession barkers sound like weary Methuselahs. Many of them have been in Coney Island since the 1920s; they have nowhere else to go. The pink stuffed prize animals seem shabby, and the Raggedy Ann dolls they give away look really raggedy. Storefronts are boarded up and eroded by the salt air. To my five-year-old, on her first trip to Coney Island, the place looks like Christmas. On my first visit to Coney Island in fifteen years, though, I am almost overcome with depression. Everything looks shrunken and dirty, like a place waiting to be knocked down by a bulldozer.

But, almost immediately, something happens to cheer me up. Two gypsy women are screaming at a married couple: The husband has refused to have his wife's fortune told or palm read. One of the gypsies shouts after them, "He's cheating on you and he's afraid I'll see." (The man does look a little guilty.)

In the amusement area, which has shrunk to the area from West 8th to West 20th Street, Surf Avenue to the boardwalk, a lot of the rides date back to the 1920s. The Wonder Wheel has carried 24 million passengers without an accident, and its manager assures me that the fear of crime is without foundation. However, as the Wonder Wheel comes to a stop, I see four huge watchdogs riding in one of its cars. The dogs seem entranced by the changing horizons of sky and sea. The manager tells me that the dogs love riding in the air-conditioned car, and when they are let out at night to stand guard over the amusement area, they can't wait to get back to their ride in the morning. There have been very few amusement-park-ride fatalities in Coney Island history—usually a drunk standing up on a roller-coaster car, or a repair worker being careless. However, it must be reported that while I was interviewing one ride owner an interesting incident occurred. As the owner was working on the machinery, the handle came off. Twenty people wheeled about in the skies as he called for a helper to fix it. While he waited, he put the handle down and continued our conversation. When the helper arrived, he couldn't find the handle. The people kept flying about in the sky, but were finally brought down safely. When I commented on what had happened, the owner shrugged and said anyone who worked in an ice cream factory would never eat ice cream again.

Surf Avenue running parallel to the boardwalk is loaded with old beer cans, soda cups, food labels and other debris. This is a weekday, a late-summer afternoon, and the boardwalk is practically empty. There are only a few hot-dog stands and pizza joints open. The food is terrible: $2.50 for a small paper cup of inedible shrimp. The hot dog is loaded with nitrites, the pizza an abomination. The beach looks like a desert.

I have no feeling of trepidation all day, even though most of the people I see there are black and Hispanic; they are mostly in family groups. The whites are more reserved, seem not to be having such a good time, and remind me of the Wasps who went to Coney Island before World War II—simply one culture being outnumbered by another. Even though I feel so secure, however, I make sure to be back home in my middle-class suburb before the clock strikes midnight.

In answer to a question about how dangerous Coney Island is today, a parking-lot attendant waves a stout wooden staff and pats a bulge in his side pocket. He informs us, "A man goes out on the streets of Coney Island after 9 P.M., his wife can have him declared legally dead."

And now to the villains. Who put Coney Island on its deathbed? Why is the safety valve of the great city of New York being destroyed? Contrary to the popular belief, it is not the fear of crime and muggings; it is not the whites' being outnumbered as customers. It really started in 1938, when Robert Moses was given control of the boardwalk and beaches of Coney Island.

Robert Moses was an impeccably honest civil servant. He was farseeing, he was dedicated. He was devoted to the interests of the people of New York, and he would do anything for them, except give them what they wanted.

Moses despised the gaudy honky-tonk of Coney Island. Moses believed in what social planners call "passive parks"—parks that people could walk in to enjoy such gentle amusements as band concerts, operettas, folksingers, and poetry readings. Moses never totally conquered Coney Island. But his thinking influenced city officials.

Jones Beach is Moses's dream come true. There is no ballyhoo, no crooked concessionaires, no gypsies to read your fortune, no boardwalk with cotton-candy stands, pizza joints, hot-dog wagons. No haunted houses, no Shoot-the-Chutes, no roller coasters. It has perhaps one of the most beautiful beaches in the world. It has the beautiful Jones Beach Marine Theater, which for decades has given New Yorkers Guy Lombardo, operettas, and musical comedies. It is so clean you could grow medical cultures. It is so honest, no respectable businessman would make an investment there. In short, it is a pain in the ass.

Any red-blooded American child would rather go to Coney Island than to Jones Beach. Any red-blooded American father would consider it a choice between Marilyn Monroe and Debby Boone.

The next villains to appear on the scene were the city planners. In the 1950s, they decided that amusement parks were not good places for our citizens. Amusement parks harbored grafters, petty criminals, concessionaires who bilked the public. The city planners begged the federal government for help in the form of housing subsidies. The federal government said, in effect, tear down the rides, turn the vacant lots into parks, and we will give you millions of dollars.

So fabulous Luna Park became a middle-income housing project. Construction firms were called in to knock down houses and buildings and amusement-area concessions. Modern housing was supposed to arise in their place. But Richard M. Nixon, in 1973, declared a moratorium on federally subsidized housing. And that is why today parts of Coney Island look like Berlin after World War II.

It is possible to argue that corruption is the very manure that makes our democratic capitalism grow. It may be that the reason communist regimes have failed to produce an affluent society is that they suppress two fundamental human instincts—the yearning for non-cerebral fun, and greed. How could we have built our vast industrial empires without the corruption of public officials? Coney Island became the greatest resort of the world in the late 1800s because of the corrupt rule of its city fathers; the entrepreneurial spirit of Americans was given full blast. Concessions were gaffed. Land leases worth hundreds of thousands were given away to cronies and bribers for as little as $500. But the profits were used to build enormous fancy restaurants, luxurious bathhouses, the extraordinary amusement parks.

Today the big corporations and the concessionaires will not invest because the city will not permit them to hustle and cheat customers in a free enough style to earn a fat profit. Yet nobody squawks when restaurants charge twenty bucks for a piece of dry veal and a few vegetables. The city doesn't realize that people don't mind being bamboozled and hustled if only they have a good time in return.

When I was a young boy of ten with what I thought was a major-league right arm, I knew that the three-for-a-dime baseballs I hurled would hit the target square, but that I would not necessarily win a prize. I knew it was crooked, but I never regretted the dimes I spent. Like everybody else, I wanted to be part of the magic world of Coney Island, with its lights, its thundering rides, and its striving for unattainable prizes. Coney Island made me happy for a day.

The owners of the lots and rides in Coney Island can't seem to get together on any plan to restore the place to its former glory. They seem to be awaiting what they consider the sure coming of legalized casino gambling to New York State. But it seems an unrealistic hope. It's unlikely that a casino-hotel complex will be built in Coney Island. There are too many housing projects. Too many low-income people. The lots available are too small and too scattered. There would be too many officials to bribe.

There are others who think that if New York City could spend over $100 million to rebuild Yankee Stadium, why could it not do the same thing for Coney Island? But Yankee Stadium is a source of pleasure to middle-income New Yorkers. Stadium-renovation money was lobbied by influential and powerful men. Money spent in Coney Island would only have encouraged the loud and vulgar amusement of the poor.

Then there are those who say, "Give me $200 million and I will build you a Coney Island that will again be the seventh wonder of the world." This, too, is unrealistic. California's Disneyland, built in 1955, cost $17 million. Disney World in Florida, built in 1971, cost $400 million. To build the equivalent today, no estimate can be given. It is enough to know that one ride in Disney World, the Haunted Mansion, with its food stands and amenities, cost $15 million. There is no way that you can get any businessman in America to invest that kind of money in Coney Island.

For almost a hundred years Coney Island has been the summer playground for New Yorkers. Like the mad Russian monk Rasputin, Coney Island has been stabbed, shot, poisoned, clubbed, and has still survived. We must realize that it is now a place for working-class blacks and poor people. That it saves the sanity of millions of harassed mothers. That it makes baby-sitting a joy to not-so-devoted fathers.

It may seem like a terrible thing to say, but the saving of Coney Island can only be accomplished by letting democratic capitalism give full rein to its worst instincts. Let entrepreneurs gaff the concessions, bribe city officials for cheap rental. Let those with capital exploit the poor in Coney Island as they do in the food industry, the movie industry, and the automobile industry. After all, Coney Island's capitalists are running a risk. The season lasts fourteen weeks, and if it rains some of those weeks, they can be wiped out. So let money be made, let there be exploitation. A small price to pay for a hot summer day in Dreamland.

I. **Suggestions for Discussion:**
   1. Discuss Puzo's use of details and statistics to paint his portrait of Coney Island.
   2. How thorough is his analysis of the factors that changed Coney Island? Explain. What evidence does he present to support his claims?
   3. How realistic is the solution he proposes? Discuss whether or not his solution is sufficiently developed to convince you.

II. **Suggestions for Writing:**
   1. Write a description of an amusement park you have visited.
   2. Propose a solution to the decay or deterioration of a park or neighborhood in your home town.

---

## JOHN RUSKIN

### Of the Open Sky

from *Modern Painters*

---

John Ruskin (1819–1900) was a distinguished English writer on art, architecture, and economics. He gained popularity with the publication of his first volume of *Modern Painters* in 1843. *The Seven Lamps of Architecture* (1849) was followed by *The Stones of Venice* (1851-1853). After 1860 he turned to unpopular attacks on the prevailing Victorian economy.

In this selection from *Modern Painters,* Ruskin describes the open sky in great, flowing sentences which record his sensations and impressions.

---

It is a strange thing how little in general people know about the sky. It is the part of creation in which nature has done more for the sake of pleasing man, more for the sole and evident purpose of talking to him and teaching him, than in any other of her works, and it is just the part in which we least attend to her. There are not many of her other works in which some more material or essential purpose than the mere pleasing of man is not answered by every part of their organization; but every essential purpose of the sky might, so far as we know, be answered, if once in three days, or thereabouts, a great, ugly, black rain-cloud were brought up over the blue, and everything well watered, and so all left blue again till next time, with perhaps a film of morning and evening mist for dew. And instead of this, there is not a moment of any day of our lives, when nature is not producing scene after scene, picture after picture, glory after glory, and working still upon such exquisite and constant principles of the most perfect beauty, that it is quite certain it is all done for us, and intended for our perpetual pleasure. And every man, wherever placed, however far from other sources of interest or of beauty, has this doing for him constantly. The noblest scenes of the earth can be seen and known but by few; it is not intended that man should live always in the midst of them; he injures them by his presence, he ceases to feel them if he be always with them: but the sky is for all; bright as it is, it is not

> 'Too bright or good
> For human nature's daily food;'

it is fitted in all its functions for the perpetual comfort and exalting of the heart, for soothing it and purifying it from its dross and dust. Sometimes gentle, sometimes capricious, sometimes awful, never the same for two moments together; almost human in its passions, almost spiritual in its tenderness, almost divine in its infinity, its appeal to what is immortal in us is as distinct, as its ministry of chastisement or of blessing to what is mortal is essential. And yet we never attend to it, we never make it a subject of thought, but as it has to do with our animal sensations: we look upon all by which it speaks to us more clearly than to brutes, upon all which bears witness to the intention of the Supreme that we are to receive more from the covering vault than the light and the dew which we share with the weed and the worm, only as a succession of meaningless and monotonous accident, too common and too vain to be worthy of a moment of watchfulness, or a glance of admiration. If in our moments of utter idleness and insipidity, we turn to the sky as a last resource, which of its phenomena do we speak of? One says it has been wet; and another, it has been windy; and another, it has been warm. Who, among the whole chattering crowd, can tell me of the forms and the precipices of the chain of tall white mountains that girded the horizon at noon yesterday? Who saw the narrow sunbeam that came out of the south and smote upon their summits until they melted and mouldered away in a dust of blue rain? Who saw the dance of the dead clouds when the sunlight left them last night, and the west wind blew them before it like withered leaves? All has passed, unregretted as unseen; or if the apathy be ever shaken off, even for an instant, it is only by what is gross, or what is extraordinary; and yet it is not in the broad and fierce manifestations of the elemental energies, not in the clash of the hail, nor the drift of the whirlwind, that the highest characters of the sublime are developed. God is not in the earthquake, nor in the fire, but in the still, small voice. They are but the blunt and the low faculties of our nature, which can only be addressed through lampblack and lightning. It is in quiet and subdued passages of unobtrusive majesty, the deep, and the calm, and the perpetual; that which must be sought ere it is seen, and loved ere it is understood; things which the angels work out for us daily, and yet vary eternally: which are never wanting, and never repeated; which are to be found always, yet each found but once; it is through these that the lesson of devotion is chiefly taught, and the blessing of beauty given. These are what the artist of highest aim must study; it is these, by the combination of which his ideal is to be created; these, of which so little notice is ordinarily taken by common observers, that I fully believe, little as people in general are concerned with art, more of their ideas of sky are derived from pictures than from reality; and that if we could examine the conception formed in the minds of most educated persons when we talk of clouds, it would frequently be found composed of fragments of blue and white reminiscences of the old masters. . . .

## I. Suggestions for Discussion:

1. Why does Ruskin choose to write about the open sky rather than another aspect of nature?
2. Comment on the accuracy of Ruskin's observations of the sky. To what extent does he rely on figurative language?

3. Compare Ruskin's descriptions of the sky with the descriptions of nature by Annie Dillard in "A Field of Silence," p. 135.

## II. Suggestions for Writing:

1. Write a description of the sky by day and by night.
2. Describe as carefully as you can some other phenomenon in nature such as a lake, a river, a stand of trees, or a range of hills or mountains.

---

# JOHN RUSKIN

## St. Mark's

### from *The Stones of Venice*

---

The following passage from *The Stones of Venice* is a lesson in how to look at a piece of architecture. John Ruskin uses comparison and contrast and a wealth of specific detail to contrast an English cathedral with St. Mark's in Venice.

---

And now I wish that the reader, before I bring him into St. Mark's Place, would imagine himself for a little time in a quiet English cathedral town, and walk with me to the west front of its cathedral. Let us go together up the more retired street, at the end of which we can see the pinnacles of one of the towers, and then through the low grey gateway, with its battlemented top and small latticed window in the centre, into the inner private-looking road or close, where nothing goes in but the carts of the tradesmen who supply the bishop and the chapter, and where there are little shaven grassplots, fenced in by neat rails, before old-fashioned groups of somewhat diminutive and excessively trim houses, with little oriel and bay windows jutting out here and there, and deep wooden cornices and eaves painted cream colour and white, and small porches to their doors in the shape of cockle-shells, or little, crooked, thick, indescribable wooden gables warped a little on one side; and so forward till we come to larger houses, also old-fashioned, but of red brick, and with garden behind them, and fruit walls, which show here and there, among the nectarines, the vestiges of an old cloister arch or shaft, and looking in front on the cathedral square itself, laid out in rigid divisions of smooth grass and gravel walk, yet not uncheerful, especially on the sunny side, where the canon's children are walking with their nurserymaids. And so, taking care not to tread on the grass, we will go along the straight walk to the west front, and there stand for a time, looking up at its deep-pointed porches and the dark places between their pillars where there were statues once, and where the fragments, here and there, of a stately figure are still left, which has in it the likeness of a king, perhaps indeed a king on earth, perhaps a saintly king long ago in heaven; and so higher and higher up to the great mouldering wall of rugged sculpture and confused arcades, shattered, and grey, and grisly with heads of dragons and mocking fiends, worn by the rain and swirling winds into yet unseemlier shape, and coloured on their stony scales by the deep russet-orange lichen, melancholy gold; and so, higher still, to the bleak towers, so far above that the eye loses itself among the bosses of their traceries, though they are rude and strong, and only sees like a drift of eddying black points, now closing, now scattering, and now settling suddenly into invisible places among the bosses and flowers, the crowd of restless birds that fill the whole square with that strange clangour of theirs, so harsh and yet so soothing, like the cries of birds on a solitary coast between the cliffs and sea.

Think for a little while of that scene, and the meaning of all its small formalisms, mixed with its serene sublimity. Estimate its secluded, continuous, drowsy felicities, and its evidence of the sense and steady performance of such kind of duties as can be regulated by the cathedral clock; and weigh the influence of those dark towers on all who have passed through the lonely square at their feet for centuries, and on all who have seen them rising far away over the wooded plain, or catching on their square masses the last rays of the sunset, when the city at their feet was indicated only by the mist at the end of the bend of the river. And then let us quickly recollect that we are in Venice, and land at the extremity of the Calle Lunga San Moisè, which may be considered as there answering to the secluded street that led us to our English cathedral gateway.

We find ourselves in a paved alley, some seven feet wide where it is widest, full of people, and resonant with cries of itinerant salesmen,—a shriek in their beginning, and dying away into a kind of brazen ringing, all the worse for its confinement between the high houses of the passage along which we have to make our way. Overhead an inextricable confusion of rugged shutters, and iron balconies and chimney flues pushed out on brackets to save room, and arched windows with projecting sills of Istrian stone, and gleams of green leaves here and there where a fig-tree branch escapes over a lower wall from some inner cortile, leading the eye up to the narrow stream of blue sky high over all. On each side, a row of shops, as densely set as may be, occupying, in fact, intervals between the square stone shafts, about eight feet high, which carry the first floors: intervals of which one is narrow and serves as a door; the other is, in the more respectable shops, wainscotted to the height of the counter and glazed above, but in those of the poorer tradesmen left open to the ground, and the wares laid on benches and tables in the open air, the light in all cases entering at the front only, and fading away in a few feet from the threshold into a gloom which the eye from without cannot penetrate, but which is generally broken by a ray or two from a feeble lamp at the back of the shop, suspended before a print of the Virgin. The less pious shopkeeper sometimes leaves his lamp unlighted, and is contented with a penny print; the more religious one has his print coloured and set in a little shrine with a gilded or figured fringe, with perhaps a faded flower or two on each side, and his lamp burning brilliantly. Here at the fruiterer's, where the dark-green water-melons are heaped upon the counter like cannon balls, the Madonna has a tabernacle of fresh laurel leaves; but the pewterer next door has let his lamp out, and there is nothing to be seen in his shop but the dull gleam of the studded patterns on the copper pans, hanging from his roof in the darkness. Next comes a 'Vendita Frittole e Liquori,' where the Virgin, enthroned in a very humble manner beside a tallow candle on a back shelf, presides over certain ambrosial morsels of a nature too ambiguous to be defined or enumerated. But a few steps farther on at the regular wine-shop of the caller where we are offered 'Vino Nostrani a Soldi 28·32,' the Madonna is in great glory, enthroned above ten or a dozen large red casks of three-year-old vintage, and flanked by goodly ranks of bottles of Maraschino, and two crimson lamps; and for the evening, when the gondoliers will come to drink out, under her auspices, the money they have gained during the day, she will have a whole chandelier.

A yard or two farther, we pass the hostelry of the Black Eagle, and glancing as we pass through the square door of marble, deeply moulded, in the outer wall, we see the shadows of its pergola of vines resting on an ancient well, with a pointed shield carved on its side; and so presently emerge on the bridge and Campo San Moisè, whence to the entrance into St. Mark's Place, called the Bocca di Piazza (mouth of the square), the Venetian character is nearly destroyed, first by the frightful façade of San Moisè, which we will pause at another time to examine, and then by the modernizing of the shops as they near the piazza, and the mingling with the lower Venetion populace of lounging groups of English and Austrians. We will push fast through them into the shadow of the pillars at the end of the 'Bocca di Piazza,' and then we forget them all; for between those pillars there opens a great light, and, in the midst of it, as we advance slowly, the vast tower of St. Mark seems to lift itself visibly forth from the level field of chequered stones; and, on each side, the countless arches prolong themselves into ranged symmetry, as if the rugged and irregular houses that pressed together above us in the dark alley had been struck back into sudden obedience and lovely order, and all their rude casements and broken walls had been transformed into arches charged with goodly sculpture, and fluted shafts of delicate stone.

And well may they fall back, for beyond those troops of ordered arches there rises a vision out of the earth, and all the great square seems to have opened from it in a kind of awe, that we may see it far away;—a multitude of pillars and white domes, clustered into a long low pyramid of coloured light; a treasureheap, it seems, partly of gold, and partly of opal and mother-of-pearl, hollowed beneath into five great vaulted porches, ceiled with fair mosaic, and beset with sculpture of alabaster, clear as amber and delicate as ivory,—sculpture fantastic and involved, of palm leaves and lilies, and grapes and pomegranates, and birds clinging and fluttering among the branches, all twined together into an endless network of buds and plumes; and in the midst of it, the solemn forms of angels, sceptred, and robed to the feet, and leaning to each other across the gates, their figures indistinct among the gleaming of the golden ground through the leaves beside them, interrupted and dim, like the morning light as it faded back among the branches of Eden, when first its gates were angel-guarded long ago. And round the walls of the porches there are set pillars of variegated stones, jasper and porphyry, and deep-green serpentine spotted with flakes of snow, and marbles, that half refuse and half yield to the sunshine, Cleopatra-like, 'their bluest veins to kiss'—the shadow, as it steals back from them, revealing line after line of azure undulation, as a receding tide leaves the waved sand; their capitals rich with interwoven tracery, rooted knots of herbage, and drifing leaves of acanthus and vine, and mystical signs, all beginning and ending in the Cross; and above them, in the broad archivolts, a continuous chain of language and of life—angels, and the signs of heaven, and the labours of men, each in its appointed season upon the earth; and above these, another range of glittering pinnacles, mixed with white arches edged with scarlet flowers,—a confusion of delight, amidst which the breasts of the Greek horses are seen blazing in their breadth of golden strength, and the St. Mark's lion, lifted on a blue field covered with stars, until at last, as if in ecstasy, the crests of the arches break into a marble foam, and toss themselves far into the blue sky in flashes and wreaths of sculptured spray, as if the breakers on the Lido shore had been frost-bound before they fell, and the sea-nymphs had inlaid them with coral and amethyst.

Between that grim cathedral of England and this, what an interval! There is a type of it in the very birds that haunt them; for, instead of the restless crowd, hoarse-voiced and sable-winged, drifting on the bleak upper air, the St. Mark's porches are full of doves, that nestle among the marble foliage, and mingle the soft iridescence of their living plumes, changing at every motion, with the tints, hardly less lovely, that have stood unchanged for seven hundred years. . . .

I. **Suggestions for Discussion**:
   1. Discuss Ruskin's use of comparison and contrast to give his readers a picture of St. Mark's Cathedral in Venice.
   2. Is Ruskin's language more specific, more concrete in this essay than in his essay on the open sky, p. 488? Explain your view.
   3. Compare a photograph of St. Mark's with Ruskin's description.
II. **Suggestions for Writing**:
   1. Compare and contrast a building on campus with an interesting building in your home town.
   2. Describe in detail the home you one day hope to own.

---

# BERTRAND RUSSELL

## The Functions of a Teacher

---

Bertrand Russell (1872–1970), noted British philosopher, mathematician, author, and educator, helped determine the course of modern philosophy with *Principles of Mathematics* (1903) and, with A. N. Whitehead, *Principia Mathematica* (1910). Lord Russell, a champion of humanitarianism all his life, was awarded the Nobel Prize for Literature in 1950.

In the following essay, Russell analyzes the role of a teacher in a modern democratic society. If democracy is to survive, he explains and illustrates, teachers must produce in their pupils a tolerance that springs from an endeavor to understand those who are different from ourselves.

---

Teaching, more even than most other professions, has been transformed during the last hundred years from a small, highly skilled profession concerned with a minority of the population, to a large and important branch of the public service. The profession has a great and honorable tradition, extending from the dawn of history until recent times, but any teacher in the modern world who allows himself to be inspired by the ideals of his predecessors is likely to be made sharply aware that it is not his function to teach what he thinks, but to instill such beliefs and prejudices as are thought useful by his employers. In former days a teacher was expected to be a man of exceptional knowledge or wisdom, to whose words men would do well to attend. In antiquity, teachers were not an organized profession, and no control was exercised over what they taught. It is true that they were often punished afterwards for their subversive doctrines. Socrates was put to death and Plato is said to have been thrown into prison, but such incidents did not interfere with the spread of their doctrines. Any man who has the genuine impulse of the teacher will be more anxious to survive in his books than in the flesh. A feeling of intellectual independence is essential to the proper fulfillment of the teacher's functions, since it is his business to instill what he can of knowledge and reasonableness into the process of forming public opinion. In antiquity he performed this function unhampered except by occasional spasmodic and ineffective interventions of tyrants or mobs. In the middle ages teaching became the exclusive prerogative of the church, with the result that there was little progress either intellectual or social. With the Renaissance, the general respect for learning brought back a very considerable measure of freedom to the teacher. It is true that the Inquisition compelled Galileo to recant, and burned Giordano Bruno at the stake, but each of these men had done his work before being punished. Institutions such as universities largely remained in the grip of the dogmatists, with the result that most of the best intellectual work was done by independent men of learning. In England, especially, until near the end of the nineteenth century, hardly any men of first-rate eminence except Newton were connected with universities. But the social system was such that this interfered little with their activities or their usefulness.

In our more highly organized world we face a new problem. Something called education is given to everybody, usually by the state, but sometimes by the churches. The teacher has thus become, in the vast majority of cases, a civil servant obliged to carry out the behests of men who have not his learning, who have no experience of dealing with the young, and whose only attitude towards education is that of the propagandist. It is not very easy to see how, in these circumstances, teachers can perform the functions for which they are specially fitted.

State education is obviously necessary, but as obviously involves certain dangers against which there ought to be safeguards. The evils to be feared were seen in their full magnitude in Nazi Germany and are still seen in Russia.

Where these evils prevail no man can teach unless he subscribes to a dogmatic creed which few people of free intelligence are like to accept sincerely. Not only must he subscribe to a creed, but he must condone abominations and carefully abstain from speaking his mind on current events. So long as he is teaching only the alphabet and the multiplication table, as to which no controversies arise, official dogmas do not necessarily warp his instruction; but even while he is teaching these elements he is expected, in totalitarian countries, not to employ the methods which he thinks most likely to achieve the scholastic result, but to instill fear, subservience, and blind obedience by demanding unquestioned submission to his authority. And as soon as he passes beyond the bare elements, he is obliged to take the official view on all controversial questions. The result is that the young in Nazi Germany became, and in Russia become, fanatical bigots, ignorant of the world outside their own country, totally unaccustomed to free discussion, and not aware that their opinions can be questioned without wickedness. This state of affairs, bad as it is, would be less disastrous than it is if the dogmas instilled were, as in medieval Catholicism, universal and international; but the whole conception of an international culture is denied by the modern dogmatists, who preached one creed in Germany, another in Italy, another in Russia, and yet another in Japan. In each of these countries fanatical nationalism was what was most emphasized in the teaching of the young, with the result that the men of one country have no common ground with the men of another, and that no conception of a common civilization stands in the way of warlike ferocity.

The decay of cultural internationalism has proceeded at a continually increasing pace ever since the First World War. When I was in Leningrad in 1920, I met the Professor of Pure Mathematics, who was familiar with London, Paris, and other capitals, having been a member of various international congresses. Nowadays the learned men of Russia are very seldom permitted such excursions, for fear of their drawing comparisons unfavorable to their own country. In other countries nationalism in learning is less extreme, but everywhere it is far more powerful than it was. There is a tendency in England (and, I believe, in the United States) to dispense with Frenchmen and Germans in the teaching of French and German. The practice of considering a man's nationality rather than his competence in appointing him to a post is damaging to education and an offense against the ideal of international culture, which was a heritage from the Roman Empire and the Catholic Church, but is now being submerged under a new barbarian invasion, proceeding from below rather than from without.

In democratic countries these evils have not yet reached anything like the same proportions, but it must be admitted that there is grave danger of similar developments in education, and that this danger can only be averted if those who believe in liberty of thought are on the alert to protect teachers from intellectual bondage. Perhaps the first requisite is a clear conception of the services which teachers can be expected to perform for the community. I agree with the governments of the world that the imparting of definite uncontroversial information is one of the least of the teacher's functions. It is, of course, the basis upon which the others are built, and in a technical civilization such as ours it has undoubtedly a considerable utility. There must exist in a modern community a sufficient number of men who possess the technical skill required to preserve the mechanical apparatus upon which our physical comforts depend. It is, moreover, inconvenient if any large percentage of the population is unable to read and write. For these reasons we are all in favor of universal compulsory education. But governments have perceived that it is easy, in the course of giving instruction, to instill beliefs on controversial matters and to produce habits of mind which may be convenient or inconvenient to those in authority. The defense of the state in all civilized countries is quite as much in the hands of teachers as in those of the armed forces. Except in totalitarian countries, the defense of the state is desirable, and the mere fact that education is used for this purpose is not in itself a ground of criticism. Criticism will only arise if the state is defended by obscurantism and appeals to irrational passion. Such methods are quite necessary in the case of any state worth defending. Nevertheless, there is a natural tendency towards their adoption by those who have no first-hand knowledge of education. There is a widespread belief that nations are made strong by uniformity of opinion and by the suppression of liberty. One hears it said over and over again that democracy weakens a country in war, in spite of the fact that in every important war since the year 1700 the victory has gone to the more democratic side. Nations have been brought to ruin much more often by insistence upon a narrow-minded doctrinal uniformity than by free discussion and the toleration of divergent opinions. Dogmatists the world over believe that although the truth is known to them, others will be led into false beliefs provided they are allowed to hear the arguments on both sides. This is a view which leads to one or another of two misfortunes: either one set of dogmatists conquers the world and prohibits all new ideas, or, what is worse, rival dogmatists conquer different regions and preach the gospel of hate against each other, the former of these evils existing in the middle ages, the latter during the wars of religion, and again in the present day. The first makes civilization static, the second tends to destroy it completely. Against both, the teacher should be the main safeguard.

It is obvious that organized party spirit is one of the greatest dangers of our time. In the form of nationalism it leads to wars between nations, and in other forms it leads to civil war. It should be the business of teachers to stand outside the strife of parties and endeavor to instill into the young the habit of impartial inquiry, leading them to judge issues on their merits and to be on their guard against accepting *ex parte* statements at their face value. The teacher should not be expected to flatter the prejudices either of the mob or of officials. His professional virtue should consist in a readiness to do justice to all sides, and in an endeavor to rise above controversy into a region of dispassionate scientific investigation. If there are people to whom the results of this investigation are inconvenient, he should be protected against their resentment, unless it can be shown that he has lent himself to dishonest propaganda by the dissemination of demonstrable untruths.

The function of the teacher, however, is not merely to mitigate the heat of current controversies. He has more positive tasks to perform, and he cannot be a great teacher unless he is inspired by a wish to perform these tasks. Teachers are more than any other class the guardians of civilization. They should be intimately aware of what civilization is, and desirous of imparting a civilized attitude to their pupils. We are thus brought to the question: what constitutes a civilized community?

This question would very commonly be answered by pointing to merely material tests. A country is civilized if it has much machinery, many motor cars, many bathrooms, and a great deal of rapid locomotion. To these things, in my opinion, most modern men attach much too much importance. Civilization, in the more important sense, is a thing of the mind, not of material adjuncts to the physical side of living. It is a matter partly of knowledge, partly of emotion. So far as knowledge is concerned, a man should be aware of the minuteness of himself and his immediate environment in relation to the world in time and space. He should see his own country not *only* as home, but as one among the countries of the world, all with an equal right to live and think and feel. He should see his own age in relation to the past and the future, and be aware that its own controversies will seem as strange to future ages as those of the past seem to us now. Taking an even wider view, he should be conscious of the vastness of geological epochs and astronomical abysses; but he should be aware of all this, not as a weight to crush the individual human spirit, but as a vast panorama which enlarges the mind that contemplates it. On the side of the emotions, a very similar enlargement from the purely personal is needed if a man is to be truly civilized. Men pass from birth to death, sometimes happy, sometimes unhappy; sometimes generous, sometimes grasping and petty; sometimes heroic, sometimes cowardly and servile.

To the man who views the procession as a whole, certain things stand out as worthy of admiration. Some men have been inspired by love of mankind; some by supreme intellect have helped us to understand the world in which we live; and some by exceptional sensitiveness have created beauty. These men have produced something of positive good to outweigh the long record of cruelty, oppression, and superstition. These men have done what lay in their power to make human life a better thing than the brief turbulence of savages. The civilized man, where he cannot admire, will aim rather at understanding than at reprobating. He will seek rather to discover and remove the impersonal causes of evil than to hate the men who are in its grip. All this should be in the mind and heart of the teacher, and if it is in his mind and heart he will convey it in his teaching to the young who are in his care.

No man can be a good teacher unless he has feelings of warm affection towards his pupils and a genuine desire to impart to them what he himself believes to be of value. This is not the attitude of the propagandist. To the propagandist his pupils are potential soldiers in any army. They are to serve purposes that lie outside their own lives, not in the sense in which every generous purpose transcends self, but in the sense of ministering to unjust privilege or to despotic power. The propagandist does not desire that his pupils should survey the world and freely choose a purpose which to them appears of value. He desires, like a topiarian artist, that their growth shall be trained and twisted to suit the gardener's purpose. And in thwarting their natural growth he is apt to destroy in them all generous vigor, replacing it by envy, destructiveness, and cruelty. There is no need for men to be cruel; on the contrary, I am persuaded that most cruelty results from thwarting in early years, above all from thwarting what is good.

Repressive and persecuting passions are very common, as the present state of the world only too amply proves. But they are not an inevitable part of human nature. On the contrary, they are, I believe, always the outcome of some kind of unhappiness. It should be one of the functions of the teacher to open vistas before his pupils showing them the possibility of activities that will be as delightful as they are useful, thereby letting loose their kind impulses and preventing the growth of a desire to rob others of joys that they will have missed. Many people decry happiness as an end, both for themselves and for others, but one may suspect them of sour grapes. It is one thing to forgo personal happiness for a public end, but it is quite another to treat the general happiness as a thing of no account. Yet this is often done in the name of some supposed heroism. In those who take this attitude there is generally some vein of cruelty based probably upon an unconscious envy, and the source of the envy will usually be found in childhood or youth. It should be the aim of the educator to train adults free from these psychological misfortunes, and not anxious to rob others of happiness because they themselves have not been robbed of it.

As matters stand today, many teachers are unable to do the best of which they are capable. For this there are a number of reasons, some more or less accidental, others very deep-seated. To begin with the former, most teachers are overworked and are compelled to prepare their pupils for examinations rather than to give them a liberalizing mental training. The people who are not accustomed to teaching—and this includes practically all educational authorities—have no idea of the expense of spirit that it involves. Clergymen are not expected to preach sermons for several hours every day, but the analogous effort is demanded of teachers. The result is that many of them become harassed and nervous, out of touch with recent work in the subjects that they teach, and unable to inspire their students with a sense of the intellectual delights to be obtained from new understanding and new knowledge.

This, however, is by no means the gravest matter. In most countries certain opinions are recognized as correct, and others as dangerous. Teachers whose opinions are not correct are expected to keep silent about them. If they mention their opinions it is propaganda, while the mentioning of correct opinions is considered to be merely sound instruction. The result is that the inquiring young too often have to go outside the classroom to discover what is being thought by the most vigorous minds of their own time. There is in America a subject called civics, in which, perhaps more than in any other, the teaching is expected to be misleading. The young are taught a sort of copybook account of how public affairs are supposed to be conducted, and are carefully shielded from all knowledge as to how in fact they are conducted. When they grow up and discover the truth, the result is too often a complete cynicism in which all public ideals are lost; whereas if they had been taught the truth carefully and with proper comment at an earlier age they might have become men able to combat evils in which, as it is, they acquiesce with a shrug.

The idea that falsehood is edifying is one of the besetting sins of those who draw up educational schemes. I should not myself consider that a man could be a good teacher unless he had made a firm resolve never in the course of his teaching to conceal truth because it is what is called "unedifying." The kind of virtue that can be produced by guarded ignorance is frail and fails at the first touch of reality. There are, in this world, many men who deserve admiration, and it is good that the young should be taught to see the ways in which these men are admirable. But it is not good to teach them to admire rogues by concealing their roguery. It is thought that the knowledge of things as they are will lead to cynicism, and so it may do if the knowledge comes suddenly with a shock of surprise and horror. But if it comes gradually, duly intermixed with a knowledge of what is good, and in the course of a scientific study inspired by the wish to get at the truth, it will have no such effect. In any case, to tell lies to the young, who have no means of checking what they are told, is morally indefensible.

The thing, above all, that a teacher should endeavor to produce in his pupils, if democracy is to survive, is the kind of tolerance that springs from an endeavor to understand those who are different from ourselves. It is perhaps a natural human impulse to view with horror and disgust all manners and customs different from those to which we are used. Ants and savages put strangers to death. And those who have never traveled either physically or mentally find it difficult to tolerate the queer ways and outlandish beliefs of other nations and other times, other sects and other political parties. This kind of ignorant intolerance is the antithesis of a civilized outlook, and is one of the gravest dangers to which our overcrowded world is exposed. The educational system ought to be designed to correct it, but much too little is done in this direction at present. In every country nationalistic feeling is encouraged, and school children are taught, what they are only too ready to believe, that the inhabitants of other countries are morally and intellectually inferior to those of the country in which the school children happen to reside. Collective hysteria, the most mad and cruel of all human emotions, is encouraged instead of being discouraged, and the young are encouraged to believe what they hear frequently said rather than what there is some rational ground for believing. In all this the teachers are not to blame. They are not free to teach as they would wish. It is they who know most intimately the needs of the young. It is they who through daily contact have come to care for them. But it is not they who decide what shall be taught or what the methods of instruction are to be. There ought to be a great deal more freedom than there is for the scholastic profession. It ought to have more opportunities of self-determination, more independence from the interference of bureaucrats and bigots. No one would consent in our day to subject the medical men to the control of non-medical authorities as to how they should treat their patients, except of course where they depart criminally from the purpose of medicine, which is to cure the patient. The teacher is a kind of medical man whose purpose is to cure the patient of childishness, but he is not allowed to decide for himself on the basis of experience what methods are most suitable to this end. A few great historic universities, by the weight of their prestige, have secured virtual self-determination, but the immense majority of educational institutions are hampered and controlled by men who do not understand the work with which they are interfering. The only way to prevent totalitarianism in our highly organized world is to secure a certain degree of independence for bodies performing useful public work, and among such bodies teachers deserve a foremost place.

The teacher, like the artist, the philosopher, and the man of letters, can only perform his work adequately if he feels himself to be an individual directed by an inner creative impulse, not dominated and fettered by an outside authority. It is very difficult in this modern world to find a place for the individual. He can subsist at the top as a dictator in a totalitarian state or a plutocratic magnate in a country of large industrial enterprises, but in the realm of the mind it is becoming more and more difficult to preserve independence of the great organized forces that control the livelihoods of men and women. If the world is not to lose the benefit to be derived from its best minds, it will have to find some method of allowing them scope and liberty in spite of organization. This involves a deliberate restraint on the part of those who have power, and a conscious realization that there are men to whom free scope must be afforded. Renaissance Popes could feel in this way towards Renaissance artists, but the powerful men of our day seem to have more difficulty in feeling respect for exceptional genius. The turbulence of our times is inimical to the fine flower of culture. The man in the street is full of fear, and therefore unwilling to tolerate freedoms for which he sees no need. Perhaps we must wait for quieter times before the claims of civilization can again override the claims of party spirit. Meanwhile, it is important that some at least should continue to realize the limitations of what can be done by organization. Every system should allow loopholes and exceptions, for if it does not it will in the end crush all that is best in man.

## I. Suggestions for Discussion:
1. What fears lead Russell to argue that teachers should stand outside party strife and instill the habit of impartial inquiry into the young?
2. How does Russell define a civilized community?
3. Discuss his criticism of civics. Were the faults he lists evident in the civics you studied in school?

## II. Suggestions for Writing:
1. Write an essay discussing the advantages and dangers of nationalistic feelings. Focus on a particular issue currently occupying public attention.
2. Compare and contrast Russell's views on the goals of education with those of T. H. Huxley in "A Liberal Education," p. 237.

# DOROTHY L. SAYERS

## Are Women Human?

Dorothy L. Sayers (1893–1957), the British novelist, is best known for mystery stories involving her detective character, Lord Peter Whimsey. Among her many books are *Whose Body?* (1923), *Unnatural Death* (1927), and *Murder Must Advertise* (1933). She was also an early advocate of women's rights, as is shown by the following essay from *Unpopular Opinions* (1939).

In the essay, she uses classification, comparison and contrast, and historical allusion to explain why women and men must be regarded as individual persons rather than as members of a class.

It is the mark of all movements, however well-intentioned, that their pioneers tend, by much lashing of themselves into excitement, to lose sight of the obvious. In reaction against the age-old slogan, "woman is the weaker vessel," or the still more offensive, "woman is a divine creature," we have, I think, allowed ourselves to drift into asserting that "a woman is as good as a man," without always pausing to think what exactly we mean by that. What, I feel, we ought to mean is something so obvious that it is apt to escape attention altogether, viz.: not that every woman is, in virtue of her sex, as strong, clever, artistic, levelheaded, industrious and so forth as any man that can be mentioned; but, that a woman is just as much an ordinary human being as a man, with the same individual preferences, and with just as much right to the tastes and preferences of an individual. What is repugnant to every human being is to be reckoned always as a member of a class and not as an individual person. A certain amount of classification is, of course, necessary for practical purposes: there is no harm in saying that women, as a class, have smaller bones than men, wear lighter clothing, have more hair on their heads and less on their faces, go more pertinaciously to church or the cinema, or have more patience with small and noisy babies. In the same way, we may say that stout people of both sexes are commonly better-tempered than thin ones, or that university dons of both sexes are more pedantic in their speech than agricultural labourers, or that Communists of both sexes are more ferocious than Fascists—or the other way round. What is unreasonable and irritating is to assume that *all* one's tastes and preferences have to be conditioned by the class to which one belongs. That has been the very common error into which men have frequently fallen about women—and it is the error into which feminist women are, perhaps, a little inclined to fall into about themselves.

Take, for example, the very usual reproach that women nowadays always want to "copy what men do." In that reproach there is a great deal of truth and a great deal of sheer, unmitigated and indeed quite wicked nonsense. There are a number of jobs and pleasures which men have in times past cornered for themselves. At one time, for instance, men had a monopoly of classical education. When the pioneers of university training for women demanded that women should be admitted to the universities, the cry went up at once: "Why should women want to know about Aristotle?" The answer is NOT that *all* women would be the better for knowing about Aristotle—still less, as Lord Tennyson seemed to think, that they would be more companionable wives for their husbands if they did know about Aristotle—but simply: "What women want as a class is irrelevant. *I* want to know about Aristotle. It is true that most women care nothing about him, and a great many male undergraduates turn pale and faint at the thought of him—but I, eccentric individual that I am, do want to know about Aristotle, and I submit that there is nothing in my shape or bodily functions which need prevent my knowing about him." . . .

So that when we hear that women have once more laid hands upon something which was previously a man's sole privilege, I think we have to ask ourselves: is this trousers or is it braces? Is it something useful, convenient and suitable to a human being as such? Or is it merely something unnecessary to us, ugly, and adopted merely for the sake of collaring the other fellow's property? These jobs and professions, now. It is ridiculous to take on a man's job just in order to be able to say that "a woman has done it—yah!" The only decent reason for tackling any job is that it is *your* job and *you* want to do it.

At this point, somebody is likely to say: "Yes, that is all very well. But it *is* the woman who is always trying to ape the man. She *is* the inferior being. You don't as a rule find the men trying to take the women's jobs away from them. They don't force their way into the household and turn women out of their rightful occupations."

Of course they do not. They have done it already.

Let us accept the idea that women should stick to their own jobs—the jobs they did so well in the good old days before they started talking about votes and women's rights. Let us return to the Middle Ages and ask what we should get then in return for certain political and educational privileges which we should have to abandon.

It is a formidable list of jobs: the whole of the spinning industry, the whole of the dyeing industry, the whole of the weaving industry. The whole catering industry and—which would not please Lady Astor, perhaps—the whole of the nation's brewing and distilling. All the preserving, pickling and bottling industry, all the bacon-curing. And (since in those days a man was often absent from home for months together on war or business) a very large share in the management of landed estates. Here are the women's jobs—and what has become of them? They are all being handled by men. It is all very well to say that woman's place is the home—but modern civilisation has taken all these pleasant and profitable activities out of the home, where the women looked after them, and handed them over to big industry, to be directed and organised by men at the head of large factories. Even the dairy-maid in her simple bonnet has gone, to be replaced by a male mechanic in charge of a mechanical milking plant.

Now, it is very likely that men in big industries do these jobs better than the women did them at home. The fact remains that the home contains much less of interesting activity than it used to contain. What is more, the home has so shrunk to the size of a small flat that—even if we restrict woman's job to the bearing and rearing of families—there is no room for her to do even that. It is useless to urge the modern woman to have twelve children, like her grandmother. Where is she to put them when she has got them? And what modern man wants to be bothered with them? It is perfectly idiotic to take away women's traditional occupations and then complain because she looks for new ones. Every woman is a human being—one cannot repeat that too often—and a human being *must* have occupation, if he or she is not to become a nuisance to the world.

I am not complaining that the brewing and baking were taken over by the men. If they can brew and bake as well as women or better, then by all means let them do it. But they cannot have it both ways. If they are going to adopt the very sound principle that the job should be done by the person who does it best, then that rule must be applied universally. If the women make better office-workers than men, they must have the office work. If any individual woman is able to make a first-class lawyer, doctor, architect or engineer, then she must be allowed to try her hand at it. Once lay down the rule that the job comes first and you throw that job open to every individual, man or woman, fat or thin, tall or short, ugly or beautiful, who is able to do that job better than the rest of the world.

Now, it is frequently asserted that, with women, the job does not come first. What (people cry) are women doing with this liberty of theirs? What woman really prefers a job to a home and family? Very few, I admit. It is unfortunate that they should so often have to make the choice. A man does not, as a rule, have to choose. He gets both. In fact, if he wants the home and family, he usually has to take the job as well, if he can get it. Nevertheless, there have been women, such as Queen Elizabeth and Florence Nightingale, who had the choice, and chose the job and made a success of it. And there have been and are many men who have sacrificed their careers for women— sometimes, like Antony or Parnell, very disastrously. When it comes to a *choice,* then every man or woman has to choose as an individual human being, and, like a human being, take the consequences.

As human beings! I am always entertained—and also irritated—by the newsmongers who inform us, with a bright air of discovery, that they have questioned a number of female workers and been told by one and all that they are "sick of the office and would love to get out of it." In the name of God, what human being is *not,* from time to time, heartily sick of the office and would *not* love to get out of it? The time of female office-workers is daily wasted in sympathising with disgruntled male colleagues who yearn to get out of the office. No human being likes work—not day in and day out. Work is notoriously a curse—and if women *liked* everlasting work they would not be human beings at all. *Being* human beings, they like work just as much and just as little as anybody else. They dislike perpetual washing and cooking just as much as perpetual typing and standing behind shop counters. Some of them prefer typing to scrubbing—but that does not mean that they are not, as human beings, entitled to damn and blast the typewriter when they feel that way. The number of men who daily damn and blast typewriters is incalculable; but that does not mean that they would be happier doing a little plain sewing. Nor would the women.

I have admitted that there are very few women who would put their job before every earthly consideration. I will go further and assert that there are very few men who would do it either. In fact, there is perhaps only one human being in a thousand who is passionately interested in his job for the job's sake. The difference is that if that one person in a thousand is a man, we say, simply, that he is passionately keen on his job; if she is a woman, we say she is a freak. It is extraordinarily entertaining to watch the historians of the past, for instance, entangling themselves in what they were pleased to call the "problem" of Queen Elizabeth. They invented the most complicated and astonishing reasons both for her success as a sovereign and for her tortuous matrimonial policy. She was the tool of Burleigh, she was the tool of Leicester, she was the fool of Essex; she was diseased, she was deformed, she was a man in disguise. She was a mystery, and must have some extraordinary solution. Only recently has it occurred to a few enlightened people that the solution might be quite simple after all. She might be one of the rare people who were born into the right job and put that job first. Whereupon a whole series of riddles cleared themselves up by magic. She was in love with Leicester—why didn't she marry him? Well, for the very same reason that numberless kings have not married their lovers—because it would have thrown a spanner into the wheels of the State machine. Why was she so bloodthirsty and unfeminine as to sign the death-warrant of Mary Queen of Scots? For much the same reasons that induced King George V to say that if the House of Lords did not pass the Parliament Bill he would create enough new peers to force it through— because she was, in the measure of her time, a constitutional sovereign, and knew that there was a point beyond which a sovereign could not defy Parliament. Being a rare human being with her eye to the job, she did what was necessary; being an ordinary human being, she hesitated a good deal before embarking on unsavoury measures—but as to feminine mystery, there is no such thing about it, and nobody, had she been a man, would have thought either her statesmanship or her humanity in any way mysterious. Remarkable they were—but she was a very remarkable person. Among her most remarkable achievements was that of showing that sovereignty was one of the jobs for which the right kind of woman was particularly well fitted.

Which brings us back to this question of what jobs, if any, are women's jobs. Few people would go so far as to say that all women are well fitted for all men's jobs. When people do say this, it is particularly exasperating. It is stupid to insist that there are as many female musicians and mathematicians as male—the facts are otherwise, and the most we can ask is that if a Dame Ethel Smyth or a Mary Somerville turns up, she shall be allowed to do her work without having aspersions cast either on her sex or her ability. What we ask is to be human individuals, however peculiar and unexpected. It is no good saying: "You are a little girl and therefore you ought to like dolls"; if the answer is, "But I don't," there is no more to be said. Few women happen to be natural born mechanics; but if there is one, it is useless to try and argue her into being something different. What we must *not* do is to argue that the occasional appearance of a female mechanical genius proves that all women would be mechanical geniuses if they were educated. They would not.

Where, I think, a great deal of confusion has arisen is in a failure to distinguish between special *knowledge* and special *ability*. There are certain questions on which what is called "the woman's point of view" is valuable, because they involve special *knowledge*. Women should be consulted about such things as housing and domestic architecture because, under present circumstances, they have still to wrestle a good deal with houses and kitchen sinks and can bring special knowledge to the problem. Similarly, some of them (though not all) know more about children than the majority of men, and their opinion, *as women,* is of value. In the same way, the opinion of colliers is of value about coal-mining, and the opinion of doctors is valuable about disease. But there are other questions—as for example, about literature or finance—on which the "woman's point of view" has no value at all. In fact, it does not exist. No special knowledge is involved, and a woman's opinion on literature or finance is valuable only as the judgment of an individual. I am occasionally desired by congenital imbeciles and the editors of magazines to say something about the writing of detective fiction "from the woman's point of view." To such demands, one can only say, "Go away and don't be silly. You might as well ask what is the female angle on an equilateral triangle." . . .

A man once asked me—it is true that it was at the end of a very good dinner, and the compliment conveyed may have been due to that circumstance—how I managed in my books to write such natural conversation between men when they were by themselves. Was I, by any chance, a member of a large, mixed family with a lot of male friends? I replied that, on the contrary, I was an only child and had practically never seen or spoken to any men of my own age till I was about twenty-five. "Well," said the man, "I shouldn't have expected a woman [meaning me] to have been able to make it so convincing." I replied that I had coped with this difficult problem by making my men talk, as far as possible, like ordinary human beings. This aspect of the matter seemed to surprise the other speaker; he said no more, but took it away to chew it over. One of these days it may quite likely occur to him that women, as well as men, when left to themselves, talk very much like human beings also.

Indeed, it is my experience that both men and women are fundamentally human, and that there is very little mystery about either sex, except the exasperating mysteriousness of human beings in general. And though for certain purposes it may still be necessary, as it undoubtedly was in the immediate past, for women to band themselves together, as women, to secure recognition of their requirements as a sex, I am sure that the time has now come to insist more strongly on each woman's—and indeed each man's—requirements as an individual person. It used to be said that women had no *esprit de corps;* we have proved that we have—do not let us run into the opposite error of insisting that there is an aggressively feminist "point of view" about everything. To oppose one class perpetually to another—young against old, manual labour against brain-worker, rich against poor, woman against man—is to split the foundations of the State; and if the cleavage runs too deep, there remains no remedy but force and dictatorship. If you wish to preserve a free democracy, you must base it—not on classes and categories, for this will land you in the totalitarian State, where no one may act or think except as the member of a category. You must base it upon the individual Tom, Dick and Harry, on the individual Jack and Jill—in fact, upon you and me.

**I. Suggestions for Discussion:**
1. Discuss the rhetorical impact of the title of Sayers' essay. What possible answers could there be to such a question?
2. What jobs formerly done by women have been taken over by men?
3. How does Sayers' extended allusion to Queen Elizabeth I contribute to the thesis of her essay?

**II. Suggestions for Writing:**
1. Write an essay discussing whether or not the kind of work you hope to do has either special attractions or special limitations for one sex or the other.
2. Compare Sayers' point of view with that of Shirley Chisholm in "Women and Their Liberation," p. 83.

---

## JEAN STAFFORD

### Con Ed and Me

---

Jean Stafford (1915-1979), was awarded the Pulitzer Prize in 1970 for her collected short stories.

In the witty narrative that follows, she recounts her winning battle over a bill with Consolidated Edison in New York.

---

On quitting New York City in 1957 where I had been living under the name Jean Stafford, I asked Consolidated Edison to send my final bill. Instead of a bill, I received a check for six cents, which represented, I supposed, what was left of my deposit. I kept it, partly as a curio, partly in the hope that in a wee way I could bollix up the company books, and partly because I thought it might come in handy some day in one way or another. Eleven years later, thanks to my mean-spirited foresight, I was able to use it as a tactical diversion in a battle I fought with and won from Con Ed.

In the spring of 1968, having spent a miserable ten months in a stygian sublet in the East 80's, calling myself Mrs. A. J. Liebling, I once again asked to settle my account with the Diggers Who Must. When the bill came, I read it with interest and in detail; I read it in artificial light and I took it outdoors and read it in the sun; I read it with and without a magnifying glass; each time I saw the same incontrovertible figures.

Over a period of 27 days I had, according to the computers in Charles F. Luce's busy concern, used up $6.32 worth of electricity and $409.28 of cooking gas, but, because I had a credit of $8.03 from the month before, the total came only to $407.57 instead of $415.60.

I had the bill and the old check for six cents Xeroxed and then I sat down to write Chief Luce a seventeen-page letter. I began:

"The originals of these unusual documents are at the frame shop. They will hang, well lit by LILCO, in some conspicuous part of my house in Suffolk County on Long Island. Let me explain that while I am Mrs. A. J. Liebling, in debt to you for your clean energy to the tune of $407.57, I am also, professionally, Jean Stafford (I am a writer and am not to be confused with *Jo* Stafford, the popular singer) to whom you owe six cents. Perhaps I could apply the latter to the former.

"I am a widow and I live alone. My breakfast consists of coffee, made in an electric percolator, and fruit. I do not eat lunch. In the city I seldom dine in but when I do, I cook something simple on top of the stove or I have 'finger-food,' as my mother would have called it, sent in from a delicatessen.

"I have a very long history (I was born in 1915) of somnambulism and it could be argued that between April 29 and May 25, I used up $401.25 of cooking gas running a short-order house and snack bar in my sleep for the operators of your pneumatic drills. The facts, however, cannot support this proposition. For example, my grocery bill for that period came to $41.77— that may seem steep, considering how little I eat, but what I do eat is always of prime quality. No matter where I live, my butcher who is also my cat's meat man is listed in my personal telephone book simply as 'Tiffany.'

"There is, of course, the possibility that there might have been a leak in my two-burner stove, but in that event, don't you imagine I would be dead?"

Chairman Luce and his subalterns had no way of knowing that the only entries I make in my engagement book are appointments with my dentist, my C.P.A., the doctors in charge of my giblets, of my eyes and my bones and my skin; and the hours of the departure of planes taking me away from my gas stove, my light bulbs and my electric blanket. So I felt free to describe, with a wealth of needless detail, where and with whom I had been each evening but two during the time in question.

My companions had all been illustrious in the world of *belle lettres,* architecture, painting, music, the natural and the physical sciences, jurisprudence, medicine and high finance. We had eaten ambrosia and drunk nectar in the smartest possible restaurants or in the dining rooms of splendidly appointed houses or apartments where Cézannes and Corots hung, where Aubussons and Sarouks lay and Chippendale and Queen Anne stood. These interiors reminded me of others I had seen or read about and I was happy to share my memories with my interlocutor—not, of course, that he was getting a word in edgewise.

I had in truth spent one weekend in Boston and another at my own house in the country, and in the course of one of those weeks, I had been in Nashville for two days and two nights. My weekend in Boston led me to nostalgic reminiscences of people I had known there and in all other parts of New England during the forties; the trip to Nashville caused me to discourse at length on the Southern Fugitive group and my association with them.

Relevant to nothing at all, I said:

"While I am writing to you, let me say a few words about a building you rent to Columbia University. It is known as Myles Cooper and is situated at 440 West 110th Street and it houses The School of the Arts where, while I was living in the city, I held a seminar. Myles Cooper is the most appalling place I have ever worked in and I have worked in some mighty appalling places. You should have seen my office at "The Southern Review" at Louisiana State University where I was my secretary . . ."

I named the distinguished editors, the distinguished contributors and described the parties held when the distinguished contributors came to call on the distinguished editors in Baton Rouge. I went into the pesky vermin of Louisiana, the tragic beauty of the antebellum houses, Spanish moss and the Long family.

Eventually I got back to Myles Cooper but then digressed, with many cross-references to colleagues, to talk of my offices on other campuses. Then back to Myles Cooper and to The Troubles at Columbia in April of 1968 when I was cooking up a storm at East 80th Street. I went into the woeful state of higher education. I concluded by wishing many years of health and prosperity for Mr. Luce and his.

My several verbose postscripts were followed by brief biographies of all the notables, in addition to those I had mentioned in the letter, to whom I was sending copies.

Ten days later I got a bill from Consolidated Edison for $407.57.

Now I was impatient. I wrote brusquely; "In my earlier letter, I told you to get your computers overhauled. Do as I say and do so instantly."

Two weeks went by and then one morning, a trembly-voiced Mr. Poltroon telephoned me from New York City and said that there had been a mistake in my Con Ed bill, that the figures had been based on an estimate.

"An estimate of what?" I demanded so loudly that my cat who had been spot-cleaning his gloves at my feet scuttered upstairs. "An estimate for Nedick's?"

The poor bloke tried to explain how the estimates were made, but the procedure is so tortuous, so idiosyncratically imaginative, that, at my suggestion, Mr. Poltroon gave up and went on to say that, in fact, Con Ed owed me 23 cents. I would not get the check, he was sorry to say, for ten days or two weeks and he sincerely hoped I would not be inconvenienced.

Two days later, Mr. P. was back on the hooter asking me to return the 1957 check for six cents. I refused. Testily. I said I thought I was to get a check for 23 cents; he said yes, but the company would like to combine the two so that I would get 29 cents. I told him nothing doing.

All through the summer Mr. Poltroon called me long distance every four or five days: If I got a bill for $3.67, I was to ignore it—it was a mistake. Had I got my check for 23 cents? Wouldn't I please turn loose my check for six cents? Each time he identified himself, I said, "Oh, Mr. Poltroon, could you hang on a sec? There's somebody at my back door."

Then I'd go out to the kitchen and make myself a bacon-and-tomato sandwich, work the daily crossword puzzle, comb the cat and sterilize a few Mason jars for canning watermelon pickles. He was always waiting for me when I moseyed back to the telephone; and before he could say a word, I'd tell him that I'd been in conversation with the plumber (I talked about sump-pumps, cesspools, elbows, Stillson wrenches, hard water, the high incidence of silverfish in the bathrooms of Monteagle, Tenn.) or the tree men (had Mr. Poltroon ever had trouble with fire-blight on his Japanese quince or powdery mildew on his mimosa?).

Toward the end of August, the calls stopped, but on the Tuesday after Labor Day, Mr. Poltroon rang up to apologize for not having been in touch for so long—he'd been away, he'd needed a rest.

Before I could compassionately inquire about his present condition, there was a knock at the back door and I had to leave him to confer with the cablevision man, to run up a batch of vichyssoise and to rearrange the spice shelf. Faithful Poltroon was still at the other end of the wire. His respiration was shallow; I didn't like the sound of it at all. Had I got my money from Con Ed yet? I hadn't? That was the limit! His voice belied the indignation of his words: It was wanting the timbre of a healthy man.

I never heard that voice again. But late in September a Mr. Bandersnatch S. Pecksniff wrote:

"Mr. C. E. Poltroon informed me of his telephone conversation in which he explained the circumstances resulting in the issuance of our inaccurate billing. We have special programing and instructions to prevent such situations. I am sorry that these instructions were not followed in this instance.

"Enclosed are the two checks which Mr. Poltroon spoke to you about. I do hope you will cash them promptly and enable us to balance your account."

There was an imploring note, I felt, in that last sentence. Although the letter was dated Sept. 24, the new check for six cents (payable to Mrs. A. J. Liebling. Why? Con Ed had owed and had paid Miss Stafford six cents in 1957 but they didn't owe Mrs. L. six cents in 1968) was dated Aug. 8 and the one for 23 cents had been made out on Sept. 6. My case had clearly consumed far more clerical time than I had consumed gas.

The three checks and the amazing bill are framed and hang in my downstairs bathroom. I'm not sure yet, but I have a hunch that by and by I'll have to make room for another set of similar testaments under glass. For I have discovered that the Long Island Lighting Company, far from being Con Ed's easy-going country cousin, is his blood brother, foxy, avaricious and, not to put too fine a point on it, uppity. If he gets too far out of line—and he seems aimed in that direction—I may have to read *him* the riot act, in no uncertain terms.

## I. Suggestions for Discussion:

1. Note how Stafford's use of details adds interest and humor to her narrative. How large, for example, are her refund checks?
2. Describe the tone of her essay. Is she amused by her experience or exasperated or angered? Does she confide in her readers in order to win their confidence and approval? Explain. How do her communications with Con Ed change as the narrative continues?
3. Describe the Con Ed employees she encounters. How fully developed are they as characters in her narrative? To what extent, for example, are you able to share Mr. Poltroon's frustrations?

## II. Suggestions for Writing:

1. Recount a dispute with a large company over a bill. Was any part of the experience amusing? frustrating? demeaning?

2. Write two letters to a customer, the first demanding payment for an overdue bill, the second to the same customer apologizing for a large error made by your employer.

---

# RICHARD STEELE

## Spectator 157—Defects in Education

---

Sir Richard Steele (1672-1729), born in Ireland, had a distinguished career in England as a poet, essayist, dramatist, and, from 1714, manager of Drury Lane Theatre. With Joseph Addison, he wrote the *Tatler* and *Spectator* papers (1710-1712). *The Conscious Lovers* (1722) is perhaps his best-known comedy.

Reflecting on the *indoles* or natural soundness and ability of English youth, Steele deplores the common practice in English schools of beating students to punish them. The essay is taken from the *Spectator.*

---

> . . . Genius natale comes qui temperal astrum,
> Naturae deus humanae, mortalis in unum Quodque caput. . . .
> Horace

> . . . That directing power,
> Who forms the genius in the natal hour:
> That God of Nature, who, within us still,
> Inclines our action, not constrains our will.

I am very much at a loss to express by any word that occurs to me in our language that which is understood by *indoles* in Latin. The natural disposition to any particular art, science, profession, or trade, is very much to be consulted in the care of youth, and studied by men for their own conduct when they form to themselves any scheme of life. It is wonderfully hard indeed for a man to judge of his own capacity impartially; that may look great to me which may appear little to another, and I may be carried by fondness towards myself so far, as to attempt things too high for my talents and accomplishments: but it is not methinks so very difficult a matter to make a judgment of the abilities of others, especially of those who are in their infancy. My commonplace book directs me on this occasion to mention the dawning of greatness in Alexander, who being asked in his youth to contend for a prize in the Olympic games, answered he would if he had kings to run against him. Cassius, who was one of the conspirators against Caesar, gave as great a proof of his temper, when in his childhood he struck a playfellow, the son of Sylla, for saying his father was master of the Roman people. Scipio is reported to have answered (when some flatterers at supper were asking him what the Romans should do for a general after his death), Take Marius. Marius was then a very boy, and had given no instances of his valour; but it was visible to Scipio from the manners of the youth, that he had a soul formed for the attempt and execution of great undertakings. I must confess I have very often with much sorrow bewailed the misfortune of the children of Great Britain, when I consider the ignorance and undiscerning of the generality of school-masters. The boasted liberty we talk of is but a mean reward for the long servitude, the many heartaches and terrors, to which our childhood is exposed in going through a grammar-school: many of these stupid tyrants exercise their cruelty without any manner of distinction of the capacities of children, or the intention of parents in their behalf. There are many excellent tempers which are worthy to be nourished and cultivated with all possible diligence and care, that were never designed to be acquainted with Aristotle, Tully, or Virgil; and there are as many who have capacities for understanding every word those great persons have writ, and yet were not born to have any relish of their writings. For want of this common and obvious discerning in those who have the care of youth, we have so many hundred unaccountable creatures every age whipped up into great scholars, that are for ever near a right understanding, and will never arrive at it. These are the scandal of letters, and these are generally the men who are to teach others. The sense of shame and honour is enough to keep the world itself in order without corporal punishment, much more to train the minds of uncorrupted and innocent children. It happens, I doubt not, more than once in a year, that a lad is chastised for a blockhead, when it is good apprehension that makes him incapable of knowing what his teacher means: a brisk imagination very often may suggest an error, which a lad could not have fallen into if he had been as heavy in conjecturing as his master in explaining: but there is no mercy even towards a wrong interpretation of his meaning; the sufferings of the scholar's body are to rectify the mistakes of his mind.

I am confident that no boy who will not be allured to letters without blows, will ever be brought to any thing with them. A great or good mind must necessarily be the worse for such indignities; and it is a sad change to lose of its virtue for the improvement of its knowledge. No one who has gone through what they call a great school, but must remember to have seen children of excellent and ingenuous natures (as has afterwards appeared in their manhood); I say no man has passed through this way of education, but must have seen an ingenuous creature expiring with shame, with pale looks, beseeching sorrow, and silent tears, throw up its honest eyes, and kneel on its tender knees to an inexorable blockhead, to be forgiven the false quantity of a word in making a Latin verse: the child is punished, and the next day he commits a like crime, and so a third with the same consequence. I would fain ask any reasonable man whether this lad, in the simplicity of his native innocence, full of shame, and capable of any impression from that grace of soul, was not fitter for any purpose in this life, than after that spark of virtue is extinguished in him, though he is able to write twenty verses in an evening?

Seneca says, after his exalted way of talking, *As the immortal gods never learnt any virtue, tho' they are indued with all that is good; so there are some men who have so natural a propensity to what they should follow, that they learn it almost as soon as they hear it.* Plants and vegetables are cultivated into the production of finer fruit than they would yield without that care; and yet we cannot entertain hopes of producing a tender conscious spirit into acts of virtue, without the same methods as is used to cut timber, or give new shape to a piece of stone.

It is wholly to this dreadful practice that we may attribute a certain hardness and ferocity which some men, though liberally educated, carry about them in all their behaviour. To be bred like a gentleman, and punished like a malefactor, must, as we see it does, produce that illiberal sauciness which we see sometimes in men of letters.

The Spartan boy who suffered the fox (which he had stolen and hid under his coat) to eat into his bowels, I dare say had not half the wit or petulance which we learn at great schools among us: but the glorious sense of honour, or rather fear of shame, which he demonstrated in that action, was worth all the learning in the world without it.

It is methinks a very melancholy consideration, that a little negligence can spoil us, but great industry is necessary to improve us; the most excellent natures are soon depreciated, but evil tempers are long before they are exalted into good habits. To help this by punishments, is the same thing as killing a man to cure him of a distemper; when he comes to suffer punishment in that one circumstance, he is brought below the existence of a rational creature, and is in the state of a brute that moves only by the admonition of stripes. But since this custom of educating by the lash is suffered by the gentry of Great Britain, I would prevail only that honest heavy lads may be dismissed from slavery sooner than they are at present, and not whipped on to their fourteenth or fifteenth year, whether they expect any progress from them or not. Let the child's capacity be forthwith examined, and he sent to some mechanic way of life, without respect to his birth, if nature designed him for nothing higher; let him go before he has innocently suffered, and is debased into a dereliction of mind for being what it is no guilt to be, a plain man. I would not here be supposed to have said, that our learned men of either robe who have been whipped at school, are not still men of noble and liberal minds; but I am sure they had been much more so than they are, had they never suffered that infamy.

But though there is so little care, as I have observed, taken, or observation made of the natural strain of men, it is no small comfort to me, as a SPECTATOR, that there is any right value set upon the *bona indoles* of other animals; as appears by the following advertisement handed about the county of Lincoln, and subscribed by Enos Thomas, a person whom I have not the honour to know, but suppose to be profoundly learned in horseflesh:

*A chestnut horse called* Caesar, *bred by* James Darcey, *Esq. at* Sedbury *near* Richmond *in the County of* York; *his grandam was his old royal mare, and got by* Blunderbuss, *which was got by* Hemsly Turk, *and he got by Mr.* Courant's Arabian, *which got Mr.* Minshul's Jewstrump. *Mr.* Caesar *sold him to a nobleman (coming five years old, when he had but one sweat) for three hundred guineas. A guinea a leap and trial, and a shilling the man.*

Enos Thomas

I. **Suggestions for Discussion**:
  1. What specific criticisms of English schooling does Steele make? Does he attempt to document his comments or is he content to let the power of his rhetoric make his case?
  2. Discuss the effectiveness of Steele's allusions. Does the reference to Alexander, for example, help clarify his point about high-spirited natural ability? Explain.
  3. Comment on the rhetorical function of the advertisement for a horse which concludes the essay.

II. **Suggestions for Writing**:
  1. Write an essay arguing for or against corporal punishment in American schools.
  2. Compare and contrast Steele's views on English schooling with those of Henry Fielding, p. 179.

# JONATHAN SWIFT

## A Modest Proposal

Jonathan Swift (1667–1745), born in Ireland, became dean of St. Patrick's Episcopal Cathedral in Dublin. In 1704 he published his first major satires, *A Tale of a Tub* and *The Battle of the Books*. An active political journalist, essayist, and poet, he is best remembered for *Gulliver's Travels* (1726) and for *A Modest Proposal* (1729), the selection that follows.

The English oppression of Ireland led Swift to adopt the mask or persona of an economist in this ironic, bitter, and disturbing plan to raise and market Irish babies for food.

For Preventing the Children of Poor People in Ireland from Being a Burden to Their Parents or Country, and for Making Them Beneficial to the Public.

It is a melancholy object to those who walk through this great town or travel in the country, when they see the streets, the roads, and cabin doors, crowded with beggars of the female sex, followed by three, four, or six children, all in rags and importuning every passenger for an alms. These mothers, instead of being able to work for their honest livelihood, are forced to employ all their time in strolling to beg sustenance for their helpless infants: who as they grow up either turn thieves for want of work, or leave their dear native country to fight for the pretender in Spain, or sell themselves to the Barbadoes.

I think it is agreed by all parties that this prodigious number of children in the arms, or on the backs, or at the heels of their mothers, and frequently of their fathers, is in the present deplorable state of the kingdom a very great additional grievance; and therefore, whoever could find out a fair, cheap, and easy method of making these children sound, useful members of the commonwealth, would deserve so well of the public as to have his statue set up for a preserver of the nation.

But my intention is very far from being confined to provide only for the children of professed beggars; it is of a much greater extent, and shall take in the whole number of infants at a certain age who are born of parents in effect as little able to support them as those who demand our charity in the streets.

As to my own part, having turned my thoughts for many years upon this important subject, and maturely weighed the several schemes of our projectors, I have always found them grossly mistaken in their computation. It is true, a child just dropped from its dam may be supported by her milk for a solar year, with little other nourishment; at most not above the value of 2s.[1] which the mother may certainly get, or the value in scraps, by her lawful occupation of begging; and it is exactly at one year old that I propose to provide for them in such a manner as instead of being a charge upon their parents or the parish, or wanting food and raiment for the rest of their lives, they shall on the contrary contribute to the feeding, and partly to the clothing, of many thousands.

There is likewise another great advantage in my scheme, that it will prevent those voluntary abortions, and that horrid practice of women murdering their bastard children, alas! too frequent among us! sacrificing the poor innocent babes I doubt more to avoid the expense than the shame, which would move tears and pity in the most savage and inhuman breast.

The number of souls in this kingdom being usually reckoned one million and a half, of these I calculate there may be about 200,000 couple whose wives are breeders; from which number I subtract 30,000 couple who are able to maintain their own children (although I apprehend there cannot be so many, under the present distress of the kingdom); but this being granted, there will remain 170,000 breeders. I again subtract 50,000 for those women who miscarry, or whose children die by accident or disease within the year. There only remain 120,000 children of poor parents annually born. The question therefore is, how this number shall be reared and provided for? which, as I have already said, under the present situation of affairs, is utterly impossible by all the methods hitherto proposed. For we can neither employ them in handicraft or agriculture; we neither build houses (I mean in the country) nor cultivate land; they can very seldom pick up a livelihood by stealing, till they arrive at six years old, except where they are of towardly parts; although I confess they learn the rudiments much earlier; during which time they can, however, be properly looked upon only as probationers; as I have been informed by a principal gentleman in the county of Cavan, who protested to

---

[1] The abbreviations for English currency are *d* for pennies, *s* for shillings, and *l* for pounds.

me that he never knew above one or two instances under the age of six, even in a part of the kingdom so renowned for the quickest proficiency in that art.

I am assured by our merchants, that a boy or a girl before twelve years old is no saleable commodity; and even when they come to this age they will not yield above *3l.* or *3l. 2s. 6d.* at most on the exchange; which cannot turn to account either to the parents or kingdom, the charge of nutriment and rags having been at least four times that value.

I shall now therefore humbly propose my own thoughts, which I hope will not be liable to the least objection.

I have been assured by a very knowing American of my acquaintance in London, that a young healthy child well nursed is at a year old a most delicious, nourishing, and wholesome food, whether stewed, roasted, baked, or broiled; and I make no doubt that it will equally serve in a fricassee or a ragout.

I do therefore humbly offer it to public consideration that of the 120,000 children already computed, 20,000 may be reserved for breed, whereof only one-fourth part to be males; which is more than we allow to sheep, black cattle, or swine; and my reason is, that these children are seldom the fruits of marriage, a circumstance not much regarded by our savages; therefore one male will be sufficient to serve four females. That the remaining 100,000 may, at a year old, be offered in sale to the persons of quality and fortune through the kingdom; always advising the mother to let them suck plentifully in the last month, so as to render them plump and fat for a good table. A child will make two dishes at an entertainment for friends; and when the family dines alone, the fore or hind quarter will make a reasonable dish, and seasoned with a little pepper or salt will be very good boiled on the fourth day, especially in winter.

I have reckoned upon a medium that a child just born will weigh 12 pounds, and in a solar year, if tolerably nursed, will increase to 28 pounds.

I grant this food will be somewhat dear, and therefore very proper for landlords, who, as they have already devoured most of the parents, seem to have the best title to the children.

Infant's flesh will be in season throughout the year, but more plentiful in March, and a little before and after: for we are told by a grave author, an eminent French physician, that fish being a prolific diet, there are more children born in Roman Catholic countries about nine months after Lent than at any other season; therefore, reckoning a year after Lent, the markets will be more glutted than usual, because the number of popish infants is at least three to one in this kingdom: and therefore it will have one other collateral advantage, by lessening the number of papists among us.

I have already computed the charge of nursing a beggar's child (in which list I reckon all cottagers, laborers, and four-fifths of the farmers) to be about *2s.* per annum, rags included; and I believe no gentleman would repine to give *10s.* for the carcass of a good fat child, which, as I have said, will make four dishes of excellent nutritive meat, when he has only some particular friend or his own family to dine with him. Thus the squire will learn to be a good landlord, and grow popular among the tenants; the mother will have *8s.* net profit, and be fit for work till she produces another child.

Those who are more thrifty (as I must confess the times require) may flay the carcass; the skin of which artificially dressed will make admirable gloves for ladies, and summer boots for fine gentlemen.

As to our city of Dublin, shambles may be appointed for this purpose in the most convenient parts of it, and butchers we may be assured will not be wanting: although I rather recommend buying the children alive, and dressing them hot from the knife as we do roasting pigs.

A very worthy person, a true lover of his country, and whose virtues I highly esteem, was lately pleased in discoursing on this matter to offer a refinement upon my scheme. He said that many gentlemen of this kingdom, having of late destroyed their deer, he conceived that the want of venison might be well supplied by the bodies of young lads and maidens, not exceeding fourteen years of age nor under twelve; so great a number of both sexes in every country being now ready to starve for want of work and service; and these to be disposed of by their parents, if alive, or otherwise by their nearest relations. But with due deference to so excellent a friend and so deserving a patriot, I cannot be altogether in his sentiments; for as to the males, my American acquaintance assured me from frequent experience that their flesh was generally tough and lean, like that of our schoolboys by continual exercise, and their taste disagreeable; and to fatten them would not answer the charge. Then as to the females, it would, I think, with humble submission be a loss to the public, because they soon would become breeders themselves: and besides, it is not improbable that some scrupulous people might be apt to censure such a practice (although indeed very unjustly), as a little bordering upon cruelty; which, I confess, has always been with me the strongest objection against any project, how well soever intended.

But in order to justify my friend, he confessed that this expedient was put into his head by the famous Psalmanazar, a native of the island Formosa, who came from thence to London about twenty years ago: and in conversation told my friend, that in his country when any young person happened to be put to death, the executioner sold the carcass to persons of quality as a prime dainty; and that in his time the body of a plump girl of fifteen, who was crucified for an attempt to poison the emperor, was sold to his imperial majesty's prime minister of state, and other great mandarins of the court, in joints from the gibbet, at 400 crowns. Neither indeed can I deny, that if the same use were made of several plump young girls in this town, who without one single groat to their fortunes cannot stir abroad without a chair, and appear at the playhouse and assemblies in foreign fineries which they never will pay for, the kingdom would not be the worse.

Some persons of a desponding spirit are in great concern about that vast number of poor people, who are aged, diseased, or maimed, and I have been desired to employ my thoughts what course may be taken to ease the nation of so grievous an encumbrance. But I am not in the least pain upon that matter, because it is well known that they are every day dying and rotting by cold and famine, and filth and vermin, as fast as can be reasonably expected. And as to the young laborers, they are now in as hopeful a condition: they cannot get work, and consequently pine away for want of nourishment, to a degree that if at any time they are accidentally hired to common labor, they have not strength to perform it; and thus the country and themselves are happily delivered from the evils to come.

I have too long digressed, and therefore shall return to my subject. I think the advantages by the proposal which I have made are obvious and many, as well as of the highest importance.

For first, as I have already observed, it would greatly lessen the number of papists, with whom we are yearly overrun, being the principal breeders of the nation as well as our most dangerous enemies; and who stay at home on purpose to deliver the kingdom to the Pretender, hoping to take their advantage by the absence of so many good Protestants, who have chosen rather to leave their country than stay at home and pay tithes against their conscience to an Episcopal curate.

Secondly, The poor tenants will have something valuable of their own, which by law may be made liable to distress and help to pay their landlord's rent, their corn and cattle being already seized, and money a thing unknown.

Thirdly, Whereas the maintenance of 100,000 children from two years old and upward, cannot be computed at less than *10s.* a-piece per annum, the nation's stock will be thereby increased £50,000 per annum, beside the profit of a new dish introduced to the tables of all gentlemen of fortune in the kingdom who have any refinement in taste. And the money will circulate among ourselves, the goods being entirely of our own growth and manufacture.

Fourthly, The constant breeders, beside the gain of *8s.* sterling per annum by the sale of their children, will be rid of the charge of maintaining them after the first year.

Fifthly, This food would likewise bring great custom to taverns, where the vintners will certainly be so prudent as to procure the best receipts for dressing it to perfection, and consequently have their houses frequented by all the fine gentlemen, who justly value themselves upon their knowledge in good eating; and a skilful cook, who understands how to oblige his guests, will contrive to make it as expensive as they please.

Sixthly, This would be a great inducement to marriage, which all wise nations have either encouraged by rewards or enforced by laws and penalties. It would increase the care and tenderness of mothers toward their children, when they were sure of a settlement for life to the poor babes, provided in some sort by the public, to their annual profit instead of expense. We should see an honest emulation among the married women, which of them would bring the fattest child to the market. Men would become as fond of their wives during the time of their pregnancy as they are now of their mares in foal, their cows in calf, their sows when they are ready to farrow; nor offer to beat or kick them (as is too frequent a practice) for fear of a miscarriage.

Many other advantages might be enumerated. For instance, the addition of some thousand carcasses in our exportation of barreled beef, the propagation of swine's flesh, and improvement in the art of making good bacon, so much wanted among us by the great destruction of pigs, too frequent at our table; which are no way comparable in taste or magnificence to a well-grown, fat, yearling child, which roasted whole will make a considerable figure at a lord mayor's feast or any other public entertainment. But this and many others I omit, being studious of brevity.

Supposing that 1,000 families in this city would be constant customers for infants' flesh, besides others who might have it at merry-meetings, particularly at weddings and christenings, I compute that Dublin would take off annually about 20,000 carcasses; and the rest of the kingdom (where probably they will be sold somewhat cheaper) the remaining 80,000.

I can think of no one objection that will possibly be raised against this proposal, unless it should be urged that the number of people will be thereby much lessened in the kingdom. This I freely own, and it was indeed one principal design in offering it to the world. I desire the reader will observe, that I calculate my remedy for this one individual kingdom of Ireland and for no other that ever was, is, or I think ever can be upon earth. Therefore let no man talk to me of other expedients: of taxing our absentees at 5s. a pound: of using neither clothes nor household furniture except what is of our own growth and manufacture: of utterly rejecting the materials and instruments that promote foreign luxury: of curing the expensiveness of pride, vanity, idleness, and gaming in our women: of introducing a vein of parsimony, prudence, and temperance: of learning to love our country, in the want of which we differ even from Laplanders and the inhabitants of Topinamboo: of quitting our animosities and factions, nor acting any longer like the Jews, who were murdering one another at the very moment their city was taken: of being a little cautious not to sell our country and conscience for nothing: of teaching landlords to have at least one degree of mercy toward their tenants: lastly, of putting a spirit of honesty, industry, and skill into our shopkeepers; who, if a resulution could now be taken to buy only our native goods, would immediately unite to cheat and exact upon us in the price, the measure, and the goodness, nor could ever yet be brought to make one fair proposal of just dealing, though often and earnestly invited to it.

Therefore I repeat, let no man talk to me of these and the like expedients, till he has at least some glimpse of hope that there will be ever some hearty and sincere attempt to put them in practice.

But as to myself, having been wearied out for many years with offering vain, idle, visionary thoughts, and at length utterly despairing of success, I fortunately fell upon this proposal; which, as it is wholly new, so it has something solid and real, of no expense and little trouble, full in our own power, and whereby we can incur no danger in disobliging England. For this kind of commodity will not bear exportation, the flesh being of too tender a consistence to admit a long continuance in salt, although perhaps I could name a country which would be glad to eat up our whole nation without it.

After all, I am not so violently bent upon my own opinion as to reject any offer proposed by wise men, which shall be found equally innocent, cheap, easy, and effectual. But before something of that kind shall be advanced in contradiction to my scheme, and offering a better, I desire the authors will be pleased maturely to consider two points. First, as things now stand, how they will be able to find food and raiment for 100,000 useless mouths and backs. And secondly, there being a round million of creatures in human figure throughout this kingdom, whose subsistence put into a common stock would leave them in debt 2,000,000*l.* sterling, adding those who are beggars by profession to the bulk of farmers, cottagers, and laborers, with the wives and children who are beggars in effect; I desire those politicians who dislike my overture, and may perhaps be so bold as to attempt an answer, that they will first ask the parents of these mortals, whether they would not at this day think it a great happiness to have been sold for food at a year old in the manner I prescribe, and thereby have avoided such a perpetual scene of misfortunes as they have since gone through by the oppression of landlords, the impossibility of paying rent without money or trade, the want of common sustenance, with neither house nor clothes to cover them from the inclemencies of the weather, and the most inevitable prospect of entailing the like or greater miseries upon their breed for ever.

I profess, in the sincerity of my heart, that I have not the least personal interest in endeavoring to promote this necessary work, having no other motive than the public good of my country, by advancing our trade, providing for infants, relieving the poor, and giving some pleasure to the rich. I have no children by which I can propose to get a single penny; the youngest being nine years old, and my wife past child-bearing.

## I. Suggestions for Discussion:

1. Swift carefully develops his persona, the essayist who writes this pamphlet. What kind of person is the essayist? How do you feel about him by the end of the essay?
2. Discuss Swift's irony. Having read the entire essay, for example, go back and reread the first few paragraphs to note ironic statements.
3. Discuss Swift's use of facts, figures, and financial computations. Do they lend credibility to the scheme? Explain.

## II. Suggestions for Writing:

1. Make an outrageous proposal in as reasonable and thoughtful a manner as possible.
2. Write a character sketch introducing a rounded character who is very different from you.

---

# LEWIS THOMAS

## Ceti

### from *The Lives of a Cell*

---

Lewis Thomas (1919–      ), a member of the National Academy of Sciences, has served as the president of the Memorial Sloan-Kettering Cancer Center in New York and as a trustee of Rockefeller University. *The Lives of a Cell* (1974), from which the following selection is taken, won the National Book Award. His latest book, *The Medusa and the Snail: More Notes of a Biology Watcher,* appeared in 1979.

Tau Ceti, Thomas relates, is a relatively nearby star that sufficiently resembles our sun to make its solar system a plausible
candidate for the existence of life. Thomas describes efforts to
discover and communicate with other sentient life in the universe.

---

Tau Ceti is a relatively nearby star that sufficiently resembles our sun to
make its solar system a plausible candidate for the existence of life. We are,
it appears, ready to begin getting in touch with Ceti, and with any other interested celestial body in more remote places, out to the edge. CETI is also, by
intention, the acronym of the First International Conference on Communication with Extraterrestrial Intelligence, held in 1972 in Soviet Armenia under
the joint sponsorship of the National Academy of Sciences of the United
States and the Soviet Academy, which involved eminent physicists and
astronomers from various countries, most of whom are convinced that the
odds for the existence of life elsewhere are very high, with a reasonable
probability that there are civilizations, one place or another, with technologic
mastery matching or exceeding ours.

On this assumption, the conferees thought it likely that radioastronomy
would be the generally accepted mode of interstellar communication, on
grounds of speed and economy. They made a formal recommendation that
we organize an international cooperative program, with new and immense
radio telescopes, to probe the reaches of deep space for electromagnetic
signals making sense. Eventually, we would plan to send out messages on our
own and receive answers, but at the outset it seems more practical to begin
by catching snatches of conversation between others.

So, the highest of all our complex technologies in the hardest of our
sciences will soon be engaged, full scale, in what is essentially biologic research—and with some aspects of social science, at that.

The earth has become, just in the last decade, too small a place. We
have the feeling of being confined—shut in; it is something like outgrowing a
small town in a small county. The views of the dark, pocked surface of Mars,
still lifeless to judge from the latest photographs, do not seem to have extended our reach; instead, they bring closer, too close, another unsatisfactory
feature of our local environment. The blue noonday sky, cloudless, has lost
its old look of immensity. The word is out that the sky is not limitless; it is
finite. It is, in truth, only a kind of local roof, a membrane under which we
live, luminous but confusingly refractile when suffused with sunlight; we can
sense its concave surface a few miles over our heads. We know that it is tough
and thick enough so that when hard objects strike it from the outside they

burst into flames. The color photographs of the earth are more amazing than anything outside: we live inside a blue chamber, a bubble of air blown by ourselves. The other sky beyond, absolutely black and appalling, is wide-open country, irresistible for exploration.

Here we go, then. An extraterrestrial embryologist, having a close look at us from time to time, would probably conclude that the morphogenesis of the earth is coming along well, with the beginnings of a nervous system and fair-sized ganglions in the form of cities, and now with specialized, dish-shaped sensory organs, miles across, ready to receive stimuli. He may well wonder, however, how we will go about responding. We are evolving into the situation of a Skinner pigeon in a Skinner box, peering about in all directions, trying to make connections, probing.

When the first word comes in from outer space, finally, we will probably be used to the idea. We can already provide a quite good explanation for the origin of life, here or elsewhere. Given a moist planet with methane, formaldehyde, ammonia, and some usable minerals, all of which abound, exposed to lightning or ultraviolet irradiation at the right temperature, life might start off almost anywhere. The tricky, unsolved thing is how to get the polymers to arrange in membranes and invent replication. The rest is clear going. If they follow our protocol, it will be anaerobic life at first, then photosynthesis and the first exhalation of oxygen, then respiring life and the great burst of variation, then speciation, and, finally, some kind of consciousness. It is easy, in the telling.

I suspect that when we have recovered from the first easy acceptance of signs of life from elsewhere, and finished nodding at each other, and finished smiling, we will be in shock. We have had it our way, relatively speaking, being unique all these years, and it will be hard to deal with the thought that the whole, infinitely huge, spinning, clocklike apparatus around us is itself animate, and can sprout life whenever the conditions are right. We will respond, beyond doubt, by making connections after the fashion of established life, floating out our filaments, extending pili, but we will end up feeling smaller than ever, as small as a single cell, with a quite new sense of continuity. It will take some getting used to.

The immediate problem, however, is a much more practical, down-to-earth matter, and must be giving insomnia to the CETI participants. Let us assume that there is, indeed, sentient life in one or another part of remote space, and that we will be successful in getting in touch with it. What on earth are we going to talk about? If, as seems likely, it is a hundred or more light years away, there are going to be some very long pauses. The barest amenities, on which we rely for opening conversations—Hello, are you there?, from us, followed by Yes, hello, from them—will take two hundred years at least. By the time we have our party we may have forgotten what we had in mind.

We could begin by gambling on the rightness of our technology and just send out news of ourselves, like a mimeographed Christmas letter, but we would have to choose our items carefully, with durability of meaning in mind. Whatever information we provide must still make sense to us two centuries later, and must still seem important, or the conversation will be an embarrassment to all concerned. In two hundred years it is, as we have found, easy to lose the thread.

Perhaps the safest thing to do at the outset, if technology permits, is to send music. This language may be the best we have for explaining what we are like to others in space, with least ambiguity. I would vote for Bach, all of Bach, streamed out into space, over and over again. We would be bragging, of course, but it is surely excusable for us to put the best possible face on at the beginning of such an acquaintance. We can tell the harder truths later. And, to do ourselves justice, music would give a fairer picture of what we are really like than some of the other things we might be sending, like *Time,* say, or a history of the U.N. or Presidential speeches. We could send out our science, of course, but just think of the wincing at this end when the polite comments arrive two hundred years from now. Whatever we offer as today's items of liveliest interest are bound to be out of date and irrelevant, maybe even ridiculous. I think we should stick to music.

Perhaps, if the technology can be adapted to it, we should send some paintings. Nothing would better describe what this place is like, to an outsider, than the Cézanne demonstrations that an apple is really part fruit, part earth.

What kinds of questions should we ask? The choices will be hard, and everyone will want his special question first. What are your smallest particles? Did you think yourselves unique? Do you have colds? Have you anything quicker than light? Do you always tell the truth? Do you cry? There is no end to the list.

Perhaps we should wait a while, until we are sure we know what we want to know, before we get down to detailed questions. After all, the main question will be the opener: Hello, are you there? If the reply should turn out to be Yes, hello, we might want to stop there and think about that, for quite a long time.

## I. Suggestions for Discussion:

    1. What problems in communicating with alien beings does Thomas list and discuss. Can you think of others? Discuss.

2. Discuss the kinds of information and ideas you would want to transmit to alien beings to introduce us as human beings. Compare your ideas with Thomas's.

3. Make a list of ten questions you would want to ask beings from another solar system.

**II. Suggestions for Writing:**

1. Write an essay about the potential dangers of letting alien beings know where and who we are.

2. Write a newspaper story or essay describing our first encounter with alien beings.

---

# HENRY DAVID THOREAU

## Where I Lived, and What I Lived For

### from *Walden*

---

Henry David Thoreau (1817–1862) was a philosopher and poet-naturalist whose independent spirit led him to the famous experiment recorded in *Walden, or Life in the Woods* (1854). His passion for freedom and his lifetime resistance to conformity in thought and manners are forcefully presented in his famous essay, "On the Duty of Civil Disobedience" (1849).

In the second chapter of *Walden,* which follows, Thoreau contrasts city life with the simple life of the country in which he was living. His basic themes are simplicity, self-trust, and the organic life.

---

At a certain season of our life we are accustomed to consider every spot as the possible site of a house. I have thus surveyed the country on every side within a dozen miles of where I live. In imagination I have bought all the farms in succession, for all were to be bought, and I knew their price. I walked over each farmer's premises, tasted his wild apples, discoursed on husbandry with him, took his farm at his price, at any price, mortgaging it to him in my mind; even put a higher price on it,—took every thing but a deed of it,—took his word for his deed, for I dearly love to talk,—cultivated it, and him too to some extent, I trust, and withdrew when I have enjoyed it long enough, leaving him to carry it on. This experience entitled me to be regarded as a sort of real-estate broker by my friends. Wherever I sat, there I might live, and the landscape radiated from me accordingly. What is a house but a *sedes*, a seat?—better if a country seat. I discovered many a site for a house not likely to be soon improved, which some might have thought too far from the village, but to my eyes the village was too far from it. Well, there I might live, I said: and there I did live, for an hour, a summer and a winter life; saw how I could let the years run off, buffet the winter through, and see the spring come in. The future inhabitants of this region, wherever they may place their houses, may be sure that they have been anticipated. An afternoon sufficed to lay out the land into orchard, woodlot, and pasture, and to decide what fine oaks or pines should be left to stand before the door, and whence each blasted tree could be seen to the best advantage; and then I let it lie, fallow perchance, for a man is rich in proportion to the number of things which he can afford to let alone.

My imagination carried me so far that I even had the refusal of several farms,—the refusal was all I wanted,—but I never got my fingers burned by actual possession. The nearest that I came to actual possession was when I bought the Hollowell place, and had begun to sort my seeds, and collected materials with which to make a wheelbarrow to carry it on or off with; but before the owner gave me a deed of it, his wife—every man has such a wife—changed her mind and wished to keep it, and he offered me ten dollars to release him. Now, to speak the truth, I had but ten cents in the world, and it surpassed my arithmetic to tell, if I was that man who had ten cents, or who had a farm, or ten dollars, or all together. However, I let him keep the ten dollars and the farm too, for I had carried it far enough; or rather, to be generous, I sold him the farm for just what I gave for it, and, as he was not a rich man, made him a present of ten dollars, and still had my ten cents, and seeds, and materials for a wheelbarrow left. I found thus that I had been a rich man without any damage to my poverty. But I retained the landscape, and I have since annually carried off what it yielded without a wheelbarrow. With respect to landscapes,—

> "I am monarch of all I *survey,*
> My right there is none to dispute."

I have frequently seen a poet withdraw, having enjoyed the most valuable part of a farm, while the crusty farmer supposed that he had got a few wild apples only. Why, the owner does not know it for many years when a poet has put his farm in rime, the most admirable kind of invisible fence, has fairly impounded it, milked it, skimmed it, and got all the cream, and left the farmer only the skimmed milk.

The real attractions of the Hollowell farm, to me, were: its complete retirement, being about two miles from the village, half a mile from the nearest neighbor, and separated from the highway by a broad field; its bounding on the river, which the owner said protected it by its fogs from frosts in the spring, though that was nothing to me; the gray color and ruinous state of the house and barn, and the dilapidated fences, which put such an interval between me and the last occupant; the hollow and lichen-covered apple trees, gnawed by rabbits, showing what kind of neighbors I should have; but above all, the recollection I had of it from my earliest voyages up the river, when the house was concealed behind a dense grove of red maples, through which I heard the house-dog bark. I was in haste to buy it, before the proprietor finished getting out some rocks, cutting down the hollow apple trees, and grubbing up some young birches which had sprung up in the pasture, or, in short, had made any more of his improvements. To enjoy these advantages I was ready to carry it on; like Atlas, to take the world on my shoulders,—I never heard what compensation he received for that,—and do all those things which had no other motive or excuse but that I might pay for it and be unmolested in my possession of it; for I knew all the while that it would yield the most abundant crop of the kind I wanted. If I could only afford to let it alone. But it turned out as I have said.

All that I could say, then, with respect to farming on a large scale—I have always cultivated a garden—was, that I had had my seeds ready. Many think that seeds improve with age. I have no doubt that time discriminates between the good and the bad; and when at last I shall plant, I shall be less likely to be disappointed. But I would say to my fellows, once for all, As long as possible live free and uncommitted. It makes but little difference whether you are committed to a farm or the county jail.

Old Cato[1] whose "De Re Rustica" is my "Cultivator," says,—and the only translation I have seen makes sheer nonsense of the passage,—"When you think of getting a farm turn it thus in your mind, not to buy greedily; nor spare your pains to look at it, and do not think it enough to go round it once. The oftener you go there the more it will please you, if it is good." I think I

---

[1]Cato the Elder (234–149 B.C.) was a Roman statesman who wrote about rural life and agriculture. The *Cultivator* was a magazine for farmers.

shall not buy greedily, but go round and round it as long as I live, and be buried in it first, that it may please me the more at last.

The present was my next experiment of this kind, which I purpose to describe more at length, for convenience putting the experience of two years into one. As I have said, I do not propose to write an ode to dejection, but to brag as lustily as chanticleer in the morning, standing on his roost, if only to wake my neighbors up.

When first I took up my abode in the woods, that is, began to spend my nights as well as days there, which, by accident, was on Independence Day, or the Fourth of July, 1845, my house was not finished for winter, but was merely a defence against the rain, without plastering or chimney, the walls being of rough, weather-stained boards, with wide chinks, which made it cool at night. The upright white hewn studs and freshly planed door and window casings gave it a clean and airy look, especially in the morning, when its timbers were saturated with dew, so that I fancied that by noon some sweet gum would exude from them. To my imagination it retained throughout the day more or less of this auroral character, reminding me of a certain house on a mountain which I had visited a year before. This was an airy and unplastered cabin, fit to entertain a travelling god, and where a goddess might trail her garments. The winds which passed over my dwelling were such as sweep over the ridges of mountains, bearing the broken strains, or celestial parts only, of terrestrial music. The morning wind forever blows, the poem of creation is uninterrupted; but few are the ears that hear it. Olympus is but the outside of the earth everywhere.

The only house I had been the owner of before, if I except boat, was a tent, which I used occasionally when making excursions in the summer, and this is still rolled up in my garret; but the boat, after passing from hand to hand, has gone down the stream of time. With this more substantial shelter about me, I had made some progress toward settling in the world. This frame, so slightly clad, was a sort of crystallization around me, and reacted on the builder. It was suggestive somewhat as a picture in outlines. I did not need to go out of doors to take the air, for the atmosphere within had lost none of its freshness. It was not so much within doors as being a door where I sat, even in the rainiest weather. The Harivansa[2] says, "An abode without birds is like a meat without seasoning." Such was not my abode, for I found myself suddenly neighbor to the birds; not by having imprisoned one, but having

[2] A fifth-century Hindu epic.

caged myself near them. I was not only nearer to some of those which commonly frequent the garden and the orchard, but to those wilder and more thrilling songsters of the forest which never, or rarely, serenade a villager,— the wood-thrush, the veery, the scarlet tanger, the field-sparrow, the whip-poorwill, and many others.

I was seated by the shore of a small pond, about a mile and half south of the village of Concord and somewhat higher than it, in the midst of an extensive wood between that town and Lincoln, and about two miles south of that our only field known to fame, Concord Battle Ground; but I was so low in the woods that the opposite shore, half a mile off, like the rest, covered with wood, was my most distant horizon. For the first week, whenever I looked out on the pond it impressed me like a tarn high up on the side of a mountain, its bottom far above the surface of other lakes, and, as the sun arose, I saw it throwing off its nightly clothing of mist, and here and there, by degrees, its soft ripples or its smooth reflecting surface was revealed, while the mists, like ghosts, were stealthily withdrawing in every direction into the woods, as at the breaking up of some nocturnal conventicle. The very dew seemed to hang upon the trees later into the day than usual, as on the sides of mountains.

This small lake was of most value as a neighbor in the intervals of a gentle rain-storm in August, when, both air and water being perfectly still, but the sky overcast, mid-afternoon had all the serenity of evening, and the wood thrush sang around, and was heard from shore to shore. A lake like this is never smoother than at such a time; and the clear portion of the air above it being shallow and darkened by clouds, the water, full of light and reflections, becomes a lower heaven itself so much the more important. From a hilltop near by, where the wood had been recently cut off, there was a pleasing vista southward across the pond, through a wide indentation in the hills which form the shore there, where their opposite sides sloping toward each other suggested a stream flowing out in that direction through a wooded valley, but stream there was none. That way I looked between and over the near green hills to some distant and higher ones in the horizon, tinged with blue. Indeed, by standing on tiptoe I could catch a glimpse of some of the peaks of the still bluer and more distant mountain ranges in the northwest, those true-blue coins from heaven's own mint, and also of some portion of the village. But in other directions, even from this point, I could not see over or beyond the woods which surrounded me. It is well to have some water in your neighborhood, to give buoyancy to and float the earth. One value even of the smallest well is, that when you look into it you see that earth is not continent but insular. This is as important as that it keeps butter cool. When I looked across the pond from this peak toward the Sudbury meadows, which in time of flood I distinguished elevated perhaps by a mirage in their seething valley, like a coin in a basin, all the earth beyond the pond appeared like a thin crust insulated and floated even by this small sheet of intervening water, and I was reminded that this on which I dwelt was but *dry land.*

Though the view from my door was still more contracted, I did not feel crowded or confined in the least. There was pasture enough for my imagination. The low shrub oak plateau to which the opposite shore arose stretched away toward the prairies of the West and the steppes of Tartary, affording ample room for all the roving families of men. "There are none happy in the world but beings who enjoy freely a vast horizon,"—said Damodara,[3] when his herds required new and larger pastures.

Both place and time were changed, and I dwelt nearer to those parts of the universe and to those eras in history which had most attracted me. Where I lived was as far off as many a region viewed nightly by astronomers. We are wont to imagine rare and delectable places in some remote and more celestial corner of the system, behind the constellation of Cassiopeia's Chair, far from noise and disturbance. I discovered that my house actually had its site in such a withdrawn, but forever new and unprofaned, part of the universe. If it were worth the while to settle in those parts near to the Pleiades or the Hyades, to Aldebaran or Altair,[4] then I was really there, or at an equal remoteness from the life which I had left behind, divided and twinkling with as fine a ray to my nearest neighbor, and to be seen only in moonless nights by him. Such was that part of creation where I had squatted;—

> "There was a shepherd that did live,
>     And held his thoughts as high
> As were the mounts whereon his flocks
>     Did hourly feed him by."

What should we think of the shepherd's life if his flocks always wandered to higher pastures than his thoughts?

Every morning was a cheerful invitation to make my life of equal simplicity, and I may say innocence, with Nature herself. I have been as sincere a worshipper of Aurora[5] as the Greeks. I got up early and bathed in the pond; that was a religious exercise, and one of the best things which I did. They say that characters were engraven on the bathing tub of King Tching-

[3] Krishna, in the Hindu religion, is the incarnation of the God Vishnu.
[4] Names of stars and constellations.
[5] The classical goddess of dawn.

thang[6] to this effect—"Renew thyself completely each day; do it again, and again, and forever again." I can understand that. Morning brings back the heroic ages. I was as much affected by the faint hum of a mosquito making its invisible and unimaginable tour through my apartment at earliest dawn, when I was sitting with door and windows open, as I could be by any trumpet that ever sang of fame. It was Homer's requiem; itself an Iliad and Odyssey in the air, singing its own wrath and wanderings. There was something cosmical about it; a standing advertisement, till forbidden, of the everlasting vigor and fertility of the world. The morning, which is the most memorable season of the day, is the awakening hour. Then there is least somnolence in us; and for an hour, at least, some part of us awakes which slumbers all the rest of the day and night. Little is to be expected of that day, if it can be called a day, to which we are not awakened by our Genius, but by the mechanical nudgings of some servitor, are not awakened by our own newly acquired force and aspirations from within, accompanied by the undulations of celestial music, instead of factory bells, and a fragrance filling the air—to a higher life than we fell asleep from; and thus the darkness bear its fruit, and prove itself to be good, no less than the light. The man who does not believe that each day contains an earlier, more sacred, and auroral hour than he has yet profaned, has despaired of life, and is pursuing a descending and darkening way. After a partial cessation of his sensuous life, the soul of man, or its organs rather, are reinvigorated each day, and his Genius tries again what noble life it can make. All memorable events, I should say, transpire in morning time and in a morning atmosphere. The Vedas[7] say, "All intelligences awake with the morning." Poetry and art, and the fairest and most memorable of the actions of men, date from such an hour. All poets and heroes, like Memmon,[8] are the children of Aurora, and emit their music at sunrise. To him whose elastic and vigorous thought keeps pace with the sun, the day is a perpetual morning. It matters not what the clocks say or the attitudes and labors of men. Morning is when I am awake and there is a dawn in me. Moral reform is the effort to throw off sleep. Why is it that men give so poor an account of their day if they have not been slumbering? They are not such poor calculators. If they had not been overcome with drowsiness, they would have performed something. The millions are awake enough for physical labor; but only one in a million is awake enough for effective intellectual exertion, only one in a hundred millions to a poetic or divine life. To

[6] Confucius (551–479 B.C.) was China's greatest sage.
[7] Ancient Hindu scriptures.
[8] At Thebes the statue of Memmon was said to emit music at dawn.

HENRY DAVID THOREAU, Where I Lived, and What I Lived For          537

be awake is to be alive. I have never yet met a man who was quite awake. How could I have looked him in the face?

We must learn to reawaken and keep ourselves awake, not by mechanical aids, but by an infinite expectation of the dawn, which does not forsake us in our soundest sleep. I know of no more encouraging fact than the unquestionable ability of man to elevate his life by a conscious endeavor. It is something to be able to paint a particular picture, or to carve a statue, and so to make a few objects beautiful; but it far more glorious to carve and paint the very atmosphere and medium through which we look, which morally we can do. To affect the quality of the day, that is the highest of arts. Every man is tasked to make his life, even in its details, worthy of the contemplation of his most elevated and critical hour. If we refused, or rather used up, such paltry information as we get, the oracles would distinctly inform us how this might be done.

I went to the woods because I wished to live deliberately, to front only the essential facts of life, and see if I could not learn what it had to teach, and not, when I came to die, discover that I had not lived. I did not wish to live what was not life, living is so dear, nor did I wish to practice resignation, unless it was quite necessary. I wanted to live deep and suck out all the marrow of life, to live so sturdily and Spartan-like as to put to rout all that was not life, to cut a broad swath and shave close, to drive life into a corner, and reduce it to its lowest terms, and, if it proved to be mean, why then to get the whole and genuine meanness of it, and publish its meanness to the world; or if it were sublime, to know it by experience, and be able to give a true account of it in my next excursion. For most men, it appears to me, are in a strange uncertainty about it, whether it is of the devil or of God and have *somewhat hastily* concluded that it is the chief end of man here to "glorify God and enjoy him forever."

Still we live meanly, like ants; though the fable tells us that we were long ago changed into men; like pygmies we fight with cranes; it is error upon error, and clout upon clout, and our best virtue has for its occasion a superfluous and evitable wretchedness. Our life is frittered away by detail. An honest man has hardly need to count more than his ten fingers, or in extreme cases he may add his ten toes, and lump the rest. Simplicity, simplicity, simplicity! I say, let your affairs be as two or three, and not a hundred or a thousand; instead of a million count half a dozen, and keep your accounts on your thumb-nail. In the midst of this chopping sea of civilized life, such are the clouds and storms and quicksands and thousand-and-one items to be allowed for, that a man has to live, if he would not founder and go to the bottom and not make his port at all, by dead reckoning, and he must be a great calculator indeed who succeeds. Simplify, simplify. Instead of three meals a day, if it be necessary eat but one; instead of a hundred dishes, five; and reduce other things in proportion. Our life is like a German Confederacy, made up of petty states, with its boundary forever fluctuating, so that even a German cannot tell you how it is bounded at any moment. The nation itself, with all its so-called internal improvements, which, by the way, are all external and superficial, is just such an unwieldy and overgrown establishment, cluttered with furniture and tripped up by its own traps, ruined by luxury and heedless expense, by want of calculation and a worthy aim, as the million households in the land; and the only cure for it, as for them, is in a rigid economy, a stern and more than Spartan simplicity of life and elevation of purpose. It lives too fast. Men think that it is essential that the *Nation* have commerce, and export ice, and talk through a telegraph, and ride thirty miles an hour, without a doubt, whether *they* do or not; but whether we should live like baboons or like men, is a little uncertain. If we do not get out sleepers,[9] and forge rails, and devote days and nights to the work, but go to tinkering upon our *lives* to improve *them,* who will build railroads? And if railroads are not built, how shall we get to Heaven in season? But if we stay at home and mind our business, who will want railroads? We do not ride on the railroad; it rides upon us. Did you ever think what those sleepers are that underlie the railroad? Each one is a man, an Irishman, or a Yankee man. The rails are laid on them, and they are covered with sand, and the cars run smoothly over them. They are sound sleepers, I assure you. And every few years a new lot is laid down and run over; so that, if some have the pleasure of riding on a rail, others have the misfortune to be ridden upon. And when they run over a man that is walking in his sleep, a supernumerary sleeper in the wrong position, and wake him up, they suddenly stop the cars, and make a hue and cry about it, as if this were an exception. I am glad to know that it takes a gang of men for every five miles to keep the sleepers down and level in their beds as it is, for this is a sign that they may sometime get up again.

Why should we live with such hurry and waste of life? We are determined to be starved before we are hungry. Men say that a stitch in time saves nine, and so they take a thousand stitches to-day to save nine tomorrow. As for *work,* we haven't any of any consequence. We have the Saint Vitus' dance, and cannot possibly keep our heads still. If I should only give a few pulls at the parish bell-rope, as for a fire, that is, without setting the bell,

[9]Railroad ties.

there is hardly a man on his farm in the outskirts of Concord, notwithstanding that press of engagements which was his excuse so many times this morning, nor a boy, nor a woman, I might almost say, but would forsake all and follow that sound, not mainly to save property from the flames, but, if we will confess the truth, much more to see it burn, since burn it must, and we, be it known, did not set it on fire,—or to see it put out, and have a hand in it, if that is done as handsomely; yes, even if it were the parish church itself. Hardly a man takes a half-hour's nap after dinner, but when he wakes he holds up his head and asks, "What's the news?" as if the rest of mankind had stood his sentinels. Some give directions to be waked every half-hour, doubtless for no other purpose; and then, to pay for it, they tell what they have dreamed. After a night's sleep the news is as indispensable as the breakfast. "Pray tell me anything new that has happened to a man anywhere on this globe,"—and he reads it over his coffee and rolls, that a man has had his eyes gouged out this morning on the Wachito River, never dreaming the while that he lives in the dark unfathomed mammoth cave of this world, and has but the rudiment of an eye himself.

For my part, I could easily do without the post-office. I think that there are very few important communications made through it. To speak critically, I never received more than one or two letters in my life—I wrote this some years ago—that were worth the postage. The penny-post is, commonly, an institution through which you seriously offer a man that penny for his thoughts which is so often safely offered in jest. And I am sure that I never read any memorable news in a newspaper. If we read of one man robbed, or murdered, or killed by accident, or one house burned, or one vessel wrecked, or one steamboat blown up, or one cow run over on the Western Railroad, or one mad dog killed, or one lot of grasshoppers in the winter,—we never need read of another. One is enough. If you are acquainted with the principle, what do you care for a myriad instances and applications? To a philosopher all *news,* as it is called, is gossip and they who edit and read it are old women over their tea. Yet not a few are greedy after this gossip. There was such a rush, as I hear, the other day at one of the offices to learn the foreign news by the last arrival, that several large squares of plate glass belonging to the establishment were broken by the pressure,—news which I seriously think a ready wit might write a twelvemonth, or twelve years, beforehand with sufficient accuracy. As for Spain, for instance, if you know how to throw in Don Carlos and the Infanta, and Don Pedro and Seville and Granada, from time to time in the right proportions,—they may have changed the names a little since I saw the papers,—and serve up a bull-fight when other entertainments fail, it will be true to the letter, and give us as good an idea of the exact state or ruin of things in Spain as the most succinct and lucid reports under this head in the newspapers: and as for England, almost the last significant scrap of news from that quarter was the revolution of 1649,[10] and if you have learned the history of her crops for an average year, you never need attend to that thing again, unless your speculations are of a merely pecuniary character. If one may judge who rarely looks into the newspapers, nothing new does ever happen in foreign parts, a French revolution not excepted.

What news! how much more important to know what that is which was never old! "Kieou-he-yu (great dignitary of the state of Wei) sent a man to Khoung-tseu to know his news. Khoung-tseu caused the messenger to be seated near him, and questioned him in these terms: What is your master doing? The messenger answered with respect: My master desires to diminish the number of his faults, but he cannot come to the end of them. The messenger being gone, the philosopher remarked: What a worthy messenger! What a worthy messenger!' The preacher, instead of vexing the ears of drowsy farmers on their day of rest at the end of the week,—for Sunday is the fit conclusion of an ill-spent week, and not the fresh and brave beginning of a new one,—with this one other draggle-tail of a sermon, should shout with thundering voice, "Pause! Avast! Why so seeming fast, but deadly slow?"

Shams and delusions are esteemed for soundest truths, while reality is fabulous. If men would steadily observe realities only, and not allow themselves to be deluded, life, to compare it with such things as we know, would be like a fairy tale and the Arabian Nights' Entertainments. If we respected only what is inevitable and has a right to be, music and poetry would resound along the streets. When we are unhurried and wise, we perceive that only great and worthy things have any permanent and absolute existence, that petty fears and petty pleasures are but the shadow of the reality. This is always exhilarating and sublime. By closing the eyes and slumbering, and consenting to be deceived by shows, men establish and confirm their daily life of routine and habit everywhere, which still is built on purely illusory foundations. Children, who play life, discern its true law and relations more clearly than men, who fail to live it worthily, but who think that they are wiser by experience, that is, by failure. I have read in a Hindoo book, that "there was a king's son, who, being expelled in infancy from his native city, was brought up by a forester, and growing up to maturity in that state, imagined himself to belong to the barbarous race with which he lived. One of his father's ministers having discovered him, revealed to him what he was,

[10] The English monarchy was overthrown and Charles I executed by the Puritans in 1649.

and the misconception of his character was removed, and he knew himself
to be a prince. So soul," continues the Hindoo philosopher, "from the circumstances in which it is placed, mistakes its own character, until the truth is
revealed to it by some holy teacher, and then it knows itself to be *Brahma.*"
I perceive that we inhabitants of New England live this mean life that we do
because our vision does not penetrate the surface of things. We think that
that *is* which *appears* to be. If a man should walk through this town and see
only the reality, where, think you, would the "Mill-dam" go to? If he should
give us an account of the realities he beheld there, we should not recognize
the place in his description. Look at a meeting-house, or a court-house, or a
jail, or a shop, or a dwelling-house, and say what that thing really is before a
true gaze, and they would all go to pieces in your account of them. Men
esteem truth remote, in the outskirts of the system, behind the farthest star,
before Adam and after the last man. In eternity there is indeed something
true and sublime. But all these times and places and occasions are now and
here. God himself culminates in the present moment, and will never be more
divine in the lapse of all the ages. And we are enabled to apprehend at all
what is sublime and noble only by the perpetual instilling and drenching of
the reality that surrounds us. The universe constantly and obediently answers
to our conceptions; whether we travel fast or slow, the track is laid for us.
Let us spend our lives in conceiving then. The poet or the artist never yet had
so fair and noble a design but some of his posterity at least could accomplish
it.

     Let us spend one day as deliberately as Nature, and not be thrown off
the track by every nutshell and mosquito's wing that falls on the rails. Let us
rise early and fast, or break fast, gently and without perturbation; let company come and let company go, let the bells ring and the children cry,—determined to make a day of it. Why should we knock under and go with the
stream? Let us not be upset and overwhelmed in that terrible rapid and
whirlpool called a dinner, situated in the meridian shallows. Weather this
danger and you are safe, for the rest of the way is down hill. With unrelaxed
nerves, with morning vigor, sail by it, looking another way, tied to the mast
like Ulysses. If the engine whistles, let it whistle till it is hoarse for its pains.
If the bell rings, why should we run? We will consider what kind of music
they are like. Let us settle ourselves, and work and wedge our feet downward through the mud and slush of opinion, and prejudice, and tradition, and
delusion, and appearance, that alluvion which covers the globe, through Paris
and London, through New York and Boston and Concord, through Church
and State, through poetry and philosophy and religion, till we come to a hard
bottom and rocks in place, which we can call *reality,* and say, This is, and no

mistake; and then begin, having a *point d'appui,*[11] below freshet and frost and fire, a place where you might found a wall or a state, or set a lamp-post safely, or perhaps a gauge, not a Nilometer,[12] but a Realometer, that future ages might know how deep a freshet of shams and appearances had gathered from time to time. If you stand right fronting and face to face to a fact, you will see the sun glimmer on both its surfaces, as if it were a cimeter,[13] and feel its sweet edge dividing you through the heart and marrow, and so you will happily conclude your mortal career. Be it life or death, we crave only reality. If we are really dying, let us hear the rattle in our throats and feel cold in the extremities; if we are alive, let us go about our business.

Time is but the stream I go a-fishing in. I drink at it; but while I drink I see the sandy bottom and detect how shallow it is. Its thin current slides away, but eternity remains. I would drink deeper; fish in the sky, whose bottom is pebbly with stars. I cannot count one. I know not the first letter of the alphabet. I have always been regretting that I was not as wise as the day I was born. The intellect is a cleaver; it discerns and rifts its way into the secret of things. I do not wish to be any more busy with my hands than is necessary. My head is hands and feet. I feel all my best faculties concentrated in it. My instinct tells me that my head is an organ for burrowing, as some creatures use their snout and fore paws, and with it I would mine and burrow my way through these hills. I think that the richest vein is somewhere hereabouts; so by the divining-rod and thin rising vapors I judge; and here I will begin to mine.

I. **Suggestions for Discussion:**
   1. Discuss Thoreau's observation that all memorable events transpire in morning time and in a morning atmosphere. Do you agree? Explain.
   2. Explain and discuss Thoreau's admonition to simplify, simplify.
   3. How does Thoreau feel about keeping up with the news? Do you agree? Explain.

II. **Suggestions for Writing:**
   1. After a period of solitude and reflection or meditation, write an account of your surroundings and of the ideas which have passed through your mind.
   2. Contrast the scene at Walden described by Thoreau with the scene depicted by E. B. White in "Walden," p. 580.

---

[11] A point of support or foundation.
[12] A device to measure the water level in the Nile River.
[13] A curved sword.

# JAMES THURBER

## Exhibit X

---

James Thurber (1894–1961), American humorist and artist, began contributing in 1927 to *The New Yorker,* in which most of his work first appeared. His humorous essays and short stories are collected in such books as *The Owl in the Attic and Other Perplexities* (1931), *My Life and Hard Times,* and *The Thurber Carnival* (1945).

In this delightful essay, Thurber narrates, in humorous detail, his adventures as a code clerk in Paris during World War I.

---

I had been a code clerk in the State Department in Washington for four months during the first World War before my loyalty was investigated, if you could call my small, pleasant interview with Mr. Shand an investigation. He had no dossier on Thurber, James Grover, except a birth certificate and draft-board deferment papers. In 1918, Americans naïvely feared the enemy more than they feared one another. There was no F.B.I. to speak of, and I had neither been followed nor secretly photographed. A snooping photographer could have caught me taking a code book home to study one night and bringing it back the next day—an act that was indiscreet, and properly regretted when I learned the rules—but a pictorial record of my activities outside the Bureau of Indexes and Archives in Washington would actually have been as innocent as it might have *looked* damning.

It would have shown me in the company of Mrs. Nichols, head of the information desk at the State, War, and Navy Building (a psychic lady I had known since I was six); George P. Martin, proprietor of the Post Café, and Mrs. Rabbit, his assistant; Frank Farrington, a movie actor who had played the part of a crook named Braine in "The Million Dollar Mystery"; and Jack Bridges, a Los Angeles air-mail flier and Hispano-Suiza expert. I doubt if any such photographs, even one showing me borrowing twenty dollars from Bridges half an hour after meeting him for the first time in my life, would have shaken Mr. Shand's confidence in me.

Mr. Shand called me to his office about a week before I was to sail for France and the Paris Embassy. He was a tall, quiet, courteous gentleman, and he had only one question to ask me. He wanted to know if all my grand-parents had been born in the United States. I said yes, he wished me God-speed, we shook hands, and I left. That's all there was to it. Waking up at night now and looking back on it, I sometimes wonder how I would have come out of one of those three-men inquisitions the Department was caught conducting last year. Having as great a guilt sense as any congressman, and a greater tendency to confession, it might have taken me hours to dredge up out of my mind and memory all the self-indictments that must have been there. I believed then, and still do, that generals of the Southern Confederacy were, in the main, superior to generals of the Northern armies; I suspected there were flaws in the American political system; I doubted the virgin birth of United States senators; I thought that German cameras and English bicy-cles were better than ours; and I denied the existence of actual proof that God was exclusively a citizen of the United States. But, as I say, Mr. Shand merely asked me about my grandparents, and that was all. I realize now that, as a measure of patriotism, the long existence of my ancestors on American soil makes me more loyal than Virginia Dare or even George Washington, but I didn't give it any thought at the time.

Before I sailed on the S.S. Orizaba, a passenger ship converted into an Army transport and looking rather sheepish about it, I was allowed to spend four days in Columbus, Ohio, and my mother has preserved, for reasons known only to mothers, a snapshot taken of me on the last day of my leave. The subject of the photograph is obviously wearing somebody else's suit, which not only convicts him of three major faults in a code clerk—absent-mindedness, carelessness, and peccability—but gives him the unwonted ap-pearance of a saluki who, through some egregious mischance of nature, has exchanged his own ears for those of a barn owl. If this would not be enough to cause a special agent to phone Hoover personally, *regardez,* as the French Sureté would say excitedly, the *figure* of this alarming *indiscret.* His worried expression indicates that he has just mislaid a code book or, what is worse, has sold one. Even Mr. Hoover's dullest agent could tell that the picture is that of a man who would be putty in the hands of a beautiful or even a dowdy, female spy. The subject's curious but unmistakable you-ask-me-and-I'll-tell-you look shows that he would babble high confidences to low com-panions on his third *pernod à l'eau.* This man could even find some way to compromise the Department of Agriculture, let alone the Department of State.

The picture would have aroused no alarm in the old days, however, for it was almost impossible to be a security risk in the State Department in

1918, no matter how you looked. All our code books except one were quaint transparencies dating back to the time when Hamilton Fish was Secretary of State, under President Grant, and they were intended to save words and cut telegraph costs, not to fool anybody. The new code book had been put together so hastily that the word "America" was left out, and code groups so closely paralleled true readings that "LOVVE," for example, was the symbol for "love."

Whatever slight illusion of secrecy we code clerks may have had was dispelled one day by a dour gentleman who announced that the Germans had all our codes. It was said that the Germans now and then got messages through to Washington taunting us about our childish ciphers, and suggesting on one occasion that our clumsy device of combining two codes, in a desperate effort at deception, would have been a little harder if we had used two other codes, which they named. This may have been rumor or legend, like the story, current at the time, that six of our code books were missing and that a seventh, neatly wrapped, firmly tied, and accompanied by a courteous note, had been returned to one or another of our embassies by the Japanese, either because they had finished with it or because they already had one.

A system of deception as easy to see through as the passing attack of a grammar-school football team naturally produces a cat's-out-of-the-bag attitude. In enciphering messages in one code, in which the symbol for "quote" was (to make up a group) "ZOXIL," we were permitted to use "UNZOXIL" for "unquote," an aid to perspicuity that gave us code clerks the depressing feeling that our tedious work was merely an exercise in block lettering. The Department may have comforted itself with the knowledge that even the most ingenious and complex codes could have been broken down by enemy cipher experts. Unzoxilation just made it a little easier for them.

Herbert O. Yardley, one-time chief cryptographer of the War Department, warned the government in a book published nearly twenty years ago that the only impregnable codes are those whose pattern is mechanically jumbled in transmission by a special telegraphic method that reassembles the pattern at the point of reception. To prove his point, Yardley revealed how he had broken the toughest Japanese code five years before. The government must have taken his advice. I doubt that we could have got through a second world war shouting, "ZOXIL Here we come, ready or not UNZOXIL."

The State Department, in the happy-go-lucky tradition of the time, forgot to visa my special diplomatic passport, and this was to cause a tremendous *brouhaha* later on, when the French discovered I was loose in their country without the signs, seals, and signatures they so devoutly respect. The captain of the Orizaba wanted nothing to do with me when I boarded his ship, whether my passport was visaed or not. He had no intention of taking orders from the State Department or carrying its code clerks, and who the hell was Robert Lansing, anyway? He finally let me stay on board after I had bowed and scraped and touched my forelock for an hour, but he refused to monkey around getting my trunk on board. When I received it in Paris, more than a year later, everything in it was covered with the melted chocolate of a dozen Hershey bars I had tucked in here and there.

I had been instructed to report to Colonel House at the Hotel Crillon when I got to Paris, but I never saw him. I saw instead an outraged gentleman named Auchincloss, who plainly regarded me as an unsuccessfully comic puppet in a crude and inexcusable practical joke. He said bitterly that code clerks had been showing up for days, that Colonel House did not want even one code clerk, let alone twelve or fifteen, and that I was to go on over to the Embassy, where I belonged. The explanation was, I think, as simple as it was monumental. Several weeks before, the State Department in Washington had received a cablegram from Colonel House in Paris urgently requesting the immediate shipment of twelve or fifteen code clerks to the Crillon, where headquarters for the American Peace Delegation had been set up. It is plain to me now what must have happened. Colonel House's cablegram must have urgently requested the immediate shipment of twelve or fifteen code books, not code clerks. The cipher groups for "books" and "clerks" must have been nearly identical, say "DOGEC" and "DOGED," and hence a setup for the telegraphic garble. Thus, if my theory is right, the single letter "D" sent me to Paris, when I had originally been slated for Berne. Even after thirty years, the power of that minuscule slip of the alphabet gives me a high sense of insecurity. A "D" for a "C" sent Colonel House clerks instead of books, and sent me to France instead of Switzerland. On the whole, I came off far better, as events proved, than the Colonel did. There I was in Paris, with a lot of jolly colleagues, and there was Colonel House, up to his ears in code clerks, but without any code books, or at least not enough to handle the flow of cablegrams to and from the Crillon when the Peace Conference got under way.

That tiny "D" was to involve the State Department, the Paris Embassy, the Peace Conference, and, in a way that would have delighted Gilbert and Sullivan, the United States Navy in a magnificent comic opera of confusion. An admiral of the Navy, for some reason (probably because he had a lot of Navy code books), arbitrarily took over, at the Crillon, the State Department's proud prerogative of diplomatic communication, and a code shambles that might have perplexed Herbert Yardley himself developed when cablegrams in Navy codes were dispatched to the State Department in Washington, which could not figure them out and sent back bewildered and frantic queries in State Department codes, which the admiral and his aides could not unravel. The Navy has always been proud of its codes, and the fact that they couldn't be broken by the State Department only went to show how strong they were, but when communication between the Peace Conference and Washington came to a dead stop, the admiral agreed to a compromise. His clerks, young and eager junior lieutenants, would use the State Department codes. This compounded the confusion, since the lieutenants didn't know how to use the strange codes. The dozen State Department clerks Colonel House had turned away and now badly needed were finally sent for, after a month, but even then they were forced to work under the supervision of the Navy. The Great Confusion was at last brought to an end when the desperate State Department finally turned to a newspaperman for help, and assigned him to go and get its stolen power of diplomatic communication and bring it back where it belonged. Not since an American battleship, many years before, in firing a twenty-one-gun salute in honor of the President of France, had accidentally used real shells and blown the bejeezus out of the harbor of Le Havre had the American Navy so royally loused up a situation. And think of it—a "DOGEC" for a "DOGED" would have sent me to Berne, where nothing at all ever happened.

The last time I saw the old building, at 5 Rue de Chaillot, that housed the chancery of the American Embassy when I was a code clerk was in 1937. Near the high, grilled door, a plaque proclaimed that Myron T. Herrick was our Ambassador during the first World War, thus perpetuating a fond American misconception and serving as a monument to the era of the Great Confusion. The truth is that Herrick served during only the first four months of the war, and from December, 1914, until after the war, in 1919, an unsung man named William M. Sharp was our Ambassador to France. This note of bronze fuzziness cheered me in a peculiar way. It was a brave, cockeyed testament to the enduring strength of a nation that can get more ingloriously mixed up than any other and somehow gloriously come out of it in the end.

As I stood there before the old chancery, I remembered another visit I had made to 5 Rue de Chaillot, in 1925, and for the convenience of the F.B.I., who must already have twenty-three exhibits to fling at me when I am called up before some committee or other, I offer my adventure in 1925 as Exhibit X. Myron Herrick was once more our Ambassador to France, and I was granted an interview with him, or, as Counsellor Sheldon Whitehouse insisted on calling it, an audience. I had given up diplomacy for journalism, as I used to explain it, and I needed material for an article I was writing about Herrick for an American newspaper. I decided I ought to have a little "art" to go along with the story, such as a photograph of the Ambassador's office, a large, bright, well-appointed room on the second floor, facing the street. I knew I couldn't get official permission to take a picture of the room, but this didn't discourage me. I had discovered that the same old French *concierge* lived in the same rooms on the ground floor of the chancery and controlled the opening of the great, grilled door. Remembering that Sunday had always been an off day, with a skeleton staff in charge, I picked out a clear, sunny Sabbath for my exploit. I went to the chancery and pushed the bell, and the *concierge* clicked the lock from her room. I went in, said *"Bonjour, Madame,"* went upstairs, photographed the Ambassador's office, came down again, having been challenged by nobody, said *"Bonjour, Madame"* to the *concierge,* raised my hat politely, and went away.

The Republicans were in charge of the Embassy then, not the Democrats, as in my code-clerk days, but things hadn't changed much. I am a pretty good hand at time exposures, and the photograph came out well. There is still a print of it in the art morgue of an American newspaper, or ought to be, but it is merely a view of a room in the home of whatever French family now lives at 5 Rue de Chaillot.

We probably learned a lot during the recent war, and I doubt if tourists with cameras could get into any of our Embassies today. If this belated confession makes it a bit harder for them, anyway, I shall be very happy indeed. I must close now, since somebody is knocking at the door. Why, it's a couple of strange men! Now, what in the world could *they* want with me?

I. **Suggestions for Discussion**:
1. Discuss the sources of Thurber's humor. Were you amused, for example, by the confusion between DOGEC and DOGED? Comment.
2. Comment on security measures during World War I as Thurber depicts them. When do you detect his use of exaggeration in his account.
3. Discuss his tone in this sketch. How does he communicate his whimsical, bemused good nature?

II. **Suggestions for Writing**:
1. Write a humorous essay exposing and illustrating bureaucratic bungling.
2. Describe a security system you have encountered in a home, store, or business. What was effective about the system and what wasn't? What recommendations can you make for its improvement?

# JAMES THURBER

## The Split Infinitive

In the whimsical essay which follows, which James Thurber seems barely to be able to keep under control, he moves innocently and humorously from split infinitives to food fights and back again.

Word has somehow got around that a split infinitive is always wrong. This is of a piece with the sentimental and outworn notion that it is always wrong to strike a lady. Everybody will recall at least one woman of his acquaintance whom, at one time, or another, he has had to punch or slap. I have in mind a charming lady who is overcome by the unaccountable desire, at formal dinners with red and white wines, to climb up on the table and lie down. Her dinner companions used at first to pinch her, under cover of the conversation, but she pinched right back or, what is even less defensible, tickled. They finally learned that they could make her hold her seat only by fetching her a smart downward blow on the head. She would then sit quietly through the rest of the dinner, smiling dreamily and nodding at people, and looking altogether charming.

A man who does not know his own strength could, of course, all too easily overshoot the mark and, instead of producing the delightful languor to which I have alluded, knock his companion completely under the table, an awkward situation which should be avoided at all costs because it would leave two men seated next each other. I know of one man who, to avert this *faux pas,* used to punch his dinner companion in the side (she would begin to cry during the red-wine courses), a blow which can be executed, as a rule, with less fuss, but which has the disadvantage of almost always causing the person who is struck to shout. The hostess, in order to put her guest at her ease, must shout too, which is almost certain to arouse one of those nervous, highstrung men, so common at formal dinners, to such a pitch that he will begin throwing things. There is nothing more deplorable than the spectacle of a formal dinner party ending in a brawl. And yet it is surprising how even the most cultured and charming people can go utterly to pieces when something is unexpectedly thrown at table. They instantly have an overwhelming desire to "join in." Everybody has, at one time or another, experienced the urge to throw a plate of jelly or a half grapefruit, an urge comparable to the inclination that suddenly assails one to leap from high places. Usually this tendency passes as quickly as it comes, but it is astounding how rapidly it can be converted into action once the spell of dignity and well-bred reserve is broken by the sight of, say, a green-glass salad plate flying through the air. It is all but impossible to sit quietly by while someone is throwing salad plates. One is stirred to participation not only by the swift progress of the objects and their crash as they hit something, but also by the cries of "Whammy!" and "Whoop!" with which most men accompany the act of hurling plates. In the end someone is bound to be caught over the eye by a badly aimed plate and rendered unconscious.

My contemporary, Mr. Fowler, in a painstaking analysis of the split infinitive, divides the English-speaking world into five classes as regards this construction: those who don't know and don't care, those who don't know and do care, those who know and approve, those who know and condemn, and those who know and discriminate. (The fact that there was no transition at all between the preceding paragraph and this one does not mean that I did not try, in several different ways, to get back to the split infinitive logically. As in a bridge hand, the absence of a re-entry is not always the fault of the man who is playing the hand, but of the way the cards lie in the dummy. To say more would only make it more difficult than it now is, if possible, to get back to Mr. Fowler.) Mr. Fowler's point is, of course, that there are good split infinitives and bad ones. For instance, he contends that it is better to say "Our object is to further cement trade relations," thus splitting "to cement," than to say "Our object is further to cement trade relations," because the use of "further" before "to cement" might lead the reader to think it had the weight of "moreover" rather than of "increasingly." My own way out of all this confusion would be simply to say "Our object is to let trade relations ride," that is, give them up, let them go. Some people would regard the abandonment of trade relations, merely for the purpose of avoiding grammatical confusion, as a weakneed and unpatriotic action. That, it seems to me, is a matter for each person to decide for himself. A man who, like myself, has no knowledge at all of trade relations cannot be expected to take the same interest in cementing them as, say, the statesman or the politician. This is no reflection on trade relations.

## I. Suggestions for Discussion:

1. Does Thurber offer any serious advice on the use of the split infinitive? Account for the title of his essay.
2. Discuss Thurber's attempt to explain how he moves from his discus-

sion of a food fight back to the split infinitive. Does he handle the transition well? Explain.

3. Compare his humor in this essay with that in "Exhibit X," p. 543. Would you know that both essays were by the same author? Explain. Is the humor more or less personal in this essay?

**II. Suggestions for Writing:**

1. Write a humorous essay about the complexities of a subject you have studied.

2. Using your own experiences or observations, write a narrative account of the origins, progress, and consequences of a food fight.

---

# SHEILA TOBIAS

## Who's Afraid of Math, and Why?

---

Sheila Tobias is a feminist and educator instrumental in founding the Math Clinic at Wesleyan University. The selection that follows is taken from her book, *Overcoming Math Anxiety* (1978).

In the essay, she analyzes reasons why women have traditionally suffered from "math anxiety" and concludes that psychological conditioning is more likely the cause than any biological difference between men and women.

---

The first thing people remember about failing at math is that it felt like sudden death. Whether the incident occurred while learning "word problems" in sixth grade, coping with equations in high school, or first confronting calculus and statistics in college, failure came suddenly and in a very frightening way. An idea or a new operation was not just difficult, it was impossible! And, instead of asking questions or taking the lesson slowly, most people remember having had the feeling that they would never go any further in mathematics. If we assume that the curriculum was reasonable, and that the new idea was but the next in a series of learnable concepts, the feeling of utter defeat was simply not rational; yet "math anxious" college students and adults have revealed that no matter how much the teacher reassured them, they could not overcome that feeling.

A common myth about the nature of mathematical ability holds that one either has or does not have a mathematical mind. Mathematical imagination and an intuitive grasp of mathematical principles may well be needed to do advanced research, but why should people who can do college-level work in other subjects not be able to do college-level math as well? Rates of learning may vary. Competency under time pressure may differ. Certainly low self-esteem will get in the way. But where is the evidence that a student needs a "mathematical mind" in order to succeed at learning math?

Consider the effects of this mythology. Since only a few people are supposed to have this mathematical mind, part of what makes us so passive in the face of our difficulties in learning mathematics is that we suspect all the while we may not be one of "them," and we spend our time waiting to find out when our nonmathematical minds will be exposed. Since our limit will eventually be reached, we see no point in being methodical or in attending to detail. We are grateful when we survive fractions, word problems, or geometry. If that certain moment of failure hasn't struck yet, it is only temporarily postponed.

Parents, especially parents of girls, often expect their children to be nonmathematical. Parents are either poor at math and had their own sudden-death experiences, or, if math came easily for them, they do not know how it feels to be slow. In either case, they unwittingly foster the idea that a mathematical mind is something one either has or does not have.

## Mathematics and Sex

Although fear of math is not a purely female phenomenon, girls tend to drop out of math sooner than boys, and adult women experience an aversion to math and math-related activities that is akin to anxiety. A 1972 survey of the amount of high school mathematics taken by incoming freshmen at Berkeley revealed that while 57 percent of the boys had taken four years of high school math, only 8 percent of the girls had had the same amount of preparation. Without four years of high school math, students at Berkeley, and at most other colleges and universities, are ineligible for the calculus sequence, unlikely to attempt chemistry or physics, and inadequately prepared for statistics and economics.

Unable to elect these entry-level courses, the remaining 92 percent of the girls will be limited, presumably, to the career choices that are considered feminine: the humanities, guidance and counseling, elementary school teaching, foreign languages, and the fine arts.

Boys and girls may be born alike with respect to math, but certain sex differences in performance emerge early according to several respected studies, and these differences remain through adulthood. They are:

1. Girls compute better than boys (elementary school and on).

2. Boys solve word problems better than girls (from age thirteen on).

3. Boys take more math than girls (from age sixteen on).

4. Girls learn to hate math sooner and possibly for different reasons.

Why the differences in performance? One reason is the amount of math learned and used at play. Another may be the difference in male-female maturation. If girls do better than boys at all elementary school tasks, then they may compute better for no other reason than that arithmetic is part of the elementary school curriculum. As boys and girls grow older, girls become, under pressure, academically less competitive. Thus, the falling off of girls' math performance between ages ten and fifteen may be because:

1. Math gets harder in each successive year and requires more work and commitment.

2. Both boys and girls are pressured, beginning at age ten, not to excel in areas designated by society to be outside their sex-role domains.

3. Thus girls have a good excuse to avoid the painful struggle with math; boys don't.

Such a model may explain girls' lower achievement in math overall, but why should girls even younger than ten have difficulty in problem-solving? In her review of the research on sex differences, psychologist Eleanor Maccoby noted that girls are generally more conforming, more suggestible, and more dependent upon the opinion of others than boys (all learned, not innate, behaviors). Being so, they may not be as willing to take risks or to think for themselves, two behaviors that are necessary in solving problems. Indeed, in one test of third-graders, girls were found to be not nearly as willing to estimate, to make judgments about "possible right answers," or to work with systems they had never seen before. Their very success at doing what is expected of them up to that time seems to get in the way of their doing something new.

If readiness to do word problems, to take one example, is as much a function of readiness to take risks as it is of "reasoning ability," then mathematics performance certainly requires more than memory, computation, and reasoning. The differences in math performance between boys and girls—no matter how consistently those differences show up—cannot be attributed simply to differences in innate ability.

Still, if one were to ask the victims themselves, they would probably disagree: they would say their problems with math have to do with the way they are "wired." They feel they are somehow missing something—one ability or several—that other people have. Although women want to believe they are not mentally inferior to men, many fear that, where math is concerned, they really are. Thus, we have to consider seriously whether mathematical ability has a biological basis, not only because a number of researchers believe this to be so, but because a number of victims agree with them.

## The Arguments from Biology

The search for some biological basis for math ability or disability is fraught with logical and experimental difficulties. Since not all math under-achievers are women, and not all women are mathematics-avoidant, poor performance in math is unlikely to be due to some genetic or hormonal difference between the sexes. Moreover, no amount of research so far has unearthed a "mathematical competency" in some tangible, measurable substance in the body. Since "masculinity" cannot be injected into women to test whether or not it improves their mathematics, the theories that attribute such ability to genes or hormones must depend for their proof on circumstantial evidence. So long as about 7 percent of the Ph.D.'s in mathematics are earned by women, we have to conclude either that these women have genes, hormones, and brain organization different from those of the rest of us, or that certain positive experiences in their lives have largely undone the negative fact that they are female, or both.

Genetically, the only difference between males and females (albeit a significant and pervasive one) is the presence of two chromosomes designated X in every female cell. Normal males exhibit an X-Y combination. Because some kinds of mental retardation are associated with sex-chromosomal anomalies, a number of researchers have sought a converse linkage between specific abilities and the presence or absence of the second X. But the linkage between genetics and mathematics is not supported by conclusive evidence.

Since intensified hormonal activity commences at adolescence, a time during which girls seem to lose interest in mathematics, much more has been made of the unequal amounts in females and males of the sex-linked hormones androgen and estrogen. Biological researchers have linked estrogen— the female hormone—with "simple repetitive tasks," and androgen—the male hormone—with "complex restructuring tasks." The assumption here is not only that such specific talents are biologically based (probably undemonstrable) but also that one cannot be good *at both* repretitive and restructuring kinds of assignments.

## Sex Roles and Mathematics Competence

The fact that many girls tend to lose interest in math at the age they reach puberty (junior high school) suggests that puberty might in some sense cause girls to fall behind in math. Several explanations come to mind: the influence of hormones, more intensified sex-role socialization, or some extracurricular learning experience exclusive to boys of that age.

One group of seventh-graders in a private school in New England gave a clue as to what children themselves think about all of this. When asked why girls do as well as boys in math until the sixth grade, while sixth-grade boys do better from that point on, the girls responded: "Oh, that's easy. After sixth grade, we have to do real math." The answer to why "real math" should be considered to be "for boys" and not "for girls" can be found not in the realm of biology but only in the realm of ideology of sex differences.

Parents, peers, and teachers forgive a girl when she does badly in math at school, encouraging her to do well in other subjects instead. " 'There, there.' my mother used to say when I failed at math," one woman says. "But I got a talking-to when I did badly in French." Lynn Fox, who directs a program for mathematically gifted junior high boys and girls on the campus of Johns Hopkins University, has trouble recruiting girls and keeping them in her program. Some parents prevent their daughters from participating altogether for fear that excellence in math will make them too different. The girls themselves are often reluctant to continue with mathematics, Fox reports, because they fear social ostracism.

Where do these associations come from?

The association of masculinity with mathematics sometimes extends from the discipline to those who practice it. Students, asked on a questionnaire what characteristics they associate with a mathematician (as contrasted with a "writer"), selected terms such as rational, cautious, wise, and responsible. The writer, on the other hand, in addition to being seen as individualistic and independent, was also described as warm, interested in people, and altogether more compatible with a feminine ideal.

As a result of this psychological conditioning, a young woman may consider math and math-related fields to be inimical to femininity. In an interesting study of West German teenagers, Erika Schildkamp-Kuendiger found that girls who identified themselves with the feminine ideal underachieved in mathematics, that is, did less well than would have been expected of them based on general intelligence and performance in other subjects.

## Street Mathematics: Things, Motion, Scores

Not all the skills that are necessary for learning mathematics are learned in school. Measuring, computing, and manipulating objects that have dimensions and dynamic properties of their own are part of the everyday life of children. Children who miss out on these experiences may not be well primed for math in school.

Feminists have complained for a long time that playing with dolls is one way of convincing impressionable little girls that they may only be mothers or housewives—or, as in the case of the Barbie doll, "pinup girls"— when they grow up. But doll-playing may have even more serious consequences for little girls than that. Do girls find out about gravity and distance and shapes and sizes playing with dolls? Probably not.

A curious boy, if his parents are tolerant, will have taken apart a number of household and play objects by the time he is ten, and, if his parents are lucky, he may even have put them back together again. In all of this he is learning things that will be useful in physics and math. Taking parts out that have to go back in requires some examination of form. Building something that stays up or at least stays put for some time involves working with structure.

Sports is another source of math-related concepts for children which tends to favor boys. Getting to first base on a not very well hit grounder is a lesson in time, speed, and distance. Intercepting a football thrown through the air requires some rapid intuitive eye calculations based on the ball's direction, speed, and trajectory. Since physics is partly concerned with velocities, trajectories, and collisions of objects, much of the math taught to prepare a student for physics deals with relationships and formulas that can be used to express motion and acceleration.

What, then, can we conclude about mathematics and sex? If math anxiety is in part the result of math avoidance, why not require girls to take as much math as they can possibly master? If being the only girl in "trig" is the reason so many women drop math at the end of high school, why not provide psychological counseling and support for those young women who wish to go on? Since ability in mathematics is considered by many to be unfeminine, perhaps fear of success, more than any bodily or mental dysfunction, may interfere with girls' ability to learn math.

## I. Suggestions for Discussion:

1. What is the principal reason for math anxiety in women, according to Tobias?
2. On what grounds does Tobias discount a biological argument for differences in mathematical ability? Does her argument satisfy you? Explain.
3. Compare her observations on psychological conditioning with Dorothy Sayers's emphasis on developing individual potential in "Are Women Human?", p. 504.

## II. Suggestions for Writing:

1. Write a personal essay comparing your experience in learning math with your experience learning another subject.
2. Write a brief introduction to the study of a subject you know and in which you have done well. Offer the new student advice on how to approach the subject.

---

# BARBARA W. TUCHMAN

## The Missing Element: Moral Courage

---

Barbara W. Tuchman (1912–    ), the distinguished American historian and journalist, won the Pulitzer Prize in 1963 for *The Guns of August,* her account of the origins of World War II. Her other books include *The Proud Tower* (1966), *Notes from China* (1972), and her latest bestseller, *A Distant Mirror: The Calamitous 14th Century* (1978).

In the following essay, she argues vigorously for a return to standards in education, government, and the arts. She calls upon her readers to have the moral courage to exercise independent, informed judgment, taste, and values.

---

What I want to say is concerned less with leadership than with its absence, that is, with the evasion of leadership. Not in the physical sense, for we have, if anything, a superabundance of leaders—hundreds of Pied Pipers, or would-be Pied Pipers, running about, ready and anxious to lead the population. They are scurrying around, collecting consensus, gathering as wide an acceptance as possible. But what they are *not* doing, very notably, is standing still and saying, *"This* is what I believe. This I will do and that I will not do, This is my code of behavior and that is outside it. This is excellent and that is trash." There is an abdication of moral leadership in the sense of a general unwillingness to state standards.

Of all the ills that our poor criticized, analyzed, sociologized society is heir to, the focal one, it seems to me, from which so much of our uneasiness and confusion derive is the absence of standards. We are too unsure of ourselves to assert them, to stick by them, or if necessary, in the case of persons who occupy positions of authority, to impose them. We seem to be afflicted by a widespread and eroding reluctance to take any stand on any values, moral, behavioral, or aesthetic.

Everyone is afraid to call anything wrong, or vulgar, or fradulent, or just bad taste or bad manners. Congress, for example, pussyfooted for months (following years of apathy) before taking action on a member convicted by the courts of illegalities; and when they finally got around to unseating him, one suspects they did it for the wrong motives. In 1922, in England, a man called Horatio Bottomley, a rather flamboyant character and popular demagogue—very similar in type, by the way, to Adam Clayton Powell, with similarly elastic financial ethics—who founded a paper called *John Bull* and got himself elected to Parliament, was found guilty of misappropriating the funds which his readers subscribed to victory bonds and other causes promoted by his paper. The day after the verdict, he was expelled from the House of Commons, with no fuss and very little debate, except for a few friendly farewells, as he was rather an engaging fellow. But no member thought the House had any other course to consider: out he went. I do not suggest that this represents a difference between British and American morality; the difference is in the *times*.

Our time is one of disillusion in our species and a resulting lack of self-confidence—for good historical reasons. Man's recent record has not been reassuring. After engaging in the Great War with all its mud and blood and ravaged ground, its disease, destruction, and death, we allowed ourselves a bare twenty years before going at it all over again. And the second time was accompanied by an episode of man's inhumanity to man of such enormity that its implications for all of us have not yet, I think, been fully measured.

A historian has recently stated that for such a phenomenon as the planned and nearly accomplished extermination of a people to take place, one of three preconditions necessary was public indifference.

Since then the human species has been busy overbreeding, polluting the air, destroying the balance of nature, and bungling in a variety of directions so that it is no wonder we have begun to doubt man's capacity for good judgment. It is hardly surprising that the self-confidence of the nineteenth century and its belief in human progress has been dissipated. "Every great civilization," said Secretary Gardner last year, "has been characterized by confidence in itself." At mid-twentieth century, the supply is low. As a result, we tend to shy away from all judgments. We hesitate to label anything wrong, and therefore hesitate to require the individual to bear moral responsibility for his acts.

We have become afraid to fix blame. Murderers and rapists and muggers and persons who beat up old men and engage in other forms of assault are not guilty; society is guilty; society has wronged them; society beats its breast and says *mea culpa*—it is our fault, not the wrongdoer's. The wrongdoer, poor fellow, could not help himself.

I find this very puzzling because I always ask myself, in these cases, what about the many neighbors of the wrongdoer, equally poor, equally disadvantaged, equally sufferers from society's neglect, who nevertheless maintain certain standards of social behavior, who do *not* commit crimes, who do not murder for money or rape for kicks. How does it happen that they know the difference between right and wrong, and how long will they abide by the difference if the leaders and opinionmakers and pacesetters continue to shy away from bringing home responsibility to the delinquent?

Admittedly, the reluctance to condemn stems partly from a worthy instinct—*tout comprendre, c'est tout pardonner*[1]—and from a rejection of what was often the hypocrisy of Victorian moral standards. True, there was a large component of hypocrisy in nineteenth-century morality. Since the advent of Freud, we know more, we understand more about human behavior, we are more reluctant to cast the first stone—to condemn—which is a good thing; but the pendulum has swung to the point where we are now afraid to place moral responsibility at all. Society, that large amorphous, nonspecific scapegoat, must carry the burden for each of us, relieving us of guilt. We have become so indoctrinated by the terrors lurking in the dark corridors of the guilt complex that guilt has acquired a very bad name. Yet a little guilt is not a dangerous thing; it has a certain social utility.

[1] To understand all is to forgive all.

When it comes to guilt, a respected writer—respected in some circles—has told us, as her considered verdict on the Nazi program, that evil is banal—a word that means something so ordinary that you are not bothered by it; the dictionary definition is "commonplace and hackneyed." Somehow that conclusion does not seem adequate or even apt. *Of course,* evil is commonplace; *of course* we all partake of it. Does that mean that we must withhold disapproval, and that when evil appears in dangerous degree or vicious form we must not condemn but only understand? That may be very Christian in intent, but in reality it is an escape from the necessity of exercising judgment—which exercise, I believe, is a prime function of leadership.

What it requires is courage—just a little, not very much—the courage to be independent and stand up for the standard of values one believes in. That kind of courage is the quality most conspicuously missing, I think, in current life. I don't mean the courage to protest and walk around with picket signs or boo Secretary McNamara which, though it may stem from the right instinct, is a group thing that does not require any very stout spirit. I did it myself for Sacco and Vanzetti when I was about twelve and picketed in some now forgotten labor dispute when I was a freshman and even got arrested. There is nothing to that; if you don't do that sort of thing when you are eighteen, then there is something wrong with you. I mean, rather, a kind of lonely moral courage, the quality that attracted me to that odd character, Czar Reed, and to Lord Salisbury, neither of whom cared a rap for the opinion of the public or would have altered his conduct a hair to adapt to it. It is the quality someone said of Lord Palmerston was his "you-be-damnedness." That is the mood we need a little more of.

Standards of taste, as well as morality, need continued reaffirmation to stay alive, as liberty needs eternal vigilance. To recognize and to proclaim the difference between the good and the shoddy, the true and the fake, as well as between right and wrong, or what we believe at a given time to be right and wrong, is the obligation, I think, of persons who presume to lead, or are thrust into leadership, or hold positions of authority. That includes—whether they asked for it or not—all educators and even, I regret to say, writers.

For educators it has become increasingly the habit in the difficult circumstances of college administration today to find out what the students want in the matter of curriculum and deportment and then give it to them. This seems to me another form of abdication, another example of the prevailing reluctance to state a standard and expect, not to say require, performance in accord with it. The permissiveness, the yielding of decision to the student, does not—from what I can tell—promote responsibility in the young so much as uneasiness and a kind of anger at *not* being told what is expected of them, a resentment of their elders' unwillingness to take a position. Recently a student psychiatric patient of the Harvard Health Services was quoted by the director, Dr. Dana Farnsworth, as complaining, "My parents never tell me what to do. They never stop me from doing anything." That is the unheard wail, I think, extended beyond parents to the general absence of a guiding, reassuring pattern, which is behind much of society's current uneasiness.

It is human nature to want patterns and standards and a structure of behavior. A pattern to conform to is a kind of shelter. You see it in kindergarten and primary school, at least in those schools where the children when leaving the classroom are required to fall into line. When the teacher gives the signal, they fall in with alacrity; they know where they belong and they instinctively like to *be* where they belong. They like the feeling of being in line.

Most people need a structure, not only to fall into but to fall out of. The rebel with a cause is better off than the one without. At least he knows what he is "agin." He is not lost. He does not suffer from an identity crisis. It occurs to me that much of the student protest now may be a testing of authority, a search for that line to fall out of, and when it isn't there students become angrier because they feel more lost, more abandoned than ever. In the late turmoil at Berkeley, at least as regards the filthy speech demonstration, there was a missed opportunity, I think (however great my respect for Clark Kerr) for a hearty, emphatic, and unmistakable "No!" backed up by sanctions. Why? Because the act, even if intended as a demonstration of principle, was in this case, like any indecent exposure, simply offensive, and what is offensive to the greater part of society is anti-social, and what is anti-social, so long as we live in social groups and not each of us on his own island, must be curtailed, like Peeping Toms or obscene telephone calls, as a public nuisance. The issue is really with more self-confidence, quite simple.

So, it seems to me, is the problem of the CIA. You will say that in this case people have taken a stand, opinion-makers have worked themselves into a moral frenzy. Indeed they have, but over a false issue. The CIA is not, after all, the Viet Cong or the Schutzstaffel in blackshirts. Its initials do not stand for Criminal Indiscretions of America. It is an arm of the American government, our elected, representative government (whatever may be one's feelings toward that body at the moment). Virtually every government in the world subsidizes youth groups, especially in their international relations, not to mention in athletic competitions. (I do not know if the CIA is subsidizing our Equestrian Team, but I know personally a number of people who would be only too delighted if it were.) The difficulty here is simply that the support was clandestine in the first place and not the proper job of the CIA in the second. An intelligence agency should be restricted to the gathering of intelligence and not extend itself into operations. In armies the two functions are distinct: intelligence is G2 and operations is G3. If our government could manage its functions with a little more precision and perform openly those functions that are perfectly respectable, there would be no issue. The recent excitement only shows how easily we succumb when reliable patterns or codes of conduct are absent, to a confusion of values.

A similar confusion exists, I think, with regard to the omnipresent pornography that surrounds us like smog. A year ago the organization of my own profession, the Authors League, filed a brief *amicus curiae* in the appeal of Ralph Ginzburg, the publisher of a periodical called *Eros* and other items, who had been convicted of disseminating obscenity through the mails. The League's action was taken on the issue of censorship to which all good liberals automatically respond like Pavlov's dogs. Since at this stage in our culture pornography has so far gotten the upper hand that to do battle in its behalf against the dragon Censorship is rather like doing battle today against the bustle in behalf of short skirts, and since I believe that the proliferation of pornography in its sadistic forms is a greater social danger at the moment than censorship, and since Mr. Ginzburg was not an author anyway but a commercial promoter, I raised an objection, as a member of the Council, to the Authors League's spending its funds in the Ginzburg case. I was, of course, outvoted; in fact, there was no vote. Everyone around the table just sat and looked at me in cold disapproval. Later, after my objection was printed in the *Bulletin,* at my request, two distinguished authors wrote privately to me to express their agreement but did not go so far as to say so publicly.

Thereafter, when the Supreme Court upheld Mr. Ginzburg's conviction, everyone in the intellectual community raised a hullaballoo about censorship advancing upon us like some sort of Frankenstein's monster. This seems to me another case of getting excited about the wrong thing. The cause of pornography is *not* the same as the cause of free speech. There *is* a difference. Ralph Ginzburg is *not* Theodore Dreiser and this is not the 1920's. If one looks around at the movies, especially the movie advertisements, and the novels and the pulp magazines glorifying perversion and the paperbacks that make de Sade available to school children, one does not get the impression that in the 1960's we are being stifled in the Puritan grip of Anthony Comstock. Here again, leaders—in this case authors and critics—seem too unsure of values or too afraid of being unpopular to stand up and assert the perfectly obvious difference between smut and free speech, or to say "Such and such is offensive and can be harmful." Happily, there are signs of awakening. In a *Times* review of a book called *On Iniquity* by Pamela Hansford Johnson, which related pornography to the Moors murders in England, the reviewer concluded that "this may be the opening of a discussion that must come, the opening shot."

In the realm of art, no less important than morals, the abdication of judgment is almost a disease. Last fall when the Lincoln Center opened its glittering new opera house with a glittering new opera on the tragedy of Antony and Cleopatra, the curtain rose on a gaudy crowd engaged in energetic revels around a gold box in the shape of a pyramid, up whose sides (conveniently fitted with toe-holds, I suppose) several sinuous and reasonably nude slave girls were chased by lecherous guards left over from "Aida." When these preliminaries quieted down, the front of the gold box suddenly dropped open, and guess who was inside? No, it was not Cleopatra, it was Antony, looking, I thought, rather bewildered. What he was doing inside the box was never made clear. Thereafter everything happened—and in crescendos of gold and spangles and sequins, silks and gauzes, feathers, fans, jewels, brocades, and such a quantity of glitter that one began to laugh, thinking that the spectacle was intended as a parody of the old Shubert revue. But no, this was the Metropolitan Opera in the vaunted splendor of its most publicized opening since the Hippodrome. I gather it was Mr. Bing's idea of giving the first night customers a fine splash. What he achieved was simply vulgarity, as at least some reviewers had the courage to say next day. Now, I cannot believe that Mr. Bing and his colleagues do not know the difference between honest artistry in stage design and pretentious ostentation. If they know better, why do they allow themselves to do worse? As leaders in their field of endeavor, they should have been setting standards of beauty and creative design, not debasing them.

One finds the same peculiarities in the visual arts. Non-art, as its practitioners describe it—the blob school, the all-black canvasses, the paper cutouts and Campbell soup tins and plastic hamburgers and pieces of old carpet—is treated as art, not only by dealers whose motive is understandable (they have discovered that shock value sells); not only by a gullible pseudocultural section of the public who are not interested in art but in being "in" and wouldn't, to quote an old joke, know a Renoir from a Jaguar; but also, which I find mystifying, by the museums and the critics. I am sure they know the difference between the genuine and the hoax. But not trusting their own judgment, they seem afraid to say no to anything, for fear, I suppose, of making a mistake and turning down what may be next decade's Matisse.

For the museums to exhibit the plastic hamburgers and twists of scrap iron is one thing, but for them to *buy* them for their permanent collection puts an imprimatur on what is fraudulent. Museum curators, too, are leaders who have an obligation to distinguish—I will not say the good from the bad in art because that is an elusive and subjective matter dependent on the eye of the time—but at least honest expression from phony. Most of what fills the galleries on Madison Avenue is simply stuff designed to take advantage of current fads and does not come from an artist's vision or an honest creative impulse. The dealers know it; the critics know it; the purveyors themselves know it; the public suspects it; but no one dares say it because that would be committing oneself to a standard of values and even, heaven forbid, exposing oneself to being called square.

In the fairy story, it required a child to cry out that the Emperor was naked. Let us not leave that task to the children. It should be the task of leaders to recognize and state the truth as they see it. It is their task not to be afraid of absolutes.

If the educated man is not willing to express standards, if he cannot show that he has them and applies them, what then is education for? Its purpose, I take it, is to form the civilized man, whom I would define as the person capable of the informed exercise of judgment, taste, and values. If at maturity he is not willing to express judgment on matters of policy or taste or morals, if at fifty he does not believe that he has acquired more wisdom and informed experience than is possessed by the student at twenty, then he is saying in effect that education has been a failure.

I. **Suggestions for Discussion:**
1. How does Tuchman account for an absence of standards in our society? Do you agree? Explain.
2. Discuss her belief that there is a widespread desire for standards and a structure of behavior. Test her observations against your own beliefs and experiences and your observations of others.
3. Discuss her views on pornography. Do you agree? Explain.

II. **Suggestions for Writing:**
1. Write an essay agreeing or disagreeing with Tuchman's belief that permissiveness among educators is an abdication of responsibility. To what extent should students participate in making decisions about such matters as curriculum and deportment?
2. Write an essay comparing Tuchman's views with those of Marya Mannes in "How Do You Know It's Good?", p. 347.

# MARY-CLAIRE VAN LEUNEN

## Scholarship: A Singular Notion

Mary-Claire van Leunen is an American essayist who has contributed to *Atlantic Monthly*.

In the essay that follows, she gives dozens of examples of bad scholarly writing and proposes that scholars use the first person singular (*I, me, my, mine, myself*) to give vitality and personality to their writing.

Someone recently suggested to me (I think waggishly) that the best way to improve scholarly writing would be to stop the subsidies for all the academic journals. As a serious proposal, the idea would be misguided. Cutting off your nose to beautify your face is madness. But it is a tempting madness, isn't it? Especially when the nose in question is so enormous, so distended and cartilaginous, so warty—but it's the only nose we have, or the only excuse for scholarship, as the case may be.

I have a much humbler suggestion, which has to do with the first person singular, the set of pronouns *I, me, my, mine, myself.* It's true that my plan will not transform the face of academic writing overnight. It's a suggestion in the form of a powder puff rather than a scalpel. But it might help; it might help a little; it really might do a small bit of good. My suggestion to scholars about the first person singular is that they use it.

If you haven't looked at any scholarly prose lately (and who would blame you?), you may not be able to appreciate just how radical my suggestion is. A reader can work his way through feet and yards and miles of the stuff without encountering a single *I* or *my* or *me.* You or I might write "my paper on turnip ambury," for instance, or "my work on Pierre Louys," or "my book on peninsular formation" (supposing, that is, that we had done some work on turnip disease or naughty writers or geophysics and wanted to talk about it). But would a scholar ever write that way? Not on your life. "Our paper on turnip ambury"—as if he were Siamese twins. "The work of the present writer on Pierre Louys"—as if he were only distantly, and rather coolly, acquainted with himself. "The book of the above-signatured author on peninsular formation"—no comment. Your average scholar would rather hand in his hood than call himself *I.*

Many of the devices that scholars use to avoid the first person singular have a sort of lunatic charm. Learned illiteracies, for example, tickle my fancy, and there's many a scholar who gets hanged by a dangling participle in trying to avoid responsibility for his own thoughts:

> Contemplating Stubbs's career, he seems to be a painter almost more of our age than of his own.

> Reasoning backward from these outcomes, the parameters must be large.

In the ordinary way, the passive voice is a burr, a bramble; unless there's some good reason for it, "Y is done by X" is nothing but a prickly version of "X does Y." But your dedicated *I*-dodging scholar can weave passives together till they form an impenetrable thicket, a regular hedgerow of passivity:

> It has been noted that these symptoms can be found to be presented by the persistent investigator even when it was initially thought that they were not able to be detected.

Most scholars are anglophilic enough to be deaf to the overuse of *one,* even to an extent that would make any of the rest of us seem hopelessly affected:

> If one were to hazard a guess at the origins of this prejudice against back-formations, one would have to guard against the possibility of projection of standards from one's time and class to other times and classes not one's own.

This *one* can sometimes combine with the other kind to comic effect:

> These terms are so badly matched that one might wish for the authors to discard one.

Another splendid maneuver around the first person singular is the allegation with buttress verb:

> It is not commonly recognized that sphygomography holds the key to the nation's energy problems.

Recognized, realized, known, understood—those are the verbs that prop up the loose and flapping structure. The lay reader cannot detect this device; for all he knows, the sentence may mean (allowing for professional chauvinism), "We sphygmographers should take a larger role in determining national energy policies." Only the author's fellow specialists know that the sentence actually means, "I've had a brainstorm about a possible connection between consuming energy and measuring pulses." This device seldom appears in a main clause. Usually it's smuggled by in a kind of subordinate false-bottomed suitcase: "Although it may not be widely known that . . ."

And then there's *we, we* the panacea, the godsend *we*. Where would scholars be without their *we*? "We must then conclude"—we the assistant professor. "It has therefore seemed to us"—us the non-ladder post-doc. "It is our hope"—our the second-year graduate student's. No amount of mumbling about the editorial *we* and the royal *we* can explain this nonsense away. A scholar who happens also to be an editor may call himself *we* in his editorials if he likes; and I suppose that a scholar who happens also to be a king must use *we* for his edicts. But in their scholarly works both should revert, like the rest of us commoners, to the plain, unadorned singular.

Of course, there are other varieties of *we*.

The *we* of joint authorship is never offensive. It solves the problem with *I* so neatly that a scholar who wants a cheap out might decide to publish only in collaboration. The genuinely plural *we* does have its awkward moments, of course:

> We hope now to be able to enlarge on the work that one of us began as a graduate student at the Institute for Sacred Music.

But they are few.

The *we* of common knowledge gives offense only when the knowledge is arcane:

> Naturally, we all know that the Hargrave conjecture laid the foundation for melodic intonation therapy.

The confederate *we*, the *we* that joins the writer and the reader in a common enterprise, can be bracing and attractive:

> These objections may seem at first almost insurmountable, but we can get around them with a little deviousness.

But it can fall flat when the reader remains unpersuaded:

> Thus we have seen that the strengths of Elizabeth's reign arose
> from the essentially masculine aspects of her psychology, and the
> weaknesses from the corresponding feminine aspects.

Oh yeah? The author of this drivel is sadly mistaken if he thinks that his *we*
means "I the writer and you the reader."

I have the idea that the twittering qualifications characteristic of
scholarly writing may also result from *I*-avoidance. Take the sentence above,
for instance. Now, if you or I wanted (heaven forbid) to say any such thing
about Elizabeth, we would do it this way:

> I think that the strengths of Elizabeth's reign came from the
> masculine side of her character, the weaknesses from the feminine
> side.

The scholarly writer, however, feels that this option is not open to him.
No matter how personal, singular, eccentric, even deviant a thought may be,
the scholar feels he ought not besmirch it with an *I*. I think, I feel, I conclude,
I consider, I recall—hot stuff. The trendy young academic may wear waist-
length greasy hair, a nose ring, and a silver-studded motorcycle jacket, but his
prose is still strictly spats and fawn-colored gloves. "My idea is that Elizabeth,
etc."? He wouldn't dare.

Denied, he thinks, the privilege of labeling his opinions openly, the
scholar starts to hedge:

> It is probable that the strengths of Elizabeth's reign arose . . .

Too strong. It's not at all probable; it's just a notion he has. So:

> It is perhaps probable . . .

Too weak. This is, after all, his pet theory, he doesn't want to wash it down
the drain. So, once again:

> It is perhaps quite probable . . .

Fifteen minutes of this, and he has achieved a fully rounded masterpiece of
scholarly mitigation:

> It may then perhaps be quite probable that what we might term
> the strengths of Elizabeth's reign can be said to have arisen from

the, so to speak, very largely masculine aspects of what was almost indubitably her psychology, and those weaknesses so rightly identified by many of our more reputable authorities in some probability from those aspects which, on some consideration, we may say were nearly incontrovertibly feminine.

There is still one other form of *I*-evasion, and it's the most troublesome of them all:

The chimpanzee grin of fear twitches at the edge of every human smile.

By my lights, that's a nearly perfect sentence. It has real words, it doesn't talk about "anthropoid phobic rictus," it has a verb, it's physical, it moves, it says something—what more could you ask? Of any given sentence, nothing. But an author who relies on flat statements alone for avoiding *I* through the course of a whole article or a whole book is in bad trouble. His work begins to smell of what scholars call journalism, by which they mean not newspaper and magazine writing but presenting opinions as facts. The stronger and finer this scholar's writing, the worse the journalistic stink. How sad, if you believe as I do that the occasional first person singular, the occasional mild personal reference, would be enough to sweeten the air.

But by this point, one or two of my readers may be twisting about in agony. What about objectivity? What about impartiality? What about the scientific method; what about detached, dispassionate, unbiased investigation; what about disinterest? If scholars start putting themselves forward, giving in to ego and self and the cult of the personality, what happens to rigor and method and the harsh ascetic demands of inquiry? Today it's *I* and *me;* tomorrow, self-important, self-serving rot.

This solicitousness about the scholarly endeavor is admirable. It is idealistic, generous—and, I'm sorry to say, hopelessly amateur. I understand that at one time scholars did think of their calling as a mighty composite engine, something almost like an impersonal force, the sort of thing that called for capital letters, like Progress or Truth.The idea was rich and complicated: sometimes the scholar was a stone cutter on a Great Pyramid of Truth; sometimes he was a lineman or a switch hand on the Railway of Knowledge; sometimes he was a quarrier in the Mineshaft of Discovery. The beauty and the power of those images resonates still for those of us on the edges of the scholarly community. But among scholars themselves, the inhuman truth-munching machine of scholarship is at best a fond, funny memory, at worst an anachronistic nuisance.

No equally protean replacement for the old vision of scholarship has yet materialized, so far as I know, but I get the feeling that one is taking shape. Richard Ohmann, in *English in America,* condemns the old engine-of-knowledge idea as inappropriate for the humanities, although he seems to think that it's still the way science works. Most of the historians and social scientists I know reject the model, again labeling it scientific or pseudo-scientific. But my friends in the sciences and in math don't see their work that way at all. From them I get the same sort of thing that I hear from the humanists and the social scientists: The scholar is a maker, a shaper. The scholarly community is not a work crew or a chain gang, but something more like a tribe around a campfire. Truth is like a common cook pot, something burnished bright by sharing, or, even better, like a folk song, refined and heightened by each new singer, sung with no sharp distinction between composing and performing. If the old-style scholar saw himself in momentary dreams of glory as Cecil Rhodes, the new might substitute Woody Guthrie; or, in a humbler mood, to match the old mason-trainman-miner tradition, as the anonymous singer who first put "The union is behind us" to the tune of "We Shall Not Be Moved."

The feeling I have is only a feeling. But I can't help connecting it to my sense that there is no longer any reason for scholars to dodge *I* and *me* and mine. As long as they believed in the impersonal engine of progress, it was quite proper for them to avoid the first person singular. Tough luck if the avoidance caused stylistic difficulties; it was the scholar's duty to tackle them and an honorable failure if he tried without success. But if the leading image of scholarship changes, then the attempt to follow the old ideal is no longer honorable, and the scrapes and bruises incurred in its service merely laughable. The upright scholar had better ignore convention, stiffen his spine and write *I.*

I. **Suggestions for Discussion:**
   1. Comment on the effectiveness of van Leunen's examples of stilted academic prose. Try rephrasing some of them.
   2. What reasons are usually offered for avoiding the first person singular in academic prose? Discuss the validity of these reasons.
   3. Compare her advice on writing with that offered by Benjamin Franklin in "On Literary Style," p. 189 and by George Orwell in "Politics and the English Language," p. 437. To what extent do these writers reinforce one another's opinions?

II. **Suggestions for Writing:**
   1. Use the first person singular in writing a critical review of a short story or of a film or television program you have watched recently.

2. Drawing on your own experience and your reading, write an essay offering your fellow students advice on improving their writing.

---

# GORE VIDAL

## Drugs

---

Gore Vidal (1925–    ), the American essayist, novelist, playwright, and writer of screenplays, has published more than twenty books. His satirical wit and insight are notable in such works as *Julian* (1946), *Washington, D.C.* (1967), *Myra Breckenridge* (1968), and *Homage to Daniel Shays* (1972), from which the following selection is taken. Vidal has remained active in Democratic-Liberal politics in New York.

In this brief piece of persuasive prose, Vidal argues that all drugs should be made available at cost and labelled with a precise description of what effect the drug will have on the taker.

---

It is possible to stop most drug addiction in the United States within a very short time. Simply make all drugs available and sell them at cost. Label each drug with a precise description of what effect—good and bad—the drug will have on the taker. This will require heroic honesty. Don't say that marijuana is addictive or dangerous when it is neither, as millions of people know—unlike "speed," which kills most unpleasantly, or heroin, which is addictive and difficult to kick.

For the record, I have tried—once—almost every drug and like none, disproving the popular Fu Manchu theory that a single whiff of opium will enslave the mind. Nevertheless many drugs are bad for certain people to take and they should be told why in a sensible way.

Along with exhortation and warning, it might be good for our citizens to recall (or learn for the first time) that the United States was the creation of men who believed that each man has the right to do what he wants with his own life as long as he does not interfere with his neighbor's pursuit of happiness (that his neighbor's idea of happiness is persecuting others does confuse matters a bit).

This is a startling notion to the current generation of Americans. They reflect a system of public education which has made the Bill of Rights, literally, unacceptable to a majority of high school graduates (see the annual Purdue reports) who now form the "silent majority"—a phrase which that underestimated wit Richard Nixon took from Homer who used it to describe the dead.

Now one can hear the warning rumble begin: if everyone is allowed to take drugs everyone will and the GNP will decrease, the Commies will stop us from making everyone free, and we shall end up a race of Zombies, passively murmuring "groovie" to one another. Alarming thought. Yet it seems most unlikely that any reasonably sane person will become a drug addict if he knows in advance what addiction is going to be like.

Is everyone reasonably sane? No. Some people will always become drug addicts just as some people will always become alcoholics, and it is just too bad. Every man, however, has the power (and should have the legal right) to kill himself if he chooses. But since most men don't, they won't be mainliners either. Nevertheless, forbidding people things they like or think they might enjoy only makes them want those things all the more. This psychological insight is, for some mysterious reason, perennially denied our governors.

It is a lucky thing for the American moralist that our country has always existed in a kind of time-vacuum: we have no public memory of anything that happened before last Tuesday. No one in Washington today recalls what happened during the years alcohol was forbidden to the people by a Congress that thought it had a divine mission to stamp out Demon Rum—launching, in the process, the greatest crime wave in the country's history, causing thousands of deaths from bad alcohol, and creating a general (and persisting) contempt among the citizenry for the laws of the United States.

The same thing is happening today. But the government has learned nothing from past attempts at prohibition, not to mention repression.

Last year when the supply of Mexican marijuana was slightly curtailed by the Feds, the pushers got the kids hooked on heroin and deaths increased dramatically, particularly in New York. Whose fault? Evil men like the Mafiosi? Permissive Dr. Spock? Wild-eyed Dr. Leary? No.

The government of the United States was responsible for those deaths. The bureaucratic machine has a vested interest in playing cops and robbers. Both the Bureau of Narcotics and the Mafia want strong laws against the sale and use of drugs because if drugs are sold at cost there would be no money in it for anyone.

If there was no money in it for the Mafia, there would be no friendly playground pushers, and addicts would not commit crimes to pay for the next fix. Finally, if there was no money in it, the Bureau of Narcotics would wither away, something they are not about to do without a struggle.

Will anything sensible be done? Of course not. The American people are as devoted to the idea of sin and its punishment as they are to making money—and fighting drugs is nearly as big a business as pushing them. Since the combination of sin and money is irresistible (particularly to the professional politician), the situation will only grow worse.*

I. **Suggestions for Discussion:**
1. Discuss Vidal's deceptively simple proposal. Consider various problems that might arise if his plan was adopted.
2. What arguments does Vidal use to defend his proposal for the relaxation of current drug laws? Does he convince you? Explain.
3. Discuss Vidal's cynicism in this brief essay. What is his attitude toward the government and toward the American people?

II. **Suggestions for Writing:**
1. Write an essay expressing your own views on drug availability.
2. Write an essay discussing drug use and abuse on your own campus.

# EUDORA WELTY

## The Point of the Story

Eudora Welty (1909–   ), the noted Southern novelist and short-story writer, won the Pulitzer Prize for her novel, *The Optimist's Daughter* (1972). Her other volumes include *A Curtain of Green* (1941), *Losing Battles* (1970), and *The Eye of the Story* (1978).

Welty uses her analysis of a short story called "A Worn Path" to argue that "the path," "the journey," "the way to get there" is the all-absorbing problem for writers.

---

*Response to this sensible proposal was not as shrill as I had anticipated. Currently, the Commissioner of Police in New York seems to be moving toward my view. (1972)

A story writer is more than happy to be read by students; the fact that these serious readers think and feel something in response to his work he finds life-giving. At the same time he may not always be able to reply to their specific questions in kind. I wondered if it might clarify something for both the questioners and myself, if I set down a general reply to the question that comes to me most often in the mail, from both students and their teachers, after some classroom discussion. The unrivaled favorite is this: "Is Phoenix Jackson's grandson really *dead*?" It refers to a short story I wrote years ago called "A Worn Path," which tells of a day's journey an old woman makes on foot from deep in the country into town and into a doctor's office on behalf of her little grandson; he is at home, periodically ill, and periodically she comes for his medicine; they give it to her as usual, she receives it and starts the journey back.

I had not meant to mystify readers by withholding any fact; it is not a writer's business to tease. The story is told through Phoenix's mind as she undertakes her errand. As the author at one with the character as I tell it, I must assume that the boy is alive. As the reader, you are free to think as you like, of course: the story invites you to believe that no matter what happens, Phoenix for as long as she is able to walk and can hold to her purpose will make her journey. The *possibility* that she would keep on even if he were dead is there in her devotion and its single-minded, single-track errand. Certainly the *artistic* truth, which should be good enough for the fact, lies in Phoenix's own answer to that question. When the nurse asks, "He isn't dead, is he?" she speaks for herself: "He still the same. He going to last."

The grandchild is the incentive. But the journey, the going of the errand, that is the story, and the question is not whether the grandchild is in reality alive or dead. It doesn't affect the outcome of the story or its meaning from start to finish. But it is not the question itself that has struck me as much as the idea, almost without exception implied in the asking, that for Phoenix's grandson to be dead would somehow make the story "better."

It's *all right,* I want to say to the students who write to me, for things to be what they appear to be, and for words to mean what they say. It's all right, too, for words and appearances to mean more than one thing—ambiguity is a fact of life. A fiction writer's responsibility covers not only what he presents as the facts of a given story but what he chooses to stir up as their implications; in the end, these implications, too, become facts, in the larger, fictional sense. But it is not all right, not in good faith, for things not to mean what they say.

The grandson's plight was real and it made the truth of the story, which is the story of an errand of love carried out. If the child no longer lived, the truth would persist in the "wornness" of the path. But his being dead can't increase the truth of the story, can't affect it one way or the other. I think I signal this, because the end of the story has been reached before old Phoenix gets home again: she simply starts back. To the question "Is the grandson really dead?" I could reply that it doesn't make any difference. I could also say that I did not make him up in order to let him play a trick on Phoenix. But my best answer would be: "Phoenix is alive."

The origin of a story is sometimes a trustworthy clue to the author—or can provide him with the clue—to its key image; maybe in this case it will do the same for the reader. One day I saw a solitary old woman like Phoenix. She was walking; I saw her, at middle distance, in a winter country landscape, and watched her slowly make her way across my line of vision. That sight of her made me write the story. I invented an errand for her, but that only seemed a living part of the figure she was herself: what errand other than for someone else could be making her go? And her going was the first thing, her persisting in her landscape was the real thing, and the first and the real were what I wanted and worked to keep. I brought her up close enough, by imagination, to describe her face, make her present to the eyes, but the full-length figure moving across the winter fields was the indelible one and the image to keep, and the perspective extending into the vanishing distance the true one to hold in mind.

I invented for my character as I wrote, some passing adventures—some dreams and harassments and a small triumph or two, some jolts to her pride, some flights of fancy to console her, one or two encounters to scare her, a moment that gave her cause to feel ashamed, a moment to dance and preen—for it had to be a journey, and all these things belonged to that, parts of life's uncertainty.

A narrative line is in its deeper sense, of course, the tracing out of a meaning, and the real continuity of a story lies in this probing forward. The real dramatic force of a story depends on the strength of the emotion that has set it going. The emotional value is the measure of the reach of the story. What gives any such content to "A Worn Path" is not its circumstances but its subject: the deep-grained habit of love.

What I hoped would come clear was that in the whole surround of this story, the world it threads through, the only certain thing at all is the worn path. The habit of love cuts through confusion and stumbles or contrives its way out of difficulty, it remembers the way even when it forgets, for a dumb-founded moment, its reason for being. The path is the thing that matters.

Her victory—old Phoenix's—is when she sees the diploma in the doctor's office, when she finds "nailed up on the wall the document that had been stamped with the gold seal and framed in the gold frame, which matched the dream that was hung up in her head." The return with the medicine is just a matter of retracing her own footsteps. It is the part of the journey, and of the story, that can now go without saying.

In the matter of function, old Phoenix's way might even do as a sort of parallel to your way of work if you are a writer of stories. The way to get there is the all-important, all-absorbing problem, and this problem is your reason for undertaking the story. Your only guide, too, is your sureness about your subject, about what this subject is. Like Phoenix, you work all your life to find your way, through all the obstructions and the false appearances and the upsets you may have brought on yourself, to reach a meaning—using inventions of your imagination, perhaps helped out by your dreams and bits of good luck. And finally too, like Phoenix, you have to assume that what you are working in aid of is life, not death.

But you would make the trip anyway—wouldn't you?—just on hope.

## I. Suggestions for Discussion:

1. To what extent does Welty clarify the meaning of her story? Is her explanation easy to grasp? Explain.
2. Does she make you want to read her story? Explain.
3. Discuss the tone of her essay. Is it clear, for example, that she likes and respects her readers? How do you know?

## II. Suggestions for Writing:

1. Drawing on mystery or detective stories you have read and liked, discuss Welty's statement that it is not a writer's business to tease readers.
2. Describe an experience or an incident you observed that you think might be the beginning of a good short story. How might the story develop? Can you write it?

---

# E. B. WHITE

## The Decline of Sport

---

Elwyn Brooks White (1899–    ), the American essayist, novelist, and short-story writer, began contributing stories and sketches to *The New Yorker* and later to *Harper's* in the 1920s. Among his many collections are *One Man's Meat* (1942) and *The Second*

*Tree from the Corner* (1953). His most highly praised children's book is *Charlotte's Web* (1952). With William Strunk, Jr., he is the author of the enormously successful *The Elements of Style* (1959, 1972, 1979).

In the parable that follows, White uses hyperbole and satire to make his point about the impact of the proliferation of sporting events on contemporary life.

---

In the third decade of the supersonic age, sport gripped the nation in an ever-tightening grip. The horse tracks, the ballparks, the fight rings, the gridirons, all drew crowds in steadily increasing numbers. Every time a game was played, an attendance record was broken. Usually some other sort of record was broken, too—such as the record for the number of consecutive doubles hit by left-handed batters in a Series game, or some such thing as that. Records fell like ripe apples on a windy day. Customs and manners changed, and the five-day business week was reduced to four days, then to three, to give everyone a better chance to memorize the scores.

Not only did sport proliferate but the demands it made on the spectator became greater. Nobody was content to take in one event at a time, and thanks to the magic of radio and television nobody had to. A Yale alumnus, class of 1962, returning to the Bowl with 197,000 others to see the Yale-Cornell football game would take along his pocket radio and pick up the Yankee Stadium, so that while his eye might be following a fumble on the Cornell twenty-two yard line, his ear would be following a man going down to second in the top of the fifth, seventy miles away. High in the blue sky above the Bowl, skywriters would be at work writing the scores of other major and minor sporting contests, weaving an interminable record of victory and defeat, and using the new high-visibility pink news-smoke perfected by Pepsi-Cola engineers. And in the frames of the giant video sets, just behind the goalposts, this same alumnus could watch Dejected win the Futurity before a record-breaking crowd of 349,872 at Belmont, each of whom was tuned to the Yale Bowl and following the World Series game in the video and searching the sky for further news of events either under way or just completed. The effect of this vast cyclorama of sport was to divide the spectator's attention, oversubtilize his appreciation, and deaden his passion. As the fourth supersonic decade was ushered in, the picture changed and sport began to wane.

A good many factors contributed to the decline of sport. Substitutions in football had increased to such an extent that there were very few fans in the United States capable of holding the players in mind during play. Each play that was called saw two entirely new elevens lined up, and the players whose names and faces you had familiarized yourself with in the first period were seldom seen or heard of again. The spectacle became as diffuse as the main concourse in Grand Central at the commuting hour.

Express motor highways leading to the parks and stadia had become so wide, so unobstructed, so devoid of all life except automobiles and trees that sport fans had got into the habit of travelling enormous distances to attend events. The normal driving speed had been stepped up to ninety-five miles an hour, and the distance between cars had been decreased to fifteen feet. This put an extraordinary strain on the sport lover's nervous system, and he arrived home from a Saturday game, after a road trip of three hundred and fifty miles, glassy-eyed, dazed, and spent. He hadn't really had any relaxation and he had failed to see Czlika (who had gone in for Trusky) take the pass from Bkeeo (who had gone in for Bjallo) in the third period, because at that moment a youngster named Lavagetto had been put in to pinch-hit for Art Gurlack in the bottom of the ninth with the tying run on second, and the skywriter who was attempting to write "Princeton 0-Lafayette 43" had banked the wrong way, muffed the "3," and distracted everyone's attention from the fact that Lavagetto had been whiffed.

Cheering, of course, lost its stimulating effect on players, because cheers were no longer associated necessarily with the immediate scene but might as easily apply to something that was happening somewhere else. This was enough to infuriate even the steadiest performer. A football star, hearing the stands break into a roar before the ball was snapped, would realize that their minds were not on him, and would become dispirited and grumpy. Two or three of the big coaches worried so about this that they considered equipping all players with tiny ear sets, so that they, too, could keep abreast of other sporting events while playing, but the idea was abandoned as impractical, and the coaches put it aside in tickler files, to bring up again later.

I think the event that marked the turning point in sport and started it downhill was the Midwest's classic Dust Bowl game of 1975, when Eastern Reserve's great right end, Ed Pistachio, was shot by a spectator. This man, the one who did the shooting, was seated well down in the stands near the forty-yard line on a bleak October afternoon and was so saturated with sport and with the disappointments of sport that he had clearly become deranged. With a minute and fifteen seconds to play and the score tied, the Eastern Reserve quarterback had whipped a long pass over Army's heads into Pistachio's waiting arms. There was no other player anywhere near him, and all Pistachio had to do was catch the ball and run it across the line. He dropped it. At exactly this moment, the spectator—a man named Homer T. Parkinson, of 35 Edgemere Drive, Toledo, O.—suffered at least three other major disappointments in the realm of sport. His horse, Hiccough, on which he had a five-hundred-dollar bet, fell while getting away from the starting gate at Pimlico and broke its leg (clearly visible in the video); his favorite shortstop, Lucky Frimstitch, struck out and let three men die on base in the final game of the Series (to which Parkinson was tuned); and the Governor Dummer soccer team, on which Parkinson's youngest son played goalie, lost to Kent, 4–3, as recorded in the sky overhead. Before anyone could stop him, he drew a gun and drilled Pistachio, before 954,000 persons, the largest crowd that had ever attended a football game and the *second*-largest crowd that had ever assembled for any sporting event in any month except July.

This tragedy, by itself, wouldn't have caused sport to decline, I suppose, but it set in motion a chain of other tragedies, the cumulative effect of which was terrific. Almost as soon as the shot was fired, the news flash was picked up by one of the skywriters directly above the field. He glanced down to see whether he could spot the trouble below, and in doing so failed to see another skywriter approaching. The two planes collided and fell, wings locked, leaving a confusing trail of smoke, which some observers tried to interpret as a late sports score. The planes struck in the middle of the nearby eastbound coast-to-coast Sunlight Parkway, and a motorist driving a convertible coupé stopped so short, to avoid hitting them, that he was bumped from behind. The pileup of cars that ensued involved 1,482 vehicles, a record for eastbound parkways. A total of more than three thousand persons lost their lives in the highway accident, including the two pilots, and when panic broke out in the stadium, it cost another 872 in dead and injured. News of the disaster spread quickly to other sports arenas, and started other panics among the crowds trying to get to the exits, where they could buy a paper and study a list of the dead. All in all, the afternoon of sport cost 20,003 lives, a record. And nobody had much to show for it except one small Midwestern boy who hung around the smoking wrecks of the planes, captured some aero news-smoke in a milk bottle, and took it home as a souvenir.

From that day on, sport waned. Through long, noncompetitive Saturday afternoons, the stadia slumbered. Even the parkways fell into disuse as motorists rediscovered the charms of old, twisty roads that led through main streets and past barnyards, with their mild congestions and pleasant smells.

I. **Suggestions for Discussion:**
   1. Discuss White's satiric look at various aspects of contemporary life. Has he chosen deserving targets for his satire?
   2. Discuss White's use of hyperbole in the essay. Cite specific examples.
   3. Compare and contrast White's parable about sports with Heywood Broun's "A Study in Sportsmanship," p. 62.
II. **Suggestions for Writing:**
   1. Write a parable about the decline of some other aspect of our society such as education or politics.
   2. Write an essay discussing whether or not the American public spends time watching and participating in sporting events at the expense of more significant activities.

---

## E. B. WHITE

### Walden

---

In this humorous letter to Henry David Thoreau, E. B. White describes in great detail the changes which have come to Walden Pond since Thoreau's day.

---

Miss Nims, take a letter to Henry David Thoreau. Dear Henry: I thought of you the other afternoon as I was approaching Concord doing fifty on Route 62. That is a high speed at which to hold a philosopher in one's mind, but in this century we are a nimble bunch.

On one of the lawns in the outskirts of the village a woman was cutting the grass with a motorized lawn mower. What made me think of you was that the machine had rather got away from her, although she was game enough, and in the brief glimpse I had of the scene it appeared to me that the lawn was mowing the lady. She kept a tight grip on the handles, which throbbed violently with every explosion of the one-cylinder motor, and as she sheered around bushes and lurched along at a reluctant trot behind her impetuous servant, she looked like a puppy who had grabbed something that was too much for him. Concord hasn't changed much, Henry; the farm implements and the animals still have the upper hand.

I may as well admit that I was journeying to Concord with the deliberate intention of visiting your woods; for although I have never knelt at the grave of a philosopher nor placed wreaths on moldy poets, and have often gone a mile out of my way to avoid some place of historical interest, I have always wanted to see Walden Pond. The account which you left of your sojourn there is, you will be amused to learn, a document of increasing pertinence; each year it seems to gain a little headway, as the world loses ground. We may all be transcendental yet, whether we like it or not. As our common complexities increase, any tale of individual simplicity (and yours is the best written and the cockiest) acquires a new fascination; as our goods accumulate, but not our well-being, your report of an existence without material adornment takes on a certain awkward credibility.

My purpose in going to Walden Pond, like yours, was not to live cheaply or to live dearly there, but to transact some private business with the fewest obstacles. Approaching Concord, doing forty, doing forty-five, doing fifty, the steering wheel held snug in my palms, the highway held grimly in my vision, the crown of the road now serving me (on the right-hand curves), now defeating me (on the lefthand curves), I began to rouse myself from the stupefaction which a day's motor journey induces. It was a delicious evening, Henry, when the whole body is one sense, and imbibes delight through every pore, if I may coin a phrase. Fields were richly brown where the harrow, drawn by the stripped Ford, had lately sunk its teeth; pastures were green; and overhead the sky had that same everlasting great look which you will find on Page 144 of the Oxford pocket edition. I could feel the road entering me, through tire, wheel, spring, and cushion; shall I not have intelligence with earth too? Am I not partly leaves and vegetable mold myself?—a man of infinite horsepower, yet partly leaves.

Stay with me on 62 and it will take you into Concord. As I say, it was a delicious evening. The snake had come forth to die in a bloody S on the highway, the wheel upon its head, its bowels flat now and exposed. The turtle had come up too to cross the road and die in the attempt, its hard shell smashed under the rubber blow, its intestinal yearning (for the other side of the road) forever squashed. There was a sign by the wayside which announced that the road had a "cotton surface." You wouldn't know what that is, but neither, for that matter, did I. There is a cryptic ingredient in many of our modern improvements—we are awed and pleased without knowing quite what we are enjoying. It is something to be traveling on a road with a cotton surface.

The civilization round Concord to-day is an odd distillation of city, village, farm, and manor. The houses, yards, fields look not quite suburban, not quite rural. Under the bronze beech and the blue spruce of the departed baron grazes the milch goat of the heirs. Under the porte-cochére stands the reconditioned station wagon; under the grape arbor sit the puppies for sale. (But why do men degenerate ever? What makes families run out?)

It was June and everywhere June was publishing her immemorial stanza; in the lilacs, in the syringa, in the freshly edged paths and the sweet-ness of moist beloved gardens, and the little wire wickets that preserve the tulips' front. Farmers were already moving the fruits of their toil into their yards, arranging the rhubarb, the asparagus, the strictly fresh eggs on the painted stands under the little shed roofs with the patent shingles. And though it was almost a hundred years since you had taken your ax and started cutting out your home on Walden Pond, I was interested to observe that the philosophical spirit was still alive in Massachusetts: in the center of a vacant lot some boys were assembling the framework of a rude shelter, their whole mind and skill concentrated in the rather inauspicious helter-skeleton of studs and rafters. They too were escaping from town, to live naturally, in a rich blend of savagery and philosophy.

That evening, after supper at the inn, I strolled out into the twilight to dream my shapeless transcendental dreams and see that the car was locked up for the night (first open the right front door, then reach over, straining, and pull up the handles of the left rear and the left front till you hear the click, then the handle of the right rear, then shut the right front but open it again, remembering that the key is still in the ignition switch, remove the key, shut the right front again with a bang, push the tiny keyhole cover to one side, insert key, turn, and withdraw). It is what we all do, Henry. It is called lock-ing the car. It is said to confuse thieves and keep them from making off with the laprobe. Four doors to lock behind one robe. The driver himself never uses a laprobe, the free movement of his legs being vital to the operation of the vehicle; so that when he locks the car it is a pure and unselfish act. I have in my life gained very little essential heat from laprobes, yet I have ever been at pains to lock them up.

The evening was full of sounds, some of which would have stirred your memory. The robins still love the elms of New England villages at sundown. There is enough of the thrush in them to make song inevitable at the end of day, and enough of the tramp to make them hang round the dwellings of men. A robin, like many another American, dearly loves a white house with green blinds. Concord is still full of them.

Your fellow-townsmen were stirring abroad—not many afoot, most of them in their cars; and the sound which they made in Concord at evening was a rustling and a whispering. The sound lacks steadfastness and is wholly unlike that of a train. A train, as you know who lived so near the Fitchburg line, whistles once or twice sadly and is gone, trailing a memory in smoke, soothing to ear and mind. Automobiles, skirting a village green, are like flies that have gained the inner ear—they buzz, cease, pause, start, shift, stop, halt, brake, and the whole effect is a nervous polytone curiously disturbing.

As I wandered along, the toc toc of ping pong balls drifted from an attic window. In front of the Reuben Brown house a Buick was drawn up. At the wheel, motionless, his hat upon his head, a man sat, listening to Amos and Andy on the radio (it is a drama of many scenes and without an end). The deep voice of Andrew Brown, emerging from the car, although it originated more than two hundred miles away, was unstrained by distance. When you used to sit on the shore of your pond on Sunday morning, listening to the church bells of Acton and Concord, you were aware of the excellent filter of the intervening atmosphere. Science has attended to that, and sound now maintains its intensity without regard for distance. Properly sponsored, it goes on forever.

A fire engine, out for a trial spin, roared past Emerson's house, hot with readiness for public duty. Over the barn roofs the martins dipped and chittered. A swarthy daughter of an asparagus grower, in culottes, shirt, and bandanna, pedalled past on her bicycle. It was indeed a delicious evening, and I returned to the inn (I believe it was your house once) to rock with the old ladies on the concrete veranda.

Next morning early I started afoot for Walden, out Main Street and down Thoreau, past the depot and the Minuteman Chevrolet Company. The morning was fresh, and in a bean field along the way I flushed an agriculturalist, quietly studying his beans. Thoreau Street soon joined Number 126, an artery of the State. We number our highways nowadays, our speed being so great we can remember little of their quality or character and are lucky to remember their number. (Men have an indistinct notion that if they keep up this activity long enough all will at length ride somewhere, in next to no time.) Your pond is on 126.

I knew I must be nearing your woodland retreat when the Golden Pheasant lunchroom came into view—Sealtest ice cream, toasted sandwiches, hot frankfurters, waffles, tonics, and lunches. Were I the proprietor, I should add rice, Indian meal, and molasses—just for old time's sake. The Pheasant, incidentally, is for sale: a chance for some nature lover who wishes to set himself up beside a pond in the Concord atmosphere and live deliberately, fronting only the essential facts of life on Number 126. Beyond the Pheasant was a place called Walden Breezes, an oasis whose porch pillars were made of old green shutters sawed into lengths. On the porch was a distorting mirror, to give the traveler a comical image of himself, who had miraculously learned to gaze in an ordinary glass without smiling. Behind the Breezes, in a sun-parched clearing, dwelt your philosophical descendants in their trailers, each trailer the size of your hut, but all grouped together for the sake of congeniality. Trailer people leave the city, as you did, to discover solitude and in any weather, at any hour of the day or night, to improve the nick of time; but they soon collect in villages and get bogged deeper in the mud than ever. The camp behind Walden Breezes was just rousing itself to the morning. The ground was packed hard under the heel, and the sun came through the clearing to bake the soil and enlarge the wry smell of cramped housekeeping. Cushman's bakery truck had stopped to deliver an early basket of rolls. A camp dog, seeing me in the road, barked petulantly. A man emerged from one of the trailers and set forth with a bucket to draw water from some forest tap.

Leaving the highway I turned off into the woods toward the pond, which was apparent through the foliage. The floor of the forest was strewn with dried old oak leaves and *Transcripts*. From beneath the flattened pop-corn wrapper (*granum explosum*) peeped the frail violet. I followed a foot-path and descended to the water's edge. The pond lay clear and blue in the morning light, as you have seen it so many times. In the shallows a man's waterlogged shirt undulated gently. A few flies came out to greet me and convoy me to your cove, past the No Bathing signs on which the fellows and the girls had scrawled their names. I felt strangely excited suddenly to be snooping around your premises, tiptoeing along watchfully, as though not to tread by mistake upon the intervening century. Before I got to the cove I heard something which seemed to me quite wonderful: I heard your frog, a full, clear *troonk*, guiding me, still hoarse and solemn, bridging the years as the robins had bridged them in the sweetness of the village evening. But he soon quit, and I came on a couple of young boys throwing stones at him.

Your front yard is marked by a bronze tablet set in a stone. Four small granite posts, a few feet away, show where the house was. On top of the tablet was a pair of faded blue bathing trunks with a white stripe. Back of it is a pile of stones, a sort of cairn, left by your visitors as a tribute I suppose. It is a rather ugly little heap of stones, Henry. In fact the hillside itself seems faded, browbeaten; a few tall skinny pines, bare of lower limbs, a smattering of young maples in suitable green, some birches and oaks, and a number of trees felled by the last big wind. It was from the bole of one of these fallen pines, torn up by the roots, that I extracted the stone which I added to the cairn—a sentimental act in which I was interrupted by a small terrier from a nearby picnic group, who confronted me and wanted to know about the stone.

I sat down for a while on one of the posts of your house to listen to the bluebottles and the dragon flies. The invaded glade sprawled shabby and mean at my feet, but the flies were tuned to the old vibration. There were the remains of a fire in your ruins, but I doubt that it was yours; also two beer bottles trodden into the soil and become part of earth. A young oak had taken root in your house, and two or three ferns, unrolling like the ticklers at a banquet. The only other furnishings were a DuBarry pattern sheet, a page torn from a picture magazine, and some crusts in wax paper.

Before I quit I walked clear round the pond and found the place where you used to sit on the northeast side to get the sun in the fall, and the beach where you got sand for scrubbing your floor. On the eastern side of the pond, where the highway borders it, the State has built dressing rooms for swimmers, a float with diving towers, drinking fountains of porcelain, and rowboats for hire. The pond is in fact a State Preserve, and carries a twenty-dollar fine for picking wild flowers, a decree signed in all solemnity by your fellow-citizens Walter C. Wardwell, Erson B. Barlow, and Nathaniel I. Bowditch. There was a smell of creosote where they had been building a wide wooden stairway to the road and the parking area. Swimmers and boaters were arriving; bodies plunged vigorously into the water and emerged wet and beautiful in the bright air. As I left, a boatload of town boys were splashing about in mid-pond, kidding and fooling, the young fellows singing at the tops of their lungs in a wild chorus:

> Amer-ica, Amer-i-ca, God shed his grace on thee,
> And crown thy good with brotherhood
> From sea to shi-ning sea!

I walked back to town along the railroad, following your custom. The rails were expanding noisily in the hot sun, and on the slope of the roadbed the wild grape and the blackberry sent up their creepers to the track.

The expense of my brief sojourn in Concord was:

| | | |
|---|---|---|
| Canvas shoes | $1.95 | |
| Baseball bat | .25 | gifts to take back |
| Left-handed fielder's glove | 1.25 | to a boy |
| Hotel and meals | 4.25 | |
| In all | $7.70 | |

As you see, this amount was almost what you spent for food for eight months. I cannot defend the shoes or the expenditure for shelter and food: they reveal a meanness and grossness in my nature which you would find contemptible. The baseball equipment, however, is the kind of impediment with which you were never on even terms. You must remember that the house where you practiced. the sort of economy which I respect was haunted only by mice and squirrels. You never had to cope with a shortstop.

## I. Suggestions for Discussion:

1. White uses many specific details to contrast the Walden of the mid-twentieth century with the Walden of Thoreau's day. To what extent does he expect his readers to be familiar with Thoreau's *Walden*? In what particular respects would a knowledge of *Walden* enhance your understanding and appreciation of White's essay?
2. Compare his use of hyperbole in this essay with the hyperbole in "The Decline of Sport." Explain how this exaggeration brings humor to the essays.
3. Discuss what Thoreau's reactions to the scene depicted by White might have been.

## II. Suggestions for Writing:

1. Write an essay identifying environmental problems in your own community and offering possible solutions.
2. Using many specific details, describe a bustling tourist attraction near your college or home.

---

## TOM WOLFE

### Mauve Gloves & Madmen, Clutter & Vine

---

Tom Wolfe (1931–    ), the American essayist and novelist, focuses on the manners and mores of contemporary society. His wit and personal style are evident in such works as *The Kandy-Kolored Tangerine-Flake Streamline Baby* (1965), *The Electric Kool-Aid Acid Test* (1968), *Mauve Gloves & Madmen, Clutter & Vine* (1976), and his latest work about the United States Project Mercury space program, *The Right Stuff* (1979).

In the following sketch, Wolfe describes the chaotic social and financial life of a major American writer, not himself. Wolfe's gift for choice details and his highly idiosyncratic prose style enliven the essay.

---

The well-known American writer . . . but perhaps it's best not to say exactly which well-known American writer . . . they're a sensitive breed! The most ordinary comments they take personally! And why would the gentleman we're about to surprise be any exception? He's in his apartment, a seven-room apartment on Riverside Drive, on the West Side of Manhattan, in his study, seated at his desk. As we approach from the rear, we notice a bald spot on the crown of his head. It's about the size of a Sunshine Chip-a-Roo cookie, this bald spot, freckled and toasty brown. Gloriously suntanned, in fact. Around this bald spot swirls a corona of dark-brown hair that becomes quite thick by the time it completes its mad Byronic rush down the back over his turtleneck and out to the side in great bushes over his ears. He knows the days of covered ears are numbered, because this particular look has become somewhat *Low Rent.* When he was coming back from his father's funeral, half the salesmen lined up at O'Hare for the commuter flights, in their pajama-striped shirts and diamond-print double-knit suits, had groovy hair much like his. And to think that just six years ago such a hairdo seemed . . . so defiant!

Meeting his sideburns at mid-jowl is the neck of his turtleneck sweater, an authentic Navy turtleneck, and the sweater tucks into his Levi's, which are the authentic Original XX Levi's, the original straight stovepipes made for wearing over boots. He got them in a bona fide cowhand's store in La Porte, Texas, during his trip to Houston to be the keynote speaker in a lecture series on "The American Dream: Myth and Reality." No small part of the latter was a fee of two thousand dollars plus expenses. This outfit, the Navy turtleneck and the double-X Levi's, means work & discipline. *Discipline*! as he says to himself every day. When he puts on these clothes, it means that he intends to write, and do nothing else, for at least four hours. *Discipline,* Mr. Wonderful!

But on the desk in front of him—that's not a manuscript or even the beginnings of one . . . that's *last month's bank statement,* which just arrived in the mail. And those are his canceled checks in a pile on top of it. In that big ledger-style checkbook there (the old-fashioned kind, serious-looking, with no crazy Peter Max designs on the checks) are his check stubs. And those slips of paper in the promiscuous heap are all unpaid bills, and he's taking the nylon cover off his Texas Instruments desk calculator, and he is about to measure the flow, the tide, the mad sluice, the crazy current of the

money that pours through his fingers every month and which is now running
against him in the most catastrophic manner, like an undertow, a riptide,
pulling him under—

—him and this apartment, which cost him $75,000 in 1972; $20,000
cash, which came out of the $25,000 he got as a paperback advance for his
fourth book, *Under Uncle's Thumb,* and $536.36 a month in bank-loan pay-
ments (on the $55,000 he borrowed) ever since, plus another $390 a month
in so-called maintenance, which has steadily increased until it is now $460 a
month . . . and although he already knows the answer, the round number, he
begins punching the figures into the calculator . . . 536.36 plus . . . 460 . . .
times 12 . . . and the calculator keys go *chuck chuck chuck chuck* and the
curious little orange numbers, broken up like stencil figures, go trucking
across the black path of the display panel at the top of the machine, giving a
little orange shudder every time he hits the *plus* button, until there it is,
stretching out seven digits long—11956.32—$12,000 a year! One thousand
dollars a month—this is what he spends on his apartment alone! and by May
he will have to come up with another $6,000 so he can rent the house on
Martha's Vineyard again *chuck chuck chuck chuck* and by September another
$6,750—$3,750 to send his daughter, Amy, to Dalton and $3,000 to send his
son, Jonathan, to Collegiate (on those marvelous frog-and-cricket evenings up
on the Vineyard he and Bill and Julie and Scott and Henry and Herman and
Leon and Shelly and the rest, all Media & Lit. people from New York, have
discussed why they send their children to private schools, and they have
pretty well decided that it is the educational turmoil in the New York public
schools that is the problem—the kids just wouldn't be educated!—plus some
considerations of their children's personal safety—but—needless to say!—it
has nothing to do with the matter of . . . well, *race*) and he punches that
in . . . 6750 . . . *chuck chuck chuck chuck* . . . and hits the *plus* button . . .
an orange shimmer . . . and beautiful! there's the figure—the three items,
the apartment in town, the summer place, and the children's schooling—
$24,706.32!—almost $25,000 a year in fixed costs, just for a starter! for lodg-
ing and schooling! nothing else included! A grim nut!

It's appalling, and he's drowning, and this is only the beginning of it,
just the basic grim nut—and yet in his secret heart he loves these little sessions
with the calculator and the checks and the stubs and the bills and the march-
ing orange numbers that stretch on and on . . . into such magnificently huge
figures. It's like an electric diagram of his infinitely expanding life, a score-
board showing the big league he's now in. Far from throwing him into a
panic, as they well might, these tote sessions are one of the most satisfying
habits he has. A regular vice! Like barbiturates! Calming the heart and slow-

ing the respiration! Because it seems *practical,* going over expenses, his conscience sanctions it as a permissible way to avoid the only thing that can possibly keep him afloat: namely, more writing . . . He's deep into his calculator
trance now . . . The orange has him enthralled. Think of it! He has now
reached a stage in his life when not only a $1,000-a-month apartment but also
a summer house on an island in the Atlantic is an absolute necessity—precisely that, absolute necessity . . . It's appalling!—and yet it's the most inexplicable bliss!—nothing less.

As for the apartment, even at $1,000 a month it is not elegant. Ele-
gance would cost at least twice that. No, his is an apartment of a sort known
as West Side Married Intellectual. The rooms are big, the layout is good, but
the moldings, cornices, covings, and chair rails seem to be corroding. Actually,
they are merely lumpy from too many coats of paint over the decades, and
the parquet sections in the floor have dried out and are sprung loose from one
another. It has been a long time since this apartment has had an owner who
could both meet the down-payment nut *and* have the woodwork stripped and
the flooring replaced. The building has a doorman but no elevator man, and
on Sundays the door is manned by a janitor in gray khaki work clothes. But
what's he supposed to do? He needs seven rooms. His son and daughter now
require separate bedrooms. He and his wife require a third one (a third and
fourth if the truth be known, but he has had to settle for three). He now
needs, not just likes, this study he's in, a workroom that is his exclusively.
He now *needs* the dining room, which is a real dining room, not a dogleg off
the living room. Even if he is giving only a cocktail party, it is . . . *necessary*
that they (one & all) note—however unconsciously—that he *does* have a dining room!

Right here on his desk are the canceled checks that have come in hung
over from the cocktail party he gave six weeks ago. They're right in front of
him now . . . $209.60 to the florists, Clutter & Vine, for flowers for the hall-
way, the living room, the dining room, and the study, although part of that,
$100, was for a bowl of tightly clustered silk poppies that will become a
permanent part of the living-room decor . . . $138.18 to the liquor store
(quite a bit was left over however, meaning that the bar will be stocked for
a while) . . . $257.50 to Mauve Gloves & Madmen, the caterers, even though
he had chosen some of the cheaper hors d'oeuvres. He also tipped the two
butlers $10 each, which made him feel a little foolish later when he learned
that one of them was co-owner of Mauve Gloves & Madmen . . . $23.91 to the
grocery store for he couldn't remember what . . . $173.95 to the Russian Tea
Room for dinner afterward with Henry and Mavis (the guests of honor) and
six other stragglers . . . $12.84 for a serving bowl from Bloomingdale's . . .

$20 extra to the maid for staying on late . . . and he's chucking all these fig-
ures into the calculator *chuck chuck chuck chuck* blink blink blink blink
*truck truck truck truck* the slanted orange numbers go trucking and winking
across the panel . . . 855.98 . . . $855.98 for a cocktail party!—not even a
dinner party!—appalling!—and how slyly sweet . . .

Should he throw in the library stairs as a party expense, too? Perhaps,
he thought, if he were honest, he would. The checks were right here: $420
to Lum B. Lee Ltd. for the stairs themselves, and another $95 to the customs
broker to get the thing through customs and $45 to the trucker to deliver it,
making a total of $560! In any event, they're terrific . . . Mayfair heaven . . .
the classic English type, stairs to nowhere, going up in a spiral around a central column, carved in the ancient bamboo style, rising up almost seven feet, ·
so he can reach books on his highest shelf . . . He had had it made extra high
by a cabinetmaking firm in Hong Kong, the aforementioned Lum B. Lee . . .
Now, if the truth be known, the stairs are the result of a habit he has: he goes
around the apartment after giving a party and stands where he saw particular
guests standing, people who stuck in his mind, and tries to see what they saw
from that position; in other words, how the apartment looked in their eyes.
About a year ago he has seen Lenny Johns of the *Times* standing in the door-
way of his study and looking in, so afterward, after Lenny and everyone else
had gone, he took up the same position and looked in . . . and what he saw
did not please him. In fact, it looked sad. Through Lenny Johns's eyes it must
have looked like the basic writer's workroom out of *Writer's Digest:* a plain
Danish-style desk (The Door Store) with dowel legs (dowel legs!), a modernistic (modernistic!) metal-and-upholstery office swivel chair, a low-slung
(more Modernismus!) couch, a bank of undistinguished-looking file cabinets,
a bookcase covering one entire wall but made of plain white-painted boards
and using the wall itself as its back. The solution, as he saw it—without
going into huge costs—was the library stairs—the stairs to nowhere!—an object
indisputably useful and yet with an air of elegant folly!

It was after that same party that his wife had said to him: "Who was
that weepy-looking little man you were talking to so much?"

"I don't know who you're talking about."

"The one with the three strands of hair pulled up from the side and
draped over his scalp."

He knew she was talking about Johns. And he knew *she* knew Johns's
name. She had met him before, on the Vineyard.

Meeting Lenny Johns socially was one of the many dividends of
Martha's Vineyard. They have been going there for three summers now,
renting a house on a hill in Chilmark . . . until it has become, well *necessity*!

It's no longer possible to stay in New York over the summer. It's not fair to the children. They shouldn't have to grow up that way. As for himself, he's gotten to know Lenny and Bill and Scott and Julie and Bob and Dick and Jody and Gillian and Frank and Shelly and the rest in a way that wouldn't be possible in New York. But quite aside from all that . . . just that clear sparkling late-August solitude, when you can smell the pine and the sea . . . heading down the piney path from the house on the hill . . . walking two hundred yards across the marshes on the pedestrian dock, just one plank wide, so that you have to keep staring down at it . . . it's hypnotic . . . the board, the marsh grass, your own tread, the sound of the frogs and the crickets . . . and then getting into the rowboat and rowing across the inlet to . . . the *dune* . . . the great swelling dune, with the dune grass waving against the sky on top . . . and then over the lip of it—to the beach! the most pristine white beach in the world! and the open sea . . . all spread out before you—yours! Just that! the sand, the sea, the sky—and solitude! No gates, no lifeguard stands, no concessions, no sprawling multitudes of transistor radios and plaid plastic beach chairs . . .

It is chiefly for these summers on the Vineyard that he has bought a car, a BMW sedan—$7,200—but very lively! It costs him $76 a month to keep it in a garage in the city for nine months of the year, another $684 in all, so that the hard nut for Martha's Vineyard is really $6,684—but it's a necessity, and one sacrifices for necessities. After three years on the Vineyard he feels very possessive about the place, even though he's a renter, and he immediately joined in with the move to publish a protest against "that little Albanian with a pickup truck," as he was (wrongly) called, some character named Zarno or something who had assembled a block of fifty acres on the Vineyard and was going to develop it into 150 building lots—one third of an acre each! (Only dimly did he recall that the house he grew up in, in Chicago, had been on about one fifth of an acre and hadn't seemed terribly hemmed in.) Bill T— wrote a terrific manifesto in which he talked about "these Snopes-like little men with their pickup trucks"—Snopes-like!—and all sorts of people signed it.

This campaign against the developers also brought the New York Media & Lit. people into contact for the first time with the Boston people. Until the Media & Lit. people began going there about ten years before, Martha's Vineyard had always been a Boston resort, "Boston" in the most proper social sense of the word. There wasn't much the Boston people could do about the New York people except not associate with them. When they said "New York people," they no doubt meant "Jews & Others," he figured. So when he was first invited to a Boston party, thanks to his interest in the anti-developers campaign, he went with some trepidation and with his resentment tucked into his waistband like a .38. His mood darkened still more when he arrived in white ducks and an embroidered white cotton shirt, yoke-shouldered and open to the sternum—a little eccentric (actually a harmless sort of shirt known in Arizona as Fruit Western) but perfectly in the mood of standard New York People Seaside Funk—and found that the Boston men, to a man, had on jackets and ties. Not only that, they had on their own tribal colors. The jackets were mostly navy blazers, and the ties were mostly striped ties or ties with little jacquard emblems on them, but the pants had a go-to-hell air: checks and plaids of the loudest possible sort, madras plaids, yellow-on-orange windowpane checks, crazy-quilt plaids, giant houndstooth checks, or else they were a solid airmail red or taxi yellow or some other implausible go-to-hell color. They finished that off with loafers and white crew socks or no socks at all. The pants were their note of Haitian abandon . . . weekends by the sea. At the same time the jackets and ties showed they had not forgotten for a moment where the power came from. He felt desolate. He slipped the loaded resentment out of his waistband and cocked it. And then the most amazing thing happened—

His hostess came up and made a fuss over him! Exactly! She had read *Under Uncle's Thumb*! So had quite a few of the men, infernal pants and all! Lawyers and investment counselors! They were all interested in him! Quite a stream—he hardly had to move from the one spot all evening! And as the sun went down over the ocean, and the alcohol rose, and all of their basted teeth glistened—he could almost see something . . . *presque vu*! . . . a glimmer of the future . . . something he could barely make out . . . a vision in which America's best minds, her intellectuals, found a common ground, a natural unity, with the enlightened segments of her old aristocracy, her old money . . . the two groups bound together by . . . but by what? . . . he could *almost* see it, but not quite . . . it was *presque vu* . . . it was somehow a matter of taste . . . of sensibility . . . of grace, natural grace . . . just as he himself had a natural feel for the best British styles, which were after all the source of the Boston manners . . . What were the library stairs, if they weren't that? What were the Lobb shoes?

For here, now, surfacing to the top of the pile, is the check for $248 to John Lobb & Sons Ltd. Boot Makers—that was the way he wrote it out, Boot Makers, two words, the way it was on their bosky florid London letterhead—$248!—for one pair of shoes!—from England!—handmade! And now, all at once, even as *chuck chuck chuck* he punches it into the calculator, he is swept by a wave of sentiment, of sadness, sweet misery—guilt! Two hundred and forty-eight dollars for a pair of handmade shoes from England . . . He thinks of his father. He wore his first pair of Lobb shoes to his father's funeral. Black cap toes they were, the most formal daytime shoes made, and it was pouring that day in Chicago and his incomparable new shoes from England were caked with mud when he got back to his father's house. He took the shoes off, but then he froze—he couldn't bring himself to remove the mud. His father had come to the United States from Russia as a young man in 1922. He had to go to work at once, and in no time, it seemed, came the Depression, and he struggled through it as a tailor, although in the forties he acquired a dry-cleaning establishment and, later, a second one, plus a diaper-service business and a hotel-linen service. But this brilliant man—oh, how many times had his mother assured him of that!—had had to spend all those years as a tailor. This cultivated man!—more assurances—oh, how many yards of Goethe and Dante had he heard him quote in an accent that gripped the English language like a full nelson! And now his son, the son of this brilliant, cultivated but uneducated and thwarted man—now his son, his son with his education and his literary career, his son who had never had to work with his hands more than half an hour at a stretch in his life—his son had turned up at his funeral in a pair of handmade shoes from England! . . . Well, he let the mud dry on them. He didn't touch them for six months. He didn't even put the shoe trees (another $47) in. Perhaps the goddamned boots would curl up and die.

The number . . . 248 . . . is sitting right up there in slanted orange digits on the face of the calculator. That seems to end the reverie. He doesn't want to continue it just now. He doesn't want to see the 6684 for Martha's Vineyard up there again for a while. He doesn't want to see the seven digits of his debts (counting the ones after the decimal point) glowing in their full, magnificent, intoxicating length. It's time to get serious! *Discipline*! Only one thing will pull him out of all this: work . . . writing . . . and there's no way to put it off any longer. *Discipline*, Mr. Wonderful! This is the most difficult day of all, the day when it falls to his lot to put a piece of paper in the typewriter and start on page 1 of a new book, with that horrible arthritic siege—writing a book!—stretching out ahead of him (a tubercular blue glow, as his mind comprehends it) . . . although it lifts his spirits a bit to know that both *The Atlantic* and *Playboy* have expressed an interest in running chapters as he goes along, and *Penthouse* would pay even more, although he doesn't want it to appear in a one-hand magazine, a household aid, as literary penicillin to help quell the spirochetes oozing from all the virulent vulvas . . . Nevertheless! help is on the way! Hell!—there's not a magazine in America that wouldn't publish something from this book!

So he feeds a sheet of paper into his typewriter, and in the center, one third of the way down from the top, he takes care of the easy part first—the working title, in capital letters:

RECESSION AND REPRESSION
POLICE STATE AMERICA
AND THE SPIRIT OF '76

**I. Suggestions for Discussion:**
   1. What is the significance of Wolfe's title? Can you suggest an alternative title?
   2. How does Wolfe's choice of details help characterize the lifestyle he portrays?
   3. In what ways do Wolfe's sentences help convey the state of mind of his principal character?
**II. Suggestions for Writing:**
   1. Use your bills or cancelled checks for the last month as the basis for an essay about your activities during this period. To what extent does your documentation show the period to be typical or atypical of your lifestyle?
   2. Describe a frantic moment you have experienced recently.

# MARY WOLLSTONECRAFT

## Introduction

### to *A Vindication of the Rights of Woman*

Mary Wollstonecraft (1759–1797), whose husband was the radical William Godwin and whose daughter married Percy Bysshe Shelley, was a schoolteacher, governess, and member of a publishing firm. Her *Vindication of the Rights of Woman* (1792), from which the following selection is taken, was an extraordinary defense of the rights of eighteenth-century women.

In the "Introduction" to her work, she clearly sets out her plan to persuade and convince women to become more respectable members of society.

My own sex, I hope, will excuse me, if I treat them like rational creatures, instead of flattering their *fascinating* graces, and viewing them as if they were in a state of perpetual childhood, unable to stand alone. I earnestly wish to point out in what true dignity and human happiness consists—I wish to persuade women to endeavour to acquire strength, both of mind and body, and to convince them that the soft phrases, susceptibility of heart, delicacy of sentiment, and refinement of taste, are almost synomymous with epithets of weakness, and that those beings who are only the objects of pity and that kind of love, which has been termed its sister, will soon become objects of contempt.

Dismissing, then, those pretty feminine phrases, which the men condescendingly use to soften our slavish dependence, and despising that weak elegancy of mind, exquisite sensibility, and sweet docility of manners, supposed to be the sexual characteristics of the weaker vessel, I wish to shew that elegance is inferior to virtue, that the first object of laudable ambition is to obtain a character as a human being, regardless of the distinction of sex; and that secondary views should be brought to this simple touchstone.

This is a rough sketch of my plan; and should I express my conviction with the energetic emotions that I feel whenever I think of the subject, the dictates of experience and reflection will be felt by some of my readers. Animated by this important object, I shall disdain to cull my phrases or polish my style;—I aim at being useful, and sincerity will render me unaffected; for, wishing rather to persuade by the force of my arguments, than dazzle by the elegance of my language, I shall not waste my time in rounding periods, or in fabricating the turgid bombast of artificial feelings, which, coming from the head, never reach the heart. I shall be employed about things, not words! and, anxious to render my sex more respectable members of society, I shall try to avoid that flowery diction which has slided from essays into novels, and from novels into familiar letters and conversation.

These pretty superlatives, dropping glibly from the tongue, vitiate the taste, and create a kind of sickly delicacy that runs away from simple unadorned truth; and a deluge of false sentiments and overstretched feelings, stifling the natural emotions of the heart, render the domestic pleasures insipid, that ought to sweeten the exercise of those severe duties, which educate a rational and immortal being for a nobler field of action.

The education of women has, of late, been more attended to than formerly; yet they are still reckoned a frivolous sex, and ridiculed or pitied by the writers who endeavour by satire or instruction or improve them. It is acknowledged that they spend many of the first years of their lives in acquiring a smattering of accomplishments; meanwhile strength of body and mind are sacrificed to libertine notions of beauty, to the desire of establishing themselves,—the only way women can rise in the world,—by marriage. And this desire making mere animals of them, when they marry they act as such children may be expected to act:—they dress; they paint, and nickname God's creatures. Surely these weak beings are only fit for a seraglio!—Can they be expected to govern a family with judgment, or take care of the poor babes whom they bring into the world?

If then it can be fairly deduced from the present conduct of the sex, from the prevalent fondness for pleasure which takes place of ambition, and those nobler passions that open and enlarge the soul; that the instruction which women have hitherto received has only tended, with the constitution of civil society, to render them insignificant objects of desire—mere propagators of fools!—if it can be proved that in aiming to accomplish them, without cultivating their understandings, they are taken out of their sphere of duties, and made ridiculous and useless when the short-lived bloom of beauty is over,[1] I presume that *rational* men will excuse me for endeavouring to persuade them to become more masculine and respectable.

Indeed the word masculine is only a bugbear: there is little reason to fear that women will acquire too much courage or fortitude; for their apparent inferiority with respect to bodily strength, must render them, in some degree, dependent on men in the various relations of life; but why should it be increased by prejudices that give a sex to virtue, and confound simple truths and sensual reveries?

Women are, in fact, so much degraded by mistaken notions of female excellence, that I do not mean to add a paradox when I assert, that this artificial weakness produces a propensity to tyrannize, and gives birth to cunning, the natural opponent of strength, which leads them to play off those contemptible infantile airs that undermine esteem even whilst they excite desire. Let men become more chaste and modest, and if women do not grow wiser in the same ratio, it will be clear that they have weaker understandings. It seems scarcely necessary to say, that I now speak of the sex in general. Many individuals have more sense than their male relatives; and, as nothing preponderates where there is a constant struggle for an equilibrium, without it has naturally more gravity, some women govern their husbands without degrading themselves, because intellect will always govern.

### I. Suggestions for Discussion:

1. Why does the author urge women to reject their conventional image of weakness? How do her diction and style contribute to her plea?

---

[1] A lively writer, I cannot recollect his name, asks what business women turned of forty have to do in the world?

2. Discuss her views on education for women and on marriage. How does the vocabulary she chooses enhance her views?

3. Compare her views on the education of women with those of Daniel Defoe in "An Academy for Women," p. 112 or Margaret Fuller in "A Vindication of the Rights of Women," p. 193.

## II. Suggestions for Writing:

1. Write an essay explaining some of the current controversies in the women's liberation movement and indicating your own stand.

2. Drawing on essays in this anthology and on other reading you have done, write an essay showing that the call for rights for women goes back at least two hundred years.

---

# VIRGINIA WOOLF

## Professions for Women

### from *The Death of the Moth*

---

Virginia Woolf (1882-1941) was an English novelist and critic known for her experimentation with the form of the novel. Her works include *Mrs. Dalloway* (1922), *To the Lighthouse* (1927), *Orlando* (1928), and *The Death of the Moth* (1942). *A Writer's Diary,* not published until 1953, contained her reflections on her own works.

Using her own experiences in becoming an author as illustrations, she argues in the following essay that women must overcome formidable phantoms and obstacles in order to succeed as professionals.

---

When your secretary invited me to come here, she told me that your Society is concerned with the employment of women and she suggested that I might tell you something about my own professional experiences. It is true I am a woman; it is true I am employed; but what professional experiences have I had? It is difficult to say. My profession is literature; and in that profession there are fewer experiences for women than in any other, with the exception of the stage—fewer, I mean, that are peculiar to women. For the road was cut many years ago—by Fanny Burney, by Aphra Behn, by Harriet Martineau, by Jane Austen, by George Eliot—many famous women, and many more unknown and forgotten, have been before me, making the path smooth, and regulating my steps. Thus, when I came to write, there were very few material obstacles in my way. Writing was a reputable and harmless occupation. The family peace was not broken by the scratching of a pen. No demand was made upon the family purse. For ten and sixpence one can buy paper enough to write all the plays of Shakespeare—if one has a mind that way. Pianos and models, Paris, Vienna and Berlin, masters and mistresses, are not needed by a writer. The cheapness of writing paper is, of course, the reason why women have succeeded as writers before they have succeeded in the other professions.

But to tell you my story—it is a simple one. You have only got to figure to yourselves a girl in a bedroom with a pen in her hand. She had only to move that pen from left to right—from ten o'clock to one. Then it occurred to her to do what is simple and cheap enough after all—to slip a few of those pages into an envelope, fix a penny stamp in the corner, and drop the envelope into the red box at the corner. It was thus that I became a journalist; and my effort was rewarded on the first day of the following month—a very glorious day it was for me—by a letter from an editor containing a cheque for one pound ten shillings and sixpence. But to show you how little I deserve to be called a professional woman, how little I know of the struggles and difficulties of such lives, I have to admit that instead of spending that sum upon bread and butter, rent, shoes and stockings, or butcher's bills, I went out and bought a cat—a beautiful cat, a Persian cat, which very soon involved me in bitter disputes with my neighbours.

What could be easier than to write articles and to buy Persian cats with the profits? But wait a moment. Articles have to be about something. Mine, I seem to remember, was about a novel by a famous man. And while I was writing this review, I discovered that if I were going to review books I should need to do battle with a certain phantom. And the phantom was a woman, and when I came to know her better I called her after the heroine of a famous poem. The Angel in the House. It was she who used to come between me and my paper when I was writing reviews. It was she who bothered me and wasted my time and so tormented me that at last I killed her. You who come of a younger and happier generation may not have heard of her—you may not know what I mean by the Angel in the House. I will describe her as shortly as I can. She was intensely sympathetic. She was immensely charming. She was utterly unselfish. She excelled in the difficult arts of family life. She sacrificed herself daily. If there was chicken, she took the leg; if there was a draught she sat in it—in short she was so constituted that she never had a mind or a wish of her own, but preferred to sympathize always with the minds and wishes of others. Above all—I need not say it—she was pure. Her purity was supposed to be her chief beauty—her blushes, her great grace. In those days—the last of Queen Victoria—every house had its Angel. And when I came to write I encountered her with the very first words. The shadow of her wings fell on my page; I heard the rustling of her skirts in the room. Directly, that is to say, I took my pen in hand to review that novel by a famous man, she slipped behind me and whispered: "My dear, you are a young woman. You are writing about a book that has been written by a man. Be sympathetic; be tender; flatter; deceive; use all the arts and wiles of our sex. Never let anybody guess that you have a mind of your own. Above all, be pure." And she made as if to guide my pen. I now record the one act for which I take some credit to myself, though the credit rightly belongs to some excellent ancestors of mine who left me a certain sum of money—shall we say five hundred pounds a year?—so that it was not necessary for me to depend solely on charm for my living. I turned upon her and caught her by the throat. I did my best to kill her. My excuse, if I were to be had up in a court of law, would be that I acted in self-defence. Had I not killed her she would have killed me. She would have plucked the heart out of my writing. For, as I found, directly I put pen to paper, you cannot review even a novel without having a mind of your own, without expressing what you think to be the truth about human relations, morality, sex. And all these questions, according to the Angel in the House, cannot be dealt with freely and openly by women; they must charm, they must conciliate, they must—to put it bluntly—tell lies if they are to succeed. Thus, whenever I felt the shadow of her wing or the radiance of her halo upon my page, I took up the inkpot and flung it at her. She died hard. Her fictitious nature was of great assistance to her. It is far harder to kill a phantom than a reality. She was always creeping back when I thought I had despatched her. Though I flatter myself that I killed her in the end, the struggle was severe; it took much time that had better have been spent upon learning Greek grammar; or in roaming the world in search of adventures. But it was a real experience; it was an experience that was bound to befall all women writers at that time. Killing the Angel in the House was part of the occupation of a woman writer.

But to continue my story. The Angel was dead; what then remained? You may say that what remained was a simple and common object—a young woman in a bedroom with an inkpot. In other words, now that she had rid herself of falsehood, that young woman had only to be herself. Ah, but what is "herself"? I mean, what is a woman? I assure you, I do not know. I do not believe that you know. I do not believe that anybody can know until she has expressed herself in all the arts and professions open to human skill. That indeed is one of the reasons why I have come here—out of respect for you, who are in process of showing us by your experiments what a woman is, who are in process of providing us, by your failures and successes, with that extremely important piece of information.

But to continue the story of my professional experiences. I made one pound ten and six by my first review; and I bought a Persian cat with the proceeds. Then I grew ambitious. A Persian cat is all very well, I said; but a Persian cat is not enough. I must have a motor car. And it was thus that I became a novelist—for it is a very strange thing that people will give you a motor car if you will tell them a story. It is a still stranger thing that there is nothing so delightful in the world as telling stories. It is far pleasanter than writing reviews of famous novels. And yet, if I am to obey your secretary and tell you my professional experiences as a novelist, I must tell you about a very strange experience that befell me as a novelist. And to understand it you must try first to imagine a novelist's state of mind. I hope I am not giving away professional secrets if I say that a novelist's chief desire is to be as unconscious as possible. He has to induce in himself a state of perpetual lethargy. He wants life to proceed with the utmost quiet and regularity. He wants to see the same faces, to read the same books, to do the same things day after day, month after month, while he is writing, so that nothing may break the illusion in which he is living—so that nothing may disturb or disquiet the mysterious nosing about, feelings round, darts, dashes and sudden discoveries of that very shy and illusive spirit, the imagination. I suspect that this state is the same both for men and women. Be that as it may, I want you to imagine me writing a novel in a state of trance. I want you to figure to yourselves a girl sitting with a pen in her hand, which for minutes, and indeed for hours, she never dips into the inkpot. The image that comes to my mind when I think of this girl is the image of a fisherman lying sunk in dreams on the verge of a deep lake with a rod held out over the water. She was letting her imagination sweep unchecked round every rock and cranny of the world that lies submerged in the depths of our unconscious being. Now came the experience, the experience that I believe to be far commoner with women writers than with men. The line raced through the girl's fingers. Her imagination had rushed away. It had sought the pools, the depths, the dark places where the largest fish slumber. And then there was a smash. There was an explosion. There was foam and confusion. The imagination had dashed itself against something hard. The girl was roused from her dream. She was indeed in a state of the most acute and difficult distress. To speak without figure she had thought of something, something about the body, about the passions which it was unfitting for her as a woman to say. Men, her reason told her, would be shocked. The consciousness of what men will say of a woman who speaks the truth about her passions had roused her from her artist's state of unconsciousness. She could write no more. The trance was over. Her imagination could work no longer. This I believe to be a very common experience with women writers—they are impeded by the extreme conventionality of the other sex. For though men sensibly allow themselves great freedom in these respects, I doubt that they realize or can control the extreme severity with which they condemn such freedom in women.

These then were two very genuine experiences of my own. These were two of the adventures of my professional life. The first—killing the Angel in the House—I think I solved. She died. But the second, telling the truth about my own experiences as a body, I do not think I solved. I doubt that any woman has solved it yet. The obstacles against her are still immensely powerful—and yet they are very difficult to define. Outwardly, what is simpler than to write books? Outwardly, what obstacles are there for a woman rather than for a man? Inwardly, I think, the case is very different; she has still many ghosts to fight, many prejudices to overcome. Indeed it will be a long time still, I think, before a woman can sit down to write a book without finding a phantom to be slain, a rock to be dashed against. And if this is so in literature, the freest of all professions for women, how is it in the new professions which you are now for the first time entering?

Those are the questions that I should like, had I time, to ask you. And indeed, if I have laid stress upon these professional experiences of mine, it is because I believe that they are, though in different forms, yours also. Even when the path is nominally open—when there is nothing to prevent a woman from being a doctor, a lawyer, a civil servant—there are many phantoms and obstacles, as I believe, looming in her way. To discuss and define them is I think of great value and importance; for thus only can the labour be shared, the difficulties be solved. But besides this, it is necessary also to discuss the ends and the aims for which we are fighting, for which we are doing battle with these formidable obstacles. Those aims cannot be taken for granted; they must be perpetually questioned and examined. The whole position, as I see it—here in this hall surrounded by women practising for the first time in history I know not how many different professions—is one of extraordinary interest and importance. You have won rooms of your own in the house hitherto exclusively owned by men. You are able, though not without great labour and effort, to pay the rent. You are earning your five hundred pounds a year. But this freedom is only a beginning; the room is your own, but it is still bare. It has to be furnished; it has to be decorated; it has to be shared. How are you going to furnish it, how are you going to decorate it? With whom are you going to share it, and upon what terms? These, I think are questions of the utmost importance and interest. For the first time in history you are able to ask them; for the first time you are able to decide for yourselves what the answers should be. Willingly would I stay and discuss those questions and answers—but not tonight. My time is up; and I must cease.

I. **Suggestions for Discussion**:
1. Explain why Virginia Woolf needed to kill the angel in the house. Describe her angel.
2. What remaining obstacles to truth did she need to overcome? How did she set about doing so?
3. Discuss the analogy of the house in the concluding paragraph. What implications does it have concerning relationships with men?

II. **Suggestions for Writing**:
1. Write an essay about an angel in the house you know.
2. Prepare and present a speech about obstacles that you must overcome to succeed in your chosen profession or occupation.

---

# VIRGINIA WOOLF

## The Death of the Moth

---

In the following essay, Virginia Woolf's detailed description of the physical appearance and activities of a hay-coloured moth at her window lead to a reflection on the power of death.

---

Moths that fly by day are not properly to be called moths; they do not excite that pleasant sense of dark autumn nights and ivy-blossom which the commonest yellow underwing asleep in the shadow of the curtain never fails to rouse in us. They are hybrid creatures, neither gay like butterflies nor sombre like their own species. Nevertheless the present specimen, with his narrow hay-coloured wings, fringed with a tassel of the same colour, seemed to be content with life. It was a pleasant morning, mid-September, mild, benignant, yet with a keener breath than of the summer months. The plough was already scoring the field opposite the window, and where the share had been, the earth was pressed flat and gleamed with moisture. Such vigour came rolling in from the fields and the down beyond that it was difficult to keep the eyes strictly turned upon the book. The rooks too were keeping one of their annual festivities; soaring round the tree-tops until it looked as if a vast net with thousands of black knots in it has been cast up into the air; which, after a few moments sank slowly down upon the trees until every twig seemed to have a knot at the end of it. Then, suddenly, the net would be thrown into the air again in a wider circle this time, with the utmost clamour and vociferation, as though to be thrown into the air and settle slowly down upon the tree-tops were a tremendously exciting experience.

The same energy which inspired the rooks, the ploughmen, the horses, and even, it seemed, the lean bare-backed downs, sent the moth fluttering from side to side of his square of the window-pane. One could not help watching him. One was, indeed, conscious of a queer feeling of pity for him. The possibilities of pleasure seemed that morning so enormous and so various that to have only a moth's part in life, and a day moth's at that, appeared a hard fate, and his zest in enjoying his meagre opportunities to the full, pathetic. He flew vigorously to one corner of his compartment, and, after waiting there a second, flew across to the other. What remained for him but to fly to a third corner and then to a fourth? That was all he could do, in spite of the size of the downs, the width of the sky, the far-off smoke of houses, and the romantic voice, now and then, of a steamer out at sea. What he could do he did. Watching him, it seemed as if a fibre, very thin but pure, of the enormous energy of the world had been thrust into his frail and diminutive body. As often as he crossed the pane, I could fancy that a thread of vital light became visible. He was little or nothing but life.

Yet, because he was so small, and so simple a form of the energy that was rolling in at the open window and driving its way through so many narrow and intricate corridors in my own brain and in those of other human beings, there was something marvellous as well as pathetic about him. It was as if someone had taken a tiny bead of pure life and decking it as lightly as possible with down and feathers, had set it dancing and zigzagging to show us the true nature of life. Thus displayed one could not get over the strangeness of it. One is apt to forget all about life, seeing it humped and bossed and garnished and cumbered so that it has to move with the greatest circumspection and dignity. Again, the thought of all that life might have been had he been born in any other shape caused one to view his simple activities with a kind of pity.

After a time, tired by his dancing apparently, he settled on the window ledge in the sun, and the queer spectacle being at an end, I forgot about him. Then, looking up, my eye was caught by him. He was trying to resume his dancing, but seemed either so stiff or so awkward that he could only flutter to the bottom of the window-pane; and when he tried to fly across it he failed. Being intent on other matters I watched these futile attempts for a time without thinking, unconsciously waiting for him to resume his flight, as one waits for a machine, that has stopped momentarily, to start again without considering the reason for its failure. After perhaps a seventh attempt he slipped from the wooden ledge and fell, fluttering his wings, on to his back on the window-sill. The helplessness of his attitude roused me. It flashed upon me that he was in difficulties; he could no longer raise himself; his legs struggled vainly. But, as I stretched out a pencil, meaning to help him to right himself, it came over me that the failure and awkwardness were the approach of death. I laid the pencil down again.

The legs agitated themselves once more. I looked as if for the enemy against which he struggled. I looked out of doors. What had happened there? Presumably it was midday, and work in the fields had stopped. Stillness and quiet had replaced the previous animation. The birds had taken themselves off to feed in the brooks. The horses stood still. Yet the power was there all the same, massed outside indifferent, impersonal, not attending to anything in particular. Somehow it was opposed to the little hay-coloured moth. It was useless to try to do anything. One could only watch the extraordinary efforts made by those tiny legs against an oncoming doom which could, had it chosen, have submerged an entire city, not merely a city, but masses of human beings; nothing, I knew, had any chance against death. Nevertheless after a pause of exhaustion the legs fluttered again. It was superb this last protest, and so frantic that he succeeded at last in righting himself. One's sympathies, of course, were all on the side of life. Also, when there was no-body to care or to know, this gigantic effort on the part of an insignificant little moth, against a power of such magnitude, to retain what no one else valued or desired to keep, moved one strangely. Again, somehow, one saw life, a pure bead. I lifted the pencil again, useless though I knew it to be. But even as I did so, the unmistakable tokens of death showed themselves. The body relaxed, and instantly grew stiff. The struggle was over. The insignificant little creature now knew death. As I looked at the dead moth, this minute wayside triumph of so great a force over so mean an antagonist filled me with wonder. Just as life had been strange a few minutes before, so death was now as strange. The moth having righted himself now lay most decently and uncomplaining composed. O yes, he seemed to say, death is stronger than I am.

## I. Suggestions for Discussion:

1. Woolf's detailed descriptions of the flight and death of a hay moth lead to what generalizations?
2. Discuss Woolf's use of simile and metaphor to characterize the activity of the moth.
3. Compare Woolf's description of nature with Annie Dillard's in "A Field of Silence," p. 135.

## II. Suggestions for Writing:

1. After careful observation, write a description of the appearance and activities of an insect or small animal.
2. From something you have experienced or observed, draw a generalization about the human condition.

# GLOSSARY

**ABSTRACTION, levels of** distinguished in two ways: in the range between the general and the specific and in the range between the abstract and the concrete.

A general word refers to a class, genus, or group; a specific word refers to a member of that group. **Ship** is a general word, but **ketch, schooner, liner,** and **tugboat** are specific. It must be remembered, however, that the terms general and specific are relative, not absolute. **Ketch,** for **example,** is more specific than **ship,** for a ketch is a kind of ship. But **ketch,** on the other hand, is more general than **Tahiti** ketch, for a Tahiti ketch is a kind of ketch.

The distinction between the abstract and the concrete also is relative. Ideas, qualities, and characteristics which do not exist by themselves may be called abstract; physical things such as **house, shoes,** and **horse** are concrete. Notice, however, that concrete words not only can range further into the specific (**bungalow, moccasin,** and **stallion**), but they also can range back toward the general (**domicile, clothing** and **cattle**). In making these distinctions between the abstract and the concrete and between the general and the specific, there is no implication that good writing should be specific and concrete and that poor writing is general and abstract. Certainly most good writing is concrete and specific, but it is also general and abstract, constantly moving from the general to the specific and from the abstract to the concrete.

**ALLUSION** a reference to a familiar person, place, or thing, whether real or imaginary: Woodrow Wilson or Zeus, Siam or Atlantis, kangaroo or Phoenix.

The allusion is an economical way to evoke an atmosphere, a historical era, or an emotion.

**ANALOGY** in exposition, usually a comparison of some length in which the unknown is explained in terms of the known, the unfamiliar in terms of the familiar, the remote in terms of the immediate.

In argument, an analogy consists of a series of likenesses between two or more dissimilar things, demonstrating that they are either similar or identical in other respects also. The use of analogy in argument is open to criticism, for two things alike in many respects are not necessarily alike in all (for example, lampblack and diamonds are both pure carbon; they differ only in their crystal structure). Although analogy never **proves** anything, its dramatic quality, its assistance in establishing tone, its vividness make it one of the most valuable techniques of the writer.

**ANALYSIS** a method of exposition by logical division, applicable to anything that can be divided into component parts: an object, such as an automobile or a watch; an institution, such as a college; or a process, such as mining coal or writing a poem. Parts or processes may be described technically and factually or impressionistically and selectively. In the latter method the parts are organized in relation to a single governing idea so that the mutually supporting function of each of the components in the total structure becomes clear to the reader. Parts may be explained in terms of their characteristic function. Analysis may also be concerned with the connection of events; given this condition or series of conditions, what effects will follow?

**ARGUMENT** often contains the following parts: the **proposition**, that is, an assertion that leads to the issue; the **issue**, that is, the precise phase of the proposition which the writer is attempting to prove and the question on which the whole argument rests; the **evidence**, the facts and opinions which the author offers as testimony. He may order the evidence deductively by proceeding from certain premises to a **conclusion**; or **inductively** by generalizing from a number of instances and drawing a **conclusion**. Informal arguments frequently make greater use of the methods of exposition than they do of formal logic. See Deduction, Induction, Logic, and Analogy.

The attempt to distinguish between argument and persuasion is sometimes made by reference to means (Argument makes appeals to reason: persuasion, to emotions); sometimes to ends (Argument causes someone to change his mind; persuasion moves him to action). These distinctions, however, are more academic than functional, for in practice argument and persuasion are not discrete entities. Yet the proof in argument rests largely upon the objectivity of evidence; the proof in persuasion, upon the heightened use of language.

**ASSUMPTION** that part of an argument which is unstated because it is either taken for granted by the reader and writer or undetected by them. When the reader consciously disagrees with an assumption, the writer has misjudged his audience by assuming what the reader refuses to concede.

**ATTITUDE** towards subject, see Tone. Toward audience, see Audience.

**AUDIENCE** for the writer, his expected readers. When the audience is a general, unknown one, and the subject matter is closely related to the writer's opinions, preferences, attitudes, and tastes, then the writer's relationship to his audience is in a very real sense his relationship to himself. The writer who distrusts the intelligence of his audience or who adapts his material to what he assumes are the tastes and interests of his readers compromises his integrity.

On the other hand, if the audience is generally known (a college class, for example), and the subject matter is factual information, then the beginning writer may well consider the education, interests, and tastes of his audience. Unless he keeps a definite audience in mind, the beginner is apt to shift levels of usage, use inappropriate diction, and lose the reader by appealing to none of his interests.

"It is now necessary to warn the writer that his concern for the reader must be pure; he must sympathize with the reader's plight (most readers are in trouble about half the time) but never seek to know his wants. The whole duty of a writer is to please and satisfy himself, and the true writer always plays to an audience of one. Let him start sniffing the air, or glancing at the Trend Machine, and he is as good as dead although he may make a nice living." Strunk and White, **The Elements of Style** (Macmillan).

**CAUSE AND EFFECT** a seemingly simple method of development in which either the cause of a particular effect or the effects of a particular cause are investigated. However, because of the philosophical difficulties surrounding causality, the writer should be cautious in ascribing causes. For the explanation of most processes, it is probably safer to proceed in a sequential order, using transitional words to indicate the order of the process.

**CLASSIFICATION** the division of a whole into the classes that comprise it; or the placement of a subject into the whole of which it is a part. See Definition and Analysis.

**COHERENCE** literally, a sticking together, therefore, the joining or linking of one point to another. It is the writer's obligation to make clear to the reader the relationship of sentence to sentence and paragraph to paragraph. Sometimes coherence is simply a matter of putting the parts in a sequence which is meaningful and relevant—logical sequence, chronological order, order of importance. Other times it is helpful to underscore the relationship. An elementary but highly useful method of underscoring relationships is the use of transitional words; **but, however, yet** inform the reader that what is to follow contrasts with what went before; **furthermore, moreover, in addition to** continue or expand what went before.

Another elementary way of achieving coherence is the enumeration of ideas—"first," "second," "third"—so as to remind the reader of the development. A more subtle transition can be gained by repeating at the beginning of a paragraph a key word or idea from the end of the preceding paragraph. Such a transition reminds the reader of what has gone before and simultaneously prepares him for what is to come.

**COMPARISON AND CONTRAST** the presentation of a subject by indicating similarities between two or more things (comparison); by indicating differences (contrast). The basic elements in a comparative process, then, are (1) the terms of the comparison, or the various objects compared, and (2) the points of likeness or difference between the objects compared. Often comparison and contrast are used in definition and other methods of exposition.

**CONCRETENESS** See Abstraction, Levels of.

**CONNOTATION** all that the word suggests or implies in addition to its literal meaning. However, this definition is arbitrary and, from the standpoint of the writer, artificial, because the meaning of a word includes **all** that it suggests and implies.

**CONTRAST** See Comparison.

**COORDINATION** elements of like importance in like grammatical construction. Less important elements should be placed in grammatically subordinate positions. See Parallelism and Subordination.

**DEDUCTIVE REASONING** in logic, the application of a generalization to a particular; by analogy, in rhetoric, that development which moves from the general to the specific.

**DEFINITION** in logic, the placing of the word to be defined in a general class and then showing how it differs from other members of the class; in rhetoric, the meaningful extension (usually enriched by the use of detail, concrete illustration, anecdote, metaphor) of a logical definition in order to answer fully, clearly, and often implicitly the question, "What is——?"

**DENOTATION** the literal meaning of a word. See Connotation.

**DESCRIPTION** that form of discourse whose primary purpose is to present factual information about an object or experience (objective description); or to report the impression or evaluation of an object or experience (subjective description). Most description combines the two purposes. **It was a frightening night.** (An evaluation with which others might disagree.) **The wind blew the shingles off the north side of the house and drove the rain under the door.** (Two facts about which there can be little disagreement).

**DICTION** style as determined by choice of words. Good diction is characterized by accuracy and appropriateness to subject matter; weak diction, by the use of inappropriate, vague or trite words. The relationship between the kinds of words a writer selects and his subject matter in large part determines tone. The deliberate use of inappropriate diction is a frequent device of satire.

**DISCOURSE, FORMS OF** traditionally, exposition, argument, description, and narration. See entries under each. These four kinds of traditional discourse are rarely found in a pure form. Argument and exposition may be interfused in the most complex fashion. Exposition often employs narration and description for purposes of illustration. It is important to remember, however, that in an effective piece of writing the use of more than one form of discourse is never accidental. It always serves the author's central purpose.

**EMPHASIS** the arrangement of the elements of a composition so that the important meanings occur in structurally important parts of the composition. Repetition, order of increasing importance, exclamation points, rhetorical questions, and figures of speech are all devices to achieve emphasis.

**EVIDENCE** that part of argument or persuasion that involves proof. It usually takes the form of facts, particulars deduced from general principles, or opinions of authorities.

**EXPOSITION** that form of discourse which explains or informs. Most papers required of college students are expository. The **methods** of exposition are identification, definition, classification, illustration, comparison and contrast, and analysis. See separate entries in glossary.

**FIGURES OF SPEECH** a form of expression in which the meanings of words are extended beyond the literal. The common figures of speech are metaphor, simile, analogy.

**GENERALIZATION** a general conception or principle derived from particulars. Often, simply a great statement. See Abstraction.

**GRAMMAR** a systematic description of a language.

**IDENTIFICATION** a process preliminary to definition of a subject. For the writer it is that vastly important period preliminary to writing when, wrestling with inchoate glimmerings, he begins to select and shape his materials. As a method of exposition, it brings the subject into focus by describing it.

**ILLUSTRATION** a particular member of a class used to explain or dramatize a class, a type, a thing, a person, a method, an idea, or a condition. The idea explained may be either stated or implied. For purposes of illustration, the individual member of a class must be a fair representation of the distinctive qualities of the class. The use of illustrations, examples, and specific instances adds to the concreteness and vividness of writing. See Narration.

**IMAGE** a word or statement which makes an appeal to the senses. Thus, there are visual images, auditory images. **etc.** As the most direct experience of the world is through the senses, writing which makes use of sense impressions (images) can be unusually effective.

**INDUCTIVE REASONING** in logic, the formulation of a generalization after the observation of an adequate number of particular instances; by analogy, in rhetoric, that development which moves from the particular to the general.

**INTENTION** for the particular purpose or function of a single piece of writing see Purpose. Intention determines the four forms of discourse. See

Exposition, Argument, Description, Narration. These intentions may be explicitly or implicitly set forth by the writer.

**IRONY** at its simplest, involves a discrepancy between literal and intended meaning; at its most complex, it involves an utterance more meaningful (and usually meaningful in a different way) to the listener than to the speaker. For example, Oedipus' remarks about discovering the murderer of the king are understood by the audience in a way Oedipus himself cannot understand them. The inability to grasp the full implications of his own remark is frequently feigned by the satirist.

**ISSUE** the limitation of a general proposition to the precise point on which the argument rests. Defeating the issue defeats the argument. Typically the main proposition of an argument will raise at least one issue for discussion and controversy.

**LIMITATION OF SUBJECT** restriction of the subject to one that can be adequately developed with reference to audience and purpose.

**METAPHOR** an implied comparison between two things that are seemingly different; a compressed analogy. Effectively used, metaphors increase clarity, interest, vividness, and concreteness.

**NARRATION** a form of discourse the purpose of which is to tell a story. If a story is significant in itself, the particulars appealing to the imagination, it is **narration**. If a story illustrates a point in exposition or argument, it may be called **illustrative narration**. If a story outlines a process step by step, the particulars appealing to the understanding, it is designated as **expository narration**.

**ORGANIZATION, METHODS OF** vary with the form of discourse. Exposition uses in part, in whole, or in combination identification, definition, classification, illustration, comparison and contrast, and analysis. Argument and persuasion often use the method of organization of inductive or deductive reasoning, or analogy. Description is often organized either around a dominant impression or by means of a spatial arrangement. Narration, to give two examples, may be organized chronologically or in terms of point of view.

**PARADOX** an assertion or sentiment seemingly self-contradictory, or opposed to common sense, which may yet be true.

**PARAGRAPH** serves to discuss one topic or one aspect of a topic. The central thought is either implied or expressed in a topic sentence. Paragraphs have such a great variety of organization and function that it is almost impossible to generalize about them.

**PARALLELISM** elements of similar rhetorical importance in similar grammatical patterns. See Coordination.

**PARODY** mimicking the language and style of another.

**PERSPECTIVE** the vantage point chosen by the writer to achieve his purpose, his strategy. It is reflected in his close scrutiny of, or distance from, his subject; his objective representation or subjective interpretation of it. See **Diction, Purpose, Tone.**

**PERSUASION** See Argument.

**POINT OF VIEW** in description, the position from which the observer looks at the object described; in narration, the person who sees the action, who tells the story; in exposition, the grammatical person of the composition. First person or the more impersonal third person may be used.

**PROPOSITION** See Argument.

**PURPOSE** what the writer wants to accomplish with a particular piece of writing.

**RHETORIC** the art of using language effectively.

**RHETORICAL QUESTION** a question asked in order to induce thought and to provide emphasis rather than to evoke an answer.

**RHYTHM** in poetry and prose, patterned emphasis. Good prose is less regular in its rhythm than poetry.

**SATIRE** the attempt to effect reform by exposing an object to laughter. Satire makes frequent recourse to irony, wit, ridicule, parody. It is usually classified under such categories as the following: social satire, personal satire, literary satire.

**STYLE** "The essence of a sound style is that it cannot be reduced to rules—that it is a living and breathing thing, with something of the demoniacal in it—that it fits its proprietor tightly and yet ever so loosely, as his skin fits him. It is, in fact, quite as securely an integral part of him as that skin is . . . In brief, a style is always the outward and visible symbol of a man, and it cannot be anything else." H. L. Mencken, **On Style**, used with permission of Alfred A. Knopf, Inc.

"Young writers often suppose that style is a garnish for the meat of prose, a sauce by which a dull dish is made palatable. Style has no such separate entity; it is nondetachable, unfilterable. The beginner should approach style warily, realizing that it is himself he is approaching, no other; and he should begin by turning resolutely away from all devices that are popularly believed to indicate style—all mannerisms, tricks, adornments. The approach to style is by way of plainness, simplicity, orderliness, sincerity." E. B. White from **The Elements of Style** (Macmillan).

**SUBORDINATION** less important rhetorical elements in grammatically subordinate positions. See Parallelism and Coordination.

**SYLLOGISM** in formal logic, a deductive argument in three steps: a major premise, a minor premise, a conclusion. The major premise states a quality of a class (All men are mortal); the minor premise states that X is a member of the class (Socrates is a man); the conclusion states that the quality of a class is also a quality of a member of the class (Socrates is mortal). In rhetoric, the full syllogism is rarely used; instead, one of the premises is usually omitted. "You can rely on him; he is independent," is an abbreviated syllogism. Major premise: Independent people are reliable; minor premise: He is independent; conclusion: He is reliable. Constructing the full syllogism frequently reveals flaws in reasoning, such as the above, which has an error in the major premise.

**SYMBOL** a concrete image which suggests a meaning beyond itself.

**TONE** the manner in which the writer communicates his attitude toward the materials he is presenting. Diction is the most obvious means of establishing tone. See Diction.

**TOPIC SENTENCE** the thesis which the paragraph as a whole develops. Some paragraphs do not have topic sentences, but the thesis is implied.

**TRANSITION** the linking together of sentences, paragraphs and larger parts of the composition to achieve coherence. See Coherence.

**UNITY** the relevance of selected material to the central theme of an essay. See Coherence.